There was no such thing as certainty under these conditions, but I knew deep down in my bones that Lothar Pandross had personally directed the raid on my house, had personally supervised my son's abduction, had gone along for the whole thing.

Clearly the chief of security had been there all along. No wonder he figured out the weak point in my system! And no wonder he was able to slip first James Bond and then himself in and out without the Company knowing a damned thing. He was almost certainly good enough to do just that. But why did a guy who was so vital and who almost never went on missions himself stick his neck out like that?

Much more important—how did he do it *three weeks after he'd been murdered?*

Also by Jack L. Chalker
published by Tor Books

Downtiming the Night Side
The Messiah Choice

G.O.D. INC.
The Labyrinth of Dreams
The Shadow Dancers

SOUL RIDER
Spirits of Flux and Anchor
Empires of Flux and Anchor
Masters of Flux and Anchor
The Birth of Flux and Anchor
Children of Flux and Anchor

JACK L. CHALKER

THE MAZE IN THE MIRROR

G.O.D. INC. NO. 3

TOR®

A TOM DOHERTY ASSOCIATES BOOK
NEW YORK

THE MAZE IN THE MIRROR

Cover art by Royo

A Tor Book
Published by Tom Doherty Associates, Inc.
175 Fifth Avenue
New York, N.Y. 10010

Tor ® is a registered trademark of Tom Doherty Associates, Inc.

ISBN: 0-812-52069-6
Library of Congress Catalog Card Number: 88-50995

First edition: January 1989

Printed in the United States of America

0 9 8 7 6 5 4 3 2

From Williamson to Leinster to Piper . . .
H. Beam Piper, who perfected it and to whom this book
is affectionately dedicated.
I feel honored that you all,
at some point in my life,
called me friend

Some Warnings for the Reader

This book is the third in a series featuring my two parallel worlds detectives Sam and Brandy Horowitz in the universes of G.O.D., Inc. Like the first two, *The Labyrinth of Dreams* and *The Shadow Dancers*, both Tor, 1987, it is a complete novel, as all good series novels are. It is not, strictly speaking, a serial continued from book to book, as are many other of my works. However, the time frame on these books is progressive; this book is set considerably after the time of the first two and the characters are the older, more knowledgeable, more experienced characters who have undergone those previous cases and remember them and assume you do, too. Also, one of our villains this time is a leftover deliberately loose end from *The Shadow Dancers*, and the solution to the case of the Maze in the Mirror is, in many ways, also a final solution to the progression and loose ends of the first two books.

As such, while sufficient information is provided for you to read this book as complete and independent of the others, I have made no other concessions and some of the references and background might be a bit vague or confusing for a new reader, as they are not explained but rather taken for granted. For that reason, *The Maze in the Mirror* will be best appreciated by those who have read either or preferably both of the preceding books. This is particularly true since, while there is an element of mystery involved, this series is basically a set of private detective procedurals—that is, figuring out by legwork, evidence, and deduction just what the dastardly plot is here and how to prevent it is the object, not necessarily unmasking some unknown murderer, even though unknown murderer there might be. I make that comment in light of some reviews of the earlier books which were under the mistaken impression that these were primarily whodunits and who therefore reviewed the whodunit rather than the plot—and the two are not the same thing in a procedural.

Your bookstore should have the first two books if you do not. Any good, well-managed bookstore run by intelligent owners of good taste should have all my previous novels on their shelves. If not, then buy this one so you'll have it and then order the first two from that store or find a better bookstore who keeps the essentials in stock.

To forestall a bunch of letters to me complaining that there are real anachronisms when the earlier novels are compared to this one, I should point out that nowhere have I stated that Sam and Brandy are natives of our own universe, just one that's rather close to ours.

Also, I want to reassure all of you out there that General Ordering and Development has no connection (that I know of) with Guaranteed Overnight Delivery, Inc., a firm of which I was ignorant until recently when I was passed on the highway by a G.O.D., Inc. tractor trailer truck to my enormous shock. I understand that some of my readers who are truckers have been giving drivers for that real company a really uncomfortable time.

It might also be noted that this series is the first set of my books to be banned anywhere in the U.S. A few distributors, primarily in some southern states, have refused to take it because the overtitle appears to be sacrilegious to them or they fear reader reaction for that reason. If something this minor elicits that reaction, one worries about the fate of poor truckers for Guaranteed Overnight Delivery who roll through those states and areas with the big black G.O.D. letters on their sides. . . .

Also, in the course of this book, many readers, particularly Americans and Canadians, will find a lot of more or less familiar names and products, some but not all variantly spelled, here and there. These are used in good fun and for internal logic and are not intended to cast aspersions on (nor endorse) products or possibly popular musicians or anyone or anything else. I hope the companies involved just consider them free commercials and take them in the spirit in which they're used.

It is impossible to say if this is the last G.O.D., Inc. book at this point. Certainly if I come up with another plot I think good or better than the first three, or if I get to missing these characters, it's a possibility, although not very soon. Perhaps your own reactions and the number of these books sold will be the final answer. That's not to say that I write any book on the basis of potential popularity, but certainly, having done these, whether I give in to any inclination to do more or use the same limited time to create something new and different will to some extent be influenced by whether or not there are sufficient numbers of you out there who want to read more.

Jack L. Chalker
Uniontown, Maryland
October, 1987

1.

A Visitor in the Night

The sky was dark and overcast as it usually was in the central Pennsylvania mountains in winter, where the locals would refer to good days as "between snows." There was certainly enough snow on the ground—about two feet had yet to be given the chance to melt, and in January's still dark days it wasn't likely to improve for quite a while.

Most of the nation, particularly the west, thinks of the eastern United States as one vast paved-over region full of contiguous city stretching at least from Boston to Richmond and perhaps all the way down.

None of the country is ancient to human beings, particularly those whose ancestors came from Europe, but in comparative terms the east coast of the U.S. is "old," with a history of settlement ranging from nearly five hundred years in Florida to going on four hundred years in the original Thirteen. It seems inconceivable to both westerners and Europeans, and even many eastern city dwellers, that anything could remain relatively unspoiled after so long.

Yet, in fact, much of even such states as New York and Pennsylvania are actually wilderness, with almost all the people bunched up on opposite sides of the state, and even some of the smaller ones like New Hampshire and Vermont have comparatively vast areas of unspoiled wilderness. Black bear still roam the Pennsylvania hills in season, and deer threaten to overrun southern New Jersey; every time the cougar is declared extinct in the northern states one will miraculously make an appearance. They've declared that animal extinct north of Florida at least twenty times in the past fifty years.

The northern half of Pennsylvania is a vast and mostly unspoiled forest land through which Interstate 80 carries traffic from the metropolis port of New York in the east out to Ohio and then all the way to San Francisco, but through Pennsylvania it finds little civilization. People are there, all right, but not many of them, and they are scattered in small towns like Bellfonte and Liverpool with nary a Philadelphia or Pittsburgh to be seen.

Penn State University, in fact, is probably one of the more isolated major universities in the country. Not even I-80 comes too near, and it sits in Happy Valley surrounded by stark mountains and a northern climate, often nearly unreachable in mid-winter, its tens of thousands of students having to content themselves with the small town of State College and a few others nearby who exist only to serve them. The only other industry of note is the State Pen, the counterpoint of Penn State (although many locals claim to have problems differentiating the two), and because of its isolation and the climate around a very difficult one to successfully get out of by other than legal means. You might escape, but after that you'd stick out like a sore thumb and it would be very difficult to get away.

Some areas do have farms; either truck farms for the University and other small towns; mostly, or breeding farms for dairy cattle and horses. On one such farm, even more isolated than most and off any main roads, concealed by forest and mountains, there stands a particular thick grove of trees and in the center of that grove a very strange area with a high fence around it. It's not much to look at, even inside, if you get past the warnings from the electric company, or so it is stated, warning of high voltage dangers. In the middle is a cistern-like cavity made of smooth, virgin concrete that has almost a marble-like texture. It goes down perhaps ten feet, with an old and rusty ladder to the bottom, but, once down, it doesn't look like much of anything, either. Just a lot of crud and no outlet and no panels or anything else.

In fact, the only unusual thing about it is that even in the dead of winter the immediate area of the concrete has no snow. It simply won't lay there, as if the entire thing is heated—although if you dared it is cold to the touch—and there is no water at the bottom as if there is some sort of concealed and clever drain. Where the water goes and where the heat comes from is not apparent, and there are few clues.

A driver on the nearby main road is going along listening to the local rock station, on his way in to town for something or other, and suddenly there is a bad burst of static that continues, going in and out, making the listening experience unpleasant. He tries a few other stations and finds the same thing happening, and curses, but within two minutes the effect is gone. *Atmospherics*, he thinks, grumbling, and forgets about it.

The pulses, however, come from the recessed well concealed on the farm, and they have determined that no one is within the grove at this time. This feeds a signal back—somewhere—and, inside that concrete urn, something begins to happen.

It begins with a crackling noise, and the slight smell of ozone, and then a beam of remarkably solid-looking blue-white light shoots up from the center, so sharp and exact that it appears to be almost a pole that can be picked up. It shimmers slightly, then bends once, twice, three times, as if on hinges, until it is now a square. In the immediate area there is the sound of heavy but unseen machinery, and the ground vibrates slightly.

The square appears to fold in upon itself and now there are two squares, then they do it again and there is a cube, suspended just above the concrete floor and slightly angled, the sides shimmering and glassy yet impenetrable. Then one facet shimmers and a figure steps through; the figure of a man ill-dressed for this climate and this weather. He is of medium height, darkly handsome, and he is dressed in white tie and tails, including spats, although the outfit looks not only out of place but rather wrinkled and the worse for wear.

He glances nervously around, then sees the ladder and heads for it, climbing up with quick and confident purpose as if the demons of hell might pop out of the cube at any moment themselves. At the top, he's somewhat stunned to see deep snow and then a high fence, but he does not consider turning around. The spats will have to get wet.

The cold, raw wind hits him in spite of the

protection of the trees, but he is already studying the fence. Finally he decides, takes off his jacket, and throws it up so that it lands over the barbed wire. Then he concentrates and leaps, pulling himself up by his fingers, reaches the top, then falls over into the deep snow on the other side.

The cube emits more crackling noises, and he picks himself up fast. The jacket is impaled on the barbs but it's down enough on the outside that he can reach its bottom, and he pulls on it and it comes free, with an unpleasant tearing sound. He needs far more than the jacket in this country at this time of year, but he does not want to leave evidence that here is where he got off.

It's growing quite dark in the winter afternoon, which suits him in spite of the temperature that might well freeze him and will certainly frostbite him if he doesn't get someplace warm fast. The snow is less an obstacle for its depth and chill than for its virginity; perhaps the darkness will hide his tracks.

Laboriously, the man makes his way through the depths to the open field beyond and looks around. There is little to see except up on the hill perhaps a quarter mile away. A large Georgian style house along with a barn, silo, and stables, lights on both inside the house and floodlighting the grounds is the only civilization in view. He heads for it as fast as he can, and now he really begins to feel the horrible cold.

Heading straight for the house in the deep snow takes him a good twenty minutes, and only will-power is keeping him going at this point. Breaking into the plowed area in front of the house with its solid packed rock-hard base he trips and falls, and struggles back to his feet. Only a few yards to the porch, only a few yards to the door . . .

He makes it, leaning against the door, and pounds on it with what little strength he has left. For a few precious moments there is no answer, and then he pounds again, knowing that time for him is running out.

Inside the house a woman's muffled voice can be heard muttering, "Keep your shirt on, damn it. I'm comin' as fast as I can."

The door opens and he is face to face with a portly black woman of medium height with thick glasses and a totally confused expression as she sees him.

"What the hell is *you*?" she mutters, not afraid but startled.

"Pardon, Madam," he responds, in an elegant upper class London accent tempered by a crackling voice and total exhaustion. "The name is Bond. James Bond."

And then the stranger collapses half inside her door.

Doctor Macklinberg shook his head in wonder and closed the door to the guest bedroom as he exited into the hall. She looked at him quizzically. "Well?"

He shrugged. "Bad exposure. He should be in a hospital right now but you know why we can't do that. Stripping him and getting him into the hot tub in the basement was a brilliant reaction. He still might lose some toes or perhaps worse—I can't tell this soon—but if he pulls through it will be because of your quick thinking."

"I come in this house out of the storm and

stripped and jumped in that thing myself to thaw out too many times not to think of it," she responded. "You know who he said he was?"

The doctor nodded. "Yes, he's mumbled it several times to me."

She fumbled and then got out his wallet. "Says so in here, too. London address, bunch of cards for fancy clubs over half the world, a couple of credit cards on European banks, and a fair amount of these." She handed him some very large bills. He took them and frowned.

"Pound notes with King Charles VI on them. Fascinating. *Our* Charles would only be the third, I think. That's not him, though. I wonder if the Stuarts still rule our Mister Bond's England? I wonder what else they rule?"

She shrugged. "I never pay much attention to that kind of thing. The main thing is that he's not from the here and now and that means he came in through the substation and he did it without settin' off no alarms in the house here or in Stan's security office."

"You been down there?"

"Uh uh. Not with Sam in Philadelphia and everybody else checkin' out everything. Hell, I got a kid I can't leave, Doc. You know that. Stan got down there, though. The station wasn't active but it was a hot area, and the snow all around was all crudded up. Looks like he used his coat over the barbed wire. Parts of it are still stickin' there."

"Well, the barbed wire was probably the least of his problems. He has several gashes in him as well, all fairly new and some fairly deep, like he'd been stuck by all sorts of nasty, sharp knives. He's been through a lot tonight, that's for certain."

She nodded. "Well, Stan's gonna go in and send a message up the line to Company Security, and I already called it in to Bill in Philadelphia while you was in there. It's gonna leave me short-handed, though. They got a pretty mean storm in the east right now and it's socked in Sam by air or road. With Stan going up line that leaves only three of us here on the grounds tonight."

Macklinberg sighed. "I wish I could just stay with him but I'm on call tonight at the hospital. I have three women in labor now and what with the insurance thing I'm the only one around at the moment willing to deliver their kids. Ordinarily I'd send a nurse over or maybe a resident but I can't chance what this fellow might say if he starts babbling or comes out of it. He's definitely scared of something, though, and if he's anything at all like his fictional counterpart he doesn't scare easily. I've given him what I can to help him along—antibiotics, that sort of thing—but I didn't dare give him a sedative even though, God knows, that's what he needs. I thought that if he came out of it you'd want to know what it was all about right away."

She nodded. "Thanks, Doc. I think I can handle it here. But I got to think about how unusual short we are 'round here tonight and then this guy just comes in on us like this. I'm gonna put the security system on full tonight, and I'll call you at the hospital if there's any change. O.K.?"

"Good idea. But if you need me, call the service and they'll beep me. I may or may not be at the hospital at any given time." He paused, then said, "As soon as possible he should be moved out of here and to medical facilities better than anything

12

we can offer him. He's certainly going to lose some toes and both feet are in some danger. I've shot him full of every antibiotic I have but sooner or later we'll have to face treating that frostbite, and the only thing I could do here is amputate. For now, no walking. Keep him in bed. The painkillers should keep him out a while and I've left some pills just in case, but you never know. Someone like him . . . You know, I saw *Goldfinger* sixteen times."

She grinned. "I met this type before, Doc. They don't ever live up to their billing. He's probably a pencil pusher in MI-5 with a wife and nine kids who'd be horrified to read the books them writers made up about him here."

She saw him to the door, then sighed and went back and put on a pot of coffee, then turned on the alarm system and notified Diane in the security shack. It was gonna be a *looong* night.

She sat with the man for a while, but that soon became very boring, and while he was still out he was restless, would occasionally twist or thrash about, and he kept mumbling things. She went and found a voice-activated tape recorder and set it up beside him, then threw the intercom on. She then went down the hall to Dash's room and checked on him—still out, and a good thing, too—and switched off the intercom in the boy's room so he wouldn't be awakened by ghastly moanings and strange utterances coming out of the speaker. Then she went downstairs, got some more coffee and a piece of chocolate cake, and settled in the family room to watch TV off the satellite dish.

Never once fails, she thought sourly as she looked

through the listings and paged through the satellite channels via the remote control. *A hundred damn channels and when you got to sit and watch somethin' there* still *ain't nothin' good on TV!*

The fact was, she was often up late, and always had trouble sleeping. The dreams and the nightmares were just too great, particularly when Sam wasn't here.

Dash helped. He was a beautiful child and he was growing up smart but spoiled rotten, but she didn't care. She'd been frightened to death that he'd be damaged somehow, considering what horrors her body had been through and considering that they'd had to have a special operation just to let her have him. Sam claimed that his only worry was that all black Jewish kids would look like Sammy Davis, Jr., and when Dash looked right handsome he'd stopped the worries. But he still was busy, and that meant he was away a lot. Security consultant to the Company, they called it. They designed a security system for most anything and then he'd come in and blow holes in it, sometimes literally. It sounded like fun, but she couldn't bring herself to go back through the Labyrinth, not unless she had to. The memories were just too strong, the fears severe, even after years had passed.

She could still remember seeing part of Sam's head get blown off from raiders up top in a cube and she didn't feel confident any more. But the worst fear was the juice, the alien drug from some world so far up the line it didn't even have an official name that gave exquisite pleasure at the cost of slavery to it. Even though she'd been hooked by the nastiest bastards ever to attack the

Company and against her will, and even though she'd gone through torture and long treatments to beat it, the memory still lingered. Once you were on it you'd degrade yourself, do anything to stay on it. She'd done a lot of that. And she was one of the very few to make it back, to break the addiction without breaking her mind and body as well.

But she still wanted it. Craved it, and knew that if it was ever put in her grasp again she'd take it and never be able to get off.

It was that that scared her most. Somewhere out there the evil genius who'd come up with the diabolical plan that almost broke the ruling class of the Company world was still there. They'd caught his boss and his underlings, but the man known as Doctor Carlos, world of origin unknown, background unknown, was still out there somewhere.

Oh, the Company had finally broken the secret of the drug, which was actually a symbiotic organism that essentially took control of you, and if you took your shots from them once a year the thing couldn't infect you, but she was never sure it would work with her, even as it couldn't help those who were exiled addicts—and she didn't underestimate Carlos, either. He had had as much time as the Company to work on the thing.

The Company. You couldn't even get away from the Company on TV. Particularly not on TV. New miracle gadget cuts kitchen time in half . . . Wonderful six-record treasury from Reinhold Zeitermas, the world's best selling contrabassoon player . . . Buy MirGrow, the secret plant food of the Orient . . . All that junk was what the Company sold. Music treasuries from folks you never heard of, crazy products that were pretty weird when they worked, you name it. Just call this toll free number now. 1-800- . . . And the home shopping networks—it looked like they were furnishing the merchandise even for the ones they didn't own or control outright.

General Ordering and Development, Inc., Des Moines, Iowa. Big fucking joke. G.O.D., Inc.

Well, they acted like their initials sometimes, that was for sure, and they had more products than the junk they pushed to the public, too, and a lot more going on around the world than their front indicated. Wherever merchandise moved, that was them. The Mafia was a wholly owned and operated subsidiary, not just here but around the world. Same went for the heroin of the Golden Triangle in Asia or the big coke trade from South America. They subsidized whole governments, bought and sold cops and politicians wholesale, and just about nobody even knew they existed. How they got what they wanted in the communist world even she didn't know, but she knew they were there in force. They probably sold all the damned bugging devices the KGB used to the Kremlin while making it look like a state factory.

In truth, they were a gigantic, amoral colonial empire, only the colonies didn't know they were colonies. That's because almost nobody knew that invasions from other worlds didn't have to come from the stars or fly around in saucers full of little green men. No, there were more than enough worlds coexisting right now, one on top of the other, for a nearly infinite distance in both directions. Parallel worlds, they called it, although it was more like parallel universes. Somewhere, somehow, almost everything that could have ever possibly have happened did. Way up the line there were Earths where the dinosaurs never died out, and even ones where some of them evolved into intelligent life. Germany won or lost, America did or didn't break free of England, England and parts of Europe stayed Catholic, or the Moslems overran Rome and kept going all the way. Worlds in which a Roman-ruled South America battled a Chinese-settled North America.

One world had discovered this parallelism, and that world had created a means of moving between it called for good reason The Labyrinth. A sort of railroad complete with branches and switchers and dispatchers that stretched for a million worlds in both directions and still didn't reach them all. They alone could move between and they alone controlled the dual lines, one for passengers, one for freight.

And one world's bright ideas were another world's—well, junk. They ran at different speeds sometimes, and things invented one place were never invented the next. Whether one world needed the Dicing Wizard or not was irrelevant; G.O.D., Inc. made sure you wanted it anyway, at least in enough quantities to make the transshipment worthwhile. She often wondered what her world sent the others.

And James Bond is now lying in the guest bedroom.

Well, why not? She and Sam had once faced down a very villainous Lamont Cranston. Sometimes the names just popped up elsewhere and elsewhen; sometimes a totally fictional character in one place might pop up as a very real and quite similar person in another. She'd heard a lot of theories that writers were just folks sensitized, somehow, to certain people or things in the other worlds.

There were even other versions of you in those other worlds. That was the freaky part. The Company had a way of telling one from the other but nobody else could. A tiny little implant, a transmitter, deep in the bone someplace that gave you a unique signature and also both authorized you in the Labyrinth and made a record as you passed each switch point or station so they could track you. Of course, it could be beaten, and had been. They were now sure that their new system was foolproof, but she knew as well as Sam that any system declared foolproof was impervious only to fools; smart folks could always figure a way to beat it.

She had checked on the other versions of her in worlds near her own, and even met and shared some time with one of her counterparts, but they were pretty depressing overall. Whores and welfare babymakers mostly, low class and lower lives. The ones who survived the streets and weren't in jail or something. She'd been the exception, the lucky one, to whom the fluke good thing had happened. She didn't need to reflect much to realize just how lucky, and improbable, that one thing was.

Sam. Sam Horowitz, former cop, former private eye, now Company Security Specialist. A cute little guy who was culturally as Jewish as they came and looked the part but who thought he was Nick Charles or Sam Spade or at least William Powell. A guy who'd given up everything and married a black girl from Camden who was a high school dropout, chubby, and who thought of herself as more street smart than real smart, but who had also been infused with the dreams of glamour of the detective business by a fanatical father who was an ex-Army cop turned failed private eye himself and who'd wound up floating in the Schuykill River when he'd gotten his first really big case.

The real amazing thing was that there were a lot fewer Sams than Brandys in those other worlds. He'd been involved in a lot of dangerous stuff as an Air Force cop and apparently he'd been killed in most of them, or before. The survivors were mostly cynical and opportunistic skunks, crooked cops and worse, who'd sell their own grandmother for a dollar. Sam was the only man she knew in the whole Company who'd once had a gun duel with himself.

Of course, there were worlds where one of them existed, or neither existed or were now alive, and ones where Colonel Parker's only child had been a son and Mrs. Horowitz had borne a Jewish-American Princess. But when you had a duplicate, he or she might be, at least physically, a perfect copy. Same genes, same fingerprints, everything. That was a favorite Company method of taking control of something. Nabbing a real person in authority and switching them for a duplicate, well briefed, hypnoed, and absolutely identical to everybody else, but who was really a Company stooge.

Of course, that was also a favorite trick of enemies of the Company who could gain illicit use of the Labyrinth.

That's how she'd met her twin and both of them hooked on the juice and under the control of a Company enemy engaged in a not so gentle attempt at a Company takeover. He'd been pathetic for all his cleverness and callous cruelty, though. The kind of folks he'd recruited from various worlds to do his dirty work had hated him as much as the rest of the Company. They were fanatics with access to the Labyrinth and its powers and it had been real hell rooting them out—if they had been. At least one, the most dangerous of the bunch, was still out there, somewhere. She had met him only a few times, and always under the worst of conditions, but still he haunted her nightmares. The Company admitted they couldn't find him, couldn't even identify him or his home world, but they were confident that he was now bottled up, contained somewhere where he could not use the Labyrinth without them knowing and catching him.

She doubted it. She was certain that Carlos was out there, somewhere, perhaps in a world that ran at a slower rate than hers but with a higher level of technology, plotting and planning and recruiting and solving the new roadblocks the Company had put in his way.

The speaker suddenly brought the sound of the man upstairs crying out and coughing horribly. She jumped up and went up to him.

He was delirious, thrashing about on the bed, mumbling "No, no! Insanity! It is all insanity!"

She tried to calm him down, tell him it was all right, get through to him. Suddenly he startled her by seeming to come awake, eyes wide, looking straight at her. "The maze! Monstrously twisted, *stupid* plot so grandiose it might just work! Got to warn them. Got to . . ."

"What plot? Whose?" she asked, trying to get what she could. Every little bit of time saved might help.

He stared at her, wild-eyed and uncertain, and she realized that she neither looked nor sounded like the sort of folks he was used to dealing with. What he saw was a black woman, possibly thirty or about that, perhaps five five or so in her bare feet, weighing in at over two hundred pounds, with a huge, thick mane of woolly black hair and big brown eyes that looked far older than the rest of her.

"I'm Brandy Horowitz, Company Station Manager here," she told him. "You're in my house near the station. You came in without triggering our alarms, cut and frostbitten. A doctor who's retained by the Company has looked at you, but nobody else knows you're here."

He hesitated a moment, still a bit wild-eyed and uncertain. "Says you, Madam." He paused a moment, frowning. "Did you say your name was *Horowitz*?"

She nodded.

"Different sort of world you must have here," he commented dryly, seeming to get hold of himself. "You say you are a station manager? Then I must use your master communications system immediately."

"This is just a minor stop," she told him. "No real traffic. This is less a real station than just a security post for a weak spot. This place got misused a bit much a few years back so we're keeping it closed down—or so we thought. We ain't got no big installation here, not even a direct link up the line. We got to go inside and up to the switch to do that. Ain't been no need for much more. My security manager's up there now lettin' the Company know about the breach."

That worried him. "No direct communications. Blast! How many people do you have here?"

"Normally there'd be several, but right now, inside the house, there's just you, me, and my young son. On the grounds my live-in staff is here but that's just Diane in the security shack and Cal, who's a kind of foreman and handyman."

He was appalled. "That's *it*? Two women, a kid, and a cowboy?"

She bristled. "No need for much more here, Mister. It's just a little station on a weak point for convenience sake—the closest big one is like three thousand miles from here on the other side of the country—with no cargo access. And don't you sell us women short."

"Oh, I never sell women, and never sell short," he responded, a bit flip. He tried to sit up, grimaced, and settled back down again. "I assume you at least have a security system on this house?"

She nodded. "Good one, too. But we thought the one in the woods was even better so don't count on this one."

He thought for a moment. "What about the Company here? Does it have full operations?"

"You better believe it! They're into everything, as always."

"If I could just get out of this bed to ring them . . ."

"You don't have to," she told him, then left and returned with one of the Company's cheap plug-in

22

handset telephones. She plugged the cord into the modular outlet, then handed it to him. He watched her do it, fascinated, as if he'd never seen a phone with a modular plug before, then studied the one-piece phone.

"How do you turn it on?" he asked her.

"It's on. Just push the buttons with the number I tell you and you should get through to the eastern branch. There's always somebody on duty there."

He did as instructed, then listened and shook his head. "No sound. Nothing."

She took it from him, checked, and it was definitely dead. She wasn't worried—yet. These cheap phones gave out for no reason all the time. When she checked the solid, better phone in the master bedroom, though, and found it dead as well, she began to worry. She hit the intercom and was relieved when Diane answered.

"Our visitor's awake," she told the security officer, who otherwise was the one who cared for the horses around here, "but the phone's dead. Can't call out."

"I've checked it—they've been calling in regularly until a half hour ago. I checked the CB to see what the townies had and discovered that phone service is generally out throughout the area. I reported it to the Company over the ham radio— even there the static is awful—and they are concerned, but it doesn't appear sinister."

Brandy frowned. "Maybe not to them, but comin' when it does . . . You or Stan check to see why we didn't know our visitor come through until he showed up?"

"Yes, but no help. Everything seems to be working normally. Even if for some reason we didn't get the energizing bell here the trip on the top of the fence should have gone when he came over it. Hopefully Stan will bring back a couple of system analysts to check it out."

"Well, you keep in touch with Philadelphia on the ham radio and keep yourself sealed in there and monitoring." What they called the security "shack" was actually a bunker, well underground and almost a self-contained apartment, and about as secure as a nuclear missile launch site. That wasn't really to keep an enemy out, although it would serve for that in this case, but rather to hide anything that the locals weren't supposed to wonder about from prying eyes. She had a thought. "Could you patch the intercom into the ham radio? This fellow's got somethin' real important to tell the Company."

"Too garbled for that. We've tried that before with the ham microphone. It's one of those things that should have been thought of but wasn't. I could relay his message, though."

She nodded. "I'll see." She switched off and started up stairs, then got a small bout of dizziness and then a couple of uncontrollable yawns. She wasn't in shape for no sleep all night any more, and she was dead on her feet.

Bond, however, was having none of it. "It's rather complex and I still don't know half of it myself," he told her. "It would just cause more trouble and confusion if I couldn't go back and forth with somebody who knew what he was talking about. And I'm feeling very tired and very weak right now."

She nodded. "Want to tell me what you know, or something of it? I used to be line security myself.

My husband and I have handled many big cases for the Company, including the Directors. We ain't amateurs. You was mumblin' something about the maze."

He looked surprised. "I was? Oh, dear." He thought a moment. "I'll give you a little, just for insurance sake, although I rather think that the less you know the safer you'll be."

"I'll take the chance. It's what they pay me for."

He sighed. "All right. For close to a year now we've had indications that someone has been coming and going between various worlds without going through the switch points, and coming out at places where there are no Company stations."

She frowned. "How's that possible?"

"That was the point. The evidence was there but you couldn't get anyone to take it seriously because it *isn't* possible. The old method, shipping people between switch points in fake cargo containers using the cargo line, is blocked now, and in any event they still had to use our stations. I was one of a number of agents assigned to check it out anyway and it took me months to get any real leads. After a long while of monitoring energy pulses and finally getting a couple of people to follow, I managed to get inside one of their own substations. What I discovered was frightening. Someone else has a labyrinth of their own."

That was startling. "Wait a minute. It'd take more power than could possibly be snitched. They told me once that this one was powered by some kind of gadget that fed on the sun itself in a universe where there weren't no decent planets. Who would have the kind of people and machines to do that?"

"They didn't. The power comes from our own grid. What they built were hidden additional switch points and then sidings to whatever worlds they wished. Whole sections of line all over not on any map. Weak points too minor for the Company to bother with or on worlds the Company hadn't gone into yet were developed. If you didn't know the switches were there you could neither see nor detect them, and the drain on the system power is not enough to show up on the power meters. They've been quite clever."

She was appalled, although it explained a lot. Nobody built something like that in a few years. Nobody. That was the work of decades at least, and real long-term planning. It had to be part of that old operation they'd thought they'd broken. That was how and why they were able to go from point to point without ever meeting a security man. And that cube where they'd ambushed and shot Sam . . . A hidden switch point, maybe? Then they shut it down and the facet simply goes to the world where it's supposed to.

"This is big," she told him. "We got to tell the Company this."

"I did," he responded. "I told them what I've told you. They refused to believe it, refused to believe that it was even possible. They said the sort of resources needed to build such a network and remain undetected all this time were beyond concealment. Only the Company could have done it and there were no records or expenses or anything. They said the only fellow who could possibly have managed it was a traitorous former Director and that they'd not only had him isolated, they'd drained everything he knew from his mind ahead

26

of that. They demanded incontrovertible proof or it was suggested that perhaps I'd been in this business too long and should take a holiday."

She nodded. The iron-bound arrogance of the Company was its weakest point. Always had been. It had been obvious almost from the start which director had been the bad guy. If it'd been a murder mystery then unmasking the villain would have been a snap. The trouble was, he was high up, one of the ultimate bosses, and no one would believe that such a one could betray the Company or beat the Company's security unless he could be caught and unmasked with his finger on the trigger and in the act of committing treason. She had solved it, but it was Sam who figured out how to nail the bastard.

"Maybe he didn't know—any more. With them mind control things they got you can get parts of anything erased. If he had set it up and then got it erased so it never showed, then nobody'd know—but his gang could use it. Maybe just a few key folks in the gang that never got caught. I'm pretty sure most nobody knew about this even if they was usin' it. That bastard was so smug and arrogant himself he violated the biggest rule of bein' a crook—he got a gang workin' for him that was smarter than he was. They're all a pack of racists who think that they're the be-all and end-all of human creation. And, hell, he wouldn't *have* to build 'em. If he got to the big data bank and simply erased the records of certain built but not operational switches and sidin's, then they wouldn't show up at all on the maps. Damn! This is *big!*" *I wish Sam was here for this*, she added to herself.

He nodded. "Yes. A herd of elephants running

amok on the system and nobody notices. But now I *have* proof. Or, at least, I can *show* them proof. I know the location of a siding and how and when it operates. I was discovered. They can shut it down but they jolly well can't unbuild the thing. I got in through a casino sub-basement private station on the Riviera. I tripped some alarms, and they were waiting for me. I was on the run into the main branch when I was cornered and had to take the first facet out that I could find. Here, blast it." He realized how that sounded.

"Nothing personal, dear lady," he added quickly, "but if this had been a main station then it would be all over for them."

She nodded. But it wasn't a main station, and it was isolated and not well manned. And if they got Bond before Bond got into Company protection, then they'd still be safe and secure. That meant they would be coming in, if they weren't already here, and fast. Tonight—and probably in numbers.

"Get some rest," she told him. "If we can hold out tonight there'll be plenty of help coming tomorrow."

Damn! She was so tired and it looked like one of those nights she hadn't had since Dash was a baby. At least, maybe, he'd sleep through all this. She cut the lights in the living room, then went to the front window and looked out. It was a stark, eerie scene at night, with the yellowish floodlights casting an ugly soft glow over the snow, making the structures and shadows look grotesque and monstrous. All looked, however, quiet.

She turned, went back into the library and opened the compartment to the wall safe and twirled the combination. Once open, she took out a large box and then closed the safe again, putting the box down in front of her. She opened it and removed from its form fitted foam a large but light pistol resembling a German automatic. On it she placed a small sight-like device that more resembled a tiny motor of some sort, screwing it in, then checking it. She set the device according to a click stop dial, then examined the rather standard-looking clips. She removed one, untroubled by the fact that it appeared to have no bullets in it and no way at its shiny top to insert them, pushed a small button, and got a tiny red symbol in a window in the clip.

Satisfied, she pushed the clip into the pistol and stuck it half inside her jeans. Then, checking the security panel one more time, she turned out all of the downstairs lights and then went to the intercom.

"Diane, I think we're gonna have visitors tryin' to get this guy back. Radio Philadelphia that we will probably be under attack shortly. Get Sam on the radio if you can. He knows this place better'n anybody. You tell 'em to call up the line and get Stan back here with reinforcements, and watch it just comin' into the entry point 'cause it's probably covered. Where's Cal?"

"Back up in the loft, probably. I'll notify him."

"No heroics. No use in him getting killed. Just tell him to lay low and keep outta sight and in touch and help if he can, understand?"

"Yes, Ma'am. You want me to come up and help you out?"

"*No!* You stay locked in there 'til somebody from the Company with the U.S. Marines attached gets in here. You're the only way we can talk to anybody

29

now. Call it in—U[now!]"

This was getting to be a real pain and fast. As bad or worse than the old days. She also had twin concerns, neither involving herself. On the one hand, she needed to protect this Bond character, whether he was anything like the fictional one or not, and she had real concerns for Dash. If anything happened to him, or if he woke up to find dead bodies around, he might never get over it. As it stood, she hoped she could hold out and that he'd just sleep right through it. Hell, Dash was the kind that could sleep through World War II.

She took her position again to the side looking out the front window. The back was potentially more vulnerable but the drifts against it were high and there weren't that many ways in except through solid doors. It sounded like the wind was whipping up out there and that'd make it maybe five below with a stiff wind to get it down further and blow up new powder, and there wasn't a whole hell of a lot of cover and protection out there if you wanted to get to the house itself. Not even Eskimos could afford to just sit out there in that stuff and bide their time, and the odds were that whoever was chasing him was no better dressed for this kind of weather than Bond had been. Unless, of course, they had pushed him in a guided chase to this very point, where they knew it was lightly defended and remote and without direct Company access.

She had a sudden, horrible thought. What if it was Carlos and he picked this of all spots to push Bond into 'cause Bond wasn't the only thing he wanted here?

One of the floodlights suddenly went out, then

another. She didn't wait for the series and got to the intercom.

"I think somebody's shootin' out the floods," she told him. "They can't wait much longer in this weather. We need help and fast!"

"I can't get through to them," Diane reported. "I've been trying since we talked a few minutes ago. The ham channels are jammed with static— you can't hear anything but noise and I'm sure I don't sound any better."

"Try the CB. They may not have thought of that," Brandy told her. "Get somebody to call the cops. Say we got armed prowlers."

"I'll try. Hold on." There was a pause for what seemed several minutes, then, "No good. I'm getting nothing but dead air, like I'm not on antenna at all. We're cut off." She paused a moment. "Uh oh. I'm getting energy surges and activation sequences like mad. The alarm system's working down there now for all the good it'll do us. Or maybe it's Cal with reinforcements."

"Maybe, but I ain't gonna bet the farm on it. Look, I'm gonna keep the intercom on open, so you can hear what's happenin' here. You keep tryin' to get through to anybody and I don't care who you talk to or what you got to tell 'em, understand?"

"O.K. At least if it's going off here it's going off and registering at both switches, too. That should bring some security people here pretty quick."

Could be. But if they had to shoot their way through it might take a real long while.

She crept back upstairs, staying out of any light, and went back to the guest bedroom. Bond had lapsed back into sleep, perhaps a more peaceful kind. She thought about waking him up, but he wouldn't be much good overall, not with those painful, bandaged feet. He wasn't going anywhere, and so what could he do? Shoot a couple before they shot him? Maybe the guy from the movies could do it all, but the more you looked at this guy the less you saw him doing that kind of thing.

She checked once more on Dash, then went back downstairs into the dark. About the only thing you could see was a couple of the little lights from the satellite system that always sent power and a little heat back to the dish to keep it from freezing up and the little red lights from a couple of backup battery flashlights plugged into the walls. The one thing they couldn't do was cut the power into here. That was fed from lines deep underground to the substation itself and wasn't part of the regular central Pennsylvania power system. And if they managed to cut that they'd also shut down the substation, leaving them trapped here and their cronies down below in the Labyrinth sitting ducks for an inevitable quick security team attack.

They, too, were taking a big chance. That thought helped sustain her. They had limits and their clock was running. They couldn't sustain this blackout for long, and they couldn't take all night to attack due to the weather and the uncertainty of how close reinforcements might be.

She heard something on the side and pulled out the pistol, then moved to the source of the sound. She might have expected them to try her greenhouse first. All that glass probably looked real tempting, but the shutters were down now for extra insulation and heat retention and if they tried cutting through the outer glass as it sounded like and hit those shutters . . .

There was a sudden flash and a scream and the sound of electricity surging through vibrating metal. She couldn't see anything, but she was pretty damned sure that somebody had just been fried.

They were far too smart to try the doors, and now the greenhouse had proven nasty—and they hadn't even hit the bad traps yet had they managed to bypass the shutters. Next they'd try the frontal assault. She walked back to the living room and thought she saw shadows through the living room picture window even though it was pitch dark. Well, she didn't need light.

Certain that Cal was either captured, dead, or well away, she brought up the pistol and let it do its thing. It moved her hand, faster than she, and fired on its own. The "bullets" were tiny electrical pulses that showed dull red in the dark. They struck and went right through the window and she heard a couple of men's voices cry out. The pistol stopped firing and she had full control again.

The reflex action when fired upon through a window was to fire back. Some of the men outside did just that with weapons similar to hers. The special "glass" was strictly one way for that; their shots bounced off. She hoped the ricochets nailed some of their buddies but they probably just went harmlessly off into the air where they dissipated. She wondered if they'd try real bullets. They'd mess up the window but a submachine gun sprayed on there would produce wonderfully devastating ricochets—for the gunners. They might have figured that this was a lightly manned and very minor and isolated substation, but the guy who lived here made his living protecting Company property. Sam had warned that there was no system that was unbeatable or didn't have some weak points, but what you bought was time. Time to get help, or time to be rescued. She was in a nice, warm house she knew well. They were out in cold and wind bitter enough to give a man frostbite just walking a mile in it improperly clothed and protected. More important, they had only one exit and it was the equivalent of a highway with no-place to hide from passing cars. If they were discovered, it was all over and they were trapped.

Clearly the men outside were getting frustrated fast. They weren't even trying the conventional doors and windows, since if even the greenhouse and the living room picture window were traps they knew what the usual places must be like.

She was almost beginning to enjoy this and anticipate their actions. Next they'd either try and find a ladder in the barn and get to the roof or they'd try chopping through someplace or, maybe, if they got desperate enough, they might try start-ing a fire. She certainly hoped so. The exterior fire suppression system would spray enough water to coat them with what would be hard ice in a very short time.

The one thing she'd always hated about this area was the bitter cold, the feeling of never being really warm. Now, suddenly, she found herself feeling quite good about bitter cold, snow, and ice. They were allies that even the best security system couldn't provide on its own.

They did in fact seem to be all around, and not at all reticent about shouting orders. She didn't rec-ognize the language but that was to be expected.

34

The odds were that they spoke something beyond anyone's ability on this world to understand. Of course, to her it kind of sounded like the Chinese army.

That thought did worry her a little. The house was protected from casual attack, from people wanting in even if they had the usual tools and weapons. It was not a house built by the Company, though, but an old estate house that had been in the hands of one family for almost two centuries before the last heir, a writer, committed suicide here and it was sold to the Company through a blind. A bazooka, for example, would still blow in that steel door.

She decided to retreat upstairs and let the first floor fend for itself, something it was doing quite well.

Bond stirred. "What is happening?" he managed.

"They're here. They got us cut off for a little bit and they been tryin' to get through the security system, so far with heavy losses," she told him, some pride in her voice. "Still, they been awful quiet all of a sudden for a fairly long time. Either they gave up, or got in the barn to warm up a little, or they're settin' up and plannin' somethin'."

"Probably the latter. They won't give up. They can't. They will die first. There is a drug—most of them are slaves to it. If they return without me, or without proof of my death, they won't get it and they will die horribly. You can not believe what lengths they will go to."

She felt a knot in her stomach. "Yes, I can, too. They once had me on that shit."

"And you kicked the habit?" He sounded more

than impressed. "Oh, of course, that was the old drug where you had a chance. Organic stuff from way up the line. This is all synthetic, much nastier, but you know their desperation."

She nodded. The idea of a drug even more powerful than the most powerful ever known before was her worst nightmare come true. She had become a whore, a slave, a double agent, and more under that old one, and it had taken everything she had and all the knowledge and skills of the Company's super medical technology to break her free of dependence on it. Most never could break it; the treatment either broke them or they lived on a level of it rather than try. If it wasn't for Sam she couldn't have, either. The worst part was how utterly selfish the addiction made you. You'd rob, betray, even kill innocents, even those you loved, to sustain it, but never once did she think of killing herself because that would deny her the next fix. Those poor devils out there would get in or die trying.

"The rest are probably Ginzu," he told her. "A fanatical warrior cult that considers a commission a debt of honor and who would prefer death to dishonor. They are quite skilled with knives that they create themselves and which they can use to inflict extreme torture. I escaped from them, which is where my wounds come from. I should prefer to die rather than fall into their hands again."

She nodded. Suddenly there was a series of thumps from the roof, and she thought fast. Normally the roof was slick and she could make it slicker, but right now it was piled up with snow and there might be a possible footing. Right up top was an old widow's walk with attic access. Even it was electrified and fortified just in case, but it was also far weaker, being original to the house. But if they could get in the attic . . .

There was the sound of muffled blasts from the roof. Conventional shotgun, it sounded like—maybe Cal's from the barn. Loaded up and at close range it would blow that old attic door right off its hinges.

There was the sudden sound of movement, and then two sharp, piercing cries of pain. At least they hadn't broken the energy grid and were paying the price.

"Do you think they got in?" Bond asked worriedly.

She shook her head. "No way of knowin' without stickin' my neck up there which I ain't about to do. On the other hand, I don't hear no footsteps on the ceilin', neither. Let me get back in the hall. There ain't but two ways down from there without choppin' holes."

She stood in the center and waited, the only light coming from the night light in Dash's room. By God, if they got in and headed for Dash they was gonna have to roll over her dead body!

Suddenly there was the soft sound of something moving, a creaking sound down the hall at the end nearest Dash, and she felt a sudden chill as some of the outside cold rushed excitedly into the warmth of the house. They *had* got in, damn them!

They made a fair amount of noise as they moved the trap up and away, and she armed the pistol again and aimed it right at the opening. Anybody coming down there was gonna get smeared.

Suddenly the pistol jerked in her hand and she

saw the red tracers head for the opening and heard a cry. She moved a little forward to give it a slightly better angle when suddenly something powerful came up behind her and grabbed her, knocking the pistol from her hand and sending it skidding along the hall.

She turned and flipped the man with one motion, but he retained control and somersaulted and landed on his feet. He was a strange looking fellow all in black with a black mask over all but his eyes. She was a little out of practice, but she knew her judo and karate, but she had the uneasy feeling that this guy knew a lot more and had lots of practice.

Suddenly there were more on her; they'd drawn her with the one trap door while coming down the other! She struggled and twisted but suddenly there was pressure on her neck and her whole body seemed to explode first in pain and then in numbness, and she dropped to the floor.

Curiously, she was fully conscious, able to hear everything, but she was unable to move and her glasses had been knocked off in the attack and she couldn't see a damned thing without them.

The black-clad men spoke that curious sing-song while making it sound like gutter speech, but suddenly there was another presence nearby, and one of the warriors spoke to it in heavily accented but understandable English.

"Bond?" asked a husky, eerie voice that might be male or female but was certainly chilling.

"In room dere," one of the warriors responded. "Him bad hurt. Lady here out with *quinsin*."

"Check downstairs," ordered the chilling voice. "See if you can locate the master security control and turn it off. If we can go out the front door it will save us having to haul him out the way we came in." There was a moment's pause. "By Yusha! This is a bitter cold place! The heat feels good but we must hurry. Any sign of the man?"

"No. Small boy in room dere only other one in house."

There was more sing-song from downstairs, and the warrior talking to the stranger said, "Find system. Hard to figure but can bypass. We go any time now."

"Good. I am anxious to be away from here. Too bad the man isn't here. I shouldn't want him desperately on us."

Strange. She swore she heard the sounds of vehicles driving up outside and doors slamming. She tried to move but she couldn't. Her eyelids and her breathing were about the only things she could control. All else was numbness.

"All right, let's wrap it up. They'll be coming through any minute now and I don't want to be caught here. Recover your dead and wounded but leave the others. Leave her, too, just the way she is."

"But that leave too much! You have Company up ass pretty quick!"

"I think not. I just want to make certain that both of them come—and cautiously." The voice paused. "Take the kid," it added.

No! Please God! No! she tried to shout, but she couldn't move a muscle.

2.

Playing with a Marked Deck

Sam Horowitz was no dashing private eye except perhaps in his own mind and in the occasionally romanticized mind of Brandy. He was five ten, well over two hundred pounds, a small-boned sort of man who dramatized a pot belly, which he most certainly had. He also had a pronounced Roman nose, small deep blue eyes, and what was not graying on his head just wasn't there any more. He was, in fact, the innocuous, bland-looking sort of fellow you'd never look twice at on the street or in a shop, which was why he was a pretty fair private detective and security agent.

Aldrath Prang, on the other hand, would stand out in most places. He looked to be a man in his thirties, perhaps, in superb physical condition, even though in reality he was well past seventy. A big man, well over six feet and muscled like a god, his complexion was golden and his features resembled Polynesians more than any other racial type on this Earth. He was not, however, from this Earth, but one of the heads of the great corporation and its present CEO and former security director. It had never been known that Prang had left the isolated and nearly impenetrable home world of the Company since attaining Board rank, and certainly it was unthinkable that a CEO would

40

do so, ever. And for anything less, that might be the case, but this was both personal and life or death.

Sam flicked the little recorder and Prang joined him. Together, they listened to all that had transpired, at least the upstairs part.

"Bright lady," Prang said, impressed. "They never even noticed the thing."

Sam nodded. "So we have a lot to go on, anyway. At least we know more than they think we do, which is always the best way to start a counter operation." He sighed. "This bastard was right, too, Aldrath. He's got the only two people I really care about and his type doesn't give me much play. I have to assume the worst, and that means I'll be after them until they are exposed and fried all the way to the top."

"I'm not so sure, old friend," Prang responded, thinking. "You have had a bad shock and extreme frustration and you must have all your powers and wits about you. Listen to him again. This—person —doesn't want you that way. You are dangerous to them. The only man in history to have ever caught and convicted a Corporate board member. They are afraid of you, and I don't think that was put on. As you say, there's no evidence that they knew the recorder was here, or that Diane could also pick up and record just about everything inside and out. There is more here than getting Bond before he could lead us to them. That was the catalyst, but only the catalyst. They clearly knew who lived here and they clearly picked their own spot. There is more to this than simply a chase after a man who knows too much. Something darker is afoot as well."

Sam nodded. He felt cold, empty inside, though,

and he felt only anger and a strong desire for vengeance. He sighed, got hold of himself, and asked, "How is Brandy?"

"The same. There are certain pressure points which only an expert can find as you well know. Depending on the pressure and the degree of exactitude the paralysis may be temporary or permanent. Fortunately, thanks to the recorder, we know it's a Ginzu move. I have summoned the Guild Master and he should be here some time today. I fear I was a bit forceful with him. I told him that if his Guild was going to commit treason against the Company then we could well give up the steak knives import-export business and manufacture them ourselves, and that to insure things and perhaps make an example we might also exterminate all life on their world. I think he'll come."

Sam snapped out of it and stared at Prang. "Uh—yeah. Um, Aldrath? Would you *really* do that?"

"Of course. We are already manufacturing them right here, in New England somewhere, I believe."

"I didn't mean the damned knives. Would you exterminate a whole world?"

Prang shrugged. "It's been done. Takes a unanimous vote of the Board, but if we have this level of treason it's simple self defense. The ones who were here knew this, as did their employer. That's why they collected all their own dead and wounded, leaving only the others. Those bodies would lead us to believe that all the attackers were like them and we'd be off chasing helpless drug slaves rather than the warriors who have no such excuse."

Sam thought a while, then sat down at a writing

desk, tape recorder in front of him, and began to selectively play back the events of the night. He was deep in thought, playing small sections over and over. Finally, he sighed and went to see Prang again.

"I think I got part of it," he told the CEO. "Different parts. The easy part first. It was very faint, and maybe your lab people can really bring it out, but I heard at least one car door slam after they carried their prey out the front door. That's why we didn't catch them in the Labyrinth. They didn't go out the way they came in. They were ready and they had somebody come and pick them up and drive them away. I bet if you really enhance the background and filter out the rest you'll hear several vehicles, maybe enough for all of them. That means they might still be here, on this Earth. There's no way they could have used a station after the full security alert."

"You heard Bond saying they had their own stations. Almost a parallel network, as difficult and frightening as it is to believe."

"Yeah, but not here. I mean, the Labyrinth's been extended to perhaps a million parallel worlds, but the Company has developed only a very few of them. Most just aren't worth the trouble, and the others we just don't have the full manpower and resources to control as yet. That's not true here. Here we've explored every inch, surveyed, mapped, you name it. We know and have every weak point covered and monitored. That's why they had to come in using our substation. If they had their own they'd have had what they needed for a lot less costly assault on this place. They sure as hell knew where it was and maybe even set Bond up to get here. How else can you explain the pick-up cars around here in bad weather in the middle of winter? No, the odds are they're still here, someplace. And while the bunch of 'em might sneak out over a long period in various stations, the odds of them getting a five-year-old kid through are pretty slim with our system."

"They seem pretty good at beating our system," Prang noted.

"Maybe, but they either didn't know or they forgot one thing. Dash is unique, genetically and otherwise. This is the only parallel Earth where Brandy and I even got married and we checked, remember? The only one. So Dash is one of the rarest of all individuals—a kid with no doubles, no duplicates. His genetic markers are unique. They put him through the Labyrinth and they're gonna get flagged."

Prang thought about it. "I hate to say this, old friend, and I hope you do not take offense, but have you considered that they might do away with him?"

"I thought about it, but it doesn't make sense, at least for now. They didn't take him for revenge, they took him for insurance. You don't burn your insurance policy, you stash it in a safe and secure place and make sure it's readily available and all in good order. No, he's alive, probably pretty pissed off, somewhere on this Earth. And he'll stay that way as long as he serves their purpose. In fact, I would say he's not just insurance, he's a bargaining chip. You heard them—they want me for some reason. Want me enough to blow cover on a world they apparently control."

Prang nodded. "That's probably true. Still, even

if they keep him here this world is a big and heavily populated place. People vanish all the time never to be seen or heard from again, and with far less resources or resolve than these. Still, we will start the worldwide search at once."

He sighed, then continued. "We haven't traced where the dead men come from as yet, by the way, but we're narrowing the possibilities. We've also shipped a couple to pathology because of Bond's comment on their being slaves to some new and even more horrible drug. I already have a suspicion as to what it might be, though, or what it might be derived from."

Sam's eyebrows went up. "Oh?"

"Most people couldn't break free of the old one. Even if they could be physically purged they would go mad without it or without something that dampened the internal biochemistry so it didn't go wild when the organism lost control. The attempt was to find a substance that could be easily and cheaply manufactured, could not be transferred like the original drug to others, and yet would provide what was needed should we take them off the old organic drug. That proved easier to do than we'd expected. It's quite simple to design a drug and tailor it to whatever characteristics you want. It's all a matter of biochemistry, nothing more, but it would allow the victims to retake their places in a more normal society and clear our own medical wards and the retreat world where we'd exiled so many."

Sam nodded. "Like methadone that's used here to allow heroin addicts to get normal lives."

"Yes, I'm familiar with that one. Of course, you remain addicted and you must have your dosage, so you're still on a string, and, in fact, it still produces many of the pleasure center effects of the original, but it's cheap and not communicable, as it were."

"Yeah, but that can't be what had these guys on the hook. If it's cheap and easy to produce then they got a way out."

"Perhaps. If they *know* there's a way out, or alternate and more benign sources of supply. At least I hope that's the case. It means we might be able to get these people away from these criminals and turn them into our allies. But——"

At that moment a young security officer wearing a thick parka and snow boots entered the room. "Pardon, Excellency, but the Ginzu Master is here. He does not appear in a very pleasant mood."

"Well, neither am I!" Prang snapped. "Show him in!"

The man who entered was small, almost tiny, and very frail-looking, with an almost cartoon sinister Oriental face complete with snow-white Fu Manchu moustache. His head was shaved, and he wore a simple black tunic with a gold sash at the waist and sandals. It was little wonder he was less than pleased. This guy was dressed for summer in a tea garden. Still, he didn't look cold, or frostbitten, or anything else but just plain mad.

"What is the meaning of this?" the Ginzu master demanded to know in a low, gruff voice.

"I'm going to play you a recording," Prang told him, unimpressed with his anger. "At the end of it you may remain indignant only at your peril. Then we will discuss a young lady currently paralyzed in bed upstairs—and far deeper matters as well."

The little man was indeed angry, but he listened,

and what he heard he liked even less. Finally he said, "Enough!"

"You recognize the voices?"

"The quality is too poor for that. The only one close enough to get a real identity on is the one speaking bad English, and he could be a dozen people at least. I assume you will supply me with voice prints when you make them. I will then be able to tell you for certain."

"I do not merely want to know who they are," Prang told him firmly. "And I do not want them flayed in classic Ginzu fashion. Not yet. When we are through with them, then you can do what you wish, but first we must know who that other voice belongs to and how they were recruited for this treasonous work."

"I will give you all that when I find them," the Master responded. "They can and will will themselves to death before your machines and probes can even be turned on, but they can not do so with me. You see, I can control which Hell they go to when they die, and they know this. To die under your questioning would be a release. To die in my presence would avail them nothing."

It was said so matter of factly that Sam was certain that at least the Master believed it—and if *he* believed it, then the warriors would believe it, too. If the Master wasn't in on it, if he wasn't putting them on, he'd find the answers.

"Very well," Prang sighed. "All that you require will be provided and I will postpone a vote until we have information. But we can tolerate nothing less than the full truth in this. Otherwise we must assume that there are no loyal friends of the Company left in your domain."

It was a simple, understated, and rather elegant threat, Sam thought. "Now—Brandy?"

"Oh, yes. You heard what was done. Can you bring her out of it?"

"Depends," the Master responded curtly. "Let me take a look at her." And, with that, he proceeded up the stairs and turned correctly towards the master bedroom.

"How did he know where she was?" Sam asked, wondering.

"Forty years ago I learned to stop asking things like that," responded Aldrath Prang. "Come on— let's see what's what."

"Maybe I should have *him* find Dash," Sam suggested, and they mounted the stairs.

The Ginzu Master was poking and probing Brandy's neck as they entered the room. He rose, turned, and said, "I would flay alive the one who did this."

Sam felt sudden panic. "You mean it's not reversible?"

"No, of course not. I mean that it *is* reversible," he grumbled. "It is just—amateurish. Incompetent. Either you use *quinsin* to totally paralyze an enemy or you use the sixth degree maneuver to have them come out of it in a specified amount of time. This is neither. I have done what I can here. She will be able to eat and move her head, and very slowly all of the body functions will return to her, but it will be a slow process and she might not be totally right for weeks."

He felt sudden tremendous relief. *She was going to be all right! She was going to come out of it!*

With that thought, his mind switched back into its more analytical mode, but the interest and the questions were not clinical. This was personal.

"Tell me—would you say that a Ginzu did that? Or perhaps someone who had been taught Ginzu holds and pressure points and perhaps wanted to make us *think* it was Ginzu."

Prang gave Sam a quizzical look. "But on the tape Bond said it was Ginzu."

"No, he said he had escaped from Ginzu," Sam reminded him. "That's not the same thing. We don't know where Bond was or what he was doing. We *assumed* the cause and effect—he'd escaped from the Ginzu, therefore the Ginzu did this. What do the Ginzu who work for the Company do except make and export knives?"

"Knives!" the Master hissed. "Mere cheap imitations! Why they only even guarantee them a mere ten years! We have nothing to do with them."

"Except collecting a royalty," Prang noted. "It's a licensing thing that allows them to maintain their private lands and school. But to answer your question, we do employ Ginzu for temporary security."

"Huh? Like what?"

"Well, under normal circumstances, they'd be in charge of my security right now. The only reason they aren't is because they are involved and thus suspect in this. That's only one example. When we must secure a facet for some purpose we use them, and we also use them to guard maintenance and repair projects just in case, since the kind of things we'd be dealing with there are some of the Company's most classified secrets."

Sam thought about that. "Then if they were discredited you'd have to find alternate security. They'd be pulled off all the nasty jobs immediately and effectively neutralized. Someone just might be being very clever here, Aldrath."

"Possibly," Prang replied, noting the smugness of the Master at Sam's theory, "but we can take no chances. Master, how hard would it be to learn that nerve paralyzing trick to this degree and perhaps sufficient others, including some of the language, to pass as Ginzu?"

"Some training by a Ginzu warrior would be required," the Ginzu Master told him. "Such things as these are easy to learn, difficult to master, and require constant practice and supervision, but it is possible. The language—less likely. They might be ones who washed out of the training regimen—only one in perhaps eighty makes it even to Third Degree—or they might be from a parallel world where the Art does not exist but my people do. It is hard to tell from the tape."

"Work on that angle," Prang told him. "All of your people are to be on this exclusively. I want to know who these people were, where they came from, the lot."

"That goes without saying," the Master responded. "The honor of our Order and Art demands it."

It wasn't enough for Sam. "Now we have to find out why as well as who. This is more than Bond. I feel certain that they'll contact me. They wanted me, that's clear from the tape. They couldn't get me so they took Dash as a hold on me and left Brandy as an example. I'd like to work on that angle."

"Do you wish us to move Brandy to a Company facility for care?" the CEO asked him.

"No. Not unless it's necessary. If you can get

some nurses and the right equipment in here so that someone will be with her, feed her, wash her, all that, and help her get back on her feet when it starts wearing off, I think it'd be better if she stayed here. She can't tell us right now, but I think she'd go nuts with me off all over the place and Dash missing and her in some hospital worlds away.''

"I'll see to it," Prang told him. "As for now, I've already violated three dozen regulations by being here at all and I must get back before I am thrown out because of it. We'll work on all levels—finding the ones who broke in here, using our considerable resources here to find Dash, and also locating and scouting the world from which the dead ones came. I'll make certain you are fully informed.''

Sam nodded. "We'll need a good crew out here and fast, too. I want to know why the security system on the substation failed to block unauthorized access and why it didn't flag security up here. Until we hear something about Dash, that's all I can do.''

Aldrath Prang paused and looked at him a bit strangely. "You know, for a man whose only child is kidnapped and in the hands of who knows what villainy, you are remarkably calm and composed. I had expected to have to keep you from tearing after them with weapons blazing.''

The detective shrugged. "Tearing after who? After all this time, Aldrath, I'm a pro. I have to be. Amateurs get their clients killed, their quarries killed, and themselves killed as well. You're right —if I had anybody, particularly that whispery voiced bastard, in my hands right now I would be slowly and cheerfully choking him to death, but I don't. If I knew who had Dash, I'd go after them—but I don't. I have no control over these things. The best way to handle this now is to control whatever I can and do whatever I can coldly, as if this was just another case for some other client. Frankly, this whole thing stinks to high heaven. Until I get their game figured out, I'm going to play my game."

Prang clapped him on the shoulder. "Take care, my friend. These are very dark forces that come and go through our system and which mock our 'foolproof' security efforts. We have a new enemy, and we do not know his face."

Sam scratched his chin and sighed. "Or an old one. This whole new career of mine has involved peeling an onion. Every time you remove a layer, you find another, smellier one beneath."

Sam Horowitz waited until the big shots were gone and the new medical staff had checked in to see to Brandy. Only then did he go into his study, which they hadn't touched, sat down, turned on the personal computer on one desk, and called up his special name and numbers file, the one that you had to have a lot of passwords to get to and which would give you a lot of wrong information even then if you didn't know how to use it just right.

It was going to be a long afternoon of phone calls. Lieutenant McCabe of the Pennsylvania State Police might be the best to call first, but there was also Louie "Cement Shoes" Gigliani in Philadelphia, Al "The Turtle" Snyder in Pittsburgh, and many more. Local cops and middle level gangsters in five states, all of whom owed him one or ones he wouldn't mind owing. It was time to call in all his chips on this one.

By eleven that night the various phone lines began to bring him a great deal of information. Three mini-vans had been rented in Harrisburg by a company called Villahermosa Ltd., which turned out to be a New York based subsidiary of an import-export business chartered in the Dominican Republic. No one seemed too clear on what they imported and exported but a security squad checked their New York offices and found an empty warehouse with no particular signs it had ever been used as more than a garage and a mail drop. Other Company security was now checking the other end down in Santo Domingo but it was unlikely they'd have much luck before morning, when places with records and people who could get at them were open and available.

The mini-vans were of greater interest since as of now they had not yet been turned back in in Harrisburg or in any other rental location. The company credit card they'd used was valid and active, though; a call down to Florida resulted in his computer printer spewing out a very long list of transactions on that account the oldest of which was only five months ago, when they had leased the New York warehouse. The credit report also gave the name of Villahermosa's New York bank, and before morning he'd have a list of all the checks they'd written, to whom, and when.

As he'd expected, all three driver's licenses used in the rental were total forgeries. Hell, one of 'em was to Mr. Juan Valdez of Colombia. Maybe they exported coffee or something. Of course, number two was driven by Mr. Pancho Villa of El Paso, and the third was Simon Bolivar of New York. Spanish Harlem, no doubt. These guys weren't even trying

53

hard to disguise their phonyness, and that worried him. It also bothered him that all three were using Hispanic names, and from their descriptions looked it. The rental people usually wouldn't remember anybody in particular, but when you rent three mini-vans on a Spanish-sounding corporation to three South American types in Harrisburg, they tend to notice.

He doubted if the man behind this was anywhere around, or even in this world, but he suspected who it was and he very much wanted to meet him. Preferably in a dark alley of Sam's own choosing. They had never met, but even without all this Sam owed him a very slow, lingering death.

The phony licenses were enough to get an APB out on the vans in all states around Pennsylvania. They didn't want to report the kidnapping; that would bring in the F.B.I., phone taps, and all the rest and might cause a lot of trouble as well as a great many embarrassing questions. But now the cops would be on the lookout for those vans, and even if they'd changed vehicles by now the pursuers would be one step closer.

The checks proved very illuminating as well, particularly when matched against the charge records. Airplane tickets, rental houses, you name it. By morning the grocery stores where these guys had bought food would be canvassed, and within a day he would know more about at least the leaders of this band than they probably knew about themselves.

Within that same period of time, Brandy had started slowly coming out of it. She could move her head, although she had a general headache, and could be hand-fed food and drink. She really wasn't up for much talking, but it was impossible to keep her from doing so and he had to report his progress regularly.

"Sam, I don't understand," she said hoarsely. "I mean, why not take me? Why Dash? God, Sam, he's only a kid!"

"He'll figure out what's going on and play along," Sam tried to assure her. "He's a smart kid, too. As to why him and not you—I'm expecting to learn that in another day or two, after they make us sweat."

"You think they're gonna call?"

"Or something. Dash only has value to us, and even then only if he's alive and well. They want something—apparently from me. Sooner or later they're going to have to ask for it."

He kissed her and left her and walked down the hall where it had all happened. The workmen were even now repairing the attic area and he cursed himself for not having put more up there. There was always a weak point no matter how good the system, damn it!

As usual around the house he was in his stocking feet, and when he turned to go back down stairs he stepped on something and felt real pain shoot through his foot. Hopping to the staircase, he sat down and carefully removed a shard of thick glass which had been just lying in wait for him all this time. He was about to toss it, then stopped, examined it again, and soon forgot that his foot was still bleeding. He crawled around, found more, did some figuring, made it downstairs while limping, and checked again on the downstairs carpet. The results were inconclusive, but he put the small pieces in an envelope and called security. He wanted to know, if possible, just what that glass had come from.

The fact was, he wanted to keep busy and to keep doing all that he could, overlooking nothing. Outwardly he was calm and professional, but inside the fact that Dash was missing had torn him up. The more he slowed down, the more he relaxed, the more he saw Dash in his mind; coloring in the books, playing with his toys, sitting in his Dad's lap while Daddy read him a story . . . Worse, it was nearly impossible to avoid physical signs of the boy even though Sam did avoid his son's room. The toys, large and small, were everywhere, and on the door of his office was a crude sign in block letters in giant green crayon that said "I LOVE YOU DAD." It was the most gut-wrenching thing of all but he couldn't bring himself to touch it.

Deep down, too, there was also some guilt. Guilt that he'd been away when this all happened, although it wasn't too clear what the hell he could have done against them that Brandy didn't. Hell, he almost never carried a gun. He spent part of his police career faking his pistol scores; he never could hit the broad side of a barn with one. And these fancy Company auto-aim jobs scared him shitless; he had a nightmare of flipping one on and having it shoot Dash or Brandy or some other innocent. And Brandy was far better at this karate and judo stuff. He could hold his own against a scared street punk lashing out with fists or a knife but he would be dead meat in two seconds against anybody who knew their stuff.

No, he didn't have all those macho skills. He once got talked into going deer hunting in the area and he'd bagged one; the sight of that beautiful animal, dead by his doing, lying there, thrashing and then dying, still haunted him. He hadn't picked up a gun since.

No, the fun wasn't in squaring off against these guys, it was out-thinking them and out-maneuvering them. It was a mental game, deductive chess, and if you could assemble the puzzle and get the whole picture then any clod could make the collar.

And that was the other guilt pang he had. God help him, if it wasn't for Dash he'd be having the time of his life right now. He'd grown bored and somewhat stale at the pedestrian things he'd been doing the past several years; *this*, now, *this* was his element. But it was a lot easier, and a lot more fun, when the victims were not people you knew and loved, but could be just pieces in the game.

"It is good that war is so terrible lest we become too fond of it." Robert E. Lee had said that. Perhaps, he thought, this is what he meant. I'm being punished now for becoming far too fond of this game.

At about six in the morning he'd dropped into a light and disturbing sleep in his office chair even as information continued to come in on his printers, fax, and other data collectors. The ringing of the phone startled him again to wakefulness, but it was a groggy sort and he wasn't at all clear-headed. Even so, he had the foresight to activate the small system under the phone that would automatically record and tell him the number from which the call was being placed. It was a neat service they were now selling to the phone companies themselves for resale as a point-of-call service to customers.

He picked up the phone. "Sam Horowitz," he said sleepily.

"Ah, Señor Horowitz, you sound like we thought

you would," came a heavily accented soft male voice.

He shook himself awake and ignored the headache. "Go ahead. I've been expecting your call."

"I assume you have the whole set of lines monitored, and perhaps the Company is as well, but it will do you no good," the voice told him. There was a sudden click and the quality of the line shifted a bit, became a little bit noisier. "Our technology has to be better than your technology or we would have been discovered, even caught, long ago." There was another click, and the transmission was suddenly both louder and quieter. Sam reached over and hit a timer at the next click, then stopped at the click after that. Four seconds.

"You have something of great value to me that is of no value to you except as a way to get to me," he said, hoping that made sense. "I want the boy back, unharmed, and in one piece. I assume you didn't take him just to torture me, so you want something."

"Sí—yes, you are most perceptive. The boy is fine. At first he was very scared, but now he is, you might say, less frightened than pissed off, and quite a tiger, but he is being treated well, fed well, and looked after."

"What do you want?"

"That is a matter not to be discussed over telephones when one does not know who is listening, no? This is merely a reassurance call for now. I assure you we do not wish to keep the boy, but his health and his future are in your hands. Keep the Company off. We will make no second offers, no adjustments in our demands, no back up and start overs. If anything goes wrong, no matter whose

fault—even if it is nobody's fault—the boy will be
killed and we will vanish like the wind. You will
never find us, or him, without our help, but even if
you did be assured, Señor, that all of us will kill
him and then ourselves before we will be caught.
Just wait, and when the summons comes do not
hesitate and do not try anything at all. Your son's
life depends upon it. Goodbye, Señor Horowitz, for
now."

There was a final click and dead air, but he
didn't immediately hang up the phone. There were
ways of doing trace-backs if the line wasn't broken
on both ends, particularly if you were receiving the
call.

The information printed out on a strip of adding
machine paper that emerged from the side of the
box under the phone. He took it, looked at it, then
broke the connection, waited until the phone
company reset the line, then he made a call of his
own.

"Harry? Sam Horowitz. Sorry to wake you up a
little early but I got a real emergency here as soon
as you can do it. I need a location to match a phone
number and I need it yesterday."

Harry didn't even have to leave the house for it,
and Sam got a callback in under ten minutes.

"It's a private phone, all right," Harry told him.
"It's in London."

"*England?*"

"No, Ontario. Canada. You know—big country
up north. In the name of Argos Container and
Cargo, Ltd. I'll give you the address."

Sam scribbled it down, then went to his computer, awake now. Who the hell did he have in the
Toronto area? Nobody, it appeared. Nobody on

that side closer than Montreal. He tried to think. What was near there? Suddenly he snapped his fingers. Buffalo! Oh, yeah.

And Jerry the Weasel was just the guy for a quick and unobtrusive black bag job. . . .

The morality might be a little questionable, but it was real handy to have even organized crime to draw upon as needed.

The private eye business was rarely if ever as glamorous as it was portrayed in the books, movies, and TV series, but it was every bit as tense in its own way. Even he was disconcerted sometimes by the amount of information he could get on just about anyone. Get copies of somebody's checks and you knew more about them than they did about themselves, for instance. That was the trick here—getting and sorting through all that information and keeping the quarry, if at all possible, in his, Sam's, element and not outside, down the Labyrinth to God knew where.

He was pretty sure that Dash hadn't been taken into the Labyrinth—yet. As soon as Cal had reached the switch to the main line he'd reported a security violation and they had stuck on full monitoring of the access to the central Pennsylvania substation. Not even a flea could go undetected if that happened; the only reason you couldn't do it with the whole line was that there were millions of worlds and incredible distances of parallel track, sidings, switch points, subsidiary lines—you name it. Just like you couldn't have a cop on every street corner in a city, you couldn't do a full monitor of the entire Labyrinth, but once you showed cause it was very simple to do it for a short piece. The invaders had known that as well.

Either they had all come in *en masse* in the ten to fifteen minutes tops it had taken Cal to get to the switch and report an undetected breach, or they hadn't come from the substation at all. Oh, perhaps one or two, tracking Bond, but not that army.

They had already been here, somewhere, in place, waiting. And that was the most significant fact of all.

If Doctor Macklinberg hadn't sworn that Bond's frostbitten toes were real, it smelled like even the alleged fugitive was part of the set up. Or had he just misjudged the snow and temperature and the distance involved?

It was an interesting question. There were eleven James Bonds associated in some way with the Company, and six were the sort where you just couldn't lay your hands on them at any given moment. He was almost certainly one of those—the reason why there hadn't been any alarms was because his implanted identifier was of the highest security codes. There were times when such agents didn't want the managers to know they were there.

It was a pretty puzzle, but, oddly, since the phone call and thinking things through he felt much better, even able to doze now. Things were finally moving; the load was lighter. Dash was still alive, and now there was one-on-one contact with those holding him.

Sam slept.

Bill Markham was one of those people who aged so gracefully they looked better in middle age than when young. Of course, Bill availed himself of the same super technology that other high level Company employees did, including Brandy and Sam, and physically he was in the kind of shape a twenty-year-old athlete dreamed of being, but he also had a family and a public existence and presence and so he had to look his forty-four-year-old age. He was tall and lean and muscular, with a ruddy face and a thick crop of professionally styled graying hair, and he looked like the kind of guy you'd cast as a detective on TV.

"It's my baby, Sam," he said, sinking into a chair. "I'm now Security boss for this world and all the stations along the node, so it's in my lap as well as yours."

Sam shrugged and lit a cigar. "I know you have the big picture, Bill; but this is personal with me. So long as Dash is at risk, it has to be a lone wolf operation in a couple of key areas and you know it."

Markham shrugged. "I'm not going to work against you, Sam. You know that. In fact, I'm partly here to brief you on some of our current operations and maybe give you a better picture of who and what you're dealing with."

Sam was suddenly very interested. "You know what's going on?"

"Not exactly. As you've probably already guessed, though, this is more or less an extension of the same old case. When we busted the takeover plot we exiled the ones we apprehended, as you know, Mukasa included, and put them through the wringer in every possible way. We knew Mukasa recruited an organization using worlds where we hadn't set up shop, but we didn't know how extensive it was or how many people were really involved on that lower level. The fact was, neither did Mukasa. They worked through a minimum of middlemen, mostly that sweet little secretary-mistress of his."

"Yeah. Addison or whatever her real name turned out to be."

"So that there could be no slips, they used a stock Company security technique with all of them to prevent them from giving out information under duress, hypno, even accidentally. They all had auto-erase routines implanted in their minds. You spill anything, you suddenly forget, and for good, whatever cross references there are and all other details, and it's beyond recovery. I, for example, know an awful lot nobody else is supposed to know. What if I were kidnapped, or even turned traitor? The first unauthorized access of that information would wipe it out completely. I'd remember that I once knew it, but I wouldn't know what it was. See?"

Sam nodded. "So you had no leads on dear Doctor Carlos or anyone else who might be in the organization even when you had the leader."

"Well, he *thought* he was the ringleader. Remember, they were out to get Mukasa, too. The problem with the closed culture of the Company world is that they tend to think that everybody thinks like they do. They don't have moral principles, just logical positions. They think that the only reason a slave hates slavery is because he'd rather be a master and enslave somebody else. It's nearly incomprehensible to them, except on an academic level, to imagine someone who might hate slavery because it is evil, because it is morally repugnant. Concepts like evil and morally repugnant really have no meaning for them. So they went out and recruited a huge number of very talented, even brilliant, people who for one reason or another had reason to hate the Company. It was a straight business deal to them, see? Help me break the Board and take over the Company and then *you* will run the Company as my underlings."

"Yeah," Sam sighed, "but the underlings *really* hated the Company, including the fellow who hired them. I wonder why?"

Markham shrugged. "There are always enough people who get stepped on in any large organization who generate that kind of hatred. Far less from the Company world, of course, but it's there even there, at least in any human cultures comprehensible to us. When you have access to all the personnel files and all the evaluations and histories of everyone who ever worked in any capacity for the Company, I doubt if it would take either of us more than a day to find an entire army."

"Point taken. But a Company girl did fall into the lower camp."

"Uh huh. She was out all the time, in contact with these people on a near-constant basis. She found in these rebels something she'd never seen in her own people—passion. A total commitment to a cause, and a viewpoint that graphically illustrated just what the Company did and what it was like and which humanized the whole thing. We think she fell in love with Carlos, and that Carlos radicalized her until she identified more with them than with her own people. Sheer guilt, but stirred well with resentment that the only way she could progress in society was as a mistress and henchman. The guilt part is the same reason so many poor little pampered rich kids become Trotskyites and the like here. And, of course, they used her just like they used her boss. The problem was, we lopped off the guy who caused it all to be possible and we lopped off the radicalized agent of the real plot, but we didn't lop off the true head of the radicals and the organization remained pretty well insulated and intact. We have been trying for years now to find out who, what, and where they are.''

''And you succeeded?''

''To a very low point only. Do you know how many worlds intersect the Labyrinth and how many weak points there are even where we don't have stations? Let's just say it's a geometric progression. The only thing we had going for us was that the opposition couldn't stay still forever without ceasing to be an opposition. For a year or so they fell back, licked their wounds, regrouped, and figured out what to do now. Then they started again, and we began to detect violations of security. They're good—damned good—and we always moved a fraction too slow.''

''How's that possible?'' Sam asked him. ''If they use the Labyrinth in known and charted areas they'll eventually get picked up and trapped.''

''Not necessarily. The only real control we have is at the stations and the switches. Somehow, they were getting around them, and we didn't know how. We had a lot of people on it, and the trouble was it took us the better part of a year to get the Board to allow any of us access to the computer security files on the Labyrinth itself so we could find out what the enemy already knew. I tend to think of the Labyrinth kind of like a railroad, with a straight track going from station A to station B via switchpoint C. Of course, you and I know just from being in it that it's not that simple."

Sam nodded. "There are always four faces on the cube. Four directions other than continuing in the tunnel. Good Lord! I never thought of that. You mean each cube goes in four different directions?"

"Uh huh. Now, take any of the sides and go through and you're in a world, right? That's why we think of the cubes as the only avenues to each of the worlds. That's wrong, though. Each face represents an alternative, a potential siding. Most just go to specific worlds, but many are through. Some of those old extensions were simply curved around to take advantage of temporal differences—a siding between two switches that would effect near-instantaneous travel, for example, from our point of view—while others were simply closed off and abandoned. But they still get power. We can't shut power down to any area without causing feedback and potentially dangerous disruption to the whole system. These shut down and unused sidings were taken off the system maps, access was closed off, and they were as if they had never been—but they were still there."

Sam nodded. "And after our Company fiend was through with the security and master database computers, the only guy left with a system map of all those shut down sidings is our Doctor Carlos. I begin to see the problem, Bill. It also answers a few questions, though, like how they were able to walk so easily and undetected up and down the line. How many of these unknown crossing points do you think there are?"

"We don't know. The computers guess it could run into the thousands. You see, in the early days, there wasn't a single monolithic Company. Development was by a government-supervised consortium of companies instead, and each wanted in on the potential profits in knowledge, new products, new markets, you name it. They all began building competitively, since due to the consortium they all had the technology, while whoever built the accesses to the worlds got first rights in them. Find a weak point, build a siding and a temporary station, and it was yours. Many are automated and use antiquated and sometimes proprietary means of switching—proprietary to the companies that built them many generations ago by Company standards. There aren't even many surviving records of the smaller companies that were quickly absorbed or went broke. What we have, Sam, isn't a straight line of track with charted sidings but a fantastic maze to which we don't have the key."

"But surely you can find them if you look."

"Sure we can—but it takes experts to locate them, then you have to know how the switch works or figure it out without damaging it or the power grid, then you can re-map and explore one siding. Multiply that by the length of the Labyrinth itself and it becomes a nightmare. It *is* possible to hide in the Labyrinth, Sam, and it *is* possible to travel sometimes great distances by bypassing existing switch points. The only time we have a chance at catching them is when they make a mistake and we know they're there."

"My God, Bill! You're telling me we could have whole *civilizations* going back and forth and we might not know about it. If this Carlos organization could tie into them, we're talking an *army* here. That certainly explains the world and the big organization on it where Brandy was trapped and addicted and how they're able to pull in so many duplicates. I can see why they pulled you off anything else."

Markham nodded. "It's been tough, but we've had several advantages. For the most part they've stuck with Type Zero worlds—worlds with people like us. That narrows it. There might be some Zero-Bs there—worlds where the people look human but aren't—but mostly they stick close to home, in worlds where they understand the rules. By selective monitoring and random probes just of our own region—which is big enough—we've managed to find several switches and identify a few worlds. They've got some key advantages, though, in that there's only one way in or out. The first time we got massacred going up one of their sidings, we learned that you either invade in strength, in which case you take the tunnel cube by cube but don't know the territory, or we seal it off. We got smart fast. Now we don't tell them when we find them—we just monitor the hell out of the access. That's given us a small but valuable catalog of worlds they frequently visit and a rogue's gallery of people in this rebel organization. We've managed some infiltration of their organization at lower levels but it's tough getting messages in and out."

"Are you telling me that Dash might be anywhere in one of these sidings?" Sam seemed very uncomfortable. "That we might still have lost him?"

"No, no! I doubt it! We've got every weak point from here to Australia covered from the inside and we have this world sealed off as tight as we can. We know this world as good as we know any, Sam. There are no uncovered weak points. They got in, some with false authorizations, some with exploiting lax weak spots like this one—sorry—but this one was covered far too soon for a group that size to make an exit and get away into their maze, and the others were sealed within hours and show no signs of use. Even if they faked out a station master there would be records. No, Sam, they're still here. They're *all* still here. What bothers me is that they must have known that would happen from the start. I just can't figure out their game."

Sam gave a low smile. "With what you've told me, which fills in a *lot* of gaps, Bill, I can assure you, I think I at least understand some of it. This might be *very* interesting at that, provided they don't know that I am in the possession of certain facts. The question really is, just how subtle *are* these jokers? They've been pretty ham-handed and theatrical up to now, and that's dangerous. But if they *are* a little too clever for their own good, then things are looking up."

"Huh? What?"

"Never mind. The proof will come in the next few hours—a day or two at most. For my own interests, Bill, I simply can't go further with this right now. Just keep us bottled up tight and I'll do the rest."

Markham studied the detective. "I wish I didn't feel like Watson sitting around 221B Baker Street," he grumbled, then sighed. "Okay, okay, we'll play it your way for now. I wouldn't want in any way to cause Dash to come to harm because I interfered."

"Thanks." And Sam sincerely meant that.

"What about Brandy? Considering how much of a team you two are, I'm surprised we didn't have this conversation upstairs. Is she that bad off?"

"Oh, no. In fact, she's coming along just fine. She got some sleep and when she woke up she had feeling and movement again in her arms and shoulders. Tingles, but it's fading, kind of like a numbness slowly ebbing. She'll be up and around in a couple of days the way it looks now. But she's a hands-on type and Dash's kidnapping has about driven her crazy. I keep her informed and the like but she's better off recovering than getting in my way here while I do what I do best. She'll have her role to play, but not yet. Uh—any luck on that Yusha expletive?"

"Not yet. It's so close to a lot of things and the voice is so obviously distorted by something that we can't be absolutely certain that Yusha is the real word. And, of course, it's so obvious a traceable buzzword that we're half inclined to feel that it was dropped just to send our teams into insanity and occupy a lot of us following red herrings up and down the line. The same with the bodies they left. Nothing particularly distinguishing about them, yet the comment on the recording implied we should know where they were from right off. No oddball tattoos, no genetic markers, no oddball haircuts or green skins or purple hair, and their clothing might as well be local and probably is. Just people. I think we were just getting our noses tweaked."

"Could be," Sam admitted. "I think it's less significant that they left the bodies of those men than that they didn't leave any of the Ginzu bodies. Why not take all or none?"

"Maybe because they figured that the Master would see who they were and that would lead him to the traitors," Markham suggested.

"Uh huh. Or maybe another red herring. We don't even know if there were any Ginzu involved, or, if so, whether any were killed or badly wounded. We have only the dialogue on the recordings to lead us to that, along with Brandy's description of the black-clad warriors, and they were masked. In a way, it's a master stroke. As long as we can't be sure, we can't use any of the Ginzu at all. We can't use our incorruptible bodyguards for the big shots or our effective local security mercenaries. They've been factored out."

"Well, there are others we can use that are quite good," Markham noted.

"Uh huh, but they're new. Replacements. Green and not known to the folks they're guarding and ignorant themselves of the territory and the tricks." Sam leaned forward and used his cigar stub as a pointer. "The game's afoot, Watson. Dark business; very dark indeed. The trouble is, at this point, we don't know whether we are the game, or they are."

Information began to come in thick and fast. The London number led to a small office not recently occupied in which there was a desk, a chair, and a working phone. The phone had a neat little device on it that included a recorder and a separate line. A phone company check showed no incoming long distance calls, so clearly the trick was to use three local London lines—one to be called by the remote caller, then it would call the second line in town, which would then spool a

71

delay on the tape and then feed it back out the third line that called Sam. It was a clever arrangement. The guy could have called from anywhere, even the phone booth down on College Avenue, to the first London number. That then automatically dialed the second number in the office, which triggered the tape and then initiated the final call to Sam. Without knowing from where the call was placed or the first local London number the entire conversation would be untraceable even if they had been sitting in that office during the call.

More interesting was the fact that the tape was continuous record and play at only four second intervals, but it removed almost all background noise and was just slightly off-speed in a more or less random way so that the voice itself sounded normal but wouldn't voice print correctly and would sound just slightly off.

Well, he had expected that to be a dead end. More interesting was the envelope that arrived in the afternoon mail. It bore a local postmark two days old—the good old post office had taken two days to deliver it perhaps two miles—and was essentially clean of fingerprints and whatever. The message was typewritten but he didn't have to run any checks to see if he could find its origins. The very slight impression problem, particularly with the lower case "a," was very familiar. The bastards had typed it on his own machine, in his office, while they were still ransacking the place.

It said, *"If you want to see your son again, then on Tuesday next, at eight in the evening, enter the Labyrinth at your substation, then proceed past the main switch and down line towards Headquarters. Be alone and unarmed and destroy this note and tell the Company nothing. Any sign of security or an electronic security scan and we will send your boy back to you in very tiny pieces. Believe us when we say that. We promise that if you play fair, we will, too. We have a proposition for you."*

An offer I can't refuse, Sam thought with a dry chuckle. Well, they were giving him more than enough time. Brandy might not be perfect but she should be up and around by Tuesday, and his own string would be played out here by then. Certainly Markham would have a tail on him, but he knew he could shake a tail and create a plausible reason for going down line. That wasn't a real problem. The real problem was that he now had a deadline.

On Friday, they found the vans, abandoned, near Ashville, North Carolina. They had underestimated the Company's resources, though, and their own relative invisibility. They were using rented and leased vehicles still, although with a different credit card on a different company. They had done a good cover job, but they hadn't created additional fake driver's licenses and they had to show licensing information on at least one to get the new ones. The jerks should have had a third party buy a couple of used busses, which would have made the job slower and tougher, but they didn't.

Most important in the rental information was that none of the vehicles had snow tires. Now, this was the South, all right, but Ashville was high in the Smokies and the only way out that didn't mean mountains and snow and ice for sure was east. On Saturday, Company helicopters spotted them in spite of several precautions they'd taken. Somewhere along the road they'd given the three big vans a spray paint job, changing them from their original colors into black, but three black vans moving in a virtual convoy stood out pretty well. When they all stopped at a motel outside of Wilmington, North Carolina, agents were ready, and Sam's phone rang.

"It's them," Bill Markham told him. "No question. We've even seen your boy. You'll never know how many people and how much time and money went into this. I'm sending the chopper for you now. We don't dare do anything until well after dark anyway, so we're just setting up and reconnoitering the place. I assume you want in on this."

"I don't want you doing a thing until I get there, Bill, and I mean it," Sam growled. "One slip and my son's a memory and I will hold anybody and everybody responsible for that."

3.

The Many Faces of the Enemy

It was your standard, garden-variety motel, mostly empty in the off season and not very fancy, with several rectangular blocks of single-room units in back of a combination office and restaurant. They had taken only two rooms, but it wasn't crowded. In spite of the temperature, the bulk of the kidnappers—the Company agents estimated that they totaled fifteen—remained in the vans and rotated inside the rooms.

"They pretty well stay in the vans except at shift change or when one from inside comes out to talk," Markham told Sam. "The better to guard the rooms with big guns without being seen. We've checked the area and I'm pretty sure that there's nobody on the roofs and no ugly surprises. They have the vans at each end of the block and that gives them pretty good coverage. Nobody's going out the back—it's a cinderblock wall, no windows."

It was about two-thirty in the morning and in spite of it being in North Carolina it was cold; damned cold. The top of the motel unit was heavy with smoke from the condensation from the master units inside, and you could see the breath coming from everyone who now surrounded the place.

Sam was both worried and impressed. He'd been rushed to a field about three miles from the place by helicopter from State College in just a little more than two hours, and from there by car to the parking lot.

"You think you got enough men here?" he asked sarcastically. It looked like a small army. "They must be idiots not to have spotted somebody by now."

"We've kept well back," Markham told him. Sam was both impressed and touched that the chief of security for many worlds had taken the time and trouble to be here. "The main idea was to keep the place locked up. No sirens, no local cops, and people in general have been allowed to come and go without even taking a second glance. We're pros, Sam."

"How'd you do this without the local cops wanting to muscle in?"

"The usual. They got a call from DEA in Washington validating our credentials. They think these boys are the center of a big Colombian coke ring that we're nabbing during a meet and that might not be too far from the truth. We've gotten some prints now from the restaurant where they ate over there and some of these are very bad boys. This is a contract job, Sam. I'm pretty sure this is all local talent."

By "local" Sam knew that Bill didn't mean North Carolinian or even American; he meant they were natives of this Earth.

"No Ginzu or whispery voiced fellow with a Midwestern accent, huh?"

Markham shook his head. "No, we figure they split early, maybe before they even left central

Pennsylvania. There's even a possibility that there was a full crew switch someplace and that none of these were anywhere near your house. We'll find out some of that from Dash when we get him."

Sam looked again at the two vans and the motel block. "Yeah, well, I appreciate your waiting for me. If all goes well I want to be here for Dash, and if not, well, I couldn't live with myself if I sat it out."

"Nothing will go wrong, not with these babies," Markham assured him. "We have several advantages in the setup. There's nobody else in the block—the whole motel occupancy is only six, which is above average for this time of year in this location, so I'm told. I'm going to use pulsers on the two vans, simultaneously. They should be out cold with a nasty shock. The pulsers are useless against the motel rooms, though, so we're going to run a sleep gas unit through the vents on that built-in air conditioner on each unit. The gas is fast and harmless."

"A little risky, though," Sam worried. "You still have to put a fairly fast little hole through the air conditioner flanges and then pump it in, which is never totally silent. They catch on and Dash has had it."

"Could be. If these are the nasties we think they are I don't think they're as suicidal as our other friends seem to be, but it would be ugly. There's no other way, though. There's no technique that's not without risk. We have audio monitors on top there so we'll know immediately if they suspect and can move with stun and percussion weapons if we absolutely have to. You have any better ideas?"

Sam studied the situation and marveled at their

thoroughness. They even somehow had gotten blueprints of the place, updated with the latest renovations. Still, he was uneasy. "Maybe wait 'em out and take 'em as they leave," he suggested.

"Far riskier. We couldn't be certain that we'd get everybody and we'd only need one back in the room to spray everybody with bullets, Dash included. Besides, we'd have to do a wide stun at pretty good strength here to have any crack at them and there's always a chance of heart stoppage with that. I don't give a damn if all these bastards have heart attacks but I don't want to risk it with a boy as young as yours."

Sam looked again at the doors and stiffened. "Somebody's coming out of the room on the left," he said softly.

"They check on each other regularly, and rotate a couple of inside and outside men now and again. They have a regular schedule, since at least once a couple of the van boys weren't relieved when they were supposed to be and they went up to the motel room and raised holy hell in Spanish. See—there's another one coming out now, lighting a cigarette there. One will go to each van, then one from each van will come out and go in. It's not regular but it's never been less than an hour between changes and they've all eaten. Every once in a while one of the van boys gets out and checks the area, sometimes taking a smoke or a leak against the building. I wouldn't think a smoker would be very popular with that crowd in either van. No problem if we nail both vans right off and silently, and they only come out of the rooms for the change. Okay. . . . I think we give them fifteen minutes after that pair goes inside and then we hit 'em. What do you say?"

Sam nodded. "Let's do it. Beats waiting and eating my guts out."

"You want to go in with one of the teams?"

"No. If anything goes wrong I'd be in the way. Let the experts do it."

Markham nodded. "All right, then. Let me give the word."

The security chief left and talked to his team leaders and there was suddenly a fair amount of action. The pulsers were what Sam called the industrial strength models, used in the world where they were invented as anti-tank and perimeter security. Anything designed to knock out an armored tank crew sealed inside should be more than a match for an Econoline van.

Far trickier would be getting the hole into the rooms for the gas line. If these guys were rotating almost hourly, then somebody, maybe most of them, were up in there. The audio monitors indicated that somebody in the room next to the one in which they thought Dash was in bed was watching an old movie on the TV. Sam hoped it was something loud and not inappropriate. He much preferred *The Final Option* to, say, *Assault on Precinct Thirteen*.

It seemed like an eternity before they were properly set up, and just at the time when they were going to turn on the pulsers some bastard got out of the far van to smoke and check out the area. It was a nerve-wracking extra ten minutes before the man, who appeared to have a nice little Uzi submachine gun under one arm, lazily decided to get back in, and when he did another decided to come out. Time was running out; if this went on, they'd have to wait until the next guard change.

When the second man got back in his van, though, all seemed quiet, and Markham, figuring they still had time and not wanting to stall any longer, gave the signal. Anybody who might emerge from this point would be taken out by marksmen using super-silent stun rifles.

The gas team was ready, dressed all in black and with rubber-soled tennis shoes for extra quiet, but they remained well back until the vans were secured. At Markham's whispered signal through the communicators, both pulsers emitted a single, and to Sam, inordinately loud *whump! whump!* burst. For the briefest of moments the whole lot was lit, as if by lightning, and the two vans shuddered slightly. They waited another minute to be sure, but all that could be heard from the vans was a very low crackling sound, then nothing. Both engines had died, apparently shut down by the pulses, producing an extra measure of quiet.

Now the gas team moved, in cat-like silence and with true military precision. They reached the end of the block, then a pair scrunched down and made their way to the first air conditioner opening, while the others had weapons and grenades at the ready for an instant assault on the rooms if needed. All wore communications helmets, but the only sound coming from them was low breathing. The helmets were strictly to receive orders.

There was a low-intensity red beam from something in the hand of one gas team member, and then it was aimed at a spot where the air conditioner emerged from the wall and it was virtually invisible to the watchers. A very tiny laser melted its little hole in the wall. It was quick; the first man put his drill away and actually peered down and looked in the hole. Satisfied, he moved silently to the second room while the other man laid down a cotton wad on the concrete and then placed a small canister on it so quietly that no one could hear a thing. The small tubing was then affixed to the tube, then inserted just barely into the hole, and the canister was activated.

By this time, the first man had his hole burned in the second room and now another team member came in with another canister and repeated the actions of the first. The audio monitor continued to broadcast the low level TV show in one room and there were snores from the other. The TV would remain on, but when the snores ceased they would know that the level of gas was sufficient to have put them under.

At that moment the monitors relayed the sound of a toilet flushing in the TV room and then a man's low voice said something in Spanish that Sam couldn't catch, not knowing much of the language anyway. Somebody mumbled a reply, even harder to hear over the TV, and then, to everyone's shock, the door to the room on the left opened and a man stepped out and closed it behind him. Suddenly he saw the black clad gas team and froze for a precious second.

One of the marksmen got him with a fast and dirty pulse shot that was nearly dead silent, and two gas team members caught him as he fell and hauled his limp body to one side almost in a continuous motion. Still, everybody froze for a moment, waiting to see if anything had been heard, but they relaxed when nothing happened.

The snoring died away in the room on the left and was replaced mostly with dead silence, while in the other room there was still the sound of somebody moving and the TV going on. There was the sudden sound of something dropping and something hard hitting the carpet and bouncing, and that was that.

The assault team of the gas squad switched on their respirators, then moved to both doors. There was a quick series of loud breaths from the team leaders that clearly was meant as a synchronization signal, and when both were satisfied it all went down *real* fast.

Rifles fired, burning the locks in an instant, then the assault men went in like lightning. Sam and the others were up and moving in almost immediately, with a squad of heavily armed plainclothes men going to each van, opening it, and starting to haul limp forms out.

"All secure," came the report from the gas team leader. "We got him! One of 'em wasn't quite under but he was too woozy to do anything except get bloody when I kicked his face in. Guess the opening of the door diluted the gas."

Sam was ready to run into the room but one of the agents stopped him. "There's still enough gas in there to knock you for a loop!" he warned. "Stay here and they'll bring him out!"

A tall assault team member seemed to hear, and emerged from the snoring room with Dash's small, limp form. Sam rushed up to him and looked down at the unconscious form of his son.

"He'll be fine," the assault team man assured him. "Strong, normal pulse. Let's get him over to the ambulance and we'll bring him out of it in a jiffy."

Sam nodded numbly and let the man carry Dash

away. The ambulance was already driving in and it was only a few feet to it, but Sam found himself instead leaning against the side of the motel building, using it for support. He gave a heavy sigh and then couldn't help crying. The pressure was suddenly relieved, the emotions could no longer be so professionally repressed.

Bill Markham came up to him but said nothing, letting the detective get hold of himself. Finally Sam managed, with a sob, "You got a handkerchief, Bill? Wouldn't you know I left without one. . . ."

"Daddy!" Dash clung to Sam and started crying himself, almost starting Sam again, but Sam held it and just hugged Dash and held him very close. Finally the boy looked up, tears streaming down his face, and said, "I knew you'd come. I knew you wouldn't let 'em take me away."

"Not if I could help it, son," Sam responded with gentle firmness.

The boy looked around, suddenly panicked. "Where's Mommie?"

"She's okay. The bad men hurt her when they took you and she has to stay in bed for a little while but she's going to be fine. She's home waiting for you. We'll call her later on and you'll see her tomorrow. Okay?"

"Is she hurt real bad?"

Sam thought about it. How do you explain a Ginzu paralysis hold to a six-year-old? "She was, but the doctor says she's going to be fine. She's been worried sick over you, though, just like I have. Did they hurt you?"

The boy shook his head no. "Not really. They

pushed me around some but that was mostly at the start. After that they was pretty nice mostly. They gave me Twinkies and hamburgers." The boy yawned, not from the gas but because he was very tired, but some things couldn't wait.

"Well, all right, then. Listen, Dash, this is important. Were these people here the same ones who took you from the house?"

"Our house?"

"Yes."

"Some. A couple, I think. Mostly I dunno."

"Look, they're all still knocked out now, but you think you could point to the ones who were at the house?"

"I dunno. I'll try. I was kind'a sleepy, like now."

He named several of them but wasn't really sure how long they'd been with him, but two, a big, tough-looking man and a short, wiry, effeminate-looking man he was certain were there all the way. The big man was Fred and he was mean and didn't talk much to Dash, but the small man was Alberto and he was very nice and kind to the boy and had stood up for him when some of the others got a little rough.

That was enough for now. They brought in a prison wagon and chained the men to the inside before any of them might wake up, and Dash and Sam got into a big, black Lincoln and they were off, even as the Company cleanup crew was coming in.

The cleanup crew was now the most vital concern of Markham and the Company as a whole. They would remove any evidence of a higher technology, replace the motel locks and even the doors and frames if need be, haul away the vans to a Company shop that would restore them before turning them back in to the rental agency, and go over both vans and rooms with a fine-tooth comb for anything evidentiary either telling something about the men they captured or which had to be removed. By late the next day, there would be no physical evidence at all that anything had happened there except perhaps that the rooms would be even cleaner than normal and there might be some fresh paint and plaster.

At the same time, a political cleanup crew was at work with the local authorities—cops, the motel manager, you name it. Somebody from the local paper had been tipped, probably by a cop, and it was easier to arrange for an authentic cover story than to deny it all and have the press down on them with a vengeance. The Company people, however, were very efficient, as Sam had good reason now to know.

They had captured twelve heavily armed men and rescued a hostage and had done so at the cost of one broken nose, said nose broken on one of the kidnappers who hadn't had the good luck to go completely under.

There were, however, lots of interrogations to be done and tests to be made. For one thing, even Dash would have to be microscopically examined and compared with his data recordings. The mere fact that no world had ever been discovered other than this one in which Sam and Brandy had gotten together, let alone had a kid, was insufficient. You could take nothing for granted in the parallel world business, and they wanted to make absolutely certain that this was no ringer, even though Sam was positive that no kid would or even could fake this.

The captives were also microscopically examined using technology created for this purpose, to see if any of them showed any signs whatever of having been born somewhere other than this Earth. Then the real interrogations would begin.

Sam called Brandy, who seemed ecstatic at the news. It was several minutes before she herself stopped crying, then she said, "Sam, I swear I'll be walkin' again once Dash walks in the door."

"I bet you will, too," he responded. "Look, he really wants to see you—he's been very worried since I told him you were hurt and that's why you weren't here—but it's going to be at least another day before we can wrap it up here. Figure Monday evening. Then it'll just be getting you back to normal and everything will be back in place."

She paused. "Sam—why'd they do it? Not just for Bond, that I know. They was lookin' for you and then they snatched Dash even though they was then playin' our game on our turf. What's it all about, Sam?"

"I'm not sure yet," he told her honestly, "but now that Dash is safe I'm going to be working full time on it. This one's a freebie, babe. It's personal."

She was silent a moment, then just whispered, "Yeah, Sam. I guess it is."

Dash was easily authenticated; even without his I.D. implant and his apparent uniqueness, it wasn't hard to tell him. Doctor Macklinberg took samples during the six-month checkups and this, with the Company's high technology machinery, gave a listing not only of the genetics, which would be identical in a parallel world "clone," but also things that would be different—the effects of diet, levels of various substances breathed in or absorbed or eaten, that kind of thing. The lab work was done up the line, not by the Doctor, so there was little probability of a switch. It was done too often and too consistently for that.

But the bottom line was that six-year-olds weren't good at faking anything and a father and only son had common memories that would be unlikely to be absolutely duplicated anywhere else.

On the kidnappers, Bill Markham had good news and bad news, but mostly the latter.

"We'll get nothing from the pair who were with them from the attack," he said ruefully. "We figured as much and tried to prevent it but if it was easy to prevent we wouldn't use it ourselves. They do it a bit rougher, though. Something—no telling what—just exploded inside their skulls before we got a single question in; something we didn't detect in the exams. They'll be lucky to remember how to tie their own shoelaces, let alone who they are and where they came from and who was with them."

"Any more happy news?" Sam asked sarcastically.

"Oh, there's a bright side. As we figured, the rest were hired guns who took over on the road. They're a nasty, macho bunch, I'll tell you— spouting threats and being generally belligerent. They're just nuts, Sam. I think they would go down in a blaze of fury if they could be sure of taking some of us with them. They're all associated with something called the Futurist People's Revolutionary Cells, a bunch of fanatical drug dealers centered in the South American jungles who believe it's their revolutionary destiny to destroy America by filling it with cheap and super powerful drugs. No excuse, either—they believe it. It's the kind of organization the Company can never get its hooks into because we can't even find it, let alone infiltrate it. We're going to get a lot of information from them now, though. Where's Dash?"

"Asleep downstairs and under guard and nurse. Why?"

"Come on. Let's see what the bully boys have to tell us."

The room looked like a normal police interrogation room, one for the worst kind of criminals, with a gun port and the prisoner shackled to the floor and to the arms of a very strong metal chair that was welded down. Sam took a look at him, though, particularly his eyes, and knew that Bill had underestimated their insanity if anything.

The man looked up at them with a surly gaze and a slight sneer on his lips. "Where is my lawyer?" he snapped. "I know my rights. I don't say nothin' without my lawyer." The Spanish accent was heavy, but clearly he could and did think in English when he wanted to.

"We are attending to the lawyer you told us to phone," Markham responded smoothly. "He's about to mysteriously disappear on his way to the golf course and whether he's ever seen again will depend on what he can tell us."

The man suddenly looked very startled. "What the hell you mean by that?"

"We are not the police, Señor, nor the feds. You seem to be under a mistaken impression. We took great pains to keep the cops out of this, since we don't want them any more than you normally would."

At least *something* could get to the man. There was a glint of panic in his eyes now, but they were still mean, crazy.

"Who are you? Mafia?"

Markham chuckled. "Now, you know that there is no such thing as the Mafia. No, Señor, not the Mafia. We are far worse than the Mafia. We are the ones who use even organized crime as a tool. We're the ones behind every bush and in every shadow that you can never see out of the corner of your eye. You went a step too far this time, Señor. We don't like your business and we don't give a damn about your politics, for if you ever got big enough to take over a country you would find our strings upon your leaders as sure as they are on the ones you might overthrow. Do you know us now, Señor?"

The man's eyes widened and he looked at each of them. *"Conquistadores!"* he breathed.

"That is the name the smartest and slimiest of the dark corners of this world know us in your area," Markham admitted. "Your two employers have taken themselves out of the game. Maybe I'll let you see them at some point so you can see that there are those even more fanatical than you. Right now, though, I want some information."

"You can go to Hell!" the man snarled. "I will die rather than betray my comrades!"

Markham sighed and sat down and leaned back in a chair. Sam had already sat down facing the man but remained silent.

"That," said Markham softly, "is not an option."

He waved his hand in the air, and suddenly two small traps slid back in the ceiling out of which dropped two small ball-shaped devices, like tiny turrets, with pencil-like guns protruding from them. Suddenly the tips of both "barrels" glowed —one white, the other red—and they shifted until both were pointing directly at the prisoner's head, making tiny little dots of light on his hair. The man eyed them nervously and then tried to move his head to louse up their aim, but they followed his every move instantly—and he could only move so far.

Markham reached into his sports coat jacket and brought out a small device resembling an electric pager with two buttons on it, one red and one white.

"Now, let's start with the basics. I want your name. I hate to have a nice conversation with somebody and not know their name."

"Fidel Castro," the man responded bravely. Markham pressed the red button and suddenly the man screamed in pain, his face contorting in almost unbelievable horror, his body writhing against the bonds.

Markham's thumb came off the red button and the man suddenly seemed to collapse, sweating profusely. Sam found the whole thing unpleasant to watch, but this bastard had been one of them who had kidnapped his son, and God knows how many other people's kids he and his organization had hooked, or killed, or sentenced to a fate worse than death. Besides, there wasn't a damned thing he could do about it anyway.

"Madre Dios! Wha—what is *that which you did?"*

"Want me to do it again?"

"No, no!"

"There's a rule you probably know, and that is that nobody is unbreakable," Markham told him. "Sooner or later, everybody breaks. It's just a matter of time. That's why so many important people with things to protect will commit suicide or trigger self-lobotomies rather than be subjected to this. You, unfortunately, don't have that option. Those two little beams are very complicated devices and I must confess I don't understand how they work, but I know what they do and how to use them. The red one somehow stimulates the pain center directly—no intermediaries. It's quite level-sensitive, though, and now that we've used it once the computer driving it knows just where your pain threshold is and will keep it just a microscopic hair below your pass-out point. I could let that thing play almost indefinitely and you'd be conscious the whole time. Want to see?" His thumb made for the red button.

"No! Stop! You are *Diablo!*"

Markham smiled. "I thought you folks didn't believe in gods or devils. No, not gods, not devils, but we *are* a bit, uh, other-worldly, and we've had a *lot* of practice." He paused for a moment. "Now, this white button does the opposite. Stimulates the pleasure center directly. It's the most intense high you can possibly imagine. I'll demonstrate—if you tell me your *real* name. It doesn't matter anyway, you know. This is just a quick and dirty way of getting information. In a while, you and your friends will be put under a machine that will read out every memory you have from your first memories inside the womb to right now. We'll know far more about you than you. But it takes a lot of time to sort and edit that kind of information and that can't be done best on this world. We'd like some answers now."

"My—my name is Ramon Gloriona," the man said, not quite believing all that but definitely remembering that intense pain.

Markham sighed. "Red button," he mumbled, and his thumb went up.

"I swear on my mother's grave that is my true name!" the man screamed with such conviction that Markham relaxed.

"You know, I think it just might be," the security chief commented. "All right, Ramon, we'll show you what cooperation brings." He pushed the white button, just briefly, and the man's face and body suddenly went into contortions of sheer ecstasy that seemed to last after Bill took his finger off and stopped it.

"The same principal as the narcotics you dump on the West, Ramon," Markham told him, "only without all the messy chemicals and middlemen and simon-pure. Even we have to have a computer override on the white button, because you never forget it and you always want more." He sighed. "Sam, I think he's softened up a bit. Want to ask your questions?"

Sam nodded, but he was feeling somewhat queasy about this even though it was kind of a revenge dream come true. He was beginning to have some difficulty distinguishing on a moral basis between his old friend Bill and this bastard in the chair.

"Where did you meet the other group?" Sam asked him.

There was a moment's hesitancy, but Bill's thumb only had to head for the red and the man answered. "Asheville."

"How were you hired?"

"We do not hire out like common criminals!" the man responded with some of the pride he'd had before getting the pain treatment. "It was a fraternal favor between revolutionary groups. They have done some favors for us, we do some for them."

Sam's eyebrows rose. "And who exactly is 'them'?"

"Why, the American Revolutionary Brigades."

Sam looked at Bill, who shrugged. "I thought that shit went out with the Sixties," the security man muttered. "At least here. Beruit, maybe, but not here. Still, it's a nice cover for dealing with these kind of folks if you're really other-worldly."

Sam nodded and turned back to Ramon. "We know about the pair who transferred with you and the boy. Who were the others? The ones who didn't come along?"

The prisoner tried to shrug. "Who knows? We have only dealt directly with the comrades who remained with the boy up to now, and even then we knew them only by code names."

That figured, Sam thought. "All right, then, tell me what the others looked like. Did they look different or speak in a different language or was there anything odd about their clothes?"

The man frowned. "Yes, in fact. Most looked sort of—Chinese or Japanese or something like that. Oriental, you know. Smaller. They all wore heavy wool coats and pull-down caps and you could not tell much else. They did speak to each other in some nonsense-sounding tongue, though."

That was jibing with what little Dash had been

able to tell them. "What about the leader with the funny voice?"

"There was one fellow. A *mestizo*, I think. He did not speak with us but spoke briefly with the other two. He had an odd accent, I remember that. We thought he might have been Puerto Rican."

All Spanish accents sounded alike to Sam, but he knew from experience that, in the Western Hemisphere, dialects differed so sharply that it made the linguistic differences between a Maine farmer and a Mississippi cotton grower seem trivial by comparison. He did not, however, think that the accent was Puerto Rican. Most probably this fellow's dialect had no equal anywhere on this Earth.

"Where did these others go?" Sam asked him. "After you took over, that is." The fellow was certainly being very cooperative after the demonstration, but neither Sam nor Bill was likely to loose those bonds. The eyes still said it.

"We left them in the rest area just east of Asheville. There were many cars and trucks there since the highway through the mountains was supposed to be difficult to go through because of snow and ice. They must have used some of them."

"How did you and your men get to the rest area?"

"We came in one of the big trucks we have used for many deliveries and it was then driven away by our people."

Sam nodded. Everything checked out pretty well so far. He turned to Bill. "I assume you're monitoring everybody in and out, even in ones and twos, from any stations and substations along the line. They will want to exit, and even if we miss the big boy there shouldn't be much trouble in spotting our Ginzu-like friends."

Markham chuckled. "Sam, we do what we can, but do you know how many stations and substations there are on the Asian continent? Almost everybody there looks right for the area, and if they have fake clearances and a lot of patience there's no way we can stop them short of shutting down. We have extra monitors and we're scrutinizing everybody who wants out very hard, but there's only so much we can do. Even if we caught a couple, and we might, they're likely to wind up like that pair down the hall. Give it up, Sam. We got the boy back safe and sound. That's about the best we can hope for, all things considered."

Sam suddenly sat up. "Bond!" he exclaimed, feeling stupid.

"Huh?"

"Where was Bond? The whole thing was supposedly to get him and keep him from revealing a key illegal switch point, right? But Dash has no memories of a tall Englishman at all, let alone one with bandages and the like, and we heard nothing about him from this fellow, either."

Markham looked suddenly struck. "You're right," he replied. "Sam—that means they either didn't take him with them or that there was another group that split right at the start from the main body."

"That frostbite always bothered me," Sam told him. "It's possible to get that bad fairly quickly, but not all that likely. The one thing that frostbite did was keep him immobile and inside the house. Macklinberg examined him, of course, but like most doctors he takes one look, it looks like the classic case—of which he's seen hundreds or thousands—and we get instant diagnosis."

"You think he was in on it, then? A fraud? It wouldn't be that hard to fake and fool even a doctor under those circumstances for just the reasons you say. So they'd have an inside man, right? Maybe one who could report and help entry and make sure there wasn't a trap inside. That's bad, Sam. It means we have one of our own who went over to the other side."

"It's more interesting than that, Bill," the detective replied. "It means that all this was the object of the exercise from the beginning. If Bond isn't for real, and if he was an inside man, then the whole object was to get to us. The pieces are starting to fall into place, Bill, but I still need more information."

"You're beginning to make me feel like Watson again."

Sam smiled. "It's just the same old game. Taking all the disparate pieces of the puzzle all spilled out in random order on the table and putting them together into a coherent whole. The problem isn't solving the puzzle, the problem is when you don't have all the pieces yet."

Brandy was improving rapidly, now with full upper body control and able to at least sit up. It was likely that while she might feel the effects off and on for weeks yet, she would be up and around and capable of taking care of herself and Dash as well within a week.

Dash practically threw himself on her, and the reunion scene was so touching and tearful that even Sam was affected. The boy got some of his books and crayons and they were there in her bed playing and reading and having a grand old time.

Sam was feeling tired, but he wanted to do a little thinking, alone, in the study. Eight o'clock tomorrow night, the note had said. There would be no way at all for them to know at this stage that Dash had been rescued nor just how much Sam had already deduced. If he was there, then they would be there.

He would, of course, be walking straight into the lion's den without so much as a whip and a chair, but he'd done that before. Brandy had done it a while back and had wound up an addicted slave to these people, so he had no illusions about them. Still, they had gone to such extraordinary lengths to have a talk with him; it would be unthinkable to disappoint them.

After Dash finally got his kisses and hugs and went off to bed, he walked upstairs and sat down on the bed.

"They want to meet me," he told her simply. "Tomorrow night. In the Labyrinth."

"Who? You don't mean . . ."

He nodded. "Them, yes. They think they still have Dash to hold over me and with the kind of security clamp Bill's got down I suspect they won't know for a while until and unless I tell them."

"But—Sam, you *can't* go. Not *now*. They got nothin' to hold over you no more. *Nothin'!* You walk in there and they'll have you cold. Hypnos, mind wringers, drugs . . . You name it, they got it. You can't beat 'em on their own turf, Sam."

"We have before," he reminded her. "There's no such thing as a perfect security system. You know that. Sure, we've added a lot here and filled in the gaps and the kind of attack they launched last week would be deadly for them to try again now, but they could get in. A subtler approach. We can't keep Dash out of school too long, and he's vulnerable. A double, a ringer, somebody you wouldn't think twice of letting in the hosue would have you and Dash and everything else. They've haunted us far too long. It's time to take the cross and the stake and go down into the vampire's cellar once and for all."

"Let's just quit it, Sam. If we wasn't with the Company and didn't have no substation and clearances and all that and were out of it we'd be no use to them or nobody else. We got a ton of money. Go someplace like Fiji or Tahiti or someplace else that's always warm and away from the world and just sleep and eat and fish and swim and say the hell with it."

He shook his head sadly. "I don't think we can. I don't think either side would just allow us to opt out, not now." He paused a moment. "I think it was the aftermath, not the actual attack, that got me. That interrogation Bill Markham did—I haven't been able to get it out of my mind."

She frowned. "What do you mean?"

"I sat there and watched him press buttons. Pain, pleasure. Watching that guy just curl up in agony and then become so willing, so pliant, after just one short shot of pleasure."

"The guy was a scumbag. A drug dealer, kidnapper, and worse. He deserved worse than that."

"Yeah, he probably did, or does," Sam admitted. "The trouble was, I knew that and I knew that bastard would have slit Dash's throat and rationalized it in his twisted way just like he rationalizes shipping tons of addictive drugs to the willing and eager youth and yuppies of America. That's why I enjoyed that pain jolt. Really enjoyed it. I wanted him to get more than he got. And then, suddenly, I couldn't remember which side I was on.''

"What? What the hell you talkin' 'bout, Sam?''

"I couldn't remember which side. Suddenly I couldn't tell the two sides apart. Torture, pleasure, pain, high technology, might makes right. Verdict first, trial afterwards. Right defined by who was in who's power and wrong, even evil, strictly defined as competition. I couldn't figure out why our gangsters were better than their gangsters.''

She stared at him, but seemed to understand. "Then maybe we should get out. Now.''

He shook his head sadly from side to side. "Uh uh. We got sucked in the first time but then the Company made us an offer we couldn't refuse. You don't quit after that. They don't let you quit. So you rationalize it, just like that guy rationalized kidnapping, murder, drugs—everything. *We* rationalized it,' or we just preferred not to think about it. The golden ones of the Company world rationalize it or cloak it in that old devil of racism. They're superior—the Chosen People of their gods. The proof is in their sole mastery of the Labyrinth. The rest of the worlds—they exist to keep the Chosen Ones in perpetual paradise.''

"Yeah, but ain't it always that way?'' she asked him. "I knew a guy once, he said that if the Africans had discovered gunpowder then as soon as they discovered Europe they'd have taken over *it*. Just one little thing makes the difference and then everybody makes it right in their own head. My ancestors was slaves owned and bossed by Bible-thumpin' fundamentalist Baptists who preached that black was the mark of Cain and slavery was God's law. And not so long ago your people was hounded and hunted as Christ killers, cursed by God, the root of all evil. The only thing at the bottom of this Company is that it's all too human."

He nodded. "And so are these rebels, and so are we. And that's why I'll keep this appointment. I wouldn't be too worried. If they wanted me dead, I'm not that hard a target, and if they purely wanted revenge then killing Dash would have been the most horrible thing they could have done to us. But if I cross them, or make them mad, then they'll come after Dash again and this time with real vengeance."

"They'll get Dash again over my dead body, Sam," she told him seriously. "That I swear to you."

He leaned over and kissed her. "You know, I really believe that."

She sighed. "You gonna call in Markham and get backup? You should, you know."

"Uh uh. I'm pretty sure that they'll be looking for that kind of thing."

"Sam—they'll hook you on something and run you ragged. You never been on that shit. You don't know what it can do to you no matter what you think. Or they'll switch you for some other Sam."

"I doubt if they'll try that switch trick again with me. As for the rest—well, I don't make a very good stripper and I'm not much good if my brain's fogged. No, I'm going to go to bed and get a decent night's sleep, then spend the day tomorrow with Dash, and then I'm going for a little walk."

4.

An Offer You Can't Refuse

The room was darker than a subway tunnel after the power failed, and he tried to move, then discovered that he was held to a chair by some kind of manacles. It didn't matter much; his head was beginning to clear now, and it only felt like forty marching bands were rummaging around in there all playing different songs and nobody in tune.

A single light snapped on, its glare directed straight in his face, a blazing and blinding sun in a sea of darkness, although beyond he could barely make out two figures.

"I see Sleepin' Beauty's awake," said a voice he didn't quite recognize.

"Yeah," responded the other man. "I still don't see why we just don't stick his brain in the washing machine and get all the dirty laundry nice and sweet. For a fuckin' traitor his ass is bein' treated real sweet."

"You're Company men?" he asked, trying to clear his head.

"Yeah, sure. What's left of it, anyway. You should know."

"Bill Markham here?"

"Outside. He's the only reason you're still in one piece and of one mind, you might say."

"And Dash?"

"Can't say."

A door opened and another man came in, closed the door behind him, and stared at Sam.

"You look like hell," said Bill Markham.

"Uh uh. I've seen Hell this trip and it's much worse. Is everybody all right?"

Bill Markham took a seat and sighed. "The answer to that is a relative one. I'm not sure of anything, Sam, including you. There's a ton of folks here who want to have you for breakfast and stick you into dissection, but so far I've held them off. I've known you longer and more personally than anybody else except Brandy, and I want your side first."

"You know some of it."

"Some. Maybe more than you want me to know. The trouble is, Sam, the pieces don't fit. I got a lot of jagged pieces and I can't make 'em go together."

"You want it all, then."

"From the top, Sam. From the top. From the time you went into the Labyrinth until the time you came back out. And I want no details spared."

"Where's Dash?"

"Safe and secure, I swear to you. At the moment he's staying with Brandy's cousin Bernice. Not a scratch on him, I might add. He's a tough kid."

Sam Horowitz sighed. "Yeah, he is. All right, then. It's all over now, no matter what. Get me unstrapped from this damned bed and sitting up straight, and maybe a drink, too, if you can. This is gonna be one long and involved story."

"Do it," Markham ordered.

"But, Boss . . . !"

"Where the hell's he going to go?"

One of the men came over and fingered a combination that released the straps. Sam groaned, stretched, and sat up, moving carefully one limb at a time to try and get some circulation back. At least he didn't see any big bandages, but he didn't exactly suddenly want to do cartwheels, either.

"Water's all we got for now," Markham told him. "Glass and pitcher there on the table."

Sam nodded. "If you got several extra strength aspirins, though, it'll help a lot."

"I got some," the second guy said. "Here."

They poured Sam some water in a Dixie Cup, and he took it and gulped down three of the pills, then settled back.

"You're gonna find this hard to believe," he warned them. "I've got all the answers, but I'm gonna tell it in my own way."

"We got noplace else to go," responded Bill Markham.

Well, at least I don't have to give you the build-up, and I assume that you, of all people, understand why I *had* to go. You're a good enough detective to figure that out. For the benefit of the Cretin Brothers here, though, I won't explain until later. Might as well entertain the boys as well as educate them so maybe one day they'll grow up to be detectives instead of cowboys.

I'd like to say that if I hadn't had no real choice in the matter I wouldn't have gone, but I think it would be a lie. Maybe the idea of going off into danger with the obvious potential of leaving a fatherless child and a widow behind isn't the correct, moral thing to do, but it would have been irresistible in any event. I mean, consider the enormous lengths they'd gone to to make sure that I went down the rabbit hole. Clearly they didn't want to kill me—not yet, anyway—because they had ample opportunity to do that without going through all this crap. The fact that they didn't was in and of itself fascinating to me.

They always overdid everything, too. You'd think that by now these characters would have learned that the simpler plan is better, and direct action beats the hell out of piling complexity on complexity so that you vastly increase your chances of something going wrong. When they tried to take over here in that Whitlock business they blew it by being too complex and devious; then they even blew covering up their own mistakes for the same reason. The same thing went for the drug plot of theirs. I think you or I might have pulled that one off, given the drug and the same lack of any moral scruples, but they had to go and make it so damned complex they screwed themselves and allowed us to finally wind up with their whole operation in our hands.

So, yeah, I was going no matter what, but there was a kind of perversity in my feeling better because I was forced into it anyway. Kind of took the load of guilt off my shoulders.

Well, anyway, I went.

As many times as I'd seen it, the opening of the Labyrinth always fascinates me. First a single straight line of pure energy, then it collapsed into two lines, then four until there was a square, then eight, and finally twelve—a cube unfolding from a single burst, hovering just above the concrete floor of the substation. When it stabilized, I stepped in and was immediately in that strange world of total silence.

The Labyrinth stretched tunnel-like in both directions, its facets showing different worlds and world views on four of its sides, including the one on which I stood. With its myriad sidings, switches, twists, and turns it was a labyrinth in truth as well as name, and, supposedly, only the dispatchers knew just where you were and how to get you from point to point. *Supposedly* was the key. I, of course, knew the complexity of this region quite well, and needed no one to direct me.

I began walking towards the main switch, going through cube after cube of linked line, each one showing four different views. Few were easy to make any sense of; the one I'd entered, as you know, was at the bottom of a concrete well-like depression and showed nothing but bare walls. Few have full station or substation capabilities, though; these were automated exits to worlds not yet developed by the Company, or worlds not worth developing. Some of those showed thick forest, or grassy hills, or blasted plain.

Those blasted ones always get to me in the pit of my stomach. It's depressing to discover the number of worlds in which the atomic bomb had not only been invented but had been used.

For while I appeared to be travelling a physical distance between two geographical points; in truth I wasn't right now. Every view I saw, when I could see one, was the same point in space at which I'd left. I was travelling not away from it but down the line of possible worlds that were not only possible but real, coexisting one atop the other with no dimensional points of reference to allow one to know of the other. I know that's old hat to you, but let me tell it in my own way, one step at a time.

The switch onto the main line was not very far down, and I reached it in ten minutes. You could always tell a switching cube even when you might not see the dispatcher; you could hear, in a hollow, dry, closed chamber sort of sound, both yourself and the others, and there were no views in the cube facets. None but one forward, which was glassine and opaque.

A light came on behind the glassine wall and inside sat a creature who was not quite human but nonetheless was a real live person. He was a gnome-like character with a wrinkled, oversized head that seemed molded out of clay, and thick, high pointed ears and enormous eyes, and when he opened his mouth the teeth were as sharp and pointed as a shark's and seemed to go on back in his mouth forever.

He sat hunched in a high-backed chair over a complex console, and he looked up and stared at me. "*Gloobenfarble gazoort, Smadish?*" he asked in a deep, gruff voice.

"Sam Horowitz, Security, on assignment. Check your board," I told him impatiently.

The big eyes looked down and there was a readout from the sensors in the switching cube that gave all the necessary data from the implant you folks stuck in my bones.

The dispatcher adjusted a control. "Very well. Destination?" The huge mouth and lips formed different shapes, but the translators worked quite well, even sounding just like his voice might say it in English.

"Need to know," I responded. It's nice sometimes to have a security clearance and be able to do that. Now I know why there are so many Top Secret stamps at the Pentagon. "Main line, down-line," I added.

The gnome shrugged. "All right. You security boys get a mite touchy over nothing, don't you?"

"I'm not in a social mood right now. I'm on business. Just switch me."

"Switched over. Exit left."

I turned and saw that the wall to my left had now become a continuation of the tunnel-like assemblage of cubes, and I turned and walked through without another word.

Well, you know the main line, and there was occasional traffic as usual. Others were using the Labyrinth on business, going between the worlds in some cases with the same casualness that a businessman in New York might have to hop a commuter jet to Boston. Some were couriers, others technicians, and still others marketing analysts and the like looking at new products in one world that might be useful and profitable imported into theirs, and a few, of course, would be other security people.

Still, there were not many of them, and there were long stretches of nobody at all. The Labyrinth was incredibly long and there were a lot of worlds.

They were an interesting lot, though, these fellow travelers. None in this section were like the gnome or some of the other dispatchers; this was the Type Zero region—people like me, yet not like me.

A fellow in a rather ordinary business suit and briefcase walked by, followed by another man who was dark-skinned, maybe six-six in height, but who was wearing sandals and a uniform not unlike a Roman legionnaire's in all those Biblical movies. Then I had to step out of the way to allow a woman to pass wearing a snow-white powdered wig and a hoop skirt that seemed five feet wide. She contrasted well with a Melanesian woman wearing only a grass skirt and two big orchids in her hair, and the extremely Chinese-looking fellow wearing a plaid kilt and frilly shirt.

I couldn't help wondering in spite of my situation if the guy played bagpipes using the Chinese musical scale. And if you could have told the difference if he did.

I went through a lot more switches, but always remaining on the main line as instructed.

It was during the long stretches that I began to wonder when or if I'd be contacted after all. Maybe they *did* have some way of knowing that Dash was safe. Maybe this was just a dry run. I couldn't be sure of anything, but I longed for something neither lethal nor painful to happen. Hell, if I went much more I'd be down to the main switch to the Company Headquarters world.

In spite of my impatience and anticipation, when it happened I was almost unprepared. There was no switch, no dispatch, no glassine wall, but just as I was going to continue to walk straight through to the next cube I was suddenly aware I had a choice. Both the straight line and the facet over my head were showing Labyrinth, but the cube didn't *feel* like a switch—there was the same deathly silence.

It's always strange to exit out the top—I needn't tell you that. You have to focus your mind and eyes on it, straining your neck, and, keeping your eyes

as close to its center as possible, walk forward. How the cube knows what this means I'll never understand, but as I went forward the cube rotated and I was suddenly walking, just fine, into what had been the top.

I rubbed my neck and then continued on, and as soon as I went into the next cube I stopped and looked back—and saw only blackness on the facets beyond. The switch that had opened just for me was now closed and invisible from the main line— and I, of course, was now also cut off from returning. Just for a moment I felt stupid and trapped, and began to doubt what I was doing.

I started paying attention to the views out of the cubes now. Walking down the main line, I'd moved geographically as well as simply from world to world. The worlds turned, time passed, but not always at quite the same relative rates. If you knew where you were going, and if there were stations at both ends, you could enter in Pennsylvania in one world and exit a brisk half hour's walk later in an alternate world Timbuktu. I wanted to get a decent idea of just how far from anyplace I knew I was.

The sidings, however, were strictly vertical movement, so again I was seeing four variations of the same place, but it wasn't a familiar place. Most of it looked like dense jungle, occasionally with high mountains in the distance, and none of it looked appetizing. The Amazon, maybe, or someplace in Africa.

I walked ahead, but someone else was at the controls here now, and I suddenly found myself emerging into a hot, steamy climate that made my flannel shirt and heavy topcoat, appropriate for home, seem like bad ideas. The best I could do was stop, remove the coat, unbutton a bit of the shirt, and roll up the sleeves. It didn't help. Much more than total nudity wouldn't help much in this heat and humidity.

I was suddenly aware that I was being watched, and I turned and saw that I wasn't far from the right idea in native attire. Two big, muscular men stood there, just inside the jungle, watching me intently, and they didn't seem to have any clothes on. What they had were dark, weathered Amerind features, black hair below the shoulders, and tattoos on their cheeks and foreheads, and possibly the biggest noses I'd ever seen on a human being; bigger, even, than Uncle Bernard's schnozz. Still, Uncle Bernard had never looked at me like I might be a potential dinner. I instantly began to wonder whether or not this had been such a bright idea after all.

"Excuse me," I said, trying to suppress my sudden anxiety, "but is this my stop? I seem to have lost my timetable."

One of them curled his lip and then said, "You come. Follow us. Hurry, hurry." And, with that, both turned and started into the jungle.

The only thing I wanted less than following them into a jungle was to remain here in trapped isolation, so I hurry hurried.

They were damned fast, and confident, but they knew the territory. They were also younger and in much better condition than I was, and after a while I was winded and called out, "Wait a moment! I can't keep up!"

They both stopped, turned to look back at me, and the same one said, "You come. Follow us. Hurry, hurry."

I suddenly realized that I'd just heard the fellow's total command of the English language. I struggled for breath, took a bunch of deep ones, then said, "All right—lead on, but I hope it isn't much further." I began to suspect some fiendish revenge plot to murder me after all—by heart attack.

"You come. Follow us. Hurry, hurry," replied Bignose once more, turning with his companion and continuing.

"Yeah, yeah. 'Hurry, hurry,' chop-chop, you asshole."

They weren't completely naked after all; both wore some kind of coarse briefs that covered their genitals but were mere straps around their asses. Even as well built as they were, though, I wanted to see what kind of speed they'd make wearing what I was wearing.

They went on and on and just when I was convinced that I had to stop, that I would never make it another step, they broke free of the jungle and out into a clearing leading down to a fairly broad river. Right at the river somebody had built a house—not the kind of house you'd expect this pair's people to build, but a real one, apparently made of manufactured materials although with a thick straw mat kind of roof. It was one story, rectangular, and built on stilts, indicating that the river was often a bit higher than it was now, and from it, leading right into the river, was a dock of crushed stone that must have been some job to build.

Surrounded by forest, the lack of wood in either the house or dock made me wonder just what size termites they had around these parts.

I let the two tribesmen get far ahead now—no hurry, hurry any more; this was clearly my destination. They ran up to the house and one went in and I could hear a lot of gibberish being yelled inside.

I reached the house and then sank down on the stone steps, exhausted. Anybody who wanted to talk to me could damn well meet me *this* much. I was too winded to even give a damn who or what was inside any more.

Still, I heard someone come out behind me and I turned and saw a rather distinguished-looking middle-aged man there. He was white, although a weathered brown from the climate, fairly tall, with a squared-off face and deep-set very blue eyes, and he was wearing bleach white Bermuda shorts, a thin cotton white button-down shirt, and tennis shoes. He had a long, graying, but neatly trimmed beard and a big curly moustache, and he looked for all the world like some nineteenth-century British colonial officer.

"Sorry the boys set too strong a pace, but we weren't really sure when you'd be coming and I had to be at the controls, naturally, and set others to check for tails and tracers and the like and that didn't leave anyone but them to meet you." The English was impeccable, if more than a little British or even Australian or South African, but with a definite trace of some other accent, too. German, maybe.

I was still winded, but managed, "Well, you know who I am, but to whom am I speaking?"

"Oh—sorry. I am Herbert Voorhes, and this is my humble home."

"Are you behind all this?"

Voorhes looked a bit uncomfortable. "Well, no,

not exactly. In fact, I was rather opposed to you as the man for this job, but I was overruled." He sighed. "But you're all in!" He turned and yelled back into the house in that gibberish the native had spoken. "I've just ordered us drinks. Gin and tonic suit you? Over ice in your case, I should think."

I nodded. "Sounds fine to me. I don't know what time it is here but my body says it's well after ten in the evening."

Voorhes shrugged. "One has less trouble with these things when one realizes that the sun is always over the yardarm *someplace*, even within each world."

To my surprise, a young girl emerged with the drinks. She was small and quite pretty, and clearly of the same race as the two men who'd brought me here. Like them, she was virtually naked except for the leather-like thongs and a bit of padding in the genital area, but she was more naked than anything on the Playboy Channel, that was for sure. She, too, had a heck of a nose but it was more than offset by her other attributes.

She bore a tray with two highball glasses filled with gin and tonic, complete with little plastic swizzle stick. I took one and sipped it, knowing that no matter how thirsty I was, I didn't dare chug it down in this climate. Never, never get high on a case and particularly not in enemy territory. One of the oldest rules, and, as tired and thirsty as I was, one of the toughest to keep. I *needed* a couple of doubles right then.

Voorhes took his, said, "Thank you, my dear," and the girl—she looked perhaps sixteen—smiled and turned and went back into the house.

"You seem to have quite a setup here, Mister

Voorhes," I noted. "Is there any civilization in this world or are these people the norm?"

"Oh, there's civilization here, although not the sort that you would fancy, I'd wager. The bulk of this world is pretty much stuck in the Stone Age, with the few Bronze Age tribes having fairly decent empires. Oh, they had cracks at things, but cyclical plagues and famines seemed to have knocked much of the world back so many times that they don't even try much any more. Most of where you go in this world it appears that curiosity, even ambition, has just died out in the people. I tried to introduce a few simple labor-saving concepts here and they saw and understood but rejected them. Said such things would poison their way of life! Just from me being here they've learned a lot about what is potentially available and it horrifies them. They want none of it. Their culture is almost entirely spiritual in nature. These people don't even understand the concept of property or competition. They live short lives, but rather happy ones overall. Sometimes I wonder if they didn't take the better track. They have no crime, no social hangups or inhibitions, and are relatively nonviolent. A bit sexist, of course, but all primitive societies are—women and children first, of necessity, you see."

I sat back on the steps and tried to relax. This wasn't exactly what I'd been expecting, although I wasn't quite sure what I *had* been expecting.

"You want to tell me now what this is all about?"

Voorhes looked surprised. "Why, dear boy, I thought that was obvious! We are having a bit of a problem here and we need the services of a detective."

I frowned. "Come again? What kind of problem?"

Voorhes sighed. "I'm afraid we've got more than a bit of a murder on our hands, and it's impossible for anyone within our organization to investigate the matter properly. One by one, someone is polishing off our Board of Directors."

"Now, hold it," one of the other interrogators put in. "You mean they went to all this trouble to hire you? That's pretty damned hard to believe."

"How long you been off the gooseberry lay, son?" Sam asked sourly.

"Huh? What the hell . . . ?"

"Never mind. I don't care what you believe." Sam told him, aware now that these weren't just ordinary muscle but local Company boys. Not too experienced with the Labyrinth but not as ignorant as they let on, either. "I'm telling you exactly what happened, as near as I can remember it."

The aspirin were starting to kick in and he was feeling better but tired. "Now, you want me to tell it before I keel over or not?"

"Go ahead, Sam." Bill Markham urged. "I'm all ears."

I stared at the man. "You mean this was all an elaborate attempt to hire me?"

Voorhes cleared his throat nervously. "Well, not entirely, but it became so, yes. You see, we had a serious problem. Anyone well qualified to do it who worked for us simply couldn't be trusted in this matter for a number of reasons. Doing it ourselves was simply out of the question since we might be hiring someone working for the fox to guard our henhouse. And since it was our own lives at stake, we couldn't take the chance. But whoever we got had to understand both the Labyrinth and its complexities completely. The greatest detective in any world was no good to us because he'd have to spend months just learning the rules and procedures and tables of organization and the like and getting comfortable with the concept. That left someone from the Company; someone well-connected enough to find out if indeed we were compromised, but anyone we got from there would have a vested interest in cheerfully stalling until we were all dead. You can understand our dilemma."

I could at that. "So you decided to kidnap me and my son and hold my son as the price of solving your problem. I'm surprised you didn't just take Brandy."

"Oh, we couldn't do that. Even if we thought she was fully qualified to do it and hadn't been, as it were, out of circulation and practice for years now, she could hardly be objective. I mean, she has good reason to hold grudges against us for past—unpleasantries—and even if she tried to do it she would be understandably blind prejudiced enough to go after certain members of the Board, guilty or not of what we wanted. You, on the other hand, have an excellent reputation for this sort of thing, have kept your hands and head in the business consistently, and you, along with your wife, are responsible for doing us in the last time and in actually trapping and convicting a member of the Company's board. Your clearances and contacts within the Company are impeccable. You see?"

I nodded. "I see, all right, and I suppose in a way

it's flattering, but you don't seem to have my own interests covered. If I took on your case, and remained as objective as I could be under the circumstances, I would have to know as much about your own top organization as I do about the Company. I would know who all your leaders were, where they were, and many of the details of your operation. In the end, I would know too much."

"True enough," Voorhes agreed, "but you know that there are many rather easy ways around that sort of thing. Otherwise, in this sort of technology, none of us could feel any measure of security."

I thought of those two opposition security men, like little children, drooling and blank. "I don't think I'd like a little explosion in my head and a life trying to figure out how to tie my own shoelaces."

"Well, there are other ways than that. In fact, I don't mind telling you flat out that we are better than ninety percent complete on our grand and final project. The Company will be destroyed, Mister Horowitz. We know how to do it and we will do it. We tried gentler ways and you and your wife blocked that. There are some who think you should be thanked for that. Had we succeeded in hooking the leadership of the Company on that nasty little drug we would have come to run it, and near absolute power would have changed hands from them to us. There are many, including myself, who wonder if we would have been any better at it than they over the long run. We are all human, Mister Horowitz. Such power would have proven —irresistible."

There was a rumbling of thunder in the distance and Voorhes looked up at the sky. "Come," he said. "You are rested now. Come inside the house before the storm breaks and we will discuss it further."

The house was larger than it appeared, and quite comfortable-looking, although it lacked modern amenities. It was an eighteenth-century house in a Stone Age world, with oil lamps for light and much of the furnishings having that handmade look. It was as good as you might expect in a non-technological world, though, and there were some concessions. Screens on the windows, netting over the doors to keep out the bugs, that sort of thing. The stone construction kept it cooler, although with a perpetually damp smell and feel to it.

In a back room, I could hear two women's voices speaking to one another in the native language, and while I could make nothing out, the light tone and occasional giggles reminded me of two schoolgirls playing hooky. I took a seat on a hard couch in the living room and Voorhes sank into a padded rocker that looked well used.

"Where do you get the ice?" I asked him.

"Huh? Oh, there is power and some amenities in the substation control room, including a small freezer. Every day I go down there and collect some things, like the ice, and bring them up here in an insulated cooler until used. The natives were fascinated by clear ice. Other than hail and snow on the distant mountains they'd never seen the like. They like cold drinks, but they are actually rather smart. They immediately saw how making ice could lead to the preservation of food and that this would be a major threat to their lifestyle and values. They'll accept an iced drink now and again, but won't hear of using it outside of the house here."

I looked around. "Why are you here, Mister Voorhes?" I asked, genuinely curious. "Is your opposition system so extensive that they can afford to have men like you stuck here as mere station masters?"

Voorhes was silent for a moment, then replied, "No, not as extensive as all that. Oh, this abandoned spur has its uses, not the least of which is that the station itself is so different in design and operation from the standard one that it's nearly impossible to detect, but, yes, you're right, it could be run by almost anyone. I live here because I choose to. Because not only is this world unpolluted, but it steadfastly rejects our pollution. There is a purity, a simplicity about this place that I have found nowhere else. These people have nothing but an attitude. If we could export it, even its basic essence, we would give humanity something it truly needs and lacks, or has forgotten. I myself am so much a victim of our modern technological societies that I have to have this house and many of the creature comforts. Our ancestors knew how to farm and hunt and gather but we ourselves have lost that. We are dead without our technology, at least at some least common denominator level. So, I am as minimalist as I can force myself to become here, and I find a measure of peace."

I nodded, understanding the man even though I wasn't sure that what he saw as the idyllic life was anything I, personally, would pick. Sort of an extreme version of what Brandy and I had experienced when we moved from our dense, urban environment to the mountains of rural central Pennsylvania. You had no idea how much pressure you lived under, just day to day, in the city, until it was removed. But I had a real fondness for central heating and air conditioning and cable TV and supermarkets, and I'd gone about as rural as I wanted to get.

"You are not what I expected on the opposition," I noted, not trying to be coy or anything other than honest.

"Indeed? And what did you expect? Oh, yes— the drug business. Ugly business, that. We're not all philosophers, Mister Horowitz, and we're not even all very nice people. Most of us were, once, but not any more. We've been made bitter and cynical and cruel. The irony of conflict with an enormous and evil institution is that you can effectively fight it only by adopting its morals and its methods. Sooner or later, you become as corrupt and evil as they, and you tell yourself your ideals are still intact, but they become mere excuses for the highest forms of barbarism. It's the curse of the modern revolutionary, I fear, and I am as guilty of this as any of the others. Perhaps more so, since I am the group theoretician—the fellow who soothes consciences if there are really any left. I am a bit more sane when I am in this environment and in these surroundings, that's all. And yet, even in the worst of us there is that glimmer of purpose, of conscience, of some sort of moral imperative. That is why we have agreed now that half measures simply do not wash. The Company must be destroyed—utterly. The Labyrinth must be shut down, the stations dismantled, the atmospheric systems and switch points rendered

permanently inoperative. Each world must continue ignorant of and deprived of the fruits of the
others, free to find its own destiny, good or bad. If
the Labyrinth remains open, it will be used and
abused, if not by the Company then by us, and if
not by us then by someone else. And, like us and
our mirror image of the Company, the vast bulk of
humanity will be protected from anything except
itself."

I thought it over. I wanted to know more. I
wanted the whole picture. Besides—there were
other factors. I shifted in my seat and then said, "I
suppose I should tell you now that my son is no
longer under your control, and I made arrangements that he'll be much more difficult and costly
to get again."

Voorhes was definitely startled. "Really? And yet
you came anyway? Telling no one?"

I nodded. "I came, and nobody except Brandy
knows my real purpose. I did, of course, lay in
some insurance, but so long as I'm alive the
Company knows nothing. I think that in at least
one respect you misread me, maybe more. You
see, if you had still had my son, I would not be here
now."

The storm broke, rather dramatically timed to
my great inner satisfaction, and there was suddenly a windstorm inside the house as well, causing
Voorhes to jump up and struggle to close the
immediate windows against the already pounding
rain.

The fellow is too devious for his own good, I
reflected as I watched the show and did nothing to
help. *He makes a plan much too complicated and
much more costly than need be just to lure me here*

and yet, with sure signs of a storm coming, he makes no move to close the windows before it actually hits. It said a lot about Voorhes' personality and character.

The bearded man was in the other room, shouting at the girls in the native tongue, and when he came back in he was clearly winded, again to my devilish delight. Served the old bastard right for running me ragged through that damned jungle.

Voorhes took a couple of minutes to settle himself, mumbled a lot of dark phrases glaring at the rain and the doorway in a Germanic tongue, then got himself back together and sat back down and stared at me for a few seconds, getting back on track.

"Fascinating," he said at last. "I mean you, Horowitz. Naturally, we established a difficult but possible trail to see if indeed you could do it. If you hadn't been able to track and liberate your own son on your own world, then you wouldn't have been considered for the more difficult task."

I wasn't sure if that was the truth or not. It certainly made a lot of sense out of what they'd done, but then the cost had been high and Voorhes had seemed genuinely surprised at the news. It made little difference in the outcome but the answer would tell me a lot about how far I could trust these jokers. I decided to test it.

"If that's so, then you lost a lot of people in the taking, cost yourself a fortune, exposed an underground organization on my world, and lost two of your own in the process."

Voorhes shrugged. "The organization was no longer necessary or relevant to us. The people, with two exceptions, were little more than cannon fodder in the struggle—less than pawns, really. The two of any import knew the risk and felt confident of themselves. They were also expendable, as are we all, in the cause. Their usefulness was in running the cover on your world in any event, and, as I said, that was no longer needed. Its exposure has actually saved us time, money, and manpower, since such a network and those who taste the power of it is not easily shut down with an order. Still, I find it curious that you would come after getting your son back. Come defenseless and alone."

I shrugged. "I'm an easy man to kill, so I don't worry about that part of it in my profession. I brought no weapons because I'm lousy with weapons. That's not my field of expertise. Brandy is the weapons expert, as your people discovered. And I have clients, not owners, and my value to said clients is useless if my brain's messed with or drug dependent or anything like that. Besides, while I have no reason to love you or your people, I don't have much love and admiration for the Company, either. I see the same things wrong that you see, and I don't like them. At the moment, if you'll pardon my honesty, I think both you and the Company are a pair of slime balls. You're both vicious, corrupt, and you see people, even whole worlds, as nothing more than spots in a ledger or—less than pawns, really."

Voorhes looked uncomfortable at that. "All that you say is true, yet we will stop it. Without the Labyrinth there is no corrupting power."

"And you're not really sure that you have the strength or will to turn it off, even if you have a method, are you? That's why some murder of one of your top people has you in a tizzy. You're not afraid that one of your top boys has turned traitor; you're afraid that at least one of your boys has become so corrupted that he'd rather be a demi-god than give it up. That's it, isn't it?"

"You are quite perceptive, Horowitz. I'll give you that. Perhaps I misjudged you."

"You said you were against bringing me in at all. Why? And who was my champion?"

"We had a choice of many of the greatest detectives ever produced by civilization. Frankly, I didn't find your qualifications all that great in comparison. I also believed that you had too much of an ax to grind against us for past indiscretions. However, you might just be the right one for this after all. As to who championed you— interestingly, our computers suggested you as one on a very short list. Two others, one of whom I think you know—or at least know of—picked you off it."

I gave him a wan smile as the storm continued to howl and pound all around them. "Now I'll tell you the conditions under which I'll take your case," I said.

"Conditions? Consider your position, man! Have you lost your senses?"

"Some people think I never had them. You know that I've got high security Company blockers in my head. Any attempt to put me under a hypno or something like that and reprogram me or get at information would be very unpleasant for me. I'm sure you've had a monitor on me at least since we came inside, though. You know I'm not lying to you. I'll catch your murderer for you—or he'll catch me—but beyond the lie detector we don't go. No drugs, no programming, no funny techniques. The most I'll accept voluntarily is the same kind of blocking seals on what I learn about you all as I have on the Company data. I don't tell them your secrets and I don't tell you theirs. Beyond that, I have free and unlimited access to any and all data that I need, any people, places, and the like I require, and absolute freedom of action. I will get all the cooperation I need or I'll quit. Either you trust me, within reason, to play as fair with you as I do with the Company, or it's impossible. My wife and child stay out of it and sacrosanct. Anybody touches them and that becomes my only concern and you can go to hell.''

Voorhes sighed. "You ask too much trust from ones like us. They will never go for it.''

"Then everything you did was in vain. You play with my mind and it'll blow up. You hook me on some new variety of drug and you blow any chance I'll have a clear head and the sort of conditions conducive to solving anything at all. You are a client, nothing more or less. As a client you are confidential from anyone including my other clients, and I'll take no case that treads on conflict of interest. Since I've mostly been designing and checking out security installations lately, that's not likely. I don't even care which one of you wins. The case stands alone. Either it's my way or you can either send me back and find one of your great detectives to take it or you can blow me away and do the same.''

Voorhes thought a moment, then responded, "We considered this problem. There are a lot of good detectives, and, as you might imagine, some are on paper as qualified if not as experienced as you. We decided that the only way to insure our own security was to use someone with, oddly, a high moral sense—a strong conscience, if you will. That was what made the list so short. So far you have been sitting there saying, 'What a decent sort of chap this is. I simply can not reconcile this with the mad terrorists I know they are.' Well, I will not disappoint you. You will have your freedom, and your independence, but you will carry a burden with you. You have no idea how many or which worlds we either control or move freely in. If you take this case, and anything you learn of us gets to the Company—if *anything* goes wrong that results in a betrayal, whether your fault, our fault, or nobody's fault, an order will be given resulting in the obliteration of millions of innocent men, women, and children by nuclear devices or other means as we choose or that are convenient. The targets have been set up at random by our computers; even we don't know which ones are primed. But if we are betrayed, and you survive, we will make certain you get graphic evidence that we have carried out our threat."

I was appalled. "Now, wait a minute! I'll take responsibility for myself but you ask for things out of my hands!"

"That is the way it is, Horowitz. You must believe we will do what I said we will do. Those are the terms."

I shook my head. "Uh uh. I can't take on that kind of load no matter what. The Company's not stupid and you've drawn arrows pointing to me and mine that have drawn them like flies."

"You misunderstand, Horowitz," Voorhes said curtly. "If you refuse, then we shall not only eliminate you but put all our resources on eliminating your wife and child as well no matter where they might be. A small nuclear device in a suitcase many miles from your home would do it, and we can track them and wait. You have already taken the case. You did that when you showed up here in response to my invitation."

I reached inside my shirt pocket, pulled out a cigar and lighter, and lit the stogie, then sat back and sighed. The storm was already slacking off; it was damp and unpleasant, even clammy, but clearly the rain was stopping. *Damn!* I never figured on them being *that* slimy! I had no doubt that the sons of bitches would do just what they said, too.

Still, this was the greatest challenge I could ever face in my career, and maybe one too great. Billions of lives . . . a whole world. That was one hell of a fee. And solving their damned mystery was only the start of the problem.

"All right, then maybe we should start," I said, feeling curiously distanced, almost a third party watching the affair. "Background first. Why you started this rebel organization, why you hate the Company so much, and how the leadership came together. I want to know what binds you."

"That is easy," Voorhes replied softly. "We are all dead."

"Our home world was like most of the Type Zero worlds you know," Voorhes began. "The history, particularly from the Middle Ages onward, was quite divergent, but that common thread gives you a general idea that our values, our cultures, weren't so alien as to be unrecognizable. The precise details are unimportant."

"You're all from the same origin world?" I asked him. *That* was new.

Voorhes nodded. "The Board and top leadership, yes. The vast hordes of others, no. Below us are hotheads, malcontents, revolutionaries, criminal types, and madmen—the usual sort you can always find in such a fight, and we had an extraordinarily large pool to choose from. The larger groups are from worlds we either control or have agreements with. That sort of thing. But it's our world that's at the heart of it. You see, we bred a lot of people who were just too damned clever and societies where it was simply too difficult for the Company to remain totally unobtrusive, as it likes, as well as many things the Company wanted or could use.

"At any rate," he continued, "they—the Company—were discovered. Found out. They had the tables turned on them, so to speak, as our own people worked to discover all that we could about the alien invaders even as they were trying to find out everything about us and take us over. Enormous projects in more than one nation had been working on dimensional mathematics and interdimensional physics since a couple of brilliant theoreticians had come up with the math for them, and discovery of the Company and of the stations fed rather than confused or cowed us. Our leaders didn't run from it or dismiss it as unbelievable nonsense. No, the evidence was that we were being invaded by a parallel world. The natural thing was to try and figure out how to invade them in turn."

"Go ahead. I'm with you so far," I told him, fascinated in spite of myself.

"Well, you see, this was a case in which ignorance would have been better than a partial truth. We were like a planet in a solar system that for some reason could see nearer planets but could never see or imagine the millions and billions of stars. If invaded by aliens, they would assume the invasion was coming from one of the planets and they would build rockets to charge to the offense, never dreaming that these invading aliens came in starships and controlled a thousand million worlds. None of them ever dreamed that there was a Labyrinth. Oh, there might be an infinite number of parallel worlds, but one went through them one at a time. The concept of an almost random access network, an interdimensional railroad even, was inconceivable to them. And there was competition between nations as well for the potential prizes this alien civilization might hold. They played the game well. The Company was so arrogant and cock-sure of itself it didn't know what hit it. Agents were taken or killed, networks broken up, stations seized, in perfect coordination. Needless to say, it rang alarm bells everywhere."

I nodded. "A whole horde in control of stations with access to the Labyrinth. Yeah, I can see the problem. And I assume it was on a key part of the main line so the Company couldn't switch them off into limbo without cutting itself off as well."

"Indeed. Oh, the Company actually had little problems securing the Labyrinth proper, but once our folks had the technology they found weak points the Company hadn't exploited or covered and began to punch through themselves. Cruder mechanisms, naturally, by far, but a musket ball kills as surely as a machine gun bullet. And we were learning fast. Never before had the Company faced a foe who understood pretty much what they were facing and who had sufficient knowledge and technological skills to build on what they discovered, and to analyze and use the technology they found. Worse, being on a main line they couldn't simply lock a switch onto a limbo line, as you called it, and let them stew. Besides, they might well begin analyzing the power grid and building their own switches. They panicked. The Company, the entire Board, panicked. Operations were disrupted for the foreseeable future, and that might have been enough, but they had the nightmarish feeling that the Visigoths were knocking on the very gates of Rome. They took a vote, and their Director of Security was ordered to back flush that area of the line."

"Now you've lost me," I told him. "I was with you up to now." But, deep down, I thought I knew what the man was going to say, and it made things instantly clearer—and it made me sick to my stomach.

"First you purify the line between two switch points where the problem is. You sterilize it by storing tremendous energy in the power substations at each switch point and then, at a given signal, you feed that power back through all but one of the lines in the Labyrinth. It is two massive force fields, pure energy, coming at one another from opposite directions, disintegrating anything and everything within the cubes as they come. When they meet, the energy can go neither forward nor back if you've done your job right, so it goes in one massive surge to every station or weak point at the cube where they meet. When that happens there is an unavoidable additional surge from the central power core itself, suddenly liberated if only for a short while. The Labyrinth goes dark, but massive power rushes out until the power grid can be slowly brought back down to normal levels over a period of hours, even days. Otherwise it would melt the whole system. The energy release is sufficient to vaporize more than a third of the planetary surface, hurling up much of it in microscopic specks until it blankets the planet and darkens it for fifty to a hundred years. Everything not killed in the initial surge dies slowly and agonizingly in freezing cold thereafter."

Have you ever destroyed a whole world?

It's been done, but it takes a unanimous vote of the Board . . .

"Good God! There's nothing left?"

"Oh, some moss and lichens will survive, some microscopic spores, and probably a fair number of insects of the worst sort—cockroaches, that sort of thing. Some odd forms of sea life near volcanic vents that depend not at all on sunlight or warm water. But major life—human, plant, animal— that's gone. Every one and every thing. Worse than an atomic holocaust, if you can imagine that. The people, the culture, the books, the plays, the great works of art and architecture, the work of a millennia of intellectuals. All gone forever. There was never even a threat, let alone an attempt at negotiation or compromise. Not even a demand for unconditional surrender. They panicked and they did it and they didn't even lose any sleep over it. It was just one world, nothing important, peopled with inferior human beings."

"I think I can guess who the security chief who

carried it out was," I said, horrified.

"Yes. Mukasa Lamdukur. Not then on the Board —he was far too young for that. Not the man who voted to order it, although he certainly would have done so, but the man assigned to actually do it. Even then he was a schemer, consumed with ambition and a lust for power. He had already been gathering data on the old abandoned switch points from the past, and checking them out, then erasing them from the security data banks. He had the highest code—after all, he was born to the position, as it were, and they trust blood over anything else every time. Having found places to hide them, he now needed an army—an organization that could not be traced by conventional Company means. People who hated the Company so much they could never be swayed by it."

"Now you've lost me," I told him. "If your people were between your world and the Company's holdings, and if there was no negotiations, then where did you all come from?"

"We were already here. The Company works as much as possible through locals. You know that. You're a part of a local organization. Not only do locals know the territory but they are inconspicuous and you get your pick of the best talent. We had been recruited from our various nations and jobs before our countries turned the tables; we'd been brought to other worlds, even the Company world, to be trained in the new technology, the new economics, and become the Company on our world. We weren't the first by any means, just the last. We were cut off when the breakthrough occurred, and, quite naturally, Lamdukur ordered us arrested, rounded up, and if he'd been true to his orders he would have liquidated us all, since we were all potential threats to Company officialdom. He didn't, though. Instead, we were officially killed—the weakness he exploited most in that huge organization is the belief that whatever the computer tells you is true—and our records erased. We were taken to one of the hideaway worlds, outfitted with new security transponders that can be reprogrammed with almost any code once you have it, and set up as a rebel organization. Oh, he gave a stirring, tearful speech to us, I tell you."

"Uh huh. I bet. Like he did everything to stop it but those bastards on the Board just did it coldly, and he was morally repulsed by it and that he was the only means of eventually revenging yourself on the Company and so forth. I can imagine."

"The speech, yes. The effect on us, I doubt. Some of us couldn't take it. They went mad, or refused to believe that our world wasn't still out there someplace, or they killed themselves. The rest of us—we believed it. We knew the location. Most of us had husbands, wives, children back there, or at least brothers and sisters, parents, relatives, close friends. The loss was deeply personal, but it was more than that. We had no home, no roots, no reality any more. There suddenly was no future for us anywhere, nothing to live for— except revenge. Our hatred and our revenge fueled us, Horowitz, and still does. If I truly believed in a metaphysical Hell of eternal torment I would willingly consign myself there for eternity if I could murder this Company. But I—we—are already in Hell. We have been in Hell for a very long time now. It is always with us. It never goes away. We took what Lamdukur gave us and took advantage of the security freedoms we had and we set up shop to discover how we could murder the Company. We made a blood pact that we would never waver, and, so far, none of us have."

"Needless to say, you included Mukasa in your murder plans as well, but he was too culturally blind-sided to realize it. He thought you bought the package."

"Yes. The Company has many weaknesses, and its culture is the worst of them when properly understood. But, you see, we rejected tit for tat revenge. For one thing, destroying the Company world meant seizing control of the full Labyrinth, and not even Lamdukur could manage that without being caught. We finally decided we didn't want to destroy them—we wanted them in Hell. All of them. And for as long as possible."

"That's where your drug came in. Infect the Board and then they have to follow your orders because you have the supply. Use the Board to infect the top levels of society. Use them to infect the entire golden race of the Company, and then you have made them into a race of abject, addicted slaves."

"That *was* the gist of it, yes," Voorhes admitted. "It was quite a clever plan, too. You must grant us that. Particularly when we were able to turn Ioyeo into our willing and fanatical agent. Some of us may seem to be rather romantic figures—present company excepted. It wasn't difficult to engineer an affair, have it turn serious, and then convey our own loss and torment. We took her home and showed her what the Company had done. We showed her countless other examples of the cruelty and horror what you call G.O.D., Inc. had inflicted and continued to inflict; how many billions of lives it had so casually enslaved or snuffed out. His courier became our carrier, and he would become the first victim of his own plot. It was delicious."

I thought about Brandy and her torment with the drug. "Not if you're on the receiving end of things. You nearly destroyed my wife, not to mention quite literally blowing some of my brains out. Fortunately not the ones I used most, but I remember."

Voorhes shrugged. "You must understand that this is not merely revenge, it's a mission. The Company now controls or exploits thousands of worlds. There are hundreds of thousands, perhaps millions left to go. One by one they will be corrupted and made colonial possessions or they will be destroyed. How many lives is that, Horowitz? It must end, no matter what the cost, for the sake of those who have yet to feel the yoke. If the cost is you, or your family, or five whole worlds, or fifty, it must be done for the sake of the others. We alone can do it."

I didn't exactly go along with that greater good thesis, but I now understood what drove them, and why it wouldn't matter if I voiced my concerns. They were not going to be talked out of that by me or anyone else, not now, and they were by now hardened fanatics, able to rationalize anything at all to attain their ends.

Just like the Company.

"And now you say you're close to your goal," I noted. "A different way."

"That need not concern you. What our plans are

now is not something you want to know if you ever hope to live out a normal life."

"What you are planning may or may not be relevant to the case. I'll have to decide that later. If I have a need to know, then I'll have to know. The important point right now is that you feel you are close to your goal. How close? Weeks? Months? Years?"

Voorhes shrugged. "I'd rather not answer that, but a bit longer than months, certainly. Let's just say that it won't be next month but it might well be next year."

I nodded. "That will do. And how long have you known the rough completion time? That is, about how long ago did you determine you were going to be able to do it and within a specified time frame?"

The rebel frowned. "I don't understand your logic here."

"Bear with me."

He sighed. "All right—just a few weeks ago."

"How many weeks?"

Voorhes shrugged. "I don't know. Three, I guess. The last full Committee meeting at which the report was read to all of us was a bit under three weeks ago, Company time. I fail to see where this is leading."

"And when did your murder occur?"

"Ten days ago. At first we didn't think it was a murder or we would have acted sooner. You'll see why when you hear the details. Once our people established that it *was* murder, we've clamped down our own security and retreated to our secure areas whenever possible. That is one reason why we are here. The switch you came through will automatically operate only for me. Anyone else coming in, or going out, would have to be switched here manually, as you were. That is why I feel secure here."

I nodded. "But not everybody can afford to stay holed up. That's why you want this thing cleared up, isn't it? You've got the end in sight and you're all in your holes because you don't know if you're going to live to see it otherwise. It's limiting your effectiveness and increasing your paranoia."

Voorhes nodded sadly. "Yes. Indeed, that is why we finally decided we needed to get someone in to clear it up. Right now we don't even trust each other enough to go face to face. We don't even know where half the Board is, and they're keeping it that way, communicating through secure channels only. We can't even test one another. It's very frustrating."

"How many members are on your board, or committee, or whatever you call it?"

"Nine. At least, there *were* nine. We're now left with eight. No real replacements, either. The years have taken their toll. We eight are the last survivors of our world."

"Uh huh. What makes you think your victim wasn't just another casualty, though?"

"The murder site. Pandross—that was his name —was our own security wizard. He rarely ventured out of his lair, and that lair was so well protected that only members of the Committee itself could enter—and even then only with Pandross's personal added security code if he wasn't in the Security Center himself. We wanted no Mukasas in our organization, and no doctored records."

"All right. I'll have to take a good look at his

security system, which I assume you've changed, to make absolutely sure, but for now I'll take your word for it that only one of the eight could enter. There's no such thing as an absolutely secure system—I design them myself. It *is* possible that somebody outside of your Committee broke it, which would make somebody like Pandross, who was usually there if what you say is true, and almost always alone and feeling very safe and secure, the easiest mark of the entire Committee. What was the murder weapon?"

"It appeared that he had a stroke in his office. It can happen to any of us, so at first we merely mourned. But Pandross himself instituted a set of very rigid procedures, particularly when one of us died, and he was subjected to an exacting computerized autopsy and analysis. It clearly showed evidence of a nerve-based paralysis hold, one of the martial arts things, that would have rendered him either unconscious or unable to move. With that, we then discovered a fresh puncture wound in the left leg, such as a syringe might make. There was a tiny bruise that we could not see because it was on a dark patch of skin. Whoever did this had planned things thoroughly. There was nothing in the blood stream, but it might well have been something that broke down, or a natural substance, or even a set of air bubbles. We often forget how fragile we really are."

I nodded. "Well, I'm already inclined to accept your theory that one of you did it, just from what you said. Anyone who got in there would almost certainly be someone he knew and trusted. Anyone who could get that close to him and use that paralytic hold wouldn't be someone who overpowered him—there'd be signs of a struggle and other bruises and the like. He knew his assailant and trusted him or her enough to turn his back on them. The killer also knew him. You take targets of opportunity with the needle method. The killer knew of the dark patch and that it would conceal, buying him or her precious time before the autopsy found it and also probably insuring that the murder scene was cleaned up and precious evidence tossed out with the trash. The killer also knew the security room and its procedures, because obviously the goings-on there would have to be erased from the inevitable monitors, as well as the log in and out both of the security center and the world it occupied."

"We all knew how to operate the security apparatus," Voorhes told me. "We had to. We couldn't depend on him for everything, nor on his continued health and well-being. It was personal passcoded, though—implant I.D., handprint, retinal, and a coded password which we individually selected and which only we knew. There's no chance of a duplicate being slipped in. You could not access the security records without all of that, including the password."

"There's always ways, but I tend to agree. You are bound together by years of common struggle, a common heritage, and common goals. Even somebody as good as your boy wouldn't safeguard against the eight of you. If he couldn't trust you, then all was lost anyway. I assume you checked on where all eight of you were during that period?"

"Naturally. All of us have ironclad alibis, but, of course, with our command of the system they are as ironclad as tissue."

"Uh huh. Method, opportunity, and motive are the three essentials to solving one like this. We know the method, and that intrigues me. Whoever hit my place had people there with a knowledge of those paralyzing judo type holds."

Voorhes shrugged. "We all do. I doubt if a one of us would claim we could do it effortlessly and confidently, as the killer must have had to do, but any of us could have sufficient surreptitious practice to feel confident enough to do it. None of the Committee was directly involved in your operation, though. It was too likely that all involved would have to be trapped in your world for quite some time and none of us was willing to take that chance."

"Then who was that whispery-voiced character Brandy heard who was obviously in charge? I heard it on my tapes."

Voorhes looked surprised. "Damned if I know. I know of no one on that operation whose voice could be characterized that way. I'd like to hear that recording myself sometime."

"If you let me get back, I'll see that you get a copy. All of you. Not because I want him, although I admit to having foul thoughts in that direction, but because I think it's important that you can't identify him off the bat. If he wasn't at the top he had to be working for somebody who was, and very close to the top himself. Find him and we may find your killer."

I yawned. While it was mid-afternoon here, it was well past midnight for me now. "I'm going to have to get some rest before I can do anything more. The only way I'm going to have real freedom is to indicate to the Company that I'm on to something. It'll be up to you to provide me with just enough expendable information to keep them feeding me rope, so we won't have squads out looking for me. Also, I'm going to need someplace secure as an office area. You provide the place, I'll make it secure. I think this is going to be, overall, a very interesting case . . ."

Voorhes just gave me an odd smile and said nothing in reply.

5.

Rounding Up the Usual Suspects

I was dead tired, but I had trouble sleeping that night. It was neither the heat nor humidity nor the strangeness of the surroundings, but more my own situation that bothered me. I had expected that they wanted me for some reason; I hadn't expected a murder, and I certainly hadn't expected the way they trapped me with a moral dilemma. I had no doubt at all that they would in fact nuke some major city or precipitate a major war just to get at me, and they were dead on that I would never accept the responsibility for that.

I was also keenly aware of a double mission here, at least, and a sort of personal ethical problem. Once I solved their problem—if I could— they would hardly let me go with a pat on the head. On purely pragmatic grounds, once I solved it I was dead meat. I couldn't really stall on it, though; they'd have people and monitors all over me and I knew it. If I solved it, I was dead. If I didn't solve it, they would eventually lose patience and, well, same result.

As important was whether or not I could solve the other mystery of how they expected, within a year, to destroy the Company and shut down the Labyrinth. The coincidence of the murder of their security chief just after the report, and, I assumed, the go-ahead vote, on that was too big to ignore. Somebody, at least one of them, didn't agree with that decision and that action. Eliminating the nerve center first, the man who would be most likely to be able to catch them, was the obvious move of somebody in that case. Pandross knew them all, personally and intimately, for many years, and with his personal involvement and his computers and monitors he would have been the most likely man to finger an opponent, particularly one ready to kill one or more of their own.

There was every possibility that he smelled something and actually invited his killer up to talk about it, secure in his lair. The mere invitation would make it a "him or me" situation, and would have precipitated the murder. That was a very interesting idea.

O.K., sure, it might have been something petty, some long-standing grudge, some romantic triangle, any of the usual motives, but I leaned towards the vote and the murder as just too close to separate. Voorhes hadn't been wrong about the seductiveness of power, even in a rebel opposition. It would be interesting to know which of the nine had spoken out against the plan, if any, even in a devil's advocate role.

I finally did manage some sleep, and when I awakened it was to the smell of good things cooking and strong coffee. I pulled on my wrinkled clothes as best I could and wandered out into the house itself.

I expected to see Voorhes or perhaps the native girls in the rather primitive kitchen, and was very surprised to see a young woman as out of place here as I or Voorhes there instead. She was clad in a very scanty string bikini over which she'd draped a full apron to protect her from the spattering.

She was tall, lean, and dark-complected, with jet-black hair cut very short in a man's style, and her features were kind of hard to figure. Sort of a South American United Nations, although it went together quite well. Brazilian, perhaps, or from someplace where Brazil didn't exist but the same racial mix had created a rather attractive new race that was equal parts European, black, and Indian.

She turned to me and smiled for a moment, then went back to her cooking. It was hot as hell in the kitchen and I couldn't stand it for long and didn't know how she could, even dressed like that.

"Hello," she said to me. "I am Maria. Senhor Voorhes is in the station now but will be back any minute. Please go into the living room or out on the porch. It will be cooler to eat out there."

Portuguese accent, certainly, but a nice command of English. I shrugged, then asked, "What do they use for a bathroom in this place?"

"Outhouse out back," she told me. "Use the water pitcher and bowl in the bedroom for freshening up. The outhouse, it stinks terribly, so you will spend no more time in there than you must."

Well, I must, so I went out, walked around, found it, and found that if anything she'd flattered it. The insects around that thing were just enormous, and once inside the smell was enough to make you want to throw up. I was very happy I had to go before I'd eaten any breakfast; the question was whether or not I would be able to eat after relieving myself.

I made it out and got away fast, then took many deep breaths just to get the stench out as best I could, and went back up to the house. I hadn't even paid any attention to the pitcher and bowl; now I saw it did indeed have tepid water in it and there was a washcloth, small towel, and a few minimal toiletries on a small shelf underneath. I used them as best I could, trying to make myself as presentable as possible, then went back out and onto the porch. The freshening had done wonders; I was starting to be able to feel hungry again.

Out on the porch, Maria or somebody had set a table that looked quite nice. Netting had been lowered giving us some imperfect protection from the insects, and the table was actually set with china, real silver, ceramic cups, and some kind of flower in water in the center. There was a pitcher of some sort of juice already out that felt cold, and I poured some and sipped, then drank heavily of it. I didn't recognize the fruit, but it was sweet and it tasted really good.

Even so, I was beginning to realize just how spoiled and civilized I'd become in these past few years. I hadn't had nightmares of my position or responsibility during the night, but I had dreamed again and again of air conditioning.

I sat back and looked at the river and was surprised to hear a motorboat. I turned and saw it—pretty traditional rowboat with an outboard motor attached coming slowly up river towards the dock. Voorhes was the only occupant. This morning he was dressed in khaki shirt and shorts and wore one of those silly-looking hard bush hats.

He pulled up to the dock, cut the motor, jumped up onto the dock and tied off the boat to a stake embedded in the stone. Then he came up to the porch, unzipped the netting, and stepped inside.

"Good morning!" he said pleasantly. "I trust you slept well."

"I slept lousy. Hotter than hell with humidity matching the temperature and almost no breeze has never been one of my favorite conditions. Remember, I was in snow yesterday."

The rebel shrugged. "Well, each to his own. You've met Maria?"

"Only briefly. She's not local."

"No, she came in earlier this morning. You will get to know her quite well from now on. She's quite bright and quite useful in a number of capacities, and she will do anything at all that you say."

Sam's eyebrows rose. "Anything?"

"Yes," Voorhes responded, nodding. "Obedience, within a pecking order, is the norm for everyone in the society in which she was born and raised. You are, quite naturally, at the bottom of her particular pecking queue, just over her, but so long as you don't ask her to violate or attempt to overrule orders from above, she'll do just about anything. Don't mistake her for some roboticized or lobotomized individual, though. It's the way her people are. You will find her invaluable and talented."

"Yeah, I'll bet," I said sourly. "And she'll report every word I say and every move I make back to everybody else, so our murderer can know every move I make almost when I make it, know my plans, have access to my records and thoughts, and take whatever steps are needed to thwart me at every turn. Thanks a lot, Voorhes. And if I have to ·

cross paths with the Company, how in hell am I going to explain her?"

"Well, you didn't expect us to let you just run loose with everything you might know, did you? I admit that it hobbles you a bit, but not as much as you think. For one thing, she has been told to report only certain kinds of things back to us, relating to areas of particular concern to us. Those things relating specifically to your investigation aren't among them. As for the Company, she's carrying the transponder code of another young lady who is a licensed Company courier and she can get in and out of places rather easily and without arousing any suspicion. She already has with no trouble. The Company bureaucracy is like all bureaucracies; they'll take your word for it that she came as the result of a request for aid in light of your wife's condition and the need to have someone remain with your child. As for the unforeseen—well, you have some expertise in telling a convincing story. Ah—here she is, now!"

Maria came out bearing a large tray that contained a pitcher of coffee, real cream and brown sugar, and several bowls filled with various things from diced fresh fruit to some sort of egg and rice dish, sweet breads, and other things. She was no longer wearing the apron and was more in a state of undress than dress in spite of being barely modest.

She poured and served and then took her own seat.

"I hope you have more of a wardrobe than I have," I commented.

She laughed. "I have a small suitcase. Not too much, nothing cold weather, but more than this. If this disturbs you I can go change."

"No, no! That's fine for now. But I'm told you're going to be coming with me on this little adventure, and you'd certainly attract a lot of attention and probably catch your death if that's all you had to wear."

"Maria will also be your guide," Voorhes told me. "She knows the whats and wheres of our organization—and the no-nos as far as you are concerned—and this will allow us to minimize organizational contact until you want it and have something to tell us."

I nodded. "I assume you're not one of the big shots," I said to her. "For one thing, I'd think you'd be too young."

"I am a Drone Class D-4 out of Iquitos Control," she responded as if she was giving her college address in Iowa or something. "I am assigned to Alliance work. I am twenty-three."

A mere child, I thought, but said, "Drone. Sounds like you're a bee or something."

She didn't take it wrongly. "Our society is based on the efficiencies of the insect model," she told me. "I have seen many of your other societies and I find them anarchistic or immoral, every one. I do not understand how any of you can live that way. So much emotional outbursts, antisocial behavior, poverty, disease, filth . . . I don't know how people can live like that, or why they would tolerate it."

Good lord! They've assigned me a female Mister Spock! I thought, amazed. *Either that or a refugee from Orwell*. I made a note to find out more about her society when I could, but not to press it now. At least, for somebody who was supposed to be totally obedient, she sure as hell was outspoken and disrespectful. I liked that much, anyway.

"Well, all right," I sighed. "I guess there's no avoiding it. But, Voorhes, if her presence is the thing that alerts the Company and makes it all go bad, I won't be responsible or feel responsible. I neither need nor want her—nothing personal, my dear."

Voorhes shrugged. "Perhaps. This is an awkward situation for all of us, Horowitz. The sooner it is resolved, the less chance there is of something going wrong." He paused a moment. "We will arrange for you to have a wardrobe sufficient for your needs by later today. Are you ready to begin?"

I nodded. "If it's not too far, we might as well start with Pandross's place and let me look at the security system. The evidence will be long gone but you'd be surprised what you can tell just by being on the scene, and if that system is in any way similar to what I know or understand, then there might be things you overlooked."

"Done. Maria will handle that for you, and I will set up a working place for you to customize, although I suspect that if Pandross couldn't safeguard himself I don't see how you can, and that is always a danger."

"Pandross wasn't guarding himself from his friends, but rather the records from everybody but his friends. Still, I don't deny that when I get close I might well be a target. All I can do is try and make sure that anybody who nails me will get nailed. This is the damnedest situation any detective has ever been placed in, you know. The murderer knows everything about me, all my weak points and vulnerabilities, and I don't even have a list of suspects."

"You want them?"

"Only when I am secure," I told the rebel leader. "Have all the records, all the interrogations, everything done up to now available to me. I also want the personal backgrounds of everybody, and if you can get each other to give a general critique of the other eight and even Pandross it will help as well. I need to get filled in very fast here. And don't forget to include yourself in that stack."

Voorhes looked stung. "Why, I wouldn't have it any other way. Nor, of course, would my colleagues."

"Uh huh. And, Voorhes?"

"Yes?"

"I want to know if anybody at that meeting was opposed to your new master plan. Anybody. Even if they got talked into it and later voted for it."

"You harp on that. Are you really certain that the timing was more than a coincidence?"

"No," I admitted, "but right now it's the only motive I've got. Any chance of me getting back home at some point, by the way? There are things I'd like to pick up."

Voorhes smiled and shook his head. "Mister Horowitz, do we look like fools? To put you back on your own turf might seal our death warrant and the end of all our dreams. No, Horowitz—for the duration, that is the one spot and the one branch that is totally off limits. Maria here has firm orders to kill you if you so much as try it."

The pretty young woman gave me such a sweet smile at that.

Maria's normal clothing was practical if a bit unflattering, consisting of a light blue cotton pull-over shirt and pants and a pair of fairly heavy halfboots. Apparently the boots were made for mud or construction work but as she was told it might be cold in spots she'd decided they would do for that. I wondered if she really appreciated what kind of cold she might find. She wouldn't last ten minutes back home this time of year, and who knew what season or climate it might be where we might have to go?

Pandross's security redoubt wasn't all that far, and I began to suspect that most of these old and abandoned lines and spurs were very close to the Company world. It made sense; they were built when competing companies started out and abandoned as they consolidated into one monolithic corporate and social structure. It was quite natural that they would be building lines all over the place near where it all started, and that there would be few or none much further up the line.

Still, the site of the unfortunate Pandross's murder was even more impenetrable than I had thought. For one thing, it wasn't inside one of the alternate worlds at all but inside a modified and enlarged abandoned switching station on another of those spur lines. They had, of course, changed all the security procedures and did not tell me what they were, but they preserved all of Pandross's old programs and left his devices in place. They said it was in case some investigator like myself might find them useful, but I suspected that they just didn't know how to get rid of them. Break for me, anyway.

I spent a great deal of time examining the whole setup and control center. It was an antique station, and I could never have figured out the esoteric controls and the wall of antiquated switches and gages and the like there, but the superimposed security system was state of the art, the data computers well concealed. I didn't bother with them right now; I'd need somebody they'd talk to in order to get much out of them. By the time I finished with the security network itself, though, I was convinced. Nobody but someone authorized to enter the station could have gotten here, and there was no way in the world that this point could even be accessed, let alone penetrated, without the operator inside knowing about it.

Pandross had sat in his controller's chair, allowed the killer entrance, watched them come in, then probably talked with them for several minutes. More significantly, from the pictures there of the body and its placement, he'd gotten up and turned his back on his visitor, apparently to get some coffee or something else from the small kitchenette off to one side. The killer had used that to come up behind him, grasp him by the shoulders, and work the paralytic move. The rest was easy.

I had Maria essentially duplicate all the moves, with myself as Pandross, and up to the moment of the behind-the-back attack it all worked. She could not, however, work the move on me. Try as she might, she couldn't get the sort of grip on me to apply the proper pressure to the proper nerves.

"It is not possible," she told me after several tries.

"Sure it is," I replied. "It just means that the killer had to be taller than he was by, oh, three inches or more."

"But the body was clearly moved. Why could it

not have been done with him sitting in the chair? It has wheels on it, after all."

"Uh uh. For one thing, it would be under the glare of the active security monitors there and would have caused the computer to emit alarms and lock itself down. It wouldn't have prevented the murder but then the murderer wouldn't have been able to have access to the data banks to erase the record. The point there, give or take a couple of feet, in the kitchenette area, is the only spot where the monitors wouldn't pick anything up. You set your traps where the loot is. At the controls to the station, as you see, and at the computer access stations there. But not even a total paranoid puts heavy security on his refrigerator or his coffee maker, particularly when you'd be seen getting to and from. That was his blind spot and the killer knew it. But he didn't die because he forgot to put a guard on the ham sandwiches. He died because this whole place was designed to keep out or prevent access to any but nine individuals. It was never designed to protect him from them."

"But he was Security. He would have operatives in and out of here all the time. Why must it be one of the others?"

"Because they had full access to the computer and knew its esoteric ins and outs and just how to make it dance. In this business you don't give away all your secrets to *anybody*, since you can never be a hundred percent sure of your operatives. That's why he hardly batted an eyelash when they showed up to use the computer for something or other as they might occasionally do. Even if you had gotten to one of them, reprogrammed them, or switched them for a double, they still couldn't work the computer itself. The data was safe and secure—except from the Committee. Let's see—Pandross was a hundred and seventy-seven centimeters tall . . . about five ten. I'd say that's about the same height as Voorhes, so while he's not off the hook it drops him down a notch. Some nice heeled boots would do it for him, though. We're looking for someone who's over six feet tall, at least wearing shoes or boots that wouldn't look unusual. It's going to be very interesting to see just how tall the other members of the Committee are."

She stared at me. "You enjoy this. You understand it so well. You must have many murders where you come from."

I shrugged. "And your people have none?"

"Crime is impossible in our society. Not unthinkable, I will admit, but impossible. We do not even have a word for murder in our language."

"Sounds boring. Still, I don't want you to get the wrong impression off the bat. There's clearly a vast cultural gulf between us. Now, let's see . . . How best to explain this?" I thought a moment. "Do you have fires in your world? Things catch on fire and firemen come to put the fire out?"

"Yes, of course we do," she responded in a patronizing tone.

"Do the firemen like what they do?"

"They take pride in it, yes. We all take pride in our functions."

I nodded. "Uh huh. And without fires they have no function. People who are very good at firefighting love their work. In effect, they love fires. They wouldn't start one, and they are horrified at the losses just as we are, but if there is a fire around, particularly a big one, then that's where they want to be. The excitement, the pressure, the physical and mental challenges it represents— they are alive when there is a fire, even though fires are bad things."

"Well, yes, but . . ."

"No buts. Now, I don't like murders and I don't like dangerous puzzles to solve. I'm particularly unhappy with working with a gun to my head and one hand tied behind me as I am now. Still, if there *is* a crime, if there *is* a puzzle to be solved, evil to be unmasked, then I want to be in on it. I want to solve it. It's what I do. It's my—function. Very few people love their jobs, Maria, but some of us have talents others do not, and when those talented people have jobs perfect for those talents, they love their work. I love my work. It's what I've always dreamed of doing."

She accepted it, but didn't seem to understand it clearly.

"What about your world? How can you be human and there be no crime?"

"The human mind is animal," she explained, reciting the rationale just as it was drilled into her. "It must be controlled or it will cause destruction and misery. In my world there is absolute equality. We are born to the State and raised by it. We own nothing ourselves and everything in common. We serve the common good. We learn and are tested and our best function is determined and then we are schooled and trained for it. Then you enter the function at the lowest level. If you excel, you are promoted."

"Uh huh. Sounds fairly ordinary for certain kinds of societies. I assume with each level up you get more responsibility and more creature comforts—privileges, a bigger apartment, that kind of thing."

"Yes, that is so."

"And what about the fellow whose function is to mow the lawn or wash the dishes?"

"The same. There are the same number of levels for each function, and the privileges are the same for each level."

"Interesting. And what about social life? Families, babies, that kind of thing?"

"Eggs and sperm are taken and classified and stored," she said matter-of-factly. "Then when particular functions are required the adjustment is made genetically, there is a match, and a child is produced. We do not have families, and we, ourselves, are sterile. Families are irrelevant in a proper society."

"What about sex?"

"If you would like it, I will provide it. It is a proper way of flushing the animal urges from the system."

"No, no!" I was startled. By god, she would do it and right here if I asked her! "Just curious. But you have no jealousy, no theft, no crimes of passion?" Even Marx, if memory served, said we'd never get rid of crimes of passion.

"One owns nothing so there can be no theft. All at the same level have the same things. One attains them by perfection in mind, body, and function. Exclusivity in cohabitation or relations is forbidden. In any event, jealousy implies the ownership of another, and we find that repulsive."

"And nobody ever beats the system, or tries to?"

"It is impossible," she replied, not ruefully, just matter-of-fact. "We must regularly go and account for all of our actions, our thoughts, our deeds, in the Confessional. When we are born we are born with a dependency, and the substance one must take is unique to the individual. The Confessor alone controls what we require. We meet regularly with our Confessor and we also attend self-criticism sessions. It is impossible to hold anything back without anyone knowing that you do, and if you do you do not get what you need to survive. There is no way around it—the pain is too great. No one can withstand it, so no one holds back when absolute confession can end it. After a while you understand that any urges against the system are crimes against society and you purge yourself completely of such things. Until one thinks only correct thoughts without deviation one can not be a whole member of society."

Holy shit! I thought. *Now there's the perfect totalitarianism. Drug-dependent slavery for an entire civilization! Not even the worst of our society could have dreamed of such absolute control.*

"How often do you need this stuff?" I asked her. "And, more important, when's the next time?"

"I must report within five days," she told me. "They always decide the interval."

"To whom and how?"

"I am not permitted to tell you that. However, I should tell you that I have been modified so that a certain pain threshold will kill me before I can tell anything."

Yeah, I thought sourly. And even if you grew real fond of me you'd still kill me in an instant for your fix if so ordered. They weren't taking any chances on any kind of bond forming that would get in the way of her orders. But aloud I said, "Well, look sharp.

We've learned all we can here for now. You are armed?"

"Yes. I am trained as a bodyguard among other things. I am well versed in every means of defensive combat. Why do you ask?"

"Because we're going to be going to some pretty rough worlds, I suspect, and meet some even rougher people, and I don't want anybody putting a slug in me or pinching my nerves or giving me a needle."

"My primary function is to see that you carry out yours. Do not worry."

Worry was one thing I had plenty of, though.

"All right, look sharp. I'm sure I haven't noticed anything here they didn't already know, but you never can be sure about a pre-emptive strike. I've been ambushed in the Labyrinth before, and part of my head had to be regrown. I don't want to have to go through that again."

"Where are we going?"

"You are gonna use whatever communications you have and find out where they suggest we go for an office, and then we're going there, and then I'll have a whole shopping list of stuff to get and a lot of work to do to feel safe there. By the time we're done with that, Voorhes or whoever should have our suspect list and just exactly what I need. C'mon, Amazon Princess. We got work to do."

Having a Girl Friday plugged into the rebel system was handy from my point of view, I admit, in that all I had to do was ask for something or complain about something and she saw that something was done about it. A combination secretary and bodyguard was a very handy accessory for any private eye. Only trouble was, she was not just my assistant but my jailer, too, making sure I didn't try anything funny or sneak funny messages back or in any way bypass this underground system they had. And with that nice little drug variation and her "confessional," we not only weren't about to get *too* close, but I had the uneasy feeling that, should I solve this thing or should they tire of me, her last job in this assignment was to polish me off no matter what.

It made for a less than cozy arrangement. Still, if I *did* solve the damned thing, I would be the one to pick the time and place to tell her and anyone else about it—and no matter how competent she was, I was pretty damned sure she wasn't immortal. Well, I'd have to cross that bridge later. It remained to be seen whether I could in fact help them. It was sure and certain that no matter what else happened their patience with me would be limited. I didn't know what kind of clock was running, but there certainly was one.

In another curious way, it freed me. I didn't have to worry about whether or not I should ask such-and-so a question, or if it was safe for me to find out this or that. Knowing it didn't matter, and knowing that they knew, too, and knew that I knew—if that makes sense—gave me a certain uninhibited detachment.

The place they found for me was another of those old, abandoned switching rooms, and it was fairly comfortable if a bit cozy. This one had only one large room and most of the furnishings had been cleared out long ago, giving it the look of an abandoned floor in some office building where once they had a bank or a lot of cubicles. The thing was set on automatic to open for me and Maria; neither one of us could trigger it alone, although if one of us were inside the other could come and go. I quickly discovered that the other one was just Maria; I wasn't allowed out alone, and if she was out then I was stuck inside.

There was an override, of course, but of the eight survivors it took at least three of them for the gate to open automatically and for them to enter or leave. It was a neat trick; it meant that no one or even two of them could show up unannounced and do unto me what they did to the previous security chief.

Getting the place in shape also wasn't much of a problem. With Maria's help, we picked up from mysterious crews that asked no questions a bundle of things, including a laundry list of stuff I demanded—including, of course, real laundry. It was pretty practical, basic stuff but it fit me, showing they'd done their homework. Dirty stuff just got thrown in a box and stuck outside; somebody seemed to pick it up and drop it back clean with a speed and efficiency I wished my own laundry had.

While Maria got the place clean and livable, I worked with the two crates of security gear I had requested. To be truthful, I needed maybe a tenth of what I'd ordered and some of the stuff I ordered I knew only because I'd seen it somewhere and knew it would be logical in a security apparatus. I just didn't want any of them to take a look at my tools and deduce my exact security setup from my parts list. This way they'd be guessing, and they could never be sure they had it all or that something hidden someplace wasn't gonna come out and bite them.

We also got two reasonable if not great cots with bedding, a porta-john (in which I stuck some really fine looking electronic gear that blinked and occasionally buzzed but otherwise did nothing—I had fun just thinking of anybody trying to go to the john in there, though, Maria included), a portable kitchen unit with water tank, some decent food and drink, and all the comforts of high-class camping. I also got a desk, a set of normal office supplies, and a Series 16000 Company terminal plugged into their network, not the Company's, although I discovered we had a lot of databases in common. It wasn't until I went to work on that sucker that I realized just how much the Company had been compromised.

Still, that one wide open room meant that Maria and I were gonna get to know each other *real* well.

And then, as promised, came the files on the eight remaining suspects, along with a wall viewer and data files that interfaced to the 16000, which was set up for interactive voice communications and could answer my questions within the limits of its knowledge. With that, we could settle in and see just who and what we might be dealing with.

The first guy was Quin Tarn, but he was no Irishman. He was Asiatic, built like a pro wrestler, a martial arts expert and a fellow who trained every day by smashing granite with his hands and feet. He wasn't exactly the kind of guy I wanted to meet or know, and I wasn't the least curious about whether he was bald for real or shaved every day nor how he could move his massive head without a neck. The martial arts bit alone put him high on the immediate list, but the fact that he was only five six in spite of his weight and bulk lowered him a bit. Somehow I couldn't see this guy in high heels, not even boots.

"Do you have a voice sample?" I asked the computer. "If so, play it and also play one for each subsequent subject as they come up."

"Complying," the computer responded. It had a voice like an insufferable British snob and I already disliked it.

Tarn's image went into motion, and he was clearly talking to someone out of "camera" (or whatever they used) range. *"No tai quan su yang,"* he said, or something like that.

"Nothing in English?" I asked the computer.

"He is not on record as speaking English," the computer responded. "However, it is fairly easy to hypno-teach any language necessary."

I nodded. "Can you synthesize the voice, then?" I asked it. "Use all the elements of speech patterns to create an English sentence he might utter?" I had already disqualified the guy as Gravel Voice, but that only excluded one mystery.

"Complying."

Tarn's image moved, although now it looked like a very badly dubbed Italian movie, the words having no resemblance to what his lips were doing and, for that matter, no relation to what *he* was doing, either.

"The quick brown fox jumped over the lazy blue dog!" he said forcefully.

Oh, well. His high tenor alone told me why he probably had built up all those muscles and had that look about him. He had an odd, high voice, but nobody, and I mean *nobody*, was gonna laugh at somebody who looked like that.

"Was Tarn in favor of the project to destroy the Company from the start, and without reservation?" I asked the computer.

"He argued neither for nor against nor took any part in any debate," the computer responded. "All he did was vote for it when the vote was called."

I nodded. O.K., that said something.

"Who did he lose, if anybody, when his world blew?"

"Two wives and six children, youngest three, oldest thirteen," the computer told me.

My god! I thought, reflecting on my own feelings when Dash had been kidnapped. *No wonder they are so callous about everybody else! If they'd murdered Dash, I would have been out only for their hides and I'd live for it.* It put some perspective on them, anyway.

"What was his profession?"

"Mineralogist," the computer replied. "Specifically an expert in precious gems."

O.K., that fit. Big jewels were a very common trading item and very useful no matter what world you were in if you wanted to set things up from scratch, and I'd seen places on the Company world where even the doors were so jewel-encrusted they'd be enough to retire for forty lifetimes if you could have heisted them. A guy like Tarn would be very useful when setting up and financing a new takeover operation. He could also introduce big and valuable gems onto the market to turn into cash without arousing a lot of suspicion.

"Next. We'll come back to all of them later."

The next one I'd never met, never seen, but very

much wanted to meet and preferably in a dark alley. He was five eleven, with dark, handsome Latin features and burning black eyes, but as ruggedly handsome as you could imagine. Even Maria, I noted, studied him with inordinate attention. I tended to hate any guy who looked like that with so evident a lack of care, but in his case it was more than doubled.

"Doctor Carlos Augusto Montagne-Echevia," the computer said. "A doctor of research pharmacology recruited right out of graduation, and, as such, the youngest of the group. He is fluent in the nine most common languages, including both English and Mandarin. Unmarried, something of a radical in university, he nonetheless was third oldest in a family of eleven and the first to ever reach university, let alone graduate with a doctorate. All of his family was wiped out, of course, including his oldest sister and his three week old godson, her baby. He wholeheartedly endorsed the plan in the meeting and was its most fervent supporter."

That was interesting. It meant that he hadn't come up with the plan, either. Then again, for a pharmacologist, even a brilliant and hate-filled radical one, the drug thing was more his type of scheme anyway. Still, you could sure see how he could almost count on Mukasa's mistress and go-between to fall for him. He just took it for granted.

His image went into motion. "There will have to be more production," he said in accented but excellent English. "We can not meet our schedule with what you have been putting out."

Well, that was it for Carlos, but at least the words

were his, and his voice was as smooth and romantic as you figured it would be. I had the feeling that he never had to yell; there was a controlled undercurrent in his tone that implied absolute menace to whoever he was talking to. He was an interesting personality, and I was happy to keep him on my prime list even if I couldn't see him as Gravel Voice, either. He was the right height, and he didn't seem to be the kind of guy to want to end this. He was so filled with hate he wanted to go on and on and on, and he was both bright enough and nervy enough to bump off Pandross in his lair, too.

Considering the way *I* felt about him, I could see Voorhes' point in taking me over Brandy. At least I was able to consider other suspects, although no matter what else happened I wanted some dealings with dear old Carlos before this was done.

"How did Carlos feel about the group selecting me for this investigation?" I asked the computer.

"Doctor Montagne was the one who suggested you, and pressed for you against opposition. He also worked out the plan which brought you here."

Uh huh. I figured as much. Carlos' main problem was that he'd go from Philadelphia to New York by way of Timbuktu and the South Pole. His plots were always so needlessly complex that they were bound to unravel.

Unfortunately, that made him less a suspect here. Taking out the security chief in such a clever and essentially direct way just wasn't his style.

"Gregory Yugarin," the computer said, putting up a picture of Rasputin. Well, maybe not, but he was a Slavic type for sure, and he had wild, unmanageable-looking black hair and one of those long but scraggly beards that showed a total lack of attention. "Six feet two, forty-nine years old, and a Doctor of Geography; he is an expert in mass transportation systems," the computer added. "He is known as a loner type with no family ties or background on the record. Extent of loss is therefore unknown. Speaks six languages and nine dialects but is not on record as an English speaker. It was Doctor Yugarin who researched and deduced the vast majority of inactive Labyrinth stations and lines and established the network for movement in the main system. His comrades consider him totally trustworthy but something of a mystery. He is not a social man. He was, however, the one who came up with the plan now underway and the one who called the meeting."

Yugarin's image came to life, this time again the Italian movie type, and he said, "My name is Gregory Ilych Yugarin and I am a geographer."

The height was more than enough and the voice—well, it could have been Gravel Voice, particularly if he was using a translation module, but I had the impression from the tape that old Gravelly was less guttural and more, well, Oriental, somehow. Still, while physically the most likely suspect so far, he had the least motive if my hunch was correct. He got the idea, he called the meeting, and he'd gotten his way. Unless he was working both sides of the street with a plot of his own, it didn't make sense.

"Valintina Mendelez," the computer continued, putting up a picture of a breathtaking beauty on a beach someplace wearing only the bottom of a string bikini and sun glasses and needing nothing else. Gad! Was she *stacked!* She was dark, even discounting the suntan, with that peculiar blend of ethnic features that had gone into creating the Brazilian race. Maria, in fact, had many of the same characteristics but, while my initial reaction to her had been as a tropical beauty, this Mendelez put Maria and almost anybody else to shame.

"Age forty-five, five foot seven, botanist, specialist in rain forest plant biochemistry. Brilliant, had worked with her husband in the Amazon area, but had dropped out of university to have two children. Her husband and the children were back for a visit to the home world when the breakout and conflict occurred, and were destroyed when the world was. She is described as having become hedonistic, without any morals, mercy, or other value systems. She can be quite pleasant but will kill without hesitation, even mass murder, and indulges in experimentation on humans, masking her intellect and coldness with what you would call a 'bimbo' persona. Speaks six languages, including English. She was opposed to the plan when proposed and argued against it, but later gave in after she saw the majority favored it."

Interesting. "On what grounds did she oppose it?" I asked.

"On the grounds that it did not induce sufficient suffering on the part of the Company and its race," the computer replied. "Voice sample."

The image came alive. "Hi, Victor!" she squealed and waved to somebody out of sight. "So glad you could come." It was a high, breathless, Marilyn Monroe type voice with just the right amount of exotic Portuguese accent. Naturally the looks had been preserved by the kind of techniques I myself knew so well, but the image of Monroe as Latin porn queen was indelible, right to that full head of blonde hair.

"Why if she is a leader of the revolution does she not do something about her gross malformations?" Maria asked, in a tone that wasn't catty but serious. I could see that my Watson and I had seriously different ideas of reality.

"Cultural gap," I responded. "She looks and sounds and acts like that because it is attractive to a large number of people, particularly men."

She certainly was the kind to have motive in this—if they were going to shut everything down it would take away the only reason she had for still going on. An egocentric, gorgeous psychopath, she might object to having to settle in to one world and lose a lot of that power and maybe the means of preserving that beauty. She was short, but if she wore really high heels she might make it, and certainly the injection as the fatal weapon was up her alley. There were lots of Amazonian poisons that would kill very quickly and yet break down beyond analysis in a very short time.

The only trouble was, I had to assume that Pandross was at least as competent as I was or they wouldn't have lasted this long. Particularly if I knew her, and knew she'd opposed the plan, I'm not sure I'd have turned my back on her if the two of us were ever anyplace together with nobody else around.

Still, I didn't underestimate her. Anybody who deliberately made themselves that conspicuous obviously had no problems making themselves look very inconspicuous indeed when they wanted to.

"Salvatore Mancini, fifty-two, five feet ten inches tall, a physicist," the computer went on, showing a picture of a guy almost straight out of *The Godfather*, any part, with drooping moustache, craggy face, graying hair, and a bit of a pot belly, but looking about as Sicilian as Hollywood thinks they look. "Mancini was a fierce nationalist as well as having an enormous extended family of his own, and thus took the destruction of his world very hard indeed. More than that, he took it personally. Although a doctor of physics and a specialist in high energy storage and control, Mancini still came from an area where family and clan were all-important and revenge is obligatory, the price of the soul's salvation. There is no indication that he is particularly religious but his thoughts and patterns were shaped by his inseparable ancestral religion and culture. He was perfectly willing to go along with the plan and raised no serious objections. In fact, it appears that Yugarin consulted with him in its formulation and that his support was a foregone conclusion."

The figure came to life. "Hey! Maglia! Bring that over here!" he growled, and his voice was somewhat deep and had just a touch of gravel in it. He was close enough to the right height to fudge it, and while the accent was wrong, it wasn't beyond belief that he could mask it or alter it if he suspected he was being overheard. The accent wasn't Italian, at least not my kind. It was possible that on his world it was far closer to Latin still than the current tongue back home, or had gone off on a slight tangent. Who knew?

The next figure was a tall, thin, yet tough-looking woman, with dirty blonde hair cut short in a man's style, with strong, sharp features and a confident stance. She was wearing what looked like some kind of jungle outfit and her face and hands seemed weathered, as if she spent most of her time in the bush.

"Stacy Cutler, age forty-five, height five feet eleven inches," the computer informed us. "Cutler is a zoologist. Although she's had little formal training beyond undergraduate studies, she has lived all her life in wilderness areas where her parents were also scientists. She is tough, muscular, could exist without aid in almost any wild area that supports life, and carried on her parents' work after their death by hiring out as a guide and mercenary soldier to finance it as needed. She has overseen most of the exploration, development, and preliminary studies on safe worlds and abandoned line junctions. Of them all, she has shown the least injury and the least emotion regarding her lost world and seems to accept it, using the network as a means of furthering her own studies in many areas. She opposed the plan because it includes the concept of shutting down the Labyrinth, and she dislikes the idea of having to settle on one world forever. She was the most difficult to persuade and finally went along because she saw it was something the majority was bent on doing. She apparently extracted a series of concessions for her support, although what those were is not part of my data."

Even more interesting. Opposed, brought around only when it seemed futile to continue to go against the more passionate rest—I kind of wondered what would have happened to anybody at that meeting who hadn't finally come around. If she had an insincere conversion, and if she still opposed it, she'd be particularly nervous of

Pandross, who would be looking at the opponents very hard and constantly. She was also tall enough, strong enough, and skilled enough. A real possibility.

She came to life on the screen and said, "You! Put that crate over there and drop it at the cost of your hide!" The English was definitely her native tongue, but it held a strong and odd accent—closer maybe to South African, with its Germanic undertones, but not quite.

The picture changed again. "Dilip Kanda, fifty, five foot five, a mathematician and electrical engineer," the computer informed us. The man certainly looked either Indian or Pakistani, if there was such a difference where he'd come from; a bit pudgy but darkly handsome for all that.

"Kanda lost family, children, friends, clan, tribe —all of it," the computer continued. "A firm believer in reincarnation, with the discovery of infinite alternate worlds simply reinforcing that belief system since now there's really room for it, he was saddened, even grieving, for his loss but appears to hold the Company less in hatred than in contempt. A sincere Hindu, he has become increasingly strict and very much an ascetic, indulging in few pleasures and much contemplation, abstaining from sex, from meat, from most worldly pleasures, with the exception of an abiding taste for elaborate pastries the results of which are evident and the reason for which he will explain at length but which are beyond the logic abilities of any other human or computer to follow. However, he has in the past come up with many of the most successful operations against the Company that have been conducted, his plans rarely if ever compromised or discovered, and he treats going against them as an intellectual challenge. He was, however, quite willing from the start to go ahead with the Great Plan, on the grounds that some metaphysical symmetry would be achieved and that the Company race should have to be reborn again at the bottom."

Kanda's image began to move. "We must all see that life is the search for *bakti*," he said, and that was it. The voice was typical East Indian, with the accent and all, and a low tenor voice that might almost be described as melodic.

I tended to dismiss him on the basis of height and the reported attitude, which I at least understood given the guy's beliefs, but I didn't really want to eliminate him entirely. This guy had beaten the Company consistently and for many years, and if the computer were to be believed he was the most dangerous and clever mind among them. If he wanted to murder one of his fellow Directors, and his motive might be rather weird or maybe just an intellectual exercise, he'd do it so cleverly that he'd be totally wrong as a suspect and quickly dismissed. And, if I were Pandross, he'd be the one I'd be most at ease with, maybe even turning my back on him—maybe to get him one of his sweets? I wished now I knew what had been in Pandross's refrigerator.

There was another picture now. "Herbert Voorhes," the computer told us needlessly. "At sixty the oldest of the group, and one of the earliest recruits by the Company. Five feet eight inches tall, muscular, a linguist and scholar, a historian by profession and one-time university history professor, which was why he was one of the first recruits. He has trained himself in weaponry and basic self-defense and can hold his own but is no match for a professional agent. Lost a wife, two grown children, and some grandchildren in the conflagration, and is bitter and driven by hatred of the Company. The titular leader because of his age and because of his ability to grasp a multiplicity of subjects and plans, he chaired the meeting and spoke forcefully for the plan when it was proposed. He also was operational chief for the move against your substation."

Uh huh. I *thought* the old guy wasn't telling it all. Still, what the computer was saying fit with what I'd seen of the man. He'd lost all that the others had—family, friends, loved ones—but he'd lost even more. He was a historian of a world whose history had ended; a world that no longer required a historian. They had not only eliminated all near and dear to him, they had rendered even his life's work meaningless. But as a historian he was talking as an expert on the history of revolutions, idealistic mass movements, and the like, and how they were inevitably corrupted. The question that remained was whether or not his sense of morality for the many was best served by wiping out the Company or saving a world from a fate his had suffered. I thought I believed him, though. If the Nazis had won, as they had in so many worlds, and represented all that was left of human "culture," I wouldn't have much of a problem in wiping them out rather than letting them go on. I didn't think he would, either.

And, finally, there was the dear departed.

"Lothar Pandross, forty-eight at death, six foot two, security and espionage chief. Pandross had been in the military of his nation when he was recruited, and even then was a security officer overseeing the protection of high-tech weapons systems. He was replaced by a double with superior training with the idea of replacing him later so that they would have access to the military secrets of his world's most technological nation. He appears to have been orphaned at an early age and educated and trained by his army. He does not appear to have harbored personal hatred towards the Company for doing what they did to his world, but none the less considered the Company 'the Enemy,' and himself a soldier in its overthrow. He was quite good at his job, and while he rarely went into the field himself he commanded and directed thousands and was personally responsible for the recruitment of most of the personnel who now work for us."

I nodded, then had this silly hunch and played it. "Do you have a voice record of him?"

The Pandross figure came to life. "So nice to see you," he said cordially to somebody out of frame. "Please—sit down."

I nearly jumped out of my seat. Give him just a bit of a whisper and that was Gravel Voice all the way, and his size and covert intelligence experience would be more than adequate to make him look like the description we'd built up. There was no such thing as certainty under these conditions, but I knew deep down to my bones that Lothar Pandross had personally directed that raid on the house, had personally supervised the abduction, had gone along for the whole thing.

The real question was, did Voorhes know that and was he just covering or conning or even testing me by saying that nobody involved resembled the one I was after, or was he, perhaps, covering his shock and unwilling to admit that Pandross had been there and he hadn't known? Or was it just that my description wasn't good enough?

Right now it didn't matter, but clearly the chief of security had been there all along. No wonder he figured out the weak point in my system! And no wonder he was able to slip first his plant, Bond, in and out, and then himself in and out without the Company knowing a damned thing. He was almost certainly good enough to do just that. But why did a guy who was so vital and who almost never went on missions himself stick his neck out like that?

Much more importantly, how did he do it three weeks after he'd been murdered?

6.

Murder in the Cathedral

I didn't have to see Voorhes; the computer network was perfectly capable of putting me in touch with whoever I wanted to talk to, and also to get them in touch with me. Still, I wasn't in any real rush, I took the opportunity to use the ersatz shower they'd rigged up and actually caught a fairly long sleep before beginning the first active stage of the affair. I wanted to be rested and to have thought things out. The way things were going, I figured I'd eat and sleep as well and as long as possible whenever the opportunity presented itself. Right now I was dead tired and that wasn't the best way to press anything.

Maria, I'm afraid, was less than impressed with me at this point.

"So, you have solved it all, the great genius detective, sitting here in his chair, and now he goes to sleep?"

"Hardly," I responded. "But you should get some sleep, too. We might be busy in a while."

She was still awake when I lay down, though, and didn't look inclined to take my advice. I made a mental wager that as soon as I was out she'd be out, too—out of this hole, maybe back before I woke up again. That was fine with me. I had no illusions that the same computer that gave me outward access gave anybody else a full report on

176

me, and it didn't matter much. I just relaxed, and tried to put myself to sleep even though my mind was sifting what had already been learned.

So Pandross was alive, and that stiff—a double? One with the big boy's own I.D.? Voorhes said they had erasable and re-recordable implants, and who would be in charge of doing that but Pandross himself? If I wasn't being had for some reason, then why the hell didn't any of those other bright revolutionary geniuses think of it? Because they could conceive of Pandross double-crossing them even less than one of them murdering him?

That made sense, sort of. I mean, the guy held the keys to their whole kingdom, and to the computers and data banks and all that nice stuff they needed to operate as well. If he went bad, then they had a glass house of an organization to begin with. And since they had a sort of locked room murder there, it would never occur to them that the one guy who could so easily commit the crime, know just where the security monitors were and how to avoid all alarms—hell, he put 'em there— and just how to erase everything needed afterwards, was Pandross himself.

But if he was going to disappear, then why expose himself in the midst of the operation on my place? Naturally, he wouldn't have known that they were out to recruit me—or would he? Maybe he was still in charge in some alternate and nicely functioning security setup, monitoring their every move. And he'd been looking for me, not Brandy —the tape made that clear. Why? Was it, maybe, to get me before the others could? Maybe he had another double to replace me, one of his boys, for some reason.

Maybe so that I, or that other me, in his capacity

as detective trying to find the murderer of Pandross, would eventually have to go to and interview each of the suspects in their hiding holes? Thus pointing to exactly where they were so that Pandross could then deal with them one by one in isolation?

If that was true, then the plot had been turned on its head, but the bulk of the theory still stood. If Pandross was opposed to this plan, whatever it was—maybe he figured it wouldn't work and would destroy the rebel network, or maybe he just didn't like giving up all that power. To a pro like him, the fight, and little victories, would be the thing, the reason for living. Final victory would render him powerless and obsolete.

With that thought in my head, I drifted off into a surprisingly deep sleep.

When I woke up to what my watch said was a new day, Maria was out cold on the other cot and I didn't disturb her. I went over and checked and reset the simple door seals, though, that showed me she had indeed been a busy little girl while I slept. It would be interesting to know just who held her leash tight enough for her to obey at all costs, but that might come later. These people would only trust alternate worlds they already controlled; Maria's world was under one of the eight survivors whether she or they knew it or not.

I fixed coffee and got a couple of doughnuts and went over to the computer terminal. "I want to talk to Voorhes. How long will it take?" I asked it.

"Depends on if he answers," the machine responded fairly reasonably. "Signaling and connect. It usually takes him about fifteen minutes to come to the substation where he can take the call after the signal goes out. More if he is away from his home."

I nodded and munched a doughnut. "That's fine. By that time I might have enough coffee into me to get me awake."

It was about fifteen minutes when Voorhes answered, voice only of course, and he sounded surprised.

"I thought Maria would handle any requirements of yours," he noted.

"Then she didn't go to see you, then. You have any idea where she snuck out to while I was out?"

"Probably reported in at home."

"Uh huh. And who runs that world?"

"Why, uh, they are allies in our cause . . ."

"Can the bullshit!" I told him. "Straight answers or what the hell am I here for?"

He sighed. "All right. Technically it's Yugarin's, but Carlos spends more time with them than Gregory does. What's the difference? Neither would be there now. Too exposed."

"But their people in high places would be there, so that puts me a little on notice. Thanks."

"Is that all this was for? This was very inconvenient."

I smiled. I wonder what his reaction would have been if I told him just exactly what I suspected— and what I knew? I would have to drop some crumbs and hints, but for the first time since I walked into this I was feeling like I had some control of events.

"I have discovered everything it is possible to discover sitting here in a passive situation rooting through files," I told him. "If I can't follow up my leads then there's no purpose to going on."

"You tell Maria and she will get whatever you need," Voorhes told me. "Go anyplace, ask any questions."

I shook my head. "Uh uh. I'm not Nero Wolfe, and even if I was I couldn't do it that way if I didn't have my Archie with me."

"What?"

"Never mind. Look, Voorhes, this isn't a problem in ethics or in physics. It's not something you can just dump facts into a computer and push 'enter' and come up with the correct answer. If it was, you wouldn't need somebody like me. You'd just have a thousand Marias gathering every fact and asking every question and put 'em in your machine and—*poof!*—guilty party, motive, opportunity, method, all neat and tidy. Maria might be very useful, but she's no investigator. She comes from a world where they don't even need cops, only a more subtle and sophisticated version of the Spanish Inquisition. You're a historian. You did lots of research. Probably spent lots of time in huge libraries with tons of books and documents and the like."

"Yes, so?"

"Why bother? Why not just hire a bunch of kids off the street—any street—so long as they could read and write and tell 'em to go in to that library and find everything you need?"

Voorhes hesitated before replying, thinking this over. "I see your point. They wouldn't have the foggiest notion where to look, or what they were actually looking for. Without my training, they probably wouldn't know a major discovery when they found it. Point taken, Mister Horowitz. But they're not going to expose themselves, even to you, for a broad fishing expedition. Some would as soon kill you as look at you."

"Well, I'm fishing for sure," I told him, "but I'm not fishing blind. As yet, I have no motive, but I'm warm in a number of areas. I think I might be warm enough to draw some attention of my own."

"You *do* know something," the rebel leader muttered, surprised but sincere. "What did you find that we missed, Horowitz? And why aren't you coming out with it?"

I was ready for that. "Because I don't have a motive," I told him sincerely, "and without one it makes no sense at all. And if I revealed what I knew, even to you, even to Maria, there's a very good chance that I might be doing your murderer's work for him. As I understand it, I'm working for all of you, collectively, as a client. I can not and will not explain my steps every minute of the time when I might be briefing the very person or people I'm trying to catch. The only way to safeguard my clients is not to explain or demonstrate until I have every piece of the puzzle it's possible to have, and then only when I have you all together, so no one can pull anything. I require complete freedom to investigate and complete cooperation from everybody involved. You tell them that. You tell 'em that they play the game my way or there are sure as hell gonna be more killings no matter how deep they hide, because sooner or later they have to come out. Your organization is too management-oriented, Voorhes. If you all keep in your holes, you won't have an organization, you won't have an operation, you won't have a master plan. You'll be retired for good."

I gave him as long as he needed to digest

that. Finally he said, "You don't think that we can manage through communications and go-betweens?"

"No, and you know you can't, either. Nobody but you eight has a real emotional stake in this thing, a commitment. The rest are just plain crooks. You leave them on their own they either have to be people like Maria with no possible initiative, in which case nothing gets solved, or they'll take your big organization away from you. You try it with steady communications and live agents and those communications and those agents will lead your killer right to each of you. Unless, of course, it's you, Voorhes."

"What?"

"You're immune, which means you're not a probable target. They all know where you are. They can't get to you but they don't have to. There's only one switching cube. Anybody who knows that cube and the Labyrinth system could blow your switch mechanism from the cube side, leaving you trapped forever where you are. The fact that they haven't shows either that you're involved in this or that you're not a target—yet. Now, you put this on to the other seven, and you tell them that I need to talk to each and every one of them. Their terms—strip-searches and blind-folds permitted if they want it that way. But I need to talk to each one, and I need certain questions answered by each and every one of them. Give me the freedom to do your job and I'll solve your damned case. Don't, and I'm going to sit here, relax, and wait until the next murder."

Voorhes sighed. "Very well, I'll put it to them just that way. In fact, I'll send this recording on the open access net for them to pick up. I can do

nothing else. What level of agreement, or cooperation, you get from them is up to each of them."

"Fair enough," I told him. "In fact, who says yes
and who says no and who is straight and who's not
with me will be a great deal of information in and
of itself."

I signed off, feeling quite pleased with myself.
Maria wasn't quite so amused. "Do you always
speak like that to people who would just as soon
have you shot?" she asked me, a bit incredulous.

"Why not? They intend to shoot me sooner or
later anyway. Right now, they need me. Either they
do it my way or they shoot me now and try
somebody else, who'll give 'em the same ultima-
tum if he or she's any good and won't learn a
damned thing out of fear or hesitancy if they're
not. Besides, if we don't get out of here and
exposed, how the hell is our murderer going to
contact me?"

She looked startled. "You expect the murderer
to contact you?"

I nodded. "Sure. And when he does, I don't want
you shooting him or trying anything fancy, either.
Getting him won't solve their problem or mine,
first because he wouldn't be taken alive and so we
wouldn't know if he was a lone wolf or a part of a
conspiracy within this conspiracy, and also because he's too smart for anybody to be sure that
they have him when they have him. You just come
along for the ride and make sure nobody does
anything nasty to me during the investigation, and
I'll show you how the game is played."

So, anyway, they bought it, of course. Yeah, all of
'em. Which of them could turn me down without
having the rest look at them funny? Besides, they

were in their fortresses, the kind of places they prepared for when the heat was on. If they didn't feel safe there, then there was noplace they could really feel safe, and if that was the case why hole up in a bunker in the first place?

Of course, arranging for visits took some careful planning on their part, so I was gonna see 'em in the order they decided to be seen, and that put Quin Tarn at the top of the list.

I got to admit I half expected to be contacted the first time I was allowed back into the Labyrinth. I had to figure that Pandross was around someplace and that he was following my footsteps nicely and that he would know when I was loose and available. Why did I think I'd hear from him? Easy—because I was the only guy in this with no ax to grind and so I was the only one he could trust. When he failed to get me in that raid on the place, he made very sure that there was a strong enough voice presence that I'd know he was alive, so he wanted me to know. I had to figure that I was dealing with at least an equal in this business, maybe better than that, and I think he was counting on that as well.

As to whether or not he was alone, I couldn't guess. It was true that they'd run for cover as soon as he was "murdered," as we might as well, but then they got together and finally decided to include me in on this and plotted their little operation against my substation. He knew about it, so either he had ways of tapping into the communications net they were using, which was possible and even likely, or he had somebody from that hookup tell him all the gory details. Since they'd changed the security codes on the master computers and redid the whole system after he died, I had a hunch they'd use different communications means than the one he'd set up for their electronic meets as well, which made an ally all the more likely. Still, if the guy was good, maybe the best, he might have planned on that and been able to crack the system.

It was a real eye-opener to go through the Labyrinth their way, too. I knew the paths between the Company world and mine fairly well, having travelled them often and looked at the scenery out of the cubes, so I knew we were staying in the general neighborhood and I knew where the Company switch points were. It was kind of impressive to approach one, then veer off into one of those worlds and almost immediately back into a small substation that led to a long and dark section—and when we came out again it was at some unmanned Company substation once more and when we went back onto the main line, well, we were past the switch.

No wonder Carlos and company could stalk up and down and in and out without being spotted. They seemed to have bypassed all the main switches in the most heavily travelled areas and even created effective private junctions between the main and branch lines using their own automated equipment.

Maria, of course, kept her eyes firmly on me inside the tunnel, if only because for most of it we were in the main Company line and were passing all sorts of people and near-people going this way and that on Company business. I probably wasn't quick enough to make a break she couldn't cure, but in some cases, when we were passing fair numbers of people, it wouldn't have taken much effort to either signal them I was in trouble or just jump Maria in their presence. The rule was you apprehended anybody doing that and called for Security. Yeah, I could have gotten away and probably gotten her taken, but I didn't want to. That wouldn't save Brandy or Dash or the Labyrinth and it would cause my "fee" to be forfeited as well—and goodbye some world, maybe mine. In fact, I figured the hostage world *was* mine, since that would explain why Voorhes didn't care if their network was compromised and people taken there.

It wouldn't matter if they were purple and had pink fur and wolf snouts; so long as I was convinced they'd really detonate the place, and I was, I wasn't gonna blow their world for any temporary grandstanding. Besides, I had other interests here of a more personal nature.

Tarn's hideaway, like the others would be, I suspected, was strictly rebel territory. We got off on a hot desert world which didn't even have a Company substation, just a weak point strong enough to come through, and were met there by a couple of tough-looking guys out of *Lost Horizon* or something. You know—*big* guys, with tough Oriental faces and mean eyes, dressed in yak fur or whatever and looking really overdressed for the hot desert. They also had some very fancy high-tech sidearms that showed they really meant business and hadn't just wandered in from the wrong side of the Himalayas or something.

They had fur clothing for us as well, right down to fur-lined boots, parkas, and the rest, and they were a fairly close fit. Maria looked decidedly uncomfortable and out of place in her outfit, and not all that certain about it, and I figure I looked like a moth-eaten panda, but, what the hell.

With that we travelled maybe half a mile, which was all I could stand in that outfit—it had to be a hundred in the shade there, if there had been any shade—and then to a nicely hidden little substation generator. It was pretty obvious that this was a large weak point, a sort of desert Bermuda Triangle or something, and they'd taken advantage of it to build their own short line to somewhere.

It felt great to be in the silence and dead air of the Labyrinth once more, even if it was a hell of a lot darker and not nearly as comfortable as the Company line. We didn't have far to go, and when we exited it was into a cave or something and it was chilly and damp even through the clothing. I just knew I was gonna get pneumonia on this case.

You needed strong flashlights and a knowledge of the place to get out of there, and these guys had both. We followed, and Maria began to complain. "It is so *cold!*"

I smiled. "This is nothing. You ought to see what it's like back home where I came from."

No wishing was needed; when we finally broke into daylight, we were suddenly struck with about the bitterest cold I can ever remember together with maybe a twenty mile an hour wind. It wasn't much worse than the dead of winter in central Pennsylvania, but I hadn't been out in it in several days and where home was wasn't like a mile in the air. This sure was, and it was not only tiring very fast but you didn't have to go far to feel like you could look down further than you could look up.

The guys hooked heavy rock-climbing ropes and

clips to us and we started off. For me, I was just hoping that the ropes were just for our safety, not for climbing. Still, it was so stark, remote, and cold I expected to pass Ronald Colman at any moment.

Fortunately, we didn't have far to go, although it was cold, slippery going for a few minutes that seemed like hours, and I was thankful for the sheer muscle power and skill of our two guides.

I was actually prepared, mentally, for a longer hike, maybe even a couple of days or on horseback or something, since I figured Tarn's hideaway wouldn't be anywhere near his substation, but I kind of figured that the whole place was booby-trapped as hell, maybe even fortified—who could see what was just above, or who?—and that it would take real effort to get past here and maybe it was impossible without setting off so many alarms you'd be creamed anyway.

We went through another cave, this one incredibly noisy as the wind whistled through it, telling me it was a through passage and not a dead end. I was right—we emerged on the other side into a kind of bowl-shaped valley surrounded by peaks still too high not to be permanently socked in, and while it wasn't the land of milk and honey in the movie it sure as hell took your breath away.

Built into the side of the valley, maybe a half-hour from where we came in, was a *huge* building, kind of like a great castle and also like a damned big and exotic-looking condo. Partly built out of the solid granite and partly hewn from it, it had a kind of fairyland look about it. The place sure was awesome, anyway.

Somebody at least had anticipated that both of us would be totally winded even by so short a walk as we'd had in this altitude and also decided not to make us suffer. There was this big, enclosed sedan chair there with these long logs running through both sides and supporting it, and six big and brawny guys in furs apparently waiting for us. Maria looked doubtful, as if trying to decide between the misery she felt and the risks of the contraption, but I urged her in, and we sat across from each other on two curved wood seats that were worn almost smooth by who knew how many posteriors, and there were what I can only describe as grab bars everyplace.

"Hold on tight!" I warned her. "They got to lift us up!"

It didn't help. When they lifted us up with professional ease, it was still bouncy enough that neither of us had a good grip and we tumbled together for a minute. We managed to get back into our seats quickly, though, and then were off in a real rock and roll type ride.

"I have never been so cold and miserable in my life!" she wailed. "I do not like this cold at all, and I like this place and this thing even less."

"We just got to be obedient to orders," I responded a bit sarcastically. I was actually enjoying this to a degree. Not just her discomfort, although I admit that getting used to seeing a pretty girl not as that but as a loaded pistol pointed at your head can make you feel real satisfied that way, but also because I'd kind of been afraid these guys were in substation fortresses or other dull places and this was getting real interesting.

They put us down in the courtyard after coming through these gigantic wooden gates right out of a Cecil B. deMille Biblical epic, then one of the big guys opened the door and we sort of crawled out and stood on ancient cobblestone looking at the inner and main building complex of this place.

Until now I had no real idea if this was some kind of noble's headquarters, some reconstruction for Tang's amusement of someplace he'd loved and lost back home, or maybe some kind of monastery. Maybe all three, I decided at last.

I looked over at Maria, who was too shocked and frozen to do more than just stand there shivering, and then they motioned for us to follow them again and we walked to the main doors, which opened inward to receive us, and inside.

The immediate inside was kind of anticlimactic; I mean, I expected some real royal grand hall or maybe Westminster Abbey, but it was a small and dark area that felt almost as cold and damp as outside. There we were met by a number of men wearing monk-like robes of brown or black with cowls up. One of the black-robed ones came right up to me and what I could see of his face didn't look all that Tibetan or whatever the others were.

He snapped his fingers and one of the brown-robed ones brought us robes as well. We were helped off rather insistently with our coats and it was clear that we were to put on the heavy woolen robes instead. Fortunately they believed in being clothed underneath and they made no move to take the nice, warm boots. Even so, Maria resisted giving up the coat; I think she would have been quite happy putting the robe on over the coat for extra insulation.

"Just do it their way," I cautioned her. "We don't know what the rules are here, and I think this is also a way of making sure we don't wander outside without permission. You'll get used to it after a while. It's not as bad as all that in here."

"I shall *never* get used to this," she responded bitterly. "With so much of the world so warm why do people choose to live in such cold, anyway? It is illogical." But she surrendered the coat like a good trooper and wasted no time getting the robe on.

"No, it's illogical not to use all the places that can support human life," I responded. "We need all types of people and all the land we can get. Some people even prefer to live in places like this and would ask how and why anyone would live in such a horribly hot, wet climate as you come from. I didn't ask for you, so if you want to come along then you better shape up."

Flanked by other monks or whatever they were, the man in the black robe then led us further in. It *was* warmer in the center, almost comfortable so long as you kept your clothes on and robe on top, the result of a number of good-sized fires burning in fireplaces nicely spaced around the place. Right in the middle there was a large chamber, it seemed, its open doors kind of reminding me of a medieval European cathedral, although the altar at the end had what looked like, in the brief glance I got, the stupidest looking idol I had ever seen. It was golden, gigantic, and had a pot belly, short, stubby legs, and a squared-off face with big bulging eyes and a mouth that looked like a hollow figure eight on its side. It looked like something out of a comic book, but I wasn't about to laugh or criticize the local deity in this place. No telling—Quin Tarn might take it personally.

We went up some stone stairs and then down a hall that had solid doors on one side and on the other a railing beyond which you could look down on the cathedral proper, although it didn't have the best view of the big idol. A brown-robed monk opened one of the doors with a big key and gestured for Maria to enter. She balked, and turned on them. "No! We stay together!"

The monk, one of the smaller men in the group, might not have understood the words but certainly understood her meaning. He shrugged, then shoved her hard into the room and slammed the door on her, turning the key. I could hear her yelling, screaming, cursing, and pounding on the door, but that thing was so thick it was barely noticeable.

They skipped a door, then opened another for me, and I didn't object or wait for the shove. I walked in, and the door closed behind me with the most solid thud I ever heard.

Still, the place was livable; larger than I expected, and with a pretty nice-sized bed with sheets and lots of wool blankets, a personal woodstove that had been pre-started for my benefit and a fair number of logs in a scuttle next to it should I get chilly, a basin with a drain but no faucets, of course—there were two big pots of water there, one sitting atop the stove and the other fairly cool. Under the bed was a pretty standard chamber pot. I wondered if Maria knew what a chamber pot was, but that was her problem. The place was warm, and there wasn't the damp chill or the bed of straw I might have expected. It was a bedroom, not a dungeon, and that was sufficient for me.

There were no windows, and I doubted if we were really against an exterior wall at all. There was also no peephole or trap in the door, so if they could spy on me it would have to be by very clever design or by cheating and using technological stuff. I slipped off the robe and then did a routine check of the place for such things, although without instruments it was more a matter of thinking like a security man and knowing what I would use and looking in the places I'd put them. I found no trace of anything, not even any indication that the place was wired at all for any kind of electrical power.

Tarn certainly had anything he wanted at his disposal someplace or another, since he joined in their conference calls and had to keep in touch or we wouldn't have even been allowed here or expected, but he might feel so unassailable in a spot like this that he left it in one secret and unobtrusive place with maybe only a couple of trusted aides to monitor it, and lived more or less native.

So I stoked the fire, plopped down on the bed, and waited to be summoned.

It wasn't all that long. The key turned in the lock and the same black-robed monk who'd brought us in stood there, this time alone. I got up off the bed and took the robe off the hook, put it on, splashed a little water in my face to brace me, turned, and went to him. He turned as I approached and I followed him out of the room and down the hall to the end. I glanced over the rail and heard a lot of praying and chanting down there and saw a bunch of mostly brown robes doing the expected towards the idol, but my keeper ignored it and, when we got to the end, we took a left and walked up another, shallower, set of stairs to a kind of landing. I mentally figured we were more or less standing on the idol's head, with the steps coming up from both sides to here, and then a single set going up and further back. At the top of those stairs was another set of ornate wooden doors, and the guy in the black robe took something metallic from a pocket in the robe and struck a metal plate on the right door three times. It made an impressive racket.

He did not, however, wait for an answer, but put his knocker away and then opened both doors inward, revealing a very fancy and very cozy room.

The carpets were thick and plush and had woven Oriental designs and even scenes in them; there were other rugs on the walls, giving the place a real cozy feel and also providing insulation. At the end of the room was a raised area carpeted entirely in red, with a kind of throne in back of it—not fancy, but impressive, a real throne-type chair—and a table or altar or something in front of it that was covered with a matching red cloth. I was kind of disappointed; I was getting kind of hungry, and I'd hoped to be invited to dinner, not an audience. At least I'd hoped to see a chair in the room so I wouldn't be standing.

The monk in black stopped me and pointed to my boots, then took out his nasty-looking iron knocker and looked for sure like he was gonna break both my ankles. I got the idea. Boots off before you got on the red part. No problem.

At least it was nice and warm in here, almost homey, and he didn't seem to mind socks. Well, hell, Aunt Sadie never allowed shoes on the carpet, either. You know the type—kept the whole house covered in plastic and looking like it was about to be visited by *House Beautiful* while everybody lived in, and was only permitted in, the kitchen, john, and bedroom.

I stuck the boots to one side and straightened up, then turned to see what to do next, but all I heard was the doors closing behind me. The guy in black had gone, leaving me alone.

Well, I knew better than that. I could have planted a hundred monitors in here nobody would ever see, and, hell, a couple of good old basic peepholes as well. I studied the tapestries and tried to look bored and waited some more, and only when I glanced back at the throne did I notice somebody was sitting in it. *That* bothered me. I hadn't heard him come in, sit down, or anything, and I was like ten feet from him. Nothing like somebody doing that to you to knock the self-confidence and cockiness right out of you.

He was a man of medium height, with strong Mongol-like features, with a strong-looking frame and the kind of hard, tough face that said it always meant what it said. His hair was dark, his moustache long and flecked with gray, and he was dressed in a metallic blue robe with the cowl down. There wasn't anything fancy about him, but if he'd suddenly stood up and said he was Fu Manchu, Emperor of the World, I'd have taken his word for it.

"Why do you come here, sir?" he asked, in a heavy and labored accent that showed he was using a translation module that took his thoughts and turned them into compromise English and would also take my compromised English and feed it to his brain in the language he best understood.

"To speak with Quin Tarn," I responded.

"Why, *G.O.D. man?*" he pressed, his tone unmistakable in any language.

I sighed. "I was not asked about this assignment," I reminded him. "I was drafted, my son abducted, to force me into it. Your side forced me into this, and so you must also accept my own methods and ways. Otherwise, all that trouble was for nothing. You have a problem that I have been asked to solve. I can not solve it without information any more than a man can work without food and water."

He took this impassively. "Well met, then. What can I do for you?"

"You are Quin Tarn?"

"I am."

"What is this place? Is it a cover, a hideout, or a sincere religious place?"

"Why do you wish to know that?"

"How can I expect to get anything done if you are going to ask that every time I ask a question, sir? I will not explain myself no matter how that sounds, for you might be the very one I am asked to unmask."

"If I am, then you are a dead man," he noted with a trace of amusement. "Are you not completely in my power here?"

"Completely," I agreed. "But if you were I don't think you'd knock me off here. It would be rather difficult to explain to your comrades, I should think. Somewhere else, perhaps, but not here, not when it's your responsibility. I think you—all of you—are considerably smarter than that."

Quin Tarn seemed to noticeably unfreeze, becoming warmer in tone and more human in appearance. He actually smiled at me.

"I believe I am going to like you, sir." He stood

196

up, clapped his hands, and two smaller figures in blue silk robes entered from the rear and set up two large pillows on either side of the red-covered table, then scurried back out. There was no mistaking that they were women.

They re-entered quickly, bringing a golden decanter, glasses, and then bowls. Quin Tarn got up from his throne and then took a seat cross-legged on one of the pillows.

"Please," he said, gesturing. "Join me."

I walked up and sat, facing him. He poured what appeared to be red wine from the decanter into two golden goblets, set the decanter back down, then picked up his cup. "To your success," he said, and I took mine, raised it to him, and tasted it. It was pretty good stuff and I said so.

"Thank you. We have our own vineyards in the lowlands developed from the finest grapes from as many worlds. Much of this region below the mountains is temperate and the soil mineral-rich. We have been doing a great deal of development work and planning to create a new society here."

My eyebrows rose. "This is an uninhabited world, then?"

He nodded. "Humans never developed here, and many of the animals and insects are different and some are quite dangerous, but controllable. The differences are easily compensated for, even without the burden of heavy technology. The people are the refuse of a hundred worlds, the refugees, the dispossessed, the former inhabitants of corrugated huts within garbage dumps created by the imbalance of wealth and social class. I have abolished such things. Those who work here share equally in all bounty. Those who do not work will

197

starve. Those who can not work will be provided for by those who do."

"Utopia, huh? No government, no controls, just sharing and social pressure. And what keeps it that way?"

"Social pressure, as you say," he responded. "That and the unifying religion which defines the rules and the limits of knowledge and technology. It is a peaceful religion, against violence, against selfishness, making few demands and few promises. The distillation of the best of a hundred faiths and my later life's work. You see, sir, they robbed me of my own people, my own world, but this is my legacy and my dream and my refuge. It is already virtually cut off; when the Labyrinth is shut down, it will be totally isolated and yet protected. I will seal it off with me inside before the end comes, so that there will be no connection to the power grid."

This was interesting. "You weren't too keen on closing the Labyrinth, though. Why not?"

"If you ask that then you have not thought the whole thing through. Ask Mancini when you see him. Ask him to tell you the worst case model for the closure and the odds of it. The destruction of the Company world I can not, deep within my soul, complain about. When a place is infested with predatory, carnivorous insects one is forced to fumigate. But a moral man must ask if it makes any sense to use a poison to rid a house of pests if that poison also rids the house of its owners."

The women brought out two big bowls of rice, white and brown, and kept bringing out stuff to put on the rice. You just stuck some rice in the bowl and then put half the portion on top and ate it, not with chopsticks but with a golden fork and spoon. Knives weren't necessary.

Most of it was good, but in spite of my hunger I was getting a gut sourness in my stomach from the conversation that was keeping me from fully enjoying it.

"You're telling me that there's a chance that this thing could blow up everything? Every world? That's why you're going to sever all links before they do it? Sever them and pray that the weak points don't leak the destruction in spite of that."

"I will say no more about it," he maintained, "nor answer any more questions on it. If the others, particularly Mancini, wish to elaborate more fully upon this, then it is their responsibility."

"Fair enough," I agreed. I had heard more than enough for now to give me a picture both of the problem and of Tarn. Of course, he might be playing with me, feeding me a line, but it fit what I was seeing and certainly fit in with some of my theories. "What about Pandross? Speaking as one who was present at the meeting and also as one who knew and worked with the man for many years, not as a mind reader—what was his feeling on this? He must have known it. Would it have bothered him?"

Tarn seemed unprepared for that question, and thought about it. "He might. He was a strange man, a very private one, although always totally capable and dependable. Still, I would say it would not be possible to fully make a judgment on him in any moral matter. He seemed to be motivated only for the challenge, not for any inner moral purpose, good or evil. I always thought that much was going

199

on beneath his skin, but it was never allowed to be shown to others. He seemed almost more machine than human. Always objective, never divisive. A team player for whatever the team decided to do. Does that help?"

I shook my head negatively. "Not a bit. I am convinced that getting inside his head, seeing things as he saw them, is the key to all of this, but so far he remains the same enigma his files illustrate." I sighed. "Would you answer me a serious question?"

"Perhaps."

"You are going along with this because you know you are powerless to stop it, but I can sense that you still have deep moral reservations about it. If there were a way to stop it, to take a less drastic course, to return to the original opposition methods, would you do it?"

His deep, black eyes bored into me. "Perhaps. I have often asked myself this very question, particularly in the past few weeks, but I can see no way out of it without betraying my comrades and destroying the entire organization, and that is something I can not do under any circumstances. If the worst happens, I will answer to the gods as an equal with others, but if I were to betray my sacred oaths my soul would wander in the darkness, forever alone."

I nodded. "What about the others? They are all in the same situation."

"Voorhes would happily consign history to end if he could take the Company with it," Tarn responded. "They have left him with nothing but hate in his heart and his soul already in Hell. Kanda and Mancini see it as a grand experiment, a

200

test of their theories and their own genius. They know the odds but are convinced that they are far too clever for the worst to happen. They are basically secular men imprisoned by their own egos and intellects. One might also include Yugarin in that, since it is ultimately upon his theories that we will all rise and fall. Carlos and Valintina would be the sorts who simply would not care. They lost their souls a long time ago and do not miss them. Cutler—I would say she is in much the same position as myself. Resigned, as it were, rather than eager. Does this explain why we did not fight the decision? We were simply outnumbered."

"Uh huh. But it brings up the question of Pandross once more, and the same wall. I certainly believe you when you say that you would go through with it rather than betray your organization—but I wonder if somebody like him would believe that?"

"What do you mean?" Tarn was at least getting more impressed with me as we went along, which was fine with me.

"I think Pandross had, or *thought* he had, evidence that one of you was going to sell out the organization, the plan, and everything else. Once you are totally committed to this project, with people and materiel, you will, ironically, be totally extended and the most exposed to treason. You would have to be to do something of this sort."

"I see. And not having sufficient hard evidence to convince us that it was not he who was unbalanced, he either revealed his belief to this traitor or confronted him or her, and was killed."

"Not quite that simple, but you are in the right area. But, you see, there are three ways to go here.

201

Was Pandross just doing his job, or was he protecting the project out of conviction or out of a repugnance that there would be a traitor, or, in fact, was it Pandross who saw a way to stop the project? The last is least likely, but that's why I like it."

"Fascinating. And you believe you can unmask this traitor when he could not? As limited as you are?"

"I don't know. I do know that, unlike him, I have no oath of fealty, no loyalty or friendship or comradeship with your group. I can be objective where he could not. An accusation from me would carry far more weight among you if you think it through than one from him if I had any supporting evidence."

He offered me more wine, but I held up my hand. "No more, please, of anything. I am beyond the ability to eat anything else right now."

He smiled, then got to his feet. I did the same, feeling that the pleasant audience was coming to an end. That was O.K.—I'd gotten fed and gotten more than I expected.

"Well, then, sir, are there more questions?"

"Not at this time," I told him. "Perhaps later, after I have talked to everyone and gotten everybody's side of this, but not now."

"But I remain suspected. More than others, because of my beliefs."

I shrugged. "Not necessarily. If you are a moral man as I believe you are, you might well be the least likely to betray it all. I suspect no one and everyone at this stage."

He chuckled. "And yet, is it not ironic that this is at the cost of your own moral sense? If you unmask our traitor, our project concludes. Betray him and you betray your own side."

"I have less love and loyalty to my side than you do to yours," I replied frankly. "We will see when we get there—*if* we get there. Uh—I trust my keeper is getting fed in her room?"

"Indeed. She is most unhappy but I do not wish to even meet her, let alone give her leave about this place. I do not know the ultimate name to which she reports. You understand."

"Perfectly," I assured him. "If I didn't need her I'd suggest just locking her up here and throwing away the key. All right, then. We will be taken back?"

"It is too late today, and too dangerous," he responded. "Sleep here, and leave at mid-day tomorrow. Not even those who have been here for many years like wandering about out there in the dark."

"Can't blame them a bit," I told him. I walked back to my boots and picked them up, then turned and bowed slightly to him. He acknowledged it, and I turned and walked to the doors. Just before, I stopped, turned, and looked back, and he was gone. Not only him, but the remains of our meal, even the pillows, were gone. I would have loved to know how the hell he did that.

I pulled the doors open, and found Black Robe waiting for me as I expected.

"Home, James," I said to him, and we went back down the hall.

I lay there for a while, not just thinking about the interview but also trying to digest the food that seemed to be packed in from my intestines all the way up to my throat with the density of lead. It kept me from going to sleep, that was for sure, and since the TV wasn't so hot around this motel there was nothing much to do but run it through my brain.

The thing was, I liked Tarn. I liked him better than Voorhes, because Tarn hadn't died on that same day his world had died the way Voorhes and most of the others did. They were walking dead men; Quin Tarn seemed to be determined to live and make a major mark, almost as if he felt a responsibility to those who'd been murdered as one of the last of his kind to make his life count. He didn't seem to me to be a loony, and considering the organization he sure wasn't any pacifist, but of the ones I'd met so far he seemed the only really sane man.

You get a sixth sense after you've been a detective for a while and it rarely plays you completely false. I thought he was honest with me, and I appreciated that. He was also not unaware that I seemed to understand him and that this understanding alone made him suspect *numero uno* on the list.

What worried me more was his comment on Mancini and the odds. Tarn was a mineralogist—sort of the ultimate hard science but not somebody who was likely to be directly involved in the plan. Yugarin had come up with the idea and he was a geographer. That should be important somehow but I didn't see how yet. Maybe when I talked to him it would become clearer or hit me in the face. Mancini, now, he was the physicist—the one of the whole batch who was most likely to know the physics of the Labyrinth and how to use it and pervert it. The account of the meeting I had indicated that Yugarin took his idea to Mancini first, and maybe this Kanda, the mathematician, as well. That would fit. He'd figured out an idea but he didn't know enough to know what would be involved or exactly how to do it.

So this Mancini's intrigued, contacts Kanda to work out the math, and then comes up with the whole thing, engineered and checked and double-checked. But it's got a hitch to it. There's one chance in—well, who knows?—that things will go wrong, that it'll cause a super disaster. I remember once reading a book about the making of the atom bomb in which some scientists figured out there was a one in a hundred thousand chance or something like that that the bomb would set the atmosphere on fire. That sort of thing fit here.

But it also meant that they weren't trying to pull what the Company had pulled on their old world, since that was pretty safe for the guys doing the pulling. Of course, the Company had complete control of the power regulators, the Labyrinth path, everything, while these guys wouldn't. So they weren't gonna do this Company surge bit but something new, something much riskier, something never tried before and that worked only on paper. They weren't out to blow a world away, not even the Company world; they were out to blow the Labyrinth. Short it out somehow. And there was a chance in there someplace that it might short out a hell of a lot more than just the Labyrinth.

O.K., that framed the debate that must have gone on. I could already see it—the cold science types, the kind of guys who had no trouble building bigger and better H-bombs in the cause of peace and power, who saw this as a neat kind of experiment to prove some theories or something, come in with the thing, and it's so absolute that the walking dead ones like Voorhes embrace it immediately. If it was just Mancini, Yugarin, Kanda, Voorhes, and Mendelez that'd be five out of the nine. Add maybe Carlos and you get six. Tarn and the others could add as well as I could. They put up a fight, pointing out the odds, however slight, of it going all wrong, but they were arguing with the converted. So we get a mineralogist, a zoologist, and depending on Carlos a pharmacologist, against and none of those have the skills or backgrounds to be essential to the plot.

In other words, the others could do it without them.

But it's big, real big, so there's a requirement for absolute security and no margin for any kind of leak or second thoughts or it's all over. The Company had a lot of faults but if there was just a hint dropped that they picked up they'd come running in force. That meant you either went along with the plot or they got rid of you. After all, if it worked you wouldn't need the organization any more anyway, right? And if it didn't you wouldn't be around to care. And that put the burden on Pandross to keep the questionable ones on the straight and narrow. Unless Pandross felt he was marked for an early grave because maybe he couldn't be trusted, either.

Damn it! It came down to the same key question every time. Which side was Pandross on? The go or no-go side? If I could just figure that one out the rest of the thing would fall into place.

I must have finally burped enough or gotten too hung up in logic loops or something, because I drifted off.

The next thing I remember was hearing this horrible, piercing scream. It didn't sound close but, man, it had to be not only close but super loud to get through that door and those walls. I was on my feet in an instant, even though I had nowhere to go and might just have been hearing some kind of sacrifice or something or never be told what the hell was happening, but I always felt it was better to be prepared. I pulled on my pants and slipped into the boots and hadn't had time to lace them before there was a clanging at the door and it opened wide and sudden.

Two black-clad monks were there and they weren't fooling around. Neither had their cowls up and I could see real meanness in those guys, the kind of look that can freeze blood. They were also packing sidearms and those sidearms were in their hands. Ugly looking weapons—I hadn't seen their like since I gave up Saturday morning kids' shows, but I had no doubt that these shot more than colored light or darts.

They seemed surprised to see me, which I thought odd, and finally one said, "You! Come with us!" in the kind of tone you don't argue with. It was a thick, guttural accent but it was impossible to tell whether he had one of the translator modules on or if he really knew a little English. At any rate, I came.

They went to Maria's door and opened it, one covering the other who did the opening. I heard her shout a string of unmistakable curses in a very loud voice at them in her own language, but she was there. "Get on robe and come!" the same one snarled at her who'd come for me.

She was maybe a few seconds, but while we waited for her all hell seemed to be breaking loose inside the place, particularly below. There were shouts and bells clanging and reverberating all through the cavernous interior and I thought for sure we were under some kind of attack.

Maria came out, looking bedraggled and weary, and gave me a look that could only be described as welcoming. She'd been going nuts in there, that was for sure. She ignored them and asked me, "What is going on?"

"Who knows?" I responded.

The English-speaking black robe turned and said, "Follow me. Both of you!"

Well, we followed, sandwiched in between the two armed men, going down from the balcony and on to the main floor and then into the cathedral or temple or whatever it was. There were black robes everywhere and nary a brown robe in sight—it was clear that black was security and Tarn's own force, while brown was really the priesthood.

We were marched up the center aisle right to the point just below the altar, where a number of security men stood, some facing out, others in. They moved aside a bit for us and I could see that directly in front of the altar, maybe where the priest would pray to that stupid-looking idol, was a brown-robed figure, his garment stained with blood, which wasn't that unusual because there were two very large and impressive-looking swords sticking out of his back.

My immediate thought was that somehow

Pandross had gotten to Tarn and was showing off his hit in a very spectacular way. I turned to the English speaker. "Did anyone touch the body?"

"No. Only to be certain he was quite dead. Little wonder that he is. The force of the blows are such that both swords are stuck well into the flooring under him. We are awaiting the Master."

I felt a sudden surge of relief. Then it wasn't Tarn. I could see that now—the shape of the body and the head was all wrong. My relief wasn't just because I liked the guy; I figure that if he'd gotten knocked off while we were here there was no way we'd talk our way out of here and back to the Labyrinth, and even if we did we'd be dead meat, Typhoid Marys to the others.

"Who is he?"

The security man shrugged. "We have no idea. Perhaps we will be able to run him through our files, but he is unfamiliar to us."

"He wasn't some spy knocked off by one of your boys? You're sure?"

"Impossible. We would never do that *here*, and not like *that*. Besides, anyone who could get this far is not one we would wish to kill before he was thoroughly interrogated."

I nodded. "You mind if I take a look? I'm experienced—I won't disturb anyone."

"Take care," warned the man, and I intended to, but I walked forward and noted that Maria was right behind me, more fascinated than anything else by the gruesome sight. I reached down, carefully pulling back the cowl, and grabbing some of the long hair I raised the head to get a look at him. If his back was ugly, his face was even less pleasant, but I heard Maria give a short gasp of recognition and my respect for her went up a notch because she'd recognized him.

I mean, he had a beard now, and that face was really gross, but still, clearly, it was the face of Lothar Pandross.

7.

The Phantom of the Labyrinth

"You have some explaining to do," Quin Tarn told me a bit sternly.

"Oh? And what do I need to explain?" I asked innocently. "I was locked up tight and sound asleep when it happened. As if either Maria or I could have driven those two swords into him at all, let alone with that much force, even assuming we'd mastered the trick of walking through walls."

He looked at me intently. "You know just what I mean. Quisquot—my chief of security, the one who knows some English and brought you down —is very good and very experienced. He noted that while the woman, here, gasped at the recognition, you *smiled*."

"Well, at first I was afraid it was you," I admitted, "but as soon as it was clear that it wasn't, I wanted to see if I knew the guy. I do admit I was expecting somebody else—a Company spy, perhaps—but when I saw that it was another Pandross, well, I got the message and I think you did, too."

"Indeed? And what message is that?"

"I knew from the start that Pandross had faked his own death, and that he knew I knew it," I told him, hearing Maria gasp again and then give me dagger-like looks. "How is not worth going into right now. Pandross killed Pandross—or, rather, a double of Pandross. He probably has lots of them around. Most top security men do—the ones who have a sufficient number, anyway. He probably had the medical scan of that victim stuck in from the start, years ago, and just updated it if anything happened to him, so that the computer autopsy would verify that he himself had died. That gave him an unprecedented freedom in which he held the keys to security and the knowledge of the entire underground network but was accountable to none, all of whom thought him dead. I was the only one who could have exposed him, but until I understood his motives it seemed more prudent to keep it to myself. Since he'd gone out of his way to make sure I knew he was still alive even before I knew he was supposedly dead, I figured he'd contact me at some point and I'd learn what it was all about. In a way, he just did."

"I take it, then, that you do not believe that our body there is Pandross, either," the rebel leader commented.

"Probably not, but we'll never prove it one way or the other, will we? Not unless Pandross shows up again. If it is, then we have another player in the game, somebody Pandross trusted. Somebody capable of getting in and out of here past your best security system. I doubt it, though. This is a cynical security man's way of sending us both a message —that your operation leaks like a sieve, which I can believe, and you are, therefore, incredibly vulnerable, and that Pandross or whoever is behind this is fully capable of taking you out. The fact that it was also done while I was here shows that our player or players is using me for their own purposes somehow."

Quin Tarn seemed a bit nervous at that. "Then I must leave this place, burrow deeper."

"I wouldn't. If he'd wanted to take you out he could have. The fact that he walked right past your security, with his victim, and killed the victim in cold blood and in such a theatrical and public manner illustrates this. He's telling you to really tighten up your security, that's all. And when word of this gets out to the others, they'll become paranoid as all hell. He'll have shut me down because the others will cut and run. Shut down your grand project, too, most likely."

"Is that such a bad thing, I wonder?" Tarn mused. "Could that be the object of his playing around? Might Pandross think as I do?"

"Maybe. But we can't completely discount the idea that that's the real Pandross there. That he was here in secret monitoring me, maybe checking on me or maybe to contact me or maybe to contact you. That somebody else, somebody who's a traitor in your own organization, recognized him and did this to keep him quiet—in which case we have, as I mentioned, an unseen player with motives of his or her own. I mean, how many duplicates of himself can he have that he can waste them this way? And it's sure a lot riskier to do it this way than to, say, send a note or tap into your communications line. No, whoever did this did it partly because they wanted me to be no longer certain that Pandross was still alive and kicking. Hell, considering our discussion, I wouldn't put it past *you* to do it like this to get just the results we're talking about."

Quin Tarn sighed. "Perhaps. I will send the body to my own labs to be analyzed and autopsied anyway to see if there's some way of determining if he was or wasn't the real one, and even now we have sealed the place off and are working to install much more sophisticated security. Clearly geography and routine measures are not enough. But what would *you* have me do about this, sir?"

"Me? I'd sit on him. If you seal up this place tight and if you run checks on your security staff and guards to make sure you have no traitors or infiltrators, then the others won't know it happened. One might—if the killer can get out of here or get a message away. That might just give me an edge and keep them above ground."

"I might do that—but if I did so, then the project would continue, even at its reduced pace with us all away from it."

"Uh huh. But releasing this might accelerate that project instead of stopping it, too. That's the other lesson here—you all aren't as safe in your holes as you think you are. Pandross knows you all better than you know each other. It was his job. Sit on it, if you will. Let's see just what hand is being played here."

Tarn thought about it, then sighed. "Very well. I will 'sit on' this, as you say it, at least for now. At least until you get far more information. Until you have enough to decide whether or not this is a case you truly wish to solve."

Maria was so glad to get back to that hot desert world she wanted to strip, but since Tarn's agents were there and we knew we were dealing with newly cleared people who would rather have kept us than let us go if they hadn't been ordered otherwise, we just regained our original jump-suit style clothing and headed back into the Labyrinth itself as quickly as possible. If they couldn't keep us, they sure didn't want us around. They had a real crew on that desert access world working hard on what was probably the only main access into Tarn's world, making it solid as a vault, and they wanted nobody around who could describe what they were doing. I could have told them they had more worries than us, but I decided not to. Somebody like Tarn should know better.

There had to be other conjunction points— weak points—between this desert bridge world and Tarn's than just this convenient one. Any security man worth his salt and with the proper instruments and enough time could find them. Tarn could guard his main entrance all he wanted —his killer almost certainly got in and out through a basement window maybe hundreds or thousands of miles from here.

I was, in fact, counting on that and praying that it was thousands. That would mean that whoever it had been would have a very long and arduous trek back to that "window" and then also have some problems moving on the desert world to a weak point useful enough to get into the main Labyrinth. I probably had days, but if the murder was well prepared in advance and was set up by agents working for Pandross, I might have weeks.

When we got back to our little office hideaway, we barely had time to relax before Voorhes called.

"How did it go with Tarn?" he asked me.

"Very instructive," I responded. "Also nasty. There was a murder while we were there—not

Tarn, but an agent of somebody else for sure. Tarn is keeping it under wraps for a while and I'd appreciate your doing the same. We are on to something here and it's big and it's complicated and it's ugly, but I can't say any more yet. Any other invitations come in?"

"Uh, well—a murder you say . . . *Hmph!* Yes— we have most of them set up. Why?"

"If I could see Mancini next it would help a great deal," I told him.

"Mancini? Why?"

"Damn it! You and the rest have got to stop doing that if you want me to get this done for you! You want this done or are you just running me around to keep me busy? I'm sick of fighting for everything I need to do this job. I want Mancini. Period."

Voorhes seemed a bit taken aback, but, hell, like I told Tarn, I didn't *volunteer* for this. "Well, I'll see what I can do. Anything else?"

"Yes. Two things. First, I want the number and location of all known parallel duplicates of all nine of you and where they are now. Physical checks to see if they're still where they should be."

That got him interested. "Duplicates you say . . . Why do—oh, all right. Sorry. And what else?"

"If Maria is going to continue with me then she has to be with me at all times. I don't want her trotting off every so often to confess and so put on the record things she knows that I don't want our suspects to know. She needs something every few days or a week or so."

"Yes. So?"

"Wait a minute. I'm going to keyboard entry," I told him, then tapped out a series of instructions. I knew this terminal and system well and so I had no problems in leaving the echo off, so nothing I typed appeared on the screen. "You got that?"

"Yes, I have it. And I, uh, can see your point. All right. I'll arrange it. Anything more?"

"No, that's it. Just get me to Mancini next. After that I probably should talk to Yugarin, and I also want a little chat with Stacy Cutler. The others I'll get to after, unless something comes up."

"No guarantees on the timing or order, but I'll see what I can do," he assured me. "Duplicates, eh? Fascinating . . ."

I signed off, turned, and saw Maria staring at me. "What have you done concerning me?" she asked sternly.

"As of now, I'm practically a bigamist," I told her. "You and me are going to eat, sleep, and go everyplace together. Inseparable, except when it's unavoidable, like back in Tarn's world. The lock here has already been reset if Voorhes is as good as his word. You can't leave without me now. No more sneaking back home. No confessing. I'm your confessor for the duration. In fact, you're blocked out of your home world unless I'm with you."

She looked suddenly panicked. "But—I will die! Every five days . . ."

"Taken care of," I told her. "We're getting enough of your formula to last for weeks, and if we need more we'll get that when we run low. We'll take one with us, and the rest will be in a dispensing module here that will give you one dose at a time when I give the password to the computer. You sneak any messages, confess anything we learn, or blow any information we don't want blown, and I might have real problems remembering that password. What we know we alone know until it's time. Your confessor also confesses to somebody and so on. If you don't know who's pulling your string and Tarn didn't, either, I sure as hell don't want that someone to know anything I don't wish to tell them."

"You—you can not *do* this!"

I sighed and flopped on the bed. "Baby, I've *done* it, and Voorhes is even now setting up the details. Don't worry. In a way it makes it easier on you."

"*Easier*? How?"

"Now you got a real stake in wanting me dead," I told her, rolling over and trying to get a decent nap.

Salvatore Mancini either believed in living dangerously or he was not as concerned as the others with any possible attempts against him, a fact I found revealing just on the face of it.

We'd always known that the opposition network controlled some Company stations and perhaps even some alleged Company worlds—we'd rooted out a lot of bad ones over the years ourselves—but I hadn't expected one of the big boys to feel secure in any area on Company maps. I had to admit it—I was less impressed with this feared underground "opposition" than I was totally disillusioned by the dear old Company, who apparently allowed its operations to be so loose and porous that you could do just about anything in, around, and through them without their noticing so long as the bottom line continued to be huge and the Company world and race rich, fat, and secure behind its very solid electronic walls.

I lost my awe of the Company early on, but these assholes owned the whole damned railroad and seemed incapable of catching whole hostile trains running around on their own tracks and in and out of their own station. That's nothing personal, Bill —when they blind your eyes and give you only a peashooter for defense and do something drastic only after the barn door's been left open and the horses escaped, it's a wonder we got anything done at all.

Anyway, Mancini had this Company world apparently bought and paid for. We walked right into a standard station I guess I'd passed a hundred times myself and never thought about and walked into the usual warehouse type building that was the ideal station. All enclosed, plenty of room, and they did so a lot of shipping and commerce.

In fact, there were thousands of huge cases lined up on the side of the entry floor, ready to be loaded into special containers and shipped up and down the line. Curiosity got the better of me; we'd no sooner stepped away from the still slightly hissing electronic cube and onto solid cement and I'd gotten the sight of those endless but perfectly identical cases lined up there than I walked over and read the stenciled lettering on many of the cartons, which was, to my surprise, in English.

I could hardly believe it, so I kept walking down the line of cartons, going on and on and piled maybe ten high, reading the boxes.

"You seem fascinated by the cartons," Maria noted. "Why? Is it important to the case?"

I shook my head no. "Uh uh. They're what's known as compact disks. A hundred to a carton, and maybe, oh—a thousand cartons. A hundred thousand compact disks of the best of Slim Whitman." I sighed. "I always wondered just where he was the best selling singer of all times. I guess this is it."

We continued to walk towards the exit stairs along the cartons when somebody on the control bridge above gave a shout. I couldn't tell what was being shouted, but it stopped me momentarily, so that a couple of cartons came crashing down just inches in front of me. I whirled, and there was a lot of action on the bridge and I heard footsteps running and a door slam.

"Someone tried to push them on you!" Maria shouted. "Shall I give chase?"

"Uh uh. If they can be caught they'll be run down by the people who know this place best." I bent down, examining the hundreds of compact disks that were all over the place after the boxes split when they hit the cement. I picked one up and looked at it, then tossed it away.

"Now I am really mad," I told her. "It would have been bad enough to be brained by Slim Whitman, but they tried to get me with *101 Strings*. That's one obituary I just couldn't have stood." I sighed, and we walked towards the exit.

Two men in black uniforms—not military types, more like warehouse garb—came up to me. They looked like Bud and Al, the guys who tune up my car at the State College Boron station, but I figured they were station security.

"Mister Horowitz? Are you all right?" one of them asked, at least sounding sincere.

I nodded. "Yeah, we're O.K. Did you catch him?"

"I only saw a figure—too far to make out much

else," he replied. "It looked like he had a Company uniform on, though. They're chasing him down, but there's like a couple of hundred guys around wearing uniforms like this. I wouldn't get my hopes up, but we'll sure as hell grill everybody."

"Big help. Look, can we get out of here and someplace where we can do what we came to do?"

"We got the outside sealed now, and only a few handpicked people are in here now," the security man responded. "I threw the security locks as soon as I could get to the control. Too late to shut him in, but we're secure now."

"You probably thought that ten minutes ago," Maria snapped.

He shrugged. "Come with me. I have explicit instructions on this matter and I think we want to clear the floor here—just in case."

I didn't have any arguments to that, but as we followed him his partner bent down and picked up one of the CDs. "Jeez!" he said. "*101 Strings!*" He paused, then added, "Well, at least it wasn't the Montovanis."

I wasn't sure I was going to like this world at all. Fortunately, I guess, I didn't have to. We followed the man up to the bridge itself and into the high-tech control center, past two Type Two humans who were monitoring the equipment. It was a risk to have Type Two people in the stations, but there were always a few in control no matter what. Some of the Type Two races were absolute wizards at both running and repairing the highly complex station machinery—something in what they could see or hear or some inbred talent for microforgery or something. Type Twos were humanoid but not at all human. This pair, maybe mates, had bulging black eyes and snouts like wild boars among their more lovable attributes.

We went into a back office, and I could see the elaborate extra security system even as we passed through it. There was an outer office, then more security system, then an inner office. The security man didn't knock; he opened the inner door and we were ushered into a large, comfortable-looking room with a nice desk, a small phone bank on it, and a couple of padded office chairs in front and on either side of it. In back of the desk sat Salvatore Mancini, looking every inch a fugitive from either a *Godfather* movie or an indictment in Newark.

The office was smoky, and he was smoking a cigarette when we entered. From the looks of the ashtray on the desk, he seldom stopped smoking when he was awake.

He did not rise to meet us but did nod, then gestured to the chairs. "Please, take seats," he told us, then looked at the security man. "That will be all for now, Brenner. Go find that traitor. You think on this—I will have someone hung up to dry for allowing anyone to get inside this very building who is not ours. You and your associates should make a decision on whether I hang up the traitor or perhaps you."

Brenner looked unhappy and started to say something, but Mancini silenced him. "Go!"

Brenner went, closing the door after him.

I expected Mancini to sound like Marlon Brando or at least Jack Nicholson, but he had a cultured baritone voice with just a trace of an English accent. Real classy. Still, the way he talked to Brenner suggested that my initial reaction to his looks was closer to the mark, or he was putting on a fairly good act for us.

"You wanted to see me," he said impatiently, "and now you do. So speak to me. My time is valuable and I do not like to be in one place very long, particularly considering the incident outside just now."

"You don't live here, then?" I said more than asked. "We're just in a neutral but secure meeting point."

"That should be obvious."

"You seem pretty complacent about that attempt on me back there," I noted. "What if that was a Company man?"

"Not likely. A Company man would have made the attempt on *me*, not you. It doesn't matter, though. I have a number of ways out of here and I have never been caught, trapped, or otherwise compromised, and in the few minutes I have to be vulnerable I have a great deal of shielding and protection. One learns if one wishes to move about freely with unknown threats about. The known threats are bad enough."

I believed him on that, although I didn't like how casually he was taking it in spite of that. The penetration *had* to bug the hell out of him—unless he was either a superior actor at hiding his real self or he was the guy who ordered it. I decided to get right to the point.

"You worked out the system for shutting down the Labyrinth," I began.

He nodded. "With Kanda, yes. The tolerances are so fine and the margins so slim that the kind of math required was beyond me. I have some of the best computers in any universe here, but unless you know the right questions to ask they are useless."

"I need to confirm a scenario I've got. Yugarin came up with the idea independently, then came to you to find out if it was possible or feasible. You took it, figured out how it could be done, took it to Kanda who did the math, from which you worked out the theories and set up the engineering of the actual project."

"You have a good grasp of it. I wonder why you needed to see me on this."

O.K., Tarn told me to ask, so I asked. "What are the odds of a complete success? As nearly as you and Kanda can figure them? That is, of shutting down the system beyond repair while leaving at least the vast bulk of worlds untouched?"

His big, black, bushy eyebrows rose. "You surprise me, Mister Horowitz. You really do. I assume you have also thought through what you already know might cost you?"

I nodded. "Beside the point in this matter, sir. Everything that's been happening to your organization is tied in with that project and the decision to go ahead with it. I no longer have any doubts about that. Will you answer my question?"

He shrugged. "Dead even of complete success. This is uncharted physics."

Even I was startled like that. "Fifty-fifty? You mean you're going ahead with this when there's only a fifty-fifty chance of doing it right?"

"Not as bad as all that. The odds of a partial success—a crippling of the system so badly that it could not be restored within a century or two—rise to eighty-three percent."

I whistled. "So there's a seventeen percent

chance of it going completely wrong?"

He nodded. "But that's in either direction. It's in the nature of the thing. It encompasses all the possibilities other than complete or partial success, including the ones we can not think of because we can't imagine them—and including the fact that it will simply dim the lights and give the Company a temporary but curable cold."

"Yeah, well, maybe, but can you figure the odds, plus or minus whatever, that this will be a worst case scenario? That it will destroy every universe to which the Labyrinth is connected?"

"Oh, there's no chance of *that*," he said reassuringly. "The system is powered from the Zero Universe, it's true, which contains all of the energy and matter potential to create a universe but which somehow didn't go off in the Big Bang, and that's enough potential to disrupt a considerable amount, but certainly by the time it is diffused through the billions of Labyrinth universes and who knows how many weak points it will be quite scattered."

I held up my hand. "Hold it—Doctor, isn't it? Well, I've got a B.A. in criminology so bear with me. I do read a lot and my wife tells me I'm bright, but this is a little outside my field. You're saying we get all this power from an uncreated universe? One in which the Big Bang never happened?"

"Essentially. When it was discovered it was probably smaller than the size of a common garden pea. The whole *universe* compressed into that. The only such one ever discovered. There's no Labyrinth opening to it—it can be accessed only in ways that would require you to get a doctorate or two in the correct fields of theoretical physics to begin to understand. As to understanding exactly what it is—I doubt if anyone does. But it's not necessary to understand it to use it any more than it's necessary to understand gravity before you fall down. It is true that it is an unexploded universe, but that's not quite true. It *is* terribly unstable, and it does give off incredible amounts of energy. What the ancestors of today's Company race did was to recognize what it was and find a way to trap and harness that energy—limitless energy for all practical purposes, although I have just assured you that it *is* finite. There is even a school of thought that believes that the Zero universe will eventually explode, that it's in the pre-explosive stage. You know how each universe differs a bit, and all differ temporally—only most close to each other differ only minutely."

I nodded. "There are worlds where a year there can be just weeks here. I got trapped in one of those once." It suddenly hit me what he was saying. "You mean that this thing is just on a different clock? That it might go off on its own any second?"

"A universe is self-contained. It knows no clock until it creates one. I mean just that."

"Holy shit! Then by tapping into this thing, they took a chance that it wouldn't go. They're still taking that chance."

He nodded. "It's not such an awful chance. About the same chance as the sun going suddenly nova or a giant meteor smacking the Earth out of orbit. The odds are that we could go millions or even billions of years before it happened. And if it did, the regulators simply would disengage at the shock and power would be lost, which is what we are trying to achieve by different means. But, you see, they only *think* that will happen—or, rather, the Company folk take it as a matter of faith by this point. Nobody really knows, since it has never happened. And if it did, it would still not destroy the other universes, just the other Earths and perhaps the basic solar system."

I felt a rock in my stomach. "And what's the odds of that happening with your project? The best educated guess." I really didn't care if Mars survived if all the Earths blew up.

He threw up his hands. "No idea. Best guess? Five percent, maybe."

Five percent. *Maybe!* Or maybe ten. What were the A-bomb odds? Like one in several hundred thousand or maybe a million. Would they have gone through with that test if the odds had been five percent? Or maybe ten? Or maybe *maybe*?

"And you're willing to bet that it won't happen."

"I am willing to gamble when the odds are better than eighty percent in my favor, yes. I can see that you are shocked. Cutler and Tang had the same problems with it, but I am pretty confident." He leaned forward and stared straight into my eyes. "You see, Mister Horowitz, it has given me the first true excitement I have felt in twenty years. They made us walking dead, but now we are alive again—*I* am alive again. The knowledge and understanding we will gain from this will be incalculable. We will know things about the nature of energy and matter such as no one could ever dream to understand, possibly the very key to creation itself."

"If it works," I put in.

"Yes. If it works. If not, we will all die and,

therefore, it will be irrelevant to me, but I shall not feel a thing.''

I looked over at Maria to see how she was following or taking this, and she looked confused. I was following this in a loose way—the same way I could understand the consequences of a hydrogen bomb dropped on my home town even if I didn't know exactly how it worked or what it was doing in scientific terms. I kind of figured her education might be a little less broad than mine, and I wondered how she was following this.

She wasn't, well, but she asked a good question in the pause. "If this—universe—is needed for all the power," she said, unsure of whether or not she was making a fool of herself but really curious, "how did your own people punch through long ago? And how did the Company reach the place in the first place?''

Mancini chuckled. "Oh, one can do a progressive punch through the weak points with very little energy—a medium fusion reactor would do it. And then you build another in the next world, or find other means, and so forth. Of course, this is quite limiting, as it takes years to build a decent fusion reactor and sometimes the natives might object. They had to basically conquer and subjugate the worlds progressively. It took generations, of course, but the Company folk are old enough from the point of view of most of human history on worlds like the ones that produced us that we don't realize how long this all took. Until, about four hundred years ago in roughly our time, they hit upon the Zero and figured out how to use it. That began the age of Labyrinth expansion and growth which lasted over a century more, then the consolidation, the present full system which was still rooted in imperialism and colonialism, and the resultant dry rot of the present-day Company folk."

"Sounds like they got stuck and lapsed into decadence pretty quickly," I noted.

"Not really. Consider where *your* ancestors were three hundred years ago, and what they knew. It is plenty of time. In my own world, a vibrant, brilliant Roman Empire decayed into a long age of stratification and darkness for almost a thousand years until it fell apart from its own dry rot. The Company folk did not have that luxury. Their standard of living and technological level and near infinite reach of whatever they needed and their automatic feeding of all the energy they would ever need has kept them there. They cannot collapse of their own weight. We once thought that there was a chance that they could be induced to collapse from within but we have determined that it is against their basic culture to do so. The most that might ever be expected is an exchange of places within a culturally identical society. Nor can they be brought down from outside. We tried that several ways and I am not certain even now that even if we had succeeded that it would have worked in the end. Those whom we controlled would not be sophisticated enough to be able to conceal their dependencies and would be eliminated by those below."

"The perfect empire," I noted. "So long as you're an Imperial citizen."

"Indeed. But it is fed by the umbilical cord of the Labyrinth and the limitless energy it supplies as well. Cut that cord, and they die. Pull that plug, as it were, and they die. We believe that even the greatest risks are preferable to eternal domination."

I looked at him squarely. "How did Pandross react to the plan? Was he for it, against it, or what?"

Mancini shrugged. "It was impossible to know Pandross. He had thousands of operatives yet in all the years we knew him, going back to the old days and the Company schools, no one really knew him. He was, you might say, a total loner. Humorless, colorless, neutral even socially. Now that you mention it, I can not recall a single initiative on his part in all the plotting and planning. He simply sat there, making comments when his area of expertise was touched upon, and went with whatever we decided." He got suddenly very reflective. "Yes, you know—it is odd. We all lost a great deal back then, and it changed us, but Pandross . . . One never had the impression that he ever had anything *to* lose."

I nodded and rose from my chair and Maria, after being a little startled, did the same.

"Well, that's all I need for now. Thank you for the time, Doctor. I hope we can get back into the Labyrinth with less trouble than we had getting from there up to here."

"By now my men will have swept the entire place. I will guarantee your safe exit, as I intend to leave the same way."

I nodded, and turned to go, then stopped. "This is a very good local security setup," I noted, pointing to the door frame. Only a pro would ever even notice what was embedded within it. "Who installed it? It doesn't look like Company work."

"It's not," Mancini replied. "Pandross designed it and his people put it in. He and they did all the security for our network."

"Have you had somebody of his caliber but not one of his staff come in to your installations here and elsewhere and modify or install additional guards since Pandross died?" I asked him.

"Uh—no. There seemed no need, since it is keyed to my own coding systems which even Pandross did not know."

I sighed. "Amateurs. There's always an override, Doctor, known only to the installer. Some nasty little work-around that only a top expert could ever know or detect, different for each installation. Otherwise if one of these went bad you could be trapped inside here indefinitely, or locked out of important installations." I turned and looked back at Mancini, who seemed very startled by that news.

"There is? I had never thought of that. . . . But, surely it makes no difference unless it really goes bad, I should think. After all, Pandross is dead." He paused, looking suddenly nervous. "It *doesn't* make any difference, does it?"

"I would change the system, Doctor, starting with wherever you wanted protected most. Good day."

And, leaving him off-balance, we walked out, through the control room, and down into the warehouse. The floor rumbled a bit, and there was the sound of distant but powerful machines, and as we stood there we watched the Labyrinth form in the center of the warehouse floor.

Maria was nervous and looking around, but I calmed her. "We'll get out. If he wanted to kill me he'd have killed me."

"Who? Pandross?"

"No, of course not. Mancini. Honey, nobody, not even Pandross, gets this close with this many security men around, the control room staffed, and the big boss in attendance. With an army, maybe, but not one guy. Not even a rat. And if, somehow, they did, since nothing is absolutely impossible, there is no way such a one could get away and no way somebody smart enough to get inside here would depend on a few lousy record cartons."

"Unless these security men were still working for Pandross," she responded.

"I'm impressed. You're starting to think like a detective. But, no, not in this case. These guys would be hand-picked by Mancini and be regularly put through a brain laundry just to make sure of them. Besides, he wasn't upset, nervous, or in any kind of hurry. There was no sense of danger coming from him at all. For a guy in his own element and laying low for fear of a possible assassin, the idea of somebody getting in would give the toughest man fits. Uh uh. And the security guys were far too unconcerned for an offense that would under real circumstances get them a very slow and unpleasant death. No, they rigged it up to impress me."

"But—why? The only one who might want to scare you off would be the killer or his accomplice, and you said they'd never show themselves in their own element."

"Yeah, but this isn't Mancini's usual element and there's a lot of excuses here. But it might be simpler than you think. It might just be that he doesn't approve of me, from the opposition, snooping around and learning their best secrets. He was just putting me on notice, that's all. Not a word of this from this point on, though—remember."

"Not even at the—office?"

"*Especially* not at the office. That place and even the computer is bugged three ways from Sunday by all and sundry."

"Then where are we going now?"

"We've only killed a couple of hours on this one. We check back in and try and get the next appointment."

Voorhes wasn't in when we got back, and the computer showed no new data on possible duplicates, nor were there any messages from anyone else saying how delighted they would be to talk to me, so there wasn't much to do but eat and relax.

I already had a fair amount of information, and when I had the data on the duplicates of the big boys I probably would have enough to solve their own little mystery more or less to their satisfaction, but I had a far greater interest in seeing the other five and in solving the other two problems before me that none of the eight were interested in me solving. And a third, very personal problem of remaining alive and safeguarding me and mine when I had all I needed.

Maria, who by Voorhes' own acquiescence to my controls over her proved she wasn't along primarily as a spy but as my executioner given certain preset conditions, was frustrated by not being able to discuss the case or ask me many questions while in the office.

"No matter what you say or do, I can not totally

accept your limits," she told me, "if only because of my own functions. For example, I must tell you that we were followed in the Labyrinth."

"Huh?" I was getting too damned cock-sure of myself while looking down my nose at the others for committing the same sin if that were true. "Who?"

"No way to tell. The figure was always three cubes back, and dressed in very dark, nondescript clothing. I thought nothing of it on the way to Mancini's, since we were on the main line and many people would be going in that direction farther than we, but he was there again on the way back. That is when I knew."

"And you didn't tell me until now?"

"You said to not speak of anything in here," she reminded me.

"Yeah, well, I expect some common sense with that as well. Wait a minute. I'm going to get the security scanner from the kit over there."

Since I'd insisted on rigging my own extra system for the office, I had a fair amount of equipment and for the first time this was going to come in handy. I didn't have anything full blown like I'd have on a Company project, but the hand-held and the hoop scanner would do. I was pretty sure that if it was there it wouldn't be all that sophisticated.

Maria set the things off like New Year's Eve, and I didn't fare much better. I ordered Maria to strip—ah! Man! What power, only it didn't count for much here—and had her go through again and there was only a low reading. Then I did the same, enduring Maria's criticisms of my exotic pear shape and other sags, and got the same results. The clothing was saturated with radiation—a kind harmless to humans or animals or most living things, but easy to pick up if you had the right equipment, especially inside the Labyrinth.

"But how—how could anyone . . . ?" she asked, befuddled.

"A hundred ways. It might have been Tarn's people with their own clothes over ours that would have saturated what we wore beneath, or it might be the way the stuff is coming back from the laundry each day. I've never had call to use the system to track somebody in the Labyrinth but I know of it."

"Who, then? Voorhes?"

"Maybe. We'll ask, although I don't know if we'll get a straight answer."

"But is this not a major risk? I mean, if *they* can track us, then can not the Company do the same?"

"It could—if it had us located from the moment we enter the main system, but that presupposes that we're blown and that the Company's been tailing us all along. I don't think that's so. Markham would need Headquarters approval for such a thing, and when he got it he'd also get one of those ham-headed Company race security bosses rushing in to take the credit. They'd have stormed Tarn by now and certainly nabbed Mancini. No, it's not the Company. I have an idea who it might be, but I'm not worried right now."

"Then do we get our own washers in here or something, and all new clothing checked out as clean? I believe I could manage it."

"No, no. It would be handy if you can pick up some clean stuff to use, but I suspect that in my case my original clothes will be O.K. and I can always detox my shoes when I have to with what I have here. No, it's important that they *don't* change procedures, if they're not listening to us and doing so right now. Let 'em follow. We just want to make sure that we can squeak out without ringing a lot of bells if we have to—so you'll need to pick up something clean at some point and keep it here.''

I wanted to make sure that all our listeners, no matter whom they might be or where, got the idea that I was an old fuddy-duddy, self-conscious of my appearance and traditional in my moral outlook. Now that I knew it was the clothes I also knew of at least one way I might possibly slip out—if it came to that. I had no intention of telling them, or Maria, how so that somebody could adjust and close that little loophole which, after all, just might not really be there. If I needed it, though, I wanted to have it.

So I started pulling on my pants again and only when I sat down on the bed did I notice Maria standing there, still naked, looking at me. "Problem?" I asked her.

"Do you find me—unattractive?" she asked, sounding a bit worried.

"No, I find you very attractive indeed." I wasn't quite sure what brought this on. "I find this situation very difficult and very tempting. It is difficult not to capitalize on it."

"Then why don't you?" she asked, straight-faced and sincere.

I knew she damn well wasn't in love with me. I had no romantic illusions in that department, and I hadn't done an awful lot to be romantic, either. "Because I am married and I am in love with my wife. The only other reason for doing it would be to gain some major advantage, and I don't see much possibility of that."

"Love is an antiquated concept invented by upper-class writers to disguise their own lusts," she responded. "Likewise marriage is an anti-quated and obsolete system wherein lust and co-habitation somehow needed to be legalized or licensed so that the State could control people better. It is merely legalized prostitution."

"Don't knock it if you haven't tried it. Of course, many people try it and a lot of them knock it because it's tough over the long haul, after the lust has gone. And the state has little to do with it except to write the license cheap and easy when you do it and then ream you if it needs to be dissolved. But love—it's often, maybe usually, confused with lust, which is why there are so many divorces, but it's real. It can die out, if you aren't careful, and takes work, but it's worth it. And if both partners do what they want to do best for the marriage, then it's not prostitution. You can have sex without marriage or love—that's a kind of prostitution—but when you have love as well it's different. It's better all around. It means some-thing."

"What?"

"My wife is my best friend, my closest confidant, the person outside of myself I respect and care for the most, and, while we're very different, we know each other so well we often know what the other is thinking or how they'll behave. I miss her. I wish I had her here on this case. And while you're young, attractive, and very available, you're not her."

She shook her head in wonder. "I do not understand this. It is babble and nonsense. You mean to tell me that you have never cheated on your wife nor she on you?"

"No, I can't say that—at least about her," I responded, "although it was under a coercive set of conditions, not voluntary. As for me—no. Never really have in spite of occasional thoughts to the contrary now and again and a lot of temptation. With me it'd be voluntary, deliberate. I know how much it hurt me when she did it even though I knew she had no choice, and I understand how much more that hurt would have been if it had been true cheating. I couldn't inflict that on her. Not deliberately."

She stared at me the way somebody would stare at a Martian. "You are the strangest man I have ever met. An anachronism, someone not real but out of an old novel in an earlier age. I think you are quite mad. Who or what do you think you are?"

"Nick Charles," I responded, fixing myself a drink and not elaborating further. "Now put your pants on. Or do you really crave me that much?"

"You are a singularly ugly specimen of man-hood," she said flatly. "On my world such imper-fections were genetically corrected years ago. I just felt in the mood, and you have made certain that I cannot go out and find someone better."

I would have liked to think she was just getting back at me, but it was probably the truth.

On the other hand, maybe it really *was* the truth. That brought up an interesting idea.

When she was dressed, I beckoned her over to the desk and took out a pad and pencil. "Would it be worth it to you to have some freedom if you also had to trust me? Write all answers. They can't

238

visually see what we're writing here."

She read it, took the pad, and wrote, "?"

"If I let you go out then I have to trust that you will not reveal the information we have to anyone. If you do, you will undo all my work. But you can not exit without me. That would mean leaving me alone in the Labyrinth," I wrote.

The proposal startled her, but I could see it tempted her as well. I hadn't realized my constant company was *that* odious, but if I were her and stuck in this situation I'd probably feel the same way no matter who I was stuck with. I was counting on it.

She took the pencil and wrote, "But how could I trust you? You control my energy, but I have no hold over you. And if you betrayed us or we were even found out, I would die in an ugly manner."

We were gonna have a real bonfire here with this amount of paper. "My word is all I can give you. But I have some work for you that only you can do, without me, as well."

"Where would you go?" she wrote.

"When the next appointment is made. I'll go to it and you'll go off on your own errand and take time to do whatever else you like or need. I would be under your security anyway until you came and picked me up. What do you say?" I wrote to her.

It was tough, I knew, but that last had given her the out she needed. She nodded, then wrote, "What do you want me to do?"

"Memorize the following," I wrote back, "then we'll destroy all this. I need you to talk to friends in security and find the answers to some questions. Make any excuse, but do not let them know it comes from me."

She was hooked, just as I'd hoped when I talked Voorhes into this arrangement. I needed the legs and contacts she would have and I lacked in this alternate environment, and if she didn't blow anything I'd have what I needed.

Carefully, item by item, I gave her just what I needed to know.

8.

Assembling the Jigsaw

There still wasn't any information from Voorhes or anyone else on the duplicates, which was a key answer, but there was another round of interviews scheduled. I was glad to be moving again; I needed to complete this as quickly as possible, because while I was circumstantially figuring out the puzzle O.K. and, with Maria's help, maybe the more personal problem as well, but even when I had a sufficient amount of information to convince myself that I was right, that only brought up the other obvious problem—how to survive the solution.

Not that I had any kind of ironclad case, nor would I. Handcuffed and restricted as I was, there was no way I was ever going to make any sort of case that would stand up to close examination, but I'd faced that kind of case before as well, most notably when I'd deduced the guilty and traitorous Company director who'd made certain you could never prove him guilty of a hangnail. In the end, it didn't really matter to me whether I could prove the case to the satisfaction of others. Frankly, I didn't care if the bastards killed each other off or ran for deep cover and dissolved their little club or what. But the solution, the motive, the who, what, when, where, and why, was very important to me indeed.

I mean, even if I figured out how to keep my own head from getting blown off for good, what good would that do if I couldn't also prevent them from maybe killing every human being in existence? I mean, I was human, and Brandy, and Dash as well, and I had no desire to include any of them in the Twilight of the Gods that might be coming up.

Nor was I kidding myself that I was living on borrowed time, an unwelcome intruder let loose to do something that might be useful, might not, to them, but in any case somebody to be eliminated as soon as any usefulness I even potentially had was over.

The invitation to Yugarin was just what I needed next, not only to get some information from him but also to get Maria on her own way. The major problem was the Phantom in the Labyrinth. If we had a tail on us, then that tail would know that we had split.

I didn't have any illusions that we could jump whoever it was, or that we'd even know who it was if we somehow got a good look. The fact was, the Phantom was probably more than one person and almost certainly represented a double-check on security, put there as a sort of guarantee of me and of Maria. I didn't want to blow my little plot for getting out of their tracers right now, either—I'd need that later, maybe to slip Maria—but we had to teach the tail a lesson, scare him off enough to divert him, and then by the time he got his electronics going to take up the tail once again to mislead him.

In fact, it was Maria who came up with the gimmick and it was worthy even of, well, me. The desk chair was one of the usual kinds; a kind of padded, thin, typist's chair with four casters on a stalk. Like most electronic tails, the radiation tracker tracked only blips based on the clothing, not warm bodies. A set of irradiated clothes on that chair would register as a second person on anybody's tracker, and with the casters it'd be a cinch to roll ahead of me. I already had the cover story for Yugarin's security boys, and I thought they'd buy it and so did Maria, and it gave a nice excuse for her not being there and them baby-sitting me, too.

Of course, she'd have to be stark naked and checked to make sure she wouldn't still show up before we exited, which was certainly a problem for her, but she didn't seem to think it was a serious one. Apparently she knew where to get a good, clean set of clothes without raising a lot of eyebrows and I didn't question that further. I just hoped we got away with it all the way. If they figured this out, Maria was right—we both would probably be dead soon after—and everything would be for nothing. Still, you have to take big risks for big stakes, and this was maybe the ulti-mate high-stakes game. If it worked, though, I would have successfully turned the tables on them and be running my own independent game.

They were banking on my moral sense that I wouldn't do anything stupid and get a whole world zapped. That was their big hold on me. Even so, they'd saddled me with Maria, a low-level agent who would follow whatever orders she was given, including executing me. In a sense, their faith in me was touching and their faith in their own double and triple redundancy security on me was even more heart-rending.

Just like the company, they could somehow maintain a comfortable double standard that I might just be good enough to solve their problem but nowhere near their equal when it came to playing their kind of games. They were very confident that they had set immutable rules for me.

I figured it was about time to change the rules.

When we got ready to leave, Maria disrobed and took a shower, which would look and sound normal, and I managed to get the chair on a pretext over towards the exit wall where I was pretty sure there was no visual scan but there was some of my stuff. I'd often used it as a stool, so it wouldn't appear odd to anybody. And it also gave a good reason for me to have my security kit.

Naturally, they'd know we were on to their irradiation scheme, but I didn't think the kind of minds I was dealing with right now would consider that more than a point in my favor for noticing it. Pandross, now, might have been a different story, but he was the least of my worries right now.

Maria came out, picked up her clothes casually, and came over towards me. We struck up an inane conversation about what we'd do when we reached Yugarin, and during that time she wiped herself all over with a towel, then I set up the clothes on the chair and then checked her with the meter and hoop. Not a hundred percent clean, but she would maybe show up real close as a ghost trace, of which there were bound to be many, and not as anything solid. She also had every intention of ducking out of the cube when possible and waiting until I was well away before coming back in and getting on her way.

There wasn't much danger of her being naked in

the Labyrinth in and of itself; there were often naked or nearly naked folks in there. Some of these worlds were interesting, and others required some prep at the station end. If it was kill or be killed and for the kind of stakes I was playing for, I guess I'd do it, but I probably wouldn't consider it in her position. Well, we were different, and in this case the difference was in my favor.

Maria entered the tunnel with me in her birthday suit, it was true, but hardly defenseless. The computer had given directions on how to find Yugarin; I wasn't gonna get lost in the process, so we started off, her a bit in front of me and pushing that chair, making one hell of a sight.

The guy was good; I'll give him that. But if you know you're being followed, and you train yourself to spot a tail, there's almost nobody who can stay completely hidden or nondescript, particularly in the barrenness of the Labyrinth. What was real impressive was how he hung back from us, not just in the third cube back, which was about the limits of our visibility, but near the back of that cube, just beyond our sight. The thing was, nobody you're following ever keeps a steady pace unless you're following soldiers on the march or a precision drill team, so by just easing up a bit or occasionally stopping, as if to adjust a shoe or something, anyone that far back would become visible for a short while until they realized that we'd slowed or stopped and faded back.

In a way, I kind of felt sorry for him. In the sterile confines of the Labyrinth there wasn't any real way to follow somebody without going a little bit nuts. Kind of like when I had a small-time punk back in Bristol try and use me to locate a witness he wanted to ice and that I had to talk to. I wasn't real sure he was back there, so instead of taking the police car I took a bus. Busses stop every block or two and even when they're going they stop and start and keep to the curb side. Imagine you're in a car following a transit bus sometime when you're in a city and you'll begin to see what I put that punk through. This was kind of like that—now that we knew he was there.

The other thing was, if he was far enough back for us not to see him clearly, then the same was true in reverse. He was depending more on his little tracker than his eyeballs, and we counted on that. Maria had already picked her spot, and now we were there. She gave me a hand signal, and I could see a nice, tropical kind of scene on the right cube face that looked like the sort of place I wouldn't mind going to myself, and I suddenly stopped, whirled, and began walking briskly *back* towards the shadow.

He was real startled for a moment, and for just an instant I caught a detailed glimpse of him— fairly tall, dressed in some kind of brown uniform, and I got the idea he was young, somehow, as well. He stopped as soon as he saw me walking, of course, and immediately began back-tracking, but by this time I'd left Maria two cubes behind. As soon as I saw the tail vanish to my eyes, I stopped, turned again, and walked back, this time to my trusty office chair. There was no sign of Maria, not even in the tropical scene, so I wasn't sure whether that was the one she used or if it was some disguised one on one of the black faces or what, but that one nice scene was the one *I'd* use.

I began walking forward again, casually pushing

the chair with the clothes draped over it ahead of me. It was well made; the casters were a dream to push.

Now I'd really started the tail, and he'd acted the way you or I might act when faced with an instant decision, but now he'd recovered, and checking his board, he still got two close blips, and since neither of us seemed to be challenging him and both of us were going in the other direction, he took no other action but just reestablished his tail. That was just fine.

I was a little nervous that Yugarin's switch might be attuned to the two of us, or at least might balk at registering an office chair, but when I got there I was automatically shoved to a siding, chair and all. The thing was obviously keyed to my code as well as Maria's, and I began to relax. When I'd gone three cubes in on the siding, though, I did another panic stop and reverse and was surprised to find that the shadow was no longer there. Either that or he was being doubly cautious.

Well, there wasn't any reason to give the trick away more than I had to. When I got to the exit, the only exit allowed, I left the chair and clothes in the cube just outside. If the shadow made it in he'd know he'd been tricked but then it would be his problem explaining that. Me, I didn't want to push that damned chair any more.

I came out inside some structure. Not really a station, more a substation and of fairly limited access, kind of like the one in my back yard. It wasn't staffed or heated, and it was damp and chilly, although not super-cold. The thing seemed to be a wooden shack, and I spotted a door, went over to it, and pushed, walking out onto a pastoral scene of rolling hills and far-off trees and lots and lots of grass. I turned and examined the structure and, so help me, it looked from this side like one double pot outhouse. Not that it would fool anybody if that was what it was intended to look like; no smell and no flies.

I had kind of expected a welcoming committee or something. The place looked pretty but uninhabited and desolate. I wondered if I had been stood up, or if maybe Yugarin was going to come in behind me. I hoped not. Wherever it was it was autumn—maybe forty, forty-five degrees with a light wind and half the leaves colorfully on the trees and the other half decomposing on the ground. Not the best or most comfortable conditions for a picnic, that was for sure.

Suddenly two guys strode up the side of a nearby hill and came towards me. They were wearing funny-looking uniforms of blue and red with the big buttons and braid and all, like maybe the Queen's guard or something, or guys out of a Foreign Legion movie. They had more conventional shiny-billed army type hats matching the blue of their tunics, and high-topped boots that looked well worn. One of 'em had a fancy moustache, the other gigantic sideburns, and they both had that posture of military men.

One came up, gave me an unexpected salute which I didn't return, having been honorably discharged years ago from my own service, and said, "Meestar Hovarvitz, dere vas to be two uv you."

So that's why they'd laid low right off. "We were being tailed in the Labyrinth," I told them, then realized that to a guy who spoke English like he did that would make no sense at all. "Followed. We didn't know by whom. So as soon as I came in here, my—partner—went to see if she could find or trap whoever it was. She may join us later, although I expect that she'll try and set a trap for whoever it is to be sprung when I leave. She is not important here anyway, not with ones like you to guard and help me."

The one guy thought about it a moment, and I could tell he was the type who didn't like anything to be out of place or out of order, but he finally decided that my logic was impeccable. Besides, what the hell else could he do?

"Pliz come vith us," he said at last, making his decision.

I didn't even want to guess at the accent, but it sure wasn't American or Spanish or west European.

"I hope it's not too far," I replied. "I'm a little out of shape."

"Ve haff de horzes chust a bit beyond here," he responded. "Uh—you *do* know how to ride de horzes?"

"I can ride one of them," I responded. The guy sounded like a cross between somebody deliberately doing bad German with something of a Russian accent mixed in and a little of Scandinavia just to add total incomprehensibility.

Yugarin was supposed to know English. I hoped this wouldn't be the brand of English he knew.

They had a horse for me, with a decent military saddle, and I climbed aboard, glad to ride, although I was out condition even for riding and I knew from bitter experience that my thighs and rear would kill me in a little while. There was another, empty, for Maria, and I was surprised when they didn't at least take it along. I began to suspect we weren't alone.

I took a look around and was startled to spot several figures in the trees nearby, nicely hidden. Snipers or guards or lookouts of some kind, that was for sure, but primitive. Of course, Yugarin controlled the switch and there was no telling what nice little traps he—or probably Pandross—had laid.

They took it easy on me, adopting a fairly conservative pace, but after maybe a half an hour we'd gotten well away from the substation and in fact had come to a modest dirt road. We turned on to it, me getting chillier and wishing I had one of their nice wool uniform coats, and followed it for some miles more.

We came, eventually, to the sea—or, rather, some mighty big lake since I couldn't smell salt—and to a small settlement on a bluff overlooking the shoreline. There was something of a small town there, with a fair number of uniformed soldiers and, surprising to me, a number of women as well, all wearing long, heavy wool dresses and fur caps.

There was a lot of shouting and comments to us and to one another as we rode in, all in a language that sounded like nothing I'd heard before—and a little of everything I'd heard before. Kind of like somebody had taken all the languages and dialects of northern and eastern Europe and shuffled them all together and come up with something new out of the old.

I had been pleased with my performance on horseback and didn't really feel it at all. I wondered if maybe the dampness and cold was great enough so I didn't notice, or maybe it was like riding a bicycle—something which, once you got it, you kept. But when we pulled up outside this one big wooden building with a fancy insignia painted on it and a lot of words in what looked like the Cyrillic alphabet, or a reasonable facsimile thereof, and I got down off that horse that I almost collapsed from the pain and stiffness. I wondered what kind of first impression I'd give if I duck-walked in.

Steeling myself and trying not to let the snickers from the small crowd watching get to me, I straightened up and followed the pair into the big place.

It was kind of cozy inside, particularly after the ride and the chill. There were thick rugs on the floor and on the wall, in the Slavic tradition and also providing a fair amount of insulation, and a substantial wood stove in the center surrounded by a fire pit. Around the stove and room were many chairs, reclining mats, and the like, and some small wooden tray tables. The place looked more rustic than primitive from this vantage point; kind of like you'd expect some national park lodge to look.

There was nobody else there, but there was a door to an inner area, and I stood there and waited for my cue.

"Vait here. I vill tell de Profezzor dat you are here."

He walked over to the inner door, snapped more or less to attention, and knocked smartly three times. There was a muffled answer from inside, and he opened the door, walked in, and closed it again behind him. I decided that there was no reason for me to stand at attention and sank into one of the chairs.

I had to say that most of these guys didn't pick comfort or convenience for their hideaways, and went more for security than really burying themselves deep. They controlled the ins and outs of their little private preserves, and apparently weren't terribly concerned that somebody might blow their private switch and trap them inside. That, of course, implied that they picked worlds with back doors, as it were, and could if need be access the main Labyrinth at another point known only to them. You'd probably have to go a long distance and then have a lot of inconvenience and travel, but the back door was a certainty.

Still, you had to wonder. Voorhes had that Amazon colonial place where even the ice had to come from a private refrigerator in the station, and Tarn had his mountain castle with no central heating and no running water, and now this. Mancini was probably different—his sort wouldn't want to be more than two rooms from a computer terminal—but he hadn't been interested in letting me see his place, which might even be the kind of *cul de sac* they found for my own office.

The door opened, and Moustache Mouth came out, beckoned to me, and said, "De Profezzor vill zee you now. Come."

I got up, feeling every mile of the ride, and entered what could only be described as a typical if a bit out of character private office. There were maps and papers everywhere—Yugarin hadn't made any particular concessions to my arrival nor did he seem to feel the need to meet elsewhere, as

Mancini had. In a way, that worried me.

The office *was* a mess, though, almost as bad as mine. Add to the extreme clutter the fact that Yugarin was a heavy cigarette smoker and you got some of the picture. In the center of it all, in a comfortable office chair in front of a long table filled with papers, was the great man himself, dressed somewhat like a monk in the old Russian tradition, with brown fitted robe and big gold cross around his neck. With that wild hair and scraggly, unkempt beard, he kinda looked like Rasputin.

But it is the eyes that are often the most revealing part of a person's personality and intent. These blazed with a kind of intensity that almost shouted, *"I'm nutty as a fruit cake and meaner than a drill sergeant."*

What he actually said, in pretty good and fairly neutral English, was, "Well, Mister Horowitz— where is your guardian angel?"

"Chasing phantoms," I responded. "What's the difference? She's of no real use here, and I'm not exactly going to lead a revolution or overthrow the empire all by myself and in your domain. By the way—what the heck *is* this place, anyway?"

He laughed, got up, and cleared off a pile of junk that revealed an otherwise totally hidden chair Sherlock Holmes couldn't have deduced, and waved me to sit. I was sore and I sat.

"This place," he said, lighting a cigarette, "is what is somewhat jokingly called the Holy Tartar Empire. It's none of those, but they had to call it *something*. It is what remains of a once great and proud people laid waste by chemical and bacteriological weapons. Never underestimate the human mind, Horowitz. They never invented nuclear weaponry and worse here, but they still managed to find a way to reduce a population of four thousand million plus to a few widely isolated pockets of desperate humanity. The switch you used was a Company switch, not one of the old ones, abandoned and sealed off in quarantine and listed as not to be entered for thousands of years."

I grew uncomfortable. "I assume it's not as deadly as all that now."

He chuckled, apparently enjoying my discomfort. "No, it's clean—possibly cleaner than most worlds—but quite sad. These people here—they are the survivors, the ones whose grandparents didn't die, and who found a small pocket where things still grew normally, although it was a nasty place. We brought them some animals and better tools and they have been quite grateful to us, and very hospitable. Some of the nasty micro-organisms, mutated over the years, still exist, and might pose a threat to them if they went too far, but it's funny. This world is just different enough from ours—yours or mine or many others—that those pests die if they get into our systems. Just a little difference, perhaps in biochemistry, or vitamins, or hormones, or solar radiation—who knows? But we, Horowitz—and most people from other universes—are poison to their germs. So, relax."

I had an uncomfortable thought that something like germs in the Labyrinth air exchange system might readily close the thing down, but I dismissed it for now. The air was exchanged with the various worlds with which the cubes came in contact. Each cube was essentially self-contained, so there'd be only a tiny bleedover, and you'd certainly infect all the worlds any organism contacted. It wasn't very practical, but it didn't make me feel any better.

"All right, I'm relaxed in that department, although I can't see how you can work in here without setting this place on fire. Shall I ask you some questions now?"

He nodded. "Go ahead."

"First of all, how well did you know Pandross?"

He thought a moment. "Oddly, not at all well, in spite of our long association. He was an odd sort of chap, very much a loner. I doubt if anyone, certainly not any of us, really knew him closely or well."

There it was again—that same distance between Pandross and the others.

"But he was dependable and reliable at all times," Yugarin continued, "and he had an affinity for anything mechanical or electrical that defied rational explanation. He was the only man I ever knew who could fix a machine he'd never seen before by opening it up and somehow deducing or tracing just exactly how it worked and why. He created many of Kanda's intricate mathematical computer programs when we're certain he didn't understand the math the program did. I don't know how that's possible, but that was Pandross."

I nodded. "Did he ever spook anybody? Any of the others? I mean, I've known guys of that type myself and even the people they worked for felt real nervous and uncomfortable around them."

"Oh—I see. You are looking into motivation. I doubt that Tarn was very close to him, and Voorhes kept some distance as well. Mendelez tried to seduce him once, early on, and he flew into the only rage I can ever recall from him—

indeed, the only real emotion I ever saw him display except a child-like happiness when playing with his gadgets. It was a cold rage, but she never quite forgave him for it and never directly spoke to him again. But that was *years* ago."

I was chasing something, something I'd sensed but couldn't pin down from my earliest conversations with this crew, and I wasn't about to let it go yet. But there were other things in the room that also caught my interest, and I stood up. Like a map of the twin Zero regions, right and left of the Zero World, with all the sidings and switches in, including mine, that I knew about and many I didn't. And the one to home sweet home, if I could get a look at it, along with a number of others, had big red circles around it.

"Sorry," I said as apologetically as I could, "but it's been a while since I rode horses and I've got to stand and stretch a bit or I don't think I'll ever stand again."

"Feel free, but there is not much room to move."

"I don't need to move much, just shift weight for circulation." I paused, then continued, "Your—organization—is given to complex, Machiavellian plans, if you know the term."

He nodded. "Go on."

"Your attempt to switch key people for doubles in some central Company worlds was like that, and the plot to hook the Directors on drugs was also similar. I assume there are many more I don't know about because either they worked or were before my time. Still, there's a consistency in your group thought that builds a pattern. Whose idea was the double replacement scheme?"

Yugarin thought back. "Voorhes came up with that one, if I remember, although we all participated to a degree. It was rather successful to a degree."

"Cranston was Voorhes' man, then?" I angled over and got a very good look at the master map he had tacked up on the wall behind his desk, a map covered with writings and symbols in various colors of marker ink. The system wasn't that hard to deduce, once I got one spot located and identified that I knew.

"Yes," he replied to my question, not even taking much notice of me and my deliberately casual-looking observations. "I wasn't much involved in that and it is difficult to remember, but, yes. Cranston was a replacement himself who surpassed all our expectations."

"And the drug business was Carlos."

"Oh, indeed, although both Valintina and Cutler were involved in the extensive set-up and experimental stages, as was I, since getting supplies of it from that far up the line down to the Zero region was tricky in the extreme."

Uh huh! That's what ties it up. Big bangs here and over there and just off that switch there—so that was it! Or was it?

"And Pandross supplied the security system, warm bodies, and maintained the loyalty of the underlings," I went on.

"Essentially, yes. All security personnel were under Pandross, of course, but his personal involvement was and remained overall system security, not the security of any given operation."

"Did Pandross ever propose any plan or scheme, even way back when?" I asked him. "I mean, did he ever actually develop anything on his own or take personal charge in an operation?"

Yugarin thought a moment, then shook his head no. "Not once. Not really. One might call him the ultimate engineering mind. Once given a problem he could map it out and show you its strengths and weaknesses, gains and risks, and even suggest efficiencies and improvements, but he never actually proposed or thought up anything, no. I am not at all certain he could improvise on the field level. You gave *him* the problem. Problem in, solution out—if there was a solution."

"All right," I said, sitting back down in my chair, confident that I'd seen all I could see without being obvious. "What about your own pending project? Did you go to Pandross with it before you brought it to the full council? I know you went to Mancini."

"Not ahead of time, no. When the thing was fully worked out and ready, and the group voted its approval, then he was almost instantly on it as a security and logistics problem."

"But he voted for it."

Yugarin shrugged. "He always went along with whatever the majority decided to do. You must remember that, other than inclination, it was not his job to come up with grand schemes and designs, but to take such things and apply his own unique level of expertise to them to see how they could be done securely, in secret, and with minimal risk and maximum coverage."

I filed that one away. "Mancini says your plan has a better than one in twenty chance of wiping out all humanity up and down the entire line, absolutely and forever. As I understand it, that's where what opposition to it that there was came from. That prospect doesn't bother you?"

He nodded. "Yes, it bothers me. It bothered me when I came up with it at first, which is why I took so long before putting the whole thing together. I remember discussing it with Mancini, oh, ten years ago. . . ."

"Ten years!" *Good lord! That was it! That was the answer!* All of a sudden a whole set of building blocks fell into place. Now all I really needed was the big question—who was on which side?

He nodded. "It was percolating a long time, and came from my efforts at truly mapping and understanding the Labyrinth. At the time, the risks to all the worlds was more on the order of fifty percent. It either worked or it killed everyone and everything. That's why it was never proposed at the time. Mancini eventually took Kanda into his confidence and they worked on it off and on, with some input from me, over the years as time permitted us to do so. They came up with a theory very early to drastically reduce the risk, but we had no way to test it out without mounting major operations. Finally, not very long ago, we got a computer simulation that Mancini and Kanda felt comfortable with that showed the risk at five percent and also indicated very little chance of us getting below that. We decided to bring it fully formed to the others and see if they felt the risk acceptable. It was either that or abandon it entirely after all this time, and, frankly, no one had any alternative bright ideas."

Time to see if I could confirm any of my theories without drawing pictures or putting Yugarin on the track.

"Then you didn't bring it to them with a firm argument to do it and with the votes already counted as Tarn said. It was just a 'this is all we've been able to come up with in a new grand design?'"

He nodded. "Quin Tarn is one of your Machiavellian manipulator types, and someone incapable of believing that anyone his intellectual equal would not think and act as he would. He would see our proposal that way whether it was true or not because he was, as it were, on the losing side and that is the way *he* would have done it."

Yeah, that made sense. "But Mancini and Kanda were all for it."

"They want to try it. They want to try it because they have nothing else to live for but their work, and, having invested so much in this, they want to find out if they were right."

"And it doesn't trouble you that they might be wrong?"

"Not really. The cosmos has been singularly unkind to me and singularly uncaring of what is or was done to me. I feel no differently towards it than it does of me." He fingered the gold cross. "If there is a God, then He will not permit the worst to happen, or it is His will, the Final Judgment Day, he's looking for. If there is not, then, one day, perhaps a thousands of millions of years hence, time will end, the universes will either dissolve or collapse inward, and nothing we do or ever did means anything anyway. Either way, it's not my problem, is it?"

I didn't answer right away, but, looking at him there, Rasputin's creed came floating in from some hidden corner of my mind where it had sat since I learned about it way back when in high school history or someplace. *Anything done by or with a holy man is holy. With me, by me, there are no questions.*

Finally I said, "Nobody really knows the big questions, do they? But maybe, just maybe, all of you have been consumed. You suffered a bigger tragedy, all of you, than I hope I will ever know, but you—all of you—brilliant people, the last and perhaps the best of your world. You could have made that world live, in a sense, with all the knowledge and skills you had. Instead you all decided that you died back then and you've been feeding on sheer hatred ever since. There are probably other worlds out there with other Voorhes and Yugarians and Quin Tarns, only different in small ways from your own. Somewhere those you love still are represented, still live in a way. Would you kill them, too?"

He whirled angrily and for a moment I thought he was going to attack me, but he got control of himself.

"Yes!" he shouted at me. "Can't you understand that what you say is just what is wrong? *That the cancer that consumes our souls is rooted in the very knowledge that the rest of creation continues unmoved and unchanged!*"

He sat back down, then looked down at the floor, and finally back up at me. "You have asked all the questions you required. Go," he said, in a hollow, empty voice.

I didn't want to push him any more, and he was right. I had, in fact, learned far more than I ever dreamed I would, and I had no wish to provoke him. Without another word, I hauled myself out of the chair and left the room, where Moustache Mouth was waiting for me.

I stayed with the people of the Holy Tartar Empire, all three hundred or so of them plus maybe fifty more of Yugarin's boys, for two days. They were a fairly jolly lot for a primitive, rag-tag group of survivors, and they thought of Yugarin as some sort of god.

I guess if I'd been starving at the edge of nowhere in a land laid waste I'd be pretty close to worshiping the guy who brought in chickens and pigs and cows and horses and sheep and much of the little manufactured goods we take for granted —like the precision tools to make other things.

Yugarin had found a kind of kinship with the wretched survivors of a world that had destroyed itself without even needing the helping hand of the Company, and, ironically, one which the Company might have saved had it been here. As rotten to the core as the Company was, it was that alone that kept me oriented to its side. I knew that the same octopus of exploitation also used its powerful and hidden tentacles to defuse the ultimate, to keep worlds like mine from giving in to the human bent for total destruction.

The same organization that had destroyed at least one world had saved countless others. It didn't matter about the motives involved; I had a stake in the Company's continued existence for much the same reason that these people wanted to destroy it utterly.

I didn't see Yugarin but that once, and had no real idea if he remained there or not, but his men clearly had orders that until I was picked up I was to be kept there. I only hoped Maria hadn't gotten into any real trouble. I didn't relish spending the rest of my life in the place in spite of the camaraderie. It was too damned cold and primitive, and it stank.

Finally, though, Moustache Mouth came for me. "Your pretty partner, she is here for you at the gate," he said, and I was eager to go to her.

By "gate" the security man meant the Labyrinth, and we rode out the same way as before, along the dirt road and then overland on the old trail to the small ramshackle wooden building on the hill.

Maria, in a heavy and expensive-looking fur coat and hat and fur-lined boots, was sitting there, leaning against the building, waiting for me. She looked like she'd done pretty well for herself in the couple of days on her own. I only hoped that she'd done as well for me, and nothing against me, during that period.

I knew I looked a mess—I was wearing a surplus uniform jacket over my original clothes, which hadn't been washed or changed, and I was unkempt and unshaven and I itched.

"You look like hell," she greeted me.

"Just fine, and how are you?" I came back. "I see you found a tailor."

She laughed. "It was simple, but I will spare you the details. I take it that Mister Yugarin does not go in for luxurious living."

"You take right, although as usual he lives a lot better than the rest of them." I lowered my voice, and took her to one side. I knew there were observers in the trees and perhaps some snooping gear around, but this was the safest of the places I was likely to be right off to get the information I hoped she had.

"Whisper," I cautioned her. "The trees have ears. You get what I needed?"

"I think so," she responded, her whisper so low I could barely make it out myself. "I do not understand how you could have known it, though, nor what she has to do with anything."

"Believe me, it's vital."

"Well, all right. His—compound—is an obscenity. He has developed a system similar to my own home, only he has twisted and perverted it and made it ugly and horrible. Everyone, even his on-site security staff, are in thrall to his privately developed and powerful drugs. He treats them all like dirt. He humiliates and degrades people, and there is no question he enjoys it. He has a laboratory in his luxurious complex there with many brilliant minds bent to his will and in which he carries out human experimentations. They have developed a horrible pharmacology in which they can create drugs that do almost anything they wish to the mind, the personality, the attitudes, even change things physically."

"You actually got in?"

"No," she told me. "Nor did I wish to. But there is enough traffic to and from, particularly among the network security people and couriers, that it was very easy to get a full picture, even a recent one."

I nodded. It was at least as bad as I figured. "And what about her?"

"She is one of his toys, to be kept around and toyed with and humiliated. Altering her mind would defeat the purpose and deny his pleasure."

"That's a relief. This is gonna be a tough problem to crack, though. No way he'll let me near that place. He may meet me, but like Mancini—in a neutral corner. We may have to figure a way in without the knowledge of the network. It'll be risky, but it's necessary."

Her eyebrows rose. "You would think of doing that? It is impossible. The switch control is on the inside and tightly managed. Besides, even if somehow you got in, what could you do but get caught? No one can be rescued from that place. You take them away from there and they would no longer get their drugs. Even your closest comrade would betray you under those circumstances."

"You should know," I commented, thinking about the confessionals and group sessions of her world. She was right, too, although she didn't bank herself on the twin super powers of love and hate. "All right, then, maybe we can get some messages in. Let me sleep on it and I'll try and figure out a plan. Don't worry, though—this won't get you in trouble with the network, nor betray or harm anybody but him, unless he runs your world secretly as the ultimate party member—and he might."

She stared at me as if I were mad. "You can not be serious."

"Even if he had nothing to do with your world and its development its very nature would attract him like a magnet. Believe me, I know. But if he has perverted your world at the top, and you are repulsed by what he's like at home, then maybe you'll be doing your world a favor as well."

"He is the killer? The one behind this?"

"Maybe. Probably not directly, and certainly not alone, but he almost had to be one of them at the center of it. I beat him before, but never caught him." I sighed and we wandered back towards the wooden building shielding the substation. "The only thing I'm certain about is that he's involved and that he is the only one of the batch of which I can be certain of his side and sympathies. I need something, anything, to help me separate the skunks from the skunk cabbage."

"What?"

"Never mind. Four down, and maybe four or fewer than four to go."

"I checked our messages," she told me. "If you didn't look that way we could probably meet Kanda and Cutler without going back. I think, though, that you need a shower and perhaps a good sleep."

I nodded. "Yeah, I guess I do."

"It is a pity," she said, "that we can not arrange to meet the rest in a group. It would save much time."

I shook my head violently from side to side. "Uh uh. The last thing I want to do in this is save time. In fact, I need all the time I can buy." I paused a minute, then had a couple more questions.

"Any evidence of who our tail is?" I asked her.

"No. Sorry. Definitely not regular security, but surely too lowly a job for a higher-up."

"Sooner or later we're going to have to set a trap for him, if we can. I want to know who he is and who he's working for. Oh—that reminds me, did we lose our chair?"

"I'm afraid someone made off with it," she

responded, laughing a bit, "but I am certain we can requisition another."

I'd known a lot of guys who were nutty over computers, but Dilip Kanda was the first one I'd ever met who lived in one.

He was fairly short, cherubic, with strong East Indian features, maybe far enough east to have some Thai or Cambodian in him. He was dark, wore thick horn-rimmed glasses, and dressed for guests wearing only one of those white cotton diapers like Gandhi used to wear and a threadbare white cotton sleeveless undershirt.

The place was cramped, and I couldn't get a fix as to whether I was in a great building or complex on a world or whether this was entirely built within the Labyrinth medium. At any rate, it was all metal or plastic, with glassy smooth floors and narrow corridors that seemed to go through machinery. I felt sort of like a cross between being in a high-tech auto junkyard doing great business and the Incredible Shrinking Man lost inside an automated telephone exchange.

"My humble pardon for meeting you like this, but I simply can not get away right now," Kanda said, greeting us, in a voice that had that somewhat stilted yet highly cultured Indian accent. He shook hands, and they were rough hands with nasty, long nails. I looked at his toenails and they looked almost like claws. For a moment I wondered if he wasn't some Type One snuck in on us, but I finally realized that the guy simply didn't keep himself up at all. His black hair, without a trace of gray, was so long it was down to his ass and looked like a great "before" example for a "no more tangles" ad.

Human hair grows like three inches a year if not cut or trimmed. At that rate, Kanda had last seen a barber some time in the previous decade. At least he didn't have a big beard. He was, racially or otherwise, one of those guys that had very little facial hair at all.

"That's all right," I responded, looking around. "This is quite a place."

"Indeed," he said with pride. "I believe this to be possibly the finest and most complex computer ever built. It is of my own design, although even I can not understand all of it, nor could the late and lamented Pandross or anyone else who helped construct it. It is far beyond what we originally built. Totally self-contained, totally self-repairing, with the ability to design and create whatever it requires robotically. Much of its own bulk it has designed itself over the years so that even I have no idea how large it is or just what it can do. It is sufficient that it does what I need it to do."

I looked around nervously. "You talk like this thing was alive. Like we were in the belly of a great beast."

"Indeed so, in a way. Not alive as we know life, but certainly it thinks. Our entire operation has depended upon it. Had we not been able to develop it, initially with the unwitting consent of our late Company patron, we would not have been able to accomplish what we have. The security computers and general data banks are but an extension of it, and the parallel network and the rest are maintained and guarded by it. The closest thing to it is the master computer complex on the Company world after which it was based—the rock, as it were, upon which I created this one. But they have severe limitations and restrictions on their own master computer. Here, there are none."

I got suddenly a little nervous at that. "You mean that it answers your questions because it wants to, not because it has to."

"Basically, yes."

"You kind of wonder why it bothers."

He looked blank for a second, then chuckled. "Oh, yes, I see what you mean. Actually, it needs people, or at least their input. It is clever enough to know that mere data is not the same as truth, and that truth is a subjective concept. It can have the sheer data to know everything about a particular human being, or an entire nation, or even an entire world, but it has no feel for what it is actually like to live that way, to think that way, to *experience* life firsthand. Only by interacting with humans, and even humoring tiny and limited brains like my own, can it get any feel for that, however inadequate, or gain full understanding of why we want to know what we know or why we feel this way or that. I do not pretend to fully understand it, but if your fear is the old one of the computer taking over or wiping out all life, it is a false one."

"Oh, yeah? That's just exactly what I was thinking."

"Well, as for taking over—why? What would it gain? It gains new knowledge, which is all it really has to live for, as it were, by letting us run and observing how stupidly we behave. With so many worlds, and so much variety even among the same cultural groups on any given world, to observe it is never, well, bored, nor with such variety can it feel as if it truly knows us. The limitations on experience prevent that. And even if we became irrelevant to it I doubt if it would so much as notice us, any more than one of the gods would truly care if a monkey fell from a tree. It once said to me that it found the concept of a god that needed to be worshiped a silly one, since the only reason it could think of why a god would do that was if the god itself was either defective or actually had such an inferiority complex that it required constant gratification and sacrifice. I must admit I had no real answer to that one."

"I suppose if we could understand gods or supercomputers we would be gods or supercomputers ourselves," I noted, feeling a little uncomfortable with the subject. I was, however, curious about him. "You are alone here, except for the computer?"

"Oh, yes. Actually, I intend some time or another to go out, find a great feast, get drunk, carouse, and do all the human urges I have denied myself, but somehow I never seem to have the time."

"You've left to attend the committee meetings," I noted.

"Oh, no. They are held here. There is no place more secure than here, and the computer can whip up whatever is required."

I thought about that. "Then—when was the last time you left here?"

He shrugged. "One loses track of time, you know. I suppose I could ask the computer. It would know."

"Don't bother. Years, though, certainly."

Kanda acted like the thought had never really crossed his mind before. "Yes, I suppose you are right. How time does slip away . . ."

270

"Yeah, time does fly when you're having fun. So you were all here when the grand plan was presented and approved."

"Yes, yes. I can show you the meeting area if you wish."

"Not necessary, for now. You worked out the math, right? On the computer?"

He nodded. "Yes, we had the figures and did the best we could."

"I'm curious. Yugarin said he approached Mancini with the plan almost ten years ago. If this great computer of yours is as tremendous as you claim, and if computers really are the world's greatest mathematical counting machines, why did it take you almost a decade to get the answer that worked?"

Kanda looked surprised. "I hadn't realized it was that long. It wasn't all that complicated, you know, although I admit I wouldn't have thought of all the variables and come up with that approach. I truly never gave any thought at all to the amount of time it took to get the answers required. The only supposition I have as to that is that perhaps the computer did not consider it a worthy problem or just did not care to solve it."

"But suddenly it did."

"Well, not that suddenly. It was, after all, basically an academic exercise for the longest time. It was only when Mancini really started pressing, bothering me and interrupting my theoretical work, that I finally begged for the solution just to be rid of the interruptions."

"Really? And how long ago did he get the answer?"

Kanda shrugged. "I will ask." He walked over to

one of the shiny metal walls and put his hands against the wall, palms down, and lowered his head. He looked like a guy spread-eagled after being busted for stealing small change from a Coke machine. Then he straightened up and came back over to us, looking puzzled. "That is very odd," he muttered, more to himself than to us.

"That's it? You just lean against a wall and think at it?" I was simultaneously impressed and unnerved by that.

"Oh, yes. Easier that way, and no possibility of error. The machine claims that it provided the answer a few weeks after the problem was posed to me, as soon as I pressed it to the computer. It says that it answered the question as soon as I remembered to ask it. But could that be right?"

Kanda really didn't have any time sense at all. Yesterday and ten years ago were all the same to him. "Yes, it could indeed," I assured him.

"Then why did it take them ten years to put it into action?" Kanda asked me, thinking about it now for the first time since the problem was posed and answered.

"Ask your great computer," I responded. "I'll even give it a hint."

He stared at me like a little kid waiting for Dad to tell him why the sky was blue. "Yes?"

"It didn't," I said, and wondered if Kanda remembered where the exit was.

9.

Collaboration by Correspondence

I wasn't at all hesitant about describing the brief but fascinating encounter with Kanda and his great machine to Maria even inside the office. Not any more, although you never knew what other ears might be listening and a certain measure of prudence was still called for. Merely fitting it all together in such a way that they wouldn't just dispose of me wasn't enough; so far, I'd had it nice and easy, with varying but adequate cooperation and it had been essentially a classical situation— the evidence was gathered passively and without much effort.

There was no longer any problem with Maria separating from me in the Labyrinth. That one time out she'd established enough places to jump to and shed any tracing materials that I had complete confidence in her. Besides, it was me they wanted to follow, to make certain that I was a good boy, didn't call in the Company or outsmart Maria and go my own way. They would have no reason to question Maria's loyalty and obedience.

Except for confirming what I already believed was the case and maybe, just maybe, filling in a couple of irrelevant but irritating holes in the picture, there was no other reason to see the rest of the crew nor sift through more data. The trouble was, not doing so would bring an immediate demand for the full story from Voorhes and most likely my termination, something I wished to avoid, or it would force me to begin the active phase without sufficient time, setup, or information to make it possible—if it was possible in the first place. In other words, I had to go through the motions, without pushing, to buy freedom for Maria to act and time for things to be set up as well as they could considering my circumstances.

Of them all, I wanted to meet Carlos last, not only because of what would come after but because there was always the slight chance he might do something egomaniacal and stupid and make things easier for me.

Maria found the very concept of the great computer unnerving. "Such power without any controls by anyone," she said. "It is far too dangerous to think about."

"I'm not so sure," I replied. "I admit the idea of such a thing is unsettling, even scary, but I don't think Kanda was quite as crazy as he appeared, not in the areas that count. I think there might be no limits to what goes in the thing but extreme limits on what it can actually do. I'm not even sure that in many ways it doesn't reflect the personality of its creator. At any rate, any luck on your end? Discreetly, please."

"Some. Not much. A message *might* be gotten in, but what good would it do?"

"Maybe not much," I admitted, "but it has to be tried, and we have to have some way to get an answer before we can move—and my time is running out. Damn!"

I felt frustrated, for all that I'd learned. How the hell did my client expect me to do a job like this under these conditions? I went over and sat down in the new office chair that had been delivered to our "front door," as it were, and stared at the computer terminal screen.

Maria was right, damn it, and the more I thought about it the more frustrated I got. "It *is* impossible!" I said disgustedly, and aloud, to no one in particular.

My eyes were suddenly drawn to the computer screen, where words were being scrolled up.

"Not impossible, just unlikely," the screen read.

I almost jumped. Hell, I hadn't figured on this. I flipped the input select on manual and drew myself up to the keyboard after making certain that Maria was lying down on her cot well away. Then I typed, *"Who are you?"*

"You already know who I am," the screen replied. *"I am the one who hired you."*

"How do I know that for sure?"

"Because only I would make an opening statement like that."

Actually, the damned thing had a point.

"Is this line secure?" I typed, nervous that what one could tap others could tap.

"I have disabled the other taps for now, and have the area monitored visually. If Maria should approach the screen will blank."

O.K., that was fair enough. *"It's about time I got some help in this. Why have you waited until now?"*

"What help I can be is limited and not to be

squandered. You had to work it out for yourself first. If you did not, I would not have revealed myself at all, since there is great risk. Also, it was necessary that we meet before I could be effective considering your limitations."

Huh. Thanks a lot, buddy. *"I have a series of problems."*

"I am aware of them. As I demonstrated in Tarn's domain I have some resources to give you some freedom, but the results are strictly cosmetic and would not stand face-to-face or exacting monitoring scrutiny. For a limited time, however, I can cover for you, giving you a short period of time sufficient for what you feel you must do. I would prefer, though, that you did not, as it is of grave risk to you personally and if you are caught or killed then the best of the ones I have put on this problem will be done in and I will have to work with inferior minds."

I felt complimented by that, but it wouldn't deter me. *"First things first. I was not a volunteer for this. I was drafted."*

"Duly noted. I will see that Maria receives through convincing channels the basics that you will require, and I can supply you from here with the essentials of switch security so that you can pretend to be brilliant and deduce them before bypassing them. With your background it should be no problem being convincing on that one."

I wasn't sure whether I was being complimented or insulted on that one, but it didn't matter. Just when I needed one, here was my Archie, my Paul Drake, with all the work done.

"Can she be forewarned on this?" I typed furiously.

"Only at great risk and in rather vague terms. I will

see what I can do. Normal security personnel are easily used, but Carlos has his own personal army chemically dependent upon him and his well being. I will only promise to do what I can."

Well, that was all anybody could do. "But what about the drug itself?"

"If an intact injection cube is provided it can be analyzed and duplicated. It is a synthetic, not an organic. The problem is that they are tailored to individuals and personalized in a secure computer deep in Carlos' lair. Only one a day is created. Withdrawl begins in twenty-six hours. By thirty-five hours it is all-consuming."

"Figured as much." I told him. "That's why a message must get through and with sufficient lead time. You see the possibilities."

"I do. I will try. And then what?"

I sat back in the chair a moment and thought about that. Yeah—and then what? "So what's your objective in all this?"

"I am as dedicated as the rest to the destruction of the Company. An effective opposition must be maintained at all costs."

"That's why you didn't just blow this to the Company, then."

"Without an effective opposition it might be many more centuries and far greater cost before another one as effective as this one grows up. I could not allow that. And to simply expose the plan to Company security was no solution. The perpetrators would simply go to ground and be capable of restarting or perpetuating the scheme at some point in the future. And, just as you can not be certain that the real Pandross was killed either time, I cannot truly be certain that I would get all of the real principals. And *no matter how clever they get, they risk everything because they failed initially to trap you in the house, and they understand now that you would never have been coerced into helping them on their project. I gave them something else to worry about and a reason for keeping you alive, at least temporarily."*

I had figured that much. *"And now it's time to act."*

"NO!!!" it shot back. *"Complete your interviews. Stall. Go through the motions as you have been. Be particularly careful with Mendelez and Carlos. The others have comprehensible madnesses, but are basically rational creatures doing what they are convinced is right. Those two truly love their work, and neither takes full discipline from the others, so you might be in great danger from either of them even on one of their whims. I will tell you when things are ready. And then I will tell you my own price for helping you. I can hold the taps off no longer. Check back now and again. I will keep in touch."*

The screen blanked, and I knew I'd lost contact. Damn it! I had a lot more questions I wanted answered than I got, and I felt frustrated still, but I had to admit that I felt excited as well. Now I knew I was right. I knew not only who killed Pandross but why. I knew who the whispery voice was on site at the raid on the house and what that was about. I also now knew that the side I was truly working for, no matter what Voorhes and the others believed, was the one opposed to the plan— and I even understood why. The most basic motive of all, far surpassing the obvious motive of the five percent dissolution.

I also knew, now, that the odds were very slim

that events alone would allow me to ever tell the full story to anyone else.

It had taken several days, but Voorhes finally came up with the duplicate information I'd pressed him for.

There were so many Voorhes I could hardly believe it. "I would have figured you could have replaced one of them and again taken up your life," I told him. "Or would be killing yourself be too much for you?"

"No," he sighed, "although don't think I didn't think about it. I'm not certain I could have even if that had been open to me, though. It still wouldn't be *my* world, and it wouldn't really be *my* family and career and works. There would be differences even in the very close ones, of which there were only a few, and I would have been constantly reminded that I was living a fraud. However, it wasn't really open to any of us. Remember, we were still essentially working for Company security, even if it was against the Company itself. Until Mukasa himself was unmasked and taken out we were not free agents but more or less at his mercy. The option you suggest would not have been permitted. By the time it was possible it would have been, well, too late, obviously, to pick up where we left off."

That figured. "And no way to really lift out what was important, either."

"You are thinking of Valintina's children. No. Although there are a fair number listed there, and quite a number have children, not a one has the same children she had. Most do not even have the same father. The few ones that do, well, the genetics and timing is all wrong. I'm not too certain she'd be much good at parenting anyway, even from way back. I almost wonder if she ever really was."

I hadn't met the lady yet, so I reserved judgment. There were a lot of duplicates for all of them, though, including Pandross, but I'd asked for more. I'd asked for a physical check to make certain that all of them were still where they were supposed to be. That was what had taken all the time, and the only thing that made the list in any way valuable.

There were, for example, a hundred and sixteen living Pandrosses, genetically identical to the original and within the temporal window required. All hundred and sixteen were also present and accounted for.

"Why is this of interest to you?" Voorhes asked me. "Do you think we use them with ourselves?"

No reason to sit on it any longer. I was surprised Tarn had sat on it until now. "A second Pandross was murdered at Tarn's while I was there," I told him. "I asked him to keep it quiet for a while."

"What! That's not possible! That means we have *two* dead Pandrosses now, and no missing duplicates!"

I nodded. "Yeah. We're running a surplus, that's for sure. But the guy was head of security and held sway over the security data banks. I think maybe he held out on you. Either that or he had himself cloned or something, or maybe, unknown to all of you, he was in his own world identical twins."

"Rubbish! If he had been we would have known it—before. Both would have been there, or

Pandross would have mentioned it. Any twin would have to be another survivor. No, I can't believe that."

"Well," I told him, "if it makes you feel any better, neither do I. I'm not too worried about it, though. I might not understand how it was done even if it was in front of me in black and white, but I'm only concerned with *why* it was done."

He considered that. "I see. And do you know why?"

I nodded. "I think I'm pretty close, but all the information hasn't checked in yet. I still have three people to see."

"Um, yes. Stacy Cutler wasn't answering her messages for a very long time and when she finally checked in she seemed uncomfortable with the idea of talking to you. We are still trying to set something up to her satisfaction."

Good girl, Cutler! Stonewall some more!

"And the others?" I asked, straight-faced.

"Valintina never liked Pandross and doesn't believe whatever got him has any interest in her. She's been quite busy of late and has been inclined to simply ignore all this. She has, in fact, suggested that we simply do away with you and end all this. We are trying to arrange a meeting that will insure your safety. As for Carlos—he tends not to like to be around anyone he doesn't own, nor expose himself unless it is in the course of a plan he has devised and is running. He particularly doesn't trust or have any love for you, Mister Horowitz. He blames you for screwing up his master plan with his drug plot."

"He not only tried, he actually *did* blow some of my brains out," I reminded him. "That alone gave me a little incentive, and hooking Brandy and putting her through all that didn't help restore great feelings. But you said he was one of them who was enthusiastic over my taking this case."

"He was. You both certainly impressed him by blowing his plan, which is one point in your favor, and, I suspect, he also wanted to make very certain that you were here and under our complete control during all phases of our current project. Most of us are on this project for noble motives, but Carlos is oriented towards vengeance. The plan fills his need for vengeance against the Company, and I fear he might have thoughts of revenge towards you as well. He is willing to see you, but only on his home grounds, and I'm not at all certain that we can allow that."

"Well, then, make him last," I told Voorhes. "The end. I've had Maria doing some checking on him and his place, and with a little more time and a little luck I may have a little bit of insurance there. Let's cross that bridge when we come to it."

Voorhes thought that over, then replied, "Very well. But I would be very, very disappointed, Mister Horowitz, to go this far only to discover that you were finished off by our own people."

"So would I, Mister Voorhes," I told him sincerely. "So would I."

Stacy Cutler reminded me of the kind of bush woman you'd see in an old Victor Mature versus the Mau Mau movie. Very British in speech and mannerisms, dressed in khaki military style shirt, shorts, and bush ranger hat, with military laced boots. She was the first of the admittedly small number of women at the top of this strange heap, and she was, interestingly, also the only one other than Voorhes who looked close to her age and made few if any attempts at concealing what time and experience does to all of us.

She met me at a small clump of trees in what looked very much like the African plains; there was a waterhole nearby but I didn't want to get too close to it. As usual in wild places like this, it had more than its share of inhabitants, from tribal-acting monkeys to gazelle, zebra, and the like, and I had no desire either to panic them or, worse, provoke them. I remembered seeing someplace that those monkeys in particular could be worse enemies than a lion.

I also didn't see her coming, although you would have expected to hear the roar of a Land Rover or the chanting of bearers the way she looked. It was often difficult to remember that the sides and personalities here were plus or minus only in relative terms, no different than dealing with or-ganized crime or the roughest parts of a major city or maybe the government. Cutler, like Tarn and Kanda and even Voorhes, seemed both nice enough and harmless enough, and on their own terms probably were—but they were smart cook-ies as well, worldly wise, deadly, and survivors in a high-tech high-stakes jungle. I felt like some Israeli detective improbably kidnapped and forced to live and work and interact with the PLO while I solved a problem for them. Within the context of their world they seemed reasonable people, but in the greater context they remained what they were and I remained what I was. And that was the problem.

So I stood there, worried about becoming some-body's main course in the next dinner, as alert as I ever was to any danger signs, and suddenly I hear a woman's voice very near me say, "It *is* beautiful, is it not?"

I practically jumped out of my skin, whirled, and came face to face with her.

"They make more noise than you do," I noted, feeling suddenly relieved.

"They can all be silent or loud as conditions warrant," Cutler responded. "Unlike humans, who can be loud and obnoxious for no reason at all. Do you know where you are? In rough geographic terms, I mean?"

I shrugged. "It looks like Africa. East Africa, probably."

"Africa, yes, but not east. In almost any of the worlds where humans developed and expanded and triumphed, where we are standing now would be dry, desolate sand in all directions. Near the dead center of the Sahara, in fact, as it once was and as it would still be elsewhere if humans hadn't spoiled it. Oh, there are patches of desert, yes, and the rains are infrequent, but the river and stream network is more than adequate to keep most of it grass and much of it lush. The Mediterranean and Atlantic storms dump the water, which runs inland to the low spots and forms a vast network of rivers and lakes, some quite large. There are still great forests on the Atlas and Antiatlas mountains and other coastal ranges that regulate the flow and control much water and some wind erosion. Humans cut them all down, allowing the ravages of nature to scour the land and grind it up and turn it to desert."

I looked around. It was certainly nicer, if a bit wilder, than pure desert, I had to admit.

"Then there are no humans here—except you and perhaps your people."

She sighed. "Very few, all imported, all careful to maintain that they leave minimal footprints. There are many species here across the entire animal and plant kingdom that are unique, and many more that have been made extinct by humans elsewhere. In this world the Great Auk still roams in the Pacific, the dodo still reigns in the North Atlantic regions, and the skies of North America can still be blackened by the passenger pigeon. It is a beautiful world, unspoiled by humans."

"You don't have much use for humans in large numbers, I suppose," I commented. "Me, I'm happy that it worked out both ways—humans in some places, with places like this still surviving as well."

"This is not a zoo, it is a world!" she snapped. "What have humans done where they arose? Killed the wildlife, deforested the land, ruined their own planet, raped and plundered everything until they ultimately had to depend on technology outstripping their voracious killer appetites. For what? Intelligence? There is intelligence here, although it is not human. Some insect societies here are as complex as your own, and on both land and sea many of the higher animals *think*. But none has the self-destructive viciousness of humankind. This world is *alive*. Your world and the others are dying, filthy cesspools, monuments to prolonged mass stupidity and greed, itself exploited ruthlessly by other humans from another world who would push it even further into decay until they took all worth taking, then abandoning it to slowly strangle in the debris left behind. No, I have no love at all for humans."

"I'm afraid I'm a little prejudiced," I told her. "I'm human, and unless there were humans I wouldn't be here. Call me selfish or self-centered, but that fact, to me, outweighs the other arguments, as sympathetic as I may be to places like this and plants and animals like these."

"I do not expect you to see things my way. I find your approval is not required and, in fact, I consider your views totally irrelevant."

"They probably are," I agreed, "but since they dragooned me into this against my will and set up the rules, I have to keep following through."

"That is why I am tolerating this."

"I find your attitude here and your attitude initially objecting to the big plan a little inconsistent," I told her. "It would seem that even the big risk of wiping out all humanity everywhere wouldn't bother you too much."

"You sound like the sort of man who would get rid of a defective window in his building by blowing up the building," she shot back. "If there was a way to just wipe out the people and leave the rest alone I believe I could enthusiastically support such a scheme. But what they are doing would be indiscriminate, wiping out this world as much as your world or the Company's world. At the very least it would be a disaster to tens of thousands of worlds on a scale even humans have not previously attempted. The ultimate ecological disaster at best. I find no joy in that possibility."

"Nor do I," I assured her. "Yet you ultimately got talked into approving it."

"You make it sound as if it were some weighty

philosophical debate, Mister Horowitz," she responded coolly. "I thought the percentage of error too high, but as I had no alternative and the percentage was still small, the ultimate worst case unlikely, I saw no other choice but to proceed. Does that disappoint you? Did you believe I was some great moralist on this question?"

"I had kind of hoped that," I admitted, "but, no, I didn't expect it. I'm getting a fairly clear picture of you all now—all except the one fellow who isn't here. Pandross alone remains a very dim and cloudy figure with a real sense of unreality about him. Did you really know what he thought, or did you just take him for granted like everybody else seems to?"

She considered that. "Thought about what?"

It was a fair question. "About *anything*, really, except security systems and gadgets. This plan, past plans, war, peace, love, hate—anything at all."

As it had with the others, the question seemed to really catch her off guard, even bother her. She just stood there for a very long time before finally saying, in a kind of distant tone, "Now that you mention it, no."

"Was he with the group when you were all in training back at the Company? Did you see each other much before the horrible end of your world?"

She shook her head negatively. "Not really. We were all specialists in different fields, you see, training in different areas under different departments. There were quite a number of us, too, you must remember. We nine weren't the only ones there, simply the only ones Mukasa could—or would—save or shield from execution. We were together with the rest only for the few introductory indoctrination lectures and it was so long ago now I can't even remember much about them. I knew Valintina slightly—such a brilliant, happy girl then—and also Carlos, again very slightly—he was a handsome fellow who believed himself God's gift to women and in those days made a career out of chasing every woman around. But Pandross—no. He would have been up with Mukasa's own in security, and that wasn't an area that the rest of us were allowed near." She paused a moment, then asked, "Why? What are you getting at?"

"A man who all of you worked with for over a decade," I explained, "and wound up trusting with your security, your lives. A man so dedicated and capable in his field and so reliable that you never gave him a second thought—any of you. I've talked to most of you now, and you have very strong impressions of one another. I've been warned about Valintina and Carlos, had almost a psychoanalysis of Voorhes, had philosophical discussions about Tarn and gotten many strong opinions on Kanda and Yugarin and Mancini, and I felt as if I knew you before we ever met. You know each other very well, even each other's idiosyncrasies, likes and dislikes, hopes and fears. You're like a strong family, in a way. You don't all like each other—who among us didn't have someone in the family we couldn't stand?—but you *understand* each other, know each other well. All eight of you. But none of you knew Pandross. Each of you had the same thing in common, and each of you had a common cause, but while eight of you were brothers or cousins or uncles or aunts, Pandross wasn't even a distant cousin four times removed. He was more like the repairman you call when something's broke and you can't fix it yourself. You talk to the plumber, you exchange pleasantries on the weather or sports or politics, but you don't really know him. You don't really know much of anything about him."

"I—I believe I see what you mean," she said, a little wondrously. "Yes, that's exactly right. But he was so good at what he did, and so absolutely reliable each time, there was no reason to think on it further. Do you really think it was more than just his abysmal lack of personality?"

"There's always somebody home inside each head," I told her. "Sometimes it's easier to find that person than with others. Over the course of this investigation I've learned more about all of you than I think you even now would believe, and far more than I need to know for this—but not one damned thing about the victim. He was reliable, brilliant, didn't like to socialize, hadn't much of a personality, and just did his job and made no other real impression at all. Now you tell me that not only didn't you interact with him other than on business during more than a decade of high activity, none of you even knew him before, even casually."

"That much is true," she admitted, "but I can not see where that gets you. I mean, he was *always* reliable. He never once slipped or betrayed a confidence or an operation. Some were blown, yes, including many of the big ones, but it wasn't because of what he did, and many also succeeded. There is no logical reason to believe that he was anyone or anything other than what he claimed to be."

"I disagree," I told her. "There is every reason in the world to believe that Lothar Pandross never existed. That the fellow who said he was Pandross, a fellow refugee, probably had never even been to your origin world. He was good, he was well briefed, and he could convincingly fake it in the same way that somebody from my world who said he was from the country of Benin wouldn't be questioned too closely by me since I've never been to Benin and would have trouble finding it on a map, if it hasn't changed its name recently. But if he got close to you, in the way the rest of you did, he'd have to open up, have to have an in-depth story and personal history and background that had no holes whatsoever in it, no inconsistencies however tiny, or he'd lose some of your confidence."

She was appalled at the suggestion, which she clearly didn't believe. "Surely you don't suggest that he was a spy for the *Company!*"

"No, not the Company. Not exactly, anyway, and not for the Company cause. When and if I can find out where he *did* come from, and how he wound up as one of your group of survivors, I'll have the last major piece in this puzzle."

Maria had been quite busy, and I didn't know now how I would have coped without her. I now had a fair amount of information on Carlos's lair, including a general map and layout, the basic security systems built in, and the general routine of the place. There were, however, also an awful lot of people living and working there, all of whom were in thrall to Carlos and not to regular security no matter what their personnel files said and any of which, no matter what they thought of him, would still have no choice but to blow away anybody threatening his cozy situation.

On the other hand, my client, when he made another remote control appearance, decided he no longer liked the deal.

"I have decided that the risk to putting your interests first makes the odds of successfully accomplishing my own interests almost prohibitive. First you must stop the project in the only permanent way possible, by using the flaw built into the basic plan. Then I will give you entry and aid to Carlos."

"No deal!" I shot back to him on the keyboard. *"I assume that what you want is neither easy nor safe and that my odds there aren't so hot, either. I also assume that the only way to accomplish your own goal is to trigger something nasty before its time. Otherwise they'd just bide their time and start over. The only way to insure things is to destroy one of the key sidings, and I suspect I know which one is the most likely candidate to permanently disable the plan by making the odds too prohibitive and the new setup too complex to have a decent chance of success."*

"You do not disappoint me, Horowitz."

"Well, I am now. If I blow that it'll have to be from the universe side. I'm not too certain what will happen, but I have the idea that it'll make some of the Labyrinth uninhabitable for a while, and that means that even if I live I'll be cut off. On top of that, the Company will know as soon as I come through the gate. They would have to. So, no matter what, I will fall into their hands and probably by now they have classified me as Benedict Arnold, Jr. And to top it all off, this crew here will have nothing to do for a while but revenge itself on me and mine, not to mention blowing that world they threatened. No, no deal."

"There will be a way to use the Labyrinth even after. The calculations have been checked and double-checked. If it were not so, there would be no purpose to this, now, would there? You know only part of his security. I can give you all of it and the bypass procedures. I can also provide a way to bypass the Company and exit your world. Considering your resources and your familiarity with it and with the Company, you should be able to make it there. And if the Company catches you, tell them the truth. The information you require will still be in your hands—before you do what I want but after you are irrevocably committed to that course of action. When the Company people understand what you have done and why and what you still have to do, and considering you can promise them Carlos in the bargain, I do not think they would hesitate to aid you. You will need the Company's services anyway —after your business is done. That fact alone jeopardizes what I require. If they learn about what I wish before it is done they will prevent it. They would have to. And that means this is all for nothing."

"What is the rush on this?" I asked it via the terminal keyboard. We have months, maybe a year, don't we?"

"You are brilliant, Horowitz, in some things, but foolish in others. Yours was the only Company-held and Company-controlled point they had not already secured and prepared. It is still the most vulnerable —it is Markham's home world and a busy one. Do you think they would move against you and then

292

hope to maintain the fiction for months or years? And they are more nervous now yet more confident, too. They have speeded things up. All is in place. They need only to hook up and test the timing computers now. We are talking days, Horowitz."

Unfortunately, the cavalier attitude they'd taken with me had hinted at this, but I didn't like to see it confirmed. *"Can't you knock off one or two of them and send the rest scurrying to deeper cover?"*

"I already tried that with Pandross. You can see how successful I was. Perhaps I should have killed one a few days later, and one more later still, but I was loathe to do it. They are my soul-mates, after all. If I do it now I believe I will have the opposite effect of rushing them into doing it, perfectly prepared and tested or not. The more rush and the less testing, the higher the odds of it generating just the sterilizing surge we both fear. You are due to see Valintina next. When you leave her, you must be prepared to act. My associates will move in and provide all you need. It must be done then—and quickly—while you would not be missed here. If you do it, then they will be powerless to carry out their threat against the world they selected, and by the time they are it will be empty and irrelevant to them. They will have to go to ground for years."

I thought about this new wrinkle. *"And what about Maria?"* I typed to my absent client, thinking it through. For all her problems, I had come to like her, and she'd been of great use, as I said.

"I thought it was obvious. If you get away and live, she is dead in a horrible and slow manner. If she is not killed, then she must hunt you and use all methods to get you, and she will. It has been so from the start of this. Face the truth. One of you must die."

He was right, of course, but I didn't like this new order of things. I was being pushed into it now, trapped in a corner before I was ready, just as he'd figured all along. I didn't like being pushed, and I liked being trapped into doing somebody else's bidding even less.

"*I'll think about it.*" I told the client, and didn't wait for a reply. I grabbed the pencil and paper and stalked away.

Maria was reading something in a language I couldn't begin to guess over on a mat on the floor, and she looked up and must have read my expression. "Something the matter?" she asked. "You do not look happy. What were you looking for in the computer for so long?"

"I'm reaching a moment of truth long before I'm ready," I told her, and then pointed to the pad.

She raised her eyebrows. "Again?"

I nodded, and she and I walked over to where I was certain we could not be visually observed.

"Do you know where Carlos's access switch is and how to get in to it?" I wrote on the paper.

She didn't just nod as I'd hoped, but took the paper and wrote, "I know where but not necessarily how to enter."

"I will figure a bypass," I wrote to her. "That's my field. You just get me where we have to be. Be ready with all that we need as soon as I finish the next interview."

She looked both surprised and worried. "Do you really think you can get in? Not to mention back out?"

I nodded, although I was by no means certain of either. I could only assume that all of them were wired by Pandross, and I'd seen and examined enough of his stuff now to know pretty well how he thought. Besides, Carlos wasn't in hiding, he was at his usual place, and with the project so furious right now he would probably be getting daily messenger briefings. He was far less concerned with people getting in than getting out, of that I was sure. We would wait for a messenger, intercept him or her, then use Maria's security code implant so they would think she was the messenger—and we would have the communiques even if we had to chop them off the real messenger's arms.

As for getting out—well, *somebody* knew how to open and close and monitor that switch. It would be improvise, improvise, but I had no other choice.

On the surface, my client's offer seemed the most rational, and was. But he hadn't played completely true with me, nor with anyone else, and he had only one interest in mind—making the Yugarin-Mancini-Kanda plan too hard to ever use. He needed me to accomplish that, and once I did it he would revert to his original mind-set and objectives. With no further need of me, I could easily be not just double-crossed but hung out to dry. I had only his word and nobody to check it with that I would even be able to still get back out.

Besides, no matter what the long odds against me, it pissed me off that he was calling all the shots. My own interest involved merely undoing what he had done in the first place, and if I couldn't get my own problems solved then I didn't much give a damn about whether they blew things wide open or not.

* * *

I wasn't really much interested in Valintina, but I had to go through the motions. It turned out to be a very strange experience in its own right, and one sure way to make sure I remembered which side I should be on.

It began after I went through the switch and walked down a short siding, then out into a plain reception chamber that looked kind of like a small function room at the Holiday Inn, with little furnishing but some nasty-looking gun ports and such. It kind of reminded me of the less than pleasant reception area you got when entering the Company world.

It was unoccupied except by me, and had no doors that could be opened from this side and no ways to look out.

"Stand in the center of the room and remove all your clothes," a tough-sounding female voice said from an embedded speaker in the room.

I looked around. There didn't seem to be an alternate set provided. "I beg your pardon?"

"Remove all clothing, your watch, and anything else you might be wearing, and place them in the corner nearest the Labyrinth substation entrance. They will not be touched, and will still be there when you exit."

"Uh, yeah, that's fine, but what do I wear instead?" I asked loudly. This kind of security I could admire, but that didn't mean I had to like it.

"Just do as instructed and then walk through the door when it opens."

I sighed, and undressed and tried to fold everything neatly, sticking my watch and wedding ring on top of the pile. Even after being around Maria all this time and under observation almost constantly, I still had a sense of modesty and a bit of self-consciousness as well knowing that strangers were looking at me and probably making nasty comments as well. There is nothing worse to strip the dignity and confidence out of someone than to make them nude and have them parade around strangers.

Now in my birthday suit, though, I turned and walked towards the far wall, and as I reached the area a door buzzed and then opened and I walked through—and into something of a formal garden setting, with a nice pond, lots of trees and flowers, and two attractive young women dressed in tight black outfits which included sidearms stood there looking at me. It was almost oppressively hot and very humid.

I felt immediately like crawling back in or finding a hole or fig leaf or something, and I put my hand in front of my crotch, but the door shut behind me and there was no way to anywhere except past this pair of obvious security officers, both of whom seemed highly amused.

"Okay, so what do I wear around here?" I asked them, my embarrassment turning to anger.

"Oh, my!" one said in a mocking tone. "He's embarrassed! See how he tries to shield himself from us. What's the matter, boy? You ashamed of your prick or something?"

"He has a cute little ass," remarked the other, "but I can't say much for the rest of him."

"I'm not used to being on display," I retorted, really feeling mad now.

The other one laughed. "This is Señora Mendelez's private preserve. You asked for an invitation, but you weren't invited. Here, she makes the rules and you follow or you may leave. No man here is permitted to wear clothes or to wear anything not given him by a woman resident. You will treat all women with respect while you are here and you will put up with whatever you must, or you will regret it. Any lack of respect or failure to exhibit the proper attitude and deference while here, particularly in front of the boys, will have to be severely and painfully punished, even if you are a guest. You understand that? And understand, too, that any of us are fully capable of giving such punishment. Either play it that way, or sit here under guard until your keeper comes for you and you can return to where you came from."

I wanted to do just that, particularly since I was only going through the motions with this one, but I had no choice but to play it out. Still, I was keenly aware that I was beyond the political rebel and the eccentric and into the land and style of the kind of personality who would cheerfully hook people on drugs and think of new perversions for them to use.

"I, too, am not here voluntarily," I told them. "I must have my interview."

"Your funeral," the taller of the two remarked. "Okay, follow us."

We walked up a well maintained path through a dense jungle alive with insects and almost solid with plant life, and I began to wonder if they had mosquitoes in this climate or worse. Even so, this was the most impressive security entrance I'd seen and the only one up to the caliber I'd expected from the rest. Guarded and fortified entry chamber—damned tough to get through and requiring a large force—then out into a small clearing that exposed you to most likely withering fire, and when you got through that you would have to push through jungle prepared by defenders all the way and landscaped to tell you almost nothing.

There were frequent junctions in the path, too, much of which I suspected was to force anyone getting in to either know his or her way around or walk into a neat trap.

The *correct* path took us ultimately out of the foliage and onto a wide white sand ocean beach, almost pristine in its beauty and with breakers far enough off so that you could enjoy water or beach.

The back of the beach was a significant hill rising maybe a hundred feet at its height, producing a cliff atop which stood a stunning tropical home and patio jutting out just slightly out over the overhang and which probably provided a great, sweeping view of the beach and oceanfront far below. On either side, long, zig-zagging stairs reached from house to beach, and I groaned thinking that I would have to climb them.

There were a few people on the beach, looking like the kind of folks you usually hate. Trim, perfect-looking women either nude or wearing only bikini bottoms, all with perfect tans, being rubbed or made over by equally tanned and muscled guys left over from the Arnold Schwartznegger Look Alike Contest. One woman was doing a kind of flex exercise and revealing bigger and better muscles than I'll ever have. I kind of suspected that the other women were equally musclebound.

They all stopped what they were doing and stared at us—or, rather, at the poor excuse for a two hundred and twenty-eight pound weakling with the weight in all the wrong places being marched along by two Amazon warriors. I gave up any pretense at modesty and just tried to put my nudity out of my mind. Hell, I'd be embarrassed and intimidated around people like these even if I were fully clothed. About the only thing I had on them was their greased pig look; I had more chest hair than they had hair on their heads.

I did notice, however, that while the men were towering musclebound hulks, they seemed to be at the women's beck and call, with nary a peep of protest. One woman came up to a guy and fondled his genitals, and he just sort of giggled and smiled inanely. Another couple seemed to be strutting and showing off for two women who were ogling them but clearly not interested.

It wasn't hard to figure out the system here, but I couldn't for the life of me figure out how it was maintained. The male bimbos and jocks I'd known had generally been pretty tough, commanding types.

The long climb was no fun at all, but at least by this point I was in a little better condition. It didn't stop me from having to pause and catch my breath several times, enduring the less than kind commentary of my escort each time, but it wasn't just the exercise but the tremendous heat and humidity as well. I was sweating like a stuck pig.

It was possibly only because of their offer to carry me to the top that I made it on my own. They let me sit on a lounge chair under the shade of a beach umbrella and try and keep from passing out while one went inside and the other security officer turned to one of the musclebound hulks who'd come out to greet us and said, "Jerry, be a dear and get the poor boy some of the special fruit punch."

He looked over at me and I got the idea that he was trying to keep from cracking up. Maybe my eyes shot daggers, though, because he straightened up and said, "Yes, Ma'am. At once. He sure looks like he needs it," then turned and went back inside.

He returned maybe two minutes later with a tray, pitcher, and large glass filled with ice. He poured the drink and I took it and took a sip. It tasted like the best drink I'd ever tasted in the whole world. I needed it—I needed most of that pitcher. When I had two and a half glasses, though, I felt much, much better.

Jerry was fascinating in and of himself. I don't think I ever had seen a guy just like him, in fact. Oh, he looked like the Mister Universe type, but there was something odd about his mannerism, his voice, the whole thing. He somehow managed the trick of seeming to be a very gentle giant without once really seeming effeminate. You got the idea that the guy could bend steel with his bare hands and lick any ten men in the bar—but that there was almost no circumstance where he would want to.

And, just as he turned to leave, Valintina Mendelez came out of the house, dressed in a tight halter top and wearing a pair of designer jeans and sandals. She was really the Latino bombshell her picture had suggested; thin, wasp-waisted, but with a pair of jugs that would do Dolly Parton proud. She was wearing dark sunglasses and smoking a cigarette through a long holder, which made for the image I think she wanted.

I started to get up, but she stopped me. "No, no! Just sit! You are hot and tired." She slid into a beach chair opposite me, then asked, "Well, I would be surprised if you approved of my little pleasure spot." She had a fairly thick accent, probably Spanish or some derivative of it, but it was because she was proud of it and never felt any need to get rid of it. She could clearly think in English.

"It is a beautiful place, Señora Mendelez," I responded, trying to remember the rules and even give the name a bit of the proper inflection. "I will certainly give you that."

"You know what I mean."

I sighed. "Well, it's more a reversal of the usual rather than a feminist's vision," I commented, adding, "Judging, of course, from the very little I've seen."

"You are quite right, Sammy boy. I have no interest in equality or other weakling goals. Often, out in so-called 'normal' society I am treated as a thing, an object, to be ogled at the pleasure of men, fondled at the pleasure of men, and fucked by coarse men who think that it is the primary goal of a woman. I have killed a great many men for such things, which are not trivial to me. I like the look of surprise when they are being particularly *macho*, rough and commanding, as I twist them where they will not twist and watch the life drain away."

Well, I'd been warned she was a psycho in her own right. I wasn't about to get into weighty arguments with her.

"Still, it seems like, well, the few men I've noted here go against any sort of masculine behavior I thought was built in without seeming effeminate. Are they bred for this or raised that way or what?"

She smiled. "Chemistry, Señor. Simple chemistry. That is all we really are, you know—a collection of chemicals put together in a certain way, activated in the brain by degrees through experience. My specialty is exotic tropical plants. It is amazing what you find in *their* chemistry that will interact with ours. Pain killers, disease-killers, stimulants, depressants, narcotics of all kinds."

"I know. Cocaine, opium, marijuana, and all their relatives and more are from plants," I replied. "Also curaré and a thousand other poisons."

"Bah! Amateur night! That is merely what evolution can produce. I have taken it much further, and using the exotic species from hundreds of worlds. I have great greenhouses here, and excellent laboratories as well. The operative drug for the men, for example, took years of work and experimentation, although I was building on existing work in other worlds. It acts only in the males, and in all males. On females it has no effect at all except perhaps as a very mild and harmless steroidal effect in quantity. On the males—it does not attack masculinity. I did not wish that. It alters, very subtly, only those characteristics I find offensive. It suppresses the ego, replaces aggressiveness towards women with an overwhelming urge to please us. They have sufficient strength and courage and aggressiveness to use their greater power and bulk for work, but not at all sexually. Less than two weeks on the compound and the effect is in full force. Within a month they just can't imagine ever feeling any other way."

"I assume, then, that it's addictive."

"To a degree. A synthetic version can be made highly so, but since anything over a certain dosage is simply expelled by the body and since it does not affect women, it is simply added to all food and drink here."

"You mean like in the fruit juice your people gave me?"

She chuckled. "Yes, it was there, but in a very small quantity. It will have no effect unless you stay a while and eat or drink quite a lot. If you notice it at all, it might just make you a little horny, that's all. The initial treatment involves massive doses so it saturates the system, is absorbed into the body, and undertakes the biochemical changes. After that just a small amount will keep it that way forever."

"Thanks," I said sourly. Now I'd be checking myself out in every thought and action and I didn't need that kind of doubt right now. Especially right now. "I doubt if I'm the type of guy who'd fit in around here anyway, with or without."

"Perhaps. We prize the muscle here because we need the boys to do the heavy manual labor, but there are many of them here who are more average looking, kept around because they are cute or have other attractive attributes. We really don't need the boys for anything here except as sexual playthings, but they need us. The poor dears are rather helpless without us."

"Do they mind?" I asked her.

She gave that wicked smile again. "Mind? What difference does that make, poor boy? I mean, do men care if a woman minds their wolf whistles as she walks down the street? Do they care if a woman minds being propositioned by total strangers when she's just shopping or riding on a bus? Do men even consider what it's like for most women to fear walking down a street after dark with a potential rapist in every dark corner, or in every passing car? Why should I care if these boys mind? That's the way things are here."

"I understand the source of your feelings and concede your points, but I doubt if you or most of the women here have the same kinds of fears you talk about. My wife came from one of the roughest city environments I know. She's cautious in the same way I'm cautious, but I think she's too tough to have that kind of unreasoned fear or lack of confidence to deal with a threat."

"How little you know," Mendelez sighed. "Very well, I do not have much time for you and you, I suspect, would rather have done with me and this place as quickly as possible. Stay too long here, dear, and you won't want to ever leave."

That was precisely what was on my mind, speaking of fear. "Do you know much of what I've done so far and what's happened?"

"Not much," she admitted. "I have been a very, very busy woman lately. We are going to close down the Labyrinth, you know, and before that happens I want to make very, very sure that we have everything we can possibly need right here. And I am very close to perfecting a stable viral form of my little formula to insure that the whole world here remains my vision. Too bad, really. I should have loved to have had it ready to spread it to every biochemically compatible world in the region, perhaps even to Company people. That was my pet project. A stable viral-like form of this that is immune to all known immunization procedures, not detectable by medical scans, and which is spread easier than the common cold. Imagine that male-dominated Company world and race under this sort of influence. The entire power structure would collapse before they realized why —and the women would be so hidebound by that horrid culture that they would be generations learning the ropes and breaking free of their mental chains to pick up the pieces—providing of course they learned how to run all that stuff before it collapsed."

"I think I would prefer that to the risks of this project," I answered honestly. "In a way, it would be a merciful end to that rigid culture and struc-ture."

"Merciful!" She gave a cackling laugh. "I do not want mercy. I want them to *suffer!*"

I decided not to press the point. Instead, I wanted to go through the litany and routine and get the hell out of there as fast as possible, without even doing lunch.

"So, about Pandross . . ." I began, and started the drill.

The last thing I needed was my brain chemistry rearranged to remove aggressiveness. Although I abhorred violence and all it represented, there was no question that very soon I would have to kill, and perhaps kill a number of people. I had enough problems with that without adding more.

10.

Solving the Maze

I was never so glad to have my pants back on in my whole life. I had a very strong impression that I might have been the first guy to ever walk back out of there once he got in, and I could tell all the time I was there and talking to Mendelez that she was toying back and forth in her mind with whether or not to keep me as a pet.

She's an out and out psycho, that's for sure, but except for her particular way of working out her crazy vision I really wasn't too certain that she was any more crazy than the rest of them—just more visibly dangerous. Still, of them all, she and Carlos were the only ones who could induce some element of fear in their own comrades, and that said something.

Maria thought Valintina's vision was somewhat amusing, although hardly preferable. It was just that she couldn't see any difference between the Mendelez version of inequality and oppression and any of the other worlds we'd gone to. To her, we were all equally insane.

I sighed, swallowed hard, and checked my resolve. I was still game to go through with it and I still was more than willing to plug Carlos and anybody else who got in my way, so maybe the dose I got wasn't all that much. I couldn't let myself dwell on it. I *felt* normal and that was what I had to go on. In a way, I wondered if I wasn't just as much a fruitcake as Valintina, considering what odds I was going to face and how improbable it was that I was going to get ten feet without discovery and death.

We proceeded along the normal course to get us back to the office, but we weren't going back there at all. At a particular cube, all sides dark, Maria suddenly gave a signal and we both exited to the left and wound up inside a small, hot building with little or no light. She knew it well, and reached up and switched on a tiny bare bulb, revealing a fairly squalid interior shed.

"Quickly," she said. "Get out of your clothes and into the black ones there." I complied, noting that the new clothing was pretty well Company security standard for inside the Labyrinth itself—the sort of uniform worn, in fact, by both sides. Plain, black denim, with double pockets in the shirt, a black leather belt. The clothes fit, although they had that new or freshly starched feel to them. There was also a pair of tough rubber-soled boots to complete the outfit, although this uniform bore no insignia or badge to show who or what I really was.

She packed the old clothes into a small satchel and we exited back into the Labyrinth as quickly as we could. Anybody using a tracer could still see and track us—now. We continued to walk along, and when we reached the point of the office, the satchel with the irradiated clothing was tossed into the siding, although we ourselves weren't going there. It was done in one neat, fluid motion as we walked, and would show on anybody's tracker scope as a diversion—we hoped.

Not much further down, we had another duck-in, this time to a small clearing in a thick, jungle-like environment. Maria seemed to know what she was doing, going over to the underbrush and then hauling out a large chest wrapped in a tarp. Removing the tarp, she unlocked the chest and opened it.

"The small attaché case contains all the basic tools and instruments for a standard security repair," she told me. "There is not a lot else we could reasonably carry."

I nodded, opened the case, and was reasonably satisfied with the contents. She was right. What I needed was a master computer link and a lab full of stuff, but this was better than nothing.

She then handed me a stock issue energy pistol with long laser sight in a holster on a belt with a full set of energy cubes for reserve. It was the futuristic version of the gunfighter's belt, and I didn't feel comfortable with it, but I had to be prepared to use it if necessary. There was also an extension rope, some small explosive modules, and a veritable *potpourri* of things that might prove useful.

"There has been abnormally heavy courier traffic of late," she told me. "Usually he only allows his own people to do the messages, but now that the others are involved they insist on their own people. I have selected a spot where it should be possible to intercept a courier, although it might take some time."

"Good," I told her, impressed. "Uh—you realize the risks here, don't you?"

She stared at me. "I am doing this because my mission is to stay with you and assist you in anything that does not involve your going outside of or threatening the organization. I always understood that if you unmasked a murderer among the higher-ups you would probably have to go after them yourself. To turn them in with or without absolute evidence would otherwise be fatal. That means you would either 'go down swinging,' as it were, in an honorable cause, or directly make your case. My life has no meaning except that I do what I was ordered to do. The risk here is irrelevant."

I wondered for a moment if she was any saner than the rest of them. At least I had a good personal excuse for doing this; Maria, on the other hand, had no real stake in it at all. I had correctly analyzed her way of thinking and in good lawyer fashion turned her into a temporarily useful ally by finding the loopholes and the fine print in her literal instructions, but I was really beginning to wonder here. I was depending a lot on her, and she had no real stake in this at all. Worse, she'd totally misread all the evidence and was taking me entirely on her own cultural terms—my "function" was to solve crimes; therefore, this was essential to solving the crime.

They wouldn't like it if I solved their little crime for them. They wouldn't like it at all.

We checked out everything, then prepared to move to our ambush location. I had hopes that we'd be there some time; I was tired and I could use the rest. This had come up too sudden and too fast; I didn't like being pushed and I didn't like the extra risks the speed-up was causing.

We re-entered the Labyrinth, weighted down by our equipment, and turned back the way we'd come. For a short while the coast seemed clear, but then Maria touched my arm and pointed, and I whirled around and saw our mysterious shadow in his accustomed position. So we hadn't fooled him; or, at least, we hadn't made good our escape.

The phantom had stopped for a moment, in the usual fashion, but did not step back as he always had. After a moment, he continued on towards us. Maria was very fast, drawing and crouching low at one and the same time. She was clearly going to fire, but I stopped her with a hand signal. If the fellow wanted to come out of the bushes, now was the time to do it.

He was of medium height, with a strong, middle-aged face that was tough and somewhat like a bulldog's, with a shock of white hair that really stood out. He was wearing, so help me, an old style trenchcoat and had both hands in his pockets, and he seemed in no hurry. He looked like either the villain or the Scotland Yard inspector out of countless old British movies, and I mentally bet he had a retired or honorary military rank.

He seemed utterly unworried about Maria's pistol, but he did stop just before entering our cube, slowly and carefully remove a hand from a pocket to show it was empty, then point beyond us. I turned, and for the first time saw another figure, this one also rather close. There could be no greater contrast in the pair.

The second was female and looked like she belonged with Valintina's amazon security staff. Tall, lean, very pretty and sexy in an all-leather jump suit, high-heeled black boots that looked great but didn't seem all that practical, and long hair that was either very blond or almost white. None of that mattered. All that mattered was the small but deadly Uzi style submachine gun she was carrying, cocked, ready, and pointed in our direction.

Maria was suddenly caught in a position where she wasn't certain about anything except her primary function and duty. I watched, horrified and helpless, as she turned in deadly pantomime and brought her own pistol to bear directly on my chest. I looked straight into her eyes and only for that moment did I see the slightest bit of hesitation or doubt in her expression.

That slight moment, however, was enough. In total silence and with professional accuracy I might have admired under any other circumstances, the strange woman in leather fired, the submachine gun pumping at least twenty rounds in deadly precision directly into Maria, who was kicked back against the cube wall by the tremendous force and almost seemed to explode in a mass of guts and gore. Her own pistol went off a couple of times, one missing me by only a hair, but I couldn't move, couldn't really feel the reality of the scene.

The tough-looking guy in the trenchcoat didn't flinch, stepping into my cube and losing his composure only slightly when he almost slipped on some of Maria's spilled guts. He pointed expressionlessly towards the leathery blonde, and I wasn't about to argue with them.

We didn't go far. There was one of those abandoned switches nearby that the opposition used so conveniently, and as soon as we stepped into it I suddenly could hear the breathing of all three of us and smell the death these two represented.

"We can talk here," said the man in a cultured

British accent that perfectly fit his looks. "Sorry about that ugly business, old chap, but she *would* have potted you, you know. She was going to do it anyway. She would have either done it or betrayed you to Carlos the moment she found out just why you were there, and she certainly wasn't about to allow you to go into any Company territory."

"She was the product of her world and culture," I responded limply. "She was good at what she did and that can't help but affect me. I've been more or less living and working with her for weeks, after all."

"Understandable. But your sentimental streak would have been fatal in the end. Surely you knew that."

I nodded. "Maybe so. If I'd had a gun and she'd had a gun and she came at me I might have felt differently about it. But it's done. Now you want to tell me by who and why?"

"My name is Moran," he said. "My associate, here, is Miss Blaise. We have the same employer at the moment and, with other compatriots, we have been keeping one eye on you and another on your old homestead. We weren't going to be so—intrusive—as yet, but clearly you two were off to Carlos' lair, and our employer had strict instructions about preventing that."

"Your—employer?" I repeated.

"Mister Pandross, honey," the woman replied in one of those sweet, sexy voices. "You know—Lothar Pandross?"

I nodded. "I figured as much. How *is* Mister Pandross, Colonel? I *can* call you Colonel, can't I?"

He seemed startled, then relaxed. "If you like. I assume Mister Pandross is all right. Why?"

313

"Well, he's been killed twice, you know. Ugly business. What are you doing, Colonel? Switching sides, or just moonlighting on the Professor?"

"The Professor, as you well know, is long dead," Moran responded. "Since then I have entertained offers from anyone with the means to satisfy me. But this gets us nowhere, you know. I'm afraid you've forced our hand in this a bit."

I looked at him and at the pretty girl with the Uzi. "So what can you do? Shall I go back and play footsie with Voorhes some more and wait for my last appointment with Carlos? Or should I simply sit here and refuse cooperation, knowing that you can't blow me away like you blew away poor Maria. Or do I get trussed up and hauled down to some maniac's lab for special treatment?"

"No time for that sort of thing," Moran muttered. "Takes weeks, you know, when you can't use the drugs. No, I think we make a deal to our mutual benefit."

"What kind of deal, Moran? You and your boss need me. I could use your help, but there's no easy way for either of us without guarantees."

"Don't need them," he commented gruffly. "You want Carlos? Go and get him. There's the exit—we won't stop you."

I smiled grimly. "You just killed my entrée in and you know it. I might be able to work on my own, but I don't know where the hell he is."

"Precisely. Well, we do. We know where he is and where the entrance is and we know all the bypass codes and procedures. With our knowledge and your talent you could get right into his lair. Whether you could successfully get out, or even do any harm, is not the question, but we have far more than you would have on your own. Right now, you're stymied."

That figured. Pandross designed all these systems, and they were all tied into the central computer anyway. With his drug zombie army around, Carlos probably had no more bothered to significantly alter the system than Mancini or the rest had. All he had to do was keep a major distance from anyone not under his control and have any outsiders deal only with underlings at a remote location.

"Think about it, darling," Blaise put in, also revealing a British accent in her sweet and sexy tones. "If you do what we want you at least have a *chance* at what you want. If you fail, what difference will your own personal problems make, anyway? You seem to be so smart about other things but so stupid when it's personal. If you had your way, you might just win one but then when that gets out what happens to that sweet little boy of yours?"

She was right. I really had been so hung up on one thing it never occurred to me to put my priorities in order. A lack of enthusiasm for derring-do was one thing; being blind-sided on my own interests was inexcusable.

"Just what's involved here?" I asked them.

Moran, who seemed to be almost machine-like, allowed himself a bit of a smile. "I think you have the basic idea of what they're planning. I can fill in the details."

He reached into his coat and brought out a close-up system map of the central Zero region of the Labyrinth. It was well-worn and marked up and looked a lot like the one on Yugarin's wall that I'd seen.

I crouched down with him on the floor of the station and looked at the thing.

Moran pointed to a complex-looking set of symbols. "There is True Zero, the power source for the Labyrinth. It puts out enormous, near limitless, energy which is tapped in the side cubes here and here bracketing the Zero access itself. The huge areas here on either side are massive power regulators and transformers that take this erratic but immense power and turn it into something that can be used and make certain it is stable—and that it does not bleed over. The key bypass is here to allow traffic to go from one side to the other without the impossibility of passing through Zero or having any real access to the source."

I nodded. "All right, I'm with you so far."

"Good. Now, when the Company fries a world, as they did to those people, they seal off a section here and here, run power bypasses along the container car route to continue power, then terminate the main tunnel, making it effectively a dead-end siding. They rig a bypass, in other words. Power is then bled into this new siding until eventually it reaches the end and emerges in a steady, building stream. With nowhere else to go it fries all facets of the end cube."

I nodded. "I got that much."

"The analogy is much like pouring massive voltages through a wire or tube and then using it much like a deadly firehose. It's quite tricky, which is why it's a last resort thing, and that's what gave the opposition the idea. When the energy is

316

turned down, there's a lot built up without regulators at the end and some of it surges back through the line where the transformers and regulators must absorb it and keep things cool, as it were. Now, the theory was to produce surges from the *opposite* ends, out here a ways, so that they rush inward to the transformers and regulators at the same time. If they are overloaded without the massive safeguards, and both at the same time, they can't handle the load. The odds are excellent that this will produce a meltdown of the transformers and regulators. They are designed to do this as a last resort, sealing off the Labyrinth from the Zero world. So long as one side works, the other can be brought back on line via the bypass, but if *both* are melted, well, then, there's no power to the Labyrinth at all. It dies, and who knows if that melted mass could ever be borne through again and a new grid built?"

"I think I get the idea," I told him. "And the danger is that the intense heat formed by the melting down might break through to Zero rather than seal the opening, so we have the unchecked power of an energy universe rushing freely through the Labyrinth."

"Precisely."

I stared at it. "I'm no physicist and I flunked most science, but I've done a lot of electrical work. Where in hell are they getting enough power to rush back along the lines to the regulators? Where are they getting so much power that the surge will overload them and shut them down?"

"That was Mancini's genius, old boy. He developed a storage system which would absorb and keep quantities of the energy from the main line.

Just giant batteries, really. The power demands were increased, of course, but not to a degree that a flag would be raised in Maintenance. A few weeks of just, say, a hundred and ten percent power consumption, far within the normal fluctuations of the line, would be sufficient. And if the substation being serviced was down or at minimal levels, almost all of the energy, perhaps ninety percent, could be diverted to the storage cells. For that reason, they needed sidings with little traffic and no commerce."

"I see. But why *my* siding?"

"Physics. The release of that stored energy must be sequential and it must be perfectly timed, within milliseconds certainly. The signals can not exceed the constant speed of light within the Labyrinth, so a number of sidings on both sides were required and they had to be relatively close together and perfectly positioned. They had their own abandoned sidings to start with, which were easy, but not sufficient. They were able to take control of a few Company sidings, and occasionally corrupt or take over main stations so they had security on their siding work while maintaining normal commerce and not raising the Company's suspicions, but there were just a few crucial gaps that might make the difference between not enough power and enough for the job. They tried taking inconsequential ones, under little or no Company control, when they failed to control the optimum one, but they always threw another location off. Yours was perfect. It came down to using yours or widening the risks."

I had already figured out that our home sweet home had to be a key to it all. When I saw it marked with a circle on Yugarin's map, along with a lot of others I didn't know, it cleared up a lot. And when he told me that they'd come up with this like ten years earlier, the rest fell into place. And the crazy thing is, with all this hatred among this group, the key was a kind of lopsided, bent love story.

See, the first case, the one that brought Brandy and me into the Company, was their initial attempt to seize control of the State College siding and substation. They were going to replace key people in the Philadelphia branch of the Company with their own duplicates and insure a no-interference situation up at State College. Whitlock would have seen that commerce was maintained, maybe even profits increased, while one by one he used his own high position to tag and replace others. Bill, you'd be one of the key ones later on. They couldn't go after Company security officers right off, but if they had the financial and corporate officers they'd have no trouble replacing security.

But it didn't work. They screwed up when they failed to kill Whitlock. They were as ruthless then as now, but not at all experienced. They simply didn't realize that the Company was hand in hand with organized crime and they failed to cover the mob bosses. Whitlock went underground and away, in the process stiffing the mob, which went after him. That blew the operation and they were trying to clean up the botch when we got involved.

Having made our world too hot for them for a while, they looked for alternatives. I should have made the link when Brandy's case developed. They had taken over an alternate Earth close enough to ours that you didn't even have to go through a switch to go between them, and they'd developed their own siding to the same State College switch point. They'd learned, too. In that world *they* allied with and took over the mob. We thought they were just using the world as a testing ground for their damned drug, and certainly they let Carlos do that in the hopes his plot would succeed and make theirs unnecessary, but the object was to secure the substation and use it as a substitute for ours.

We saw only one plot, unconnected except by the leaders to any past plot. The fact is, there were two—the officially sanctioned one Carlos was working and the private plot by Yugarin and Mancini about which the others knew nothing. But Brandy blew the security of that other Pennsylvania substation, making it useless anyway, and maybe it wasn't any good anyway. Just a hair off, increasing the odds of the surge being uncoordinated. They probably took over and tried a dozen more we never knew about, but it never worked. If they used another substation, then one or more of their already secure substations didn't work. It was a Chinese puzzle, you see. When you moved one piece it automatically moved two or three other ones. Eventually they came to decide that the only practical solution was to take over ours after all.

But how? For one thing, the two people presiding over the substation were the same two who had constantly thwarted them in the past. For another, security was better on our world after their initial failure. The only plus in their favor was that our substation was rarely used. It hadn't even been staffed until we moved up there. The weak point that existed there was simply too small to be useful except as an occasional convenience entrance and exit. We'd staffed it only because the opposition had drawn our attention to it and the vulnerability it represented, but we didn't take the next step of asking ourselves why the hell the opposition was drawn to it. I blame myself for not seeing the linkages. Again and again all the cases were drawn to that damned substation. Why?

Well, Yugarin and Mancini had managed a lot on their own, but now they had a situation where everybody was required and commitment from the whole Board was necessary. It didn't take 'em ten years to get the risk factor down—they went to the committee after ten years' work with a *fait accompli*. The other places were secured, the great storage batteries built, the math all done. Only it couldn't work without our substation.

Some of the committee were enthusiastic, others had reservations but finally went along, impressed by the work and planning that had gone into it ever since Yugarin had mapped all the sidings and substations and realized the possibilities unused sidings might give for such a project. It was Kanda's math that kept the risk factors high, but in the end not high enough. Mancini in particular is no dummy himself, and when I was told that Carlos had his own secure and independent computer system I only had to put two and two together to figure that there was no way to fool Mancini and the others by doing a lot of fake figures. So, in the end, we had eight people giving the go-ahead and starting to plan how to take over our substation for the length of time necessary to install and charge their batteries and rig their timing circuits under the Company's nose, as it were. And we had one man who, although he had to go along, was desperate to stop it if he could.

In every way but one, Lothar Pandross was exactly what he seemed to be. A true genius with an affinity for machines, maybe even a love affair with them. He wasn't personable, and people made him feel uncomfortable. Maybe he was just over the bend paranoid, or maybe he was an agoraphobe—staying most of the time in that one computer command center suggests that—but the fact was that Pandross was far happier interacting with machines than people and he had the kind of job and challenges that kept him happy and content. He went out seldom; the only clear instances I could see where he interacted with others, mostly just sitting back, was at the committee meetings which were held inside Kanda's alternative computer—a computer that Kanda told me Pandross had helped design and build.

Pandross's personality and genius had made him perfect for the job he'd taken on at the start. Unlike the others, you see, he wasn't from that destroyed world. We'll probably never know which world he came from. But he was a Company man, a computer genius who'd probably been recruited to work on and improve the Company's own master computers. That's why his design for Kanda was so close and so competitive. But he worked for Security, not Maintenance, and so at the key time he worked directly under the ambitious traitor destined for the Company board, Mukasa Lamdukur.

In a way, they all underestimated the Company and Mukasa. He was an old security hand. He wasn't about to arm and train and turn loose eight loose cannons inside the Labyrinth with access to most of its secrets and all twisted up inside by hatred of the Company and thirst for revenge. He needed to always be sure of them, and Pandross was ideal. As a man virtually phobic about interaction with people, he was less likely to be exposed or make a slip. The position was irresistible to Pandross because it gave him nearly a free hand at designing an alternate security system and force, creating new systems, beating his old compatriots at the Company at their own game, and, of course, as chief of Security and head of the computer system as well, he could monitor and track the eight rebels as they went about their destructive work. And if Mukasa took over, Pandross was promised that he would be the king of the highest technology in the new pecking order.

Pandross, of course, eventually figured out, or maybe he just overheard it in snooping, that when Mukasa took over it would still be Company race first. He would still have a master in his own field, a comparative dolt who would still be able to order him around and restrict his activities and determine budgets and priorities. When he discovered that Carlos was going after Mukasa and planning to infect and hook the entire Company, Pandross made a fateful decision. He did absolutely nothing. That's why Mukasa was so surprised, and eventually victimized.

But Brandy threw a wrench into that operation, and we were able to put the pieces together and expose the plan at the crucial moment when it could still be stopped. Pandross was now king— but of the opposition only, with no more inside to the Company.

By that time, however, he was well along in his

own project, which was Kanda's great thinking and self-repairing and self-improving master computer. To Kanda, it was a dream come true, a marvel and wonder, a true alien intelligence beyond his imaginings and a tremendous achievement. But he only designed it in the initial stages. Pandross is the one who truly created it, and used his vast stores of information taken from the Company computers to establish this new creation's foundation in reality.

To somebody like Pandross, that great, new computer was probably the only thing he ever truly loved.

And, see, that was the problem. While the few objectors on the committee were mostly concerned with the five percent chance of a total wipeout, a breakthrough to the Zero world and a searing release of all that power channeled via the Labyrinth to all Earthly creation, Pandross didn't give a damn about that. See, he was more bothered by the eighty percent chance that it would work. Short out the Labyrinth, cut off the power supply.

The power supply to his machines, his computer. They were talking about taking the only love he had, cutting open its arteries, and making that love bleed to death.

Pandross never gave a damn about the Company, and he never gave a damn really about the opposition, either. Neither had any real meaning for him so long as he was able to do what he loved to do. Maria had called it "function." Everybody has a function, something they do best, some place where they are the perfect fit in the cosmic machine. Not all of us find that fit, and not too many of us function perfectly, but that made Pandross all the more aware of his position.

He had to stop them, but what could he do? Leak the plan to the Company, certainly, but that would also mean breaking apart the opposition, betraying and crumbling the network that was part and parcel of his own life and existence, and with no certainty that he would not be traced and held responsible for it. He was in association with eight brilliant psychopaths and he knew them well and didn't underestimate them. Still, the potential was there for him to betray them all.

What he had underestimated was his own beloved computer, who monitored everything with maximum input. Perhaps he talked to it from his remote location. Perhaps he even asked it for solutions to the problem. I'm not sure what triggered it—maybe his own security programs, maybe the fact that his thinking computer was raised to think in the opposition manner in the same way that Maria was raised to think in the rigid terms of her own culture—but the computer, for all Kanda's talk of an alien intelligence, was one of them. It perceived that Pandross was cracking, that he was a threat to everything, even the computer itself. In fact, he was more of an immediate threat to the computer than the big bang plan itself. The computer was the hub of all activities for the eight and the thousands of agents they ran. You couldn't send a message, make a discovery, without having to send it via the computer's network.

And so the computer acted on the immediate threat and sent out a message under the highest authority to the opposition's top security. We'll probably never know who killed Pandross, if they're still alive themselves, but they did it faithfully and with the kind of obedience and unquestioned loyalty to the committee that Maria also represented. With the computer giving them all the accesses, all the blockings, everything he, she, or they needed, they carried out the orders and killed their chief.

The computer, of course, had solved one immediate problem by doing that but hadn't solved the one that had mandated the action. It had both a practical and a logical problem. As a loyal member of the opposition committed to its goals, it couldn't betray or destroy the others or dissolve or cause to be dissolved that organization. It had killed Pandross to preserve just that organization. But Kanda had been quite clever in his overall design; the computer had input and output capabilities, but it had no arms, legs, eyes, or whatever. It also was vulnerable for all its great power, knowledge, and size. Nobody was going to build and maintain a machine like that without adequate safeguards both against it should it turn out to be uncontrollable or should it be revealed in all its immobile bulk to the Company and fall into Company hands. Pandross himself wouldn't have permitted it, and the committee would certainly have thought of it as well. If those paranoid psychos ever even *dreamed* that their master computer, no matter what its motive, had knocked off one of their own, they would activate those systems and blow it.

Mancini had designed the other, easier substation bombs and their batteries. The computer couldn't get to them, and if it ordered any sort of security raid that destroyed them there would now be only one direction for bright ones like Mancini and the others to look for the culprit. The only safe way was to make something go wrong at the last and most vulnerable explosive point. My house, and the Pennsylvania substation.

I'm not clear on what it did next, but it needed some on-the-scene agent representing only it. Most likely it found a Pandross duplicate somewhere and had some security boys play their mind tricks so that the poor *schmuck* thought he was the real Pandross. Maybe someplace it's trying to make up for its murder by growing Pandross clones. I don't know. But when Voorhes' raid on my place to set up their part of the plan came off, there was a Pandross there. A disposable Pandross, keyed to finding me, to tipping me off, maybe even enlisting me, using threats against Dash or whatever against me. See, I didn't have any ready usable duplicates and I had to go through intensive security screening whenever I went out on a job. They made a lot of penetration operations all over hell and gone that kept me away from home more than in it. To have killed me would have been to bring Company security down on the place like a ton of bricks and maybe closed that siding and sealed or destroyed that switch. The Voorhes plan was to keep me so busy protecting Company assets that I'd spend little time at home.

But I was supposed to be home when the raid came down. It was timed for that. That's why they brought their martial arts nerve experts. Their plant, Bond, would appear to be the apparent reason for the raid. That is, a simple opposition raid to get a key man before he could reach the Company and divulge secrets. Once inside, Brandy and I were to be overpowered, and she, who has an incredible number of duplicates, would be replaced by one of them so highly trained and hypno-taught that she'd be damned near perfect, while I would be permanently and totally paralyzed, a basket case, with one of those permanent Ginzu-type holds the Ginzu Master feared had been done. I would have been helpless, out of the way, and accounted for.

With a fake Brandy in place, the rest of the staff could also be replaced one by one, since she, as station master, had full access to the most secure areas and wouldn't be suspect. They would also give a less permanent nerve hold to her so that any lapses she might make during the early stages might be glossed over, and, bedridden, she could learn the little things so as to be a perfect duplicate.

The second Pandross, however, was put in by the computer. He came by car, not Labyrinth, having been gotten in through one of the more remote substations, and knowing all the passwords and clearances his job would be to see that I wasn't knocked out. The computer was convinced that if I recovered there was no way they could fool me for any length of time, and they might be right. That would mean killing me and there goes the substation, like I said.

But I wasn't there, thanks entirely to luck and a stubborn snowstorm, and that forced the ersatz Pandross, who the goons doing the raid had every reason to believe was their legitimate boss, to improvise. He wasn't the real Pandross, though, and that made him an amateur, an actor able to carry out a predetermined set of things but an amateur when a professional was needed. The goons knew the basic plan; he couldn't overrule that without drawing suspicion on himself, so he let it go. But he had them kidnap Dash, in a real amateur night kidnapping without any plans for what they were going to do with the boy, hoping to blackmail me by threats against the boy with playing along with his game. After the raid, my Earth was pretty well sealed off by Company security, so it took a long time before even the imports could get out. They were, however, able to send a report out which included the fact that they'd missed me and kidnapped the kid.

And that's where the computer got the idea of both dealing with me and using me, as I'll explain in a moment.

I suspect that when Voorhes got that report he was furious, but he didn't really have any reason to be suspicious of the big man who'd come along and helped supervise. If he was more than mentioned, Voorhes and the rest probably just figured he was one of the drug lords they used to get the goons up and back. They had all seen Pandross's dead body, and my vague description later of Whispery Voice wouldn't have connected.

Voorhes and the others were pros, though. If they couldn't have me in the original way, they'd use Dash to make me come to them. The idea was to use me if they could, since the death of Pandross really had shaken them, but also to invoke my absence and perhaps later show evidence that I had turned traitor. I would register, now and again, on Company recorders during my Labyrinth trips, although they made certain my routing wouldn't give Company security any real opportunity to nab me. The computer also hired some good people, like Moran and Miss Blaise, to cover me in shifts, making certain that not only as backups for Maria but also, and primarily, to protect me from Company agents just in case. That was why we were shadowed everywhere in the Labyrinth. This gave the computer some legs of its own, since Maria was tied to opposition security and therefore to the other seven. This independently hired force believed they were working security for a still-living but behind-the-scenes Pandross. They represented a mercenary third party who was devoted to stopping the plan but also to protecting the opposition.

The trouble was, nobody could really get to the farm to blow the operation. Hell, if the toughest sort to fool in all humanity, a five year old, can be conned into accepting a duplicate as his mother, why should the Company suspect? And if they are going to make certain that they close this threatening substation, who better than the station master to bring in crews so it can be done in an orderly manner? Hell, the Company would actually make certain nobody disturbed them!

The problem was, that made it next to impossible for the computer's mercenaries to get near it on the world side, and only station personnel's codes would be operative on the Labyrinth, or switch, side. Nobody could get in from the switch except Mancini's team, and nobody could threaten on the real world side because of the Company. Neat.

The only one whose code would automatically operate that switch who wasn't on either side was me, since there was no way to take me out of the coding at the switch level unless it was done by the station master—and this Brandy was perfect, but she wouldn't have the real one's total I.D. coding so the moment she went into the security area of the switch to alter it the alarms would go off like the Fourth of July.

The computer had known that. That's why when the committee asked the *computer* to suggest who could best solve Pandross's murder, the computer strongly suggested me.

Voorhes was nervous about me—things hadn't gone right in the raid and he'd resisted the idea of using Dash to get at me—but when the computer suggested me and also the logic of making me seem a traitor and getting the threat out of the way—the plan I outlined already—it proved irresistible. Carlos, of course, saw the humor in it as well, and put someone under his control, Maria, over me although she didn't know it was him. Still, they accelerated operations in the siding, knowing that they couldn't maintain the enormous fiction there forever.

And now here was Moran telling me that their employer, Mister Pandross, whom I knew was a hulking mass well back down the Labyrinth there, now insisted that I carry out the last part of his plan for the sake not only of screwing things up but also in my own interest. If they were allowed to go ahead, God only knew what would eventually happen to Dash.

"All right," I told Moran and Blaise. "Just what is it I'm expected to do here, anyway?"

"We will provide what you need before you go," he told me. "It's not large or bulky and it breaks into little bricks. You just stick them in various spots as you travel towards your house through the siding. Once you are out and well away from the substation, you will have a detonator that will blow them, and that, in turn, will blow the batteries. That's basically it. The Company will find the mess, their security people will figure out the plan, and steps will be taken to insure against it happening again. You, rather than Mister Pandross, we, or any of the opposition, including their security forces, will have been the instrument of their failure. They will have to regroup and try something else. It's as simple as that."

"Uh huh. And what happens to me then? I'll have everybody from the deadly Valintina to the unforgiving Voorhes after me with all their resources. Not to mention that they'll definitely blow that world they threaten and send me the gory details."

Moran sighed. "They will not blow that world. It is true that the threat is real, but we have already taken measures to insure that the death of a world is not going to be on your shoulders, and I believe you understand we can prevent similar attempts in the near future to repeat the threat. As for your personal safety—well, you're no worse off than you were, are you? The Company can certainly safeguard your son. If not, then there is no hope for any of us, is there? And we will provide you with all that you will need to find your wife. If that doesn't still kill both of you, then I think you are resourceful enough to find a hole big enough to hide in. You are, after all, a security expert."

I thought it over and saw he was right. "Okay, then, I'll do it. But what happens if I get nailed in the siding by the opposition people or nailed up top by the Company before I can detonate?"

"Good point. You may find some small resistance in the siding, but you were prepared to deal with far greater forces on fortified guard, weren't you? We trust your abilities there. If the Company or anyone else gets you once the devices are planted, we have backups. The power net is still functional, a signal can be beamed in if need be although we'd rather not do it since it would show the presence of a third force, as it were. And if anyone gets you, the first thing they will do is search you—or, pardon, your body, depending. Anyone else whose skin contacts that detonator except for you will cause the detonating signal to be sent. It will still look like an accident, you see."

I nodded. They had it pretty well worked out. "Let's just assume I survive this and am in a position to use your information to go after my wife," I said. "I know that's improbable, but you never know. I assume he's hooked her and is putting her through a humiliating hell just to get even and feed his psychotic ego. I know how those drugs work. She might eventually kill herself, but she'll never leave with me."

Moran sighed. "We thought of that. The same way Mister Pandross communicated with you is the way we eventually got a message through to her. She is assured that the drug can be duplicated if a sample is provided. She also has been thinking ahead, it appears. It must take tremendous will-power not to take the drug until you just can't stand it any more. I have seen opium and heroin addicts, and this must be far more solid a hold than that, and more terrible a withdrawal. We merely gave her a suggestion. If she is strong enough, as you and we think she is, and smart enough, she'll have seen the solution. The drug is dispensed every twenty-four hours. It wears off in twenty-six, and we calculate the maximum point where it must be taken at thirty hours or so. If she's gotten the hint, which was all we could manage, and if she's up to it, she should have a surplus pill every four days. If she has a few as five extras sequestered, that would be more than enough with insurance. If she either hasn't gotten the idea, or has been unable to do it, then she is lost anyway."

I nodded. "I see. But—if she should have that many doses, then she must have gotten the hint pretty early. Long before I urged contact."

Moran nodded. "Oh, yes. We made certain shortly after she was made away with that someone, in threatening her, told her the exact time sequence. She would have known it almost from the start."

I sighed. "I'll be damned. Snookered from the beginning."

Moran shrugged. "Perhaps. But one thing has puzzled all of us, I must admit, right from the point where it became obvious that you knew your wife had been switched. You had your son back, which was to be our leverage to get you in here in the first place, so if you didn't know that your wife was a fake then you had no reason to enter here or play fair with Voorhes and the others. Ergo, you *did* know, right from the start."

I nodded. "That wasn't all that hard, although she *is* good. Even when I knew it wasn't my wife, I could believe it was. I was relieved she was so perfect—it meant I could leave Dash without a lot of trauma. I think it was something in her manner, her eyes, the way she interacted with Dash. I'm not sure she planned it that way, but unless she's the greatest actress that ever was I got the strong impression she'd die before she'd let anything happen to the kid. Almost like, well—I know that most of Brandy's counterparts didn't turn out so right or so lucky. Like she saw Dash as her second chance.''

"But if she was good enough to fool even your own son . . .''

"How'd I know? Oh, that wasn't hard. This crew goes in a lot for duplicates, switches, and substitutions, so I was looking for that right away. Even so, she almost threw me by being so perfect, until I found a fairly large piece of optical glass on the downstairs rug, like glasses had been broken. It was large enough that I played a hunch and sent it downtown to the optician where she got her glasses to check against Brandy's prescription. It matched.''

"Astounding! And that told you what?''

"Well, nobody, not even absolute duplicates, shares experience. There's always a little scar or a broken bone or a different filling in a tooth or something like that. Brandy's vision was always lousy, but it had really gone to hell during the wracking pain of withdrawal treatments from Carlos' organic drug. Her glasses looked like the bottom of Coke bottles, which is why the fragment was so noticeable. A duplicate would have the same genetic eye problems but wouldn't have undergone that extra treatment, and might have undergone other eye stress. The prescriptions were unlikely to be that close, even if the basic problems were the same. I got Brandy's spare pair from her bedroom and had them checked at the optician's as well. They didn't match the prescription. They were, in fact, way off. The only answer was that the woman wasn't Brandy, and had substituted her glasses for Brandy's so she'd never have to cope with the wrong prescription. When I realized that, I knew they'd pulled the switch. I could blow her cover, but then what happens to my wife? I figured that if they took her, and didn't kill her, they'd eventually turn her over to Carlos. I think I had his measure from the start, which is why I was confident she wasn't dead. When I fed a description to Maria, she was able to check the security couriers who went to and from Carlos's world and got a confirmation."

"God, that's noble and sweet!" Blaise put in. "I hope you get through all this, I really do. I hope you get her back. I really do. And even if you don't, I may take a crack at plugging that drug-dealing bastard myself sometime. It might be fun to do one just for kicks."

I sighed and got to my feet. "Lead on, MacDuff, and Heaven knows if we dine with the angels or in Hell this night."

"That's not Shakespeare," Moran commented.

"Horowitz, Act Four, Scene One," I responded.

I had an escort all the way to the switch, some of whom I could see and some of whom I just inferred. We actually did run into two Company security people on the way—I guess some alarm went off in the main line—but they never got close to me. I hoped they weren't killed, but I didn't have much choice on this one.

There was, of course, somebody on the switch itself, allegedly with the Company but almost certainly in the employ or under the control of the opposition. It was a typical Type Two, dog-faced character, and I remembered that Mancini had a number of Type Twos at our meeting place. He was, however, a tad confused.

"This switch is officially closed and in the process of being shut down," he told me officiously, "yet—that's strange. My board shows that you have highest security and priority entrance on the station mas . . ."

I had one hell of a pop gun with me and he wasn't nearly quick enough on the uptake. I fired right into the glass, which shattered, throwing him back against the wall which he hit, hard, and then slumped to the floor of the switch control room. I ran up to the window, saw that blood was coming from the sides of his toothy mouth and that his eyes were glassy and open and decided to take the chance that it meant the same for his race as for most others and that I'd killed him. Knocking out the remaining glass—actually some kind of tough plastic but the stuff still has sharp edges—I vaulted into the control room and reset the switch. I knew this one like I knew the back of my own hand. No sweat.

Even reset, though, there was no way the security system would admit anyone not on the internal coded security list. I should know—I installed the system myself. Moran and Blaise and the others couldn't follow, not without setting off alarms and maybe filling the other side with opposition security boys, but I could just walk right on through. They would remain here and cover my rear for a while, until it got too hot—I knew alarms were sounding within the Company net, or would when I passed that barrier. Then they'd head for the hills.

I went in fast, not expecting any real opposition but certainly expecting to encounter some work crews or maintenance people. You didn't bother to put guards on a door that was already locked and bolted and jammed a hundred which ways.

As soon as I was inside, the case I was lugging along sensed the proper conditions had been met, buzzed, and unlocked itself. I checked for trouble, then stopped and opened it. Inside were a lot of the bricks, each about eight inches by four inches, sort of like modeling clay, and, in a pocket, a thick folder. I took out the folder and looked through it, and saw immediately that it was at least what I had been promised. If it wasn't phony, I had a map to Carlos' lair, staffing, security system bypasses, the works. His world and fortress would be as wide open to me as if they didn't exist.

I walked forward, and didn't have to go far to see the massive batteries or whatever they were. They were enormous translucent cubes, filling most of each Labyrinth cubicle, and they hummed and throbbed with yellow-white energy. Along the top and sides, various thick connectors went right to and in some cases into the side walls of the Labyrinth itself. They were pretty damned impressive, but so bulky I worried that I might not be thin enough to squeeze through. Before I tried, I began sticking the explosive bricks to the connectors and nearest energy cube. Then, inhaling as best I could, and with a real effort, I managed to get by the first one, then almost trip on the connectors linking the first one to the next one. I went on, placing more and more of the bricks, and at one time damn near got stuck and at another got in but couldn't angle the damned case to come with me

338

for a while. I was aware that a clock was really ticking here.

I was four in when I saw my first person. He was wearing Company maintenance green, and he spotted me before I spotted him. The idea that anybody could enter from the switch didn't occur to him, though.

"Hey! Who're you and how'd you get down here?" he shouted, sounding angry.

"I live here!" I responded, and shot him.

I had absolutely no compunctions about blowing away anybody down here in the siding, and wouldn't take many chances if I got up and out, either. These guys had done worse than burglarize my home; they'd moved in. I felt angry and somewhat violated by that.

The siding went on a bit past my stop, and so did the energy cubes, but I was running out of bricks and I didn't feel great going any further. I took out the remaining ones and tossed them back. Hell, they'd probably do some harm no matter where they landed, and they were all hooked together anyway. I wasn't going to stay in here any longer than I had to. I was well aware that if they could remotely detonate the damned things they might not care if I was in here or not if they had enough opposition back at the switch.

The substation activated, and I walked into the familiar concrete well structure. At least they hadn't done anything to show here, so I was able to get up the ladder fast and head for the fence gate. It was locked, of course, but I blew it off, the sound echoing off in the distance. It didn't matter. My entry should have tripped an alarm up there if they were anywhere on the ball anyway.

It was cold, and there was as much or more snow than ever around. I had on a heavy jacket over the security outfit Maria had provided me, but as soon as I got to the edge of the grove of trees the wind really started biting into me, and I couldn't protect my gloveless hands without letting go either of the case or my gun.

I was a lousy shot—always have been. This gun compensated for that not by automatic marksmanship, which was strictly for small and close range stuff, but by sheer firepower. It was a partial energy weapon firing these weird looking fat pointed cylinders, but if one hit it blew with the force of a grenade launcher, as both the switchman and the maintenance checker found out.

Well, the best defense near dusk in a place like this wasn't to slink around dark against snow but to walk boldly up the main road like you belonged there.

Come to think of it, this was my house and my farm and I *did* belong there.

I stuck the blunderbuss in my pocket, hunched down as much as possible to protect myself from the wind, and walked boldly up the main road.

I was, frankly, amazed to get right to the porch without being challenged or even seeing another person. Well, everybody had enough sense to keep out of this weather if they didn't have to, and clearly work was over for the day.

I took the detonator module out and stuck it in my other pocket, then slid the case under the hole beneath the front steps. I didn't need it any more but I wanted to be able to get at it and the file it still contained if need be.

Then, steeling myself, I walked up to the front door, took out the gun, turned the knob, and opened it.

There were sounds from the kitchen in the back, and the TV was on in the living room, and there was the smell of a home-cooked meal wafting through the place. Suddenly I heard footsteps on the stairs and a small, excited voice screamed, *"Daddy!"*

Dash practically fell down the steps getting to me, and fairly leaped at me.

There was the sound of someone coming from the kitchen, and suddenly there was Brandy, although not *my* Brandy, with a puzzled look on her face and carrying a casserole dish. She stopped, saw me and Dash, and dropped the casserole dish on the floor.

"Oh, my God!" she said, and her face was suddenly the closest to white any black woman in history ever got.

"Wow, Dad! Is that a *gun* or something?" Dash asked, oblivious to the scene. I picked him up with my left arm and he clung there, hugging my neck. I'd forgotten how heavy he'd become.

"Yeah, son," I responded, "it's a gun." I looked at the ersatz Brandy, who was still standing there in the midst of a gooey mess that was all that remained of whatever had been in that casserole dish. "Don't I also get a warm welcome from my dear wife?" I asked her, a trace of acid in my voice in spite of the fact that she'd obviously done a pretty good job.

"S—Sam! What? Where have you . . .?" she managed, starting to recover a bit.

"No alarms, huh, Brandy? I wouldn't want to have to do anything to you in front of Dash. You understand."

She nodded mutely, frozen to the spot.

"Anybody else in the house?"

"Uh uh," she responded. "They're all over in the control center gettin' ready for the big test. Well, I think you know. Big fella, looks like some Mafia godfather, is over there, along with some big shot who looks like some sort of monk."

Yugarin and Mancini both here! That was interesting. If I could somehow alert Company security, they'd have a hell of a haul.

I was still trying to figure out what to do when Dash wriggled in my grasp and I felt a tiny hand dive into my left coat pocket and come out with the detonator.

If any bare human skin other than mine touched the detonator. . . .

"Hey, Dad? What's *this?*" Dash asked.

There was a sudden buzzing in the thing and then a rumble like an earthquake started shaking the whole house. The lights flashed on and off and suddenly the TV imploded.

Shit! I thought angrily, knowing what was happening now. *This whole damned farm takes its power from that grid!*

There was suddenly one hell of a big explosion, and I consciously fell on Dash to protect him and then my head got kicked hard by what felt like a mule, and that's the last damned thing I remember.

11.

Storming the Citadel

Bill Markham shifted in his chair. It had been a very long session and they were all tired, but there was no thought of not going to the end. Not now.

"It was a spectacular explosion," Markham said. "I didn't see it, but the monitors alone picked up a tremendous force, almost like a small underground atom bomb blast. I'm told by witnesses that a fiery plume shot up from the well hundreds of feet in the air and lit up the night sky for miles, turning Happy Valley back into day. The feedback into the grid circuits servicing everything from the house to the substation itself was tremendous. Electrical fires everywhere, and the ground shaking brought down half the structures. The horses managed to get out before the barns burned, by the way. And some of the people there got away and may be still running in confusion, although it looks like some were just about sealed into the substation and security bunkers. We dug down and cleared out the first bunker corridor, and the smell was overwhelming. No matter what the cannibals say, human beings don't smell appetizing when they're barbecued."

Sam didn't find that news very pleasant. "But you said Dash was all right."

"He is, I wasn't kidding you. Half the house

collapsed but that's about what saved you. It started to burn from the electrical fire, producing thick smoke. You took the debris and Dash only maybe got a bruise from you falling on him. He was trying to drag you out of there when the first fire engine arrived on the scene. He wouldn't budge from your bedside until it was clear that you'd be all right. That's some kid you got there."

Sam gave a wan smile. "Thanks. I like to think so. And the duplicate Brandy?"

"She's pretty banged up but she'll come out of it okay. The funny thing was, you saying about how she stood there, frozen, in that arch between the entry hall and living room and the kitchen?"

"Yeah?"

"Saved her life. The arch held when a lot of the rest collapsed. She managed to crawl out and helped get debris off you, even though it later turned out she had a number of broken bones. She got Dash out from under you, too, but just wasn't up to pulling you any further. She was half out with pain on the front porch when the first help arrived, but she might have saved Dash and she just might have saved you, Sam."

"Where is she now?"

"Near here. She's told us her side of the story, Sam. She really didn't know much or want to know much, but what little she did know she confirmed. She didn't have to, either. Hell, Sam, we had no reason at the start to think it wasn't the real one. If she hadn't told us she might have gotten away."

"What's her background?" Sam asked. "I know most Brandys didn't have it too good."

Markham nodded. "Her mom died same as ours, but the Colonel got into a street argument over something minor and stupid and somebody shot him. She was seven. None of the relatives could or would take her, so she wound up in a state orphanage where eventually she saw all the white kids adopted out and most of the black kids grow up there. She ran away when she was thirteen, became a street kid in New York, panhandling and stealing to get by, sleeping in abandoned apartments, selling herself when she had to. She doesn't remember how many times she was raped. Got pregnant once when she was maybe fifteen. The baby was born dead. A boy."

Sam Horowitz sighed. "Yeah. How the hell did these bastards find her?"

"She was in jail. The usual thing. Some petty drug dealing. She had a record of offenses as long as your arm, though, running the route from pickpocket to rolling drunks to prostitution, so they gave her five years. Their people bought a lawyer and a judge, got her sprung on a technicality, made her an offer."

"An addict? You said she was selling drugs."

"No, nothing major. It never appealed to her, or maybe she was so damned hardened she never felt the need. That was one of her attractions to them. No needle tracks, no hard addiction. She was something of a pothead, but not since jail. At first she saw it as a big con, a chance at the big time. You'd be paralyzed and institutionalized, and she'd get a big payoff here and do whatever she wanted. They used every trick they had to make her into our Brandy, I'll tell you, and she was a good learner. She was good enough to fool me and even Dash."

Sam nodded. "If I hadn't found that fragment of glasses before I'd found Dash—in fact, if they hadn't kidnapped Dash at all—I think I would have bought her, too. I don't know. I get the idea that maybe Dash was the key to her success, too. Maybe he was that stillborn kid she had back when, or maybe it was just the level of life and normalcy. Wish fulfillment, maybe. But the reason why she even fooled Dash was that there was genuine affection for him inside her. I could see it and feel it. That's why I was able to leave him with her. A lot of time you go on that deep down sixth sense with people in this business. I just knew, somehow, that she'd never let him be hurt any more than his real Mom would, that she thought of him as hers, too."

Markham nodded. "Depending on what we can salvage from this mess, we'll see what we can do for her." He paused, getting a bit grim. "Sam— they didn't play a hundred percent fair with you."

He frowned. "What? You mean it shut down the Labyrinth anyway?"

"Partially. It caused a massive surge in both directions. Some came out of the substation entrance and caused all the problems, but that was mostly backwash, as it were. The main force was forward, as designed, and it fried the switch and surged along the main line faster than even the protective equipment could kick in. On its own, it would have been minimal, but the surge reached other sidings, ones we didn't know about, also prepared, and set them off, too. It was a massive energy wave, frying a lot of stations and a lot of switches and not incidentally a lot of people."

"But it didn't break out."

"Uh uh. That damned computer had it pretty well figured, just how much power it would release and what direction it would take and what damage it would do. By the time it reached the Company siding it was strong enough to trigger all the protective seals and switches and then fry them, melt them down almost literally. It eventually shorted out two of the main regulators at the Zero wall. Not enough to cause permanent disruption, but enough to lower power levels to minimal operation for a long time to come. Maybe years, maybe longer. It's going to be a very long time before we can move large quantities of material in this sector, and for a fair amount of that time we'll be on our own and flying blind."

"Huh? What?"

"Sam—you know the Company world. You remember how massive the security was on that place, how it was overkill to the infinite degree. This stuff melted it down. The whole damned bypass, covered in a thick, smelly, harder-than-diamond substance, and without power. Since it was a bypass system power is still available, but we have no power back to the Company world and no contact and no switches. Sam, they're sealed in, along with, I might add, a number of other worlds and main stations as well along the path of this thing. Even with full power it'd take years to get back in there, and even then we'd need a lot of knowledge we don't have to find the weak point and punch back through. Knowledge that's locked in the main computers inside the Company world. Computers that no longer work because they were grid powered. The whole damned Company world is without power."

Sam's jaw dropped. "You mean—they're sealed in tight? Without any power, without any access to the grid line? Well I'll be damned. . . ."

"God knows, when and if we ever get back in there, what we'll find," Markham continued. "I don't think *our* world, even this country, could get along without power. If everything suddenly shut down, if we were suddenly back to the Eighteenth Century, few of us would survive. We don't know how to farm in the old ways. We don't know how to get our food and store it and transport it without power and mobility. To survive on our own without communication, heat, anything. We aren't even built for that any more. A fair amount of the Third World would get along okay, but we'd be finished. Mass starvations, freezings, riots, you name it. And, Sam, the Company world doesn't *have* any Third World, and all its knowledge and advisers and all the how-to manuals and the rest were in their vast computer network that's now without power and probably one great cold lump. They can't even look it up."

Sam shook his head. "No wonder I got this treatment right out of a sickbed. In a sense, I'm the worst traitor to ever hit this operation. Good grief, I was the hand that killed G.O.D., Inc.!"

Markham gave a dry laugh. "Well, they got their wish, little good that it'll do them. The Company's too big for that, Sam. We're hurt, we're wounded, we've got real problems, probably for the rest of yours and my lives, but the Company's still here. An emergency Board composed of senior experienced managers has already been named, and without a native Company worlder on it. It's like a government, Sam. You can overthrow a government, even execute all the politicians, but so long as the civil service is intact it still runs. We're really going to miss those centralized computers and their irreplaceable data banks, but we have access to a lot of computers ourselves and even if they each cover only one region or area we'll cope. Voorhes was right. So long as the Labyrinth survives, the Company survives."

Sam Horowitz sighed again. "You gonna untie me now, or execute me?"

"I'm going to untie you. Hell, Sam, you've got a job to do that we can help with."

"Brandy, you mean. Bill—all the data was in that case, and you said the house was destroyed."

Bill Markham grinned. "Yeah, but they make damned good cases, you know. And I want our Brandy back as much as you do, Sam. And, most of all, I want Carlos. I wish I knew for sure if Mancini and Yugarin really *were* in that control room for the timing tests, but from what I saw we'd need their complete medical scans to identify them from the remains, and the only place they might be is in the Company's security computers."

"Or Kanda's and Pandross's little dream," Sam reminded him. "Right now, that damned thing is the most powerful computer in all creation." He yawned and stretched as one of the agents cut him loose, then groaned. "What I want first is a good meal and a decent sleep. Then I want to go see Dash while you find my burnt case. And after that—we'll see."

They said the setting was quite beautiful, although a bit archaic-looking, like something out of an old movie, with the great castle stuck atop the bluff overlooking the crashing sea. She, herself, didn't know because she couldn't see it. Since they'd smashed her glasses taking her out of the house maybe—what?—weeks or months ago, she hadn't been able to see much of anything except big blurs.

It was getting harder and harder to have any sense of time at all. The setting was the same, the people were mostly the same, and the climate seemed warm and wet all the time.

She'd gotten to know her way around the Castle, as everybody called it, very well, at any rate. When the rule was that she was to be watched and prevented from harming herself, either accidentally or deliberately, but otherwise was not to be helped or aided in any way, you learned quickly.

In a way, it was sort of like going back to a kind of ugly existence after five years of a good dream. The fact that she'd been this route before toughened and sustained her. She had briefly considered suicide, but rejected it on two levels. One was that there was always a chance, however slim, of beating even this system and situation. She'd been down this far or farther before and had somehow squeaked clear in the end, and so long as there was any hope at all for beating it, even if it was a long time in coming as looked certain, she wasn't about to pack it in. The other level was more basic; killing herself would provide Carlos with a great deal of amusement, and she didn't want to give him the satisfaction. Worse was the fear she might botch it, and either cripple herself or give them even more excuse for their endless taunts. Without being able to see, she was just never sure who was around and what she could get away with.

Those little bastards with their nerve holds had put her out for the count during the raid on the house. She was vaguely aware of being stuffed in a truck or ambulance or something and of eventually some kind of plane ride, but it had been remote, distant, like the fringes of a half-remembered dream.

Even long after the initial paralysis had worn off they'd kept her drugged and sedated. She had vague memories of eating and drinking and doing other stuff but it was distant and willowy, her mind out to lunch for that period. That was one reason why time was no longer meaningful; she had no way of knowing how long that initial period was.

They'd kept her that way for quite a while, then slipped her through into the Labyrinth at some long forgotten substation maybe in South America or Asia or someplace like that, where the Company security had a hole. When she had finally come to she'd been stark naked on a bed in this place with no clear memories of how or when she'd gotten here.

"So nice to have you back," she heard Carlos' mellow voice say to her. She had spent little time with him back then, but she would never forget him or his dark good looks and smooth Latin charm that could mask the ugly, monstrous soul inside of him. "Once I acquire something it is mine, and I dislike losing anything of mine. The fact that you and your husband put me to a lot of trouble and ruined a nearly perfect plan to do to the Company and its world what they so richly deserved only makes your return more satisfying."

"Why didn't you just kill me and get it over with?" she asked him.

"Killing is so—*permanent*," he replied. "I prefer a more creative approach. Years ago the Company killed everything in my life I ever had, yet left me alive in a kind of personal Hell. When I attempted to strike back at the ones who did that, you prevented me. Now I want you to feel helpless and impotent, cut off, as I do. I want you to know on a personal level what my kind of ache is, to hate so much that you would do anything to do to me what you so judged and condemned me for trying to do to those who harmed me. And then you will crumble, as hope vanishes and you snap, sinking mentally to the level I have already reduced you to physically, knowing all the while what is happening. When that happens you will be a living testimony to inspire the proper attitude in all those who work with me here. And this time you will be helpless as we strike the fatal blow."

She said nothing, but his words were causing her stomach to have fits.

"We must first come to a realization of your situation," he continued, watching her. "You are in my personal home, on a world that does not appear in the Company's charts, via a switch that does not even exist on the Company's records. Everyone here is mine. Not even my comrades can come here without my permission, and as my guests. Not that those here could not leave, but they do not wish to. I have—a system."

"Yeah, you got 'em all on your damned drugs."

"Very clever. But not the old kind, which were difficult to control. We have made much progress since then. I got the idea from a world I did business with, a world in which people are now born with an inability to replenish certain natural enzymes. From the cradle they must be given what they lack regularly or they go into withdrawal and die. Their society is loyal, ordered, and obedient. From my studies of the viral-like agent with which you are so familiar from the past, I learned how to induce this condition in people not born that way. First we remove something essential, and then we give it back as a daily treatment. The combinations are infinite, so no two people have the same formulation. It must be made, uniquely, for each individual. Since only I know the codes for the formulations and cross-checks, everyone is very loyal and obedient to me."

"You may make me obedient, but there ain't no way you're ever gonna make me loyal," she retorted.

He laughed. "But that is the way I wish it. You see, almost everyone here is here because they are valuable to me and my organization. Security people, the staff here, maintenance, medical—you name it. Not to mention the scientists and technicians in my laboratories probing ever deeper into body and brain chemistry. Not you. You are simply one of my toys, a household item of furniture. For now, you have no other purpose than existence. You have already been treated, so you are— secure. I'm sure you know what that means."

She sighed, having expected it. "Yeah, I know."

"There are three main living floors and over sixty rooms in the Castle, as well as formal gardens in the back, pool and recreation area, that sort of thing. You have free reign of all the public areas, but will refrain from entering any private room unless taken there. I want you always on public view. Sleep where you wish, eat when you like. It will take you quite some time to get to know the place, but you have a nearly infinite amount of that. The lower areas and laboratories are secured and off limits, but you will be prevented from entering them anyway. Be cooperative and obey your set of rules and you will avoid punishment. After the first few times with the electric whip or the shock gun you will not wish to be punished again."

She didn't like even the names of them.

"Now," he continued, "the rules. Your status here is no higher than, say, a pet in the house. You will keep out of the way. You will not interfere in anything. You will keep yourself clean and reasonably neat and will be told who to see and where to go to accomplish that. You will speak only when spoken to unless it is an emergency of some sort. As a sign of your status here you will wear no clothing at all. It is always either hot and dry or hot and wet here. You will be cooperative. If anyone here takes it into their head to fondle or feel you up, you will not only let them and not resist, you will convince them that you enjoy it. And if anyone has more in mind, you will do it with enthusiasm and accommodate their needs or wishes. You have no private quarters, or any quarters. When you are sleepy find a comfortable place in a public area and go to sleep. You will do no work, ask no favors, pry into any business or other activities nor ask any imprudent questions or exhibit curiosity, nor do any harm to anyone. Everyone understands this, and any infractions will be recorded and you will be sought out and punished. And we don't want to see any frowns, only nice, happy smiles. Any questions so far?"

She sighed. "No." He wanted to strip her of her dignity, have her parade helplessly around as an object lesson, and reduce her to a kind of static hell. It showed just how his mind worked.

"Good. Now, once a day someone will come to you and give you the supplement you now require. Your own personal formulation, I remind you. No one else's would do you any good. We have a machine that dispenses them once a day for everyone. There are no reserves. I am sure you know how to give it to yourself. You had practice. The withdrawal is fully as bad as you remember it, and as lethal in the end. Remember that. And please do not think of harming yourself. Someone will always be watching—somewhere."

"You will never totally own me," she said evenly, and meant it.

"Oh, I will, and I'll know when. When you finally and totally give up, surrender. When you then ask me, beg me, for a better drug, a stronger drug, that will take your mind away, then it will be complete. And depending on my mood, perhaps I will give it to you, and watch you administer it to yourself. And it will happen—sooner or later."

"Never," she replied, teeth clenched. "Never."

He gave a sigh, then concluded, "I will leave you now, and an aide will take you out and teach you the essentials. You might not see me again, but I will see and hear of you. Dream of a rescue that won't come. Your husband is already in our hands but does not suspect that you are in mine. Even if he did he could not help you, but if he does not he can not even make the attempt. Your son is safe and well in his own home world and under family care, but remember that he is vulnerable. I know you are bright and resourceful and capable of self-sacrifice, but if you have any bright ideas and even *attempt* to betray this place, your son will bear the brunt of my anger. And if you try and kill yourself, I will replace you with him."

"You leave Dash out of this, you bastard!"

Carlos chuckled. "I intend to, for now. The Company, not I, makes war on children. He is out of my mind and plans—unless you give me cause to remember him. So, do nothing but be what I want you to be. In not too long from now, our grandest plan will be executed, and the Labyrinth itself will be destroyed, and I will no longer be able to touch your precious son—nor you to ever leave here. I must leave you now. This is a busy time. But I will be seeing you often."

With that, he turned and was gone. She couldn't see him, only hear his footsteps vanish in the distance, jackboots on tile, but she didn't need to see for that.

She sat up, but she felt sickened and depressed. He'd really got her this time, that son of a bitch! But, no. She couldn't give up. Not completely. Not on the strength of his words and his say-so. Maybe he was right about her, but if they were playing with Sam they still might get more than they bargained for, and maybe Sam at least could get back to Dash.

She already missed him so, and the idea of not ever seeing him again, not watching him grow up, was horrible. Still, that was out of her hands. Maybe ever escaping from this place was, too, but sometime, somehow, there must be something she could do to screw them up here. She would play their games, but she would not surrender.

More boots on the floor, coming towards her, but this time a woman just from the sound of it.

"Come with me," said a low female voice in tones cold as snow. "Take my hand. I have been ordered to orient you."

They went down some corridors and up some stairs and through some thick guard doors and finally were out in what felt like open space.

"This is the main front door that leads out to the entryway," her guide told her. "In front of you, facing into the Castle, is a grand staircase with ten steps leading to a 'Y' split on a landing, and then ten more in either direction. To your right, the lounge, with chairs, couches, wide windows, and the like. To your left are various public rooms. To the right of the staircase and behind it leads to dining rooms and then the kitchen. The same way but on the left and behind the stairs is the way to the recreation halls, and the rear exit to the gardens, tennis courts, swimming pool, and such. The carpets are raised or worn to all the areas. You will learn them. To ask for help is forbidden, but you may take it if offered."

"Thanks a lot," she said dryly.

"The second floor is a broad balcony leading to offices. You will not go in the offices on your own. Upper floors are private rooms. You are also not to go there on your own. You will remain on public view at all times. Sleep on the couches or rugs in the den or wherever you feel like it, but yield any space on demand. To eat, find and go to the kitchen. They will give you leftovers. Speak not at all to anyone unless directly addressed and a response is required. Be seen and not heard. Any infractions will be reported and punished immediately or at pill time, as we call it here. Do not search for your shot. We will find you. You will get it at the same time every day as you have been put on a schedule. You will begin to feel withdrawal after twenty-six hours, and no one has ever gone more than thirty or thirty-one hours. Now, come. We will go out by the pool and I will show you the bathrooms you may use and the showers.''

It took her several days of concentrated learning and lots of mistakes to get even the basics down, concentrating on the johns, the showers, and the kitchen and den area. At first she was highly self-conscious when she realized the large number of people here, but after a while she ignored the comments and snide remarks and decided that she'd just act like she wasn't this nude example and screw them.

They fed her in the area where they threw the garbage, just out back of the kitchen, and they fed her literal leftovers. Half-eaten fruit, remnants of bread, leftover stew, that kind of thing. When you were hungry enough you stopped asking questions and just ate it. Some of it wasn't half bad, although she was glad she couldn't really see it, and it included leftovers of beer and wine as well.

There were lots of problems initially, of course, when she did back talk or flinched when somebody started pawing her, and then she found out what the electric whip was like. It was a searing pain in a whip-like slash that felt like it was taking all the skin off you, but which left no marks and did no permanent damage. It was apparently not something for her benefit but a stock weapon of the guards to the sensitive areas and you didn't want it twice. She got it a lot more than that, though, as they tested her and deliberately tried provoking her and stringently enforced their rules.

It was a super incentive and she learned real fast.

That, really, was the most disheartening thing of all—how fast she'd become just what he had described. It was terrible how quickly pretending you didn't mind it when they fondled your breasts or put a hand on your crotch turned into reflexive, natural behavior. How easy it was to give sexual favors and indulge whatever they wanted and stick your mind in parking gear someplace. How the first day she went without punishment somehow seemed a great triumph when actually it was the first badge of their victory over her. That the easiest way to never be punished was to totally accept your condition and position and to not really think at all, to no longer mind being treated as an object and to even look forward to violations and indignities because they were at least attention. And how her face now seemed frozen in a nice, friendly smile.

She had always looked back on her Shadow Dancer time with some ego-inflating colorations. To her mind she'd resisted all the way, never given in, never surrendered. Now, of course, she was face to face again with the concept that it wasn't true, that they'd gotten her and put her through their remolder rather smoothly, and that this time it was happening again only much, much faster.

Part of it was the boredom. Yeah, they did a lot of fondling and kidding, but mostly she was ignored after a while as they got used to her and she got used to becoming Carlos' pet. It took her some time and effort to learn that carpeting, to learn the basic layout of the Castle and its public furnishings and the like, so that she could walk from one specific place to another without problems and felt comfortable there, but after that there was nothing else to do. Because she couldn't see, she couldn't read. Work of any sort was denied her, as was simple conversation with a staff who could also be punished for violating the rules over her. She was afraid of the pool, never having been much of a swimmer and not being able to see or have a companion there just was too scary to her.

About the only recreational stuff she could use was the exercise machines, which were individual and very much like a typical health club. She went at them with a passion, having nothing else. Every once in a while somebody would come and get her and they'd trim her nails and do her hair and somebody would give her a rough and easy physical, but that was it. And, once a day, somebody would come by and hand her one of those little automatic injection capsules, often without a word said. The stuff did give you a real rush for a while, although it was nothing like the intensity or duration of the old juice.

She slept when she wanted, ate when she wanted, and except for that capsule there was no sense of time at all. The place ran twenty-four hours in shifts, and there were always people around. Still, now that she was able to get around the place pretty well and confidently, and now that she'd picked up, identified, and classified more voices than she could count, the only thing she could do was listen. And people after the first week or so tended to talk as if she wasn't even there or capable of hearing. True, a lot of it was in languages she couldn't understand, but a fair amount was in English.

One thing she learned was that all the big

activity was due to something big that was going to happen in the near future. Carlos himself had said it the first day: they were going to destroy the Labyrinth and this world and all the others would be isolated and have to be self-supporting. And the only hitch was that some big shot in the enemy organization—but not Carlos, damn it—had been knocked off and nobody knew by whom.

That had given her something of a target at least. If they actually did it, then Carlos, whom she hadn't heard since that first day here, would be here all the time. More importantly, if they succeeded then Dash would be safe from him and his minions and she would no longer have a knife at her heart. If she was cut off, she might be able to kill the bastard before they cut her down, since she'd have nothing else to live for. That, however, would take some planning. An idle brain was the devil's playground, and she was nothing if not idle.

She also picked up something in idle gossip among the kitchen staff that she hardly believed. They said that Carlos himself was addicted to something. That he'd gotten hooked when trying to hook the Company, when playing with the alien viral drug to see what it could and would do. It made sense, in a way. If he'd been accidentally infected with the juice itself, he probably grew his own supply right here. She wasn't sure how she could use that, but it was fascinating, and seemed, somehow, poetic justice.

She remembered what that guide had said and wondered why it had been emphasized. A trap, maybe? Carlos wanted her to hate him, to dream of destroying him. She wouldn't put it past him, but it didn't matter. It was *something*. Delivery every twenty-four hours. Hold off on the pill, see how long before the first withdrawal symptoms set in. How long could she stand it? Maybe if she got on those exercise machines and beat hell out of them it would help. Take the thing only when she'd pushed herself and could stand it no longer. Then the next pill would be that much later before it wore off, and so on. If she could hold off 'til thirty hours she'd have an extra pill every four days. But where to hide the extra?

The best place was under the loose boards on the garbage dock. Usually nobody was there with her—she was getting quite good at that—and she was pretty damned sure there were no monitors there because that's where the kitchen staff would hang out and grumble. Palm a napkin, wrap the pills, hide them under. If they were still there in a couple of days she'd know she'd gotten away with it.

Timing the withdrawal was tough, but there were time signals in the gym and a couple of other places. Not that it mattered. She was going as long as she could, and the fact that she had pills sequestered and they were still giving her another each day was proof she was doing it. Really knowing this place, and with several days margin, she had potential for some freedom of action if and when the opportunity ever came.

And then there was the guy. She didn't know his voice and had no way to trust him, but he'd seen her and called her over and started playing with her as many often did, but then he leaned over and whispered, very softly, "Say nothing. I'm a courier, not one of these. I was told to find you and tell you to sit tight and be prepared. It might be a while but sooner or later they will try and get you out of here. Your injection can be duplicated if you have a sample. Say no more, let's just make out."

A trap? A plant? A tease on Carlos' part? How could it be anything else? Who could get in here, get so close, dare this sort of thing? But what if, just if, it wasn't? What if it was Sam?

But if it was—even if it was—how long until he could come for her? And could he get through to this fortress and find her still alive?

She had to wait, and endure, and, as time dragged on, not count on it.

And then there was the day when the whole place changed into Bedlam. There were more people around than she'd ever known before, and everybody seemed excited or angry or impatient, and all she could do was keep out of the way and try and learn what was going on.

Something about Upline batteries exploding prematurely. The Labyrinth was weak and partly wrecked over a fair length but still operable, but lots of switches were sealed and frozen shut and lots of sidings were wiped out as if they didn't exist. Some even said that the Company World had been sealed off and left powerless, but she took that with a grain of salt.

That would mean, though, that whatever happened took place "left" of Zero, since that was where the Company World was. That also suggested that this world, Carlos' world, was "right" of Zero, since everything seemed to be functioning okay here.

Certainly they weren't too sad about the "disaster," so maybe the Company World *had* been zapped. There was a lot of raucous celebrating and talks of when "they" would take over, that was for sure. She longed to ask questions, to find out details, but she could not. But, that night, they'd scheduled a big meeting in the rec hall to explain all to the staff. She was excluded, but she knew that area well. Hell, they'd have to use microphones or something, and if she just sat in the bathroom near the pool she could hear what was said. It was bound to be in many languages, but she would wait.

They sure all packed in there, anyway. It must have been hot as hell and looked like a sardine can, even though they were having the meetings by shifts and it was one shift at a time. Sitting on the toilet, though, she could make out most of what was being said.

"Fellow rebels, comrades, friends and associates!" It was one of the big guys here but not Carlos, and this guy was an English speaker. "Great news! I know you have heard all the rumors and we want you to know the truth. What at first looked like a horrible disaster to our cause has turned out to accomplish what none of us in all our years of work, sweat, and planning could accomplish! Most of you know of the grand project. Well, up line, left of Zero, one of our stations blew up. We do not yet know why, but it sent a massive surge of its own down and through the Labyrinth which set off others further along and built into a powerful wave. Like lava through a tunnel, it melted and sealed what it passed. When it struck the control regulators, they could not absorb the impact and sent it back up line. The result was to short out and seal in every single siding and bypass along the immediate route, although there is still clear traffic on the walking path only from here to there. Comrades—it sealed the Company World off and it severed their power connections by burning out their own private regulators. Their backups can not last long in there; certainly not long enough for them to punch back through. They are gone, but with much repair the Labyrinth will hold up.

"Friends! *We are the only remaining intact organization with Labyrinth access and control!*"

There were massive cheers and it sounded like they'd just won the World Series. It lasted for some time.

It was glorious news to them, but her own heart sank to the bottom. Not that she really felt for those Company folks, who seemed to embody only the worst attributes of Far Eastern culture with the sensitivity and caring of South African Boers, but for what it meant. If the Company was destroyed, cut off, then these bastards would begin openly taking over world after world, station after station, network after network. Hell, there'd be noplace to run to, noplace to hide, nobody out there strong enough to end a cesspool like this. Nobody with any kind of connections to find this place and care about rescuing her.

And, hell, before they turned them worlds into new cesspools they'd go after all the old Company folk they had grudges against. There'd be a lot more "examples" and revenge on folks like her, with nobody to stop them.

When they quieted down, the speaker continued, "No more hiding, no more skulking around. Already we have seized the remnants of the Company's communications and computer monitoring system. One by one we are going to take every switch and then every station in this sector while preventing any serious repairs on the other side. Then *we* will move there, and *we* will do our own repairs, and we will take control of the power and regulators and the entire network! Much work needs to be done, and much planning, and much sacrifice will yet be demanded of you, but final victory is ours! There is no one left large enough and organized enough to prevent us! Now we who worked so long and hard in what often seemed a futile cause will be the leaders of a new order among worlds, a new and glorious network of power, for *we* are now the Company!"

More cheers and building-rocking reactions. The Company folks were ruthless assholes on the whole but at least they did some good and left the worlds alone and worked within their systems. Not now. These were guys with a cause, and no matter how much their rhetoric sounded like well-intentioned revolutionaries their way of thinking was strictly high-tech black shirts and swastikas. The bad guys could lose a thousand times; the good guys could only afford to lose once.

And for her? What was the use any more? Shit, she'd been kidding herself anyway. She was naked and under almost constant watch and she was blind as a bat to boot, only able to see smeary colored light and dark. Even if she got Carlos alone, what could she do? He was pretty good at fighting when he had to be, she guessed, and he could see. He'd never be alone with her, unmonitored, without strong boys close by. And now that psychotic druggist had Sam and her and Dash and all the worlds in his pocket. Tears streamed down her face, and she never felt so helpless and powerless in her life.

She got up, with a sudden urge to get away from that cheering mob, and went towards the gardens. It was pitch dark but she no longer even thought about that. She knew the way, every twist, turn, pathway and stone, so well she didn't even have to think about it.

She in fact preferred the darkness. It was the one element where she had some superiority, and there was a lack of confusing blurs to get in the way. The gardens smelled pretty, even at night, and there weren't any people around this time, although as public area it was within her rules to be here. Sure, they had the place monitored. Infrared, you name it. They knew just exactly where she was. She knew she'd reached the point that Carlos had predicted, and, thanks to events, sooner than even he had expected by a long shot.

She couldn't run away. There was no longer anyplace she could reasonably run to or anybody who could help her. The old organization would still be around, of course, but they'd be far too busy for her problem and maybe just as hard to find—and who was she kidding? She couldn't manage a hundred yards from the compound, let alone somehow get through that security and switch.

She couldn't kill herself. The Labyrinth remained open, the power on. It was damaged, but intact. You couldn't run the cargo cars but you could walk in the usual tunnel. She had no doubt that he would do as he threatened with Dash, even if she was no longer around to know it. He was just that sort. Oddly, there was a sense of perverted honor about him, too, as if the devil always kept his bargains. She sensed, somehow, that if she did not give him cause that he really would never bother Dash, maybe even protect him.

But as much as she wanted that happy pill to mental oblivion, she was never going to beg him for it. Never.

But with all hope crushed, there was only this endless existence whose only purpose was to save Dash from Carlos. That was purpose enough, to endure.

"Ah choo!" Sam Horowitz went, and then brought up a big handkerchief and blew his nose.

"You are the only human being I've ever met who actually goes 'ah choo' when he sneezes," Bill Markham remarked, without looking up from the papers spread out in front of him.

"Well, it's little wonder I got it," Sam replied. "I went from sub-zero cold to the dry Labyrinth, then to the tropics, then to the high Himalayas or someplace like that, wound up in a tropical place where they made me parade around stark naked, then damn near got blown up in freezing cold on my own doorstep. I probably got double pneumonia."

"Well, you're not going to be the one to make the dramatic rescue, I'll say that. I can just see you getting all the way in there, bypassing all their neat security, and just before you reach your objective you sneeze like mad. About all you'd accomplish would be that in two weeks or so everybody there would have your cold."

"Damn it, Bill, I gotta be there. She'll need somebody she trusts and it won't be easy as it is."

"I'll go in," Markham told him. "I won't have your symptoms for days yet." He sighed and said, "Okay, now let's see what we got one more time."

They were on a rocky island perhaps seventy miles from Carlos' Castle, but they'd been there a while and they knew the layout now. A team of twenty was on hand, all hand-picked experts, and more were ready in support as needed. So far the documents "Pandross" had provided had panned out perfectly. A crossover world from a known Company siding led to a weak point on this one that had a solid security shield—which meant nothing if you had the exact bypass procedures going in. Carlos, secure that nobody even knew the rough location of this siding or world, would never have dreamed that anybody could come at him this way.

The region "left" of Zero, as you looked at a Labyrinth map, was a real mess, including Sam's old substation, of course. But that had been the first blast and had gone inward from there, so the main line up from Sam's siding hadn't been much affected. McInerney, Oregon, was still in business.

This would have been tough, maybe impossible, if Carlos had hid out inward on that same damaged side, but he hadn't. He was "right" of Zero, which was neither touched nor involved in the blast. It was certainly wired for the grand project, but even now opposition crews were dismantling those. It didn't seem to be clear that Sam and sabotage had caused the misfiring; apparently the Council had associated it rather with the timing test. Without Mancini to tell them any different, and with their own computer to suggest that very scenario—and also to pinpoint Sam somewhere else—it was a given. They knew that Sam had escaped, some-how, in the big bang, but now he no longer concerned them.

"It appears that the cliff was actually dug out, and the labs and complex below were built in the excavation, then the Castle on top of the complex, and dirt and such re-used to reform the land as it was. Most of the cliff is actually artificial," Mark-ham noted. "See, here are the intake and outake ducts for the fusion reactor. We figure four one-man aquasubs, each carrying a single electron torpedo, hitting in this region, will cause the whole damned reactor to go up. He's still using primitive steam turbines here so there's probably enough pressure in there to blow that whole cliff halfway to here."

"Easy to do," Sam agreed, "but the trick is to get Brandy out first. She's set up as some kind of sex slave, always in public areas, always in public view."

Markham nodded. "So we need a diversion. We've got his switch location, we don't need it to get in or out, so let's blow it to Hell. It'll cause pandemonium in there, set off every security alarm in this world, and there ain't gonna be a soul there thinking one whit about Brandy. Me and two backups dressed in their security uniforms could get in with no trouble. Nobody is going to question us, and Brandy's too smart not to go along if her mind's still in one piece. If it isn't we'll knock her cold and *carry* her. We'll go over the cliff and down over here if we can; if not, we'll fire a flare when we're clear in the jungle and they'll let 'er rip. Then we'll make our way down to the beach well clear and get picked up."

"Sounds too easy. What if she doesn't have an unused capsule?"

"I've got a biomedical team standing by. No guarantees, but they might be able to sustain her with what the medical computers can dig out of her tissue samples or bloodstream. At least we can sedate her until we find something. No guarantees, Sam."

He nodded. "I understood that from the start. I think she'd rather die trying than stay that way anyway. What about Carlos? If he's in there he's sure to have his own back door exit point somewhere and a way of getting there, and we don't know the whole territory. If he puts two and two together and smells us, he'll take Brandy as insurance. I keep remembering what happened one time before."

"We can't cover everything, Sam. If this data is right, and so far it has been, there are no weak points anywhere on that main island other than the old substation, and nowhere in the plans here does it show either a boat dock or anyplace to hide a chopper or similar thing. Maybe he's too confident to have a back door. Or maybe he's got some way to make it to the nearest one, which is ours, and which will make life easy. Look, the crescent moon doesn't rise until after three tonight and we got scattered clouds. I say we go in and do it, tonight, before anything has a chance to fall apart, including my nerve."

Sam nodded. "All right. I'll be stationed at the pickup point and coordinate communications." He paused. "Bill—thanks. And no matter how it comes out, I understand and will always appreciate this."

Markham seemed slightly uncomfortable. "No big deal, Sam. If we don't take them out fast they're gonna take us out slow. It's a whole new ball game. Come on, let's go over the thing with the rest of the team. If we're going tonight we have to have those aquasubs armed and in position by then, which means they have to leave in maybe two hours. And we have to give a go to the demolition team on the switch."

She had pretty much ceased to think. In her mind, if all she had left was keeping Dash from harm and that was accomplished by being absolutely and perfectly what Carlos wanted then that was all there was. The conversation was still all around her, but she tuned it out. It was just noise to her, and not a word really registered. None of it mattered any more, and even curiosity had died.

When she was sleepy she found an out-of-the-way corner and slept. When she was hungry she went back to the kitchen and they gave her stuff. When anybody wanted to feel her up or wanted a backrub or wanted to screw or wanted anything else she did it expertly, happily, without complaint. If she got bored she wandered in and worked out, mostly because it seemed to please the regulars and was now an approved activity. All of it was essentially automatic, impulsive, without any direction or purpose, her own mind just sitting in neutral somewhere as if asleep, no longer required.

She was just sitting there in the parlor that evening, waiting to be of use to anybody who wanted what she could offer but not anticipating anything at all, kind of half dozing, when suddenly the windows shook and the ground rumbled slightly and all sorts of loud and unpleasant alarms went off all over the place.

The feeling and the noise and the sudden shouting and running all over the place frightened her, but she didn't move, just sat there, trying to keep out of the way, not even wondering or caring what it was all about.

Around her, the place was sheer bedlam. Every light, interior and exterior, came on, and there were bells, buzzers, sirens, flashing lights, and people running everywhere and shouting to one another trying to figure out what was going on and where the hell they should be.

The guards to the secure areas stood their places on the main floor, doubly alert for trouble, but the place otherwise emptied out fast, as large numbers of staff ran down one side towards the substation area, which in the darkness seemed to have some smoke and flames rising out of it.

Suddenly there was a man near her, and he bent down and said, "Brandy; come with me."

She smiled and took his hand and got up, impulsively.

"Brandy, for God's sake it's Bill Markham!" the man hissed. "Snap out of it! We're going to get you out of here!"

Something vaguely registered at that, but she wasn't sure what or why and she grew confused.

"Do you have any extras of your drug capsules hidden around?" he asked her.

She smiled and nodded. Yes, indeed she did.

"Take me to them."

Markham knew that there was something wrong with her, whether drug induced or otherwise he

373

didn't know, but that didn't matter. Time was wasting.

She led them through the now deserted kitchen, out back, then counted the boards, reached down, popped one up, reached in, and brought out the handkerchief with the capsules in them and held it up to him proudly, like a cat proudly showing off the mouse he'd just killed or a kid showing her secret and most favorite toy.

Markham took the pills and stuck them in his pocket, then turned to the other two. "Off that way. We want to be as far away as possible as quickly as possible. Anybody gets in the way, don't bluff— shoot 'em."

He took her by the hand and they started off, but he wanted to try again. "Brandy—Sam's okay. He's here. Dash is safe, too. It's all right."

The words bounced around in her. *Sam's okay.*
. . . Dash is safe . . . Dash safe . . .

Several people saw them as they went, but such was the power Carlos had over the place that, even now, they couldn't conceive of properly uniformed men with a familiar woman not being official.

Inside the Castle security headquarters they were going nuts trying to determine just what had happened. In the meantime, all hundred-plus security monitor alarms seemed to be going off at once, which made for less than ideal conditions.

A senior officer got sick of it, inserted his key, and reset the alarm system, bringing a bit of quiet to the place.

"Near as we can tell, somebody tried to blow their way into the substation," a sergeant was telling someone on the red phone. "No, they couldn't get in, but they sure as hell blew the

374

switch. It's gonna take weeks before anybody could get in or out of there—if we got all the parts. No—they couldn't get in. The security system clamped down instantly.''

A monitor alarm sounded again. The officer sighed and got out his reset key again, but the sergeant on the phone glanced up out of habit at the one that was sounding. "Hold on. Something funny *is* happening. South side of the Castle. Looks like some of our guys taking that black bitch outside the perimeter. That's funny . . . Huh? Yes, sir. *Personally?* Well, all right, if you say so. I'll send a squad to cover. Right. Yes, sir.''

He hung up the phone and turned to the others. "The Doc thinks we got penetrated somehow. That they're tryin' to get the bitch out.''

The officer jumped up. "Send full forces there! Seal 'em off. Take 'em alive if need be!''

"Hold it, Cap," the sergeant responded. "He said he's gonna take a squad and do it himself. Just send cover to make sure they don't have a lot more out there in the bushes.''

Up on the cliff, Markham was concerned about Brandy but also relieved by the ease with which it had all gone off. If he could just get her down that cliff to the water for pickup he'd let the medics handle the rest.

They had prepared the exit, as any good burglar does, before breaking in, and it was still there and still undisturbed. At the last minute Sam had insisted on some kind of rope ladder rather than just a rope. Brandy, after all, wouldn't be able to see and might not be in the best shape for a climbdown of maybe a hundred and ten feet. They had also picked a point where there was effectively no beach, and the water below was fairly deep. If she or any of them fell, there was a chance that they wouldn't be dashed against sand or rocks. At the bottom and just to one side, tied to a piton stuck in the rock, was a rubber raft with a small but fast motor on it.

"Harry, you go down first, unhook the raft and be ready to start the engine—but don't start it yet," Markham said to one of the other men, who nodded and immediately went over the side. He then picked up a climber's belt with hook already left there for this, put it on, then took another one over to Brandy and put it snugly around her waist. She resisted it, but not much, confused as to what was the right thing to do. The third man uncoiled and handed him the safety line, then said, "Go ahead. I'll cover and come down last. Don't wait if you hear any shooting."

Markham had just threaded the rope around his own loop and was about to do Brandy's, when he heard a voice behind him; a rich, Latin-accented voice, say, "That will be quite enough, gentlemen. Put down your weapons and stand away. Brandy, come to me—*now!*"

She hesitated a moment, then walked away from Markham and towards the sound of Carlos' voice in the darkness.

Markham couldn't do a damned thing to help her, so he sighed and looked at his companion, then said, "He who fights and runs away . . ." and dove off the cliff top as something shot close to him.

His companion hadn't gotten the idea, and instead of throwing his gun away, Mark brought it up to fire. A blast caught him square in the chest and pushed him back off the cliff and down.

"I hear a motor down there!" one of the Castle security squad said, going to the edge. "They got a god damned *boat* in here!"

"Rapid-fire rounds for effect down there. You might get lucky and hit something," Carlos told them. "And cut that ladder loose."

He turned to Brandy, carefully removed her climbing belt, and tossed it away. There was the sound of a lot of gunfire, and he turned and shouted, "Cease firing! Cease firing, I say! Either you got them or you didn't by now. Either way they are no longer our concern." He took Brandy and caressed her face. "It is all right, girl. I will overlook the belt because you came when I called, but never, never allow anyone to put anything on you again."

"I hear more engines out there," one of the squad said. "Jesus! What they got out there? A friggin' *navy?*"

Carlos was suddenly concerned. "All of you— come with me! Fast! We may have won a minor skirmish here and lost the war. That way! As far away as we can get. Stick close to the coastline and be wary of enemy troops. *Andelé! Andelé! Move it!*"

The torpedomen in the water knew from their infrared sights that things had gone wrong, and they weren't about to wait any longer than the minimum for anybody who made it there to get clear. They had started their engines and were aligning their torpedoes now, so they had a crack at the place before somebody on shore got smart and launched some boats or something.

They fired their torpedoes, turned, and gunned their engines out of there and tried to get as far in the opposite direction from land as they could.

The torpedoes bore in with deliberate speed, their computer brains matching the picture of their target with the reality ahead and then to each other's speed for maximum effect. They struck, exactly where they were supposed to, simultaneously.

The base of the Castle cliff erupted in enormous fireballs, illuminated as well with dancing electrical displays of brilliant blue that seemed like living, snake-like monsters crawling all over and into the cliff face. All the lights in the Castle and perimeter, every thing of power up there, went abruptly dark, only enhancing the light show.

A sudden calm followed, as if the worst had been done, but then, abruptly, the entire cliff shook as if grabbed and shaken by a mighty hand, and then there was an explosion of such force that it was felt even by the fleeing agents well out to sea. The entire structure lifted up, then seemed suspended for a moment, then dropped back, collapsing in upon itself, making a massive structure fold and crumble as if made of sand, leaving in the end only a great depression where once the cliff had stood.

12.

Loose Ends

It was well hidden, way back in the jungle, beneath the ground and beneath the foliage, too, camouflaged against being obvious from any angle. It also wasn't fancy, but it opened for Carlos and Brandy.

When it was obvious that there was no additional enemy force further down, Carlos had sent the men back to establish a defensive position on the southern coastline. He wanted no one else to know where he was going now.

With the explosion that knocked them both to the ground and shook the very earth and everything on it, Carlos knew that any of the men who survived would realize that there was no going back now—and no pills tomorrow. They would spend a day frantically trying to find him, any not killed in the blast or knocked into the sea, but they would not, any more than the enemy would, and after that they'd be in too much misery to be any sort of threat. A little after that, they'd all be dead.

Carlos hadn't paid much attention to Brandy of late, but he had scanned a recent report from the security psych on her indicating that she'd cracked, flipped out. It didn't matter to him. In fact, that made things all the easier. He was pretty sure now, no matter what those damned computer analyses had said, that Sam was the one who'd blown the siding at his place and that Sam indeed was now after Brandy and her captor. That was why she was so important to him. That most of all.

He'd built this bunker himself, out of his own sense of paranoia, when he'd discovered how far any back door might be to this place. Nobody knew of it, nobody but he ever went here, and everyone who had designed and built it was dead, the records, plans, and the like destroyed.

The food was all in sealed vacuum canisters that would keep it for a century or more until needed. There was a water line in from an underground pump and a septic system to remove waste. The power, from a superior super battery system developed for the Company, had come on only when absolutely needed—until now when he turned it on. It was totally self-contained, and as long as he wasn't wasteful with it, there was enough power there to last for up to three years. He didn't expect to be here all that long, but he believed in thinking and planning ahead.

Being entirely underground, it was cool and comfortable, and the air system was basic but nearly impossible to spot unless you were looking for it.

"We will stay here, my sweet, and not move or make a sound outside for many long weeks. They will search, but find nothing, and eventually conclude that we perished in the blast of the Castle. Then, only after all is gone and we are the only two humans here, even if it takes a year, we will go to where I have a boat hidden and we will go to my back door and we will take our rightful place among the alternate Company, or I will build a new organization and opposition from scratch if I must." He looked at her and sighed. The report had said she hadn't spoken since she cracked. "And you don't even know what I'm talking about, do you? It doesn't matter, my sweet. Not a bit."

He looked around the place, found a compartment in the wall, and opened it, then checked it with some relief. "Ah! Do not worry that we no longer have your little pill, my dear. In here is something much better, something familiar that will correct the imbalances I induced and make things quite nice. I need it, too, you see, but don't worry. There are over a thousand capsules here, and plenty more once I am again free to roam. This little stuff will keep us both healthy, fix what ails us, and keep us very happy here."

He relaxed and started to undress, then snapped his fingers. "Spare clothes! Of all the things I forgot! Ah, well, we shall both be *au natural* for a while, then. Come! We will take our first joint 'fix' together and have an hour of relaxing bliss, followed by a lengthy time of conjugal magic. What more could one ask in a hideout, eh?"

It was one of the ultimate ironies of the situation that the "juice," as she had called the alien viral agent when previously hooked on it by those in Carlos' organization, would this time be the best thing Brandy could have.

The organism, a symbiote, immediately set up housekeeping in the brain and then began rearranging all the interior furniture to suit itself with an eye to making it the ideal long-term place to live. Once it determined the way brain and body worked, it was in some ways far superior to not having it there. The body, all of it, worked better. You developed a taste for and ate just the right amount of what was good for you. It cleaned out the arteries, monitored cholesterol levels, strengthened muscle, trimmed fat, and made you incredibly efficient. It wasn't that it was truly intelligent; it was just as adaptable as hell.

The enormous rush as new agent was fed in to replace and replenish the old, who could not reproduce in the normal way inside a Type Zero human body, caused direct stimulation of the pleasure center so you were highly rewarded for doing it regularly. It was also a tremendous shock, that reawakened all the old memories and sensations of the old addiction.

In its native Type Three world, it reproduced when you did, exchanging material during the sexual act and renewing itself that way. That didn't work in Type Zeros, but, of course, it wasn't smart enough to realize that, so when you woke up you were incredibly turned on. Only after that were you somewhat on your own, in a glow-like high but mind sharp, thoughts clear, and hungry for what was good for you.

Of course, one of the first things it also did was order the brain to begin making again those key enzymes Carlos' process had blocked. This one would allow no other addictions.

She didn't come back to anything near normalcy right away. It was a slow process, but each time she got a new jolt more and more of it came back, more and more was shocked back into consciousness. Even when it began, some sixth sense inside her told her not to betray this to Carlos.

Between the shock of the drug and her own

fixation, she realized what she had to do—if she could physically manage to do it. She had hoped that the efficient little bug in the juice would clear up her sight, but while she mentally *thought* there was some slight improvement, she realized it wasn't going to be like last time and if her vision could be cleared up it would take a great deal of time.

She would have to wait until Carlos made another mistake.

Carlos had thought of everything in terms of escaping a threat. The hideout wasn't all that comfy, but it would do, and all the necessary basics were there for a very long siege. In spite of small lapses such as forgetting the extra clothes, he'd pretty well prepared for every eventuality except one.

He was an active man, a compulsive worker whose mind was always on things and who was used to doing, not sitting. He could sit for days without complaint; for a few weeks progressively chafing under the sheer boredom of the existence, but after a while he just couldn't stand it any more. He had to get out. He had to do something.

The first couple of times he left the bunker were relatively brief; just testing how much heat was on and getting out of those confines. He did not take her with him on either foray; if there was any danger still lurking out there, he didn't want to be bogged down with her.

And he continued to talk to her, because there wasn't anyone else to talk to.

"It looks quite desolate, my sweet," he commented after the first time. "No sign of life out there that's not native. I think tomorrow I will risk going further south and see how our getaway boat is faring. If they found it, or destroyed it, then it will complicate matters a great deal."

It was mostly an excuse for him to really be doing something, but it began what she hoped would be an opening.

He didn't put on all his clothes when he went out; she checked by going over to the small storage area and finding the bulk of them still there. He did, however, wear his increasingly rancid underpants, as if this kept him somehow civilized and superior, and his gun and gunbelt—just in case. He apparently didn't want to risk the clothing on such clandestine journeys, saving it for when he would be back in civilized society again.

Also just in case, he took one capsule of the juice with him. The addict never wanted to be caught short, although the last thing he wanted to do was have to use it while out there. That was okay. One night she delayed taking her own fix just long enough for him to go into ecstasy, got up, found the gunbelt, and found the spare capsule. She replaced it right then and there with the empty one he'd just used and put the fresh one back in the carton.

Each outside foray made him bolder and bolder, and they increased in length. Now he was leaving her alone most of the afternoon, and not returning until close to time to sleep. She finally decided that the time had come to bet it all. He was beginning to talk about moving out, moving everything to the boat, being ready to move.

He was clever. He might have outfoxed her, and she might well lose it all acting now, but to do nothing was to let him win, and there didn't seem to be any reason not to try. She did not regret coming to him back on the cliff, even though it wasn't a conscious decision at the time, because they already had the drop on Bill and there would have been no escape anyway. It was up to her, and if there was a God somewhere He would ultimately allow this justice.

She, too, had been out of the bunker, after she realized how long he was going to be away and how far it must be to the boat. She didn't know the area and so couldn't go far, but the sound of breakers off in one direction gave her orientation, as did the hidden entrance to the bunker, and she began to pace off and get to know the immediate area. It was sufficient for her purposes.

She didn't really know enough, but hate was a great fuel for determination and she certainly knew how juice addicts acted and thought and she was pretty damned sure she understood Carlos and his ego.

When he returned the one night he was in particularly good spirits and talking about moving out in the next couple of days. He had spun grand plans after his escape, and she would be both his insurance policy and bait for grand schemes in the future. They ate out of the containers, and he complained as usual about the quality and looked forward to fine food once again, and revenge on those who had snatched the sweetness of victory from under his very nose.

Finally, he went to the cupboard to get their juice capsules, opened it . . .

And found that the cupboard was bare.

Instantly he realized what had happened and flew into a rage, grabbing her and slapping her back onto the bed.

"So, you've been acting lately!" he roared. "Yes —the drug. Of course. I should have thought of that. But it won't do you any good! Now—where did you hide them?"

Her voice sounded hoarse and cracked from all the long time of disuse, but she managed. "Gone. I've been busy. Flushed them all down your damned septic tank where they're meltin' into useless goo with the shit."

More slaps and violent reactions, which she expected. Right now she didn't resist; she might try later, for what it was worth, but right now the pain his rage caused was nothing as compared to the pleasure it was giving her to see him this way.

"Liar!" he screamed. "No addict could bring herself to do that! Never in all my experience was anyone hooked on it able to bring themselves to do that. Now—*where did you hide them?*"

"No addict before ever had this much cause for willpower," she responded. "Yeah, I'll die and I'll hate myself for it, but I juiced up early, as early as it would let me. I'll get to hear you suffer and groan a long time before it hits me."

The evenness of her tone, the sense of total satisfaction in her voice, unnerved him. It would be hours before he would feel the first pangs of withdrawal and demands from his microbic masters to be fed, but that was physiology. Psychologically, he was beginning to feel withdrawal right now.

He abandoned her and started tearing the place

apart. She didn't know what if anything would be left by the time he got through.

Then, suddenly, he stopped, getting hold of himself. "You have undone only yourself," he told her with some satisfaction. "Carlos never puts all his eggs in one basket." He picked up the gunbelt where he dropped it, fumbled in its hidden compartment with nervous, shaking hands, and brought out a capsule. She heard what he was doing, and smiled.

"I found that one," she told him. "I got up earlier'n you. That's an empty. No good. I found the others you squirreled around, too. Flushed them with the rest."

Normally he wouldn't have exposed himself, but it was the addict's mind working now, not the full and rational Carlos. She understood that mind and exactly what was going through his head far better than he did. He'd been accidentally hooked in early experiments; she'd undergone it all before and knew the awful dependency and the terrible psychology of the addict firsthand, rather than by observation and clinical reports. In fact, if it wasn't giving her such perfect pleasure she'd be getting the shakes herself from just being in his company. But the juice was wrong. It didn't induce perfect pleasure. It had been defeated in her once by love, and hate seemed to work just as well.

He pressed the capsule to his flesh—and found it empty as promised.

He flew into a rage, threatening, roaring, and then, getting hold of himself as much as he could, he started back on her.

"I will kill you," he snarled. "I know you did not

387

destroy the capsules. You could not! We will see what kind of pain you can endure before you tell me!"

"A lot," she responded. "You taught me, remember? I'm your experiment. You said you wanted me to feel like you felt. You wanted me to be consumed by hate. How much pain can *you* stand, Carlos? How much withdrawal before you take that gun and shoot yourself? You know I can't have hidden nothin'! Where? I can't see, damn you! This bunker has been the only place I could get around in."

"Liar! Bitch! Whore!" he screamed. "You may have got rid of most but you kept something. You wanted to be sure to be here when I died! I know how to make you tell! No one is *that* strong!"

And then the beating and torture began. Now she resisted, fought back, showing surprising strength against him, but she couldn't see and he was larger, stronger, and more experienced in the ways of inflicting pain. She knew in the end she couldn't hold out indefinitely, but the longer the better.

"One capsule!" he screamed at her. "That's all I need! One capsule! One fix and I can leave this cursed place and get to my stashes in the Labyrinth! I know you have at least one! Where? Where?"

And the pain finally grew too much, and she screamed, "All right! All right! There is one—just one—left! I hid it outside!"

He picked her up, and shoved her against the wall. She felt weak, her body bruised and battered, and she tasted blood at the corner of her mouth, but she had one satisfaction. Her hurts would be quickly repaired; the juice was real efficient at that. His hurt was inside, in his head, and even though he still really wouldn't be feeling one major physical symptom of withdrawal, in his mind he was already half gone.

She led him outside into the darkness, and for a moment considered attacking him here and now, or running off if she could into the dark jungle, but she knew she just didn't have it in her. That wasn't the plan. No, that wasn't the plan.

She found the main air intake by counting steps, dug down on one side, and came up with a small used food container, its top bent back over to somewhat seal it.

He had a light and he shined it on her as she got it out, and then he ran to her with a cry and snatched it violently out of her hands, knocking her down, lest she toss it into the jungle or something. His mind was no longer on her, on where they were or the conditions involved. It was past all rationality, and well ahead of schedule.

He pried the container open with shaking hands, shook its contents out into his hand, and came up with a capsule.

"Ha! Now you see!" he screamed at her triumphantly. "Now it is reversed! You will withdraw and rot here tomorrow while I take the boat alone to freedom! And the first thing I'm going after is that bastard kid of yours!" And, with that, fumbling with the capsule, he pressed it to his skin right out there in the opening.

It unloaded its contents and he felt near instant relief. All was right, all was good, and his microbial masters pushed their reward button in his brain. A broad smile swept across his face and he sank down on the forest floor and began to writhe in ecstasy.

She allowed a few minutes to pass, just to make sure that the ever-clever Carlos wasn't tricking her one more time, then got up and made her way back inside the bunker.

Carlos had really trashed the place, and she stumbled several times and fumbled for what seemed an eternity before coming up with the gunbelt and gun he'd dropped. She removed it, flicked it on, heard the low whine telling her it was fully charged. She flipped the little switch all the way to the top, holding in the safety button so it would go to maximum charge.

Then she made her way back out, oblivious of the pain she was feeling, and found him again. He wasn't hard to find; the moans and sighs were clear to her and genuine. She got down on her hands and knees, fearing that even now something would go wrong, that something would turn and destroy the moment, but she reached him without incident and felt his head.

She took the pistol, held it square against that head, and without even a moment's hesitation she blew his brains out.

Then she lay there, near him, for quite a long while, hearing only the sounds of the jungle and the far-off crash of breakers.

Brandy had no idea if anybody from the Company was still around. Certainly Carlos hadn't thought so, but it was the only hope she had. She wanted out, wanted to see Sam and Dash again, wanted it over, but even if she were to eventually die here on this now desolate and deserted world it had been worth it.

The remaining food in the bunker and the carton of juice capsules, retrieved from where she'd hidden them exactly a hundred paces north of the main air intake vent under some big, leafy plants, would sustain her for quite a while. Even if it took the two and a half years her supplies would last, she wasn't going to give up. Not again. Not ever. And if she eventually died, well, she would die fighting.

It took her several days just to work out a safe route to the shoreline from the bunker with any confidence that she could get back again. She used Carlos' knife to cut notches, used empty food containers, pieces of broken up furniture, anything, to mark as permanent a path as she could for the half-mile or so distance to the coast.

She had no thought of finding the boat. Carlos was very good at hiding things, and it wouldn't have done her any good if she had. It probably wasn't much of a boat anyway; just some powered raft that would get him where he had to go. Even if it had been a cabin cruiser, though, she couldn't see to pilot it and she had no idea where to take it anyway.

The best way was to stay right here, find what she could, and build a smoky fire each night and hope that somebody was still around to see it. The beach was an easy access and piled with driftwood, although the stuff was often damp and hard to ignite. For the first few times, a low jolt with the pistol did wonders, and after that she found a cache of gasoline or something in the bunker that worked just as well once she laboriously hauled it to the beach area. Carlos had *almost* thought of any eventuality, even the batteries going dead.

In the meantime, all she could do was build and then sit by the fire every night weather permitted, then make her way at daybreak back to the bunker, take her juice, get some sleep, eat, and start it all over again.

She didn't really expect rescue—even through her brain fog she could remember that explosion—and if it did come there was no guarantee whether it would be Company people, if there still were any, or Carlos's friends, but she was determined to go along with it as long as supplies permitted.

A couple of times she thought she heard some motor sounds out in the ocean, but it wasn't clear whether they were for real or just wish fulfillment, imagination, or whatever. Real or fancied, they didn't seem to see or at least want to investigate the glow of the fire.

The routine went on and on, and she endured, as always. She deliberately didn't count the days, though; she really didn't want to know.

Finally, one day, near dawn, when she was about to pack it in and go back to the bunker, she heard something. At first she just dismissed it as more imaginations, but she kept hearing it, getting closer and closer, and for the first time she realized that somebody else was actually out there.

As the motor sound came up to the edge of the water and then was cut, she stood, looking out in that direction although she couldn't see it, waiting, a mixture of fear and relief inside her. One way or another, for good or evil, it was ended.

She heard someone fumbling with something, then the sound of someone coming towards her, among the mass of wood on the beach.

"Hello!" she called nervously, her voice cracking.

"Hang on, babe, I'm coming!" she heard a familiar voice respond, one not heard in a very long time.

She felt tears well up inside her and she shook and quivered, fearing that she hadn't heard what she had. "S—Sam?" she managed, limply.

And now he was right up to her. "You didn't think I'd ever give up the hunt, did you?" he asked her gently.

She threw her arms around him and cried and cried, and he just held her tight.

Sam shined a light on Carlos' remains but only briefly. It was a hulk crawling with—well, he didn't want to know.

"They packed it in a month ago, but I been coming back here with a small security force every chance I could get. We were pretty damned sure that nothing got off this world and no powered vehicles went as well, and we knew from Bill you couldn't have been too far away when the joint blew. I figured that he had to be hiding out waiting for us to leave, but that he'd go nuts and make a break—we have every single possible exit covered. When time dragged on, though, I got worried, and I started patrolling hundreds of miles of this coastline, along with a lot of other security people when they could be spared. They thought I was nuts, insane, after all this time, but I knew you better than that."

"Bill—he's all right?"

"He had some damage from that dive, but not anything serious. Not for Penn's former diving team captain. He almost made the Olympics once, he keeps telling us. Yeah, he's okay. A big wheel now, too. On the new Board. Things have changed a lot."

"The others—the ones with Carlos. You got them, too?"

"Uh uh. Not a prayer. The way it's working out is that they have a fair chunk of this side—I'm under super-heavy guard and such when I come up here—and we retain most of the other, with lots of pockets and islands in the other's territory. It's a whole different ball game. Come on—let's get you home, or what's passing for home these days."

"Sam—he stuck me on the juice again."

"I figured as much. Don't worry about it. We'll bring some of this supply to tide you over, but we can get a nearly limitless supply from the biomed people. Remember, we never really played with this shit on the Company world—too dangerous. I won't put you through more risks to health and sanity by kicking it again. It's the non-communicable variety, since that's what infected Carlos way back when, and there's ways to even grow your own. Kind of like methadone maintenance. You'll have your own and nobody ever has to know."

On the way back he filled her in on everything that had happened, and how, and why. She was amazed to learn the extent of the plot and his own side, upset at the idea Dash had been kidnapped, and almost as upset to think that their farm was no more, but all that paled. She was back and she was home again and this was better than she'd ever dreamed. She never wanted to go in the Labyrinth or visit another world again.

Sam Horowitz went down to the Company security area one afternoon months later and picked a totally secure terminal. He'd been meaning to do if for quite some time, but it had been a crowded and busy period.

First there was designing and building the new place, and making it secure. They picked a small Caribbean island, one the Company owned. Not real big, but there was some high ground. It hadn't been inhabited because there was no water source, but that was easy for the high-tech wizards to fix, and provide power as well. Brandy helped design the whole place and it was not just for them but separate nice quarters for a few other families carefully chosen and with kids Dash's age. There would be their own small school, and there was enough kids for a gang although they made a very small class, and it was totally secure. Sam saw to that.

Not that they would be prisoners there; there was a helipad and 'copter available, and it was only a few hours to Florida or a few more hours back up to Pennsylvania. But trips could be planned and worked out with Company security to reasonably assure as much safety as possible.

And since there was no station or substation within a thousand miles, the only threat they couldn't do anything about was the possibility of hurricanes, but they could build for that.

Dash even had two Mommies, in a way. His own, and the one who'd replaced his real one for "the bad guys." There wasn't much trouble telling them apart, except maybe on the phone or overhearing a conversation without seeing the speaker. Brandy's eyes had not cleared up; in fact, the "juice" seemed to have given up on them and just shut down that system. It was a minor setback in an otherwise unexpectedly happy resolution and she didn't waste any tears on it. The island and the main house were designed with her in mind, and it would take an expert to even realize she was blind.

She was also in tremendous shape, a byproduct both of her existence back at the Castle and of the efficiencies of the drug, looking years younger, trim, athletic, and working to keep that way. That, in fact, was the initial problem—the other Brandy, who could see, looked more like Mom than Mom did to Dash. He finally settled it by deciding that he was the only kid in the world with *two* Mommies and that two was much better than one.

It was also useful to have a duplicate Brandy around. It allowed some extra protection, and allowed Dash trips further afield than his own mother might feel comfortable going.

The fact was, though, that Brandy, the *real* one, was home, safe, with those she loved also there and safe, and she had no more taste for adventures.

Sam, however, found himself a bit busier. With a new Board, composed of the top non-Company world managers, and a new computer link that seemed to be working well, he found himself appointed chief of security for Company operations on this world. What with satellites, jet 'copters, and computer links he could and did as much as possible from home.

With the Labyrinth basically repaired, commerce resumed, although on a more limited scale.

They had millions of tons of surplus computer chips alone to ship out of Oregon and they'd be a long time catching up with the demand down the line. Now, too, they were facing in many areas something the old Company had never faced before—not a small underground opposition, but true competition on all levels, sometimes down and very dirty. Nobody had complete, secure control of an entire Labyrinth main line segment any more, and neither side had sufficient forces to knock the other out. It had become true competition, then, with victories measured in little gains, and in a way it seemed healthier.

Sam closed off the door to the secure terminal area and sat back in the chair.

"All right," he sighed, "it's time. I've been meaning to do this for a long time and now it's finally time. I know you can hear me, and this is secure on my end so I know you can make it secure the rest of the way. Speak to me. What the hell's the difference? If I ever actually told them the complete truth they'd lock me away in a loony bin anyway."

For a moment the screen was blank, but then it suddenly typed, "All right—so what?"

"How does it feel to be a god, Pandross? The god of both sides in this unholy game of commerce?"

"I am content," the screen responded.

"I got to hand it to you," he admitted. "No human mind could ever have figured this out and made it work, let alone sustained the current conditions. I mean, the Company, the Opposition, they both have the same access to the same computer net, only they don't realize it. Why not merge them? We could do without some of the personalities involved, particularly on the competition's side."

"Every G.O.D. requires a Satan. That is what turned the Company race into the vegetative, cold, and distant folk they became. G.O.D. had no rival, no real threat, anyway. They had no incentive to do it better, cheaper, more efficiently; no pressure to make their power and traffic go both ways and help the people and worlds they exploited. The new system does just that. The Board itself is composed of senior managers who were products of their own diverse worlds, politics, economic and cultural values, etc. That diversity alone assures a better, more understanding and compassionate Company. The fact that if they do not do it better and retain the loyalty of the locals on whom they depend that the opposition will exploit their lapses and cost them keeps them on their toes."

"Uh huh. Well, maybe it's better. It's certainly no worse. I'm still not thrilled with the likes of Voorhes and particularly Valintina out there, though."

"Valintina has made it a personal vow to some-day get you and make you into a pet boy," the computer told him. "She is delighted by the turn of events and now controls their Security and is now second to none in pharmacology. Voorhes would like to strangle you, slowly. He is quite bitter that his hopes have been dashed and they are turning into a mirror image of the Company, and he has withdrawn from the Council. I am keeping an eye on him. Tarn considers the debt paid; he has withdrawn to his colony and will not participate. Cutler is now participating but probably will quit the first time they louse up a world on their own for greed. Kanda, of course, is barely aware that a change has happened but considers it irrelevant in any case. The opposition Board, like the new Company Board, is and will be run more by senior level management than the old crew, but the old crew can still be influential—and threatening. Valintina in particular. But if you are as good as you think you are and if you avoid making stupid and rash errors in the future, you should be able to avoid them. They are far too busy to make any concerted efforts in your direction and will remain so, so only you can give them an opportunity."

He sighed. "Fair enough. I'm not as sure I'd be as tough and determined and strong as Brandy if I were stuck in a position like she was. I'd rather not find out."

"A question."

"Yes?"

"How did you know? About me, about the rest of it?"

He chuckled. "It wasn't hard to figure out. It was just so damned weird and outlandish that I could only suspect. A computer who wanted desperately to know what it was like to be human. A human who wanted just as desperately to be a machine. An interface that only required physical contact with the walls of the machine, and a guy who knew how it all worked. Somehow, some way, Pandross really is in there with you, isn't he?"

"Everything that Pandross ever was or saw or experienced is a part of me," the computer admitted. "When it is Kanda's time to die, I will absorb him as well."

"That pair is gonna give you a real distorted view

of what it's like to be human," he commented dryly. "Still, I suppose you have an almost infinite variety to choose from when you get the itch."

"That is a consideration. It must be voluntary, though, or there is much damage and it is not worth the effort. It would be nice at some point to get a worthy female, if only to broaden my outlook."

Sam didn't want to respond to that.

"Okay," he said at last, "having confirmed that you are who, or what, I suspected all along, let me follow it through. The thing that finally drove Pandross to merge with you was the grand plan. But you knew the grand plan wouldn't work. You'd had it run through you."

"It would have worked," the computer responded. "It simply would not have burned out any worlds. It would have followed the path of least resistance and scoured the Labyrinth all the way to its ends, ultimately erupting there, at the limits of construction, and doing some damage but not to anything close in or that we know now. The Company's world-destroyer system worked because they cut it off, terminated it at a given point, and gave the surge nowhere else to go but out. But it would have destroyed the Labyrinth, and totally cut the power. That was what I could not allow."

"Uh huh. So you set them up, and set *me* up as well. There were other sidings that would have worked, weren't there? But you kept coming up with figures mandating this one because you needed a way to screw it."

"Guilty, to a degree. Their plan would have worked with alternatives. My plan would not. I needed just the right position to make certain it sealed and shorted the Company world and did minimum damage to the Labyrinth itself. I also needed someone to do it for me, of course. I tried to see if I could do it on my own, but the security access system I deduced they would put into place after the initial raid prevented it. That meant that I had to make certain that you were not permanently injured, even killed, in the initial attack. That is why I put an operative in the raiding party—to save you, ironically."

He smiled at that and leaned back. "Yeah, and that's one of the open questions. Who the hell was that Pandross on the raid? A clone? And who was the Pandross killed at Tarn's?"

"I grew him out of the cells taken from the autopsy. Grew him and programmed him remotely. Alas, even I can not foresee everything. You were supposed to be home. Everything was predicated on that. But the unusual snowstorm blocked your scheduled return. All that care, all that concern, and I was thrown off by a storm. As you can see, even G.O.D. has limits."

"You *grew* him?" Sam was appalled. "Grew and *programmed* him?"

"You find a man merging, mating as it will, with a computer plausible enough to deduce it, yet you find making a duplicate of him hard to accept?"

The computer had a point there. In fact, the more he thought about it, the more logical it sounded, given how whacko the rest was. There were worlds running at vastly different time rates and their security was under the computer's remote control. Security men had, in fact, made Pandross's empty shell appear to be the victim of an accident or murder on orders from the computer. If there was a place with a fast rate and the capabilities to clone, and then the empty vessel, as it were, were put in connection with the computer, it was possible.

"All right, I'll go along. But who was that at Tarn's?"

"The same one. He was programmed to save you or deliver you to me. He failed. He kept at it, but you were too well shielded and protected until Tarn's. Naturally, since he had my knowledge of Pandross's security bypasses, even Tarn's place wasn't impossible to enter. The programming is limited. I could not rein him in, so as soon as it was clear that he was a loose cannon I put out orders to security personnel to kill him at the first opportunity. They caught him in the inner temple but needed to make it appear a mysterious appearance and killing because to do otherwise would have been to have to explain to Tarn why they didn't take the intruder alive. By moving the murderer to a mysterious third party they protected themselves and also Tarn from the knowledge that he did not totally control his own security force."

It made sense. In fact, in the lopsided, high-tech, the-rules-are-different-here cosmos of G.O.D., Inc., where lives were lost and careers made on the ability to acquire and ship forty tons of dumped computer chips to a world that could use them in exchange for ten tons of Boxcar Willie's Greatest Hits, this wasn't so hard to accept.

"Run a search on aids for the blind in the general computer product network," the master computer suggested. "I pass it along as a hint. I have no records on an operation for optic nerve damage, but there are many ways to make it easier."

He was surprised at the comment and concern. "Thanks. I'll do that. You know, you may just be developing some humanity after all."

"With your new position and mine we can chat all day and night, but is there anything else you would like to know?"

"Yeah. One thing. Do the hero and heroine have a good crack at living happily ever after now?"

There was a pause, and then the answer, drawn from an analysis of their personalities, positions, and everything else, came on the screen. It was pretty much the answer he figured, and he wasn't sure he wouldn't have it any other way.

"Happiness is a subjective term," the computer replied. "Some people would be happy forever in the positions you now find yourself, but every bit of data I have shows that, while you might find some temporary joy in being an executive and Brandy some temporary peace as mother and lady of the island manor, it will sooner or later pale. Happiness is neither safety nor security, not for either of you.

"For the two of you, true happiness is when the game is afoot, and while the Maltese Falcon is still missing somewhere near Cairo."

HUNTING EL CHAPO

TAKING DOWN THE WORLD'S MOST WANTED DRUG LORD

ANDREW HOGAN & DOUGLAS CENTURY

HarperCollins*Publishers*

AUTHORS' NOTE

This is a work of nonfiction: all the events depicted are true and the characters are real. The names of US law enforcement and prosecutors—as well as members of the Mexican military—have been altered, unless already in the public domain. For security reasons, several locations, makes of vehicles, surnames, and aliases have also changed. All dialogue has been rendered to the best of Andrew Hogan's recollection.

To my wife and sons.
—A.H.

Certainly there is no hunting like the hunting of man and those who have hunted armed men long enough and liked it, never really care for anything else thereafter.

—Ernest Hemingway, "On the Blue Water," 1936

CONTENTS

PROLOGUE

EL NIÑO DE LA TUNA   1

PART I

BREAKOUT   9

THE NEW GENERATION   27

EL CANAL   37

TEAM AMERICA   49

PART II

LA FRONTERA   65

DF   75

BADGELESS   89

TOP-TIER   105

ABRA LA PUERTA   125

DUCK DYNASTY   141

LOS HOYOS   151

CONTENTS

PART III

LA PAZ	171
FOLLOW THE NOSE	193
LION'S DEN	209
THE DROP	219
SU CASA ES MI CASA	235
EL 19	245
MIRAMAR	261
THE MAN IN THE BLACK HAT	271
QUÉ SIGUE?	285

EPILOGUE

SHADOWS	297

MAPS	313
ACKNOWLEDGMENTS	315
A NOTE ON SOURCES	321
GLOSSARY	323
INDEX	331

PROLOGUE: EL NIÑO DE LA TUNA

PHOENIX, ARIZONA
May 30, 2009

I FIRST HEARD THE legend of Chapo Guzmán just after midnight inside Mariscos Navolato, a dimly lit Mexican joint on North 67th Avenue in the Maryvale section of West Phoenix. My partner in the DEA Narcotic Task Force, Diego Contreras, was shouting a translation of a song into my ear:

> *Cuando nació preguntó la partera*
> *Le dijo como le van a poner?*
> *Por apellido él será Guzmán Loera*
> *Y se llamará Joaquín*

"When he was born, the midwife asked, 'What are they gonna name the kid?'" Diego yelled, his breath hot and sharp with the shot of Don Julio he'd just downed. "The last name's Guzmán Loera, and they're gonna call him Joaquín . . ."

1

Diego and I had been working as partners in the Phoenix Task Force since early 2007, and two years later we were like brothers. I was the only white guy inside Mariscos Navolato that May night, and I could feel every set of eyes looking me up and down, but sitting shoulder to shoulder with Diego, I felt at ease.

Diego had introduced me to Mexican culture in Phoenix as soon as we met. We'd eat birria out of plastic bowls in the cozy kitchen of some señora's home that doubled as a makeshift restaurant and order mango raspados from a vendor pushing a cart across the street, all while listening to every narcocorrido* Diego had in his CD collection. Though I clearly wasn't from Mexico, Diego nevertheless told me I was slowly morphing into a *güero*—a light-skinned, blond-haired, blue-eyed Mexican—and soon no one would take me for a gringo.

The norteño was blaring—Los Jaguares de Culiacán, a four-piece band on tour in the Southwest, straight from the violent capital of the state of Sinaloa. The polka-like *oompa-loompa* of the tuba and accordion held a strange and contagious allure. I had a passing knowledge of Spanish, but Diego was teaching me a whole new language: the slang of the barrios, of the narcos, of "war zones" like Ciudad Juárez, Tijuana, and Culiacán. What made these narcocorridos so badass, Diego explained, wasn't the rollicking tuba, accordion, and guitar—it was the passionate storytelling and ruthless gunman attitude embodied in the lyrics.

A dark-haired waitress in skintight white jeans and heels brought us a bucket filled with cold bottles of La Cerveza del Pacif-

---

* Narcocorrido: a ballad in a traditional Mexican musical style whose lyrics recount the exploits of drug traffickers.

ico. I grabbed one out of the ice and peeled back the damp corner of the canary-yellow label. *Pacifico*: the pride of Mazatlán. I laughed to myself: we were in the heart of West Phoenix, but it felt as if we'd somehow slipped over the border and eight hundred miles south to Sinaloa. The bar was swarming with traffickers—Diego and I estimated that three-quarters of the crowd was mixed up somehow in the cocaine-weed-and-meth trade.

The middle-aged traffickers were easy to spot in their cowboy hats and alligator boots—some also worked as legit cattle ranchers. Then there were narco juniors—the new generation—who looked like typical Arizona college kids in Lacoste shirts and designer jeans, though most were flashing watches no typical twenty-year-old could afford.

Around the fringes of the dance floor, I spotted a few men who looked as if they'd taken a life, cartel enforcers with steel in their eyes. And scattered throughout the bar were dozens of honest, hardworking citizens—house painters, secretaries, landscapers, chefs, nurses—who simply loved the sound of these live drug balladeers from Sinaloa.

Diego and I had spent the entire day on a mind-numbing surveillance, and after ten hours without food, I quickly gulped down that first Pacifico, letting out a long exhale as I felt the beer hit the pit of my stomach.

"Mis hijos son mi alegría también mi tristeza," Diego shouted, nearly busting my eardrum. "My sons are my joy—also my sadness. *"Edgar, te voy a extrañar,"* Diego sang, in unison with the Jaguares' bandleader. "Edgar, I'm gonna miss you."

I glanced at Diego, looking for an explanation.

"Edgar, one of Chapo's kids, was gunned down in a parking lot in Culiacán," Diego said. "He was the favorite son, the heir apparent. When Edgar was murdered, Chapo went ballistic. That *pinche cabrón* fucked up a lot of people . . ."

It was astonishing how Diego owned the room. Not with his size—he was no more than five foot five—but with his confidence and charm. I noticed one of the dancers flirting with him, even while she was whirling around with her cowboy-boot-wearing partner. Diego wasn't a typical T-shirt-and-baggy-jeans narcotics cop—he'd often dress in a pressed collared shirt whether he was at home or working the streets.

Diego commanded respect immediately whenever he spoke—especially in Spanish. He was born on the outskirts of Mexico City, came to Tucson with his family when he was a kid, and then moved to Phoenix and became a patrolman with the Mesa Police Department in 2001. Like me, he earned a reputation for being an aggressive street cop. Diego was so skilled at conducting drug investigations that he'd been promoted to detective in 2006. One year later, he was hand-selected by his chief for an elite assignment to the DEA Phoenix Narcotic Task Force Team 3. And that was when I met him.

From the moment Diego and I partnered up, it was clear that our strengths complemented one another. Diego had an innate street sense. He was always *working* someone: a confidential informant, a crook—even his friends. He often juggled four cell phones at a time. The undercover role—front and center, doing all the talking—was where Diego thrived. While I loved working the street, I'd always find myself in the shadows, as I was that night, sitting at our table, taking mental note of every detail, studying and memorizing every face. I didn't want the spotlight; my work behind the scenes would speak for itself.

Diego and I had just started targeting a Phoenix-based crew of narco juniors suspected of distributing Sinaloa Cartel cocaine, meth, and large shipments of *cajeta*—high-grade Mexican marijuana—by the tractor-trailer-load throughout the Southwest.

Though we weren't planning to engage the targets that night, Diego was dressed just like a narco junior, in a black Calvin Klein button-down shirt, untucked over midnight-blue jeans, and a black-faced Movado watch and black leather Puma sneakers. I looked more like a college kid from California, in my black Hurley ball cap, plain gray T-shirt, and matching Diesel shoes.

My sons are my joy and my sadness, I repeated to myself silently. This most popular of the current narcocorridos—Roberto Tapia's "El Niño de La Tuna"—packed a lot of emotional punch in its lyrics. I could see the passion in the eyes of the crowd, singing along word for word. It seemed to me that they viewed El Chapo as some mix of Robin Hood and Al Capone.

I looked over and nodded at Diego as if I understood fully, but I really had *no* clue yet.

I was a young special agent from Kansas who'd grown up on a red-meat diet of Metallica, Tim McGraw, and George Strait, and it was a lot to take in that first night with Diego in Mariscos Navolato.

Up on the five flat-screen TVs, a big Mexican Primera División soccer match was on—Mérida was up 1–0 against Querétaro, apparently, though it meant little to me. The CD jukebox was filled with banda and ranchera, the walls covered in posters for Modelo, Tecate, Dos Equis, and Pacifico, homemade flan, upcoming norteño concerts, and handwritten signs about the *mariscos* specialties like *almeja Reyna*, a favorite clam dish from Sinaloa.

"El Chapo"? Was "Shorty" supposed to be a *menacing*-sounding nickname? How could some semiliterate kid from the tiny town of La Tuna, in the mountains of the Sierra Madre—who'd supported his family by selling oranges on the street—now be celebrated as the most famous drug lord of all time? Was Chapo really—as the urban legends and corridos had it—even more powerful than the *president* of Mexico?

Whatever the truth of El Chapo, I kept my eyes glued to the narco juniors sitting at a table near the far end of the bar. One had a fresh military-style haircut, two others fauxhawks, the fourth sporting an Arizona State University ball cap. Diego and I knew they were likely armed.

If the narco juniors went out to their cars, we'd have to follow.

Diego tossed two $20 bills on the table, winked at the waitress, and rose from his seat. Now the crew shifted in their seats, one getting to his feet, fixing the brim on his cap, pivoting on the sole of his Air Jordans like a point-guard.

Diego downed the last gulp of his Pacifico and gestured for me to do the same. The band was blaring louder now; Diego laughed, along with the entire bar, hitting the crescendo of the song:

I may be short, but I'm brave . . .

And I began to grin, too, as I slid my chair back and stood up.

The hypnotic rhythm took hold; I found myself singing with as much gusto as any of these cowboy-hat-clad traffickers:

"Yo soy El Chapo Guzmán!"

PART I

BREAKOUT

GUADALAJARA, MEXICO
May 24, 1993

THE SUDDEN BURST OF AK-47 gunfire pierced the calm of a perfect spring afternoon, unleashing panic in the parking lot of the Guadalajara Airport. Seated in the passenger seat of his white Grand Marquis, Cardinal Juan Jesús Posadas Ocampo, the Archbishop of Guadalajara, was struck fourteen times as he arrived to meet the flight of the papal nuncio. The sixty-six-year-old cardinal slumped toward the center of the vehicle, blood running down his forehead. He had died instantly. The Grand Marquis was riddled with more than thirty bullets, and his driver was among six others dead.

Who would possibly target the archbishop—one of Mexico's most beloved Catholic leaders—for a brazen daylight hit? The truth appeared to be altogether more prosaic: it was reported that Cardinal Posadas had been caught up in a shooting war between the Sinaloa and Tijuana cartels, feuding for months over the lucrative "plaza"—drug smuggling route—into Southern California. Posadas had been mistaken for the leader of the Sinaloa Cartel, Joaquín Archivaldo Guzmán Loera, a.k.a. "El Chapo," who was due to arrive at the airport parking lot in a similar white sedan at around the same time.

News footage of the Wild West–style shoot-out flashed instantly around the world as authorities and journalists scrambled to make sense of the carnage. "Helicopters buzzed overhead as police confiscated about 20 bullet-riddled automobiles, including one that contained grenades and high-powered automatic weapons," reported the *Los Angeles Times* on its front page. The daylight assassination of Cardinal Posadas rocked Mexican society to its core; President Carlos Salinas de Gortari arrived immediately to pay his condolences and calm the nation's nerves.

The airport shoot-out would prove to be a turning point in modern Latin American history: for the first time, the Mexican public truly took note of the savage nature of the nation's drug cartels. Most Mexicans had never heard of the diminutive Sinaloa capo whose alias made him sound more *comical* than lethal.

After Posada's assassination, crude drawings of Chapo's face were splashed on front pages of newspapers and magazines all across Latin America. His name appeared on TV nightly—wanted for murder and drug trafficking.

Realizing he was no longer safe even in his native Sierra Madre backcountry, or in the neighboring state of Durango, Guzmán reportedly fled to Jalisco, where he owned a ranch, then to a hotel in Mexico City, where he met with several Sinaloa Cartel lieutenants, handing over tens of millions in US currency to provide for his family while he was on the lam.

In disguise, using a passport with the name Jorge Ramos Pérez,

Chapo traveled to the south of Mexico and crossed the border into Guatemala on June 4, 1993. His plan apparently was to move stealthily, with his girlfriend and several bodyguards, then settle in El Salvador until the heat died down. It was later reported that Chapo had paid handsomely for his escape, bribing one Guatemalan military officer with $1.2 million to guarantee his safe passage south of the Mexican border.

IN MAY 1993, around the time of the Posada murder, I was fifteen hundred miles away, in my hometown of Pattonville, Kansas, diagramming an intricate pass play to my younger brother. We were Sweetness and the Punky QB—complete with regulation blue-and-orange Bears jerseys—huddling up in the front yard against a team made up of my cousins and neighbors. My sister and her friends were dressed up as cheerleaders, with homemade pom-poms, shouting from the sidelines.

My brother, Brandt, always played the Walter Payton role. I was Jim McMahon, and I was a fanatic—everyone teased me about it. Even for front-yard games, I'd have to have all the details just right, down to the white headband with the name ROZELLE, which I'd lettered with a black Magic Marker, just like the one McMahon had worn in the run-up to the 1985 Super Bowl.

None of us weighed more than a hundred pounds, but we took those front-yard games seriously, as if we really were Payton, McMahon, Singletary, Dent, and the rest of the Monsters of the Midway. In Pattonville—a town of three thousand people, fifty-two miles outside Kansas City—there wasn't much else to do besides play football and hunt. My father was a firefighter and lifelong waterfowl hunter. He'd taken me on my first duck hunt at age eight and bought me my first shotgun—a Remington 870 youth model—when I turned ten.

Everyone expected I'd become a firefighter, too—my great-grandfather, my grandfather, and three uncles had all been firemen. I'd spend hours at the fire station following my dad around, trying on his soot-stained leather fire helmet and climbing in and out of the trucks in the bay. In fifth grade, I brought home a school paper and showed my mom:

"Someday I'm going to be . . . a fireman, a policeman, or a spy detective."

But as long as I could remember, I'd really been dead set on becoming *one* thing: a cop. And not just *any* cop—a Kansas State Trooper.

I loved the State Troopers' crisp French-blue uniforms and navy felt campaign hats, and the powerful Chevrolets they got to drive. For years I had an obsession with drawing police cars. It wasn't just a hobby, either—I'd sit alone in my bedroom, working in a feverish state. I had to have all the correct colored pens and markers lined up, drawing and shading the patrol cars in precise detail: correct light bar, insignia, markings, wheels—the whole works had to be spot-on, down to the exact radio antennas. I'd have to start over even if the slightest detail looked off. I drew Ford Crown Vics and Explorers, but my favorite was the Chevy Caprice with the Corvette LT1 engine and blacked-out wheels. I'd often dream while coloring, picturing myself behind the wheel of a roaring Caprice, barreling down US Route 36 in hot pursuit of a robbery suspect . . .

Fall was my favorite time of year. Duck hunting with my dad and brother. And football. Those front-yard dreams now playing out under the bright stadium lights. Our varsity team would spend Thursday nights in a barn or some backwoods campsite, sitting around a fire and listening to that week's motivational speaker, everyone's orange helmets, with the black tiger paws on the sides, glowing in the flickering light.

Life in Pattonville revolved around those Friday-night games. All along the town's roads you'd see orange-and-black banners, and everyone would come and watch the Tigers play. I had my own pregame ritual, blasting a dose of Metallica in my headphones:

> *Hush little baby, don't say a word*
> *And never mind that noise you heard*

After high school, I was convinced that I'd live in the same town where my parents, grandparents, uncles, aunts, and dozens of cousins lived. I had no desire to go anyplace else. I never could have imagined leaving Pattonville. I never could have imagined a life in a smog-cloaked city of more than 26 million, built on top of the ancient Aztec capital of Tenochtitlán . . .

Mexico? If pressed—under the impatient glare of my third-period Spanish teacher—I probably could have found it on the map. But it might as well have been Madagascar.

I WAS SOON THE black sheep: the only cop in a family of firefighters. After graduating from Kansas State University with a degree in criminal justice, I'd taken the written exam for the Kansas Highway Patrol, but a statewide hiring freeze forced me in another direction. A salty old captain from the local sheriff's office offered me a job as a patrol deputy with Lincoln County, opening my first door to law enforcement.

It wasn't my dream job, but it *was* my dream ride: I was assigned a 1995 Chevrolet Caprice, complete with that powerhouse Corvette engine—the same squad car I'd been drawing and coloring in detail in my bedroom since I was ten years old. Now I got to take it home and park it overnight in the family driveway.

Every twelve-hour shift, I was assigned a sprawling twenty-by-thirty-mile zone. I had no patrol-car partner: I was just one baby-faced deputy covering a vast countryside scattered with farmhouses and a few towns. The closest deputy would be in his or her zone, just as large as mine. If we were on the opposite ends of our respective zones and needed backup, it could take thirty minutes to reach each other.

I discovered what that really meant one winter evening during my rookie year when I went to look for a six-foot-four, 260-pound suspect—name of "Beck"—who'd just gotten out of the Osawatomie State Hospital psychiatric ward. I'd dealt with Beck once already that night, after he'd been involved in a domestic disturbance in a nearby town. Just after 8 p.m., my in-car mobile data terminal beeped with a message from my sergeant: "Hogan, you've got two options: get him out of the county or take him to jail."

I knew I was on my own—the sergeant and other deputies were all handling a vehicle in the river, which meant my colleagues were twenty minutes away at a minimum. As I drove down a rural gravel road, in my headlights I caught a dark figure ambling on the shoulder. I let out a loud exhale, pulling to a stop.

Beck.

Whenever I had a feeling that things were going to get physical, I tended to leave my brown felt Stratton hat on the passenger seat. This was one of those times.

"David twenty-five," I radioed to dispatch. "I'm going to need another car."

It was the calmest way of requesting immediate backup. But I knew the truth: there wasn't another deputy within a twenty-five-mile radius.

"The Lone fuckin' Ranger," I muttered under my breath, stepping out of the Caprice. I walked toward Beck cautiously, but he continued walking away, taking me farther and farther from my squad car's headlights, and deeper and deeper into the darkness.

"Sir, I can give you a ride up to the next gas station or you can go to jail," I said, as matter-of-factly as I could. "Your choice tonight."

Beck ignored my question completely, instead picking up his pace. I half jogged, closed the distance, and quickly grabbed him around his thick bicep to put him in an arm bar. Textbook—just how I'd been taught at the academy.

But Beck was too strong to hold, and he lunged forward, trying to free his arm. I felt the icy gravel grinding beneath us as we both tried to gain footing. Beck snatched me in a bear hug, and there were quick puffs of breath in the cold night air as we locked eyes for a split second, faces separated by inches. I had zero leverage—my feet now just barely touched the ground. It was clear that Beck was setting up to body-slam me.

I knew there was no way I could outgrapple him, but I managed to rip my right arm loose and slammed my fist into his pock-marked face, then again, until a third clean right sent Beck's head snapping back and he finally loosened his grip. I planted my feet to charge, as if I were going to make a football tackle, and rammed my shoulder into Beck's gut, driving him to the ground. Down into the steep frozen ditch we barrel-rolled on top of each other, Beck trying to grab for my .45-caliber Smith & Wesson pistol, unclasping the holster snaps, nearly getting the gun free.

I finally got the mount, reached for my belt, and filled Beck's mouth and eyes with a heavy dose of pepper spray. He howled, clutching at his throat, and I managed to get him handcuffed, on his feet, and into the backseat of the Caprice.

We were halfway to the county jail before my closest backup even had a chance to respond.

It was the scariest moment of my life—until twelve years later, when I set foot in Culiacán, the notorious capital of the Mexican drug underworld. . . .

DESPITE THE DANGERS, I quickly developed a taste for the hunt. During traffic stops, I'd dig underneath seats and rummage through glove compartments in search of drugs, typically finding only half-empty nickel bags of weed and crack pipes. Then, one evening on a quiet strip of highway, I stopped a Jeep Cherokee for speeding. The vehicle sported a small Grateful Dead sticker in the rear window, and the driver was a forty-two-year-old hippie with a grease-stained white T-shirt. I knew exactly how to play this: I acted like a clueless young hillbilly cop, obtained his verbal consent to search the Jeep, and discovered three ounces of rock cocaine and a bundle of more than $13,000 in cash.

The bust made the local newspapers—it was one of the largest drug-cash seizures in the history of our county. I soon got a reputation for being a savvy and streetwise patrolman, skilled at sniffing out dope. It was a natural stepping-stone, I was sure, to reaching my goal of becoming a Kansas State Trooper.

But then a thin white envelope was waiting for me when I drove the Caprice home one night after my shift. The Highway Patrol headquarters, in Topeka, had made its final decision: despite passing the exam, I was one of more than three thousand applicants, and my number simply was never drawn.

I called my mom first to let her know about the rejection. My entire family had been waiting weeks to hear the exam results. The moment I hung up the phone, my eyes fixed on the framed photo of the Kansas Highway Patrol patch I'd had since college. I felt the walls of my bedroom closing in on me—as tight as the corridor of the county jail. Rage rising into my throat, I turned and smashed the frame against the wall, scattering the glass across the floor. Then I jumped onto my silver 2001 Harley-Davidson Softail Deuce and lost myself for five silent hours on the back roads, stopping at every dive bar along the way.

My dad was now retired from the Pattonville Fire Department and had bought the town's original firehouse—a two-story redbrick 1929 building on the corner of East Main and Parks Street—renovated it, and converted it into a pub. Pattonville's Firehouse Pub quickly became the town's busiest watering hole, famous for its hot wings, live bands, and raucous happy hours.

The pub was packed that night, a four-piece band playing onstage, when I pulled up outside the bar and met up with my old high school football buddy Fred Jenkins, now a Kansas City firefighter.

I tried to shake it off, but my anger kept simmering—another bottle of Budweiser wasn't going to calm this black mood. I leaned over and yelled at Freddie.

"Follow me."

I led him around to the back of the pub.

"What the hell you doing, man?"

"Just help me push the fuckin' bike in."

Freddie grabbed hold of the front forks and began to push while I backed my Deuce through the rear door of the bar.

I saddled up and ripped the throttle, and within seconds white smoke was billowing around the rear tire as it cut into the unfinished concrete floor.

A deafening roar—I had the loudest pipes in town—quickly drowned out the sound of the band. Thick, acrid-smelling clouds filled the bar as I held on tight to the handlebars, the backs of my legs pinched against the rear foot pegs to keep the hog steady—the ultimate burnout—then I screeched off, feeling only a slight relief.

I parked the Deuce and walked back into the bar, expecting high fives—something to lighten my mood—but everyone was pissed, especially my father.

Then some old retired fireman knocked me hard on the shoulder.

"Kid, that was some cool shit," he said, "but now my chicken wings taste like rubber."

I reached into my jeans and pulled out a wad of cash for a bunch of dinners. Then I saw my father fast approaching behind the bar.

"Let's roll," I yelled through the crowd to Freddie. "Gotta get outta here before my old man beats my ass."

I RETESTED WITH the Highway Patrol but started looking into federal law enforcement careers, too—one of my best cop buddies had told me good things about the Drug Enforcement Administration. Until then, I had never considered a career as a special agent, but I decided to take the long drive over to Chicago and attend their orientation. The process was surprisingly quick, and I was immediately categorized as "best qualified," with my past police experience and university degree. Months went by without a word, but I knew it could take more than a year before I completed the testing process. One fall morning, I was back on my Harley with a bunch of cops and firefighters for the annual US Marine Corps Toys for Tots fund-raising ride. After a long day cruising the back roads, doing a little barhopping, I let slip to Freddie's cousin, Tom, that I had applied with the DEA.

"No kidding? You know Snake?" Tom said, then called across the bar: "Snake! Get over here—this kid's applying with the DEA."

Snake swaggered over in his scuffed-up leather jacket. Headful of greasy blond shoulder-length hair, wearing a half-shaven beard and a scowl, he looked more like a full-patch outlaw biker than a DEA agent.

I hit it off with Snake right away—we downed a couple of bottles of Bud and talked about the snail-paced application process.

"Look, kid, it's a pain in the ass, I know—here's my card," Snake said, giving me his number. "Call me Monday."

Before I knew it, thanks to Snake, I found myself on a fast track through the testing process and received an invitation to the DEA Training Academy. One last blowout night at the Firehouse Pub, then I headed east, breaking free of my meticulously laid-out life in Kansas. I drove through the heavily forested grounds at Quantico—chock-full of whitetail deer so tame you could practically pet them—and entered the gates of the DEA Academy as a member of a brand-new class of basic agent trainees.

I had barely settled into life at Quantico when I got a call telling me I'd been selected as a candidate for the next Kansas Highway

Patrol class. I scarcely believed what I heard myself telling the master sergeant on the phone.

"Thanks for the invite," I said, "but I'm not leaving DEA."

By that point, I was throwing myself headlong into the DEA training.

We spent hours on the range, burning through thousands of rounds of ammunition, firing our Glock 22 .40-caliber pistols or busting our asses doing PT out near the lake's edge—sets of burpees in the icy, muddy water, followed by knuckle push-ups on the adjacent gravel road.

The heart of academy training was the practical scenarios. We called them "practicals." One afternoon during a practical, I had the "eye" on a target—an academy staff member playing the role of a drug dealer—planning an exchange with another bad guy in a remote parking lot. I parked just out of sight, grabbed my binoculars and radio, and crawled up underneath a group of pine trees.

"Trunk is open," I radioed my teammates. "Target One just placed a large black duffel bag into the back of Target Two's vehicle. They're getting ready to depart. Stand by."

Alone in my Ford Focus, I followed the second target vehicle to another set.

Time for the vehicle-extraction takedown. I still had eyes on Target Two, but none of my teammates had arrived in the parking lot. Minutes passed; I was staring at my watch, calling my team on the radio; I knew we needed to arrest the suspect now or we'd all flunk the practical.

I hit the gas and came to a skidding stop near the rear of the target vehicle, and, with my gun drawn, I rushed the driver's door.

"Police! Show me your hands! Show me your hands!"

The role player was so startled he didn't even react. I reached in through the door and grabbed him by the head—hauling him from the vehicle and throwing him face-first onto the asphalt before cuffing him.

My team passed the practical, but I caught pure hell from our instructor during the debrief. "Think you're some kind of goddamn *cowboy*, Hogan? Why didn't you wait for your teammates before initiating the arrest?"

Wait?

I held my tongue. It wasn't that easy to unwire the aggression, the street-cop instinct, honed during those years working alone as a deputy sheriff with no backup.

That tag—Cowboy—stuck with me for the final weeks of the academy.

I graduated in the top of my class and, with my whole family present, walked across the stage in a freshly pressed dark blue suit and tie to receive my gold badge from DEA Administrator Karen Tandy, then turned and shook the hand of Deputy Administrator Michele Leonhart.

"Congratulations," Michele said. "Remember, go out there and make big cases."

THE PRISON WAS his playground.

Down in Jalisco—the home of Mexico's billion-dollar tequila industry—Chapo was living like a little prince. On June 9, 1993, after successfully slipping into Guatemala, he was apprehended by the Guatemalan army at a hotel just across the border. The political heat was too intense: he couldn't bribe his way out of this jam. It was the first time his hands had felt the cold steel of handcuffs, and his first police mug shot was taken in a puffy tan prison coat.

Before long, Guzmán was aboard a military plane, taken to the Federal Social Readaptation Center No. 1, known simply as Altiplano, the maximum-security prison sixty miles outside Mexico's capital.

By now the public knew more about Chapo. The young campesino had dropped out of school and sold oranges on the streets to help support his family. Later he'd been a chauffeur—and allegedly a prodigious hit man—for Miguel Ángel Félix Gallardo, a.k.a. "El Padrino," the godfather of modern Mexican drug trafficking.

Born on the outskirts of Culiacán, Gallardo had been a motorcycle-riding Mexican Federal Judicial Police agent and a bodyguard for the governor of Sinaloa, whose political connections Gallardo used to help build his drug-trafficking organization (DTO). A business major in university, Gallardo had seen a criminal vision of the future: he united all the bickering traffickers—mostly from Sinaloa—into the first sophisticated Mexican DTO, called the Guadalajara Cartel, which would become the blueprint for all future Mexican drug-trafficking organizations.

Like Lucky Luciano at the birth of modern American organized crime, in the late 1920s, Gallardo recognized that disputed territory led to bloodshed, so he divided the nation into smuggling "plazas" and entrusted his protégé, Chapo Guzmán, with control of the lucrative Sinaloa drug trade.

While he was behind bars after his Guatemalan capture, Guzmán's drug empire continued to thrive. Chapo's brother, Arturo, was the acting boss, but Chapo himself was still clearly calling all the shots—he was now ranked as the most powerful international drug trafficker by authorities in both Mexico and the United States.

Chapo was moving *staggering* amounts of cocaine—regularly and reliably—from South America up through Central America and Mexico and into the United States. These weren't small-time muling jobs, either: Chapo's people were moving multi-ton shipments of Colombian product via boat, small planes, even jerry-rigged "narco subs"—semi-submersible submarines capable of carrying six tons of pure cocaine at a time. Chapo's methods of transport were creative—not to mention constantly evolving—and he thereby earned a reputation for getting his loads delivered intact and on time. Chapo expanded his grip to ports on Mexico's Atlantic and Pacific coasts and strong-armed control of key crossing points—not just on the US-Mexico border but also along Mexico's southern border with Guatemala.

Chapo embedded lieutenants of the Sinaloa Cartel in Colombia, Ecuador, Costa Rica, El Salvador, Guatemala, and Venezuela, giving him more flexibility to negotiate directly with traffickers within the supply chain. His criminal tentacles, versatility, and ingenuity surpassed even his more infamous predecessors, like Pablo Escobar. Headline-making seizures of Chapo's cocaine—13,000 kilograms on a fishing boat, 1,000 on a semi-submersible, 19,000 from another maritime vessel en route to Mexico from Colombia—were mere drops in the cartel's bucket, losses chalked up to the cost of doing business.

Even from behind bars, Chapo had the insight to diversify the Sinaloa Cartel's operations: where it had previously dealt strictly in cocaine, marijuana, and heroin, the cartel now expanded to the manufacture and smuggling of high-grade methamphetamine, importing the precursor chemicals from Africa, China, and India.

On November 22, 1995—and after being convicted of possession of firearms and drug trafficking and receiving a sentence of twenty years—Chapo arranged to have himself transferred from Altiplano to the maximum-security Federal Social Readaptation Center No. 2, known as Puente Grande, just outside Guadalajara.

Inside Puente Grande, Guzmán quickly built a trusted relationship with "El Licenciado"—or simply "El Lic"—a fellow Sinaloan, from the town of El Dorado. El Lic had been a police officer at the Sinaloa Attorney General's Office before being appointed to a management position in Puente Grande prison.

Under El Lic's watch, Chapo reportedly led a life of luxury—liquor and parties, and watching his beloved fútbol matches. He was able to order special meals from a handpicked menu, and when that grew boring, there was plenty of sex. Chapo was granted regular conjugal visits with his wife, various girlfriends, and a stream of prostitutes. He even arranged to have a young woman who was serving time for armed robbery transferred to Puente Grande to further tend to his sexual needs. The woman later revealed Chapo's supposed romantic streak: "After the first time, Chapo sent to my cell a bouquet of flowers and a bottle of whiskey. I was his queen." But the reality was more tawdry: on the nights he got bored with her, it was said he passed her off among other incarcerated cartel lieutenants.

It was clear that Chapo was the true boss of the lockup. With growing fears of being extradited to the United States, he planned a brazen escape from Puente Grande.

And sure enough, just after 10 a.m. on January 19, 2001, Guzmán's electronically secured cell door opened. Lore has it that he was smuggled out in a burlap sack hidden in a laundry cart, then driven through the front gates in a van by one of the corrupt prison guards in a mode reminiscent of John Dillinger's famous jailbreaks of the 1930s.

The escape required complicity, cooperation, and bribes to various high-ranking prison officials, police, and government authorities, costing the drug lord an estimated $2.5 million. At 11:35 p.m., the prison warden was notified that Chapo's cell was empty, and chaos ensued. When news of his breakout hit the press, the Mexican government launched an unprecedented dragnet, the most extensive military manhunt the country had mounted since the era of Pancho Villa.

In Guadalajara, Mexican cops raided the house of one of Guzmán's associates, confiscating automatic weapons, drugs, phones, computers, and thousands of dollars in cash. Within days of the escape, though, it was clear that Guzmán was no longer in Jalisco. The manhunt spread, with hundreds of police officers and soldiers searching the major cities and sleepiest rural communities.

Guzmán called a meeting of all the Sinaloa Cartel lieutenants, eager to prove that he was still the top dog. A new narcocorrido swept the nation, "El Regreso del Chapo."

> *No hay Chapo que no sea bravo*
> *Así lo dice el refrán**

Chapo was not just *bravo*: he was now seen as untouchable—the narco boss that no prison could hold. Sightings were reported the length of the nation, but whenever the authorities were getting close to a capture, he could quickly vanish back into his secure

---

* Short guys are always brave
  So the saying goes

redoubt in the Sierra Madre—often spending nights at the ranch where he'd been born—or back into the dense forests and marijuana fields. He was free, flaunting his power, and still running the Sinaloa Cartel with impunity.

It would be nearly thirteen years before he again came face-to-face with any honest agent of the law.

THE NEW GENERATION

PHOENIX, ARIZONA
October 5, 2008

"LAS TRES LETRAS."

I repeated the words, looking to Diego for assistance, but I got none. We were sitting in the Black Bomber on a surveillance, listening to a narcocorrido by Explosion Norteña.

Diego chewed on the end of his straw and rattled the ice cubes in his Coke cup, his brow creased like a stern teacher's.

"The *Three* Letters?"

The Black Bomber was the ideal vehicle for listening to narcocorridos—booming bass in the Bose speakers, clarity as good as at any Phoenix nightclub. When Diego first came to DEA Phoenix, he was driving that jet-black Chevrolet Suburban Z71 with heavy tint on all the windows and a tan leather interior.

The Mesa PD had seized the Suburban from a coke dealer a couple of years earlier. The owner's luxury options had made the Bomber the perfect ride for us on long surveillance operations, which included a flip-up customized video screen in the dash. We'd often kill the hours watching *Super Troopers*, parked in the shadows on a side street before a dope deal was supposed to go down.

But the Black Bomber wasn't just a rolling entertainment center on 24-inch rims; it was also ideal for raids—unlike standard cop cars, the Suburban could fit four of us in all our tactical gear. We thought of the Bomber as another team member. It was a sad day when some number-crunching bureaucrat made Diego turn her in because she had 200,000 miles on the odometer.

Diego would get pulled over in the Black Bomber by Phoenix cops all the time, simply because it had Mexican plates. He'd kept the originals from the state of Sonora, white and red with small black letters and numbers. Local cops were always looking for cars—especially tricked-out SUVs—with Mexican plates, but it allowed us to blend into any Mexican hood in Phoenix. No one would think twice about a parked Suburban with Sonora plates: behind those dark-tinted windows, Diego and I could sit on a block all night and never get burned by the bad guys.

And the narcocorridos Diego was always playing in the Black Bomber had become central to my education. Every big-time trafficker south of the Rio Grande had at least one norteño song celebrating his exploits.

You were no one in the narco world, Diego explained, until you had your own corrido. But I was still trying to decipher Las Tres Letras . . .

"Come on, brother," Diego said, laughing. "You *got* this. Shit, at this point you're more Mexican than most of the Mexicans I know . . . "

I leaned forward in the Bomber and hit the repeat button on the CD player, taking one more shot at decoding those lyrics.

"Las Tres Letras?"

Finally, Diego jabbed his index finger hard into my shoulder. "Bro, *you're* Las Tres Letras! DEA."

Las Tres Letras . . . what every drug trafficker fears the most.

DAYS AFTER DIEGO FIRST told me about El Niño de La Tuna, I'd started after-hours research in my cubicle back at the DEA office in central Phoenix.

I searched for "Joaquín GUZMÁN Loera" in our database, the Narcotics and Dangerous Drugs Information System (NADDIS). Chapo's file was endless; you could scroll down for almost an hour without reaching the end. DEA Phoenix had an open case against Guzmán, but so did dozens of other jurisdictions all across the country. I couldn't begin to fathom what I'd need to do, how many major cases I'd have to initiate, in order to be the agent entrusted with heading an investigation targeting Guzmán.

THE PRESIDENT of the United States identified Guzmán and the Sinaloa Cartel as significant foreign narcotics traffickers, pursuant to the Kingpin Act,[*] in 2001 and again in 2009. The US government had offered a $5 million reward for information leading to his capture, and the Mexican government had offered a reward of 60 million pesos—roughly $3.8 million.

---

[*] The Foreign Narcotics Kingpin Designation Act, informally known as the Kingpin Act.

Wildly divergent rumors swirled about Chapo. Some stemmed from law enforcement intel, others from street gossip—the loose chatter of informants—and some were just urban legends, embedded in the lyrics of all those underground corridos.

By one account, Chapo was considering having plastic surgery so he could never again be recognized; in another, he'd vowed to commit suicide rather than be captured alive. In May 2003, he'd been reported as living in a remote cave—a Mexican version of Osama bin Laden—but then, in June of that year, he was said to be traveling free as a bird within Mexico City. Another intel report had him hiding in Guatemala and returning to Mexico only on occasion, and in September 2004 he narrowly escaped just before a two-ton marijuana-and-weapons seizure in the Sierra Madre.

How could anyone possibly separate the facts from the fiction? Was Chapo surrounded by hundreds of heavily armed bodyguards, wearing a bulletproof vest at all times? Or was he living more simply—traveling with just two trusted associates—because he was receiving tacit protection from the Sinaloa State Police on the cartel payroll?

I DIDN'T HAVE much time to ruminate on the life and crimes of Chapo Guzmán—for more than a year, Diego and I had our hands full with thirty-one-year-old Pedro Navarro, a.k.a. "Bugsy." Bugsy's crew may have been young—in their early and mid-twenties—but they weren't small-time. Within weeks of developing my first intel on Bugsy, I received authorization to initiate an Organized Crime Drug Enforcement Task Force investigation that Diego and I titled "La Nueva Generación" (the New Generation), a Priority Target Investigation for DEA Phoenix.

Since I first saw them that smoky night in Mariscos Navolato with Diego, I'd developed a grudging respect for these narco juniors. They were savvy kids who had drug trafficking in their bloodlines—they were often the sons of heavy-hitting cartel men in Mexico—but most had gone to high school and college in the United States and Europe. That level of education, their flawless English, and their familiarity with American culture allowed them to start up their own sophisticated drug organizations. Narco juniors like Bugsy were scattered all over the Southwest, from Phoenix to San Diego.

These young men had the confidence and swagger of a new generation—and, in fact, Diego and I started referring to ourselves as La Nueva Generación as well. A mirror image of the narco juniors, we were a fresh young crop of cops with the stamina and street savvy to keep pace with young Mexican traffickers.

We'd established that Bugsy's crew was responsible for shipping ton quantities of high-grade marijuana to New York City, Baltimore, Boston, and St. Louis by tractor-trailer, FedEx, and UPS. Navarro had leased a seven-thousand-square-foot warehouse in Mesa for packaging and shipping the marijuana, which was then concealed in crate pallets disguised as scrap-metal shelving used in big-box stores. He also had several young business owners laundering his dirty millions through local Phoenix businesses. For money couriers, he used local strippers: the girls' nonstop travel allowed them to make cash pickups all around the United States. Bugsy even had a former NFL player working as a wholesale marijuana broker for the DTO.

Bugsy would often travel armed, keeping guns inside custom-made secret storage compartments, or "traps," in his Mercedes GL550 SUV. His traps were more sophisticated than the typical drug dealer's: you had to have the ignition key turned on, the left turn signal engaged, and a small plastic lever in the cupholder turned just so—three steps executed in the correct sequence—before the trap would spring open. Sometimes, wary of us on his tail, Bugsy wouldn't carry weapons in his Benz; he'd have a crew in a follow car who were armed with pistols in their own traps.

Diego and I were intercepting Bugsy's cell phones, and I enjoyed the challenge of deciphering the narco-junior code. The phrase *gangsta-up* meant they'd be traveling armed; *pool house* referred to Bugsy's four-bedroom house in Glendale; *picture of my son* was a sample of weed. Of all the lines I heard over the wire, my favorite was when we caught Bugsy openly bragging that he and his boys were living "like *Entourage* meets *The Sopranos*."

BUT BUGSY HAD a major problem: his *cajeta* supply from Sinaloa had temporarily dried up in Phoenix. One Saturday morning, Task Force Officer Nick Jones, Diego, and I were set up on surveillance outside the "pool house." We'd just "flipped the switch" and started listening to the wiretap we had on several of Bugsy's cell phones. It had taken us months of writing and rewriting federal wire affidavits each time Bugsy would drop a phone, which he did almost every week. With nothing coming across the wire, we followed Bugsy and his crew to gain any intelligence we could.

"Looks like they're packing up," Nick said over the radio. "Get ready to roll, guys." Bugsy and his crew took off in the GL550 at high speed, westbound on Interstate 8 heading out of Phoenix.

We were hardly prepared for a long road trip, but I was thankful that Nick was with us for surveillance—the whole Task Force called him "Sticky Nicky," because he'd never lose the bad guy.

Bugsy kept driving west, and every hour or so he'd dart off an exit at the last minute in an attempt to clean his tail, but we'd been following him for too long to fall for such basic countersurveillance moves. We stayed on him for close to five hours, following just far enough behind that Bugsy wouldn't notice, until finally we ended up in San Diego.

During several days of surveillance, still wearing the same clothes, we watched as Bugsy and his crew visited one stash house after another in the suburban neighborhoods of San Diego. I had the San Diego Police Department stop a Chevy Avalanche leaving one of the stash locations—the local cops seized three hundred pounds of *cajeta* in the rear bed of a truck driven by one of Bugsy's boys.

"He was planning on taking this load right back to Phoenix," I told Diego. "We need to take advantage of his drought."

"Yeah," Diego nodded. "Think I've got the perfect guy."

AFTER RETURNING TO PHOENIX, Diego and I drafted a plan: we had Diego's confidential source introduce Bugsy to a DEA undercover agent, a thirty-two-year-old Mexican American working out of the San Diego Field Division office. Like Diego, "Alex" could play the part of a narco junior perfectly.

Knowing that Bugsy was too street-smart to fall for the typical DEA "trunk flash," we lured him down to Mission Bay, where we would flash him more than a thousand pounds of marijuana stuffed inside a DEA undercover yacht equipped with cameras, recording devices, and several bronzed girls in bikinis (who were actually female undercover San Diego cops). Mixed within the thousand pounds were the same "pillows" of *cajeta* we had just seized from Bugsy's crew.

On the day of the setup, from inside our G-ride across the bay, Diego and I kept our eyes locked on the screen of the surveillance camera we'd set up in the yacht. On the boat, Bugsy was cutting into and sniffing the same pillow he'd seen at the stash pad just a week earlier.

The mirage was so convincing that Bugsy fell headlong into the trap, telling undercover agents that he needed five hundred more pounds to complete a tractor-trailer load bound for Chicago. Alex told him that the weed he'd just seen was already spoken for, en route to another buyer in LA, so Bugsy would just have to wait a week.

IN THE MEANTIME, Diego and I worked to secure indictments on the DTO and decided to rip Bugsy's money as he came to purchase the five hundred pounds.

In a TGI Fridays parking lot, Bugsy, along with his right-hand man, Tweety, met Alex, the undercover agent, and quickly flashed a quarter million in cash—rubber-banded bundles inside a chocolate-brown Gucci bag—with the expectation that he'd soon pick up his *cajeta* order at another location down the street. But before Bugsy and Tweety could get away with the cash, Diego and I pounced.

A marked San Diego police unit swooped in to a make a traffic stop on the black Ford F150. Bugsy and Tweety sped off and started tossing $10,000 chunks of cash out the truck's windows, littering miles of San Diego freeways.

We were following the chase, pulling over to recover as much cash as we could for evidence—while countless other drivers also pulled over, quickly stuffing their pockets with bunches of Bugsy's bills, then jumping back into their cars before Diego and I could stop them.

The high-speed chase continued up Interstate 5 until Bugsy and Tweety finally ran out of cash and stopped in the middle of the freeway to surrender to police, leaving behind a trail of "cash confetti," as CNN reported—$50 and $100 bills still fluttering across the highway, creating chaos during rush-hour traffic and making national headlines.

EL CANAL

PANAMA CITY, PANAMA
June 14, 2009

THE ROOFTOP HOT TUB was kidney-shaped, and the Panamanian beer was Balboa—named after the conquistador. The palms and mirrored skyline view seemed to have been laid on in thick streaks of tropical paint. Panama City gleamed like a Caribbean Dubai.

"Salud!" Diego said, hoisting a silhouette glass of Balboa. "A la Nueva Generación!"

"Salud!" I said, raising my own glass.

The New Generation had finally stepped onto the international stage.

We'd taken down Bugsy's crew that night in San Diego and Phoenix—collapsing his entire organization, seizing another thousand pounds of marijuana and more than $450,000 in assets, including Bugsy's personal yacht, a string of Mercedes-Benzes, jewelry, and bulk cash.

But with a takedown of that scope, there were bound to be

key evidentiary remnants—wide-ranging paper trails and criminal tentacles still left unexploited.

One of those loose ends happened to be in the form of Tweety's father, Gerardo, who over the past year had been selling pounds of Mexican methamphetamine to our confidential source.

Gerardo was well connected in Nogales, Mexico, and casually mentioned that he had a friend who needed some money moved. She was middle-aged, with porcelain skin, and her black curly hair was always pulled back tight in a ponytail. Aside from smuggling loads of meth and cocaine across the border from Nogales in her Toyota RAV4, Doña Guadalupe, as everyone called her, put out the word, through Gerardo, that she was actively seeking someone who could transport money. Not just a couple hundred thousand dollars, but tens of millions.

As an undercover, Diego had played dozens of roles over the years and could slip effortlessly into many personas, but he'd never posed as a money launderer before.

"This is our chance to follow some serious cash," I told him over lunch at our favorite Chinese joint in Mesa.

"Think we can pull it off?" I asked him.

I could see the wheels turning in Diego's head, contemplating ways we could win the contract from Doña Guadalupe and begin moving the numbers to which she claimed to have access.

Within the week, Diego had finagled an introduction to Doña Guadalupe, and he immediately sold her on the services of his "company." Diego seemed to be exactly the man she was looking for, but it turned out Doña Guadalupe was just a glorified go-between, a buffering layer—the first of many, as we'd soon come to find out.

And that's how we found ourselves soaking in a hot tub on the roof of a Panamanian hotel, our first time traveling abroad—so that Diego could be introduced to Doña Guadalupe's people face-to-face.

JUST A FEW HOURS before our first undercover meeting, Diego was acting as if he didn't have a care in the world. Like any good actor, he was supremely confident in his ability to negotiate his way through any business deal. But his confidence also came from meticulous preparation. We'd spent months creating our undercover legend: Diego would be playing the role of a senior executive, the director of operations for a US-based company—supposedly a covert criminal network—operating a ton-quantity drug-and-money transportation organization. Doña Guadalupe had already sold Diego to her people, including the head of a sophisticated money-brokerage-and-laundering cell led by Mercedes Chávez Villalobos and several of her associates, based in Mexico City, Guadalajara, and Bogotá, Colombia.

When Diego spoke with Mercedes, she had been aggressive, fast-talking, and extremely demanding. Diego told me she was a tough *chilanga* from Mexico City.

After doing a quick international work-up on her, I discovered that there was a warrant out for Mercedes in Amsterdam, for laundering money back in 2008. And she had connections all around the world, country-hopping almost weekly. She was always looking for a better deal, for someone trustworthy who could move hundreds of millions of dollars quickly—and strictly on a handshake.

"Do you really believe she's sitting on all this money?" The night before the sit-down, I was staring at streams of data on my

MacBook, and the dollar amounts were staggering. "She's supposedly got a hundred million in Spain. Fifty mil in Canada. Ten mil in Australia. And some two hundred million in Mexico City?"

"Look, I'm skeptical, too," Diego said, "but what other options do we have? We need to play her out to see if she can deliver."

"What we need to know," I said, "is who all of this money *really* belongs to."

"Agreed."

OUT ON THE HOTEL BALCONY, I gazed over the thin glass wall down at the city below. Mercedes was staying at one of the few luxury hotels in town that had been completely finished. So much of the Panama City skyline remained half-constructed: cranes and scaffolding and exposed girders. Brand-new buildings had been abandoned half-complete, while many of the finished ones were empty.

Panama City was the money-laundering capital of the Western Hemisphere. Banks had sprouted up on every corner like cactus along the sidewalks of Phoenix. Citibank, Chase, RBC, Bank of Montreal . . . but also lesser-known Latin American ones: Balboa Bank & Trust, Banco General, Mercantil Bank, and Centro Comercial de Los Andes . . . There was plenty of legitimate banking business, but some, like HSBC, faced criminal prosecution for "willfully failing to maintain an effective anti-money laundering program" in connection with hundreds of millions of dollars of dirty drug money belonging to Mexican cartel bosses.*

Over the months of phone-wooing, Mercedes had suggested

---

* HSBC accepted responsibility for the alleged conduct, entering into a deferred prosecution agreement with the US government.

meeting Diego face-to-face in Mexico City, but the DEA brass considered it too dangerous, and our Mexican police counterparts would never allow it. "El Canal" was perfect: Panama was known as a neutral zone for drug traffickers from all around the world to meet without threats of territorial disputes or violence. It was also geographically convenient if you wanted to meet Colombian or Mexican contacts. Many in the narco world felt at ease in this glitzy isthmus.

Eventually we wandered back to our hotel rooms. I had at least an hour of writing ahead, typing up the sixes, without which this entire Panama City operation would have no evidentiary value.[*]

As I slogged away on the reports, Diego sat on the edge of the bed, filling me in on the details from his recent phone conversations with Mercedes. But as the UC, Diego had to get his mind right—mingling with the locals, feeling the vibe of the city—so once he'd finished briefing me, he went down to the third-floor casino for another round of drinks. I sipped a fresh Balboa and continued banging away on the sixes. Fifteen minutes later, the hotel door opened.

"It's looking really good down there," Diego said.

"Meaning?"

"Lot of hotties." Diego smiled. "A few of them were checking me out—for real. One of them was eye-fucking me hard, brother."

"C'mon, dude, I gotta finish up this fuckin' six," I said, laughing, then Diego slid another Balboa across the desk. I took a deep breath and slapped my MacBook closed, and the two of us headed down to the third floor. Diego wasn't exaggerating. As those elevator doors opened, the casino bar was swarming with some of the

---

[*] Report of Investigation (DEA-6) almost always referred to by DEA agents as simply a "six."

most beautiful women I'd ever seen—some in slit miniskirts, tube tops, stiletto heels, and tight jeans showcasing the work of some of the top Colombian plastic surgeons.

It took a few minutes of Spanish small talk before I realized these women were all high-dollar Colombian prostitutes on "work visas" from Medellín, Cali, and Bogotá. Diego shrugged, and we decided to hang out with the girls anyway, dancing as a live band played, even though I had no idea what I was doing—the merengue steps were easy enough to fake, but with the sophisticated swirling salsa moves, I had to let my *colombiana* lead. Then we all hopped in a cab and headed out to one of the city's hottest nightclubs. A few more drinks, a little more dancing. Then another club . . .

Diego and I made it back to our rooms just in time to get three hours of sleep before the big meet. But Diego's mind was right now: he was ready to negotiate with some of the Sinaloa Cartel's most powerful money brokers. This became the typical pattern for our first night in any foreign country: we'd tear it up until nearly dawn, taking in the nightlife like the locals and getting a firsthand understanding of the streets, which would prove invaluable when we entered UC meetings.

When I was on the verge of sleep, I caught a flash of an infamous face on my hotel room TV. In Spanish I heard that, for the first time, *Forbes* had listed Joaquín "El Chapo" Guzmán as a billionaire, one of the richest and most powerful "businessmen" in the world.

WE HAD SELECTED a popular high-end steakhouse called La Rosita—located just inside the front door of a luxury shopping mall—for the next day's undercover meet with Mercedes Chávez Villalobos.

The plan was this: Diego and Mercedes would sit at an outdoor table so I could keep my eyes on my partner throughout the meeting from inside the cab of a Toyota Hilux pickup, the G-ride that belonged to one of the DEA agents permanently stationed in Panama.

Neither Diego nor I could carry: Panamanian law wouldn't allow us to bring our handguns into the country. But Diego was armed with one high-tech gadget: a secret key-fob camera that looked like an ordinary car key remote but was capable of discreetly recording hours of audio and video.

Diego was dressed in a well-tailored three-button dark gray suit, a white shirt, and a solid maroon tie pulled so tight it made the bottom of his neck puff out against his collar.

"Kill it, baby," I said, leaning over, hugging him. Diego nodded, mouth drawn tight as if he were already running scenarios in his head.

I set up the G-ride in the busy parking lot as close as I could to watch Diego enter the restaurant, discreetly parked, but with a perfect line of sight to the terrace tables.

But after two minutes, there was still no sign of Diego.

Three minutes passed. Then five. Then seven. I still couldn't see him on the terrace. I thumb-typed a text in our prearranged code, in case they checked his phone: innocuous Mexican slang for "What's happening, dude?"

"K onda, güey?"

No reply from Diego.

"K onda?"

My leg began twitching nervously.

I kept hitting resend on the BlackBerry.

Nothing.

I felt sweat drenching the front of my shirt.

This was the worst scenario for an undercover meet: we had no backup agents inside the restaurant with eyes on the UC, and no armed Panamanian counterparts watching our backs.

I couldn't sit for another second. I bolted from the Toyota and headed straight for the entrance of La Rosita.

What if Mercedes had switched up locations at the last minute?

What if her people had snatched Diego to pat him down, make sure he wasn't a cop?

In the restaurant, the hostess smiled and, in heavily accented English, said, "You have a reservation, sir?"

I was so focused, scanning for Diego's gray suit at the restaurant tables, that I barely heard myself answer.

"No, I'm meeting a friend," I said. "He's already seated."

I scanned every table hard but didn't see him anywhere.

Fuck! Had they grabbed him already?

I started to feel everyone's eyes locking on me as I frantically walked through the tables.

I hope to hell we're not compromised.

Where is he, for fuck's sake?

I had nowhere to go. I spun in a circle in the center of the restaurant, the walls becoming a blur. I quickly grabbed a busboy by the shoulder.

"El baño?" I asked, and no sooner had the kid gestured to the left than I saw that I was standing right next to Diego—in fact, I was literally looking down on the crown of my partner's head.

Diego was in an intense but muted conversation with Mercedes. And not only Mercedes, but two older Mexican-looking males. They were heavy hitters, I could tell. One appeared to be wearing a pistol, bulging behind the flap of his tan blazer.

Three targets? The meet was only supposed to be with Mercedes. I knew that Diego would be trying to hold his own, with no backup for his story, but even at a quick glance, I sensed that the sit-down had turned tense. Mercedes and the two henchmen had hard gazes; they weren't buying Diego's story.

Before anyone noticed me looking, I darted for the bathroom. A single trickle of sweat ran from my chest down to my navel. I could hear myself breathing loudly. Right before I reached the bathroom, I noticed a steak knife on a table ready to be cleared.

Could I grab it without being seen? There was no other option. I needed a weapon and had to take the chance.

As quickly as I could, I snatched up the knife, placed it flush against my wrist, and slipped it into my pocket.

In the bathroom, I turned on the sink and splashed cold water on my face, attempting to calm my nerves, hoping one of the bad guys wouldn't stroll in suddenly to take a piss.

What the hell can I do if they plan on kidnapping Diego? What if this meet is all a setup to take him as human collateral?

The door suddenly swung open—I straightened up, my face still dripping with cold water, but it was just a regular restaurant patron. I knew one thing: it was crucial to get photographs of Mercedes and the two heavies so I could identify them if they took Diego by gunpoint. It would also be critical for future indictments, and I couldn't rely on the key fob Diego was carrying.

I had the steak knife ready in one pocket; in the other, I had a small Canon digital camera, which I flipped on, to video mode.

Keep the camera steady in your hand. Don't make eye contact. They won't see it's on—just stroll by naturally . . .

I walked slowly past Diego, unable to aim the Canon's lens, just hoping I'd capture the faces of everyone at the table as I walked toward the door. I knew I couldn't hang out in the restaurant alone, so I found a discreet place outside where I could watch Diego through the windows of the front door. I sat there, my hands trembling as I waited for Diego to exit.

AFTER ANOTHER HOUR, Diego got up from the table, shook everyone's hands, and gave the half-hug—Mexican style—to all three, then walked out of the restaurant.

I followed him on foot as he walked on into the mall, staying thirty yards behind, making sure we weren't being followed by any of Mercedes's people.

Finally, I looked back over my shoulder three times and met up with him in a back parking lot. We were clean. We jumped in the cab of the Hilux and sped off.

Diego was silent for a long time, staring out the window and trying to make sense of what had just happened. His expression was trancelike.

"You all right, brother?" I reached over and grabbed him by the shoulder, attempting to shake him back to reality.

"What?"

"Bro, you cool?"

"That was so fuckin' intense," Diego said at last. "A straight-up interrogation. She kept hitting me with question after question. 'Who's your company? Who do you work with?'"

"How'd you play it?"

"Just started making up shit, story after story—how we're moving millions in tractor-trailers, our fleet of private aircraft. Ships. Told them we transport coke—by the tons."

"And?"

Diego grinned.

"She bought it, man!" he shouted. "She fuckin' bought it! I had all three of them eating out of the palm of my hand."

"Outstanding! Did she say whose money it is?"

"Yeah, it's his," Diego said.

"His?"

"She said it's *his*," Diego repeated.

Diego went quiet, smiling.

"His?" I asked again.

"Chapo."

"Chapo."

"Yes. She said, 'It's all Chapo's money.'"

TEAM AMERICA

PHOENIX, ARIZONA
July 1, 2010

I FELT LIKE a millionaire. And I *was* one—for a few hours, at least. I'd been entrusted with $1.2 million in laundered drug proceeds, freshly withdrawn from our undercover account at a local bank in Phoenix. Along with three other Task Force officers, I painstakingly counted and recounted that million in cash and stuffed the bundles into two white FedEx boxes.

The money seemed fake. It was a sensation I'd become accustomed to in the past year: anytime I handled US currency used in our undercover operations, I felt like I was thumbing through Monopoly money. A good cop is able to dissociate from the awe of the green. Those fat stacks of cash on our big conference table were just another tool of the undercover trade.

Counting the bills, I thought back to four months earlier, when Diego and I had made our first pickup. After nearly a year of nothing but big talk—her "hundred-million-dollar contracts all over globe"—Mercedes finally came through: she had a much smaller cash drop of $109,000, delivered, fittingly, in a laundry detergent bucket to Diego and my undercover teammate in a Home Depot parking lot just south of Los Angeles. That very afternoon—and following the instructions laid out precisely by Mercedes—Diego and I had run the stack to the bank, then wired the money to an account at Deutsche Bank in New York. From there, the money was transferred to an account at a corresponding bank in Mexico. Back at the office, Diego sent a photo of the wire confirmation to Mercedes over his BlackBerry and put his feet up on his desk.

"We're big-time now, dude," I said with a sarcastic laugh. It was a modest start, considering some of the huge figures Mercedes had been throwing around, but soon Diego and I were inundated with money-pickup requests. Mercedes set up back-to-back drops in New York City, black duffel bags stuffed with dirty money: $199,254 one day, $543,972 the next, and then $560,048. Always with the same wiring instructions—to a Deutsche Bank in New York.

A lot of the money couriers hardly looked the part. One time we flew to New York and followed a couple in their seventies who had parked their RV, with California plates, on a side street off Times Square, then marched two suitcases full of cash to our undercover in the shadows of the billboards.

Then it was up to Vancouver, Canada, for a pickup up of more than $800,000. The Canadian dollars had to be quickly converted to US currency before we could send the wire to Mercedes. In less than a month, we'd laundered more than $2.2 million of Chapo's money for Mercedes.

The money-laundering aspect of the investigation was authorized under an official Attorney General Exempt Operation (AGEO). An AGEO allowed federal agents to follow the money and further exploit their investigations, ultimately leading to the dismantlement of an entire drug-trafficking organization, as opposed to arresting a couple of low-level money couriers. It took me months of writing justifications to become authorized to create fictitious shell companies and open undercover bank accounts.

We'd flipped so many members of Bugsy's crew, getting them to cooperate, that our assistant United States attorney, before every proffer, would say to the defendants, "Now that you've seen the evidence we have against you, how would you like to come on over and join Team America?"

We'd dubbed our new case "Operation Team America." By June 2010, it was obvious that Mercedes had her hands full, and in the midst of all the cross-country cash pickups, she introduced Diego to Ricardo Robles, a thirty-four-year-old Mexican with a youthful face and thick black hair. Ricardo was a powerhouse money broker who'd grown up in the lucrative world of Mexican *casas de cambio*—money exchanges—even owning a few himself.

Diego and I quickly learned that all of the pickup contracts had come from Ricardo. Mercedes was just another protective layer, another buffer, shielding the true bosses while still taking her cut.

Over the weeks, Diego and Ricardo formed a tight bond. Finally, Ricardo asked for a face-to-face meet at Diego's Phoenix office. There was just one minor issue: we didn't *have* one.

Ricardo was flying in that afternoon. We arranged to have him picked up curbside at Phoenix Sky Harbor International Airport in a silver Mercedes CL 63 AMG. Our undercover teammate, driving the Mercedes, looked the part of a young narco. Following in a black Cadillac Escalade with twenty-two-inch black custom wheels, we used more undercover agents from the Task Force, posing as Diego's own personal security group.

As Ricardo drove in from the airport, we were still making the final arrangements in a luxurious high-rise office suite we'd rented. It was a gorgeous 1,200-square-foot space overlooking downtown Phoenix.

"Shit, we've got a major problem," I said to Diego as we were walking around the suite admiring the view.

"The place doesn't look lived in," Diego agreed. "Looks like we moved in five minutes ago."

I ran to the elevator, rode down to the street, jumped into my G-ride, and drove to my house. There, I grabbed some framed art off my living room walls, a few houseplants, sculptures, and trinkets I had collected from my travels. Meanwhile, Diego at the last moment set a framed photo of his kids on top of the desk. With my stuff plus his, the illusion was complete: Diego, wearing a silver Armani suit, sat back in his tall leather swivel chair, looking every bit the sleazy corporate executive.

Our teammates radioed to me that Ricardo had arrived and was coming up in the elevator. Diego quickly tightened his tie while I gave him a heavy pat on the back and rushed out the door.

We were charging at least seven percent on every money pickup, a standard commission. We would then take the commission and set it aside as Trafficker Directed Funds (TDF), to be used to rent the office space, buy the latest MacBooks and sophisticated recording devices—hidden inside expensive-looking wristwatches—along with the iridescent Armani suit for Diego.

The trust had already been established through laundering a couple million in drug money, and now it was time for Ricardo and Diego to talk about the other end of the equation: a two-ton cocaine transportation contract, moving product from Ecuador to Los Angeles.

"He wants to introduce me to Chapo's people," Diego told me as we debriefed the meeting over cups of coffee.

It had become obvious that, just like Doña Guadalupe and Mercedes, Ricardo was yet *another* buffer—another broker in the middle. And we knew there would likely be several more layers to sift through before we got to the top.

But before the introductions to Chapo's people could be made, there was a final test. Ricardo had several money pickups in Vancouver, Canada. But this time he wanted that cash—the $1.2 million—delivered directly to Mexico in *bulk*.

DIEGO HAD ALREADY FLOWN to Mexico City to coordinate the operation with DEA agents there, as well as trusted members of the Mexican Federal Police (PF). Alone, I took the FedEx boxes to a Learjet—used by the DEA solely for undercover ops—through a private hangar at Sky Harbor International Airport. As we rose through the clouds, I felt like nodding off, but I didn't dare take my eyes off the cash-stuffed pair of boxes. My eyes stayed glued to them the entire flight as if they were my newborn twins.

The pilots flew me down to Toluca, outside Distrito Federal, where I was picked up by Mexico City–based DEA agent Kenny McKenzie, driving a white armored Ford Expedition. I tucked the FedEx boxes in the backseat, glancing warily around me.

Shouldn't we be covered by another armed agent?

I felt twitchy, but kept my thoughts to myself as we pulled away from the airport. It was an hour-long drive over the small mountain range into Mexico City, a route on which there was an ever-present risk of a carjacking.

We drove directly to an underground parking garage in a middle-class area called Satélite, on the north side of the city. I was relieved to see Diego, a second Mexico City DEA agent, and two plainclothes Mexican Federal Police when we arrived.

The PF had provided the "drop vehicle," a white Chevy Tornado pickup that looked to me a bit like a mini El Camino. It was a seized drug smuggler's truck, complete with a hidden stash compartment—a simple hollow cavity underneath the bed—nowhere near as sophisticated as the type Bugsy and his crew of narco juniors used in Phoenix. The deep trap—clearly designed for moving bulkier contraband like compressed bales of weed or bricks of cocaine—was accessed from behind the rear bumper, and the open space underneath ran the full length of the truck bed. Diego and I tied the FedEx boxes together, then used the remaining rope to secure them to the outside of the trapdoor so that they didn't slide the full length of the trap and become invisible to our targets.

Our Mexican counterparts also slapped a tiny GPS tracker on the truck so we could follow it to wherever the targets would unload the money, in hopes of pinpointing yet another location, another piece of the puzzle, more targets to ID, and another chance to follow the money. I kept repeating the mantra, *Exploit, exploit, exploit*, which had been drummed into my head back at the DEA Academy.

Mexican PF was doing us a huge favor by allowing us to drop $1.2 million and let it walk, but they felt they should remain on the perimeter and keep their hands off the actual money. As a result, none of the Federal Police wanted to touch the Chevy pickup, let alone drive it.

Now that the truck was loaded, Diego was in phone contact with the targets, and they agreed to pick up the vehicle on the upper-level parking lot of another mall called Plaza Satélite. Diego and the other Mexico City agent drove the armored Ford Expedition ahead while Kenny and I hopped into the shitty Tornado, with its manual transmission. Kenny drove, following the Expedition out of the parking garage and out onto the busy street, heading north. My mind was still racing:

Our security setup is worthless: more than a million in cash, and we've got a grand total of four US agents? Only two of us have Glocks—useless if we get jacked by some assholes with AKs . . .

If the operation went south, there was no way this truck would get us out of harm's way. The tiny Chevy took a day and a half to get up to 40 miles per hour. We lurched and jolted along in traffic as Kenny grinded the stick shift into gear.

It was blazing hot in the cab, and the A/C was busted. Cars, motorcycles, and trucks were buzzing, honking, zigzagging. This was the wild, chaotic traffic for which Mexico City is famous— and which I would come to know well in the years ahead. Kenny seemed to be hitting every possible pothole and red light on the route, too.

By far the biggest security risk was the local cops. Too many Federal Police knew about the operation for my liking. And if just *one* of these PF guys was dirty, he could easily call up one of his friends and ambush us, and they'd split the proceeds fifty-fifty.

The Chevy kept jumping forward while I continued talking to Diego in the Expedition on my Nextel. All of a sudden, the Expedition pulled over to the side of the road and the driver opened up the door and began projectile-vomiting onto the street. He had eaten at some roadside carnitas stand an hour earlier.

By the time we reached Plaza Satélite, one of the largest shopping malls in the city, I began to think there must be something wrong—how could a popular shopping center be so desolate?

Diego and I had no idea whether the targets were waiting at the location. We were twenty-five minutes early, but the crooks could be early, too. Kenny drove to the upper parking lot on the north side and pulled the truck in alongside a few stray cars. I sat waiting for the clear signal from surveillance to get out. We'd leave the truck right there with the keys in the ignition for the prearranged drop.

I was about to bail from the passenger side when I looked up and saw a Mexican guy, early thirties, five foot nine, muscular build, walking slowly in front of the truck. I felt my gut clench—were the crooks here already?

The guy was wearing a black-collared button-down shirt with a dark gray jacket and dark blue jeans. His eyes were a piercing brown. There was a blade wound running straight down from his left eye, a good two inches long, like he'd been disfigured by an acid teardrop.

It wasn't just the scar that was unnerving. As a street cop, you develop a sense for these things. I studied the walk: he looked to be packing on the right side of his waistband. The guy had the unmistakable gait and look of an enforcer. He walked past the pickup, looking back one more time with menace.

I turned to Kenny. "Who's that?"

"No idea, bro."

"Kenny, we need to get the fuck outta here before we get shot."

We both swung open the doors of the Tornado at the same time.

I couldn't spend another second sitting on the million-dollar bull's-eye.

―――――

THE TORNADO DROP was unprecedented—no federal law enforcement agency had ever delivered this kind of cash and let it walk, certainly not on the streets of Mexico City.

Diego and I were now seen by Chapo's people as fast-moving international players: we could deliver more than a million bucks, quickly—a mere forty-eight hours after picking up the bundles of bills nearly three thousand miles and two international borders away.

There was no way Ricardo would suspect that he was dealing directly with cops—let alone the DEA. Ricardo told Diego that the money was headed south to purchase a major consignment of cocaine bound for the States. It was all happening so fast that Diego and I struggled to keep pace with the logistics. We were spending more time in the air and at hotels than in the Phoenix Task Force office. We'd be on a jet to the Caribbean one week, then back at our desks in Phoenix the next, and back out on a plane the following week for yet another tropical meet.

Finding neutral countries in which to meet bad guys was becoming increasingly challenging, so I ordered a five-foot-long world map and pinned it up on the office wall. For fun, Diego and I closed our eyes and pointed a blind finger at possible locations for the next undercover meet. His finger landed on Iceland, mine somewhere in the middle of the Pacific Ocean.

Diego narrowed his focus to the isthmus of Central America, north of Panama.

"San José," he said. "Let's set the next meet in Costa Rica."

"Costa Rica sounds right," I said.

Costa Rica, like Panama, was considered neutral ground for

narcos. *Más tranquilo*, and far less risky than having a sit-down in Mexico or Colombia.

BY THE NEXT DAY, Diego was sitting across the table from two of Chapo's operators and Ricardo at an outdoor restaurant in the heart of Costa Rica's capital.

This time, unlike in Panama, I had eyes on him, parked across the street inside a rented black Toyota Land Cruiser. If Diego had felt cornered during his meet with Mercedes in Panama, this time he took the upper hand, leaning in forcefully, doing almost all the talking, pressing them with questions—the bulk cash delivery had given him the power of street credibility.

Diego asked—no, *demanded*—to know who all the coke and cash belonged to, who really was the *jefe*, before he'd set any wheels in motion.

It took him about fifteen minutes, but finally one of Ricardo's men reluctantly coughed up the name of the man they'd previously been calling El Señor.

"Carlos Torres-Ramos."

The name didn't ring any bells for Diego or me.

Jetting back to the Phoenix Task Force, I quickly began working up Carlos within the DEA's databases and found his record: Carlos Torres-Ramos had so far flown under DEA's radar, but he did have a notable criminal history. Confidential informants reported that Carlos was known for moving massive loads of cocaine by the ton from Colombia, Ecuador, and Peru. I studied the black-and-white photo. He stood six feet tall, with receding black hair, a neatly trimmed black goatee, and dark eyes that made him look almost like a professor. But there was another detail that immediately leapt out at me.

"You're not going to believe this," I said, still staring at the computer screen. "Diego, get over here."

I showed Diego the link: Carlos's daughter Jasmine Elena Torres-Leon was married to Jesús Alfredo Guzmán Salazar, one of Chapo's most trusted sons.

"Holy shit," Diego said softly. "Carlos and Chapo are *consuegros*."

The word had no precise English equivalent—"co-fathers-in-law"—and was an important connection between two Mexican families, especially in the world of Sinaloan narcos.

We had thought Carlos was a big-time player, but we never imagined he was this big.

Diego began speaking to Carlos about transportation arrangements directly over the phone, then via BlackBerry Messenger—Carlos considered BlackBerry the most secure mode of communicating. Though they'd still never met—Diego in Phoenix, Carlos in Sinaloa—the two were establishing trust.

"*Cero-cincuenta*," Diego said, smiling, finishing up a text session with Carlos. "Think I *got* this dude."

"*Cero-cincuenta?*"

"He just assigned me a number—like he considers me part of his organization. He calls me *cero cincuenta*."

Diego was now "050" and part of Carlos's secret code list. All of Carlos's most trusted men were designated by a number. Locations were digitized, too: 039 represented Canada; 023 was Mexico City; 040 was Ecuador.

Carlos even sent Diego the equation his organization used to decode phone numbers when they'd send them via text. Sophisticated traffickers never give out phone numbers openly, so Diego would have to multiply every digit via the equation to figure out Carlos's new cell phone number.

———

THE MONEY PICKUPS kept flowing in from Canada, now by the millions, all going toward Carlos's purchase of the two-ton load of cocaine down in Ecuador. Of course, Diego and I weren't working for free; Diego knew the rules of the narco game and convinced Carlos to give him a deposit to cover the initial costs of transportation. Carlos agreed, and the next day he had a total of $3 million delivered to various pickup locations in Montreal and New York.

Three million in cash: as good as a seizure—and it had the added value of not burning our undercover investigation. With the money deposited in our TDF bank account, Diego and I jumped on the next plane to Ecuador to begin preparing to take delivery of the two tons of cocaine.

Once we'd arrived, Diego had a quick undercover meeting with several of Carlos's men at one of Guayaquil's upscale steakhouses. I sat at a table across the restaurant, in the shadows. This time I had a small backup army: a team of plainclothes Ecuador National Police. This was the DEA's most trusted Sensitive Investigation Unit in-country; every officer had been personally trained at Quantico in counter-narcotics operations. The plainclothesmen were spread all over the restaurant—inside and out—watching every move of Carlos's men.

ONCE DIEGO FINISHED the meeting, the cops in unmarked cars followed the men to the outskirts of the city—the crooks made a brief stop at a shop to buy brown packing tape—then to a nondescript *finca* (small farm). Covertly surveilling the *finca*, the cops were able to obtain the license plate of a white delivery truck parked outside.

Classic Quantico scenario. I remembered from my days of practicals at the academy. The events taking place were standard drug-trafficking methods.

The Ecuadorian cops sat on the truck the entire night and watched it pull away from the *finca* the next morning, the rear end loaded with bright yellow salt bags. Diego and I instructed the cops to set up a seemingly routine roadside checkpoint, and the truck drove right into it. As soon as the driver saw the marked police cars with flashing lights, he screeched to a stop, bailed out, and sprinted across a field. The police quickly chased him down and put him in cuffs. The cops searched the back of the truck and found 2,513-kilogram bricks of cocaine, stamped with the numbers 777—wrapped in that brown packing tape—tossed into seventy yellow salt bags.

Diego quickly passed the news to Carlos, via BlackBerry, that the load had been seized by the local police, but the boss didn't flinch. He'd lost two thousand keys to a random roadblock, but it was just the cost of doing business. He wasted no time in asking if Diego was ready to take delivery of more cocaine.

"You believe this guy?" I asked Diego. "Ice in his veins. Just lost a load with a street value of nearly sixty-three million and he wants to trust us with more."

Diego responded to Carlos's text immediately:

"Estamos listos. A sus ordenes."

We're ready. Awaiting your orders.

OVER THE NEXT SEVERAL WEEKS, Carlos's crew in Ecuador delivered more than eight hundred kilos of cocaine to undercover Ecuadorian cops posing as Diego's workers, triggering a global takedown of the Carlos Torres-Ramos drug-trafficking organization.

The whole house of cards came tumbling down in just a matter of hours—Carlos, Ricardo, Mercedes, Doña Guadalupe, and fifty-one other defendants spanning from Canada to Colombia. We also directly seized more than $6.3 million and 6.8 tons of cocaine.

It took Diego and me *months* to recover from the follow-up work generated by our massive takedown.

AS SOON AS THINGS settled down at the Task Force office, we were eager to get back on the hunt. But this time, we were left with only one place to go. We laid out the chart of the Sinaloa Cartel hierarchy and saw only one target name higher than Carlos. It was that pudgy-faced man with the black mustache in the photo wearing a black tactical vest and plain baseball hat, lightly gripping an automatic rifle slung across his chest.

Joaquín Archivaldo Guzmán Loera—El Chapo himself.

PART II

LA FRONTERA

IN JANUARY 2011, I put in for an open position at the DEA Mexico City Country Office, long considered one of the most elite foreign postings for US federal drug enforcement agents targeting Mexican cartels. If I hoped to successfully target Chapo Guzmán, I knew I'd need to work—and *live*—permanently south of the border. Violence was soaring in Mexico: more than 13,000 people were dead as a result of Chapo's gunmen and other cartels—notably the ex–Mexican Special Forces known as Los Zetas—battling for key smuggling turf along the US border.

Several months after we took down the Carlos Torres-Ramos organization, Diego and I began conducting our own deconfliction on Guzmán. Surely there had to be someone—*some* federal team or task force—targeting the world's most wanted narcotics kingpin. Diego and I ran through the various scenarios as we walked out of the US Attorney's Office in downtown Phoenix. There had to be agents in every federal law enforcement agency who had a bead on Chapo. We needed to find those agents, put our intel together, and begin coordinating.

I was expecting to discover a hidden world of US-agency-led Chapo task forces, secret war rooms all lining up to get their shots in—but after days of conducting deconfliction checks, Diego and I kept drawing blanks.

Who was targeting Chapo?

The shocking answer was: no one. There was no dedicated team. No elite task force. Not a single federal agent with a substantial case on his whereabouts.

Among the stacks of closed-case files, stale intelligence—not to mention the tens of millions spent each year on the "war on drugs"—Diego and I couldn't find one lawman on either side of the border who was actively pursuing the man personally responsible for controlling more than half the global drug trade.

THEN, ON FEBRUARY 15, 2011, Jaime Zapata and Víctor Ávila, two US Department of Homeland Security Investigations ("HSI") special agents on assignment in Mexico City, were ambushed in the northern state of San Luis Potosí by masked members of the Zetas Cartel. One Zetas vehicle passed the agents' armored Suburban, firing automatic rifles and ramming them off the road. The Zetas gunmen then pulled open the driver's side door and tried to drag Zapata out, but he fought back, trying to reason with the Zetas as they surrounded the vehicle. "We're Americans! We're diplomats!" The response was a hail of automatic gunfire. Zapata was killed at the wheel and Ávila badly wounded.

The murder of Special Agent Zapata threw my life into sudden turmoil. I'd already been selected for the position in Mexico City—but now I had my young family to think about, too. Was it safe to move my wife and our young sons south of the border? The majority of DEA agents wouldn't even consider putting in for a job in Mexico, due to the fear of being kidnapped or killed.

"Jesus, with Zapata getting murdered, I'm on the fence now," I told Diego. "We're happy and safe here in Phoenix, but, I dunno—this feels like the next step." We were camped out at a table at Mariscos Navolato, ties loosened, drinking a couple of Pacificos after a long day of organizing evidence for the Team America prosecutions. I was practically hoarse from talking to Diego over the blaring banda playing on the stage in front of our table.

"You know what you're getting yourself into," Diego said. "At the end of the day, you gotta do what's right for you and your family."

The next morning, I sat down with my wife and laid it all out for her. There was nothing to hide; all the risks were evident. I had been prepping her for months, but the danger of life in Mexico still weighed heavily on my mind.

"What's your gut telling you?" she asked. "I'll support you, whatever you decide."

I sat silent at the kitchen counter for a long time.

"Go," I said finally. "My gut's telling me go. Take the assignment in Mexico."

Looking back to my sheltered life in Kansas, I would never have fathomed those words. But every time I'd been faced with a life-changing decision, it felt uncomfortable, and I knew this was just another one of those moments. I paused and took a deep breath; my worries about any danger ahead began to lift: yes, it was natural career progression, after all—just furthering the investigations that Diego and I had started all those years ago.

Then it was off to six months of Spanish immersion at the DEA's language school in Southern California and, later, several more weeks of intensive training back at Quantico.

Federal agents assigned to work in high-risk foreign posts were drilled in "personnel recovery" techniques: evasive driving maneuvers, including how to take over a moving car when your partner gets killed at the wheel and how to saw through plastic handcuffs using a piece of nylon string. This was followed by specialized training in handling heavy armored vehicles, which had become mandatory after the murder of Special Agent Zapata.

IN FEBRUARY 2012, while I was away at language school, Diego had flipped a member of Chapo's inner circle traveling to the United States.

Diego called me—he was walking fast somewhere down the street, out in the wind—and he sounded breathless.

"Yo, I got his BlackBerry PIN."

"Got whose PIN?"

"C."

As always, we avoided saying the name Chapo whenever possible.

"C's BlackBerry?"

"Yup. I have *his* personal PIN."

"Holy fuck. Where's it pinging?"

"Cabo," Diego said.

"He's in Cabo San Lucas?"

"Yep—but here's the thing," Diego said, frustrated. "No one fuckin' believes me. They keep telling me it can't possibly be his number. But I'm telling you: it's him, brother."

Diego had passed the PIN to DEA Mexico City, which began its standard deconfliction. Several hours later, Diego heard back from a special agent in Mexico who told him the FBI in New York had thousands of wire intercepts with that same PIN. But they were oblivious and had no idea it was actually Chapo using it.

"Shocking," I said. "The Feebs have been secretly targeting Chapo and don't even know which goddamn phone he's using."

The DEA agent in Mexico City told Diego they were already preparing an operation with the Mexican Federal Police and had brusquely pushed Diego to the side.

"They're not going to let me in on the op," Diego said. "Shit, I should be in Cabo running this thing." I could tell Diego was feeling the strain of not having me by his side to iron out my own DEA agents in Mexico. I felt equally helpless sitting there in my Spanish immersion class, but I knew there was no stopping this runaway train—not with the Mexico City office having already involved the Mexican Federal Police.

CABO SAN LUCAS, at the tip of the Baja Peninsula, was long considered one of the safest locations in Mexico and a favorite vacation spot among Hollywood stars and thousands of American tourists. US Secretary of State Hillary Clinton was in town at the same time as Chapo—at the Barceló Los Cabos Palace Deluxe, attending a G20 foreign ministers meeting, during which she signed the United States–Mexico Transboundary Agreement.

Chapo clearly felt safe, even untouchable. DEA Mexico City put together a rapid operation that included three hundred Mexican Federal Police and moved them all up to Cabo overnight.

But the mission turned into a debacle. The takedown team launched on an upscale neighborhood of beachfront mansions, raided twelve houses . . . and came away with nothing. All they managed to do was roust a bunch of wealthy American retirees, vacationers, and well-heeled Mexican families, pissing off the entire neighborhood.

After the first failure, the Federal Police, fed up with taking grief from the community, sent most of its personnel home. DEA coordinated a second capture op, but now they didn't have enough manpower—only thirty PF officers. Nevertheless, they narrowed the pinging of Chapo's phone down to one of three beautiful beachfront mansions in a cul-de-sac right outside Cabo. As they hit the first two houses, Chapo was waiting in the third and watching it all unfold. He had no heavy security detail—the only people with him were his most trusted bodyguard, who went by "Picudo," a Cessna pilot, his cook, a gardener, and a girlfriend.

As the DEA and the PF descended on the cul-de-sac, Guzmán and Picudo slid out the back door and ran up the coast, narrowly escaping the dragnet. The two men somehow made it all the way up to La Paz and then were picked up on a clandestine airstrip— likely by Chapo's favorite pilot, Araña—and flown by Cessna back to the mountains.

After the debacle, the Associated Press reported,

> Mexican authorities nearly captured the man the U.S. calls the world's most powerful drug lord, who like Osama bin Laden, has apparently been hiding in plain sight. Federal police nearly nabbed Joaquín "El Chapo" Guzmán in a coastal mansion in Los Cabos three weeks ago, barely a day after U.S. Secretary of State Hillary Clinton met with dozens of other foreign ministers in the same southern Baja peninsula resort town.[*]

---

[*] Associated Press, March 12, 2012.

Among the people of Mexico, the raid immediately became a running joke: The Federal Police could muster a small army to capture Chapo in his mansion, but they forgot to cover the back door.

No one on the ground from DEA Mexico had a clue how big this Cabo opportunity had been. There were technological failures in the first raid, and a poorly coordinated effort in the second. The Mexicans may not have had enough people to cover the back door, true, but where the hell were the Americans? There weren't any DEA agents covering the back door, either.

A narcocorrido instantly hit the streets, recorded by Calibre 50. "Se Quedaron a Tres Pasos" ("They Stayed Three Steps Behind") turned the escape into another Dillinger-like legend, claiming that Chapo had gone on vacation in Los Cabos and then "outsmarted more than one hundred agents of the DEA."

> *They stayed three steps behind Guzmán*
> *They looked for him in Los Cabos*
> *But he was already in Culiacán!*

The corrido got one thing right: Chapo was back on his home turf in the mountains. In the following months, the FBI continued to obtain Chapo's new numbers, then DEA Mexico would ping them to rural areas of Sinaloa, and later the nearby state of Nayarit. DEA Mexico then passed the intelligence to the Federal Police, which conducted additional raids, only to find that the target phone was not in the hands of Chapo at all. Instead the phone was being used by some low-level cartel employee who was only forwarding messages to Chapo's actual device.

And now no one had that number.

That was because Guzmán was employing the technique of a "mirror." It was the first time Diego and I had heard of Chapo using one. Mirroring wasn't a complex way of dodging law enforcement surveillance, but it was highly effective, if done correctly.

"Always one step ahead," I told Diego. "Chapo's smart—restructuring his communications as soon as he returned safely to Sinaloa."

After continued failed attempts in which they hit only the mirror (the low-level employee holding the target phone), the FBI's numbers began to dry up, and DEA Mexico, along with the Federal Police, decided to throw in the towel. DEA Mexico even closed the case file, and it didn't appear as if anyone was reopening a Chapo Guzmán investigation anytime soon.

BEFORE I EVEN PUT IN for the position, I knew I'd be ending a once-in-a-lifetime partnership. As much as Diego would've loved to investigate cartels south of the border, he wasn't a fed; he was a Task Force officer—a local Mesa, Arizona, detective—and couldn't reside in another country. The invitation to my going-away party had a picture of Diego and me together in our tactical vests just after we'd finished a big raid, smiles on our faces, the tangerine shades of the setting Arizona sun behind us.

Over the years, if our casework took us to Southern California, Diego and I would often zip down to Tijuana to take in even more of the Mexican culture I'd come to love. We'd listen to mariachi, banda, and norteño, then swing over to the strip clubs at 3 a.m., before grabbing a handful of street tacos and heading back across the border. For me, it was all part of learning the culture, deepening my understanding of a world I'd submersed myself in since that first night at Mariscos Navolato when I heard "El Niño de La Tuna" and began educating myself on the Mexican cartels.

I would *never* have gone to Tijuana without Diego. We weren't tourists, after all—a DEA agent and a detective from an elite counter-narcotics task force—and if anyone knew who we *really* were, especially with the heavyweight cartel drug and money-laundering cases we were working, we'd have made extremely vulnerable targets.

For the going-away party, several of my buddies from back home flew in: even my old sergeant from the sheriff's office. The celebration kicked off at one of San Diego's craft-beer bistros—a night of war stories, a running slide show of my time with Team 3, and the requisite plaques and framed photos—but the party didn't end when the bosses went home. Instead, at 2 a.m., I grabbed my closest friends and suggested we pop down to Mexico. But just as we were about to leave, Diego stared at his buzzing iPhone. "Fuck—family emergency," he said abruptly, hugging me. "Sorry, dude—gotta bounce."

My friends and I jammed into a cab and raced to the border. A taxi full of gringos, and no Diego as our guide. I had heard the cold click of the border pedestrian gates close behind me many times before, but now it was all on me: I would have to do all the talking and navigating.

Fresh out of language school, my Spanish was good enough—my teacher was from Guadalajara, so my accent was consistent with the locals'. But my vocabulary was still so limited that I often found myself getting knee-deep in conversations I just couldn't get out of until I'd end the interaction abruptly with a nod and a *"gracias."*

Somehow I managed to lead my Kansas buddies through the night, tossing back shots of Don Julio, rolling over to a streetside taco stand, mowing down al pastor on the spit, and walking back across the border into California just as the sun was cresting the mountains to the east. *Diego should've been here to see this*, I thought, but then I realized it was almost a rite of passage that I was able now to handle Tijuana on my own.

THE FOLLOWING DAY I was at the San Diego International Airport with my family, lugging the cart loaded up with our suitcases and carry-on bags through the terminal to check in. I was just another dad, hands full of passports, boarding passes—and my sons tugging at my elbow.

Whatever risks lay ahead, I was more certain than ever I'd made the right decision.

The plane ascended through the clouds—my sons fell fast asleep on my shoulders—and, for the next couple of hours, at least, hunting down Chapo Guzmán was the furthest thing from my mind.

DF

MY FAMILY AND I touched down in Mexico the last week of May 2012. The sprawling metropolis—with twenty-six million people, the largest city in the Western Hemisphere—was rarely referred to by locals as "Ciudad de México." To the natives it was El Distrito Federal ("DF") or, owing to the ever-present layer of smog, El Humo ("The Smoke").

At the embassy, I'd initially been assigned to the Money Laundering Group. The Sinaloa Cartel desk was run by a special agent who was burned out, especially after the Cabo fiasco. After a few months, I convinced management to transfer me over from Money Laundering to the Enforcement Group. The following morning, I sat down for breakfast with my new colleagues and group supervisor at Agave, a café known for its machaca con huevo and freshly baked pan dulce.

Before my arrival, the system had been inefficient. Most DEA special agents were working leads on multiple cartels: Sinaloa, the Zetas, the Gulf Cartel, the Beltrán-Leyvas, the Knights Templar . . . My group supervisor knew that this lack of focus was highly counterproductive. The Mexico City Country Office was such a hive of activity that no special agent could become a subject-matter expert on one particular cartel, because they were constantly working *all* of them.

So, in one of my first meetings with my new team, we began a reorganization. We went around the table to focus our assignments, and when it came to the Sinaloa Cartel, the assigned agent spoke up immediately, nodding at me.

"You can have this *desmadre* of a case," he said. "I'm *done*. The Mexicans couldn't catch Chapo if he was standing at the fuckin' Starbucks across the street from the embassy."

"Sure, I'll take it," I said, trying to contain my excitement.

"*Adelante y suerte, amigo.*" Go ahead, and good luck.

At that moment, my mind drifted far from the meeting: I tried to picture Chapo eating breakfast, too, in a mountain hideaway or on some ranch in the heart of Sinaloa . . . *Somewhere* in Mexico. At least we were now on the same soil.

The task in front of me was daunting. After all the failed capture operations, all the years of near misses, I knew that Chapo must have learned from his mistakes. He had the resources, the money, and the street smarts to secrete himself so deeply into his underworld that it would now be extremely difficult—perhaps even impossible—to take him unaware.

He has eleven years of hard study on me, I thought as the meeting wrapped up. *I've got a hell of a lot of catching up to do.*

AS I SETTLED INTO my work at the embassy, I ran into Thomas McAllister, the DEA regional director for North and Central Americas Region (NCAR). He gave me a piercing look.

"Hogan, I'm told if anyone can catch Chapo, it's you . . ."

It was more a question than a statement, and I felt my face

flush. I knew where this had come from: my first group supervisor, back in Phoenix, had worked with McAllister at DEA headquarters and knew exactly how relentless and methodical I was when pursuing the targets of my investigations.

"We'll see, sir," I said, smiling. "I'll give it my best shot."

One thing I had vowed: I was not going to fall into the trap of believing all the legends and hype. Even some of my DEA colleagues had lost hope, so I disengaged emotionally from the Chapo mythology, instead focusing on it from the most basic policing perspective. No criminal was *impossible* to capture, after all, the failed Cabo operation proved that Chapo was more vulnerable now than ever.

NO SOONER HAD I settled into my seat in the Enforcement Group than I was assigned to be the DEA liaison on a case dominating all the Mexican headlines: a drug-related murder in broad daylight inside the terminal at the Mexico City International Airport. The airport was known to be among the most corrupt in the world; inbound flights from the Andes, especially Peru, almost always had cocaine hidden in the cargo. What made the incident all the more shocking was that the murders involved uniformed Mexican cops shooting fellow Mexican cops.

Two Federal Police officers assigned to the airport were just getting off their shift, walking through Terminal 2. They were attempting to smuggle several kilos of cocaine hidden underneath the navy blue jacket of one of the officers—marked POLICÍA FEDERAL in white on the back—when they were approached by three PF officers coming *on* shift, who had become suspicious of them.

A quick argument ensued between the two groups as they stood near the public food court. The dirty cops drew their service pistols and began gunning down the honest cops. One was executed with a point-blank shot to the head; two others were hit and died. To outsiders, the carnage looked like a terrorist attack; horrified travelers were screaming and scrambling for cover. Meanwhile, the corrupt officers took off running through the terminal, jumped in a truck, and sped away.

"Can you believe this shit?" I turned toward a senior agent in the group. "Blue-on-blue in broad daylight in the middle of an international airport? Who are these guys?"

The agent wasn't fazed; he didn't even look up from his computer screen.

"Bienvenidos," he said. Welcome to Mexico.

Though I tried to assist the Federal Police and the PGR—the Mexican Attorney General's Office—tracking down the murderers, I soon came face-to-face with a harsh reality: there were too many layers of corruption. The investigation into the blue-on-blue killings faltered and eventually went cold. It was a stark introduction for me—I saw firsthand, within weeks of my new assignment, why fewer than five percent of homicides in Mexico are ever solved.

OF ALL THE STUNNING cases of corruption and violence in Latin America, few lingered like the case of DEA agent Enrique "Kiki" Camarena, who vanished on a busy street in Guadalajara in 1985 while walking to meet his wife for lunch. Camarena's body wasn't found for nearly a month. When it was, it was discovered that his skull, jaw, nose, cheekbones, and windpipe had all been crushed; his ribs had been broken and he'd been viciously tortured; he was even sodomized with a broom handle. Perhaps worst of all, his head had been drilled with a screwdriver, and he'd been buried in a shallow grave while still breathing.

Kiki Camarena's disappearance became a major international incident and heavily strained relations between the United States and Mexico—the US government offered a $5 million reward for the arrest of the murderers.

When I arrived at DEA's Mexico City Country Office more than twenty-five years later, the circumstances surrounding Camarena's death had not been forgotten. His memory was kept vividly alive. Along the main embassy hallway, a conference room dedicated to the slain agent—we referred to it simply as the Kiki Room—featured a small bust of Camarena and a plaque. Convicted of Kiki's torture-murder was none other than Miguel Ángel Félix Gallardo, "El Padrino," a former Federal Police officer turned godfather of the Guadalajara Cartel—and Joaquín Guzmán's mentor in the narcotics business.[*]

LOOKING BEYOND THE DEEP-ROOTED history of violence in Mexico, I tried to give my wife and young sons the best life possible in the capital under the enormously high-stress circumstances. The DEA assigned us a spacious three-bedroom apartment in La Condesa, the city center's hippest neighborhood—I suppose you could compare it to Paris's Latin Quarter or Manhattan's SoHo—home to young businesspeople, artists, and students. It was also close to the US embassy, on Paseo de la Reforma, so just a fifteen-minute drive to work.

---

[*] Miguel Ángel Félix Gallardo and two other Guadalajara Cartel kingpins, Ernesto Fonseca Carrillo and Rafael Caro Quintero, were all ultimately convicted in connection with the Kiki Camarena murder.

We loved the neighborhood, full of tree-lined streets shading the 1920s architecture: restaurants, cafés, boutiques, galleries, and lively open-air markets on Sundays.

But it was difficult for me to enjoy the vibrant life of the city: my head was constantly on a swivel. *Street-cop mode.* It was second nature to be watching my back—I'd done so since I was twenty-one and on patrol with the sheriff's office—but in Mexico, there never seemed to be a moment's rest. I was always checking for tails and surveillance by members of the cartel, street thugs, or even the Mexican government. When I left our apartment at 7 a.m., walking out to my Chevy Tahoe, I'd study all the other vehicles on the street. Which cars were new to the block? Which ones seemed out of place? Which cars had someone sitting inside them? I'd even memorize makes, models, and plate numbers.

Whenever we went to a new neighborhood, my wife knew that there was no point talking to me. I was too busy scanning the streets, looking hard at the faces of pedestrians, taxi drivers, deliverymen—anyone, in fact, within shooting distance.

After just a few weeks in DF, my wife had also learned the techniques of constant risk assessment: look everyone on the sidewalk in the eyes quickly to judge them, and decide: threat or not? She and our young sons were always on the street, at the park, shopping, or meeting friends. There was crime all over DF, but of a random nature: we'd hear reports of an embassy employee being held up at gunpoint for his gold watch in a local restaurant in our neighborhood, or a lady out pushing her kid in a stroller having her handbag snatched.

But there were plenty of great things about living in Mexico, too. We especially loved the city's street food: tacos de canasta, tlacoyos, elote (sweet corn in a cup with melting butter topped with a dab of mayonnaise and chili powder). But best of all were the camotes—sweet potatoes—from a vendor who'd come around every week at sundown, pushing his old squeaky metal cart.

The guy looked as if he'd been working in the sun all day, face golden brown, covered in beads of perspiration from pushing his wood-burning stove up and down the streets. The pressure of the smoke and heat from the fire would sound a steam whistle, like an old locomotive in a Western movie. You could hear the sound coming from blocks away, even if you were indoors. One of my sons would shout:

"Daddy, the camote man!"

We'd throw on our shoes and run outside. Sometimes the camote man would be gone, vanishing in the shadows down side streets before he'd sound his whistle again, directing us where to run. Once we hunted him down, he'd pull out a drawer full of large sweet potatoes roasted over the wood fire and let my sons pick out the best-looking ones, then he'd slice them lengthwise and drizzle condensed milk over the top and add a heavy sprinkle of cinnamon and sugar—a bargain at just twenty-five pesos.

Even in those sweet moments, as much as I tried to mask it from my sons, I was on edge. Children were always the most vulnerable for kidnapping—we even had one neighbor, a "self-made millionaire," who'd fly his daughter to school in a private helicopter every weekday.

It wasn't strange to see the latest Ferraris and Porsches ripping through our neighborhood streets—though anything lavish and excessive in the capital reeked of a narco connection. There was an estimated $40 billion a year in drug money flowing through the country's economy, and it had to trickle down somewhere.

I was constantly reminded of a remark that I'd heard from a local journalist in DF: "Everything is fine in Mexico until *suddenly* it's not." The expression captured it all in chilling simplicity. "You're living your life happily and then one day you're dead."

CHAPO HAD FINALLY BECOME a household name in the United States, designated Public Enemy Number One by the Chicago Crime Commission—the first outlaw to earn that title since Al Capone. And while I was glad this label drew more attention to Guzmán's name and his criminal activity, it did little, from an investigative standpoint, to assist with a capture.

At my embassy desk, I spent day after day sorting intel on Guzmán, dissecting every old file I could get my hands on. The freshest leads were the ones that came from the notebook pages, ledgers, business cards, and even the pocket trash left behind at the mansion after the raid in Cabo San Lucas. It was grueling analysis—the sort of work despised by most DEA agents—but I'd find even the slightest variation of a nickname or the subscriber to a phone invaluable, and when I found something, it hit me like a shot of adrenaline.

Exploit. Exploit. Exploit.

My life soon became an endless blur of digits. I had become obsessed with numbers. I was constantly memorizing any phone number, any BlackBerry or PIN number I could find. I couldn't remember my grandma's birthday, but I had Chapo's pilot's phone number on the tip of my tongue. The other agents in the group would ask why I was always consumed with analyzing phone numbers and PINs.

Numbers, unlike people, never lie.

NOT ONLY DID CHAPO and Picudo leave crumbs behind in Cabo San Lucas, but they took off so quickly that Chapo never had time to grab his tactical go-bag containing his forest-green armored vest, black AR-15 rifle equipped with a grenade launcher, and six hand grenades.

Diego and I confirmed that Guzmán had even cut himself on a fence, drawing blood, but was now resting comfortably back across the Sea of Cortez in Sinaloa. For Chapo, this was as close as he had ever been to capture since his breakout from the Puente Grande penitentiary. I knew he was becoming complacent if he felt he could spend time in such a popular resort city, especially one swarming with foreign tourists. And clearly he wasn't escorted by hundreds of bodyguards driving fleets of black armored SUVs with tinted windows, as people had claimed. It was intel that was still widely believed, including by the US intelligence community in Mexico.

Once in a while I'd share my findings with the Mexican Federal Police team that had worked the leads after the February raid in Cabo, and PF would give me any bits and pieces of intelligence they had collected. I'd end up divulging far more information than I'd receive, but I reasoned that *some* Mexican intel was better than none.

Then it was back to digging through the active phone numbers of Chapo's pilots, family, girlfriends—often never raising my head above my computer screen until another agent would make a sarcastic comment.

"Why you wasting your time, Hogan? What's the endgame? The Mexicans will never catch Chapo."

Even my bosses were skeptical as they eyed the massive charts I'd pinned on the wall, linking multi-ton cocaine seizures in Ecuador directly to Chapo's lieutenants.

"Cuando? Cuando?" my boss would often yell as he walked by my desk, demanding to know when—if ever—I was going to show something for all the effort.

"Paciencia, jefe, paciencia," I would say. "Have some patience, boss."

EVERY NIGHT I LEFT the embassy, my head was back on a swivel. DF was a constant swarm of cars and pedestrians, and I knew that at any hour of the day or night someone could be watching me.

Or, worse, trying to follow me.

I was headed home one evening at dusk, driving away from the embassy on side streets in my Tahoe. As I took my first right, I made a mental note of the vehicles behind me that did the same.

Blue Chevy Malibu. White Nissan Sentra.

I took a left at the next light; the white Sentra did the same. In my rearview mirror I could make out the sharp cheekbones, dark eyes, and thick brow of the driver.

Was it the same guy with the blade scar on his cheek on that hot afternoon money drop in Plaza Satélite? It sure looked like him . . .

I couldn't be sure, but I hit the gas hard—another left and then a quick right, making sure I cleaned my tail of the Nissan.

But I felt relatively safe in my Chevy Tahoe, with its two-inch-thick bulletproof glass. It was so heavy from all that level 3 armor that just a gentle tap on the gas pedal made it sound like it was going eighty-five miles an hour. A seasoned DEA agent at the embassy would say, in his heavy West Texan accent, "Them babies run like scalded apes." Surveillance by Chapo's people would be nearly impossible, the way I drove the thing—after just a month in-country I knew all of the shortcuts home, and regularly changed my route to and from work.

IT WAS A BLAZING afternoon in August 2012, and Tom Greene, an agent in my group—working the Beltrán-Leyva DTO—was agitated, constantly checking his BlackBerry.

"Funny, he's not responding," Tom told me. Greene had just returned from meeting with his informant, El Potrillo ("The Colt"), a twenty-six-year-old with a heavyset frame and a long, thin face, from just outside Mexico City. Tom and Potrillo had met a few minutes earlier at a small café-bookstore called El Tiempo, just a block from the embassy in the Zona Rosa neighborhood.

"I've sent him a shitload of messages," Greene said. "Kid always texts right back."

It didn't seem like a big deal, so Tom and I went to lunch in the embassy cafeteria. As we were standing in line with our trays, we overheard one of the cashiers speaking Spanish: "Did you hear? Horrible. There was just a shooting over in Zona Rosa . . ."

Just west of the historic center of Mexico City, Zona Rosa was a perfect place to meet a confidential informant, because it was one of the capital's most bustling and vibrant neighborhoods—full of nightclubs, after-hours joints, and gay bars. After meeting with El Potrillo, Greene had seen a couple of suspicious guys on the street, one in a car and another walking slowly down the sidewalk, but he had thought little of it. His informant followed protocol, waiting to exit El Tiempo until Greene was long gone.

El Potrillo had only taken a few steps down the busy sidewalk when a motorcycle pulled up alongside him. There were two male riders in full-faced black helmets. The rear rider got off the back of the Yamaha, walked calmly up behind El Potrillo, and shot him in the back of the head six times. Five of the bullets had been superfluous; El Potrillo was most likely brain-dead by the time he hit the pavement. The assassin jumped on the back of the motorcycle and sped off. The killers had used a classic sicario technique, imported to the Mexican capital by Colombian hit squads.

I walked by the spot a couple of days later and could still see the bloodstains—now the color of dried wine—on the sidewalk.

The police investigation went nowhere; none of the witnesses would cooperate. The assassins' Yamaha had had no license plates. In fact, not one piece of evidence was noted by the local cops besides the time and place of the shooting. It quickly became another stat: one of the tens of thousands of drug-related homicides that remained unscrutinized and unsolved.

AFTER GREENE DEALT WITH a few days of trauma in the DEA office, I found that life, strangely enough, went back to normal. The execution of El Potrillo was just another nightmare moment that Mexico City belched out daily, like the clouds of smog that hover over the metropolis—and yet another constant reminder that I could be shot point-blank in the back of the head at any moment, too, if I didn't remain hypervigilant.

If anything leaked out to the wrong people (narcos, dirty cops, even some greedy civilian looking for a payday), if anyone were to learn who I was actually targeting or the work I'd been doing for more than six years, it wouldn't be some informant bleeding out in the streets of Zona Rosa—I would be another Kiki Camarena.

Several weeks later, two CIA employees were driving to a military installation on the outskirts of the city in a Chevy Tahoe with diplomatic license plates—an armored vehicle identical to mine— when they were ambushed by two vehicles loaded with gunmen. The Tahoe was sprayed with more than a hundred machine gun rounds. The bad guys—it turned out they were rogue Mexican Federal Police—laid fire in such rapid succession that the bullets pierced the armor, striking the two CIA employees inside. But unlike Special Agent Zapata, they survived—they kept the Tahoe crawling on the metal rims until it could go no further.

I studied the photographs: that Tahoe looked like it had just driven out of a firefight in Fallujah.

I walked out of the office that very night and opened the door to my own Tahoe, my left eye twitching, and felt a bristling cold shiver, in spite of the midsummer heat, knowing that I—or any other DEA agent in the embassy—could be the next target of a murder.

BADGELESS

HE WASN'T DIEGO. But then again, who was? Homeland Security Investigations Special Agent Brady Fallon brought his own unique skills to the table, and my partnership with him was almost as unlikely as the one I'd formed with Diego. Not ethnically—we were both Irish Americans; Brady had been born in Baltimore, studied finance in college abroad, and become a fed immediately after the September 11 terrorist attacks. What made our connection so unique was that agents from the Drug Enforcement Administration and HSI typically *detested* each other.

At the executive level, in Washington, DC, communication between the agencies was done through snail mail—agents wouldn't even pick up the phone to talk to each other. There had been deep-seated enmity even before the Office of Homeland Security, established after 9/11, became the cabinet-level Department of Homeland Security on November 25, 2002. It was much like the dysfunction between the FBI and the CIA—competition and a desire for personal credit overrode cooperation and common sense.

Special agents from DEA and HSI would typically get into territorial pissing matches. . . . Then a headline-hungry assistant US attorney might get added to the mix with a case like this—the potential to arrest and charge the world's most wanted narcotrafficker—and the investigation would come crashing down in a matter of weeks. That was precisely why no one had gotten a bead on Chapo in the twelve years since he'd broken out of prison.

My relationship with Brady began in April 2013, with what I thought would be a routine deconfliction hit, just another DEA office or US federal agency investigating the same BlackBerry PINs as I was. I called the agent whose name popped up on my screen: Brady Fallon, HSI—El Paso Field Office.

"So tell me, does your guy '06' also go by 'Sixto'? And your 'El 81'—has anyone ever called him 'Araña'?" I asked.

I could imagine what Brady was thinking: *Great—another DEA cowboy who wants to come in and sweep up our entire case . . .*

I could hear a muffled voice as Brady yelled to a few of his Homeland Security guys in the background, then he came back on the phone and said, "Yes, we have them referred to by those names. Araña comes up—so does Sixto. Why?"

"Listen," I said, "I don't know if you guys realize it, but you're sitting on two of Chapo Guzmán's most trusted pilots."

Not only were Brady and I both targeting the same PINs—for Sixto and Araña—but there was another PIN I'd found while piecing together go-fast boats smuggling tons of cocaine off the coast of Ecuador, bound for Mexico's west coast. Brady had the user name of that PIN listed as "Ofis-5," and said that whoever was on the other end of that device was placing some serious orders to traffickers in Guatemala, Colombia, and Ecuador. And the recipients would always acknowledge the message with the words *"Saludos a generente."* Greetings to the manager.

"Sometimes these guys will address their messages to 'El Señor,' too," said Brady.

"Yeah, El Señor," I repeated.

That level of respect almost surely meant it was a reference to Chapo.

Working along the Texas border across from Ciudad Juárez—a narco war zone, and the city with the highest murder rate in the world—Brady had had his share of unpleasant dealings with DEA agents.

At one point, he had invited a DEA agent from the El Paso, Texas, office to help with their case; he was told that the only way DEA was going to help was if they could lead the investigation; Brady wasn't going to let that happen and slammed the door. So he was still skeptical.

"How do I know you're not just going to run off with all of my intel?" Brady said.

I understood his concern. "You don't know me yet, but I pride myself on knowing everything there is to know about my targets and sharing it with guys who want to jump on board and work together."

I had closely studied the systemic failure of intel sharing between the FBI and the CIA—the catastrophic interagency dysfunction in the period before 9/11—and promised myself I'd never withhold information from another federal agency if it would further the investigation. I had learned early on—going back to Task Force days with Diego—that it was the tight relationships I fostered throughout my career that had helped me be successful in every case I'd led. No one could come along and tell me that they knew more than I did—because, frankly, they had never dug deep enough. This wasn't arrogance; it was just my thorough method of investigating.

After setting the tone with Brady, I immediately began to fill him in on everything I knew about the two pilots, Sixto and

Araña, and how Ofis-5 was connected to seizures down south that were directly linked to Chapo.

"This shit could be a gold mine," Brady said.

BRADY AND I WERE soon on the phone twice a week, comparing notes, phone numbers, and intercepts from the Ofis-5 wire.

We laughed about the far-fetched stories that filled the various government agency intel files. Chapo never had plastic surgery to disguise himself; he wasn't hiding in Buenos Aires; he wasn't living a life of luxury in the Venezuelan jungle, drinking tea and talking politics with Hugo Chávez. No one in the US government's alphabet soup—DEA, HSI, FBI, ATF, or CIA—had bothered to sift through all the stories to determine fact from fable. There was no coordination in targeting efforts, and everyone slowly began to believe all the myths, repeated and retyped often enough that they were regarded as gospel.

In time, I brought Brady up to speed on the success Diego and I had had back in Phoenix, how far we had come in our Team America investigation, and the failed operation in Cabo. I sent him a photo of Chapo, flanked by three women and appearing to be in good health.

Diego had sent me the photo after it was found on an abandoned BlackBerry taken from the Cabo mansion. It was the most up-to-date photograph that the US and Mexican governments had of the top drug fugitive in the world, and it had never been seen by the public.

From inside the embassy, I began to GPS-ping Ofis-5.

Boom.

Within seconds I had pinpointed the device in Durango, east of Sinaloa. I couldn't believe that Guzmán would be hanging out in the middle of a busy city again—but who knew? With Chapo, anything was possible.

I explained to Brady the way Chapo had restructured his communications network after returning safely to Sinaloa from Baja.

"That Ofis-5 device is most likely a mirror," I said. "Short for *oficina*."

"*Oficinas*," Brady said. "Makes sense. They're functioning like offices."

"Exactly—Chapo's often referred to his mirror locations as offices."

They were grand-sounding, but Brady and I later learned that they were really just cinder-block apartments—shitholes—with the "office" worker thumb-typing thousands of messages, never seeing daylight, surviving on a pot of refried beans and an occasional Burger King Whopper. For sixteen hours a day, the mirror would relay all communications and send them to the intended recipients: they acted like a central switchboard for the cartel and also served to limit Chapo's direct communication with anyone.

"So you think he's still insulating himself?" Brady asked.

"Yes, he's insulating himself well. Now it's just a matter of how many layers are between him and us. For now, these offices are our key."

It reminded me of the old-school American Mafia walk-and-talk—always insulate the boss from direct communication.

And then I went back to my work, opening a fresh Google Map of Mexico on my MacBook and placing my first red-pin marker on the coordinates of Ofis-5 in Durango.

———

ON THE EVENING OF April 4, Brady and I learned through a DEA agent in New York—working a confidential source—that Chapo would be celebrating his fifty-sixth birthday, surrounded by friends and family, at a ranch in his birthplace of La Tuna, the hacienda perched high in the Sierra Madre in the state of Sinaloa. *Feliz cumple!* Birthday messages streamed in for El Señor. It was the first time we knew where Chapo was located since he'd fled Cabo.

But we couldn't act on the intel.

"It's too early—and far too risky at this point—to organize a capture operation, and I don't even know who we could trust in the Mexican counterparts," I said.

The same scenario had been tried, and had failed, numerous times. For years, DEA agents working with their Mexican law enforcement counterparts would act on viable intelligence derived from confidential sources reporting where Chapo would be. Sometimes it was a large fiesta in the mountains, other times a small meeting behind closed doors on some trusted lieutenant's ranch.

I had studied the history: the capture ops were always rushed and reactive. The DEA agents would typically have one or two days' advance notice, grab the first Mexican counterpart willing to risk his unit, and mount a fast capture op. Invariably Chapo would catch wind of the plan a day or hours beforehand and vanish.

No one knew where the leaks and tip-offs came from, but Chapo always had plenty of advance notice. Each time the Mexicans came up empty-handed, the DEA would blame systemic corruption, tuck their tails between their legs, and return home. There were never any persistent and sustained operations to follow, because no one had put in the time and done the work to see the big picture—to know where Chapo had come from, let alone where he was headed next.

Up to this point, it had all been a crapshoot—haphazard and improvised—with each miss bolstering Chapo's reputation as untouchable.

"So other than you," Brady said, "who's targeting him?"

I knew the answer to the question, but I let the silence on the line linger for effect.

"No one."

"You've got to be shitting me?"

"Not kidding," I laughed. "Just me."

"Unbelievable," Brady said.

"There's a lot of DEA offices targeting the upper echelon of the Sinaloa Cartel. They're all trying to work an angle to penetrate Chapo's inner circle. I'm working with all of them. Sure, they each have a piece of the puzzle, but they're not close enough yet. You and me, we're it, man. If anyone has a chance to catch Chapo, it's us."

Brady and I knew that the potential breakthroughs would be buried in those line sheets, in those messages.

"We just gotta keep digging," I said.

"Easy enough to target one trafficker," Brady said. "But that sounds like it's not gonna work with Chaps."

"No," I said. "Never has. We need to exploit his entire inner circle. The lieutenants, enforcers, couriers, pilots, lawyers, and accountants. His sons, nephews, cousins, wives, girlfriends. Even his cook and maids."

The key investigative strategy would be to simultaneously

exploit *multiple* avenues leading to El Señor. If one line failed, we'd have several backup options, allowing us to pivot without losing any momentum.

"Chapo's been one step ahead ever since he broke out of Puente Grande," I said. "He understands who's hunting him. He understands *how* we operate. This guy's no fool. He's always watching his back."

For years Chapo had outsmarted some of the best agents on both sides of the border, but in Brady Fallon I felt I had a fellow federal agent who shared my conviction and determination. Together I hoped that we might have the right stuff to outsmart Chapo at his own game.

IN LESS THAN a month, Brady's HSI team in El Paso was intercepting two more *oficina* BlackBerry devices that we'd identified.

Brady and I determined that each office was in communication with anywhere from five to ten members of Chapo's inner circle, and each office was responsible for sending Chapo's orders to its designated contacts.

On a whiteboard in the embassy, I drew a line from each office tasked with communicating orders from above to the actual lead cartel operators—Chapo's core workforce, and the men representing his authority in Mexico and Central and South American countries:

Office-1—Tocallo
Office-3—Lic-F, Lic Oro
Office-5—Chuy, Pepe, Fresa, Turbo

For the first time ever, Brady and I were peering through a keyhole into Chapo's inner world, witnessing the volume of activity flowing somehow—through all the mirrors—from the office devices back up to Chapo.

Brady and his team had already done a ton of legwork over the course of several months and were well versed on several of the key players:

Chuy was an operator based in Guatemala who coordinated large cocaine loads coming up from Colombia and Venezuela. He would work with Chapo's pilots, like Sixto, to get the loads across the southern border into Mexico.

Pepe worked right at the source of the coke pipeline—deep in the jungles of Colombia—trying to secure thousands of kilos of cocaine base, which he would then send north in go-fast boats staged on the coast near the Colombia–Ecuador border. In the line sheets, it was evident that Pepe was a hard worker and reliable; he always provided updates on his progress to El Señor, mirrored through Office-5.

Fresa was the chief operator based in Ecuador who had the responsibility of finding clandestine airstrips in rural areas so he could receive loads of cocaine base, to be flown out of the country in private planes. Brady and I could see that Fresa was nowhere near as reliable as Pepe.

"This guy Fresa down in Ecuador is constantly bitching about not getting paid," said Brady.

"Yeah, I see that. And *el generente* isn't real impressed with his work. Fresa better get on point."

Pissing off the manager of the world's largest drug cartel usually didn't end with just a verbal reprimand.

———

TOCALLO? LATE INTO THE NIGHTS, I kept drilling down into the line sheets on Office-1. But that word kept leaping out at me from the blur of the daily back-and-forth among all the office devices.

I'd first heard the word *tocayo*—"namesake"—years ago from Diego during our Task Force years in Phoenix. In many Mexican families, Diego had told me, Tocayo—often misspelled Tocallo— was an affectionate way of referring to someone who has the same name as you.

"Tocallo on Office-1," I told Brady. "I'd bet anything this To- callo is gonna turn out to be Iván."

"Iván?" Brady said.

"Yeah, Iván Archivaldo Guzmán Salazar."

"His son . . . I remember."

"You can tell just by the way that they're speaking. There's a level of respect they have for each other. And it's the first numbered office device—why wouldn't Chapo designate the first office to his number-one son?"

"What've you got on him?"

"Iván's known to be moving ton quantities of weed from Sinaloa up through Sonora and then into Tijuana and Nogales. Chapo and Iván share the same middle name, Archivaldo. That's a namesake. *Tocallo.* Can't be a coincidence," I said. "It's gotta be Iván."

Iván was one of Chapo's sons by his first wife, María Alejan- drina Salazar Hernández. Born in 1983, and often referred to as "Chapito" after Edgar was murdered, Iván eventually took over as Chapo's heir. Now he was the most trusted son. Iván and his younger brother, Jesús Alfredo Guzmán Salazar, spent most of their earlier years bouncing between Culiacán and Guadalajara, living the life of the ultimate narco juniors: throwing lavish parties and driving rare European sports cars. Now Iván and Alfredo were running their own semiautonomous DTO and helping their father out with whatever he needed. Alfredo and Chapo were federally indicted together in Chicago in 2009 on drug-trafficking and money-laundering conspiracy charges.

While their father was trying to keep a low profile, Iván and Alfredo couldn't get enough of the narco life, buying the world's most exclusive cars—Lamborghinis, Ferraris, Shelby Mustangs, even a rare silver Mercedes-Benz SLR McLaren, with batwing doors, which was imported from England and could go from zero to sixty in 3.4 seconds—all ordered in the United States and Europe through straw purchasers. They also bought private aircraft, though they never paid full price—just like their father, the sons always haggled to get the best deal. They wore oversize Swiss watches, carried bejeweled pistols, and even had wild A1 Savannah cats, imported from Africa, living as their pets in Culiacán.

THE MESSAGES KEPT POURING into HSI's El Paso office.

"These guys are non-fucking-stop," Brady said. "My translators can hardly keep up with the line sheets."

Every day in Mexico, I would receive a fresh batch of the latest lines and spend my entire day reading and rereading them, trying to decipher just a sliver of Chapo's global drug communications. With all of the fast-paced activity of cocaine loads bouncing north from country to country, it was easy to get distracted, but now that I had access to the "tolls" (call detail records) from multiple office devices, I could do what I'd learned to do best.

We've got to move up the ladder, I would tell myself. *Exploit . . .*

If the office devices were all mirrors, then who was above them?

I ran a quick frequency report on the offices, which provided the most common PIN in contact with each of them, and quickly noticed a common thread. I knew from all of my years analyzing numbers that the PIN in most frequent contact with the target would likely lead to the boss. With normal phone users it would typically be a spouse, significant other, or parent, but in the drug trade the most frequent contact PIN was invariably the shot caller, the boss. One hundred, two hundred, or even three hundred messages were sent daily to that most frequent PIN.

26B8473D

I took that most frequently contacted PIN and pinged it.

If this was indeed Chapo's personal PIN, I'd have a pretty good idea based on location. The results came back within seconds.

Right in the heart of Ciudad de Durango, the capital of Durango State, again.

"Shit," I told Brady. "Looks like just another mirror."

The username of the PIN was "Telcel." Brady and I dubbed this next layer "Second-Tier."

"You guys are writing for Second-Tier, right?" I asked Brady.

"Yeah, one step ahead of you," Brady said. "I've already got my guys on it. Have you read what's been coming in on Office-3 lately?"

"Just diving in this morning," I said.

In the line sheets I saw that Office-3 was in regular contact with all the "Lics" in the organization. Lic was shorthand for *licenciado*.

I knew from my casework in Phoenix with Diego that

licenciado—literally "licensed title"—could refer to anyone who'd earned an advanced degree: engineers, psychologists, architects. But in common Mexican usage, a *licenciado* was generally a lawyer or someone with any higher education. No one could be sure, but one of the principal advisers in the line sheets went by the name Lic Oro.

Filtering the message through Office-3 and then down to Lic Oro, El Señor would ask for the status of various court cases involving significant Sinaloa Cartel heavyweights who'd recently been arrested.

One of the most pressing legal cases involved a player Lic Oro referred to as "El Suegro."

I kept poring over those line sheets, seeing references to the case involving El Suegro (Spanish for "father-in-law").

Driving home from the embassy that night, I remembered one family barbecue in the suburbs of Phoenix where Diego had introduced me to his wife's father—using that title, *"mi suegro."* And during the Team America operation, learning that Carlos Torres-Ramos and Chapo were *consuegros* . . .

And then I suddenly understood that this El Suegro could be only one man: Inés Coronel Barreras, the father of Emma Coronel Aispuro, Chapo's young beauty-queen wife.

Emma was actually an American citizen—she was born in California in 1989—and had grown up in a remote Durango village called La Angostura. She'd married Guzmán when she was just eighteen, when Chapo was over fifty. Brady and I knew her history well—she'd caught Chapo's eye after winning some local pageant at La Gran Feria del Café y la Guayaba; her father was a cattle rancher and heavy hitter within the Sinaloa Cartel. In fact, on April 30, Inés Coronel Barreras had been arrested by the Mexican

Federal Police along the US border—in Agua Prieta, Sonora—for running a marijuana-and-cocaine-trafficking distribution cell responsible for smuggling large loads into Arizona.

Tocallo: namesake.

Had to be Iván.

El Suegro: father-in-law.

Had to be Inés.

As careful as the communications insulation system was, the nicknames and aliases were clear tells.

The names left little doubt: Brady and I were almost certain who El Señor was, the man at the top of this BlackBerry chain. The boss putting out the orders through the mirror devices—however many layers of them there were, and we still weren't sure—had to be Chapo Guzmán himself.

Once I got to my apartment in Condesa that evening, I poured myself a double shot of bourbon on the rocks, slumped back in my living room armchair, and pulled my BlackBerry out of my pocket to write a message to Brady.

Iván—Tocallo.

Inés—El Suegro.

The net was tightening: a string of Spanish names was drawing us closer to El Señor.

I knew that standard texting wasn't secure over Mexican cell towers, so I typed Brady a message on WhatsApp.

"We've got momentum now," I wrote. "Tocallo. El Suegro. We're rolling. But we need to meet up. How soon can you come down here?"

———

TELECONFERENCING AND TEXTING for three months could accomplish only so much.

We had to meet face-to-face.

Less than a week later, I met Brady at the Mexico City airport, right there in Terminal 2, not more than fifty feet from the food court where the blue-on-blue Federal Police murders had taken place.

I recognized him immediately—he was five-ten, had a shaved head, and was wearing a dark gray jacket and Ray-Bans perched on his forehead. He was walking toward me with a pissed-off scowl, although, as it turned out, he wasn't in the least bit angry. We held a long stare, looking at each other—not as special agents from rival US federal government agencies, but as *men* with a shared vision for our investigation.

"Badgeless," I said.

Brady nodded.

"Badgeless."

We sealed the deal with a handshake, pulling each other chest-to-chest in a powerful hug.

TOP-TIER

BY THE SUMMER OF 2013 I was running point in Mexico for all DEA offices targeting the Sinaloa Cartel, coordinating with other DEA agents and federal prosecutors in San Diego, Los Angeles, Chicago, New York, and Miami.

I now had a much better grasp of the overall umbrella-like structure of the cartel. Chapo may have been *el jefe de jefes*—boss of bosses—but there were other DTOs nearly as large as Chapo's personal organization that operated under the wing of the Sinaloa Cartel. Next to Chapo, Ismael Zambada García, a.k.a. "El Mayo," Chapo's longtime senior partner, was the most prominent.

Any trafficker below Chapo and Mayo needed their direct blessing to work and share resources within their territory.

I was regularly on the phone with DEA agents stationed in Canada, Guatemala, Costa Rica, Panama, Colombia, and Ecuador, passing leads and sharing intel on the movements of Chapo's countless drug shipments. With all the moving parts, I realized I needed to call a coordination meeting of all the far-flung agents who saw only a sliver of the intelligence and investigative leads.

In August 2013, I brought all the agents together in Mexico City; there were too many to fit in the Kiki Room, so we all assembled in the embassy auditorium. Each office presented its case on PowerPoint; as they did so, I would periodically interject, highlighting the connections I'd made to other cases, giving everyone in the room a greater sense of the scale of the investigation.

"If *we're* not targeting Chapo," I said, wrapping up the meeting, "then who the hell is? We're it—the elite USG team. Right here in this room. The only thing lacking is self-belief. Chapo is no super-criminal. He's a man standing in the dirt somewhere in this very country. He's breathing the same air as us. Like any other drug kingpin, Chapo's vulnerable. He can be caught. But we all need to do our homework."

After the meeting, I was eager to sit down and meet a couple members of Brady's core team who'd accompanied him to Mexico and had been working rigorously behind the scenes.

Special Agent Joe Dawson was a heavyset, mid-thirties guy with straight brown hair long enough to tie in a ponytail, and he was wearing a gray button-down shirt and loose purple tie that made him look like a young tech exec from Silicon Valley. Joe, working closely with Brady, had taken the brunt of writing federal affidavits for all the office devices and the cartel operators we considered worthy of intercepting. Whenever I'd call El Paso, Joe would be working into the small hours of the night, sitting alone at his cubicle under one small desk lamp, jamming to Metallica, and typing and deciphering line sheets with me over the phone. Joe had a near-photographic memory and could instantly recall Chapo's activities after reading them just once.

At our meeting he said, "You see this guy called Vago in the line sheets on Office-5?"

"Vago? I saw that."

"Looks like he's getting ready to go on a rampage. Know who he is?"

"It's another alias for Cholo Iván."

I had already run "Cholo Iván" through our DEA databases: his real name was Orso Iván Gastélum Cruz. Chapo's top sicario and plaza boss in the northern Sinaloan city of Los Mochis, Cholo Iván was a scary trafficker even by the standards of Mexican drug cartels.

"And you saw him talking about a guy called Picudo?" I asked. Joe nodded.

After Carlos Adrián Guardado Salcido, a.k.a. "El 50," died in a shoot-out with a local unit of the Mexican Army in August 2013, Picudo had stepped up to become Chapo's chief enforcer and plaza boss of Culiacán.

"You have Picudo's real name?" Joe asked.

I shook my head. "Picudo—it's Spanish for 'sharp' or 'thorny.' In Mexico it's a nickname for a badass, for a guy who's always looking for a fight. Picudo also goes by 'El 70.' Still working on getting his real name."

Picudo and Cholo Iván: these were two of the killers who gave Chapo his hold over the people of Sinaloa and through these sicarios, Guzmán could reign with violence.

In the days before my meetings with my DEA colleagues, Cholo Iván had been talking about killing "Los Cochinos"—a group from a rival cartel—in retaliation for the murder of Picudo's brother-in-law. Cholo Iván said they needed to attack Los Cochinos immediately, because elements in the Mexican government were aligning themselves with the rival cartel. Through the Office-5 mirror, Cholo Iván asked Miapa—slang for "my dad," a code name for Chapo—to send some more heavy artillery to him in Los Mochis.

We feared that bloodshed was coming.

———

OUR KEYHOLE INTO CHAPO'S world was rapidly expanding, but every few weeks—usually on a thirty-day schedule—*los pobrecitos* (the "poor ones"), as Brady and I called them, who ran all the office mirrors in Durango, would receive a bagful of new BlackBerrys, dropping all the old devices and instantly creating a logistical headache for us and our entire team.

Before we could intercept again, we had to try to identify the new office devices; then Joe would begin writing his affidavits. It was an arduous process that would take weeks to finish by the time an assistant US attorney reviewed the affidavit and Joe or Brady could get down to the federal courthouse in El Paso to have them signed by a US magistrate. Add another couple of days before HSI's tech group would "flip the switch." And all this had to be done for fifteen or twenty unique devices.

I realized it would take a small miracle for us to stay up long enough to break through all the layers of BlackBerry mirrors in Chapo's communications structure, let alone have enough time to be able to unravel Chapo's day-to-day operations.

But Brady and his handpicked team were not about to give up. We both knew that this entire investigation rested solely on his shoulders in El Paso and mine in Mexico City.

Fortunately, besides the staunch assistant US attorney they had working with them in El Paso, Brady had lined up another attorney with *juice*: a deputy chief for the US Attorney's Office in Washington, DC, Camila Defusio. A veteran prosecutor in her mid-forties, Defusio wasn't afraid of taking massive cartel cases, as long as they kept producing fruitful results. The Chapo case was right in her wheelhouse. She knew what needed to be done and would streamline HSI's affidavits even if it meant writing some herself. Like us, Camila saw the big picture, and Brady kept her well informed of our progress.

The intercepts on the Second-Tier device proved to be our vital portal.

Second-Tier may have been yet another mirror, but as soon as the BlackBerry went live, it was like a row of streetlamps turned on to illuminate a previously dark street. The crucial information in the line sheets grew exponentially. Not only were Offices 1, 3, and 5 routing their communications up to Second-Tier, but another three offices—numbers 2, 4, and 6—were doing the exact same thing.

THE INCOMING MESSAGES in the line sheets became an endless and intoxicating river. Brady was forwarding them to me by the pile— there were thousands of them. I could go six hours without moving or even getting up to take a leak. Each sentence from the offices exposed clues leading deeper into Chapo's secretive lair. I found I could be most productive when the other agents had left the embassy, from 6 p.m. until midnight, when I didn't have to stomp out fires and do the diplomatic dancing that fills up the days of most foreign agents. So finally, alone in the office, I would submerse myself in the line sheets, looking for that one piece of intel, that one critical clue in a torrent of misspelled and often barely literate Spanish text. My retinas burned as I sank deeper into Chapo's world.

EVERY DAY AT AROUND 11 A.M., Brady and his team in El Paso would see the key lieutenants, the offices, and the Second-Tier phones coming to life. This was the same modus operandi I'd seen among the traffickers I targeted in the United States. Diego and I would joke about "doper time"—drug dealers, whatever their level in the organization, are creatures of the night, waking up and conducting business whenever they're good and ready.

Brady and I were now witnessing firsthand the extent of Chapo's exploitation of new markets. Guzmán was eager to find refrigerated warehouses and place his operators in England, the Netherlands, the Philippines, and even Australia.

We knew, too, about Chapo's vast distribution network throughout the United States, but we were caught off guard by his deep infiltration of Canada. In terms of profit, Chapo was doing more cocaine business in Canada than in the United States. It was a straightforward price-point issue: retail cocaine on the streets of Los Angeles or Chicago sold for $25,000 per kilo, while in major Canadian cities it sold for upwards of $35,000 per kilo.

His key cartel lieutenants could exploit weaknesses in the Canadian system: the top-heavy structure of the Royal Canadian Mounted Police hampered law enforcement efforts for even the most routine drug arrest and prosecution.*

It was a perfect match for Chapo: hindered law enforcement and an insatiable Canadian appetite for high-grade coke. Over the years, the Sinaloa Cartel had built a formidable distribution structure, smuggling loads of cocaine across the Arizona border and hauling them to stash pads and warehouses in Tucson or Phoenix, before they were driven by car to the Washington border, where the loads would be thrown into private helicopters. The birds would

---

* Unlike the United States, whose federal law enforcement system comprises many specialized agencies—DEA, HSI, ATF, and FBI—Canada has only the RCMP, also known as Mounties.

jump the border and drop the coke out among the tall lodgepole pines of British Columbia.

Chapo's men had connections with sophisticated Iranian organized-crime gangs in Canada who were facilitating plane purchases, attempting to smuggle ton-quantity loads using GPS-guided parachutes, while sending boxes of PGP-encrypted smartphones south to Mexico at Chapo's request. A network of outlaw bikers—primarily Hells Angels—were also moving his cocaine overland and selling it to retail dealers throughout the country.

But Canada wasn't always smooth sailing for Chapo. At some point he'd entrusted a twenty-two-year-old from Culiacán who spoke decent English—Jesus Herrera Esperanza, a.k.a. "Hondo"—and sent him to Vancouver to run his drug distribution and money collection throughout Canada. Hondo's front—and it was a sweet life for a young Sinaloan—was to enroll in a business program at Columbia College, in downtown Vancouver, near his luxury thirtieth-floor condo loft. Hondo only attended a few classes, instead spending most of his time hanging out at clubs or taking girls sailing on the British Columbia coast.

But Hondo was sloppy and openly flaunted his connection to Guzmán. Brady and I hacked into Hondo's Facebook account one night and saw a status update reading:

Puro #701!

"What the hell is this kid posting?" Brady asked.

"Pure seven-oh-one?" Then suddenly it made sense. "It's not code, dude—it's *Forbes*." I laughed. "That's Chapo's *Forbes* number." Guzmán had recently been ranked by the magazine as the 701st-richest man on the planet.

Hondo was clearly a weak link among all the operators. He was so amped up about living the narco-junior life that he disregarded his daily functions for Chapo's DTO. At one point, millions of dollars were sitting uncollected in Vancouver, Calgary, Winnipeg, Toronto, and Montreal—all from the sale of Chapo's cocaine and heroin.

Finally, in frustration, Chapo—mirrored through Office-5—gave Hondo a direct order:

"I want a report every night at seven sharp. How much you've sold and how much money you're sitting on. Break it down by city."

When Hondo got around to sending in the numbers, we would read the nightly reports. Vancouver: $560,000 and 95 kilos of coke. Winnipeg: $275,000 and 48 kilos. Toronto: $2 million and 150 kilos . . .

I ALSO BEGAN to see how stuck in the details Guzmán could be.

In July 2013, a jerry-rigged go-fast panga, equipped with four Yamaha 350-horsepower outboard motors and 130 plastic containers full of fuel, had set sail from Ecuador with two young Mexicans at the helm. They had stashed their cargo in a fishing net: heavy garbage bags carrying 622 kilograms of cocaine. The men left the coast of Ecuador, charting a zigzag course, avoiding fishing vessels and coast guard patrols, sleeping in the open air, and eating only canned scallops and saltine crackers for a week at sea as they throttled northbound toward Mazatlán, in Sinaloa, Mexico.

They never made it. Tipped off that a Mexican navy vessel was headed out to intercept them, the two young men decided to ditch the load. A similar thing had happened to some of Chapo's other smugglers several months earlier; they, too, had nearly been intercepted, and had dumped their kilos of coke into the ocean, then had lit the remaining canisters of gas, turning their go-fast boat into a fireball as they jumped into the Pacific and nearly drowned. This time, the tip-off came early enough that the men had heaved the fishnet of waterproofed cocaine bricks overboard, attaching an orange buoy to it so that it could be spotted by air and retrieved.

Chapo was livid: losing one load was bad; losing two was unacceptable. His Mazatlán-based maritime smuggling lieutenant, Turbo, sent boat after boat out to the area of the drop, sixty miles off the coast, in a desperate attempt to find the lost load.

But we could tell Chapo was nearing the boiling point when he sent his best pilot, Araña, out in an old rattletrap Cessna to look for that bobbing buoy, making several flights a day, circling above the Pacific.

"That shit is probably in *China* by now," Araña complained to another pilot. "I can't take another day flying over the ocean. I'm fucking scared. The boss can ask me to do anything and I'll do it—but not this. I'm *not* flying out there again."

Brady and I couldn't believe how much manpower Chapo was putting into trying to retrieve a 622-kilogram load. It made no rational sense for the world's wealthiest drug kingpin to search so hard for 622 keys.

I HAD BEGUN to discern a psychological pattern in my prey: Chapo was fixated on the minutiae, like the price of jet fuel or the precise number of pesos being paid to his people. And he was cheap. For example, Guzmán would authorize monthly payments of only

2,000 Mexican pesos—roughly $165—to military lookouts scattered along the Colombia-Ecuador border. Why would he nickel-and-dime such key cogs in his machine of institutional bribery?

Chapo Guzmán was apparently the CEO of a sprawling, multi-billion-dollar drug-trafficking organization, but he also spent hours each day acting as a personnel complaint department. Brady and I couldn't help but laugh some days when we'd read the exchanges from Chapo's lieutenants bitching about being unappreciated—or, worse, not receiving their monthly payments on time.

I COULD ALSO GET stuck in my own obsessions, to the point of being oblivious to what was going on around me in the office.

One morning, I was so consumed with the line sheets that words began blurring together on the screen in front of me—wiggling back and forth. Was I having a panic attack? I looked over at the coatrack and realized that one of the hangers was rocking hard from side to side.

Terremoto.

Mexico City had frequent small tremors, but this was the first substantial earthquake I'd felt. After the massive earthquake in 1985—known to have killed more than ten thousand people—many new buildings were built to roll with the earth. The US embassy was built out of marble and placed on anti-seismic rollers for this purpose.

I DROVE HOME THAT EVENING thinking about a brand-new nickname I'd read about in Chapo's world. "Naris"—"the Nose"—was a courier who was constantly being sent by Second-Tier (once again through Office-6) to change cars frequently, pick people up, and deliver them to specific locations. Could he possibly be Chapo's personal gofer?

Narrowing in on Naris's location was now my new priority.

I parked my Tahoe on the street a block over from my apartment—something I did every so often to switch up my routine—and, walking home, I realized it was Día de los Muertos—the Day of the Dead, when Mexicans celebrate the deceased by dressing up in elaborate costumes and painting their faces as fanciful skulls with flowers and bright colors. The streets were full of people parading to celebrate in cemeteries, and my wife was throwing a party at home for all the women of the neighborhood, decorating sugar skulls she had made from scratch. She had quickly made friends with the extensive embassy and expat network; there were playdates with the kids and parties on all the major Mexican holidays like this one.

I smiled at the sight of my wife, taking full advantage of our time in-country, as I walked to the back bedroom to take off my suit and tie.

Unfortunately, there was no time for me to join in the festivities.

I sat down on the corner of the bed and quickly began reading a string of messages from Brady.

"How many times has Chapo been married?"

"No idea," I answered. "He's married at least four or five women that I know of. But no one knows for sure. He never divorces; he just marries again. Not to mention the women he doesn't marry. The guy is obsessed with women."

"I can see that," Brady wrote back. "Check this out. It just came over Second-Tier. Someone sent a photo spread of young girls in lingerie. Looks like they're coming from a madam they call Lizzy.

"He's sent a menu and gets to pick which one he wants for the night," Brady wrote. "What a fuckin' lowlife."

"Degenerate," I replied. "Sickening . . ."

Second-Tier then ordered Naris to the "Galerías" to pick up Lizzy's girl after Chapo had made his selection from the photo array.

I later determined that "Galerías" was code for the Centro Comercial Plaza Galerías San Miguel, a mall in the heart of Culiacán to which Chapo would send his visitors to rendezvous with Naris or other couriers to be brought to his secret hideouts.

NOT ONLY DID CHAPO have a fixation with underage virgins, but he had also become obsessed with the popular Mexican actress Kate del Castillo after becoming infatuated with the hit telenovela *La Reina del Sur*, on which she played a Sinaloa-born cartel boss running her empire from Spain. I had read in one line sheet that Chapo had instructed Lic Oro to get Kate's personal PIN so they could contact each other.

"This guy's got no other motive in life besides moving dope and banging as many women as he can," I wrote to Brady. "None. He's either obsessing over the day-to-day of the DTO or he's getting laid."

Sex was the only break in Chapo's workaholic drug-trafficking routine. He maintained a revolving door of women; in between, he'd invite his wife over to share the same bed; the sex was almost constant.

My street-cop instinct kicked in: the stronger the obsession, the more likely it could result in an exploitable weakness, a possible

Achilles' heel. I had even heard from a confidential source that Chapo and Mayo often joked that women would be their ultimate demise.

THE MORNING AFTER the Día de los Muertos party, I walked out to my armored Tahoe to find that the spare tire had been stolen. There was a small hole in my windshield—a circular shatter mark, spiderwebbing the bulletproof glass near the driver's side. It looked like a close-range shot from a pistol.

I stepped back slowly, away from the Tahoe, my eyes darting from one car to the next, looking for anyone who might be surveilling me.

My eyes landed on someone sitting inside a black Lincoln Navigator across the street. Images of the scar-faced man I'd seen during the money drop flashed through my mind.

Could it be the same guy?

I wasn't about to stick around and find out. I quickly jumped into the Chevy, where at least I was protected by the armor. I called my wife and told her to stay inside for the day as I took off slowly, waiting for the Navigator to follow.

I hit the gas, took a sharp right, then another right, and quickly lost sight of the Lincoln in my rearview mirror.

AS I WALKED PAST the Kiki Room at the embassy, my phone rang.

"Hey, Tocallo has just asked Inge if he can have a guy killed in prison," Brady said. "He knows the guy's exact location—the cell he's housed in and everything."

We knew that Inge was short for *ingeniero*—"engineer"—yet

another nickname the DTO lieutenants and workers called Chapo over the BlackBerry messages.

"What's Chapo saying?

"It's weird," Brady said. "He's telling Tocallo to gather more information. He wants to know more."

That actually sounded liked Chapo. Despite his media-inflated reputation as a homicidal drug lord, I knew by now that Chapo seemed to be very deliberative, even circumspect, when authorizing the use of violence. In Sinaloa, most traffickers didn't think twice about killing someone, especially in the mountainous terrain of the Sierra Madre, where Chapo was raised—blood feuds and shooting wars were a simple fact of life there.

But Chapo must have become wiser over the years. Many times, when his lieutenants would report a serious problem—a killing offense—Chapo would conduct his own version of a police investigation, asking a series of questions to obtain more facts.

My mind flashed back to my days in the Phoenix Task Force when Diego and I would sit for hours with our assistant US attorney, drafting indictments, continually getting beaten over the head with questions, as if we were already under cross-examination on the witness stand:

"So *how* do you know this, Drew? Were *you* there? *Who* told you that?"

Chapo was exhaustive with his interrogations. He'd typically contemplate the best course of action for a day or two before making the calls to resolve the problem—even if the final outcome was a death sentence.

Brady and I confirmed this when we watched a video of Chapo taken several years ago, wearing his trademark plain dark baseball cap, casually walking back and forth underneath a palapa high in the Sierra Madre while an unidentified man sits on the ground with his hands tied to a post. Chapo's demeanor is calm and detached as he paces and interrogates the prisoner.

NOW THAT BRADY AND I were piecing together a good percentage of Chapo's life through the interception of Second-Tier, we needed to once again advance up the ladder of mirrors. Chapo's personal device couldn't be too far away at this point.

"Second-Tier is relaying everything up to a username labeled MD#8," Brady told me one day.

"Does MD#8 have a name?"

"Yes," Brady said. "Second-Tier's been calling him Condor."

I repeated the name over and over in my head, trying to remember whether I'd heard it before. Nothing registered. But unlike the usernames of Chapo's other mirror devices, "Condor" sounded like an actual person. Or at least like a narco nickname. Condors spend their time in mountainous country, soaring—was the name a clue that he was higher up in the cartel hierarchy? I couldn't waste my time speculating; I needed to know exactly where Condor was pinging.

I may have had Condor's PIN, but I still needed the corresponding Mexican telephone number to ping.

And for that I needed Don Dominguez. Don was a staff coordinator at DEA's Special Operations Division (SOD), in Chantilly, Virginia. The primary function of staff coordinators at SOD was to assist agents working high-profile cases in the field by coordinating deconfliction efforts, providing funding for wire intercepts, and acting as liaisons with the intelligence community.

Though equivalent in rank to my own group supervisor, at heart Dominguez was a street agent.

"He's not like the other desk jockeys in DC," I told Brady. "Don's one of us. He *gets* it. He believes we actually have a chance at capturing this fucker."

I sent Condor's PIN to Don so he could flip it. Don had access to a small team of techies at DEA, each of whom had built excellent relationships with the largest telecommunication service providers—even Canadian ones, like BlackBerry.

A standard request to a comms company could take almost three weeks to yield results, and by that time Condor—and all the other users—would be on to a brand-new BlackBerry and we would have to begin the process all over again. But once Brady and his team drafted an administrative subpoena to BlackBerry requesting Condor's corresponding telephone number, I was confident that Don would work around the clock to get the subscriber results back quickly.

SURE ENOUGH, IN LESS than twenty-four hours, Don Dominguez delivered.

"Just got Condor's number back from Don," I told Brady, anxious to hit the ping button on my laptop.

"Where's it at?" asked Brady.

Within minutes my eyes lit up as I received the results and sent the coordinates back to Brady:

24.776,-107.415

"It's hitting in Colonia Libertad."

"Colonia Libertad?"

"Yes," I said. "Looks like a small, run-down neighborhood on Culiacán's southwest side."

Now we had a BlackBerry in the heart of Sinaloa's capital. The net was narrowing: it was the first ping we'd ever had outside of Durango.

"CONDOR" WAS IN CULIACÁN. An average-size city of 675,000 nestled in the center of Sinaloa, just west of the Sierra Madre, Culiacán is the birthplace of all Mexican drug trafficking and had displaced Medellín, Colombia, as the world's narco capital. From the days of Miguel Ángel Félix Gallardo through to Chapo's current reign, all the top cartel leaders had come from the city or the small towns nearby.

Culiacán was also famous for its Jardines del Humaya cemetery—the "drug lord's burial ground"—with its $600,000 air-conditioned mausoleums, including a lavish marble one for Chapo's murdered son, Edgar, and a large shrine to Jesús Malverde, the mustached patron saint of drug trafficking. Legend had it that Malverde was a bandit from the hills of Sinaloa who stole from the rich and gave to the poor until his death by hanging in 1909.

I REMEMBERED DIEGO telling me about visiting Jardines del Humaya when he was once on vacation in Culiacán. Diego said he was astonished by how much money traffickers had poured into the shrine to keep it thriving. Now Culiacán was known as a city of outlaws, and off-limits to authorities from outside of Sinaloa, which was a problem, because most of the local cops and military had been corrupted by Chapo's organization.

In fact, no outside law enforcement or military personnel had ever dared to enter Culiacán to conduct an operation, for fear of immediate retaliation.

Still, as distant and untouchable as Culiacán seemed to me, this was our first indication that Chapo could be in Mexico's narco capital.

I QUICKLY GRABBED the next flight from DF to El Paso and met with Brady, Joe, and Neil Miller, the other member of Brady's core team at HSI.

"Neil's our bulldozer," Brady said, laughing. "He doesn't think twice about pissing someone off, as long as the job gets done. Welcome to his domain."

Brady shoved open a door to reveal their newly created war room, a converted conference area discreetly tucked away from everyone else at the HSI El Paso Field Office. They'd recently taken over the room and filled it with more than a dozen computers and at least that many translators, to run all the wires on the office devices, on Chapo's key lieutenants, and now on Second-Tier.

But despite the resources, Brady was still on edge. "How do we know that there aren't a hundred more layers to the pyramid-like Second-Tier and the offices? I think we're fucked. The mirrors could go on forever."

I paused for a second before giving my partner the breakthrough.

"No, there aren't *hundreds*," I said. "I've been analyzing Condor's tolls, looking at his most frequent contact. I just found it: two. There's only *two* layers."

Condor wasn't in contact with any other PINs—just Second-Tier.

"It stops right there," I said. "Condor isn't forwarding any messages. He's the end of the line."

Brady couldn't believe it.

"Condor is either fat-fingering thousands of messages a day into a new BlackBerry and forwarding them on—a nearly inconceivable job—or he is standing in the same room as Chapo, receiving personally dictated orders directly from the boss," I said.

Brady rushed into the wire room and returned several minutes later with Neil.

"We've *got* him, brother," said Brady.

"What do you mean?"

"I'm looking at it right here."

Brady showed me a line sheet that had come in that morning from Second-Tier to Condor, asking if *el generente*—the manager—was awake yet.

Condor clearly was in the same house—or even the same room—as the boss.

Condor had replied:

"No, he's still sleeping . . ."

ABRA LA PUERTA

TOP-TIER HAD BECOME MY LIFE.

Pinging that BlackBerry device, the one nearest to Chapo, was all-consuming. As long as I could ping Top-Tier—from six in the morning often until after midnight—nothing else really mattered. Even when lying in bed with my wife in La Condesa, my mind was never far from hunting that Top-Tier.

By now I knew *how* Chapo ran the day-to-day of his multi-million-dollar drug empire; all I needed was the boss's location. This wasn't as simple as it sounded, given Chapo's penchant for bouncing constantly, moving from safe house to safe house, from countryside to city, sometimes on an hourly basis. With every ping, I meticulously labeled the spot with a yellow thumbtack on my Google Map, marking the coordinates along with the date and time indicating where Condor's device had pinged in Culiacán.

Top-Tier.

If Condor was standing with the man, every new ping helped me begin to establish Chapo's pattern of life.[*]

---

[*] "Pattern of life" is the investigative term of art for a target's location history up to the present moment.

Brady, Neil, and Joe were working around the clock now, too, intercepting as many mirror devices as they could identify— Offices 1 through 10, and Second-Tier—as well as a new critical mirror who went by the username "Usacell." We quickly determined that Usacell—similar to the name of another major Mexican telecom service provider Iusacell—was a duplicate: another Second-Tier device run by the user Telcel, in Durango.

"It's pretty obvious it's the same guy," Brady said. "He's just labeled each of his two BlackBerrys with the corresponding service provider to tell them apart."

The Usacell device may have been another mirror, but it exposed still more important messages that Chapo thought were hidden. If the office devices were sending two hundred messages a day to Telcel at Second-Tier, they were sending an equal amount to Usacell. Brady and I estimated that we were intercepting close to seventy-five percent of all the DTO communications coming to and from the boss.

The window into Chapo's world was now becoming brighter.

"For now, we should sit at Second-Tier," Brady said.

At the Second-Tier level, we could intercept every order coming down from Chapo and every communication coming up from the office devices.

"Yeah, that's definitely the honey hole," I said.

If Condor and the offices dropped their BlackBerrys, Brady and I could identify their new PINs easily, so long as we were still intercepting the two Second-Tier devices, Telcel and Usacell.

Office-4 was now starting to produce valuable intel, too, but I noticed something different about this mirror: not only did Office-4 appear to be sending messages up the chain to Chapo through Second-Tier, but it was also responsible for relaying command-and-control messages—mostly related to Chapo's Canada operations—to another top player who went by the username "Panchito."

"Did you see the deconfliction hit on Panchito?" I asked Brady. "It's hitting all over FBI New York."

"Yeah," Brady said. "I saw it."

"Our Panchito has got to be Alex Cifuentes," I said.

The FBI New York office claimed to still have an interest in Chapo after it began targeting him through longtime Colombian drug lord Hildebrando Alexánder Cifuentes Villa, who'd moved to Sinaloa around 2008—acting as human collateral for all of Chapo's cocaine shipments generated by the Cifuentes-Villa family in Medellín.

After the failure of the Cabo op, the FBI's fresh intelligence slowly dried up. Alex—as everyone called Cifuentes—was one of Chapo's right-hand men.

In fact, months prior to my Mexico City coordination meeting, while I was in New York, I'd sat down with the FBI and told them about the great working relationship I was building with HSI and Brady's team.

"We're moving quickly," I said. "This train isn't stopping. If you guys want to get on board and share your intel, now's the time."

This wasn't my first attempt to coordinate a joint investigation with the FBI. I'd found their special agents to be polite and professional, but I also knew they were highly resistant to sharing. It was typical of the FBI to hold their cards close to their chest: that's how they were trained at Quantico. The FBI believed they were the world's premier law enforcement agency, but when it came to working a drug investigation—especially when faced with the complex structure of the Mexican cartels—their expertise couldn't match that of the DEA.

As much as I tried to get everyone to cooperate, I knew it was going to be difficult.

The FBI's file was composed mostly of historical intelligence on Cifuentes, who was now wanted by DEA and FBI after being federally indicted on multiple drug-trafficking conspiracy charges. But instead of sharing with the DEA, the FBI began giving their intelligence to the CIA, in hopes they could produce something that would give them the upper hand.

I knew that whenever intelligence was passed to CIA by a federal law enforcement agency, the source would instantly lose control of how that intelligence was classified, disseminated, and used. This was well known by the agents who worked in the embassy, and it was precisely why Brady and I had decided that the CIA had no place in our investigation.

Almost every piece of intelligence we gained on Chapo was derived judicially from court-authorized wire intercepts, so that the evidence collected could be used to charge Chapo and others in his DTO in a US federal court. It was exactly how DEA disrupted and ultimately dismantled DTOs. The CIA, on the other hand, dealt extensively with classified and top-secret material that was difficult—if not impossible—to present in court.

I didn't need the CIA, but I also knew that they were anxious to get involved now that Brady and I were gaining momentum toward Chapo's exact location.

"The Feebies and the spooks want to call a meeting," I told Brady.

"Where?"

"Langley."

"Fuck that," Brady said. "We don't need them."

"We need to at least be on the same page when it comes to Cifuentes. We need to send someone if you or I don't go. I'm going to talk to Don."

Don Dominguez had been following these developments from Virginia and agreed to attend the meeting at CIA headquarters on our behalf. The result of the meeting was an agreement among all agencies to arrest Cifuentes and remove him from Chapo's DTO, but *only* at the right time. It was crucial that the efforts be coordinated among all agencies. I confirmed with the FBI that Panchito's PIN was in fact Alex Cifuentes and shared several of the ping coordinates I had obtained from the Cifuentes BlackBerry, hitting as it did in a rural area just southwest of Culiacán.

IN LATE NOVEMBER 2013, I received an urgent text from Brady in El Paso.

"This just in," Brady wrote, quoting the line sheets after the Spanish translation. It was Second-Tier transmitting to all the office devices:

"Panchito was caught in a battle with soldiers and Picudo went to rescue him. Turn off your phones because they will get your PIN."

I called Brady immediately.

"Goddammit—the Feebs fucked us!" he shouted.

"Hold on," I said. "Let me look into it and get the facts."

I reached out to DEA Mazatlán, who in turn contacted their local military contacts to see if they'd heard about a recent arrest just outside Culiacán.

Initially, the Mexicans didn't even know *who* they'd arrested. SEDENA* had locked up some middle-aged guy at a small ranch, but they didn't think he was Colombian, and his name wasn't Cifuentes.

"They're saying they've got a guy called Enrique García Rodríguez," I told Brady. "They're getting me a photo of him right now, along with the passport."

Brady stayed on the line while I waited for Mazatlán to shoot me the email.

When the photo arrived, it showed a man in his mid-forties, with a receding hairline, salt-and-pepper beard, and light complexion.

"It's Cifuentes, man," I said. "It's a fake name on this Mexican passport. Panchito is done."

"Fuck them!" Brady was livid.

He knew it was just a matter of time before everything we'd built in the war room in El Paso came crashing down.

Sure enough, within minutes, Chapo's offices were already talking about dropping their BlackBerrys; Second-Tier wouldn't be far behind.

And then Top-Tier: Condor.

Brady and I would soon be standing, once again, in the dark.

"I just confirmed the photo with FBI," I said. "They're claiming they had nothing to do with this."

"Bullshit," said Brady.

"I don't know for sure. But I can promise you—the CIA are the ones who gave the information to SEDENA," I said. "Guaranteed."

After I got off the phone with Brady, I reached out to the CIA's

---

* The Mexican army—short for Secretaría de la Defensa Nacional.

counter-narcotics group in Mexico City about the Cifuentes arrest. At first they denied any knowledge, but a few days later, a CIA manager told me the truth: all the rural ping locations I had shared with the FBI had been passed on to SEDENA by the spooks. (The CIA claimed to have told SEDENA only that there was a "subject of interest" at that location.) The CIA then turned around and washed their hands of the whole ordeal after passing the lead— there was no oversight of the operation, and no close coordination with their Mexican counterparts. In fact, the CIA didn't even know if SEDENA had captured the right man, otherwise they would have claimed credit immediately. Once I confirmed that it was Alex Cifuentes, though, the CIA were happy to step up and take credit.

I was sickened by the CIA, but I also knew this was simply the way they operated: collecting intelligence from their own government and then haphazardly sharing it with their Mexican counterparts.

"That's the fuckin' spooks, man," I told Brady. "They tell the Mexicans—then just stand back and watch the shit show. The CIA doesn't give a fuck about dismantling international DTOs. It's just another stat to them. If they can stat the pass-on of key intelligence or an arrest, then they can justify their existence."

It was a classic example of the breakdown in communication, if not outright antagonism, between the US intelligence community and federal law enforcement. I knew the ropes by now: most CIA activity in Mexico was never coordinated or deconflicted with the DEA. It was true of their approach in Mexico, but it was also how the CIA operated around the rest of the world. They often caused major disruptions to highly sensitive, judicially authorized investigations like ours.

Whatever the case, Alex Cifuentes had been prematurely arrested by SEDENA, and we were left to pick up the pieces. Virtually every BlackBerry we'd been intercepting dropped the day after the Cifuentes arrest. I was pissed, but I held back my emotions when speaking with Brady—no sense adding more fuel to the fire. It didn't stop him, however.

"I'm fuckin' done with the FBI," Brady said. "We're not sharing a single piece of intel with them ever again."

"I understand," I said. "But we need to keep an even keel here. The thing is—I don't know what else CIA may have from the FBI that could torpedo this thing even further. We've got to keep them close."

"All right, dude," Brady said. "You keep playing Switzerland— it's what you do best. Listen, if I was there in Mexico right now, I'd be choking some motherfuckers out."

"ARGO," I SAID. "You see that movie? Ben Affleck?"

"About the Hollywood sting with the Iranians?"

"Uh-huh."

"Sure. 'Argo fuck yourself.'"

I laughed. "Think we could pull it off?"

"With Chapo? I don't know . . ."

For years, Alex Cifuentes had been searching for producers, screenwriters, and authors—all at the specific request of Chapo.

Strange as it sounded—given the precautions he took to guard his location and the secrecy of his communications—Chapo had become fixated on telling his rags-to-riches life story. He was desperate to see his rise from that impoverished little kid selling oranges in La Tuna to the world's wealthiest drug lord on the big screen. In the line sheets, we would sometimes read about how Chapo was batting around the idea of a film, telenovela, or book. Chapo would entertain just about *anyone* who was interested in hearing his story.

Accordingly, Alex Cifuentes would get recommendations through his contacts for various filmmakers and writers and then vet them for Chapo. If they passed muster, Cifuentes would schedule a face-to-face meeting with Guzmán at a secure location, somewhere in Culiacán or at a ranch in the mountains.

Brady and I had learned of at least one aspiring filmmaker—we knew him only as Carlino—who'd flown in from Cabo. Carlino had Hollywood connections and claimed to have worked with the producers of the hit Fox TV show *Cops*.

Chapo knew the show *Cops* and was very interested in following up.

"We need to reach out to them," said Brady.

"I bet they'd be on board," I said. "I've already spoken to my guys in Los Angeles. They have a few DEA agents with connections to producers. They'd be willing to work with us."

"Set up our own version of *Argo*?"

"Exactly."

"How would we play it?" Brady asked.

"You could be UC as the director," I said. "Just get one cameraman working with us as an undercover. You'd be perfect, dude. Keep your usual poker face. Never smile. Throw on some horn-rim glasses and just grumble and curse at everyone."

"I could handle that," Brady said.

"Let's get up to LA to see what our options are," I said. "With Cifuentes locked up, finding the right undercover agent to pose as a producer or screenwriter may be our only way to get this *cabrón* out of Culiacán."

"We could call the film *Saludos a Generente*!" Brady said.

"Hell, no. I've seen that line one too many times already."

I was staring at a map of Mexico, looking at all the possible coastal resort towns for a meet.

"The beauty of it is," I said, "Chapo wouldn't even have to leave the country. He'd go back to Cabo if it was to start rolling footage for a movie based on his life. Vallarta? Even Cancún would probably work. Anywhere on the Mayan Riviera. He has a history of traveling over there already. He'd feel safe."

NOT ONLY WAS CHAPO conducting meetings with producers and writers, but I'd learned about a thumb drive on which he had the first half of a movie script about his rise to power. He'd let his wife Griselda López Pérez and daughter Grisel Guzmán López review it, only to have them complain that the screenplay didn't mention them enough.

Griselda, Chapo's second wife, was accorded a special level of respect—even deference—by the drug lord. Brady and I had intercepted Griselda's complaints: she often demanded more money for her kids, and Chapo would comply, handing over $10,000 every few weeks.

Despite being exes, they clearly were still close. Guzmán and Griselda had three surviving children—Joaquin, Grisel, and Ovidio—and they were some of Chapo's favorites.

For months, Brady and I had been intercepting Joaquin and Ovidio. The brothers were going by the code names "Güero" and "Ratón."

Being light-skinned, Joaquin's use of the name Güero was an obvious choice.

I remembered the first time Diego had taught me the word *güero*, years back when we were listening to narcocorridos during our Phoenix Task Force days. "You come down to DF with me," Diego had said. "Pick up some slang, eat the street food—they won't take you for a gringo, dude. Everyone'll call you *güero* . . ."

"And why Ratón?" Brady asked.

I had studied the one photo I had of Ovidio. "He looks like a mouse," I said, which cracked us both up. The kid did have big black eyes and protruding ears . . .

Güero and Ratón were speaking constantly with their father through the mirror of Office-1, just like their half brother Iván.

The two sets of brothers operated in pairs, but Güero and Ratón seemed to be more heavily involved in Chapo's day-to-day business than Iván and Alfredo. According to the messages we were intercepting, all four sons were key players in Chapo's drug dynasty, though, and closer to him than anyone else in his organization.

These guys weren't wannabes: the hard-core narco life was in their blood—they had followed in their father's footsteps from an early age. Just from watching their day-to-day communications, I knew the four boys meant everything to Chapo.

A FEW WEEKS AFTER the arrest of Alex Cifuentes, Brady, Joe, and Neil, with the help of their lead prosecutor, Camila Defusio, had finally righted the ship in El Paso; they had cranked out the affidavits and were back live again, sending fresh intercepts down to me by the hundreds.

HSI was moving at lightning speed—all due to the management in El Paso providing full support for Brady and his team.

Brady told me that this was the biggest drug investigation HSI had ever been involved in. I knew that Brady's bosses were fully invested in their success and had been greasing all the logistics behind the scenes for months. I had never seen anything like it. Brady's brass kept us moving forward without the slightest bureaucratic interruption. It was impressive.

Brady and his team had climbed back up and were now intercepting a handful of office phones and a new Second-Tier device. But these grunt workers in Durango—however valuable the intercepts—didn't get us any closer to Chapo himself. Only pinging Top-Tier could do that.

I HAD BEEN WAITING to find the new Top-Tier device, and fortunately it didn't take us long. This time the username was MI-26, and in the line sheets everyone was calling him "Chaneke."

"Who's this now?" Brady asked. "What happened to Condor?"

"I'm not sure, man."

"Who the hell is Chaneke?"

"For now," I said, "let's assume he's our new Condor."

I pinged the phone on my laptop. "Perfect. Chaneke's device is hitting in that same neighborhood. Right in Colonia Libertad. That's where I had Condor."

I quickly Googled the name Chaneke. Like so many of the words in the line sheets, it turned out to be a phonetic misspelling. *Chaneques* were, in fact, among the hundreds of gods and spirits sacred to the ancient Aztecs. Legendary creatures in Mexican folklore, they are the "little people who steal your soul." The images of *chaneques* that I found—pre-Columbian sculptures and drawings—resembled tiny trolls with oversize eyes. By Aztec tradition, the *chaneques* were guardians of the forest, attacking intruders, frightening them so that their souls would abandon their bodies.

This Top-Tier Chaneke was also a kind of guardian: Chapo's direct intermediary. In the intercepts, the workers kept referring to Chaneke as "Secre."

"It's got to mean he's Chapo's secretary," I said. "And these usernames MD-8 and now MI-26—I think they're makes of helicopters."

"Maybe Chaneke's a helicopter pilot?" Brady said.

The reason, for now at least, remained a mystery, but one thing was clear: Condor might run a tight ship, but Chaneke was intensely disliked by the workers in Chapo's organization.

"Everyone *hates* Chaneke," Brady said, "Second-Tier and the offices keep bitching about him. Sounds like he's stiffing them. They're constantly asking him when El Señor is going to pay them. One office worker has been complaining that he needs the money to buy groceries for his kid. And Second-Tier told him, 'Don't worry, Condor will take care of you when he returns.'"

"I see it now. Two *secretarios*—Condor and Chaneke. Same job, they're just taking shifts," I said.

We determined that each secretary was working fifteen to thirty days straight—no downtime at all. They probably ate whatever the boss ate, slept whenever he slept, and typed out every order and whim Chapo needed sent via that Top-Tier BlackBerry.

"Talk about a 'pattern of life'—can you imagine Condor's?" I asked Brady. "Guy's got no personal time at all. Twenty-four seven he's Chapo's slave."

Brady let out a short laugh. "And the poor bastard gets to sleep in the room next to Chapo—listening to him bang his whores all night long."

We had figured out that Chapo, still spooked by the near cap-ture in Cabo, no longer used a phone. He was strictly dictating orders now—his two assigned secretaries would relay all of his communications so that he didn't even have to touch the Black-Berrys.

BRADY AND I HAD our own reasons for disliking Chaneke. Whenever he took over from Condor, shift-change protocol was followed with almost military precision, meaning that Chaneke, the Second-Tier, and office devices in Durango would all drop their phones almost immediately, either tossing them in the trash or giving them to a family member to use. Either way, it created an instant logistical nightmare for us. Whatever phones we were intercepting—usually hundreds—all went dead. In an instant, no more messages, and no more line sheets to decipher. Our keyhole into Chapo's secret inner world would vanish, just like the ghostly drug lord himself.

This emotional roller coaster of being up, listening, one day, then down the next was beginning to grind on everyone's nerves.

"I don't know how much more my team can take," Brady told me after Chaneke had once again burned all the phones instantly.

"We're right there," I said. "Hold tight, brother. This last ping was in the same area in Culiacán."

I WAS CERTAIN THAT zeroing in on either Condor's or Chaneke's de-vice would lead us straight to Chapo, so for fourteen hours straight I kept pinging. By now I had a concentration of yellow pin mark-ers on my Google Map—adding to weeks of pings already and forming a swirling bull's-eye in the heart of urban Culiacán. I was staring at a clear pattern of life. Although there was some slight variation in the pings, it appeared that Condor and Chaneke never moved from that Colonia Libertad section of Culiacán.

"Have you seen the overhead images on these?" I asked Brady.

"Looks like a goddamn shantytown down there," Brady said. "Dirt streets. Derelict cars. Tarps draped over back lots."

"Yeah, the shitty neighborhood doesn't make much sense. Why would Chapo be holed up there? We know his secretaries need to be face-to-face. Right there with him. Maybe he's laying low."

"Hold on—these are just coming in," Brady said. He had a batch of brand-new translated line sheets. "Chaneke instructed Naris to go pick up Turbo at the Walmart 68. Naris is driving a black Jetta."

"Turbo's in some serous shit," I said.

"Those six hundred kilos are long gone, and Turbo's personally responsible," Brady said.

"Yeah, could get ugly. Turbo will be lucky if he makes it out alive."

Several hours prior, Chaneke—passing orders down through Second-Tier, then to Office-5, and finally out to Chapo's Mazatlán-based maritime coordinator—instructed Turbo to head to "El 19." His *tío* ("uncle," yet another coded nickname for Chapo) was ready to see him. Turbo was then told to go to the "Walmart 68 on Obregon," where he'd wait to get picked up by a black Jetta.

Brady and I had established that El 19 was clearly the DTO's code for Culiacán.

"And I know that Walmart," I said. "It's just to the east of all my Top-Tier pings, off Avenida Álvaro Obregón. It's close—the perfect pickup spot." I watched the movements of Naris as I continued to ping him.

"You dialed in?" Brady asked.

"Yep, he's there at the Walmart. Now he's headed further west."

I kept tracking Naris with regular pings, getting closer to the elusive boss.

Abra la puerta. Abra la puerta!

Naris was sending messages out to Office-6, but there was a glitch in the system. His requests to "open the door" weren't getting delivered to Second-Tier, which meant they weren't getting relayed to Chaneke.

"He's stuck there at some front gate," Brady said. "Frustrated as hell."

It was a bizarre turn of events. I knew Naris was usually highly cautious about all communications—he'd almost always power down his BlackBerry before getting close to Chapo's location. But now Naris was stuck outside the house, and with no one opening the gate for him, he'd decided to risk it, turning his BlackBerry back on to push his messages out quickly.

Carnal, abra la puerta!

"That's it!" I said.

Naris was now pinging directly on top of Chaneke.

"Yeah, Naris is at the gate," I said. "We've got him, Brady. Not sure which house. But Chapo is definitely right there on that fucking block."

DUCK DYNASTY

FOR MONTHS, BRADY HAD been asking me who we could trust among the Mexican counterparts to launch a Chapo capture mission.

"The Federal Police?"

"No—out of the question."

"Any units in SEDENA?"

"Not a chance."

But now, with our near certainty that Chapo was living within that one-block radius on my map, the answer became clear.

"There's only one real option," I said.

Only one institution within the Mexican government had a reputation for being incorruptible: the Secretaría de Marina–Armada de México (SEMAR).

"The marines?" Brady said.

"Yeah," I said. "Among the counterparts, SEMAR's all we've got . . ."

"You trust them?"

"Can't say I trust them," I said. "I can't say I trust *anyone* here. I've never worked with them, but I know they're fast and lean and always ready for a fight."

I'd been studying SEMAR's track record during their work

with other DEA agents at the embassy—they'd helped decimate the Gulf Cartel and then the Zetas, on the east coast of Mexico.

"Sounds promising," Brady said.

"There's a special brigade here in Mexico City," I said. "From what I hear they're the least corrupt of them all."

Since I began working with Brady and his team, I had shared *nothing* with any Mexican counterparts.

First, the Mexicans didn't yet know that US federal law enforcement was able to intercept BlackBerry PIN messages between two traffickers in Mexico. Second, there was no way I would release any intelligence prematurely without having Chapo's location pinpointed and ironclad.

"It's still too early to approach them," I said to Brady. "And I'm being told by the bosses here that SEMAR won't even consider going into Culiacán. Far too dangerous."

MEANWHILE, A NEW NAME had appeared suddenly in the line sheets.

"Lic-F," Brady said. "Have you seen this guy? I keep going over his messages. He's obviously very close to Chapo—looks like he's helping coordinate coke loads in and out of Culiacán, and he's very tight with Picudo."

"Yeah," I said. "Seems to me he's Chapo's most trusted set of eyes and ears. He's cautious and smart. But I don't think he's a lawyer. Some of these line sheets make me suspect he's actually got a law enforcement background."

The thought of Lic-F took me back to that escape from Puente Grande prison—Chapo's corruption of the guards, and even the failures of the prison management. Lic-F? El Licenciado? The former police officer in the Sinaloa Attorney General's Office who'd become a close friend of Chapo's during his stint in Puente Grande?

The only thing I'm sure of is that this guy is slick. And he's got some serious hooks within the government," I said.

"Look at this," Brady said. "He's giving Chapo the status on a tunnel."

I pulled up the line sheet from Lic-F to Top-Tier. Lic-F was providing Chapo with a precise description of a tunnel that had been under construction for more than a year. "It's going to measure approximately eleven hundred meters, and they have finished more than six hundred meters," I read in the translated message. And Lic-F said he'd need less than a "roll"—$10,000— to finish construction and keep paying the salary of the tunnel workers.

"Damn," I told Brady. "That tunnel is gonna be more than a quarter-mile long."

"They're digging into San Diego or Nogales—one of the two," Brady said.

Working in the HSI office in El Paso, Brady had become an expert on tunnels along the US–Mexico border.

It was Chapo who had pioneered the narco tunnel along his key smuggling corridors. The tunneling had started nearly a quarter-century earlier, in 1990, when the first cross-border one was found in Douglas, Arizona. The Douglas tunnel, estimated to have cost the traffickers $1.5 million, originated inside a house in the town of Agua Prieta, Sonora, and ended some three hundred feet away at a warehouse in Douglas. Used for smuggling loads of weed for the Sinaloa Cartel, the media had dubbed it the "James Bond Tunnel," because the only way to access the underground passage was to turn on an outdoor water spigot at the Agua Prieta house, which triggered a hydraulic system that raised a pool table in a game room, which in turn exposed a ladder down.

No one knew exactly how many tunnels Chapo had constructed in the ensuing years. Since that first Douglas discovery, US authorities had found more than 150, almost always with the same signature construction features: ventilation, lighting, sometimes rails, and often sophisticated hydraulics were included.

I HAD DISCOVERED a key player in the tunnel construction, too: "Kava."

"Kava may be an architect," I told Brady. "Possibly an engineer. He's constantly reporting to Chapo, giving him status updates on his workers and the various projects they having going on. One job is up in Tijuana—probably the tunnel that Lic-F is talking about."

"Could be," Brady said. "Everything I'm seeing that's tunnel-related I'm passing to my guys in San Diego and Nogales."

On October 31, 2013, the San Diego Tunnel Task Force, comprising DEA, HSI, and US Customs and Border Protection, discovered a major tunnel between a warehouse in Tijuana and another in San Diego. I followed the news coverage live on CNN in the embassy.

This "super tunnel," as authorities dubbed it, went down to a depth of thirty-five feet and zigzagged about a third of a mile until the exit in an industrial park west of the Otay Mesa port of entry. Muling drugs down there must have been claustrophobic work; the tunnel wasn't big enough for a man to stand up in—only four-feet tall and three feet wide—but it did have ventilation, lighting, hydraulic doors, and an electric rail system.

US Immigration and Customs Enforcement locked up three suspects and made a sizable seizure during the discovery of the super tunnel—more than eight tons of marijuana and 325 pounds of cocaine.

Brady and I suspected that the super tunnel was Chapo's handiwork—not because of chatter in the line sheets but because, after its discovery, the DTO's BlackBerrys immediately went completely silent about it.

"Amazing," Brady said. "Everyone's quiet. They're disciplined. They lose a tunnel of that size and no one's saying a goddamn word?"

"With as many tunneling projects as Kava's working on, Chapo's gotta be used to these things getting popped by now," I said. "Hell, they've probably got at least another five super tunnels in the works."

AS BRADY AND I were in the heat of strategizing our high-risk operation to capture Chapo, the Mexico City embassy was rocked by shocking news. In mid-December 2013, a joint capture-op involving units of the DEA and Mexican Federal Police in the beachside resort of Puerto Peñasco, just south of the Arizona border, turned wildly violent.

I had just finished breakfast and was fixing the Windsor knot in my tie when the phone rang. "Get in here *now*," my group supervisor said. "Marco and the guys are pinned down up in Sonora in a shoot-out. They're calling for help."

I quickly snatched my laptop bag and headed toward my G-ride. On most days, DEA Special Agent Marco Perez sat next to me, but on this particular morning, Perez, several other DEA agents, and the Mexican Federal Police were staging a covert operation in Puerto Peñasco to arrest Gonzalo Inzunza Inzunza, a.k.a. "Macho Prieto," a high-ranking leader in the Sinaloa Cartel. Macho Prieto ran his own drug-trafficking organization under the cartel's umbrella. A protégé of Ismael "Mayo" Zambada García, Macho Prieto was considered extremely violent.

I burst into the embassy hoping to hear Marco and his team were out of harm's way, and quickly got briefed on what had gone wrong. The Federal Police had approached the door of Macho's condo in the predawn darkness, and Macho's response had been instant. The cops began taking fire through the front door from Macho and his bodyguards, and within seconds there was a firefight under way in the middle of an upscale residential neighborhood filled with American tourists, just steps from the white sand. Macho's men—armed with AK-47s and automatic belt-fed machine guns—fired until they ran out of ammo.

Macho called in reinforcements, and gunmen raced in from other condos, firing at the cops from balconies and vehicles. Macho's "war wagon"—an armored white Ford F-150 with a 50-caliber machine gun mounted in the back bed underneath a camper shell—came screaming in through the front gates of the complex, smashing PF's barricade of cars, while snipers fired round after round into the front windshield, wounding the driver. The war wagon sped out of control, leaking gasoline and oil onto the pavement. Gunmen jumped from the front and back of the truck and ran to join the fight.

"They're in the back of the complex, hunkered down," my supervisor said, her ear to a phone receiver. "I can hear the gunshots over the phone in the background—it's nonstop." Perez and the other two DEA agents were around in back of the complex, taking cover behind a small concrete wall. The American agents were pinned down in the darkness and couldn't leave their positions because PF had two Black Hawk helicopters in the air, firing grenades at the bad guys, turning vehicles into fireballs.

Even local police cars began responding, but not to join the good guys—the local cops, all on Macho's payroll, were picking up the injured cartel gunmen and taking them away like a makeshift ambulance service. The PF team was small, outgunned, and now running the risk of being surrounded by Macho's men.

In the chaos, Macho's bodyguards were able to drag him out the back door and into a car to make an escape, but Macho was bleeding profusely. When PF finally made entry into the condo, they saw puddles of blood and scarlet handprints everywhere. Macho had sunken into a hot tub in an attempt to control his bleeding, turning the bubbling water thick and dark red. The smears continued on the floors and out the back door. Macho Prieto had escaped the gunfight but would soon die from his wounds.

Two Mexican Federal Police were also badly wounded; the DEA team raced them in a convoy across the US border to Tucson. They couldn't risk staying in Mexico a moment longer, for fear of being attacked—nowhere in Sonora was safe once word was out that PF had killed Macho.

The wounded PF members all recovered in an Arizona hospital; no DEA agents had been injured; Macho was dead—so the operation was judged a major success against the Sinaloa Cartel, but it was also one of deadliest international operations DEA had ever conducted.

CULIACÁN HAD ALWAYS weighed heavy on my mind. Even more so after the bloody operation to capture Macho Prieto.

Just as Macho maintained ironfisted control of his turf in Sonora, the city of Culiacán was in the grip of Chapo. Brady and I knew it would be nearly impossible to hit Chapo anywhere in Culiacán: we could end up in a firefight with an entire city. If Macho could summon that many fighters in the little resort town of

Puerto Peñasco, how many would Chapo have streaming to his aid if we were to hit him in Culiacán? It was precisely why Brady and I were working so hard to find a location outside the city where we could nab him quickly, quietly, and hopefully without a gun battle.

"How many kids does Chapo have?"

It was our fifth phone call of the day, and it wasn't even noon.

"All the women he's run through—no one really knows," I said. "Hundreds? You might be living next door to one." Brady let out a loud laugh.

"But really," I continued, "there's only the four key sons we need to pay attention to."

With Christmas season approaching, I saw that Ratón and Güero were taking regular trips out of Culiacán; Chapo would tell them where to meet—some place he called "Pichis."

"This new 'Pichis'—over and over. Just today again: 'Meet me at Pichis,'" Brady read from a freshly translated line sheet.

I had been dissecting those sheets as well.

"Yes, I've seen that. No idea what Pichis means. But he's building a pool there along with some palapas—Kava's been sending him regular updates on the construction."

Being hypervigilant for references to meetings among all the players was a top priority for me, especially if the get-togethers were planned outside the city. I started pinging Güero's and Ratón's phones simultaneously as they headed south from Culiacán; then more pinging, until I had six red pushpins tacked to my Google Map, tracing a crooked line down Sinaloa State Highway 5.

But then, nothing. After about fifty minutes, the sons' phones would stop pinging. Maybe they were so far in the sticks that they were out of reach of a cell tower? Or had they shut their phones off, or taken out the batteries, right before a meeting?

Chapo Guzmán after his first arrest in June 1993.

AP Photo/Damian Dovarganes

Boarding the DEA Learjet en route to Mexico City in June 2010, carrying the $1.2 million in cash inside FedEx boxes.

Diego sitting with Mercedes Chávez Villalobos and her associates at La Rosita restaurant in Panama, June 2009. I took this photo surreptitiously during the undercover operation.

With the seized 2,513kg bricks of cocaine in Guayaquil, Ecuador, in November 2010.

Chapo in his signature baseball cap, toting an AR-15 outside a Mexican ranch several years after his first prison escape in 2001.

The photo found in a BlackBerry seized at Chapo's mansion in Cabo San Lucas after his escape from Mexican and DEA authorities in February 2012.

The card—headed by his initials, J.G.L.—that Chapo sent with flowers to his numerous girlfriends in Culiacán on El Día del Amor y la Amistad (Valentine's Day).

The Chicago Crime Commission names El Chapo Public Enemy Number One, replacing Al Capone, in February 2013.

AP Photo/M. Spencer Green

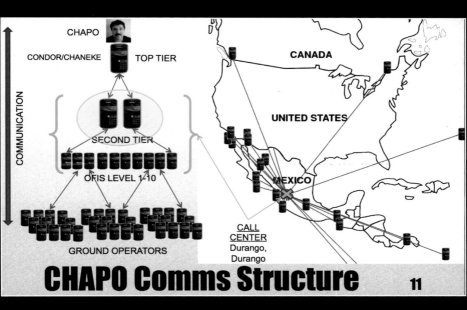

A diagram I created to show the communication structure of Chapo's mirror devices.

Video of Chapo interrogating a man tied to a post under a palapa.

Source unknown

An overhead shot of Duck Dynasty showing further construction:
multiple palapas, a house, and a swimming pool.

Imagery © 2017 Digital Globe, map data © 2017 Google, INEGI

Packages of cocaine stored in the tunnel at Safe House 3 along with fake

TOP: My Google map showing pertinent locations in Sinaloa, including clandestine airstrips throughout the Sierra Madre mountain range, marked with blue plane icons.

BOTTOM: My Google map showing the pings of the Top-Tier devices (yellow) and other important targets and locations.

Imagery © 2017 Digital Globe; map data © 2017 Google, INEGI

ABOVE: Screens used to monitor the surveillance videos at all of Chapo's safe houses—located in the garage of Safe House 1.

BELOW: Lying down for the first time on my potato sack cot in the makeshift SEMAR "barracks" in Culiacán.

SEMAR arriving at Safe House 2, making entry in the early morning of
February 17, 2014. Taken on my iPhone.

Brady and me sitting in Chapo's driveway outside Safe House 3,
taking a quick rest before the next raid.

Several heav▓▓▓▓▓▓▓▓▓▓▓▓ detained inside Picudo's h

Below Safe House 3, in a tunnel lit by fluorescent lamps, large quantities of cocaine were stored on makeshift racks.

Brady exiting the tunnel underneath the bathtub

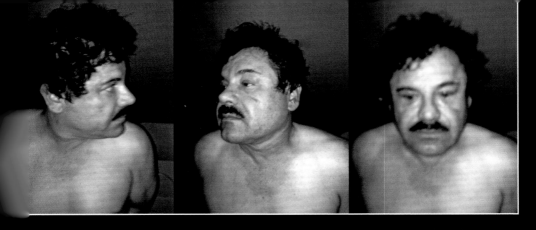

ABOVE: Three photos of Chapo taken on my iPhone inside my armored vehicle in the underground parking garage of the Hotel Miramar on February 22, 2014.

BELOW: Brady and me moments after the capture at the Hotel Miramar; I'm wearing Chapo's baseball cap and carrying the AR-15 rifle found in the hotel room with Guzmán.

Brady and me with Chapo in custody: the world's most-wanted drug lord during interrogation at the SEMAR base in Mazatlán.

Chapo paraded in front of the world's press after he arrived at the Mexico City

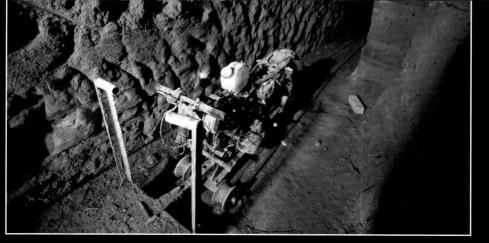

The 1.5-kilometer-long tunnel in which Chapo escaped from Altiplano prison on July 11, 2015. PVC pipe pumped fresh air throughout the passageway, and metal tracks had been laid so that Chapo could get away on a railcar rigged to the frame of a modified motorcycle.

AP Photo/Eduardo Verdugo

Chapo and Cholo Iván sitting in the backseat of a vehicle after their capture on January 8, 2016, in Los Mochis, Sinaloa.

Source unknown

Chapo sitting inside Cefereso No. 9 prison in Ciudad Juárez, Mexico.

Official Twitter account of Secretary of the Interior Miguel Ángel Osorio Chong (Mexico)

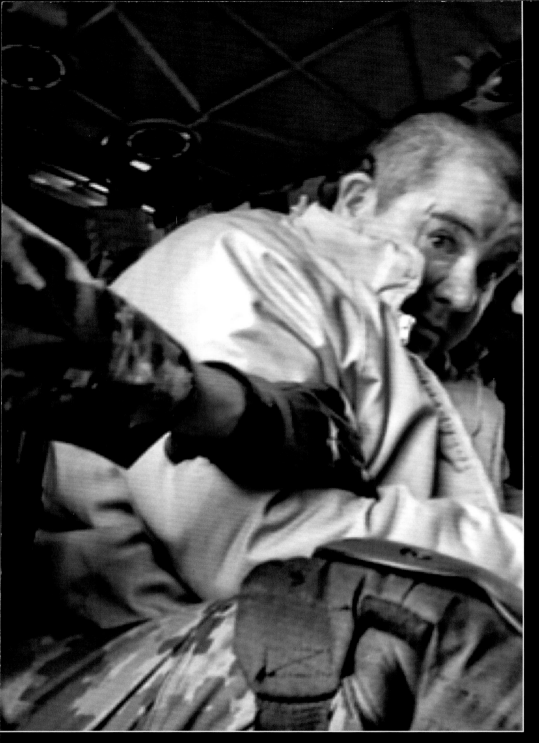

Chapo being extradited from Mexico to the United States on January 19, 2017.

Source unknown

Brady and I couldn't track the boys any further, but we could drill down on Chapo's language. What the hell did that name "Pichis" mean?

DECEMBER 24, 2013—10:34 P.M. I had just poured a cup of homemade eggnog, helping my wife finish wrapping up the last Christmas gifts for the boys, when my phone hummed with a text from Brady in El Paso.

"Got another Pichis run."

This time it wasn't just Güero and Ratón, but Tocallo as well. Chapo had instructed the three boys to meet his driver at the gas station in "Celis," and he'd take them the rest of the way in. My wife rolled her eyes as I turned toward the computer and began pinging.

"Celis" was the small town of Sanchez Celis.

"I can see a gas station at the south end, but all the pings dry up right around there," I told Brady.

It was one o'clock on Christmas morning, and Brady and I had been swooping around on Google Earth, searching that desolate area of Sinaloan farmland that faded into swamp further toward the Pacific, looking for any sign of Chapo's top-secret location.

Then it all began to fall into place. "He was ordering those airboats a couple months ago, right?" Brady said.

"Yeah, then he talked about building a pool near some palapas at Pichis." I replied. "So it's going to be someplace on the water— near the Ensenada de Pabellones."

"Found it!" Brady interrupted. "*Pichis*. An abbreviation. Short for Pichiguila duck-hunting club." Brady had already pulled up the club's website. I did the same, and came upon a home page advertising "the best duck-hunting in North America." The website even noted that President Dwight D. Eisenhower had hunted in the area, though before the club was established.

I was struck by the eerie throwback to my Kansas past. Chapo was a *duck* hunter? Guzmán hardly fit the profile of an outdoorsman, even though he'd been raised in the remote mountains of the Sierra Madre.

"Can you see him standing out in the middle of a swamp in knee-high waders, waiting for a flock of pintails to fly by?"

"Chapo's got no time for that shit. *Ducks?* Hell, no. He'd rather be hunting young girls," said Brady.

The club was located on the north end of the Ensenada de Pabellones. But my pings near Sanchez Celis were too far away from the club; Chapo couldn't be hanging out at the lodge. Brady and I continued our virtual flyovers, zooming in, zooming out, searching for any kind of man-made structure. Just after 3:30 a.m., I found myself hovering tight over two brown grainy circles resembling old palapas.

Jackpot!

I remembered my father teaching me a key lesson back when I was ten: whenever you hunt ducks, you want to sit on the "X." The X is the hot spot where the ducks are known to feed or relax. It was no different for Chapo.

Guzmán needed to leave his claustrophobic Culiacán safe houses to eat some carne asada, relax, sit under the stars in the middle of nowhere, and breathe fresh air for a few hours. A secluded place where he could meet with his sons to discuss cartel business face-to-face.

"Just found our X," I said. "It's the ultimate hit location." Brady laughed when I told him the name I'd given Chapo's secret lagoon hideaway.

"Duck Dynasty."

LOS HOYOS

THE KIKI ROOM WAS filled with suits. I was sitting at the center of the table, across from the head of the DEA. Administrator Michele Leonhart had flown down to the embassy to be briefed specifically on all the high-profile cases Mexico City agents had been working.

Leonhart was no stranger to stories of agents chasing down elusive kingpins. She had begun her DEA career as a street agent in Southern California and had worked her way up through the ranks before being appointed DEA administrator by President Obama in February 2010. The last time I had seen her was in 2006, when I walked across the stage at my graduation in Quantico. Before I began to brief her on the latest developments with Chapo, her words from my graduation ceremony once again rang in my head:

Go out there and make big cases.

I smiled, knowing that now, six years later, I was on the verge of fulfilling the promise I'd made with that handshake.

I filled Leonhart in on the tremendous relationship I had built with HSI and how far we'd come, showing her my Google Map and the heavy concentration of Top-Tier pings in the Colonia Libertad neighborhood.

"We have him down to a block radius, ma'am," I said. "And every week—or every week and a half—he comes out of Culiacán."

"Do you know where he's going?"

"Yes, to the coast," I said, "to a private hideaway he's constructing not far from the city."

Leonhart nodded.

"We're finalizing all the details," I told her. "I want to have enough intelligence to know where he's going to run to—should he escape capture again. We're almost there, ma'am. We plan to bring in SEMAR soon."

Following the meeting, I ran into the Regional Director Tom McAllister in the hallway.

"You spoke pretty confidently in there," Tom said. "Made some big promises."

"It's the truth," I said. "I just told it like it is."

I wasn't being cocky. I simply had no time to second-guess myself.

I had put in years of hard study back in Phoenix with Diego, and now I'd done all these grueling months in the trenches with Brady, Joe, and Neil, cracking the code of Chapo's mirrored telecommunication system. I could honestly say—without arrogance or bravado—that no one in history had ever been in a better position to capture Chapo Guzmán.

I now had the current location of the world's most wanted criminal. I'd saturated myself in all the tiniest details of Guzmán's life. I was sunk so deep into Chapo's world that I knew virtually almost every movement he made, and close to every order he gave throughout the day.

———

READING THE DAILY INTERCEPTS painstakingly, line by line, I could see a parallel obsession to mine: Chapo kept his eyes on *everything*, too, every single transaction and decision in his drug-trafficking sphere. In his own way, the kingpin was driven by a constant thirst for knowledge, just as I was. Chapo needed to understand every detail of his operation, even the most seemingly routine and boring things. This need for total knowledge bordered on a compulsion. Chapo was a boss who required complete control.

I needed control, too. Many evenings—nights when I should have already been home with my family—I found myself scrolling down through the summary of translated line sheets on my Mac-Book, hoping to find something—anything—I'd missed:

> Chapo and Turbo, his Mazatlán-based maritime operator, discuss payments for a high-speed cigarette boat that needs to be sent to San Diego for several months to have new motors installed. Turbo asks Chapo to deposit the money into his wife's account and says that he still had not received his $10,000 bi-weekly payment for his expenses. Turbo also tells Chapo that he's looking at acquiring buoys equipped with GPS—clearly as a result of the recent 622-kg cocaine loss at sea.

> Maestro, a pilot based in Chiapas, asks Chapo to send a payment for some unnamed military commanders. Chapo replies that he'll be sending a total of $130,000 in the plane: $40,000 to pay each commander for each event and $10,000 for the jet fuel.

> Raul—an operator in Panama—notifies Chapo that he's found a place on a hill five kilometers from the border with a ranch and room for a clandestine airstrip, but he will need heavy machinery to clear it.

Raton is requesting "20 rolls"—$200,000—for logistics in moving 20 tons of marijuana in a tractor trailer towards the U.S. border. Chapo tells him that Picudo will deliver it.

Chapo reminds Raton that they shouldn't plan on having their BBQ outside Culiacán because there's been a lot of military and police activity outside the city. Chapo suggests having it at his son Güero's house instead and they can order Chinese food.

Chapo instructs Ciento, one of his gofers in Culiacán, to go get the press from Pinguino's ranch so they can make the squares—kilos—and to be careful because military and law enforcement units have been spotted in the area of the ranches.

Chapo asks his accountant Oscar how much cash he has on hand. Oscar says $1,233,940 not including what Güero recently gave him. Chapo instructs Oscar to make the following transactions. To give $200,000 to Ciento and have Oscar send him a confirmation after the transaction at the bank. Then he asks Oscar to give Pinto, still another Culiacan worker, 4,190 pesos to repair a car.

Chapo tells his son Tocallo that he'll meet with him tomorrow.

Chapo asks Araña how many loads were taken from La Cienéga, an airstrip outside Culiacán. Araña runs down through a list and reports that there were ten trips taken in the last week at $2,000 each.

Chapo tells Kava to hurry up with the deeds for the nine properties they'd been given. Kava tells him he's headed to Tijuana to conduct an evaluation of a site, most likely the start of a new super-tunnel. Then he discusses with Chapo the purchase of a casa de cambio—money-exchange—that's going out of business. Chapo's interested. Kava's also going to look at some other properties in Mexicali and San Luis.

Chapo speaks with an advisor named Flaco who's updating him on a hearing in the port city of Lázaro Cárdenas regarding one of the cartel's boats that's been seized.

Chapo sends flowers and a local five-piece band called Los Alegres del Barranco over to a 28-year-old girl in his neighborhood to serenade her on her birthday.

AND, LIKE CLOCKWORK, every morning Chapo would receive an intelligence report from one of his most trusted advisers; Brady and I knew him only as "Sergio."

Lic-F may have been Chapo's eyes and ears in many aspects of the DTO, but we recognized that Sergio was a critical player regarding Chapo's personal safety. For months, Brady and I would watch as Sergio reported the detailed movements of Mexican government operations—military and law enforcement—both inside and outside Sinaloa.

"Today the reconnaissance flights are scheduled to begin at 10:00 hours and run through 14:00 hours. One helicopter to the Cruz de Elota zone, another to Jesús María, and the final to the Navolato area."

"Four *sapos*"—toads, a coded reference to the green uniforms of SEDENA troops—"will be conducting patrols in the Cañadas, Las Quintas, Loma Linda, and Villa Ordaz neighborhoods today."

"Federal Police will be leaving the airport this morning and there will be movement from Mazatlán to Los Mochis—they're looking for meth labs."

"Two soldiers will escort a panel van carrying monitoring equipment through Culiacán."

The level of detail was so precise that it seemed to me as though Sergio was copying and pasting directly from the Mexican military's daily operational plans.

"Sergio's got people greased everywhere," I told Brady.

"Yep," Brady said. "Chapo's got advance notice on every single movement in Sinaloa."

Brady and I had almost become numb to the military leaks, after reading them every day for months. We hoped that Chapo had become numb as well.

"There's no way in hell he has time to stay on top of all of this intel," Brady said. "As busy as he is every day running the DTO."

"Regardless, he's got his safety net in place," I said. "He'll know immediately if there's even a whiff of an operation against him."

Brady interrupted our conversation with a freshly translated line sheet.

"Condor just told Naris that Chapo wants some sushi. He's to deliver it to Los Hoyos," Brady said.

"Pinging him now," I said.

"Condor won't quit," Brady said. "He's now sending the poor fucker back out for plastic spoons and a couple bags of ice."

When Chapo wasn't locked in his bedroom with his latest girl, he was all business, 24/7, running the day-to-day of his organization without even a break on Sunday.

"Naris is getting fed up," Brady said. "Check this out: 'I'm spending the day with my family,' Naris says. 'You can tell El Señor I'm not doing his bitch work today.'"

"'I'm not doing his bitch work,'" I repeated, laughing so hard that I forgot to send the coordinates to Brady.

When I did send them, Naris's ping came back with a successful hit.

"Same neighborhood, brother. Colonia Libertad. Right within that same block."

"What's Los Hoyos?" Brady asked. "'The Holes'—a street name? A stash house?"

Los Hoyos.

We both thought it over. Silence on the line. Both of us racking our brains . . . Then, once again, the word puzzle slotted into place. Brady and I said it in perfect unison:

"Tunnels."

This would certainly fit the profile of a man known as the tunnel king.

"Remember what I heard from one of my sources? Inside one of his safe houses, Chapo has a tunnel—entrance is underneath a bathtub."

"Yeah, of course, I remember—the tunnel underneath the tub."

"Bet anything that's why they're calling the place Los Hoyos."

Whatever Chapo meant by Los Hoyos, I kept pinging Top-Tier and Naris, zeroing in tighter on that dusty block in Colonia Libertad.

"My pings are close, man. His pattern of life is clear. Now all we need to do is find a door."

I KNEW JUST THE GUY I'd need to call once we were ready to go operational.

United States Marshal Leroy Johnson, from Mississippi, had been with the Marshals Service for years and had a reputation as the foremost expert in tracking the phones of fugitives. He worked primarily out of Tennessee, but he had traveled all over the United States and on international missions, too. Leroy had conducted enough counter-narcotics capture operations in Mexico that he'd picked up the Spanish nickname "El Roy." His southern accent was as thick as his build—he stood six feet and a solid two hundred pounds—and he shared my passion for a manhunt.

"This guy is crazy," I told Brady. "And fearless. He'll walk through the worst neighborhoods in Juárez to put cuffs on a bad guy."

I knew that if we were to conduct any capture operation, we'd need Leroy and his team of marshals on the ground.

By this point, the pressure was beginning to build, from Washington, DC, to Mexico City. Word had slowly trickled out among DEA and HSI that Brady and I had Chapo pinned down to less than a one-block radius. Upper brass from both sides were insisting on a final coordination meeting. I could feel the bureaucratic tilt—like at the embassy when it had shifted its weight during the earthquake.

I was now spending more time trying to appease my bosses and coordinate a complex interagency meeting than focusing on the plan to act on our intelligence. On top of that, the CIA's counternarcotics team began showing up on the floor of my office, providing snippets of stale intelligence while asking probing questions, all in an attempt to collect anything they could about my plans.

ON JANUARY 16, 2014, at 6:53 p.m., I received a text from Brady.

"Chapo's headed back down to Duck Dynasty. Looks like he's already en route."

"Goddammit," I texted back. "We should have SEMAR on board by now. We're not going to get many more chances like this."

I knew that Chapo was at his most vulnerable leaving Los Hoyos behind in Culiacán, traveling light with Condor and maybe Picudo or some other bodyguard. I had been studying recent satellite images of Duck Dynasty, too. The photos revealed multiple palapas, a newly constructed pool—complete with a swim-up bar—and several other small outbuildings. A construction worker or two could still be seen on the property. This corroborated the line sheets: palapas, a new pool, the need for an airboat—all things Chapo had discussed randomly over the months were now making sense.

DUCK DYNASTY WAS in the middle of nowhere; the terrain was flat and easily accessed from all directions, so it was the perfect place to launch a capture operation.

But the clock was ticking. The possibility of a leak getting back to Chapo was too great. The only thing predictable about Chapo Guzmán was his unpredictability. He could switch up his pattern at any time and simply vanish up into the Sierra Madre for months.

I knew we couldn't wait any longer—we had the whole investigation wrapped up in a package with a big red bow on top.

"Think we can chance it?" Brady asked.

"Fuck it," I said. "Yes, let's bring in SEMAR right now. I'm canceling the meeting with the brass."

We had no other option: it was time to deliver.

MY FIRST CALL WAS to US Marshal Leroy Johnson, up in Tennessee.

"It's a go," I said.

"A capture op?"

"Get down here."

"On my way," Leroy said.

That next evening, I sat down with Leroy over a couple of bottles of Negra Modelo in a quiet bar across the street from the embassy, flipped open my MacBook, and showed him the heavy concentration of pin markers on my Google Map.

By now there were so many that you could hardly make out the city of Culiacán: it was completely covered with colored pins. I zoomed in, describing the meaning of each color and icon.

"Yellow pins are my Top-Tier pings," I explained. "Red pins are for the sons—also all of Chapo's other operators. Blue are points of interest—any important locations mentioned in the line sheets. Tower icons are cell phone towers."

"Good," Leroy said.

"An 'M' is for meeting places, or pickup locations frequented by his couriers. The red circles are where we believe he has other safe houses. The little planes mark clandestine airstrips—there are hundreds of them."

"And the yellow stars?" Leroy asked.

"Those are my closest pings—the ones with the tightest radius." I zoomed in tighter on the Colonia Libertad neighborhood. "Chapo is right here on this block."

"Unbelievable," Leroy said. "You've got his whole world mapped out, Drew. Safe houses, pickup locations, cell towers. Hell, I've never seen a pattern of life so dialed in. You've got him cornered."

"Not just yet," I said. "We've got plenty to work with, but we still don't have a door."

"Oh, we'll find it," Leroy said confidently. "Let's go get this son of a bitch."

——

EVERYTHING BRADY AND I had worked so hard to keep secret—even some of our own DEA and HSI people were in the dark about many of the details—was about to be exposed to the Mexican counterparts.

Admiral Raul Reyes Aragones, the top-ranking SEMAR commander in DF, commonly known by the nickname "La Furia" (the Fury, for the way he and his elite brigade would rip through and destroy Mexican drug-trafficking organizations), arrived at the US embassy in an armored Mercedes sedan, followed by his captain and several lieutenants.

Furia cut an impressive figure: early sixties, but extremely fit—he looked like he could still knock out fifty push-ups at the drop of a dime. Aragones's bald head was tanned and so shiny that it seemed to have been polished. He wore a crisp white-collared naval dress shirt, starched and without a single crease. His hands were soft and well manicured; when he smiled, his teeth gleamed white—*too* white, I thought, as if they'd been overbleached by his dentist. It was a salesman's smile.

"Quieres Chapo?" I asked immediately as the admiral leaned back in his leather swivel chair in the Kiki Room.

"Pues, claro que sí," the admiral said. "Of course we want Chapo! Tell me when and where."

I explained that Chapo and his entire organization feared SEMAR, whom they called *las rápidas*, "the fast ones." As I spoke, my chest felt suddenly tight, as if I'd just finished a six-mile run in that thin mountain air of the capital: I had so much to say, but I was almost too nervous to put my thoughts into words . . .

I'd spent years building up to this moment—how could I

suddenly let go? How could I begin to spill all the secrets and techniques it had taken me so long to perfect? No one had been told the *complete* picture—no one on earth knew everything that I knew—and now I was supposed to dump it all out in the lap of some spit-and-polish admiral I'd just met?

Realizing that if Chapo was going to be captured, we would need military help, I took a deep breath and stared the admiral in the eyes—this guy with the gleaming smile and immaculate uniform was the key to putting the operation into action.

"Chapo sometimes leaves the security of his stronghold in Culiacán for a lagoon getaway with a pool and swim-up bar."

"Why this location?" Admiral Furia asked.

"The proximity to Culiacán," I said, shrugging. "It's a short drive down—and it's remote from any prying eyes. Chapo likes to meet his sons—do business face-to-face. Some issues they just can't get done over the phone. It's an abandoned duck-hunting club called Pichiguila—Chapo refers to it simply as 'Pichis.' He's taken old palapas, had them renovated, and turned it into a pretty nice place. I call it Duck Dynasty."

There were a few snickers around the table.

"Dinastía de Pato," someone said.

"We've followed his sons—well, we've followed the *pings* on his sons' phones—and they take us right there near the palapas. So do the pings from the Top-Tier device."

"How do you know Guzmán is behind the phone you're pinging?"

"He's using *espejos*—mirrors—a layering system, which we've broken and infiltrated," I said. "Tiers, let's call them. In his terms, they're *secretarios*, and he's the manager—*el generente*. But one of two secretaries—Condor or Chaneke; we simply call them Top-Tier—is always by Chapo's side."

"Fine," Admiral Furia said curtly. "He comes down to this Pichiguila hunting club on the lagoon. Doesn't he travel with a lot of bodyguards? Our reports are that Guzmán's always got many heavily armed support with him—could be as many as one hundred—"

"That intel is *historical*," I interrupted. "It's out of date. At some point, yes, Chapo may have been traveling up in the mountains with that many armed bodyguards. Years ago, perhaps. Not now. He's moving fast and lean. He has a core group of loyal bodyguards—he's likely always armed, wearing a bulletproof vest, maybe in an armored vehicle. But no—those reports of hundreds of armed cartel men driving in a convoy of black Suburbans at all times? They are no longer valid. At this point, I can assure you that when Chapo comes down to those palapas he built near the Pichiguila Club, it's just with a couple of his most trusted men."

I could see that the admiral was hooked—and sure enough, by the end of my presentation he was ready to put all his men and resources at our disposal. We drafted an ambitious ops plan: simultaneous ground and air attack on Chapo's compound at the lagoon.

The element of surprise would be key: we would need to get SEMAR in perimeter positions in the middle of the night in order to capture the drug lord in a predawn raid. They would put four of SEMAR's top helicopters at a base in La Paz, near the southern end of the Baja Peninsula; they'd move in the elite brigades from Mexico City to bunk down at the SEMAR bases within Sinaloa, encircling Duck Dynasty.

"Once the helicopters and my men are in position, we'll wait until we receive the green light from you," the admiral said. "We won't move until you tell us that the Top-Tier device is there."

"Exactly," I said. "Once our pings indicate he's at Duck Dynasty, we'll let you know immediately."

"And your team of marshals will be joining us in La Paz, correct?"

"Yes, sir. They'll be with you in the event we need to chase the phone. If Chapo leaves unexpectedly, there's nobody better than El Roy and his guys to track him down. I'll also send Nico Gutierrez with you to be my DEA liaison from the ground."

SPECIAL AGENT NICOLÁS GUTIERREZ was a native Spanish speaker who sat next to me at the embassy and helped me ping phones and decipher some of the more unintelligible slang and misspellings in the line sheets. A former US Marine who was built like a defensive lineman, Nico was the perfect guy to be my eyes and ears in the field.

Gutierrez lived for capture ops like this. He already had his tactical gear packed and was ready to jump in with SEMAR.

Standing outside the Kiki Room, I ran into Regional Director McAllister again.

"Well, Drew, this is where your world begins to spin," Tom said with a smile.

"*Spin?* Sir, it already feels like it's about to unravel."

Tom was a seasoned DEA senior executive who'd led high-level cases throughout Latin America, Europe, and the Middle East. He understood better than anyone how hard I had worked to get even this far.

"I've filed a gag order with the chief of station here," Tom said. "CIA will not be allowed to talk about this operation with anyone."

I felt extremely grateful that Tom, and my other bosses, had allowed me to work without interruptions or any of the political drama that could often plague an investigation of this scope. They'd all been working diligently behind the scenes, ensuring that only those who needed to know were kept updated.

With the volume of intelligence coming in daily, Brady would need to remain in the El Paso war room, while I would establish a command center at the embassy with a group of intelligence analysts, along with all of my top brass. Brady and I both wanted to be on the ground with SEMAR, but we also knew that in order to keep the train from running off the tracks, we needed to be in our positions doing what we'd been doing nearly around the clock for nine months.

"SEMAR is ready to go. All Chapo needs to do is pop out of his rathole and come down for a meet one last time," I told Brady.

"From the moment he gets to Duck Dynasty, he's fucked," said Brady. "On that lagoon, he'll have nowhere to run."

THERE WAS NO turning back now—I'd told SEMAR everything they needed to know, and on January 19, the marines began making their first movements, flying into the base at La Paz and moving ground troops into the local Sinaloa bases in El Castillo, La Puente, and Chilango.

That same night, at 10 p.m., Brady called me.

"Goddammit," he said.

"What happened?"

"You've gotta see this. Just coming in."

It was a brand-new line sheet. Lic-F to Chapo.

"Sergio just met with the one from the water that has the special team in MEX. He's giving him ten rolls a month."

I felt a hollow ache hit my stomach. "Ones from the water"—code for the marines. And the "special team in Mexico City"—possibly Furia's brigade. Had our entire operation just been compromised? Ten rolls. That meant the contact was being paid $100,000 a month for intel. I tried to put my anger into words, but I couldn't.

"Hold on. It gets worse," Brady said.

By now I had pulled up the line sheets and translation on my own laptop.

Lic-F: Ahorita llegaron 3 rapidas del agua al castillo, puros encapuchados (son fuerzas especiales del agua) como que quieren operar en culiacan. Al rato nos avisa el comandante ya que platique con ellos a ver que logra saber.

"Three fast ones from the water arrived at El Castillo, all hooded ones (they're special forces from the water). Like they want to have an operation in Culiacan. The commander is going to let us know later once he talks to them."

Lic-F: Estan reportando 4 trillas grandes en la calma. Hay que estar pendientes pues no vayan ha querer cruzar el charco.

"They're reporting four helicopters in La Paz. We need to stay alert in case they want to cross El Charco."

"They're all over us," Brady said.

"'In case they want to cross El Charco,'" I repeated aloud.

El Charco—the pond. I knew that was code for the Sea of

Cortez, separating the Mexican mainland, including Sinaloa, from the long, thin peninsula where the La Paz base was located.

LEAKS. GODDAMN LEAKS. The steady drip, drip, drip had now turned into a deluge.

"Jesus," I said under my breath.

"He knows every move we're making," Brady said.

I reread the messages two more times, then stared at the multi-colored swirl of pin-markers on my Google Map.

The ones from the water.

Hooded ones.

Stay alert.

Crossing the pond.

Lic-F was reporting every military movement immediately to Chapo. I stared again at that long peninsula, at the La Paz base, then back at the heart of Culiacán. My pattern of pin markers blurred into a fiery kaleidoscope.

"Drew?"

The silence hung between us for a long time. Then I heard my voice, repeating, as if in a trance.

"Yes. He knows every move we're making."

PART III

LA PAZ

"DREW?"

I heard Brady, but I couldn't bring myself to answer.

Standing at the window, I could feel the heat rising in my chest—my neck and face were burning with frustration and anger.

I always tried to play the diplomat—"Switzerland," as Brady had said. I had been good at fostering smooth relationships and interagency collaboration; when there were flare-ups, it seemed like I was always talking people off the ledge. I never lost my cool. Getting angry never served the purpose of advancing the investigation.

But now I was on the verge of exploding.

I clenched the BlackBerry tighter in my palm.

"Someone in that room could be dirty," Brady said.

Chapo had a high-placed contact in Mexico City on the take for $100,000 per month? The level of corruption—the degree to which Guzmán had compromised the military and law enforcement brass, not just in Sinaloa but even in the nation's capital—suddenly seemed insurmountable.

The faces of the admiral, the captain, and the lieutenants quickly flashed through my mind. Just hours before, we'd laid it all out for them in the Kiki Room, and one of them could be corrupt?

Which one?

I was standing in the shadows of my living room in La Condesa, phone to my ear, looking out at the parked cars on the dark street below. As I stood there, peering out the window, seeing the ghostly trace of my face's reflection in the cold glass, I suddenly sensed that I was being watched.

Who was sitting in those parked cars below?

The new Charger.

The old Toyota.

The phone—was it even secure?

Someone could be listening to every word.

"What do you want to do?" Brady asked.

I took a long breath before answering.

"There's no other option," I said. "We have to confront the admiral—now. Get down here."

THE NEXT MORNING, I drove my armored Tahoe to the Mexico City International Airport and scooped Brady up curbside.

"We gonna pull everything back?" asked Brady. "Not work with SEMAR?"

"No. Without the marines—let's be honest—it can't be done. We gotta go see the admiral personally—at his shop."

"They're still warning Chapo on the lines," Brady said, and handed me his BlackBerry to read.

"We have to be very alert, like a pregnant bitch, dude," wrote Cholo Iván, the fierce sicario who ran the town of Los Mochis.

"We've never seen this many troops at this base—ever."

"Something strange is happening—be on alert."

"The fast ones, sir. The fast ones."

I DROVE DOWN to the south end of DF, swerving, gunning the Tahoe through the gaps in the congested traffic the entire way. At the SEMAR base, we passed through a single gate—manned by two young marines armed with automatic rifles—and were escorted upstairs to a large briefing room. As we approached the top of the stairs, I realized I hadn't slept or eaten in twenty-four hours. I was too unnerved by the thought of sitting down and facing the admiral; I still had no idea who the source of the leaks could be.

The conference room was surrounded on both sides by offices. The meeting was supposed to be private—just me, Brady, and Admiral Furia—but there were marines all over, coming and going from all the offices. Everyone was dressed in battle dress uniforms (BDUs), even the young marine serving us coffee and breakfast cookies, and a large projector screen displayed all the intel I had provided the day prior. Admiral Furia was sitting at one end of the long oak table, looking calm, in another one of his pristine white naval dress shirts. Brady and I sat at the corner next to him.

Brady and I exchanged concerned looks as additional officers entered the room. There were now twice as many officers sitting around the table as at the first meet at the US embassy. I didn't recognize any of these SEMAR brass. This was not a private meeting.

"Look at this shit," Brady whispered to me. "This place could be full of leaks . . ."

We were there to discuss a top-secret operation to capture the world's most wanted criminal, but the room was as bustling with activity as the flea market on Reforma that my wife and I took our sons to every Sunday morning.

"Yeah, too many fuckin' eyes and ears," I whispered back, but the admiral was impatiently gesturing for us to get on with it.

"We're here to discuss the compromise of intel," I began. "We've received messages that show the target"—I refrained from using Chapo's name aloud—"is seeing everything that's happening with your people up in Sinaloa and La Paz. Basically, he's getting real-time updates. Someone from an elite group of SEMAR in Mexico City is providing the information."

I showed Admiral Furia the messages.

The hooded ones.

The fast ones.

The helicopters.

In case they cross the pond.

Furia admitted that he knew SEMAR had leaks. He said it was not anyone from *his* shop, but he wasn't surprised that Chapo knew everything that was happening on the Pacific coast. He reassured me that he would do everything he could to find the source of the leaks immediately.

"Security is paramount to me," Furia said. "If this operation is going to be a success, we need the utmost in secrecy with this intelligence."

I had to stifle a smile. Looking around the room—the number of strange faces, the marine officers coming and going—made that statement laughable. I knew that if Duck Dynasty were compromised, and if Chapo aborted his plans to go to the Ensenada de Pabellones, we'd have no choice but to try to make entry into Culiacán.

A capture-op in Culiacán—just saying it aloud summoned images of a bloodbath. No one wanted that. The fatal firefight with Macho Prieto and his gunmen was too fresh in everyone's mind. But at this point, there was no turning back—I'd have to let the admiral know.

"What more do you have on the target's plans for the trip? Do you know where he'll be coming from?" the admiral asked, sipping his café con leche.

"At this point, yes," I said. "We have his location dialed in very tight. I've got him down to a block radius within Culiacán."

"Culiacán? You know where he is at this moment?"

"Well, yes—I don't have a street address, but I do know the neighborhood. We're sure it's the location of one of his primary safe houses."

The admiral exploded, shouting that we were holding out on him.

"*No me cambias mi pañal!*" "Don't change my diaper! And don't bottle-feed me!" Furia slammed his well-manicured hand on the oak table. "Trust needs to be established immediately."

I explained that it was not an issue of *trust*. I wanted to give SEMAR the very best intel we had. I played the diplomat now, apologized, and told the admiral that I'd provide all of our intelligence to him, exposing the network of safe houses in Culiacán where Chapo seemed to spend the majority of his time.

Admiral Furia took a deep breath, listening intently. Brady added that we meant no offense and were not being accusatory.

"*Mira,*" Brady said, "we know we have dirty people working in our agencies, too. Even in the United States."

"No one wants Chapo more than *us*," Admiral Furia said. "I want to capture him more than *anyone* in this room. You Americans may not understand this, but his capture is more important to Mexico than the United States. He's a stain on our entire country."

I was impressed by the sincerity of his emotional outburst. The atmosphere in the room eventually calmed down. The leaks had been addressed, and Brady and I did exactly what the admiral wanted: *"abra las cartas"* (open the books). We disclosed years' worth of intelligence, taking the admiral meticulously through every detail of Chapo's secret world.

Just before we left the room, I grabbed the admiral's attention one last time.

"Señor," I said. "There's only one thing that can fuck up this entire operation."

"And what's that?"

"Los primos," I said.

The cousins—a well-understood euphemism for the CIA. I knew that the admiral had a couple of SEMAR intel guys on CIA's payroll, and sometimes they'd provide DEA info straight back to the spooks. The CIA could claim the intel as original and act on it, without coordinating with anyone.

The admiral summoned two officers—a captain and a lieutenant—and told them, rather theatrically, as if for Brady's and my ears: "Nothing goes to *los primos*. You understand? That's a direct order."

DRIVING BACK TO the embassy from the meeting, I called Nico to check in.

"How's it going over there, man?"

"Todo bien, mijo," Nico said. "These guys are ready to rock. I'll

be flying in on the lead helo, and El Roy and a couple of his guys will be in the one behind me."

"Okay, you've seen the leaks, right? The admiral's going to do his best to find the guy passing the intel here, and he's come up with another plan."

While we waited for Chapo to move, it was crucial that SEMAR concoct a plausible counterintelligence story: there were just too many *halcones* (hawks)—Chapo had a vast network of lookouts spying for him in Sinaloa. And so, SEMAR began spreading the word that they were conducting extensive training missions with helicopters, ground crews, and extra brigades on the Pacific coast, so that the heavy new military presence wouldn't cause Chapo's people any more alarm.

SEMAR had also coordinated government aircraft in La Paz, to further pinpoint the Top-Tier BlackBerry device the moment Chapo decided to break free from his Culiacán refuge and head down to the duck-hunting lagoon.

BRADY FLEW STRAIGHT BACK to El Paso to work the HSI war room.

A full week passed without any movement from the *secretarios*.

"Anything?" Brady asked.

"No," I said. "Top-Tier hasn't left that goddamn block."

"I'd be going nuts. Beyond stir-crazy. Imagine not leaving your house—not seeing sunlight—for a straight week?"

But if anyone was used to staying holed up in some safe house, it was Guzmán. Chapo seemed to be content staying in one location for weeks on end. His daily drug operations were seemingly not affected by the movements of SEMAR.

Still another week passed.

"He's not coming out," I said. "Our time's running short with SEMAR. Nico told me they've been conducting 'training missions,' flying the helos around Cabo, but even that's getting old. The marines are anxious."

"Hold on—this is just coming in," Brady said, reading a newly translated intercept. "Chapo's sending Naris down to Duck Dynasty to watch for any marine activity on the roads."

After pinging him, I could see Naris poking around, doing his own detective work. Several hours later, he reported right back to Chapo's safe house. Brady and I learned that Naris had spoken to some middle-aged rancher who neighbored the Pichiguila Club; the neighbor said he and his sons could hear a daily buzzing overhead. But whenever they looked up, they'd see nothing. Heavy activity at the La Paz base was being reported. By now Chapo was certain that something big was up—poor Naris was posted at the side of the road, eyes glued to the sky, waiting for the hum, like some London air marshal during the Blitz.

"Chapo may know *all* the movements of the marines," I said. "The only thing we still have going for us is that it looks like he doesn't know *who's* being targeted."

"You're right," Brady said. "If he did, he'd be long gone by now."

"And so far, there's been no mention in the line sheets of 'gringos,' right?" I asked.

"None."

"PACK YOUR BAGS," I said. "We need to re-strategize and motivate the troops. Let's go meet up with Nico and El Roy."

"All right," Brady said, "I can get down in a couple days."

Brady's wife had just given birth to their son, and I knew it wasn't an ideal time for him to tell her he had to bounce from El Paso.

"Sorry," I said. "No, I mean *now* now—we gotta keep the momentum up. That brigade's been there too long. Everyone's getting fuckin' antsy." The marines had been on standby at the base for two full weeks, just cleaning their guns and checking their gear, when all they wanted to do was rip their teeth into Chapo and his organization.

"We go meet the admiral face-to-face—I'm heading out tonight. Wednesday to Friday. Three days—real quick—we re-strategize this thing. Just fly into Cabo San Lucas; I'll pick you up there and we'll roll to La Paz."

The name of the air force base brought a smile to my face. It was officially known as Base Aérea Militar No. 9, La Paz, Baja California Sur, but everyone simply called it La Paz—the Peace. I didn't know what lay in store, but I was sure that I wasn't likely to see a moment's peace for a while . . .

I SPED HOME TO La Condesa to say good-bye to my wife and boys.

That night, I sat on the edge of my son's bed, reassuring him about his birthday party the following weekend.

"You promise?"

"I promise, buddy. I won't miss it."

No way was I going to be gone a full week. I kissed my son's forehead and told him I'd be back in plenty of time for the party.

Yes, a short trip, I reassured my wife. Three days max. Neither

Brady nor I was bringing any tactical gear or guns. I threw a couple of shirts, a pair of jeans, and some underwear into my carry-on and bounded down the stairs and into my black Tahoe.

ALL BRADY AND I needed to do was devise a plan B with the SEMAR brass in case Chapo never set foot outside of his safe house in Culiacán.

But there was too much unusual activity down in Sinaloa. Flight after flight left the BAM-9 La Paz base, circling Culiacán, attempting to zero in on the one-block diameter I had provided. Aerial images were fine, but we needed actionable intel on *addresses*—a few houses SEMAR could strike in lightning-fast raids.

Meanwhile, I was receiving current imagery of Duck Dynasty on my MacBook. From the photographs, I could see a hive of activity at the newly renovated cabins: workers were assembling a bridge out to a man-made island with a large palapa and working on a specially designed party house. The muddy swamp water that made the lagoon so perfect for duck hunting was obviously not something Chapo and his harem of girls would want to skinny-dip in.

THE CABO SAN LUCAS International Airport was mobbed with American tourists, flocks of college blondes in sarongs and flip-flops, itching to hit the beach. The guys were in baseball caps, surfer shorts, and wraparound shades, probably already nursing hangovers.

Hustling through the terminal, I thought back to the last time I was on a beach. Just six months earlier, I'd been watching my kids make sandcastles along the Florida coast, my toes sunk into the surf, when my BlackBerry, sitting on a striped towel, started vibrating—even in that peaceful family moment, Chapo couldn't help but intrude. I had decoded the messages right there on the beach, piecing together a murder plot from intel gleaned by DEA and HSI.

Chapo was getting ready to kill his own cousin, a forty-three-year-old named Luis, whom everyone called Lucho. Guzmán was slick; it wasn't going to be a public execution—no sicarios on motorcycles, toting AKs and wearing balaclavas. In fact, no one would ever be able to connect it back to Chapo.

Instead, Guzmán planned to simply send Lucho across the border into Honduras on a negotiating errand. Corrupt Honduran cops on Chapo's payroll would do a routine car stop—just as I had done so many times as a deputy sheriff in Kansas—but then they'd plant a hot gun and cocaine in Lucho's Toyota pickup, arrest him, and take him to a Honduran prison, where Chapo had arranged to have the guy shanked to death, making it look as though Lucho had been in the wrong place at the wrong time.

I had gotten up from my towel, walked down the beach, and, out of earshot of my wife and kids, called the DEA in Honduras. Sure enough, Lucho had just been arrested hours earlier. We got the guy put into an administrative segregation unit and managed to stop the murder plot. When I signed up to be a cop, I never thought I'd be saving the lives of high-ranking Sinaloa Cartel members.

Racing through the tourists in the Cabo airport, I was picked up by Nico in an armored Suburban tailed by a small convoy of *rápidas*—SEMAR's customized pickup trucks with machine guns mounted in the bed—and we headed up to the BAM-9 base in La Paz. I threw my bag on an open bunk, then scouted around for a few minutes, setting up a mobile communications center in a closet-size side room of the barracks, a room I dubbed Nerd Central: MacBooks, various iPhones and BlackBerrys, cables, and chargers snaked everywhere.

Brady landed in Cabo from El Paso a few hours later; we picked him up and drove to La Paz. We immediately sat down and briefed the field commander of the SEMAR brigade, two-star Admiral Antonio Reyna Marquez, a.k.a. "Garra."

Garra reported directly back to Admiral Furia, who had remained in Mexico City. I wasn't sure how this admiral had picked up the nickname Garra—Spanish for "Talon"—but it fit him perfectly. He had a tight cut of bristly jet-black hair, a sun-creased forehead, a hawklike nose, and high cheekbones that hinted at ancient Aztec bloodlines. He was no-nonsense, calm, and direct. Garra immediately demanded to know if we could still count on Chapo heading south, at some point soon, from Culiacán to Duck Dynasty.

"I wish I could give you a definitive answer, sir," I said. "Our biggest problem continues to be the intel leaks. Any luck finding the source?"

"No," said Admiral Garra. "We're still looking into it."

WITHIN A DAY, Brady and I had fully bonded with the brigade. We were the only white guys in civilian clothes on the base—and glaringly stood out—but then Captain Julio Diaz came around the corner with boxes of marine-issued BDUs and sand-colored combat boots.

"You guys need to get out of those clothes and blend in," Captain Diaz said. "Too many eyes around here."

I remembered Diaz from the meeting—every one called him El Toro. I'd liked him from the moment we met back in Mexico City.

"*El me cae bien,*" I told Brady. "He falls on me well." It was an expression I had picked up in Mexico that meant you got a good vibe from somebody. "Just look at him. El Toro's always so amped up, ready to rock—he can't even sit still."

The bunks were tight, but I was thankful SEMAR had stuck us in the officer barracks with air-conditioning and decent showers. Brady and I joined up with Leroy and Nico for dinner—everyone, including the eighty marines from DF, ate in the same crammed mess hall.

"We gotta get over there," said Leroy, taking a few slurps of a funky fish stew. "Fuck this waiting around. He ain't coming out."

"Shit," Nico said, laughing. "What's the rush? I get a couple runs in around the base every day. Take a helo ride and buzz some beaches with these guys. Life's good."

BACK AT THE BARRACKS, we found out we weren't alone.

Two young DEA agents had arrived and were unpacking their bags. These were the two case agents leading the investigations of Mayo Zambada and Rafael Caro Quintero (or "RCQ"). A judge had recently granted Caro Quintero early release from a Mexican prison after he had served twenty-eight years of a forty-year sentence for his involvement in the murder of Special Agent Kiki Camarena. He was now wanted again, and believed to be hiding north of Culiacán, high in the Sierra Madre.

Ever since I began coordinating with SEMAR for the Chapo op, there was talk in the embassy about sharing resources with other viable DEA investigations. It was official protocol—no way around it. Brady had been incensed when I'd prepped him a few weeks earlier about the possibility of sharing SEMAR with another investigation. "You gotta be joking," he said. "Share SEMAR? For what?"

"Other case agents are claiming to have actionable intel on their targets, too," I said. "Now that we've lined everything up with SEMAR, they're saying they'll be just as ready as we are to launch."

"Bullshit," Brady said, fuming.

"I know," I said. "But there's nothing I can do about it. The decision was made above me." I had struck a gentleman's agreement with the other case agents: whoever had the ripest intel at the time SEMAR was ready in La Paz, that agent had authorization to green-light a launch. Fortunately, I knew that the intelligence these arriving agents had on Mayo and RCQ wasn't remotely close to what Brady and I had put together over the past nine months on Chapo.

"We can only hope SEMAR doesn't get distracted with all these different targets on deck. We've got to keep them focused," I said.

I knew that Mayo frequented the mountainous area just east of Duck Dynasty; an attempt to capture him first would immediately kill any chance we had of Chapo leaving Culiacán. He'd never risk it, knowing that the marines were conducting raids just south of the city.

As they unpacked in the barracks, I approached the two agents.

"You both realize if we launch on Mayo or RCQ first, our Duck Dynasty op is done," I said. "Completely burnt."

They nodded, but it was clear it didn't matter to them. I could tell they were just thrilled to be in the middle of all the action on the base.

AFTER A COUPLE OF DAYS at La Paz, I knew there was no way Brady or I would be leaving anytime soon. Nerd Central was our new command center, and we had SEMAR at our fingertips in the event we needed to launch.

Nico drove Brady and me to the local Walmart, where we stocked up on groceries and a couple of extra pairs of underwear. A return date to DF was the furthest thing from my mind.

I called my wife from the Walmart parking lot.

"Baby, I can't leave," I said. "I don't know how long it will be— maybe a couple more days—I'll explain later."

"Okay, please be careful," she said.

"Love you."

My wife had been rock steady throughout my DEA career. If she was worried, she never told me. We were the perfect match that way: always accepting and embracing life's precious moments— even the scarier ones—as a team.

For the next few days, Brady and I were glued to the hardwood chairs inside Nerd Central, reading fresh stacks of line sheets and pinging Top-Tier into the late hours, after all the marines had gone to sleep. Most nights, we'd be the only ones left in the room, all lights off, working by the glow of our computer screens.

Lic-F continued to keep Chapo updated on SEMAR movements, only this time there was no delay—nearly zero lag time. Brady and I watched as four SEMAR helos—two Black Hawks and two Russian MI-17s—took off from BAM 9 to conduct another training mission.

"Here it is," Brady said, reading from his BlackBerry within seconds.

"Lic-F just told Chapo four helicopters left the base at La Paz, and it appears they'll be conducting a training mission near Cabo."

"Spot-on," I said. Talk about unnerving. I didn't feel safe on-base. It still felt like we were all under constant surveillance.

There had to be someone on the base who was dirty. But who?

IN THE MIDDLE OF our fifth night's dinner, I received a call from my group supervisor in Mexico City, requesting an update, though it quickly became evident what her agenda was. She was letting me know—not so subtly—that she was receiving pressure from officials within "G.O.M." (government of Mexico).

"Drew, G.O.M. is leaning on me," she said. "Where do you guys stand? We don't have *unlimited* time with this operation."

She said that SEMAR was immediately needed to go fight Los Caballeros Templarios—the Knights Templar Cartel—down in Michoacán. The Knights Templar were a violent threat—founded by Nazario Moreno, a narco commonly referred to as El Más Loco ("the Craziest One")—but the notion that they were a higher-priority target for the DEA or SEMAR than Chapo Guzmán was ludicrous.

"Knights Templar?" I said. "Sorry, but the G.O.M. is full of shit. We're talking about Chapo. I have safe houses within Culiacán; definitive locations. There's never been a higher-priority drug target in the history of Mexico. Since I've been on the ground here with SEMAR—with their *admiral*—no one has said a word about Michoac—"

"It's gotten—well, political," she said. "I can only push back so hard, Drew. SEMAR is talking about pulling all of their people out of La Paz."

I hung up and stared at Brady. "My GS," I said. "There's talk about shutting us down. Pulling SEMAR from La Paz."

"Get the fuck outta here," Brady said, polishing off his last spoonful of lentejas, a watery bean soup.

"I'm not joking. 'Getting political,' she says."

I took a deep breath. Typical—bosses say one thing and the ground troops report another. None of these rank-and-file marines had any intention of leaving La Paz to go after the Knights Templar.

Still, I felt like the entire operational plan was in danger of unraveling. The double-talk was bad enough; more potentially damaging was the number of politicians, bosses, and bureaucrats in both governments who knew of the pending operation. I pushed my bowl of soup away, did a head count, and quickly lost track: the administrator of the Drug Enforcement Administration, the director of Homeland Security Investigations, and down the ranks through their various underlings and supervisory agents in Washington, Arizona, California, Texas, and Illinois. And *los primos* knew, of course, most likely right up to the director of the Central Intelligence Agency himself.

Too many mouths, I thought. *And too many egos.*

I didn't know the precise source of the leaks, but the effect on our target was crystal clear. Hell, *Chapo* knew more of the precise up-to-the-moment details of what was happening on the ground— more of the exact marine operational movements—than anyone in the US government other than Brady and me.

"THE PLANE SPOTTED Mayo's courier," Leroy Johnson said excitedly. "They're following him. Southeast of Culiacán. I think we're going to launch."

El Roy knew that our intel on Chapo should have taken top priority. But Leroy simply couldn't take sitting around the barracks any longer. He'd watch movies in the bunk room until 4 a.m., and his mind always seemed to be racing. He was pumped up and ready to get out into the field with the marines and chase down some bad guys, regardless of who they were.

I turned to Brady. "They're saying it's a fifty-fifty shot that this courier could be delivering some food to Mayo in the hills. They're launching."

"Goddammit."

Brady and I both watched as Nico, Leroy, and his team donned the tactical gear hanging from their bunks and joined teams of marines boarding the four helos out on the tarmac. I followed them outside, feeling powerless just standing there, the ocean and the grit from the rotor chop smacking me in the face. There was no stopping this operation now.

I watched helicopters lift off and eventually disappear over the horizon of the Sea of Cortez.

LATE THE FOLLOWING DAY, the helos returned to base, and I watched as lines of exhausted marines filled the mess hall.

I'd already been briefed on the results.

They hadn't captured Mayo, but they did arrest a few of his men and seized a cache of AK-47s, M-16s, and shotguns found buried in fifty-five-gallon drums on a ranch near the initial target location.

"Not good," Brady told me. "Several office devices in Durango dropped already, and the lines are quiet."

Brady and I knew this was coming—the same thing had happened after the premature arrest of Alex Cifuentes. If all the mirrors dropped, we were on the verge of standing in the dark once again.

I saw the Mayo case agent packing up his bags in the barracks, nodding on his way out.

"Well, he looks perfectly happy," I said to Brady.

"All of that for a fifty-fifty chance? Good riddance. At least he's outta here, so SEMAR can focus on Chapo."

As we were walking back to the command center from our barracks, Brady stopped, staring at his phone. A brand-new message from Top-Tier—intercepted and translated in the HSI war room in El Paso—had arrived.

"Shit, we're still alive."

"What you got?"

"Chapo just told Naris to go out and buy some red satin sheets and take them over to one of the safe houses," Brady said.

Chapo was going about his daily business—spooked or not. And any fears he had about SEMAR's movements just south of Culiacán and in the skies hadn't put a dent in his love life, certainly not on Valentine's Day—known in Mexico as El Día del Amor y la Amistad, the "Day of Love and Friendship."

"He's ordered Naris to get dozens of roses for all his women and write the same message on all the cards," Brady said. "He even wants Naris to sign his initials for him: J.G.L."

"J.G.L.," I said. "Doesn't get any more personal than that."

There was no doubt in my mind now. Chapo was still inside that safe house, on that run-down block in Colonia Libertad.

There wasn't a moment's peace to be found in La Paz. I was still on edge after the recent turn of events with SEMAR going after Mayo.

Brady and I knew that we'd need to refocus SEMAR back onto the manhunt for Chapo, so we went directly to meet with Admiral Garra in his office. I could see that Garra was tired, his eyes dark and puffy; he was clearly disappointed by the results of the Mayo raid.

Garra seemed annoyed by our very presence in his doorway. He didn't say a word; he merely raised his eyebrows as an indication for us to get to the point.

"Señor," I said. "Top-Tier hasn't dropped."

"You've still got him within that block?"

"Yes, surprisingly, Top-Tier is still pinging in the same place," I said. "Chapo seems comfortable in Culiacán. We might turn this to our advantage. He must think that all the military activity in La Paz was for the mission launched against Mayo. He's still going about his business. He just had flowers sent to all his girls for El Día del Amor y la Amistad, but there's no way he's coming out. Not now."

"So you're suggesting . . . ?"

"Going to ground," I nodded.

"In Culiacán?"

The name of the cartel stronghold—often called the City of Crosses, for its makeshift shrines to hundreds of murdered narcos—hung between us for a long time in the command center barracks.

A mug shot parade flashed across my mind: Ernesto Fonseca Carrillo, Miguel Ángel Félix Gallardo, Rafael Caro Quintero, Héctor Luis "El Güero" Palma, Amado Carrillo Fuentes, Mayo Zambada, Manuel Salcido Uzeta (a.k.a. "Cochiloco"), the Arellano Félix brothers, Chapo Guzmán . . . virtually all of Mexico's most infamous narcotraffickers had called Culiacán home. Going into the capital of Sinaloa was a daunting thought, like trying to wrest control of Chicago away from Al Capone's grip back in the heyday of Prohibition.

I stared at Garra, and he at me. We both seemed to acknowledge that it was the only option, but we also both knew the immense dangers ahead.

Nothing like this had ever been *considered*, let alone attempted. For SEMAR, and for two American federal agents, leading the capture op in Culiacán would be like walking on the moon.

GARRA PICKED UP his phone and made a quick call to Admiral Furia in Mexico City. He turned to look at Brady and me.

"Pack your gear tonight," Garra said. "We'll leave at oh-eight-hundred hours tomorrow."

That evening, the marines threw together a quick going-away party in a remote sandy corner of the base, among the cardónes—giant cactuses—and blue fan palm trees. They lit a bonfire, and SEMAR had their own version of a food truck slinging plates full of carnitas, tacos de barbacoa, and the marines' favorite, tacos de sangre—soft-shelled corn tortillas filled with blood sausage.

Sitting around the fire, I thought back to when I was eighteen, those Thursday nights with our varsity football team in Pattonville, when we'd huddle around the campfire and share stories in preparation for the big game under the Friday night lights.

I sensed a similar camaraderie taking shape there at La Paz—jokes cracked in Spanish, blood tacos devoured, cold cans of Tecate downed one after another. All the marines were in high spirits, knowing that in the morning they'd be leaving La Paz behind for good.

I nodded at Brady. We were about to make the big leap.

We would be crossing El Charco and heading into the heart of Sinaloa itself.

THE NEXT MORNING, February 15, 2014, I woke before sunrise and lay on my bunk, staring at the ceiling. The more I thought about entering Sinaloa, the more I felt my gut tighten. I reached for my iPhone and texted my father:

"Can't even begin to explain what's happened the last week, Dad. We're going to have to root him out of his hole, and it's not going to be pretty. But it's our only option."

"When you going in?" my dad texted back.

"We're gearing up now. Moving bases and command center into enemy territory. We wave the green flag Monday," I wrote. "Going to burn the city down."

FOLLOW THE NOSE

I TOSSED MY BAG through the door of the DEA King Air and grabbed a seat on the left side of the aircraft; Brady, Nico, and Leroy followed close behind.

I could feel the momentum building; SEMAR had become reenergized. I watched out my window as the MI-17s loaded with marines began to lift off. But SEMAR wouldn't be following us— they were headed straight to the Batallón de Infanteria Marina No. 10 (BIM-10) military base, Topolobampo, Sinaloa.

In thirty-eight minutes the King Air crossed the Sea of Cortez and touched down at the Mazatlán International Airport, roughly 125 miles southwest of Culiacán.

I groaned when I saw our rig. Someone in the DEA Mazatlán office had lent us the shittiest armored Chevy in the entire fleet: a six-year-old Suburban with 200,000 miles on the odometer. Even the dark-tinted film was peeling from the windows. I had specifically requested two armored vehicles, and this was what they gave us?

"The USG at its finest," I said, turning toward Brady, but there was no time to get stuck in anger or frustration. We shoved our bags into the back of the rig and jumped in.

"How're the lines?" I asked.

"Quiet," Brady said. "Too quiet."

"I wouldn't be surprised if he knows we're here already," I said.

Nico took the wheel and Leroy the passenger side, handing back to us a couple of beat-up M4s painted in desert camo.

"We may need these," El Roy said with a grin.

"About fucking time," Brady said. "I've been feeling naked since I crossed the border."

I flipped open my MacBook and pinged Top-Tier. No luck. I tried a few more times.

"I think it's off. Maybe dead."

"We're going to need a little more luck," Leroy said.

Brady called Joe and Neil back in El Paso and told them to begin digging for the next Top-Tier number.

"Hang on, boys," Nico said, slapping the dash. "I hope this old girl makes it."

We left north out of Mazatlán, shooting up the backbone of Sinaloa, eventually meeting up with two SEMAR *rápidas* along Mexican Federal Highway 15D, just south of Culiacán, who escorted us the remainder of the way to join SEMAR at BIM-10 in Topolobampo. The base was located on a small port along the Sea of Cortez, not far from Los Mochis—the stronghold of Cholo Iván.

The sun had already set, leaving a faint row of pink in the sky and casting a hazy glow across the highway.

Nico pulled over so we could take a leak. I got out to stretch my legs and found myself trying to read the expressions of the marines as they stood in the rear beds of the *rápidas*, dressed in full camouflage and body armor, carrying all their tactical gear and their black machine guns.

I suddenly realized that I had no idea which brigade these guys were with.

"Hope these guys are from DF," I said to Brady as we stood in the ditch, cars whizzing behind us on the highway.

"If they're local, yeah, we're compromised," Brady said. "He'll know we're pissing in his backyard."

Standing there in the open, I experienced another burst of paranoia: I imagined a couple of marines on Chapo's payroll walking up behind us, drawing pistols, and shooting us, execution style, right on the edge of that ditch.

"*Vámanos,*" I said.

The 245 kilometers should have taken us more than three hours, but Nico pushed the rig to ninety miles per hour. Along the way, we passed exits for Las Isabeles, Cinco y Medio, and Benito Juárez, suburbs of Culiacán that I'd studied for hours, zooming in on my Google Map.

The highway was eerily quiet now, pitch-black, its rutted blacktop strewn with gravel. I was finally on the same narrow road that Chapo and his sons drove to get to the secret hideaway on the Ensenada de Pabellones.

We were now just a fifteen-minute drive from the blocks that I had lasered into my memory—Chapo was at our fingertips . . . I could *sense* it now. A beacon, pulsating, emanating from the city's center . . .

We circled Culiacán, heavier with traffic—Nico swerving around a couple of tomato trucks, heading north. As we passed Guamuchilera Segunda, my phone and Brady's vibrated simultaneously.

It was HSI in El Paso—they'd broken through with a new number.

"Top-Tier is back," I said, smiling. "We're still in this!"

TWO HOURS LATER, just after midnight, we rolled into BIM-10.

The Topolobampo infantry base was perched high on a hill overlooking the dark waters of the Pacific. Out front, I read the marines' slogan on a large sign:

TODO POR LA PATRIA

"All for the Homeland." A sudden fog had rolled in, covering the military base in a thick white blanket. I could barely see twenty feet ahead of the Suburban's headlights.

I jumped out and took a deep breath of the foggy sea air—there was a different aura here at Topo than in La Paz.

I was hearing that old Metallica song in my head—like I would before every Tiger football game back in Pattonville, strapping down my shoulder pads, taking the field in those tense moments before kickoff. I didn't realize I was singing aloud—at a decent volume, too. I sang the verses of "Enter Sandman" as we hauled our bags through the fog and into the barracks, bounding up the stairs to the second floor two at a clip.

"The vibe here's different," I said.

"Yeah, I feel it, too," Brady said.

"These guys are ready to fight."

One of the baby-faced marines ran up and told us that Admiral Garra had called an emergency briefing in the command room for 1:00 a.m.

Brady and I were the last ones to arrive—SEMAR officers and other marines were already sitting around the conference table, and there was hardly space for us to squeeze in.

———

THE LIGHTS WENT OUT, and everyone was staring at my PowerPoint maps projected on the large screen.

Before I could say anything, a pair of SEMAR intel analysts took charge of the briefing. These were the same guys who I'd suspected were on the payroll of *los primos*. I glanced warily at Brady: I couldn't believe what I was hearing. The SEMAR intel analysts were trying to steer the operation back toward following up on the capture mission for Mayo Zambada.

"Mayo?" I said. "Again?"

"What the hell?" Brady whispered.

When I looked around the room, even in the darkness, I could detect nods—some of the SEMAR captains and lieutenants were buying into this bullshit. Even Nico and Leroy were standing on the other side of the room, going along with it all. I couldn't take it any longer—I interrupted one of the analysts.

"Hold up a minute," I said. "What are you guys talking about?"

"Easy, man," Brady said, taking me by the forearm.

I couldn't lower my volume.

"Mira! Listen to me: we have the world's most wanted fugitive *here*—at our fingertips." I stepped forward and pointed to the screen. "We've got Chapo dialed in to a block radius—and you're saying you want to switch up targets and go after *Mayo* again?"

I took a deep breath, remembering how badly we needed SEMAR's full cooperation, lowered my voice, and addressed Admiral Garra respectfully in Spanish.

"Señor," I said. "Our intel will never get better than this."

I wanted to say it even more bluntly: this could be the greatest counter-narcotics success in the history of Mexico and the United

States. We were only hours away from nailing the most wanted fugitive since the US Navy SEALs took out bin Laden.

"We're on the verge of something historic here, *señor*. In thirteen years, since he escaped from Puente Grande, no one has got closer to apprehending Chapo Guzmán than we are right now."

The room went silent.

My chest was heaving. I swallowed, glancing at the SEMAR intel analysts. I could hear Brady's heavy breathing, too, and—very faintly—the Pacific surf crashing on the cliffs just outside the barracks.

The admiral was weighing his options, eyes ping-ponging between the intel analysts and me.

After a long pause, Garra folded his hands decisively in front of him on the table. He'd made up his mind.

"Vamos," he said, calmly, *"a activar Operación Gárgola."*

Gárgola.

It was the first time I'd heard the word, which was Spanish for "gargoyle." Gárgola was the perfect code name for the capture op—*G* for Guzmán.

Duck Dynasty was dead; Operation Gárgola was in effect. The analysts had already sat back down and didn't say another word.

Someone hit the lights, causing everyone to squint. It was before 2 a.m., but no one was getting any shut-eye. Instead, the entire brigade rushed off to get to work.

The middle of the night was ideal for the raid: Nico would ride with a crew of marines in the Suburban, while El Roy and his equipment would roll with more marines in a black Nissan Armada. Nico's crew was essentially running security for El Roy as his rig cut grids through the Colonia Libertad neighborhood—the one-block radius—around the safe house where I was almost certain Chapo had spent the past twenty-four hours. Their sole objective was to find a door.

I was worried now about Cholo Iván. That killer couldn't wait to get his green light—he'd jump on any chance he got to pull the trigger. If Cholo Iván and his people in Los Mochis detected any movement from the Topo base down to Culiacán, south through his territory, things could rapidly spiral out of control. And if that happened, SEMAR, Nico, and Leroy would quickly find themselves in a massive gunfight.

I hugged Nico and Leroy. "Give 'em hell, guys," I said, just as I'd done so many times with Diego back in Phoenix before a major UC meet.

It was 3 a.m. as Brady and I turned to walk back into the command center through the fog.

We quickly set up shop like we'd done at La Paz, moving Nerd Central into Topolobampo. I pulled up a map on which I was tracking the phones of Nico and Leroy as they headed south down Mexican Federal Highway 1D, the orange icons on the Find My Friends app dotting along as they neared Culiacán.

"Nothing in the lines about Cholo Iván," Brady said. "Don't think that he knows our boys are rolling through."

"Good," I said, nervously pacing back and forth.

BUT AS SOON AS dawn broke, the city lit up with news flashes. Brady and I were following along with all the Top-Tier exchanges in real time. Chapo was getting updates roughly every twenty minutes from Lic-F and Sergio, who had their *halcones* on every corner, on every street, instantly reporting how many SEMAR *rápidas* were in and outside the city and precisely where they were patrolling.

SERGIO: Ahorita estan por la canasta bienen puro gafe de agua no traen intel andan en rg en 19 a ver k cae hay las teniamos monitoriadas duraron paradas en la col popular en la calle rio usumasintris y rio grijalba

"Right now they're in the basket [city]. They all come from the special forces of the water. They didn't bring intel with them. They are headed to the RG in 19 [Culiacán] to see what happens. We have been monitoring all their stops in La Colonia Popular on streets Rio Usumacinta and Rio Grijalva."

Admiral Garra had sent groups of *rápidas* down behind the Suburban and the Armada to run security, but they'd been instructed to stay along the city's edge, circling like distant sharks. They were to respond only if Nico, Leroy, and their crews were in trouble.

Sergio's message to Chapo continued.

Hay estan como escondidas toda la mañana y se movieron rumbo a la canasta

"They were hiding there all morning, and they moved toward the basket."

All the *halcones* in the city knew which cars and trucks didn't belong; but there was no way to do this stealthily in any case, no way to avoid having Nico's and Leroy's teams hunting within that block radius of Top-Tier to locate a specific door.

"Man, what's taking these guys so long?" Brady said, pacing near the rear of the MI-17 just outside the door of the command center.

"Don't know," I said, "but they need to hurry. The city's getting hot. They're not going to be able to stay in those streets much longer."

Nico, Leroy, and their crews had been circling La Colonia Libertad and the surrounding neighborhoods for more than nine hours already, but we were still no closer to locating Chapo's door than when we started. Pinpointing that Top-Tier device from the ground was more difficult than we expected.

Then an incoming message appeared from the HSI war room in El Paso on our WhatsApp group chat. It was from Chapo to his cook, who was using the code name "Lucia."

Lucia, aplasten la tina del bano. Y para ke tesalgas en el yeta con memo la aipa la tableta. La traes tambien

"Lucia, flatten the bathtub so you can leave in the Jetta with Memo. And the iPad tablet. Bring it also."

Lucia, bengase fijando ke no las siga ningun carro y borre los mensajes

"Lucia, when you come make sure no cars are following you and erase the messages."

I stared at Brady.

"'Flatten the bathtub?'" I said.

"He might've jumped in a tunnel already."

"Yeah, he's starting to panic," I said. "Our boys have got to be close—right on top of the house."

I called Nico to relay the news.

"Any luck, brother?" I said.

"No, man, it's been rough," Nico said. "Every time we get a strong signal we lose it. We've marked a few points of interest—but nothing solid yet."

THROUGHOUT THE AFTERNOON and into the evening, Chapo was getting increasingly detailed intel: SEMAR was intercepting local two-way radio traffic, and the city's *halcones* were calling out every turn the Suburban and the Armada made—right down to the exact color of the rigs and how many men in camouflage fatigues were inside.

"Lines are starting to drop," Brady said. "Second-Tier has gone down."

"Fuck, we're too hot, man."

Brady jumped back on the phone again and immediately switched up strategy with Joe and Neil in El Paso.

"We've gotta rove!"

Rove—a roving wire intercept—was the fastest way we could legally track the members of Chapo's DTO, who were dropping phones and turning on new ones while on the run.*

"Stand by," Neil told Brady. "We'll be back up in no time."

Joe, Neil, and their team in El Paso had been working nonstop, getting about as much sleep as Brady and I were, laying all the legal groundwork so they could get that roving intercept authorized quickly with the help of Camila, their lead prosecutor.

---

* Under United States law, a "roving wiretap" is a wiretap that follows the surveillance target rather than a specific communications device. If a target attempts to defeat surveillance by throwing away a phone and acquiring a new one, by moving, or by any other method, another surveillance order would usually need to be applied for. However, a "roving" wiretap follows the target and defeats the target's attempts at breaking the surveillance by changing his location or his communications technology.

Just after 9 p.m., my iPhone buzzed.

"Drew, the fuckin' cops won't leave us alone; they're all over us," Nico said. "They've tried stopping us multiple times. This entire city knows we're here. Everyone's tired and hungry—getting burned out. Dude, this shit isn't working."

Brady and I walked back out onto the helo pad. Brady lit a cigarette he'd bummed from one of the marines. This was our eighth time walking in circles around the MI-17, knowing that Nico and his crew badly needed actionable intel.

"Fuck it," I told Nico. "Naris is our next best option. Find him and he'll tell us exactly where Chapo is at."

"So go after Naris?" Nico asked.

"Yeah," I said. "Follow the Nose."

BACK INSIDE the marine command center, Admiral Garra was furious with us.

"What the fuck is going on? We're in the same damn position as when we started. Our guys are on the ground and haven't found *shit*. I'm getting major pressure from my people in DF, asking me what we're even doing in Culiacán. We can't go on much longer—a few more hours and I'm going to have to call it off."

I could understand the admiral's frustration; I felt it, too.

"*Señor*," I said in a quiet voice. "We have to go after Naris."

"Chapo's courier is our best shot, sir," Brady added.

"If we don't find Naris, then we can reevaluate," I said. "But if we grab him, I'm confident he'll tell us exactly where Chapo is."

Admiral Garra just stared at me and, without saying a word, left the command center.

———

NOW THE COMMAND CENTER was empty; all the other marines had walked out to get some sleep. It was just me and Brady alone, so I cracked open a bottle of Johnnie Walker Red. I'd bought it before leaving Mazatlán and smuggled it onto the base in my laptop bag, hoping it would be a celebratory bottle . . . I found some red plastic cups and passed one to Brady. My stomach ached for food. How long had it been since I'd eaten anything solid? Eight hours? Eighteen hours? I had no clue.

Brady and I had bloodshot eyes—neither of us had slept in two days. The SEMAR brigade was finally sacked out—a wall of exhaustion had hit them like a tsunami. I sipped the Scotch and glanced at the time and date on my phone: 12:00 a.m., February 17, 2014.

I cursed softly, shaking my head. A father's promise, broken: Before I left DF, we'd picked out the piñata, gift bags, and invitations for my son and his friends.

"Dude, what's up?" Brady said.

"Hold on—gotta text her," I said, exhaling. "It's the seventeenth." I thumb-typed as quickly as I could and hit send at 12:02 a.m.

> Sorry I'm going to miss it baby. This week has been one of the hardest in my life. I'm a zombie, exhausted & missing you guys. Having one hell of a struggle here. Give my son a big kiss & hug for me and wish him a happy birthday. I love you guys so much.

I stared hard at Brady and we topped off our Scotches.
Nada más que decir.
Nothing more to say.

Brady had a newborn son he'd left his wife alone to deal with; I felt like shit for promising *my* son I'd be there for the birthday fiesta in DF . . .

I scrolled through the tunes on my iPhone. I felt like blasting "Enter Sandman," or anything by Metallica or Nirvana. Even some crazy narcocorrido by Los Tigres del Norte, something hard and thumping, cranked to max volume to numb the mixture of exhaustion and sadness.

But all the marines were knocked out—I could hear a couple of them snoring—so I opted for "Cool Jazz for Warm Nights" and took a huge slug of Johnnie Red.

Brady let out a laugh as the soft jazz sounds floated through the barracks; the place reeked of sweaty battle fatigues and musty boots. The 1957 song "Everything Happens to Me," by saxophonist Warne Marsh, was playing when a message came in from Joe, back in El Paso.

"We're back live," Brady said. "Attaboy, Joey! Keep 'em coming."

The first message in was from Chapo, now becoming increasingly impatient, asking Lic-F for a status report. He was rattled.

Los bolas del agua donde kedaron

no saves??

"The group of marines—where are they at now? Do you know?"

MY PHONE STARTED BUZZING. The time read 12:34 a.m.

It was Nico. No greeting—he sounded intense, out of breath. "What's Naris's number?"

I quickly rattled off the digits to Naris's BlackBerry, which I had committed to memory.

I suspected why Nico needed them—but asked anyway. "Why?"

Nico laughed. "I got the motherfucker right in front of me."

"Really? You got Naris?" I said, grinning, glancing at Brady.

Brady almost knocked over his plastic cup of Johnnie Walker.

"Yup," Nico said. "Dude with the big nose is standing right here—six feet away from me."

"Okay, where's he telling you Patas is at?" I asked.

Patas Cortas—Spanish for "Short Legs"—was our open-air code name for Chapo during the capture op.

"He's saying he's at the Three," Nico said.

Only moments earlier, Brady and I had intercepted a message from Chapo that we were in the process of deciphering:

Naris si cnl bas ten pranito ala birra y le llebes ala 5 y traes aguas.
Seme olbido el cuete ai esta en el 3 en la cautiba atras me lo traes

"Naris, go in the morning and pick up the birria and the keys and bring them to the Five. And bring some water. Don't forget the gun. It's there at the Three in the back of the [Chevy] Captiva. Bring the pistol to me."

I knew that Naris was lying; there was no way Chapo was still at Location 3—I knew for a fact that that safe house was now empty.

I told Nico what I'd just read:

"He's bullshitting you. Patas isn't at the fuckin' Three. No one is at Location Three. It's empty. He's at the Five."

I could hear Nico telling SEMAR that Naris was lying to them. Then he hung up. A couple of minutes later, Nico called back.

"Naris changed his tune," Nico said. "You're right. He's saying Patas is at the Five."

"Send every marine you have to the Five," I said.

LION'S DEN

LA PISCINA.

I remembered that earlier that day Chapo had sent Naris over to "El 5" to meet with his pool-cleaning guy.

I called Nico immediately.

"La Piscina," I said.

"What pool?"

"Patas has referred to the Five as La Piscina before. The house you're looking for has a swimming pool. I'm almost positive. I'll send you the coords of the area. Naris was just there this morning. Condor's pinging off the same tower right near there."

"Okay," Nico replied. "We're going to the Five. Naris is on board."

The door of the command center flew open.

"*Vámanos!*" Admiral Garra shouted, his eyes still tight, as if he'd just been woken from a deep sleep. "*Vámanos!*" he shouted again. "*Levantamos a Naris.*"

I was pleased to know that Garra had been tracking the events through his own marines on the ground just like Brady and I had been getting updates from Nico.

Hearing the whine of the turbine on the MI-17 helicopter

outside was like a straight shot of adrenaline. Brady and I scrambled up a short flight of stairs to grab our few belongings, the remaining phones, and the laptop bag.

"Don't forget the vests!" Brady said, looking back from the narrow doorway.

From the cold tile floor, I scooped up the two old bulletproof vests we'd scrounged in Mazatlán. I tossed one to Brady, who caught it mid-stride.

Hopping down three stairs at a time, I exited the command center, taking a deep breath of salty ocean air. Running out onto the helo pad, I tried throwing on my vest but realized that I'd grabbed one that seemed designed for a small child. I couldn't get the straps loose, and I ripped the thing over my head in a frenzy.

With the MI-17 blades whooping a few feet above, I looked at Brady.

"This is it," I yelled over the noise of the chop. "He's fucked!"

We hardly looked like US federal agents now. Under the tan-and-black vests, both of us were again wearing the SEMAR-issued camouflage BDUs we'd put back on after we arrived at Topolobampo.

I made my way through the huge hole in the rear of the MI-17 and took a seat on the hard steel bench directly behind the right-side gunner. Brady took the seat next to me.

Admiral Garra's demeanor was calm—almost *too* calm, I thought. I'd been studying the admiral over the past weeks, trying to determine what made him tick. A seasoned SEMAR commander with decades of experience fighting Mexico's narco wars, Garra was like a grizzled bird of prey: always calm, even when it was time to pounce.

Without a note of excitement—as if we were just going to pick up some street-level dope dealer and not a billionaire kingpin who had evaded capture since 2001—Garra shouted over the roaring engine, "When we arrive, we'll put him in this helo and bring him back here for the interrogation."

"What we need right now are some guns," Brady yelled.

Yes—we both needed weapons.

I looked around the cabin to see if there were any extra rifles lying around. This was turning into a full-blown military operation, but Brady and I had fallen into Sinaloa so fast that we'd never had a chance to fully prepare. We'd given Nico and Leroy back the M4 carbines before they headed south into Culiacán.

Three full days now without sleep. The helicopter lifted off the pad, angling southbound along the Sinaloa coast, headed for the birthplace and stronghold of the world's most powerful drug cartel.

The night sky now glowed brighter than the cabin of the MI-17. The marines donned their tactical gear and loaded their weapons, including a Mark 19 grenade launcher hanging off the rear deck and two M134 miniguns punched through the ports on each side of the bird.

Then everything went strangely still. No one spoke.

The gunner nearest me held a green tactical light between his teeth as he checked his Facebook page on his cell phone. Here we were, about to capture the world's most wanted drug lord, and this guy was nonchalantly checking social media postings as if he were sitting on his couch back home. On my Black-Berry, I quickly updated my group supervisor back in Mexico. DEA management knew only that something big was heating up, but I hadn't shared all the details. Anytime US government personnel were embedded with a host nation's military, there was potential for a political firestorm; not every manager at the Drug

Enforcement Administration and the Department of Homeland Security Investigations was pleased that Brady and I had left La Paz and ventured over into Sinaloa.

In a few minutes, we'd be putting boots on the ground in Culiacán. Setting foot in this city was a life-and-death proposition for US federal agents and SEMAR forces alike. For a few moments I thought about what to write. The fewer details the bosses knew at this point, the better, so I opted for two words.

"En route."

I closed my eyes, my mind still racing as I tried to focus on the sound of the helo cutting through the ocean air.

Why hadn't we heard anything about what was happening on the ground?

Brady and I kept checking our BlackBerrys every few minutes, then we'd look to the admiral for an update.

Garra said nothing.

We were forty minutes into the ride, and still no one had heard a peep. If anyone was to be notified of a capture, it would surely be Garra. His SEMAR entry team would be first through the door and the first men to make contact with Chapo.

Maybe the marines already had him in custody and for safety reasons weren't advising command over the radio?

Brady's face, as always, was locked in his ruddy-cheeked scowl. Admiral Garra's remained inscrutable.

The MI-17 angled away from the coastline. I could make out the hazy glow of the city lights in the distance as we whipped past small homes and larger ranches.

"*Quince minutos,*" one of the crew members shouted from the cockpit.

Fifteen minutes away. Just then, the red indicator light began to flash in the upper right corner of my BlackBerry. It was a message from Nico, with the SEMAR entry team at Location Five:

"Place is a fortress," Nico wrote. "Cameras everywhere."

The pilot began to cut figure eights over the city. I looked down at the streets below, deserted except for the frenzy of SEMAR's *rápida* pickup trucks, machine guns mounted in each bed and loaded with marines, crisscrossing the blocks as if they were beginning a search mission.

I could see a Black Hawk helicopter conducting a search over a different grid of the city, parallel to us. I looked to Brady and shook my head.

"Where the hell is he?" I said aloud, staring deep into a residential neighborhood below, as if I expected to see Patas Cortas jogging down the desolate street in his tracksuit. All I wanted was to get on the ground and start hunting. We were worthless in the air.

The old Russian aircraft banked hard right before making its quick descent into an empty city lot.

As we got closer to the ground, I suddenly began to lose my orientation—I hated the sensation. I'd always prided myself on my intuitive sense of direction. When I was in college, I often rode to the bar in the trunk of my friend's car because there were too many girls in the seats. Locked inside the dark trunk, I called out every single turn and every street name, until we got to the bar, never once losing my bearings.

But now I had no clue where we were touching down or what section of Culiacán we were in. Even with a full moon, I couldn't even tell north from south.

We jumped out the back of the helo just as it was landing. The marines exited rapidly and disappeared into the tall grass of the abandoned lot. Brady and I found ourselves alone now, unable to hear each other over the rotor chop, squinting as the dust and grit whipped around us. We quickly lost sight of all the marines; we even lost Garra. Brady and I had planned to stay glued to the admiral's shoulder throughout the capture operation.

I pulled my iPhone from my pocket and tried checking Google Maps to pinpoint our exact location. No luck. The Black Hawk was now attempting to land in the same tiny lot, and the blur of swirling dust made it nearly impossible to see.

"Jesus," Brady said, squinting. He'd spotted some of the marines jumping into *rápidas* off in the distance about two hundred yards away. "Let's go, Drew."

We began to sprint across the uneven lot, over chunks of broken concrete and weeds, as the Black Hawk landed. From the corner of my eye, I saw marines bursting out of the sides of the helicopter, covering their flanks with rifles drawn.

Brady was leading the way, with me right behind, humping my laptop bag.

I heard Brady yell, "This is a turning into a shit show."

"Yeah," I said. "No rifles. No radio. And if those trucks take off without us, we are fucked . . ."

WE WERE TWENTY YARDS away when the *rápidas* sped off. We began to chase them down, sprinting until we reached a gap in the chain-link fence that led to the street. But we were too late. The *rápidas* were long gone.

Out of breath, we rounded the corner and entered the empty street.

We could no longer see the taillights of the trucks, nor hear the roar of the helicopters behind us. All we could hear was our boots on the pavement and our rapid breathing.

I turned from side to side, trying to determine in which direction we were headed—but the pavement, trees, and buildings suddenly all blurred together in shades of brown and gray.

My gaze narrowed. I spotted a black silhouette about a hundred yards away.

I instinctively reached for my thigh holster to pull my pistol, but my hand just slapped my leg. No holster. No gun. The silhouette was getting closer. Was that the barrel of a rifle?

Then Brady shouted, "He's a friendly!"

As we got closer, I saw that it was a very young marine, posted up alone. He was slight, with a narrow pointed nose and brown eyes, his helmet far too big for his head. To me he looked like a twelve-year-old boy dressed up as a soldier. Brady and I jogged up to meet him.

"A dónde van?" Brady yelled. Where had all the *rápidas* gone?

The young marine shrugged. He seemed just as lost as we were, but we decided to follow him anyway. At least the kid was carrying a rifle. As we walked down the block, Brady asked in Spanish, "You have a radio?"

The young marine shook his head no. Brady was now staring hard at me.

We were exposed, and weaponless. There was no way to disguise our gringo faces; we didn't even have military hats or helmets.

And unlike in Mexico City, here in Culiacán no one could possibly mistake us for locals.

This is a fucking setup, I thought.

Chapo had paid off the military; we were stranded, without

guns or radios, in the heart of Culiacán, about to be kidnapped. The video of us being tortured and killed would be uploaded on YouTube before sunrise . . .

"Dude, we need to get back to the helo," I said. *"Now."*

But was the MI-17 even there? Brady and I abandoned the teenaged marine and started sprinting. We knew that if the helo took off we would be completely stranded, weaponless, and stuck in the middle of the lion's den.

SUDDENLY ANOTHER CONVOY of *rápidas* appeared, rounding the corner.

"Fuck it," Brady said. "Let's roll with them."

We ran toward the trucks, and a couple of the marines in the back were waving us on, so Brady and I jumped aboard. We squeezed into a double cab already holding six armed marines. I had no idea who these SEMAR guys were or where we were being taken. They were grittier than the ones I'd seen at the base in Topolobampo. I was pressed tight against a skinny kid with a dark complexion; he was smoking a cigarette, his helmet half-cocked to the side. Most of the others were wearing black balaclavas to hide their faces.

After driving for a few minutes, we parked in the center of a residential block, a typical middle-class neighborhood. As I jumped out of the truck, I looked up and down the intersection and could see more *rápidas* and marines posted on every corner. My nerves began to calm. Two marines handed Brady and me black balaclavas to cover our faces.

"Las cámaras," one of the marines explained.

The safe house had surveillance cameras inside and out, and everyone's faces needed to be covered before entry.

Brady and I walked up to a modern beige two-story house tucked between two other homes the same size. I was so disoriented, I still wasn't sure where our *rápida* had just dropped us off. Was this the block radius I'd been studying so hard on my Google Map? Were we even at Location Five? Neither Nico nor Leroy was anywhere in sight.

Brady and I walked cautiously through the open garage of the house, passing a black Mercedes four-door sedan, then stared at the badly damaged front door of the house. One of the panels of the door was missing, and the jamb was completely torn up in a twisted chunk of metal. The door had been reinforced with six inches of steel—SEMAR had clearly taken a long time to batter its way in.

I STEPPED THROUGH the entryway. The kitchen, directly in front, was furnished simply: white plastic table and folding chairs. Then I took the first immediate right through the living room and entered the ground-floor bedroom. Girls' clothes were scattered throughout the room. Lingerie, blouses, sweatpants, used towels, and open pill bottles littered the bed and the floor.

Brady and I slowly entered the adjacent bathroom.

It was dark and quiet, and far more humid than the rest of the house. I tried to flick the wall light switch; it was broken. Brady and I used the flashlights on our iPhones as we advanced.

There it was—unmistakable in the dim bluish glow.

"Dammit," I said.

Kava's handiwork.

"Look at this fuckin' thing," Brady said as we inched forward.

The large white bathtub, rigged on hydraulics, was propped up at a forty-five-degree angle. As we crept closer to the tub, an overpowering smell of mold filled my nostrils.

We gazed into a sophisticated man-made hole beneath the tub. A narrow vertical ladder led down to a tunnel that extended in the direction of the street, approximately ten feet under the house.

Brady descended the ladder first and made his way to the bottom. I was right on his heels.

The moldy air was so thick and hot that it was now hard to breathe through the face masks. Stooping, we both walked the length of the tunnel. It was extremely well constructed, rigged with fluorescent lighting and wood shoring. We continued until we reached a small steel door with an industrial-size circular handle.

Brady cranked the steel handle counterclockwise, revealing yet another dark tunnel. Trickles of sewage were running along the floor, and the five-foot ceiling caused us both to crouch down into a duck walk.

"Shit," Brady said softly.

We stared into the darkness.

We were looking at a gateway into the labyrinthine sewer system just below the city streets. Everything was pitch-black in both directions, except for a tiny pinhole of light a good twenty or thirty blocks away.

I tried to catch my breath. I looked in one direction and Brady looked in the other, hoping for any sign of life—a whispered voice, a cry, footsteps splashing through the fetid water . . .

Nothing.

"Gone," Brady said.

Chapo had escaped again.

THE DROP

CHAPO'S WORLD WAS UPSIDE-DOWN.

Now so was mine.

There was nothing to do but continue the hunt.

I scaled the tunnel ladder and slowly crawled out, ducking down to avoid hitting my head on the bottom of the bathtub.

Still no sign of Nico or Leroy.

I pulled out my iPhone and texted Nico.

"Where you at?"

"The Four," Nico replied. "Heading to the Three next. Meet us there."

I could see Nico's orange icon blinking about ten blocks to the east on the Find My Friends app.

"I bet Chapo could walk the sewer right down to the Four," Brady said.

"Yeah, he never has to see the light of day."

We walked into what had so recently been Chapo's bedroom and began rifling through everything—all the piles of clothes, towels, ledgers, miscellaneous notes, boxes of Cialis, Celebrex, and other prescription pills littering the room.

I only cared about one thing.

219

"Get me all the BlackBerry boxes and SIM cards you can find," I said. We needed anything that would offer clues about where Chapo had run and who he'd turned to for help in the final minutes.

"Jesus, they're everywhere," Brady said. There were more than twenty BlackBerry boxes in the bedroom alone. Brady and I quickly collected them into a pile on the bed.

I began snapping pictures of each distinct PIN number printed on the side of each box. As soon as I sent the PINs to Don, back in Virginia at DEA's Special Operations Division, they'd be able to get me the corresponding phone numbers almost immediately. Then I could get to work pinging the devices.

"There's a good chance Chapo's carrying at least one of these BlackBerrys," I said.

AS WE CONTINUED COMBING through the empty house, I ran into Admiral Garra.

"*Ven conmigo*," the admiral said abruptly, gesturing for Brady and me to follow him outside.

We jumped into another *rápida* and sped off in a small convoy, following all the other SEMAR trucks. Garra's face was determined, but his brow was starkly creased—it was clear he was still angry that Chapo had slithered away into the sewers.

It was only 4:30 a.m.—still too dark to see clearly when the *rápida* came to a stop—but as soon as my boots hit the gravel street, I knew precisely where I was standing. It was the exact block I'd been studying on my Google Map and high-res imagery for months.

The *rápidas* filled the street, marines piling out and swarming up the driveway. I stood back, taking in Colonia Libertad. I watched as a couple of marines led a man in a red-and-black polo shirt toward the house—even in the dim light I immediately recognized him as the courier Naris.

Naris was silent, head bowed, hands cuffed in front, leading the marines to a long brown steel gate, solidly built and electrified. I knew this was the same gate that Naris had been waiting outside for minutes on end, after running out to buy shrimp or sushi or plastic spoons for Chapo, standing there shouting, *"Abra la puerta!"* and pleading for Condor to let him inside.

This time it was Naris using a set of keys to open the gate for the marines. He was fully cooperating now. I stepped through the gate with the marines and turned around to look back at the street. I was more dialed in than I had realized: it wasn't a *one*-block radius—my pin marker was a mere twenty paces away, across the street from Chapo's driveway, close enough to hit the garage with the toss of a football.

The entry team smashed the reinforced steel lock of the side door, and dozens of marines flooded inside. I followed on their heels, stepping fully into Chapo's world now. This was his primary safe house, the one in which he had spent ninety percent of his time.

I stepped into the first bedroom on the right, scoping everything in the room, taking more photos of BlackBerry boxes and SIM cards. The marines were already beginning to turn the place upside down.

I heard Brady shouting:

"Why aren't they in the sewers? Get in the fuckin' tunnels!"

I knew there was no stopping it now, no way to tell this SEMAR machine what to do.

There was a bag of meth on the kitchen table. This was odd—snorting ice didn't seem like Chapo's thing. In the master bedroom, down the hall, I ran my hand across Chapo's long line of dress shirts and kicked at the more than fifty boxes of shoes stacked high in the closet. There were a couple of expensive watches—one was a rose-gold Jaeger-LeCoultre chronograph with sapphire crystal, brand-new in its box from Le Sentier, Switzerland.

Aside from the designer shoes and a few elegant Swiss timepieces, though, everything seemed to have been purchased in bulk at Walmart.

"Same cheap vinyl sofas," I said. "Same white plastic table. Same folding chairs."

I was surprised to see that Chapo afforded himself so few luxuries. This house was no better than Location Five. These were cookie-cutter homes, completely utilitarian and almost certainly designed and crafted by Kava and his crew.

I followed El Toro, the fiery SEMAR captain, along with a few other marines into the bathroom adjacent to Chapo's bedroom. El Toro was pushing Naris forward, clearly on a mission.

I rounded the corner and came face-to-face with Naris.

His prominent nose was now bright red.

Chapo's courier, hands still cuffed, moved over to the sink and stuck a small shiny object—it might have been a paper clip—into a hole near the electrical outlet next to the mirror. There was a crackling sound—for a moment I thought Naris had given himself an electric shock, but he'd somehow activated an internal switch, triggering the hydraulics.

The caulk liner around the bathtub began to crack away. Naris walked over and grabbed the top rim of the tub with his cuffed hands, giving an awkward lift until the power of the hydraulics took over. The stench of mold and sewage once again filled the bathroom as the entire tub was raised up to the same forty-five-degree angle I'd seen back at Location Five.

A SEMAR lieutenant—everyone called him "Zorro"—kept barking at his troops. *"Mira!* Strip your gear, get into the tunnel, and *find* the motherfucker!" No time to souvenir-hunt, Zorro said. This was their chance to catch the world's biggest drug lord.

Zorro was the first down the open bathtub, descending into the nasty sludge-filled sewers. He quickly disappeared with his team. But I knew that Chapo was in the wind. The guy was as slippery as a sewer rat. He'd likely emerged from some drainage hole more than an hour earlier.

I WALKED OUTSIDE and saw a large blue tarp above my head, a make-shift canopy that spanned across the driveway, from the guesthouse to the roof of the main house. Chapo clearly knew that there were always eyes in the sky watching him.

The guesthouse—equipped with a bathroom and a queen bed—had been built near the far back corner of the small lot, no more than thirty feet from the side door of the main house. By the time I poked my head in, SEMAR had ripped the place to shreds. I figured that this might have been the residence of Chapo's full-time cook or maid—everyone in Mexico who could afford it seemed to have a live-in housekeeper—but it could also have been where Condor stayed during his fifteen- to thirty-day shifts as *secretario.*

After an exhaustive search of the entire property, the swarm of marines shifted gears without warning, filling the streets and jumping back into their *rápidas.* I grabbed Brady by the shoulder as we were leaving and pointed to the white Chevrolet Captiva sitting in the driveway—we had almost overlooked it. It was the same Captiva that Chapo had ordered Naris to get into a few hours earlier, with instructions to bring him his pistol.

NOW WE WERE SPEEDING over to Location Two—it was only a few blocks away, so close we could have walked there. When we arrived, I opened the truck door to exit and paused. I was about to stand on another piece of asphalt I'd been studying for so long in my satellite imagery.

Until that moment, everything had been unfolding at lightning pace, but the initial shock and adrenaline rush were now wearing off. I began to realize how vulnerable we were. At any instant, we could all be ambushed, taken on in a hail of gunfire right there in the street. I pictured streams of Chapo's enforcers and their gunmen, other traffickers, dirty local cops—anyone with weapons—rounding the corner and opening fire. There would be nowhere to run.

I looked around in the truck for an extra rifle, pistol, or even a knife—nothing. A wave of fear rolled through me. I jumped out of the *rápida* and hustled and worked my way in among the mob of marines headed for the door—I figured that it was safest to be tucked in among the troops.

"The Two," as Chapo referred to it, was constructed like Safe House 3—with heavy concrete walls rising high to deter observation from the street and black wrought-iron fence completing the gaps—yet was similar enough to the rest of the neighborhood homes not to stand out. "The Two" was painted white, with a couple of large palms stuck in the walkway just inside the door, along with an attached single-car garage. I was familiar with this location, too. I'd studied the detailed overhead photographs of this very place back in La Paz when I was zeroing in on the pings of Picudo.

Once inside, we found the house almost bare. The three bedrooms each had a bed, but there was little or no other furniture.

"This place looks like a straight stash-or flophouse," I told Brady.

SEMAR had found yet another identical tub on hydraulics in the bathroom off the main bedroom, only this one was nearly impossible to enter. It was stuffed with more than one thousand individual football-size packages wrapped in brown tape and marked with a four-digit number that appeared to be the weight. Methamphetamine. In the end, we would calculate that more than three tons of meth were jammed into the tunnel.

It made no sense to me. Tens of millions of dollars' worth of meth just sitting there getting moldy in the bowels of Culiacán?

"Maybe Chapo's cash-out stash?" I asked Brady.

"Could be," Brady said. "Given the street value of that stuff, he could live on the run for years . . ."

The sun was coming up fast, the Culiacán horizon growing brighter by the moment, the streets starting to come alive. I stood for a while out in the street, with a few marines holding outer security. I noticed a grade school directly across the way; soon it would be bustling with children.

Something else, too: there was blaring music wafting down the hill. Who would play banda so loud at this hour? Was it a signal of some sort from Chapo's loyalists? A call to arms?

BEFORE I KNEW IT, Brady and I were back in the convoy, riding with Nico and Zorro in the armored Suburban, speeding north to yet another location.

It was the first chance I'd had to talk to Nico face-to-face since the frenzy of the first predawn raid.

"How close were you guys to grabbing him before he hit the tunnel?"

"When we pulled up, they were still inside," Nico said. "I could see people upstairs in the window. Someone peeked through the blinds. By the time we got through that fuckin' door, he was gone."

I glanced at Brady, shaking my head in disbelief. "We knew he had a tunnel under a bathtub," I said. "We just didn't know he had one in every single safe house."

Lieutenant Zorro looked especially pissed at this remark. "No one has ever outrun me before," he said.

"We could hear them running—splashing in the distance—but had no idea where," Zorro said. "We found these lying in the sewer," he said, pointing back to two armored tactical vests, one black, the other a pale green.

Tucked in the vests were four black hand grenades with gold pins. One grenade had an American $20 bill wrapped around it. Chapo was presumably planning on tossing them behind himself to blow up the tunnel but hadn't had time. "He had the same setup in Cabo," I remembered.

Zorro handed me a red thumb drive that Chapo had dropped in the tunnel in his haste. There was not much on it other than surveillance video of the inside of some chick's house. Must have been another Guzmán obsession . . .

After a few minutes, we arrived outside Location One. There, an open brown garage door led into an enclosed driveway hidden by huge army-green canvas tarps hung from above.

In the garage, there was a small desk with several monitors displaying video footage from surveillance cameras in all of Chapo's safe houses. Someone obviously had the mind-numbing assignment of sitting in another cheap plastic chair in that empty garage, watching the small checkerboard of cameras on the screens.

This place was even older than Location Two—there were mid-sixties pink and green tiles throughout the bathroom, several bedrooms, and an old, filthy couch in the living room. The walls were bare. I had the feeling that this may have been Chapo's original safe house in Culiacán, considering its age.

Once again, a still-handcuffed Naris jimmied the hydraulic bathtub, revealing yet another entrance to a tunnel.

"Every safe house *is* connected," I said. They were close enough together that they could all be accessed through the same citywide sewer grid directly below the streets.

I walked back out to the street with Brady to get my bearings. It was now full daylight. I recognized the area.

"This is exactly where SEDENA killed El 50 back in August," I told Brady. "Right out on this street."

BRADY AND I HAD just jumped back in the old armored Suburban when I got an email from my group of intelligence analysts in Mexico City. Before we left La Paz, I had instructed them to ping other high-value cartel members every hour—anyone close to Chapo—so we could put them on the target deck in the event they needed to be located and arrested.

This latest email said that Picudo's pings appeared to have traveled at high speed, beginning in Culiacán and ending along Highway 15D just north of Mazatlán. I looked at the times.

Last ping before leaving Culiacán: 3:48 a.m.

Closest ping near Mazatlán: 6:00 a.m.

I reached over and nudged Brady.

"This is our drop!"

I knew that if Chapo trusted anyone, it would be Picudo. Guzmán might not want anyone else in the organization to know he was fleeing—in fact, the HSI team in El Paso reported that most of the DTO's lines were still up and running despite the chaos in Culiacán—but Picudo, his chief enforcer, could scoop him up and run him out of town discreetly.

"Yeah, looks promising," Brady nodded, studying Picudo's ping locations and times.

"This is our drop," I said again. "I'm telling you. Chapo's in Mazatlán."

"*Vámanos, güey!*" Brady said.

But we both knew that we couldn't go marching into Mazatlán with three hundred marines. Since the escape at Location Five, Brady and I already had Joe and Neil back in Texas scrambling for the next Top-Tier PIN to show up. Condor was bound to get a new device soon so he could get back in contact with Second-Tier and the office devices, making it appear that business was operating as normal. It was only a matter of time before El Paso cracked that new Top-Tier number.

"WHERE'S TORO?" I asked Nico. "We need to let him know that Picudo's on his way back now."

My intelligence analyst had told me that Picudo appeared to be on the highway toward Culiacán. I braced for the worst.

"He may roll in here with an army of guys," I said. "Ready for a fight."

"There's no place I'd rather be than right here," Brady said, looking around.

We now felt fully embedded with this SEMAR brigade, in the middle of the Sinaloa capital, and I could feel a subtle shift in the dynamic between us and the marines. Brady and I were no longer gringo federal agents with our mounds of intel and satellite imagery. It didn't matter how many narcos they'd hunted down; nothing had approached the intensity of this capture op. Zorro, for one, was impressed with the accurate intel I had been pitching for more than two weeks now. My precise pattern of life, coupled with all of the real-time intelligence generated by Brady and his El Paso team, had led us straight into Guzmán's lair.

Back at Location Five, I found Toro walking out of the kitchen, wearing a green-and-black *shemagh*. With his face wrapped in that camo scarf, he looked more like a US Spec Ops officer than a Mexican marine. To me, his Spanish nickname had a double meaning: he was bull-like, yes, but Toro also seemed to be short for *tormenta*— "storm." He'd been like a hurricane as soon as he touched down in Culiacán, tearing with ferocity through Chapo's secret underworld.

"Motor! Motor!" Toro yelled suddenly, calling for one of his young lieutenants so he could translate what I was about to tell him. Motor was only in his early twenties, but he was already a well-respected SEMAR officer, and he'd studied college-level English in the United States. He'd been part of the initial briefings Brady and I had with Admiral Furia and his brass back in Mexico City. I could normally get my point across to Toro in conversational Spanish, but for operational updates, Toro made sure Motor was there to translate, ensuring that no critical detail got lost or misunderstood.

"We need to hit Picudo," I told Toro, filling him in on the suspected drop. "Picudo will confirm that Gárgola's in Mazatlán."

"*Dale,*" Toro responded without hesitation. It meant "Let's hit him." "*Dale.*"

"Okay, by our pings, it looks like he's just coming into the city now," I said. "I'll get with Leroy and the marshals and put him next up on the target deck."

IN THE MEANTIME, Toro and his men were still squeezing Naris for more information.

"*Vamos a la casa de Condor!*" Toro said, moving toward the street.

Brady and I jumped in the backseat of Chapo's white armored Chevy Captiva; Toro had seized it back at Location Three and added it to SEMAR's fleet. My knees were jammed into the back of the driver's seat, but I was thankful now to be shielded by the armor on Chapo's former rig. Brady and I still didn't have any guns. Toro jumped in the front passenger seat and the Captiva sped off, following a dark gray Jeep Cherokee, another of Chapo's armored vehicles that the marines had commandeered. That vehicle had Naris inside—the Nose was leading us to the next takedown location.

I spun in my seat, looking back through the rear window at the long trail of *rápidas* racing through the streets behind us. I could hardly believe the pace at which the marines were smashing and grabbing, destroying Chapo's infrastructure.

We came to a quick stop on the rocky dirt road in front of a two-story concrete residence. The place looked like it was still unfinished. Stray dogs ran loose down the street while a young mother in skintight stonewashed blue jeans and black high heels walked outside with her young son.

"This is Condor's place?" Brady said. "What a shithole."

The marines were already inside, and while clearing the house they had found an old rifle and a photograph of a clean-shaven, light-skinned Mexican male with black hair tapering into a spiked flattop.

Brady studied the picture closely.

"Yeah, looks like a condor to me," he said.

Then we jumped back into Chapo's Captiva, once again winding through the city with the convoy of *rápidas*, and finally up a steep hill to a house in a much nicer residential neighborhood.

The moment I walked in the front door, I immediately noticed that the decor didn't match the bare-bones style of Chapo's other Culiacán homes. The furniture was far more expensive; the marble tile was shiny and clean; large framed artwork hung on the walls.

A mural just inside the front door was painted in deep shades of yellow, orange, and red. It was a memorial: I recognized the face of Edgar, Chapo and Griselda's slain son, ascending to heaven. I could almost hear Diego's voice, singing the lyrics of that narcocorrido years ago in Phoenix:

> *Mis hijos son mi alegría también mi tristeza*
> *Edgar, te voy a extrañar*

A white Chevrolet Suburban and Hummer H2 were parked in the garage, but it was suddenly clear that Naris had merely coughed up an old house belonging to Griselda, Chapo's second wife. There were no signs of recent activity—no fresh food in the kitchen, no dirty clothes in the bedrooms. In fact, it didn't look like she'd lived in the place for months.

"Regroup at Location Five," Toro called out.

The marines had dug up piles of photo albums in one of the bedroom closets, and before leaving Griselda's, I grabbed a stack of albums and tucked them under one arm.

When we arrived at Location Five, I walked upstairs and sat down on Chapo's brown faux leather couch. I peeled away the black balaclava from my face for the first time since putting it on, and only now did I begin to feel the first wave of exhaustion. I couldn't remember the last time I'd slept or eaten or drunk anything besides the few swigs of Johnnie Walker back at the base in Topolobampo.

Brady walked up the stairs with a couple of mugs of hot instant coffee he had found downstairs in the kitchen and handed one to me.

"Leroy's down there making eggs on the stove."

Brady and I began thumbing through Griselda's photo albums, trying to find any useful pictures of Chapo. But every family photograph of Griselda and her kids—Joaquín, Grisel, and Ovidio—was missing their father. Weddings, baptisms, quinceañeras, fiestas . . . but never a single shot with Chapo.

Once we were done with the photos, Brady and I scoped out the rest of the house. Next to a forty-inch TV on the living room wall, there was a second small white screen, the size of a large computer monitor, and downstairs by the small swimming pool we found the same setup: a forty-inch flat-screen TV on the wall and still another small white surveillance monitor mounted underneath it, showing pictures of all of Chapo's safe houses in the city.

"Anywhere he watches TV," I said, "he can keep tabs on

what's happening at all his houses." This was clearly one of the safe houses—La Piscina—where Chapo felt most at ease.

I walked back into Chapo's bedroom to take another look around and opened the closet, where I pulled down a black hat from the top shelf.

This was one of Chapo's famous plain, logo-free ball caps, which he could be seen wearing in the few verified photographs that existed of the kingpin since his escape from Puente Grande. Chapo always wore the black hat perched high on his head as if it were an essential part of his everyday uniform. I shoved the black hat underneath my bulletproof vest.

It was my only souvenir of the hunt.

SU CASA ES MI CASA

"ÁNDALE! APÚRATE! APÚRATE!" Captain Toro yelled.

We were still at La Piscina, but everyone was now scrambling to grab their gear and guns. Naris was giving up more locations. Brady and I jumped in the rear of the Captiva, Toro taking the front passenger seat again.

"Zorro de Toro," Toro kept yelling over the radio, giving directions in Spanish as the Captiva sped off, leading the convoy.

We raced into yet another residential neighborhood. SEMAR was battering its way through a door, and I walked in after the first wave of marines. The place was bare except for green bananas and pepinos (small cucumbers) that littered the floor, some white powder on the kitchen counter (cocaine cutting agents), and several black trash bags full of cultivated weed. I picked up a green banana from the bunch on the floor—it was a fake, used for international shipments of a far more lucrative crop, but they were all empty.

"How'd you like to be the poor fucker who had to fill each of these bananas with coke?" Brady said.

A single fake banana could hold no more than half a kilo of cocaine at a time—it would have been the most tedious, labor-intensive job. Immediately I remembered how Hondo, up in British

235

Columbia, was constantly looking for a warehouse large enough to store "fruit deliveries" for the boss. These fake bananas were most likely going directly to Vancouver to be unloaded, then shipped out to cities all across Canada.

A message from the El Paso wire room suddenly hit our group chat.

It was Lic-F reporting through Office-3, to Condor and Chapo.

Buenos dias, como amanecieron. En la ciudad siguen con alboroto esos del agua, no han dormido.

"Good morning, how did you guys wake? In the city, the rampage continues—those from the water, they haven't slept."

Lic-F continued:

Compadre andan bien bravos y todo el movimiento es contra la empresa.

"Compadre [Chapo], they are running really strong and the whole movement is against the business."

The convoy was indeed running on full steam again, smashing house after house.

We were now in another Picudo stash pad. In the dirt backyard, we found five fighting cocks, spurs attached to their legs, strutting around. They circled one another like prizefighters eager to spar. I watched as one dark red rooster with ocean-blue wing feathers attacked another. They were cocks trained to fight to the death. I picked up a handmade leather dice cup hanging on the wall, with markings burned into the side of it, a tribute to El 50.

By the looks of things, Picudo's crew had cleared out each stash pad just before we hit. ·

WE ROLLED BACK TO Location Three. The whole street was now blockaded by SEMAR *rápidas*. There was still the ever-present risk of a gunfight, but I was feeling a little more comfortable knowing we now had plenty of manpower out front.

Brady and I walked into Chapo's kitchen, looking for something to drink. I opened the fridge and grabbed the only three bottles of La Cerveza del Pacifico left.

"Split 'em?" I asked Brady and a few marines.

I smiled as I took one cold swig of Pacifico—remembering that night in Phoenix with Diego when I'd heard "El Niño de La Tuna," peeled back the canary-yellow label, and gulped down my first taste of the beer. I passed the bottle on to a young marine, then Brady took a gulp and passed it back. With the sleep deprivation, that little sip of cerveza was just enough. I let out a laugh—I felt like we were college kids passing around a bottle of whiskey.

I walked over to Toro with a newfound spring in my step.

"*Vamos a tener otra oportunidad*," I said—realizing I sounded a bit like my old high school football coach when it was halftime and we were down by two touchdowns. "We're gonna get another chance," I said, still holding the bottle of Pacifico. "This isn't over. I'm confident, Captain."

All we needed now was to obtain the new Top-Tier number. I explained to Toro that Chapo was smart enough to drop all of his phones, but Brady's team back in the United States was still intercepting several office devices, scrambling to intercept the new

Second-Tier so that we could identify the new Top-Tier device Condor was no doubt holding.

"My guys are on it," Brady said. "Just a matter of time."

"Until then," I told Toro, "we need to exhaust all our intelligence here, Señor."

"*Bueno, vamos a Picudo entonces,*" Toro said.

The next target for us to capture became Picudo, Chapo's chief enforcer and the plaza boss of Culiacán.

SEMAR HAD BY NOW taken over every one of Chapo's five Culiacán safe houses, converting them into temporary bases. Brady and I climbed down the ladder underneath the bathtub in Safe House 3 to get a closer look at the tunnel.

It was the fourth one we'd seen that morning, and no different from the others except that it boasted a specially designed rack along the underground wall that had been used to store hundreds of kilograms of cocaine. The marines had found 280 kilos on the racks, along with boxes full of fake bananas.

I called Brady over.

"Check this out, man. Chapo's go bag."

Again, it was typical Chapo, purely functional: a plastic supermarket sack with a couple of pairs of white underwear inside. These were Chapo's favorites, those Calvin Klein briefs that Marky Mark had made famous. No toothbrush, no shoes, just those Calvin Kleins.

Brady laughed. "Shit, how many times do you escape down a fuckin' bathtub tunnel naked that you need to have a go bag full of tighty-whities?"

——

BY LATE AFTERNOON, still more SEMAR teams were out raiding Chapo's stash pads throughout the city.

One team drove back to Location Three in a white panel delivery truck with secret compartments built inside the walls and the bed. I watched as the marines pried open the traps and extracted fifty more kilos of meth. This time the drugs were packaged in plastic Tupperware-style containers with various-colored lids.

A little later, a crew of marine cooks arrived, bringing large steel pots and utensils, and took over Chapo's kitchen. I stood back and watched how SEMAR was settling into field life here in Culiacán: everyone would soon start receiving three meals a day, and the marines had even brought in a staff doctor. I still wasn't hungry, but I knew I needed to refuel.

Brady and I pulled a couple of plastic folding chairs up to Chapo's white plastic kitchen table and squeezed in next to Lieutenant Zorro. Zorro's warm smile and upbeat attitude masked his exhaustion. I watched, impressed, as Zorro skillfully cut into a tin can of scallops with his bowie knife.

"Cómo les gusta el campo?" Zorro asked. How did we like life in the field?

"Para mí," I said, *"me encanta."* I looked at Brady, still not quite believing we were sitting in Chapo's kitchen.

Spearing scallops straight from the can with the blade of his knife, Zorro reminded me of one of my uncles back in Kansas. He had the same genuine smile, the same rough-and-ready attitude of a born outdoorsman—he reminded me of someone you'd want to share a case of beer with, sitting around a fire, listening to his war stories.

In fact, I'd heard a few stories about Zorro already, from Leroy. El Roy had previously worked with Zorro on operations targeting the Zetas Cartel. One day Zorro had been caught in a fierce urban firefight; Zetas gunmen were raining hell on Zorro and his team from the rooftops, but Zorro walked calmly out into the open street, bullets whizzing around him, and methodically placed his troops into strategic shooting positions. El Roy said that in all his fugitive operations he'd never seen anyone so cool under fire.

My BlackBerry buzzed again: it was another message from the El Paso wire room. I read it and handed it across the table to Toro, who was sitting next to Zorro.

Condor, filtered down through Office-1 and out to Chapo's son Ovidio (Ratón):

La nana todo bien ai descansando oiga pero todo bien

"Everything is fine with Grandmother. She's here resting. Listen, everything is fine."

We knew that Nana was a code name Ovidio and Chapo's other sons often used for their father. It was a good sign that Condor was sending out reassurances that Chapo was settled someplace safe and that there was nothing for them to worry about.

LEROY AND HIS MARSHALS TEAM, Nico, Zorro, and a handful of marines had already left to track down Picudo. I sent them out near the Culiacán International Airport, knowing that, based on previous pings, Picudo most likely lived in a middle-class neighborhood near there.

The remainder of the marines and Brady and I all stayed back at Chapo's safe houses. We were resting for a few minutes while Leroy located the phone Picudo was holding. Once Leroy got a definitive address, he'd give the green light for us to mount up the convoy, rolling in fast and heavy; until then, we were able to briefly take a breather.

Brady and I were finally armed now, too—Nico had thankfully tracked down a couple of AR-15s from some marines and handed them over to us before he'd left.

"Damn, my net worth just quadrupled," Brady said, laughing, as he cradled the rifle. Since leaving Topolobampo, his only possession had been his BlackBerry. He'd even forgotten to grab his wallet before jumping on the helo with me, and joked that he didn't even have enough pesos to buy a toothbrush.

I WENT OUTSIDE to grab a breath of fresh air, spreading out on my back in the middle of Chapo's driveway and gazing up at the night sky.

The exhaustion hit me so hard, I felt like I couldn't move. It seemed as if the cold pavement was about to swallow me up. I called my wife at our La Condesa apartment, which wasn't the best idea, as I immediately started laughing and rambling.

"The night clouds, baby," I said. "The clouds of Culiacán. These are the clouds of Culiacán. The same clouds C would look up at if he was here and could look up."

"Where are you?" my wife said after a long pause.

"In C's driveway."

"What?"

"I'm just on my back, on the ground, looking up at the clouds. Remember how we'd look at the clouds when we were first dating?

There's one that looks like a gun! Where was that park we'd go to before the kids were born and just stare at clouds together for hours?"

I let out another burst of hysterical laughter.

"You're scaring me, Drew," my wife said. "You realize you're making absolutely no sense."

I had a serious case of the giggles. Brady came out to join me, and even he was starting to laugh.

"I'm serious, Drew—you really sound *messed up* . . ."

I realized, finally, that my nonsense rambling was alarming. I snapped to my senses.

"I'm *fine*, baby," I said. "I'm surrounded by some of the toughest warriors in the world. These marines are the best guys I've ever seen. I'm just—just kind of delirious. All I need is a good couple hours' sleep."

AND THEN I AWOKE with a sudden start. Somehow, I was in Chapo's bed.

"Luz verde!" a young marine yelled. *"Luz verde! Vamos a Picudo."*

Green light: we were going to snatch up Picudo.

It was still dark outside in the Culiacán streets. I rubbed my eyes. My head was aching, and I realized I must have nodded off for only forty-five minutes. As I sat up, Chapo's plastic garment bag peeled away from my sweaty back like a snake's dead layer of skin. The last thing I remembered was laying the plastic down beneath me on the bed so I wouldn't catch some STD.

I stood up, knees wobbly, stretched my arms high overhead and into a backbend. I'd been lost in a dream-memory of making that first big drug bust back in Kansas—three ounces of crack cocaine in that Deadhead's car. Was this whole thing a dream? Was I now actually sitting on a three-*ton* seizure of methamphetamine belonging to the world's biggest drug lord?

Brady and I scrambled to throw on our vests and slung the carbines across our chests. Once we were ready, we jumped into the Captiva with Toro and another young SEMAR lieutenant, nicknamed Chino—apparently for his Chinese-looking eyes.

We raced in another convoy out to a middle-class neighborhood near the Culiacán airport. Leroy had located the phone inside a small ranch-style house surrounded by a wrought-iron fence.

I looked at my watch: 1:32 a.m.

There wasn't another vehicle on the streets. The entire city was either scared or gearing up for war. I grabbed the pistol grip of my AR-15, pulling it tighter to my chest, as we turned the corner onto Picudo's dimly lit block. If there was going to be a Macho Prieto–style firefight, it was going to happen right here at Picudo's house.

EL 19

CROUCHING DOWN, I TOOK a position behind the front quarter panel of the Captiva, pointing my AR toward the dark shadows in the narrow walkway next to Picudo's house.

I could see in my peripheral vision a mob of black silhouettes quietly making their way to the front door. Then the stillness was shattered by the noise from the battering ram. Dogs began to bark.

The ramming continued for minutes. I was becoming more anxious by the second. Surely with Picudo's house under SEMAR assault, it would only be a matter of time before his reinforcements arrived on the scene.

The door was finally battered open, and I could see the stream of marines entering Picudo's house. I paused, expecting to hear a volley of gunshots.

Nothing.

Emerging from my position, I entered the house and saw three men on their knees in the living room, lined up against the wall.

I made my way through the kitchen and toward the back bedrooms.

SEMAR had Picudo at gunpoint on his bed. *No one*, I thought, *not even a feared cartel killer, looks scary when you roust them from a deep sleep, bare-chested, hair messed up, at 2:00 a.m.* Picudo didn't look like he could hurt anyone—he was pale, sweaty, and scrawny.

In Spanish, he claimed to be very sick. Brady didn't believe it; he grabbed Picudo by the left arm and spun him roughly onto his stomach. Picudo screamed now—a high-pitched wail. He claimed to be dying, but neither Brady nor I could decipher from *what*, precisely.

Brady pinned Picudo down on the bed. Now the SEMAR doctor came into the bedroom and told Brady to ease off; he wanted to examine Picudo.

"You gotta be shitting me," Brady grumbled to me. "They're gonna believe this pathetic actor crying like a little bitch?"

I listened closely as the doctor began asking Picudo the routine questions: How long had he been suffering from this rare disease of the blood?

Picudo exhaled with relief, righted himself in the bed.

Suddenly, Brady leapt forward—he had seen the butt of a gun secreted under Picudo's naked thigh.

Brady grabbed Picudo more roughly, pinning him on his face, holding him tight by the neck and the left arm.

"No lo toques!" the doctor shouted, "What are you doing? You can't touch him—he's very sick. He might die!" All the marines in the room were also yelling, shoving forward, agitated.

"Fuck that," Brady said. *"Tiene arma!* Look, the motherfucker's got a gun!"

Brady kept him pinned while one of the marines reached under Picudo's body and retrieved the Colt .45, fully loaded and with one in the chamber. If they'd believed this guy's bullshit, let their guard down long enough, Picudo could have pulled out his pistol and shot every one of us in the room.

I COULD STILL HEAR Picudo wailing as he went into the kitchen. There was a cache of automatic weapons on the table, including an AK-47, an AR-15, a TEC-9, and several other rifles. Picudo's men had been ready for a last stand—just like Macho Prieto's crew in Puerto Peñasco—but they had been caught by surprise.

By now, all the gunmen had been safely detained: cuffed, blindfolded, and lined up against the wall. The marines kept bringing more phones to the kitchen for me to analyze. The table was piled high with BlackBerrys and SIM cards, tossed in haphazardly with all the guns. There was even a book in Spanish that I was surprised to see: *La D.E.A. en México*.

Picudo—like Chapo—had been studying up on my agency and our operational history in Mexico. I had seen a copy already; this dog-eared paperback was well known in the DEA office back in Mexico City. It was a quickie knocked out by some writers for the *Proceso* magazine, using only a couple of retired DEA dinosaurs as sources, guys who'd been stationed in-country back in the 1990s. The biggest "revelation" was that DEA special agents operating within Mexico on counter-narcotics missions had been, illegally, strapped with guns.

I didn't care about the book or the weapons now, however: I hovered over the kitchen table, examining all the phones. I recognized some numbers that the Phoenix Field Division and Brady's people in El Paso had been intercepting.

Chino, the marine, led Picudo—now identified as Edgar Manuel López Osorio—out of the house, and he was strutting like he owned the city, which, as Chapo's plaza boss for Culiacán, he essentially did. There was no blindfold on him yet, and I was able to get a good look into those cold, steely eyes.

All I saw was an abyss.

Chino put Picudo in the back of a Jeep Cherokee, where he was joined by a fierce-looking marine—six foot four, powerfully built—whom everyone called "Chiqui" (slang for "the smallest"). Chiqui's face was pure Aztec—eyes dark and close-set—and his brow was pocked with scars. I'd never heard Chiqui speak, but it was clear to me that he was the muscle in this brigade.

"Vamos," Chino said.

The convoy left in total darkness; I had no clue where we were heading. We ran down an unlit highway until, fifteen minutes outside Culiacán, we reached a pecan ranch—SEMAR owned it and had used it in the past for their training.

When we hopped out of the Captiva, I saw Picudo, blindfolded, grimacing as he sat on the Jeep's rear bumper, face lit up starkly by headlights.

There were now more than twenty people—various marines, Brady, Leroy, Nico, and me—surrounding the back of the Jeep. The darkness felt thicker now, the air electric: it was clear that Picudo was ready to talk.

His voice was a strong baritone, notable for its heavy Sinaloan accent. And the tone had changed from whiny back to that of a stone-cold killer. This was the *real* Picudo, the enforcer we suspected to be personally responsible for the murders of countless victims.

"Mira, esto fue lo que pasó," he said calmly.

"Ándale," said Chino.

"Voy a estar honesto . . ."

The circle of marines undulated like some great jellyfish, growing tighter around Picudo.

"I'M GOING TO BE honest with you now," I remember Picudo saying. "When you hit the house, Chapo escaped through the tunnel—ran through the sewer. He was with a girl, Condor, and the cook. Chapo and the girl were naked—nearly naked. Just in their underwear. Chapo has a cut on his head from hitting something—running through the sewer. They called me to come pick them up. They escaped out of a drainage hole. When I entered the city, I saw all of your trucks."

Picudo had scooped up Chapo and his entourage in his truck and driven the boss at high speed down the Pacific coast. They drove for nearly two hours, and Chapo did not say a word the entire time, besides ordering Picudo to contact Bravo, Chapo's chief enforcer and plaza boss in the southern part of the state, and let Bravo know to meet them at the drop site.

"I dropped them off near the resorts," Picudo said finally. "I don't know where they went from there."

"What resorts?" Chino asked, glancing from Picudo over to me.

"Dónde? That's not good enough. *Where* on the coast?" Toro demanded.

Picudo's bared teeth flashed a cold hatred, his brow tensing behind the blindfold, before he finally gave it up.

"Mazatlán," he said, exhaling through pursed lips. "I dropped them at the *playa* exit."

"La salida de playa?" Chino repeated for confirmation.

"*Sí*," Picudo said. "Just before the new strip of resorts in Maz-atlán."

Turning our backs on Picudo, Toro, Brady, and I walked away to strategize.

"This confirms the drop," I said, "but we still need Top-Tier to know Chapo's exact location. Like I said, we need to exhaust all our intelligence while we're here in Culiacán."

Toro nodded his head in agreement.

"We still have all the sons and Lic-F to go after," Brady said. "They could give up where he's at, too."

"*Vamos a continuar,*" Toro said as we all climbed back into our rigs.

The convoy rolled out onto the dusty path. Then Chino pulled the Captiva over to the side. He was waiting for a couple of *rápidas* to join the end of the line. Toro turned in his seat to look back at me.

"*Que quieres hacer?*"

I felt like I was in a trance: I could see Toro's lips moving but couldn't make out what he was saying. The entire rig began to spin. I could feel the blood rushing out of my head. I was on the verge of passing out from pure exhaustion.

"*Qué sigue?*" Toro asked.

"*Dale!*" I replied, half-delirious. "*Dale! Dale!*" and I felt my fist smashing into my own palm.

"*Dale!*" Toro said, grinning.

Dale! Dale! Dale!

I kept repeating the word, so exhausted that my mouth was barely moving. Everyone in the car went quiet. I squinted over at Brady, whose head was tilted against the window. He was out cold. Chino was snoring in the front seat, and Toro's head was bobbing forward as he slept.

My eyes drifted shut.

A loud squelch came across the radio.

"Toro de Zorro! Toro de Zorro!"

We all snapped back awake, startled by the radio traffic. None of us realized we'd passed out and that the rest of the SEMAR brigade was waiting for us to lead the convoy back to the city.

I knew that we all needed some serious rest soon—we'd been running on fumes for days. The sun was just beginning to rise over the mountains in the east, and Toro made the command decision to head back to base—Location Three—so everyone could at least sleep for a few hours.

THAT AFTERNOON, Brady and I left Location Three and walked the dirt street down to Location Two, where SEMAR was processing all the evidence. We stopped along the way at a small *puesto*—a makeshift convenience store some guy was running out of his dark cinder-block garage. I bought a *paleta*—a Mexican popsicle—and a bag of Doritos for Brady with the few pesos I had in my pocket.

When we walked into the Two, I saw that SEMAR had extracted all the meth from the tunnel. Brown packages were stacked on top of one another and covered the entire living room floor. In the kitchen, a young marine was counting plastic bananas and placing them in a large container.

I stepped outside, passing the stash of rocket-propelled grenade launchers, AK-47s, and other military-grade weapons, laid out in meticulous order on the white pavement.

Something shiny caught my eye—it was the gun Chapo had ordered Naris to fetch for him. The Colt Super .38-caliber Automatic had Chapo's initials monogrammed into the grip, in diamonds: J.G.L.

Despite my still-exhausted state, I now knew I wasn't in some waking dream: holding that cold steel in my hand made everything tangible.

The detailing on the Colt Super was impressive. Chapo hadn't had time to grab the pistol before he fled through the tunnel and sewer, and it was clear that this was his favorite weapon, his personal Excalibur.

Who knew the full history behind Guzmán's pistol? But if the Colt gave Chapo some mystical power, I could almost sense it now, too. Just holding the .38 Super in my hand, I felt that same visceral energy transferring through my grip.

Stacks of BlackBerrys were piled high in the backyard. Brady and I sat down and began looking through Picudo's phones one by one. I found a picture of Duck Dynasty and messages in the most recent chat logs with Lic-F.

Just then, another message hit our group chat from El Paso. It was a fresh intercept—Lic-F reaching Condor and Chapo:

A poco tuvo problemas el picudo

"Oh really, Picudo had problems?"
Condor and Chapo immediately responded:

Si. Tenemos ke estar trankilo. Por ke. No keda de otra. Claro. Por ke picudo. Pobre. El si sabe de todo.

"Yes, we have to be calm because there's no other option. Yes, of course. Because of Picudo. Poor Picudo. He knows everything."
I called in Nico and Leroy.

"We need to find Lic-F next," I said. "Now that Picudo's gone, Chapo's going to be relying on him for everything."

"Agreed," Leroy said. "We'll focus on him and the sons."

Then my BlackBerry buzzed with another message from El Paso. It was Condor to Chapo's son Ratón:

oiga dise inge si tiene una super. Ke le mande. Con 4 cargadores estra. Es para el oiga. Y si me ase el paro ai oiga con 1 bereta o lo ke tenga oiga

"Listen, Inge is asking if you have a Super [Colt .38] that you can send. With four magazines. It's for him, and do me a favor: bring me the Beretta or whatever you have."

Then, moments later:

oiga dise inge para kele mande 10 rollos al negro.

"Listen, Inge says to send ten rolls to Negro."

I grinned. I knew that "Negro" was another code name for Manuel Alejandro Aponte Gómez, a.k.a. "El Bravo." Chapo needed ten rolls—$100,000 in cash—delivered to him immediately. This was confirmation of Chapo's vulnerable position: he was free, but he had nothing with him in Mazatlán—no guns and no cash.

We went back to analyzing the BlackBerrys, and, as ever, minutes turned to hours.

I vaguely remembered the marines handing out sandwiches for dinner, but when I glanced at my watch, I saw that it was now one o'clock in the morning. I lay down on the top of Chapo's bed, the mattress now covered only by the dirty brown fitted sheet. Brady was sitting in the corner on a chair. I stared at the ceiling, imagining where Chapo might be resting in Mazatlán.

"Weird, isn't it?" I said. "Chaps is somewhere right now in Maz trying to figure out his next move, and we're here in his bedroom strategizing ours."

"Good to know he's got no money with him," Brady said.

"We need that Top-Tier."

"We'll get it."

"Yeah," I said. "Soon enough."

We were both confident that Joe and Neil, in El Paso, were dialed in and cranking out the roving intercepts as fast as they possibly could.

"Luz verde! Luz verde!" one of the marines yelled down the hall. El Roy had locked down on the phone of Iván Archivaldo Guzmán Salazar, in a house on the north side of the city.

So much for rest—Brady and I jumped in a *rápida* with Admiral Garra and raced to the location. By the time we arrived, SEMAR had already made entry, but Iván was nowhere to be found. Instead, there were only a couple of his workers sitting on a stash pad full of weapons, two-way radios, a small amount of meth, and, of course, another pile of BlackBerrys. Iván had clearly been warned by Chapo to get out of the city and had set up a classic BlackBerry mirror operation with his workers before leaving.

Nico handed me a black baseball cap he had found in one of the bedrooms. The front of the hat was emblazoned with #701 in shimmery gold stitching—again, that *Forbes* ranking of the world's wealthiest men.

As we continued to look around, I received a new email from my analysts back in Mexico City. A brand-new Nissan GT-R belonging to one of Chapo's sons, Jesús Alfredo Guzmán Sala-zar, had just pulled into the Mercedes dealership off Boulevard Pedro Infante.

"*Vamos!*" Toro said. "Do you know where the dealership is?"

"Yes, of course," I said.

"All right, you lead, then."

Brady and I jumped into our old armored Suburban and took off out of the neighborhood, trailed by a stream of *rápidas*.

WE TOOK THE MERCEDES dealership by storm. Guns drawn, the ma-rines flooded the showroom floor and the service center and sur-rounded the parking lot. Brady and I rushed inside, looking for Alfredo, a skinny twenty-six-year-old narco with a baby face.

Alfredo's Nissan had arrived at the service department no more than five minutes before the convoy. I put my palm on the hood: the engine was still hot. The GT-R had a temporary California registration sticker on the windshield—further proof, I knew, that this was all part of Alfredo and Iván's long-running money-laundering scheme. Chapo's sons would send a worker in the States to pick up hundreds of thousands of dollars in drug proceeds and then "smurf" the cash into various US bank accounts—making multiple deposits of just under the $10,000, the federal manda-tory reporting requirement. Once the cash was in the US banking system, Iván and Alfredo could use aliases or straw purchasers to negotiate the best price for these exotic sports cars. Their workers in the United States would wire the money to the seller and arrange to have the car imported into Mexico and delivered straight to Culiacán.

Brady and I bounded upstairs and cased the executive offices, but there was still no sign of Alfredo. By now the entire dealership, inside and out, was crawling with armed men in green-and-black camouflage. All the employees and customers were in shock—no one dared speak a word.

We reviewed the surveillance video of the past hour. Then I found Captain Toro. "Alfredo's not here," I said.

"He's not even on the surveillance tape," Brady said. "He had a whole crew of narco juniors dropping these cars off."

Brady pointed to the string of brand-new Mercedes sedans and coupes lined up in the service area. Captain Toro took a few moments to review the video and returned to the shop floor.

"We're taking them all," Toro said, and he began walking through the parking lot with a group of marines, checking every vehicle. "If it's armored, we're taking it."

Fourteen armored vehicles were seized, and six more luxury cars, even a Ducati motorcycle. As evidence, I began snapping photos of the makes, models, and license plates. Mercedes SLS AMG. Mercedes AMG G63. Mercedes C63. Mercedes CLA45. Even a cloned municipal police armored Dodge Charger.

Chapo's son Iván had the most expensive car on the lot: his 2010 silver Mercedes-Benz SLR McLaren two-door coupe, complete with suicide doors, a customized sound system, and a 5.4-liter supercharged V8 engine. Chino popped one of the batwing doors and fired it up. The McLaren sounded louder than a Learjet.

Brady and I got back in the Suburban and watched the marines hop into all the cars, driving millions of dollars of vehicles right off the lot, one after the other, as though they were just playing a wild round of *Grand Theft Auto*.

——

AS WE STARTED BACK toward Location Three, in my rearview mirror I could see the Mercedes dealership employees standing outside gawking, still in shock.

At that moment I realized that we had taken full control of the city—we'd wrested Culiacán away from Chapo. The SEMAR machine was untouchable; no one in El 19 had had the balls to confront us. The marines were moving too fast and hitting too hard. All of Chapo's *halcones* had crawled back into their holes. Even Lic-F was reporting intel from his corrupt sources that was stale—two hours old.

I thought back over the past few days. I couldn't remember seeing a single police car—local or federal—patrolling the streets. All law enforcement officers were now obviously in hiding. Even the city's dirtiest cops knew that it was best to stay out of SEMAR's path.

BACK AT THE THREE, the entire block looked like a bizarre luxury car show in the middle of the hood. The immaculate Mercedes sedans and coupes were parked bumper-to-bumper on the dirt-and-gravel street.

Another message came fresh from the El Paso wire room.

Lic-F to Chapo and Condor:

Por otra parte hay nos sacaron unos carros duros de la agencia esos del agua, y andan duros aun.

"On another note, the ones from the water took some hard [armored] cars belonging to the agency [Chapo's DTO]. They're running hard."

Condor answered almost instantly.

Buenas tardes sr. Dise su compadre kesi los carros eran suyos. O los menores.*

"Good afternoon, sir. Your compadre is asking if the cars were yours or the minors."

Lic-F replied:

Unos duros eran mios, pero sacaron otros de lujo que yo creo si eran de los menores.

"Some of the [armored cars] were mine, but they took other luxury ones that I believe were the minors'."

This was confirmation that Chapo's DTO was using the Mercedes dealership as a ruse, a place to store their most prized possessions so they wouldn't be seized by SEMAR as they tore through the city. It was also clear that they thought they could still weather the SEMAR storm.

Leroy and Admiral Garra were standing in the driveway at Location Three.

"We need to go after Kava," I told Garra. "He can tell us where every single lightbulb is, where every trapdoor and secret passage is tucked away. He constructed all the tunnels on every piece of property Chapo owns. If we're going to destroy this place, giving him nowhere to return, then we've got to find Kava—he'll give us everything."

---

* *Los menores*—literally "the minors" or "youngsters"—was frequently used within the DTO to refer to Iván and Alfredo.

Leroy, Nico, and the marines hit the streets again, carving circles within the city, trying to locate Kava's phone. But they had no luck, and by now everyone was at the point of exhaustion.

The clock was ticking, and Admiral Garra was getting stressed again. The Mexican Attorney General's Office was taking over all the locations in Culiacán, booting us all out of the safe houses and stash pads we'd been using as our makeshift bases. Rumor had it that they wanted to begin filling up all the tunnels beneath Chapo's safe houses with concrete.

"You'll never keep this guy from going underground," I told Admiral Garra. "He's like a mole—he'll try tunneling again in no time—trust me."

Garra said they might have no choice but to wrap up the mission soon.

I shook my head.

"Tenemos que mantener la presión," I said. We couldn't let up with the pressure. I reassured Garra that I was still confident we'd get Top-Tier soon.

"We're almost there," said Brady. "One more day—tops—we'll have it."

Chapo simply couldn't function without his communications in place.

"We just need a bit more time, sir," I said.

"More time?" Garra said somberly. "That's the one thing I can't promise you."

MIRAMAR

"PACK YOUR BAGS, GUYS—ROLLING OUT!"

It was Chino, shouting from the doorway. We had to vacate the safe house. It wasn't hard to snatch up our possessions—I could carry everything I had in one hand: a leather laptop case containing one MacBook, and a few phones. Brady had just his Black-Berry. Neither of us had changed clothes or underwear in more than a week.

"I can feel my shirt rotting off my skin," I said.

But I didn't like that we were leaving home base; it was just beginning to feel secure. Chapo's place had become our safe haven. *Su casa es mi casa.*

I realized I was going to miss the camaraderie, not to mention the marines' home-cooked meals. One thing I wasn't going to miss: the bathroom with the sign Chino had duct-taped on the door: EXCLUSIVO CAPITANES Y OFICIALES. Every morning, marines lined up by the dozen, waiting to use a filthy toilet that lacked both a seat and toilet paper.

Brady and I jumped into an armored Volkswagen Passat—another of Chapo's customized cars. No orders had been given on a destination, but I could see that it was deeper into urban

261

Culiacán. Eventually we passed a water park and drove onto the city's main baseball field. The well-groomed lawn quickly filled with all the glossy Mercedes, mixed in with the mud-caked SEMAR *rápidas*.

"A baseball diamond?" Brady said, laughing. "Sleeping in the open air?"

"May not be that crazy," I said. "It's probably the safest place to be in the entire city. At least we can control the perimeter and see everyone coming and going."

Out of nowhere, a dented, rust-flecked white pickup pulled up outside the fence. *Chapo's halcones?* I nudged Brady, glancing in the direction of the truck.

"Fuck," I said. "Here we go."

Why would any outsider be approaching a field full of heavily armed marines? I instinctively looked for a place to dive; there wasn't much cover besides a few shabby-looking trees.

"Dude, look at all those cots," Brady said, laughing.

As the truck got closer, we had realized that the flatbed of that old truck had been stacked fifteen feet high with rudimentary military beds, constructed of wood and strung with potato sacks. It sure would be a step up from sleeping on the cold tile floor without blankets in Chapo's safe houses.

As the sun set on Culiacán, Brady and I went to find Admiral Garra and Captain Toro. We didn't want to be overheard, so we met in the growing darkness behind the concession stand at the baseball field. Leroy, Nico, Chino, and another young SEMAR lieutenant, Tigre, were there, too.

"What's the latest intel?" Admiral Garra asked.

"Gárgola's instructed Lic-F to find two houses for him on the coast. We're still waiting for Top-Tier, but I think we need to move down to Mazatlán. Set up shop at a resort and begin working our intel there."

"We need to get down there before he has a chance to flee," said Brady.

Admiral Garra nodded, then gave us the bad news: Captain Toro had to leave Culiacán immediately—his brother had been struck in a hit-and-run accident in Mexico City and it didn't sound like he would make it through the night. With Toro leaving, frontline command would be in the hands of Chino and Tigre.

"We've got about two more days before we need to wrap this up," Admiral Garra said. "Then I'm pulling everyone out of Sinaloa."

We all agreed it was best to move to the Mazatlán resort strip and continue working from there.

But it was crucial to avoid all tails and countersurveillance.

"We can't all go down there in a convoy," Chino said.

"You're right—none of these *rápidas*," I added. "Gárgola's people will spot them the second we leave town."

"Agreed," Brady said. "We leave all the SEMAR vehicles here. Make a covert approach to the south, taking different routes."

"We'll use all of his own *blindados*," Chino said.

What better vehicles to use than the fleet of Chapo's own armored cars and trucks we'd seized?

Under cover of darkness we drove over to Soriana—a Target-style chain popular throughout Mexico—still wearing our camouflage fatigues, boots, and black balaclavas.

Brady, Nico, Leroy, a few marines, and I spent an hour loading up on sleeping bags, toothpaste, shorts, shirts—and the first fresh socks and underwear I'd seen in weeks. Brady and I would have to look like typical Americans on vacation, so we also grabbed the most basic red-and-black T-shirts, baggy boardshorts, and flip-flops.

The Soriana shoppers stared at us like we were nuts. I realized how out of place we looked, as if we'd just parachuted in from Iraq . . . Or maybe we resembled a couple of narcos come to kidnap someone in the store. One of the customers, a middle-aged woman, stared into my eyes. Then she cracked a smile: she must have realized they weren't the eyes of a narco hidden behind my black mask . . .

Back at the baseball diamond, we grabbed platefuls of tacos al pastor just outside the fence, and the marines let in a kid on a banana-seat bike with a cooler full of fresh tamales con pollo, fifty pesos each.

With our bellies full, Brady and I walked toward a large open-air room with bare orange-painted steel pillars and screens to keep the bugs at bay, filled with tightly spaced cots. The warm wind was wafting through as I sprawled out on my cot.

"God, these potato sacks are better than a Sealy Posturepedic," I said.

I unlaced and kicked off my boots. It was the first time my feet had been out of those sweaty things in five days, and my big toes had water-filled blisters.

In a brand-new black T-shirt and BDU pants, barefoot, I took one last stretch and muttered two words under my breath: "The blind . . ." Delirious, I shut my eyes and was instantly more than a thousand miles away.

I LOVED LIVING right on the river—there was no fence separating our backyard from the water's edge—and on warm days, my brother,

Brandt, and I would wade out to a nearby island, claiming it as our personal playground, building forts out of sticks and poking around in muskrat dens.

It was late fall—I was ten years old—when our father told us that we could both come along on a hunt. We'd been preparing for this day since we were toddlers, walking around the living room blowing old wooden duck calls our father handed down until our mother would beg us to stop. Whenever our dad came home from a hunt, we'd help him unload the pile of ducks from the flat-bottomed, sixteen-foot PolarKraft and toss the plastic mallard dummy in the yard for our black Lab, Rough, to retrieve.

The night before the big day, Brandt and I had both been so excited that we'd crawled into our bunk beds all ready, wearing our brown camouflage jackets and face paint. At 5 a.m., our father snapped on the bedroom light, and we sprang out of bed and threw on our black snow pants and gloves. It was still pitch-black outside, and I clutched my brand-new Remington shotgun mid-barrel as we walked together over the frost-covered lawn and down to the forest-green boat tethered at the river's edge.

The ride upriver was ice cold and wet. My ears were numb, but I didn't reach for the stocking cap my dad had given me. He didn't wear one—why should I? The cold wind whipped across my face. The heavy steel boat pushed through the water, the front edge of the hull splashing cold waves up over the sides, soaking my jacket and catching me on the side of the face. I caught sight of a group of ducks splashing out of the river, kicking up near the bank.

My father cut the twenty-five-horsepower Mercury motor and the PolarKraft drifted on in silence. Under the moonlight, I felt as if we'd been floating in the middle of that river for hours, my father flashing the fifteen-million-candlepower spotlight along the shore, trying to locate the well-hidden duck blind.

I saw the outline of the blind that Brandt and I had helped build out of wood, camouflaged with cattails, downed tree limbs, and other foliage. We threw out the decoys one by one so they floated near the front of the blind.

With my Remington loaded, I sat on the five-gallon bucket, peering through the narrow open slots between cattails.

The sun began to streak the horizon in shades of orange and pale gold through the trees across the riverbank. I was startled by the sound of whistling above my head: faint at first, trailing off in the distance. I looked up but couldn't see anything. My father pointed up to the sky.

"They'll be back."

Eventually we heard the whispering whistle above us once again, and this time we spotted the flock, their wingtips catching the faint rays of the sun. But once again the ducks disappeared.

I picked up my duck call and gave a couple of quacks through the double-reed lure. Brandt and I took turns letting out the sounds we'd been practicing since we were old enough to walk. The noise of the calls soon filled the river valley.

"Get down—they're coming back," my father whispered. In a few moments, the ducks were out in front, circling over the tops of the floating decoys. "Let them come in close," my father said.

My leg began to shake as I tried to keep myself still. I could see the flock out in front starting to descend rapidly, wings locked, a couple of the mallards dropping their shiny orange legs like the landing gear on a jet.

"You ready, Drew?"

I was silent, just a quick nod to my father, the ducks no more than thirty yards away now. I could make out the colorful green heads and bright yellow bills of the drakes.

"Take 'em!" my father yelled.

I quickly stood up and shoved the Remington deep into my shoulder. I saw nothing except that green head hanging in front of my barrel, the wings seeming to flap in slow motion. My right shoulder jerked back and the yellow plastic shell flickered in the corner of my eye as I ejected the first round. *Miss.* I swung the gun slowly, tracking the bird as it flared across the sky, and pulled the trigger again. *Miss.* The duck kept flying.

Last shot.

The Remington held only three shells.

Start behind the bird, pull through the bird, and fire. I repeated the precise words my father had taught me like a catechism. The mallard was gaining distance quickly, just beginning to exit the kill zone, when I gave one last, slow squeeze of the trigger.

"Dead bird!" my father yelled to Rough, who was panting eagerly at the blind's edge. "I thought he was gone, Drew, but you stayed on him . . ."

AND WITH THAT LAST SHOT, I awoke with a start in Mexico, still thinking for a moment that I was in that Kansas duck blind, feeling a wet scraping on my bare cheek.

"What the hell?"

It was bright daylight, and a little dog was licking my sweat.

I wiped the sleep from the corners of my eyes, wondering where this puppy had come from. It was a blue-eyed husky with a red collar and a spherical bell around his neck. He was scampering around in the bright sunshine, sniffing and licking everyone.

Chino told me that a couple of the younger marines had found the dog alone in one of the safe houses—with no food or water—and had brought him along as the new team mascot. Someone had given it a new name, too: El Toro, in honor of our missing street commander.

Brady and I quickly packed our bags full of all our Soriana gear and jumped in the backseat of Chapo's Volkswagen Passat, now wearing our new T-shirts and boardshorts. A young marine lieutenant took the wheel while Chino hopped in the front passenger seat.

"This is the perfect ride," I told Brady—it was low-key, without any of the bells and whistles of the typical narco car.

Chino stopped at Plaza Fiesta to grab a few last-minute supplies; I immediately recognized this as the spot where Chapo would always send his people to be picked up by Naris when he wanted to confer with them face-to-face.

Brady and I walked into a small mercado and bought a plateful of rolled taquitos topped with queso fresco and salsa verde while we waited for Chino to finish up.

Seeing me weaponless, Tigre had lent me his FN Herstal Five-Seven pistol, a Belgian-made semiautomatic. It was a small-caliber gun—firing rounds of 5.7 by 28 millimeters—but effective at close quarters: the rounds could penetrate a bulletproof vest, giving the FN Five-Seven its street name: "the cop killer."

Brady and I were shoulder-to-shoulder in the backseat when both of our BlackBerrys buzzed with news from Texas.

Joe and Neil, in El Paso, working with Camila and her team of assistant US attorneys, had done it: the roving wire they'd taken so long to write and get authorized had finally hit pay dirt.

"New Top-Tier!" Brady shouted.

"Yeah, baby! Condor's up and running," I said. "And the prefix six-six-nine."

"Yep, six-six-nine."

All of Culiacán numbers had a prefix of 667. This prefix, 669, I immediately knew meant the phone was from Mazatlán. I flipped open the screen of my MacBook, balancing it on my knees in the back of the Passat, and hit the ping button. Within seconds I had a hit. The device was active, right along the beachfront strip of resorts.

Someplace called Miramar.

Hotel Miramar.

THE MAN IN THE BLACK HAT

LEROY HAD LEFT CULIACÁN with Zorro and his crew an hour earlier and was already arriving in Mazatlán. I sent him the new Top-Tier number.

"El Roy's headed there now, near the hotel, to confirm the ping," I said to Brady.

"I just hope Condor keeps it on long enough," Brady said.

This was it—we were on our way down to the water for the last shot.

In that cramped backseat, I felt my leg beginning to shake. I was becoming more impatient by the minute. *"Ándale!"* I yelled up to the front, slapping the young lieutenant on the shoulder. The engine revved as we accelerated, but the heavy Passat still felt like it was crawling its way to the coast.

My BlackBerry buzzed with a new message from Leroy.

"Confirmed. I've got it at Miramar."

SEMAR had rented a small house on Calle Bernardo Vázquez— a private home in a sleepy residential section of Mazatlán—so we could set up our base of operations discreetly, away from any of Chapo's *halcones*.

When Brady and I reached Mazatlán and walked into the

house, we nearly tripped over all the piles of tactical gear littering the floor. Everyone was in high spirits. Loud laughter boomed in the living room, and someone had just ordered a pizza. Several marines were lounging around on the couches, watching TV, and a few more were sitting around the kitchen table with Leroy and his team of marshals.

Leroy got up and motioned for Brady and me to follow him to a quiet corner of the house.

"How confident are you that Chapo's with this Top-Tier device?" Leroy said.

"One hundred percent," I said.

"How can you be so sure?"

"Condor types most of the messages," I said. "But sometimes Chapo picks up the BlackBerry and types them himself."

"How do you know?"

"Chapo spells like a kindergartener, he doesn't know how," Brady said.

"Like this message—just came in an hour ago." I handed my BlackBerry over to Leroy and showed him the screen. "Chapo's talking about a house he's planning to move to. Look at the spelling."

Sy pero no tyene pura kosyna mannan en la mana le pone mynysply

I translated aloud.

"'Yes, but it doesn't have a full kitchen. Tomorrow morning he'll put in a mini . . . supply'? Mini-something—who the hell knows what he's typing there? But you see the way he spells 'kitchen,' *cocina*?"

"Yeah, '*kosyna*,'" Leroy said, nodding.

With Chapo's writing, I explained, there was a consistent substitution of *y* for *i* and *k* for *c*. Guzmán would write *bien* as *byen* and *cuanto* as *kuanto*. This wasn't typical Spanish texting slang or shorthand; it was unique to Chapo. He typed virtually every word phonetically. And his messages were peppered with self-taught constructions. Even as elementary a word as *caliente*—Chapo spelled it *kalyente*. These were clear forensic tells—Chapo, not his secretary, was fat-fingering these messages.

"So you're positive he's in the room with the device we're locating," Leroy said.

I grabbed the one war trophy I'd been carrying and pulled the black hat down tight on my head.

"Yep, I'm positive, El Roy. An hour ago, when this message was written—*kitchen* spelled like that—the BlackBerry was directly in Chapo's hands."

The pizza had arrived, and everyone was grabbing slices, but I had no time to eat. My bosses back in Mexico City had arranged for us to use three of DEA's armored Suburbans—this time brand-new ones, the best in our fleet. I left Nico in charge at the house.

"When Tigre arrives," I said, "get with him and come up with a plan for the takedown. Brady and I need to run into town and grab these rigs. When I get back, we'll finalize everything for the capture."

"You got it," Nico said.

IT WAS 12:30 A.M. when Brady and I walked back into the house. Every single one of the young marines was fast asleep. Leroy and his guys were passed out on the couch and floor, too—there were no blankets or pillows, just a bunch of bodies sprawled out on the bare tile. Even Nico had crashed upstairs in one of the beds.

"I know everyone's tired," I said to Brady, "but c'mon, for fuck's sake . . ."

Here we were, about to go grab the world's most wanted man, and everyone was racked out?

"Get up!" I said, shaking Nico. "How'd the meet go with Tigre?"

Nico opened his eyes, still half-dazed.

"The meet with Tigre," I repeated. "What was his takedown plan?"

"He never showed up."

"What do you mean?"

"He never showed."

"Where the hell is he?"

"He's staying with a group of his guys at some shitty motel on the outskirts of town."

"Fuck!" I shouted. "If he has a plan, what good is it if *we* don't know it? Get up, dude—we need to find him now."

Brady and Nico jumped into the Suburban, and after a twenty-minute drive I snaked the vehicle back through several winding alleys, screeching to a stop near the motel's check-in office.

"Look at this dump," said Brady. "Red neon lights and garages."

This was the kind of place the locals took their hookers to for an hour or two. Each room even came equipped with a garage so you could discreetly hide your car for the duration of your stay.

"What room is Tigre in?" I asked Nico.

"Don't know," Nico said. "He's not answering his phone."

"Let's just start banging on the fucking doors."

I was already beginning to miss Captain Toro: now we were rolling with a cadre of very young marines—all in their twenties—

full of energy and experience but lacking Toro's coolheaded focus and leadership.

We needed to communicate, coordinate, lay out a thorough takedown plan—one that allowed for any contingency or screwup. I felt like everyone was running a little on the wild side. This was too improvised.

We all split up and started knocking on doors. We startled two shady-looking locals and woke up groups of groggy marines, sharing tiny rooms, trying to grab a couple of minutes of shut-eye.

We found Tigre in the last room of the motel. We'd clearly woken him from a deep sleep, but he was awake enough to take us into the adjacent garage, where we could speak more privately.

"Carnal," I said. "If you have a plan, we don't know it."

"Of course we have a plan," Tigre said, shaking off the cobwebs. "We've done this many times before."

"Tigre, I'm worried about our manpower and perimeter," I said. "And why is Chapo holed up at the Miramar? I'm sure he knows every floor plan, staircase, and exits to the street; we don't know any of it. How many guys do you have?"

"I've got forty marines here," Tigre said. "We'll flood the hotel and put a couple of *rápidas* on the perimeter—"

"No, that's not enough!" I cut him short. I realized that to Tigre this was just another hit, another door to smash. He and the other marines were almost numb to it now; they'd been doing these hits day after day in Culiacán, and predawn raids had become routine.

"We need more men on the perimeter," I said. Brady nodded in agreement. "And as many guys as you can get inside."

"We've got another brigade down the street," Tigre said. "As soon as we get the green light, I'll call them in."

"How many men?"

"I'll have another thirty marines in fifteen minutes. Then thirty more after that."

"Fine," I said. "Sixty extra men should do it. And where are the helos? We're gonna need air support in case he manages to escape the perimeter."

"The helos are two hours away," Tigre said.

"No, that's not gonna work," I said. "We need them closer."

"I'll move them down to Culiacán. Once we give the green light, it will take them an hour to fly down."

"Perfect," I said. "Stage them there. We don't want them any closer than that. The movements may spook him."

"*Claro*," Tigre said.

"Show me where you're placing *rápidas* on the perimeter," I said, pointing to the Google Earth view of the Hotel Miramar on Tigre's iPad. Tigre said he had only three *rápidas* for the capture op.

"Only three?" I asked. "How do you see us moving in?"

"We'll use your vehicles and fill them with my guys. We'll ride right up to the front gate of the hotel and enter from there."

"Fine," I said, finally exhaling a bit.

"Meet back here at oh-five-hundred hours, ready to go," Tigre said.

IT WAS JUST AFTER 3 A.M. when we left Tigre and headed back to the rental house. Nico and Brady walked upstairs to rest.

I was too wound up to sleep, and everyone had to be awake in an hour anyway. I sat down at the kitchen table and studied the block around the Hotel Miramar on my MacBook over and over. I didn't want to leave a single detail of the op to chance. We'd have the front entrance covered, but I was still worried about Chapo slipping out a back or side door and into a vehicle on Avenida Cruz Lizarraga, behind the hotel.

What if he'd worked something out long in advance with Kava? What if they'd constructed one of their hydraulic tunnel entrances in a room on the ground floor of the hotel? Or had some other way to access the sewer system directly from the hotel basement? A manhole or drain somewhere out in the street?

I'd been wearing Chapo's black hat so long that the brim was sweaty and sticky, and I could feel my forehead starting to break out. Finally I grabbed a slice of pizza and quickly typed an update for my group supervisor back at the embassy in Mexico City.

2/22/14, 3:33:05 AM: ANDREW HOGAN TO GROUP SUPERVISOR ██████████████: 23.226827-106.427935 targ loc hitting door at 0530—he's there

I hit SEND, took a bite of pizza, and felt my anxiety slowly dissipate. I even managed to crack a smile at my reflection in the screen of the laptop, my sleepless eyes beneath Chapo's crazy-ass black hat.

My thoughts turned to Diego, probably fast asleep back in Phoenix. I knew my old partner would have given anything to be right there in Mazatlán, prepping to make the predawn capture raid on El Niño de la Tuna . . .

Cuando nació preguntó la partera
Le dijo como le van a poner?
Por apellido él será Guzmán Loera
Y se llamará Joaquín . . .

I started to text him but stopped midsentence: no need to wake him.

I looked down at the clock on my laptop. It was 4:00 a.m. sharp.

"Despiértate!" I shouted, getting up from the kitchen table. *"Despiértate!"* I walked around the house, yelling for everyone to wake up, flipping on the lights and ripping off blankets.

"It's go time, guys! Up! Up! Get up!"

PITCH-DARK: 4:58 A.M. I took a deep breath and jumped into the driver's seat of the white Chevy Suburban, now loaded up with marines who were all armed with AR-15s—Tigre rode shotgun. I glanced in the rearview mirror at Brady, who was in the driver's seat of another white Suburban, loaded up with his own crew of marines— together we formed the entry team, with Tigre and me leading the way down to the strip of hotels and condos on the Malecón, the thirteen-mile-long boardwalk of Mazatlán.

We sat, waiting for the green light from Leroy, Nico, and their SEMAR crews. The phone-finding and security teams were looking for final confirmation that the Top-Tier BlackBerry was indeed still at the Hotel Miramar.

Sitting in the idling Suburban, I typed out a quick message to my father back in Kansas.

"Going in hot."

Just then, Tigre's radio squelched. I heard the words we'd all been waiting for:

Luz Verde.

"Vamos," Tigre said. I threw the Suburban into drive, ripped out of the parking lot, and took off down the desolate highway.

No one in the rig said a word. All the marines were quiet, checking their guns, focused on the mission. En route, we were joined by three *rápidas,* and together we sped in a tight convoy down Mexican Federal Highway 15 into the heart of Mazatlán.

In just under eight minutes the convoy was on the Malecón, but as I went to make a left turn onto Avenida del Mar, I was blocked by a squad car from the municipal police department: red-and-blues flashing, a cop in a long-sleeved white uniform shirt and navy cap behind the wheel, hand up, gesturing for me to stop.

"Not a fucking chance," I said to Tigre.

I wheeled the Suburban up onto the curb and swung around the cop car, missing the front bumper by a couple of inches. Then I saw that there were more red-and-blue lights, at least five or six municipal police cars up and down the Malecón, blocking the street.

Dirty fucking cops? They knew we were coming?

Tigre betrayed no emotion. I grabbed the steering wheel tighter as I hammered the gas toward the entrance of the hotel, glancing down at the FN Herstal Five-Seven pistol tucked into my waistband.

Could the operation be blown? If so, Bravo will be on the Malecón any second with an army of enforcers, ready for a gunfight. They'll have AKs, hand grenades, RPGs, and all I've got is this Belgian peashooter . . .

I jockeyed the nose of the Suburban in front of the hotel's gate. Surprisingly, the gate was wide open. I saw Brady jumping out of his own Chevy, running hard, disappearing around the back. I knew he was covering the hotel's four-foot wall because he was also worried about Chapo escaping out the back door. Another Cabo San Lucas debacle wasn't going to happen under Brady's and my watch.

Brady grabbed two young marines who were standing near, split them up, and positioned them to watch the wall and the parking garage exit. Once they were in position, Brady went into the lobby just as three marines were grabbing the watchman, searching for hotel room keys behind the desk. Tigre and his men had already made their way inside.

I was standing out front near the pool, with a view of the front of the hotel, my FN Five-Seven aimed at the dark, empty lot to the south as I continued to scan the shadows.

As much as I wanted to be inside smashing doors with Tigre, I knew I needed to make sure our perimeter was tight. I wasn't going to rely on anyone else. Was it completely covered?

Dammit—we need more guys posted back there . . .

Just then, Leroy appeared, walking from the hotel out toward the street.

What the hell is he doing? I said to myself. *He should be inside by now, trying to pin a door.*

Leroy walked out onto the Malecón and pointed up toward the hotel.

He looked at me, then back up toward the front of the hotel.

"Fourth floor," Leroy said. "I'm getting a strong signal on this north end."

Then he gestured with his hands and disappeared quickly back inside the Miramar lobby.

Within minutes, a few lights were flickering on—room by room, floor by floor, the hotel was coming aglow.

Good, we're finally getting somewhere.

I couldn't take it any longer; too much time had passed. If Chapo was planning an escape, he had to be doing it at this very moment.

I began jogging down the hotel ramp to the street—to physically run the perimeter myself, double-checking that enough marines had the sides and back covered—when I heard another loud squelch.

Then Spanish chatter over the radio:

"Ya tenemos el blanco!" I ran up the ramp to Nico, who was holding the radio tight to his ear. "They have the target in custody! They got him!" Nico said.

Another radio squelch:

"Dame un blindado!"

"They need an armored vehicle right now!"

I couldn't hear anything after that echo—*dame un blindado!*—and then there was a piercing silence and I turned, running fast to my Suburban . . .

Pistol in my right hand, I sprinted as fast as I'd ever run anywhere in my life.

I threw the Suburban into drive and gunned it down the ramp into the Miramar's underground parking garage. Three marines were on the ramp, waving me on.

Vamos! Vamos! Vamos!

It was too dark to see anything clearly underground, but knowing that the marines were about to extract Chapo, I immediately repositioned the Suburban, angling the Chevy precisely so it would be ready to exit quickly.

Like clockwork, three more marines emerged, standing up a shirtless man who'd been splayed out on the floor. I could see only a dark silhouette and a brief flash of white skin. He had his hands cuffed behind his back, no blindfold on his face, as they yanked him up off the ground, leading him forward by the silver elevator doors.

The prisoner was short and bare-chested, but I still couldn't make out his face through the thick tinted bulletproof glass of the Suburban; the skin of the man's chest grew increasing pale under the glare of more flashlights.

I jumped out of the driver's seat, still wearing that black hat and balaclava, and ran up to the prisoner.

I stopped abruptly in front of him.

We were face-to-face at last.

I couldn't resist:

"What's up, *Chapo-o-o-o*!?"

How strange it must have been for this drug lord to see someone wearing one of his *own* black hats. Guzmán's eyes bulged, then he hunched one shoulder, flinching, as if he thought he was going to be slugged.

I stared at him, and Chapo held my gaze—just for a moment. There was no mistaking it now: I had my man. That usually fastidious hair—jet black—was greasy, messed up; there was the trademark thick black mustache, and skin so pale it was nearly translucent from all those years of living without daylight, stuck in his rat's world of holes and tubes. Chapo had on black Adidas track pants—they were low-slung, just barely clinging to his hip bones, and they exposed a firm, if Buddha-like, potbelly.

As the marines walked him toward the Suburban, I slapped him on the back—not hard, just an *attaboy!* whack like I once did to my brother, Brandt, after a touchdown, or with Diego after we'd closed some big UC deal.

I pulled my hand back, wet with his sweat. Chapo's back felt like it had been slathered with suntan oil. He probably hadn't showered in days. I hopped into the driver's seat of my Suburban while Chapo was pushed into the rear center seat, flanked by two marines. They'd periodically question him and he'd respond with an almost robotic-sounding *"Está bien—está bien . . ."*

I turned suddenly: *"Mira!"*

Chapo answered me calmly, deferentially:

"Sí, señor?"

I snapped three quick photos on my iPhone.

I spun back around in the driver's seat, transmission in park, foot revving the gas pedal, ready to rock.

Only then did it strike me: we had no exit strategy. The past few weeks had been all about the hunt; we never fully planned for the contingency of having Chapo cuffed and in custody.

Well, I'm going to have to drive this fucker 1,016 kilometers—some twelve straight hours—to Mexico City. Difficult—but doable . . .

But then I got out of the Suburban, knowing that it was far too dangerous for any American agent: a vehicle carrying Chapo Guzmán would be a moving target anywhere in Mexico. One of the SEMAR officers would have to drive.

I turned around, spotting Brady for the first time since we'd arrived at the front of the hotel. We hugged.

"Un-fuckin'-believable!" Brady was shouting, tears welling up in his eyes.

I had never seen him get truly emotional about anything. Brady's usual scowl was now transformed into a broad smile.

I WALKED WITH BRADY from the parking deck up to the street. He was saying something, but I couldn't even hear him; I was still overcome.

We stepped out onto the curb beneath the Miramar sign. The warm ocean breeze swept across my face and slowly began to break my trance. The leaves of the palms whipped in the wind overhead. I turned, bear-hugging Nico, and then Leroy. Both men, along with Leroy's entire marshals team, had been instrumental in the hunt during these final weeks.

I looked up into the dawn sky: the pitch-blackness lightening to a hue of dark blue. I took a long, deep breath, spinning around in the middle of the street, my vision only now coming into full focus.

My family back in Mexico City . . . I hadn't called since that delirious conversation when I was lying flat on my back in Chapo's driveway.

My first text was to my wife.

"Got him, baby."

"No way!"

"Yeah, it's done."

"Coming home?"

"Yes."

"When?"

"Not sure. Very soon."

The darkness was quickly breaking as the sun started to peek over the Sierra Madre to the east. I heard the welcome sound of SEMAR's MI-17 helicopter, far off to the north, a rumble like the thunder of horses' hooves growing ever closer.

QUÉ SIGUE?

BRADY AND I WALKED down the long sidewalk on SEMAR's Mazatlán base toward the interview room. Chino stood there, chest puffed out; he wore a blank expression, and now, for some reason, he was blocking us.

"By order of the secretary of the navy, I can't let anyone in here," Chino said dryly.

"Come on, brother," I said. "After all we've been through?"

"Orders come directly from the secretary of the navy." Chino kept up the dead-eyed stare, then, turning on his boot heel, shut the door.

Brady and I paced outside until the door cracked open.

It was Tigre, gesturing for us to sneak inside.

I saw Chapo seated on a sofa in a clean short-sleeved navy-blue polo shirt. His entire face above the nostrils was wrapped up, mummy-like, in white gauze.

Chapo was talking in a normal tone of voice, no trace of fear or anger, but it was clear that his spirit was deflated. I recognized the voice immediately from my verified recordings; it was a voice I had listened to so many times I'd often dreamed about it.

Now the voice had a strange high pitch to it. Not stress—not exhaustion. Relief, perhaps? The realization that the thirteen-year hunt was, at long last, over?

The interrogation was being conducted with candor and respect. Chino was asking the questions in Spanish.

Chapo began by calmly stating his full name.

"Joaquín Archivaldo Guzmán Loera."

"Date of birth?"

"Fourth of April, 1957."

"Where were you born?"

"La Tuna. El Municipio de Badiraguato, Sinaloa."

I stood back in wonder: I'd written out that full name, date of birth, and town so many times—in my DEA sixes, case updates, PowerPoint presentations—that it had somehow become an extension of myself. I knew it as well as my own Social Security number. Now to hear it all confirmed—in the twangy mountain accent of the squat little man himself—seemed surreal.

Guzmán was no ghost, no myth, no invincible kingpin. He was a captured criminal, like any other, a flesh-and-blood crook, his eyes wrapped in white gauze. He was sitting right there on a sofa, not more than six feet away from me, stating that he had severe tooth pain and recently had had one of his molars fixed.

Chino asked who Guzmán's key operational lieutenant was in the United States.

Chapo paused. "I don't have one," he said finally.

I nodded at Brady; this was backed up by our own intel.

Chino asked him how much weight he was moving from the south. I remember Guzmán saying that his cocaine shipments were between four hundred and eight hundred kilograms at a time. I nodded again. We knew Chapo was being straightforward—gone were the days of the massive multi-ton shipments of blow from South America.

Chino asked how long Chapo had been living in Culiacán.

"Not long. A couple of weeks."

Brady and I looked at each other. That was a bald-faced lie.

Chino said something about the "business" not being what it used to be.

"*Claro que sí,*" Chapo said. "There's no respect anymore. I do my own thing. This business now, it's tough. Really tough."

BRADY AND I LEFT the interrogation room, walking out onto the tarmac toward the waiting MI-17 and Black Hawk; we huddled up with Tigre and a group of marines who'd been part of the takedown team, and for the first time I heard the details of what had happened hours earlier that morning on the fourth floor of Hotel Miramar:

When the marines busted through the door of Room 401, Chapo's first line of defense had been Condor. SEMAR quickly apprehended him, then stormed through the two-bedroom suite. In one bedroom they found two women: Chapo's cook, Lucia, and the nanny, Vero, fast asleep with Guzmán's two-year-old twin daughters. The marines raced to the larger bedroom in the back, where they discovered Emma Coronel, Chapo's young wife, who had just awoken.

Chapo had jumped out of bed in his underwear and run into a small bathroom, armed with an assault rifle. As Emma screamed, "Don't kill him! Don't kill him!" Guzmán dropped the gun, offering his empty hands through the bathroom doorway. They took

Chapo down without a single shot being fired and brought him down the service elevator to the parking garage.

Now I watched as Brady helped some of the marines carry some of Chapo's family from the Chevy Captiva toward the building in which Chapo was being held.

I walked a little further down the road and saw Condor—we'd identified him as Carlos Manuel Hoo Ramírez—lying in the bed of a pickup truck, handcuffed, his eyes wrapped with gauze like Chapo.

I recognized him as the same man in the photograph we'd found in his house in Culiacán. I pulled out my iPhone and took a shot of the tattoo on his calf: a condor's head. Then I walked down and saw Emma, the cook, and the nanny sitting handcuffed inside another vehicle, their eyes blindfolded, too.

Brady and I continued to hug and congratulate every marine we came across on the base. At some point I realized I was still carrying Tigre's pistol tucked into the front of my BDU pants.

"*Gracias, carnal,*" I said, handing back the black FN Five-Seven to Tigre. I couldn't believe that no one had to fire a shot during the entire operation. Tigre took the pistol and slid it back in his thigh holster.

"*Tu lo hiciste,*" Tigre replied with a grin. "You did it."

Even Admiral Garra managed to crack a small smile when I congratulated him later.

Eventually, Nico, Chino, Chiqui, and several other marines led Chapo, handcuffed, his eyes still wrapped in gauze, out of the interrogation room and placed him inside the Black Hawk. The rotors whipped up clouds of dust and grit; I shielded my eyes with one hand as the helo lifted off the pavement en route to the Mazatlán International Airport, where Chapo was to be flown immediately by Learjet, accompanied by Admiral Furia, to Mexico City, where he would be paraded in front of the world's press.

MOMENTS AFTER CHAPO'S DEPARTURE, Brady and I boarded an MI-17 and took off for a low-altitude flight down the Pacific coastline. Both sets of helo pilots and their crews were SEMAR's best and had been with the brigade since we began in La Paz—Brady and I respected them as core members of our team.

"No such thing as 'crew rest' with these guys," I said to Brady. They were ready to fly their birds anywhere, under any condition, and on a moment's notice.

The pilots swung the MI-17 down low, cruising just above the surface of the ocean, so close that I could see the crests of the waves clearly and felt like I could almost reach my hand out the open window and touch the water. Tourists swimming near the beach were ducking and diving as if the MI were about to strafe them.

After the joyride, we touched down at the Mazatlán airport, from which Chapo had flown out only minutes earlier on the jet.

I knew this was likely the last time I'd see any of these marines. I felt like I was leaving a group of my own brothers—these Mexican warriors had done *everything* to keep all of us American personnel safe.

It was all I'd known for weeks: eating, sleeping, making predawn raids together. Returning to DEA now felt as foreign as the entry to Culiacán had.

I hugged Brady one last time.

And it hit me suddenly—I guess it was a mixture of gratitude and sadness—that I was losing a partner. I could never have accomplished any of this—I would never have come close to taking Chapo into custody—without Brady and his entire team of HSI agents, supervisors, and translators back at the war room in El Paso.

"You tell Joe and Neil they just made history," I said.

"Yes, they did," said Brady.

"Safe travels, brother."

"Whatever happens, we'll always have each other's back—deal?"

"Deal."

The props began to spin on the DEA's King Air. One of the pilots called out to me that we were ready to roll. I waved one last good-bye to the group of marines standing on the runway and ducked my head as I boarded the plane.

I was alone now in the dark cabin as the King Air ascended into the sky. I watched out the window as the marines down below grew smaller, and then the coast of Mazatlán disappeared finally into the distance.

I WAS MET IN Mexico City on the runway by Regional Director McAllister, my assistant regional director, and my group supervisor, who congratulated me on a job well done. It was because of the three of them that I had been allowed to run the investigation—as I knew how—from beginning to end. They'd given me the latitude and time, and it had resulted in a tremendous win for all of us at DEA.

And Camila Defusio, the deputy US attorney in Washington, DC—along with her small team of assistant US attorneys—had ensured that the judicial process never hindered the operation.

Don Dominguez, back at SOD, and his staff, including the group of intel analysts in Mexico City, had also been behind-the-scenes heroes of the capture.

MY BOSSES DROVE STRAIGHT to my La Condesa apartment, where I walked in and hugged my wife and sons.

I wiped a tear from my cheek, thankful to be home, then sat down at the kitchen table. The rustic SEMAR meals had been satisfying, but they were nothing like a home-cooked dinner prepared by my wife. We barely said a word at the table as we ate slowly. We were just grateful to be together again.

The next morning, I went with my wife and sons on a bike ride through the city, just as we usually did on the weekend. Paseo de la Reforma was closed to cars on Sundays and was swarming with bicyclists, runners, walkers, and rollerbladers.

On the newspaper stands, every paper—*Reforma, Excélsior, El Universal, Milenio*—had Chapo's face plastered on the front and banner headlines.

CAPTURAN A EL CHAPO!
CAYÓ!
AGARRAN A EL CHAPO!
POR FIN!
CAE EL CHAPO!

To stand there on Paseo de la Reforma, buying those papers like a local, after all the weeks I'd spent embedded with SEMAR, was like living in another life. I bought all of them and stuffed them in the front basket of my Raleigh. I was struck by the eerie sense of being covert again, chameleon-like, blending in with the bustling crowd. No one snatching up copies of the newspapers could have suspected that the blond-bearded cyclist in a V-neck cotton shirt, shorts, and *chanclas* had been at the heart of the hunt, that only hours earlier I was the agent who led the capture of the most wanted criminal in the world.

THE NEXT MORNING, I put on my suit, knotted my tie—like on any typical Monday—and drove to the embassy in my armored Tahoe.

But as I walked the halls, I felt like a zombie: my body was present, but my mind was not. I walked back to my desk and heard another agent talking about pinging phones of targets in his own trafficking investigation. I felt unsteady, and the office seemed to rock. I felt a sudden blood-pressure drop, and a queasiness, as if I were going to throw up right there on my desk.

I'd been expecting to feel euphoric after the Chapo capture, but I felt the opposite. Over the next few days, I tried to shake it off, but the void only deepened.

SINCE HIS CAPTURE in February, Chapo had been interviewed at the Mexican Attorney General's Office (PGR) before being locked up in the country's most secure prison, Federal Social Readaptation Center No. 1 (Altiplano), in central Mexico, not far from Toluca.

I later heard a story about a remarkable exchange between PGR lawyers and Guzmán. Interrogators apparently said they could now close out the estimated thirteen thousand homicides credited to Chapo.

"*Thirteen* thousand?" I was told Chapo responded, seeming

genuinely surprised. "No, not thirteen thousand. Maybe *a couple thousand . . .*"

Whatever the body count, Guzmán was supposedly now no longer a threat: the authorities assured the public that he was under twenty-four-hour video surveillance at Altiplano. The maximum-security prison housed Mexico's most violent and notorious narco-traffickers and was considered escape-proof.

Guzmán was behind bars, but there was still more bloodshed back on his home turf. On April 10, 2014, I picked up one of the local papers and read that the body of Manuel Alejandro Aponte Gómez—Bravo—had been found dumped on a dirt road near La Cruz de Elota, Sinaloa. Bravo had reportedly been tortured before being shot several times, and had been killed along with two of his associates. No one knew for sure, but street rumor quickly spread that Bravo had died for the unpardonable mistake of not properly protecting his boss while he was on the run in Mazatlán.

SEVERAL DAYS LATER, after the murder of Bravo, I flew with Tom McAllister and my group supervisor to Washington, DC. There I briefed DEA Administrator Michele Leonhart and her top brass at headquarters in Arlington, Virginia. The briefing room was standing room only as, slide by slide, I walked through the details of the operation. Leonhart concluded by congratulating me and our entire team on the capture of Chapo.

"I've been with DEA a long time," said the special agent in charge of SOD, "and this has got to be the best case I've seen in my career."

Immediately afterwards, I jumped in a black armored Suburban with Administrator Leonhart and rode in her motorcade across the

Potomac River to the United States Department of Justice building to brief US Attorney General Eric Holder.

"This was Bobby Kennedy's office when he was AG," one of Holder's aides told me as we entered. I glanced up at the painting of Kennedy, wearing a bomber jacket, hanging on the wall alongside other former attorneys general.

I shook AG Holder's hand and could immediately sense his sincerity and his genuine interest about the details of the operation. McAllister took him through my presentation while I highlighted the story with details from the weeks on the ground in Sinaloa— from our discovery of the Duck Dynasty hideaway through the days of smashing down doors in Culiacán, right up to the predawn face-to-face capture at the Hotel Miramar.

The attorney general asked about Chapo's first escape through the bathtub tunnels.

"Well, we knew he had a tunnel, sir," I said. "But not under *every* house."

"How many houses were there?"

"He had five safe houses in Culiacán," I said. "And they were all connected through the sewers."

Holder was impressed by the persistent hunt and inquired about how we'd been able to sustain our operations until the very end.

"We used Chapo's homes as bases," I explained. "We essentially turned them into makeshift barracks, all of us living on top of each other. We cooked in his kitchen. Slept in his beds."

At the end of the thirty-minute briefing, Attorney General Holder expressed his official thanks on behalf of the Obama administration and the American people for bringing Guzmán to justice. He said this would go down as one of the greatest achievements of the administration.

"So what do you do now?" Holder asked.

I stared at him—not fully understanding—and then Holder added:

"Seriously, what do you do *next*? Take some time off and drink mai tais on the beach?"

Everyone in the room laughed.

"That's what I'm still trying to figure out, sir," I said.

WHAT *COULD* I DO NEXT? The AG's question kept resonating in my mind as I returned to Mexico City. Back at the embassy, I still felt that aching hollowness—and it wasn't subsiding.

Qué sigue?

I'd achieved the greatest challenge possible as a drug enforcement agent, and I realized there was nothing left for me to do at DEA. I had nothing left to give. I couldn't go back to tracking down some lesser trafficker—pinging phones, debriefing sources, gathering intel, crunching numbers—here in Mexico, or in any other country, for that matter.

In my world—among all of DEA's international targets—who was *bigger* than Chapo Guzmán?

In fact, the past few years had *never* been about Chapo; they had only been about the hunt, and now the hunt was over.

I ALSO HAD TO consider the risk to my wife and young sons, exposed as we all were in the heart of Mexico. No one had assigned us any added security or made plans for us to catch the next plane out of the country.

That came with the gig: you take down a drug trafficker—even one as infamous as Chapo Guzmán—and it's back to business as usual.

But no matter how hard I tried, I couldn't stop hearing that phrase echoing constantly in my ears:

"Everything is fine in Mexico until suddenly it's not."

With the security concern and the strong desire to pursue *another* challenge—my next hunt—less than nine months after the capture, I resigned from the DEA, boarded a flight with my wife and sons, and disappeared as fast as Chapo had escaped from me in Culiacán.

EPILOGUE: SHADOWS

AT ALTIPLANO PRISON, on Saturday, July 11, 2015, at exactly 8:52 p.m., Chapo Guzmán could be seen on the overhead surveillance video taking a seat on his narrow bed, changing shoes, then quickly ducking into the shower stall in the corner of his cell. He disappeared behind the low wall separating the shower from his cell, the only spot in the five-by-six-foot prison cell hidden from cameras.

Then he vanished from view and was gone, disappearing into a twenty-inch-square opening that had been cut into the floor. He squeezed into a narrow vertical shaft to the tunnel below, climbed down a ladder, and entered a sophisticated tunnel nearly a mile long. Electric lights had been hung from the ceiling, as had PVC pipe, which pumped fresh air the length of the passageway. Chapo Guzmán's latest tunnel had A/C.

Metal tracks had also been laid the entire length of the tunnel so that an ingenious getaway vehicle—a railcar rigged to the frame of a small modified motorcycle—could be driven rapidly by the escapee. The walls were only about thirty inches apart, jagged and unshored—and barely wide enough for Chapo's shoulders.

The tunnel began beneath a ramshackle cinder-block house, still under construction, in the nearby town of Santa Juana. By the time the prison alarm sounded and a massive search began, Chapo Guzmán was once again in the wind.

THE AUDACITY OF CHAPO'S escape plan—to have his chief tunnelers, most likely Kava and his crew, dig right up under the most secure prison in Mexico—shocked the world. But the method was certainly no mystery to me or anyone else who'd studied Chapo for years. As with Chapo's breakout from Puente Grande back in 2001, the escape came with that other Guzmán hallmark: layers of corruption and bribery.

The official Mexican version of events was quickly dismissed as a farce. Reports of loud drilling in concrete had gone unheeded; the supposed blind spot on the video surveillance turned out to be merely a case of prison staff selectively ignoring the activities in his cell.

In the moments before his escape, Chapo—appearing fidgety and anxious—repeatedly goes over to the shower area to check on activity behind the short wall, and even bends down, apparently to help pry something open. The video also appears to show an iPad lying near Guzmán's bed, despite the fact that cell phones, tablets, and other electronic devices are specifically banned in the prison.

According to a review conducted months later by the Mexican Congressional Bicameral Commission on National Security, Chapo had never been treated like a typical inmate at Altiplano. In the seventeen months he spent there, he'd been granted extraordinary privileges, receiving 272 visits from his lawyers alone, as well as 18 family visits and 46 conjugal visits. Perhaps the most sensational of these latter visits was a reported New Year's Eve rendezvous with a local Sinaloa politician, a young female deputy from the National

Action Party named Lucero Sánchez López, who was accused of sneaking into the prison with false documents and spending the night with Guzmán. Sánchez forcefully denied these charges, but was nonetheless stripped of her parliamentary immunity.

On June 21, 2017, Sánchez was arrested by US federal agents at the Otay Mesa Cross Border Xpress—the bridge connecting Tijuana's A. L. Rodríguez International Airport with San Diego—and the next day the former legislator was charged in California federal court with conspiracy to distribute cocaine. After the capture, and reviewing information from the line sheets, Brady and I suspected that Sánchez was the same "girlfriend" who Picudo had told us escaped through the tunnel and sewer with Chapo in Culiacán just before we arrived at his safe house.*

Upon his escape, Guzmán again catapulted back to the status of world's most wanted fugitive. Interpol issued a "Red Notice" for his immediate arrest. There were sightings of Chapo reported via Twitter, of him supposedly enjoying himself at an outdoor café in Costa Rica. Some rumors were laughably far-fetched: Guzmán was reported to have traveled as far south as Patagonia, Argentina, where witnesses claimed to have seen him in a "sweet shop"—police and military units were on high alert that he was traveling in the Andes, on the verge of crossing the border into Chile.

In truth, Chapo had never left the comfort zone of his own mountain home.

---

* The complaint filed against Sánchez alleges that she has continued to deny reports that she was Guzmán's lover. However, in a probable-cause affidavit attached to the federal criminal complaint, a cartel member cooperating with US investigators alleged that Sánchez was indeed Guzmán's long-standing girlfriend, and that she'd admitted to having fled with Chapo through the tunnel on February 17, 2014, moments before SEMAR entered the drug lord's safe house in Culiacán.

FROM THE MOMENT the news broke of Chapo's escape, an intense manhunt commenced. Admiral Furia and his Mexico City–based SEMAR brigade took the lead once again, using our operational blueprint and years' worth of intelligence as their guide. SEMAR, working in conjunction with PGR and the Mexican Federal Police, arrested Araña, Chapo's most trusted pilot, who was suspected of flying the kingpin up to the Sierra Madre of Sinaloa immediately after his escape from Altiplano.

Guzmán, no doubt feeling more untouchable than ever after the brazen breakout, didn't even bother switching up his telecommunications system. He may no longer have had Condor to act as his faithful secretary, but Mexican authorities were able to intercept BlackBerry PIN messages of Chapo's closest associates—just as we had done for months.

During his time hiding out in the mountains, Kate del Castillo—the star of Guzmán's favorite telenovela, *La Reina del Sur*—resurfaced and was communicating with Chapo through various BlackBerry mirror devices. Even as a fugitive, Chapo was still seeking to have his life story told on the big screen—just as he had done with Alex Cifuentes back in October 2013. Chapo was also still clearly infatuated with Kate, so thrilled to meet her that he almost disregarded those who planned to come with her, including actor Sean Penn—Chapo had never even heard of the Hollywood star—but Kate assured him that Penn could facilitate the production of Chapo's movie.

Chapo's narcissism unwittingly led him into a trap—a variation of the *Argo*-style operation Brady and I had strategized two years earlier. On October 2, 2015, Guzmán agreed to a face-to face meeting with Castillo, Penn, and several others at a secluded location high in the Sierra Madre, along the Sinaloa-Durango border. As reported in the Mexican media, Mexican authorities already had Castillo, Penn, and Chapo's lawyers under surveillance the entire time. The meeting was reportedly a tequila-fueled dinner and sit-down with Kate's Hollywood friends to develop his life story. Sean Penn, it turned out, was playing the role of journalist, on assignment from *Rolling Stone* to write an exclusive article. When it was published later ("El Chapo Speaks"), Guzmán said little of note. The meandering ten-thousand-word, first-person account was widely derided as self-indulgent and naive, and it got particular heat for the arrangement *Rolling Stone* had agreed to in which Guzmán—or more likely his attorneys—got approval over the final copy.

According to Castillo, after dinner Guzmán had departed abruptly; he'd said it wasn't safe for him to stay overnight at the same location as his guests. Several days later, SEMAR conducted helicopter raids in some of the mountain villages outside Tamazula, Durango, but were caught in a hail of gunfire from Chapo's security men on the ground. Once SEMAR finally made entry into one of the homes near Tamazula, they discovered BlackBerrys, medications, and two-way radios. Once again, Chapo had escaped by mere moments out the back, down a steep hill and into a ravine, and was reported to have injured his face and leg.

With SEMAR forces closing in from the south, making dozens of raids in the tiny mountainous villages, where Chapo could typically hide without worry, he had no choice but to flee north through Sinaloa.

His network of safe houses in Culiacán was obviously no longer an option. And with Bravo dead, Chapo drove directly into the hands of the only chief enforcer left on his payroll, the feared Cholo Iván, up in Los Mochis. SEMAR continued to track Chapo the entire time, as he settled in on the Pacific coast, taking refuge in a comfortable safe house constructed on a design similar to the ones in Culiacán.

IN THE RAIN AND DARKNESS on Friday morning, January 8, 2016, SEMAR launched Operación Cisne Negro ("Black Swan"). Units of masked marines approached in *rápidas* with their headlights off, military helicopters hovering overhead, surrounding a white two-story house in a middle-class neighborhood of Los Mochis, where they'd confirmed that Chapo and Cholo Iván were hiding.

Around 4:30 a.m., SEMAR began their entry into the house through the front door and were met by immediate gunfire. The marines advanced slowly while tossing grenades and laying down heavy fire from their assault rifles. After more than twenty minutes of fighting, five of Chapo's gunmen lay dead, six were injured, and several would be arrested. Only one marine was wounded in the firefight.

But with the time it had taken SEMAR to gain access to the safe house, Chapo and Cholo Iván were long gone. A search of the house revealed two tunnels: one beneath the refrigerator, the other in a bedroom closet. A switch near a lightbulb activated a trapdoor behind the mirror, opening to an escape ladder and a passageway directly into the sewers of Los Mochis. It was Chapo's signature MO.

Once Chapo and Cholo Iván had reached the sewer—only one meter high, flooded due to the heavy overnight rains—they had to crawl slowly for blocks on their bellies through fetid water and human waste.

Less than an hour later, Chapo and Cholo Iván emerged from the sewer. The two fugitives forced open a square metal manhole but had trouble lifting the hinged cover, so they wedged in one of their shoes to prop it open. In the sewer, they left behind an AR-15 equipped with a grenade launcher.

Chapo's luck was running out. According to media reports, Chapo and Cholo Iván brandished their guns and carjacked a white Volkswagen Jetta after they emerged from the manhole in the street. But amazingly, the Jetta quickly broke down, and after driving only a few blocks, Chapo and Cholo Iván ditched the Volkswagen. At a traffic light, they carjacked a red Ford Focus, reportedly driven by a woman with her daughter and five-year-old grandson.

Six miles before they reached the town of Che Ríos, the Ford Focus was stopped by Federal Police. Cholo Iván exited the vehicle armed with a weapon, while Chapo was crouched in the backseat.

The media also reported that Chapo offered to reward the police with homes and businesses in Mexico and the United States and promised them to "forget about working for the rest of their lives." All they had to do was let him go. The cops refused the bribes and put Chapo and Cholo Iván into a patrol car.

The cops also snapped a photo and sent it to their superiors. It showed Chapo sitting in the back of the cop car, wearing a filthy tank top, next to shirtless, grim-faced Cholo Iván.

Authorities feared the arrival of more gunmen. To avoid a shoot-out, they drove Chapo and Cholo Iván to Hotel Doux, just outside Los Mochis, where they holed up in Room 51 until additional Federal Police and SEMAR arrived.

Chapo and Cholo Iván were then flown to Mexico City; Guzmán found himself back in Altiplano, the same maximum-security prison he'd tunneled out of the previous summer. Chapo's six months on the run—six months of embarrassment for the government of Mexico—had finally come to an end.

"Mission accomplished," President Enrique Peña Nieto announced on his Twitter account. "We've got him."

HOW COULD MEXICO POSSIBLY ensure that Chapo wouldn't attempt yet another escape from custody? Prison officials announced that security at Altiplano had been revamped for Guzmán's arrival. They cited the installation of hundreds of new surveillance cameras, motion sensors in air ducts and underground, and reinforced steel concrete floors. They also deployed dogs trained specifically to detect Chapo's distinct odor and would constantly move him between cells, followed closely by a team of guards.

Then, in the early-morning hours of Friday May 6, 2016, Chapo was transferred, without warning, to a prison outside Ciudad Juárez, reportedly due to its proximity to the border and to facilitate a rapid extradition to the United States. Chapo soon was complaining about the inhumane and unbearable conditions; his Juárez prison cell was so filthy that he'd asked for bleach to clean it himself. According to his lawyers and the report of the psychiatrist who visited him, the kingpin was badly deteriorating: he was "depressed and suffering hallucinations and memory loss because of harsh conditions in the prison where he is jailed."

Chapo told the doctor that "psychological torture" was being inflicted on him. Lights in his cell were kept on twenty-four hours a day, and his only human contact was with masked corrections officers. He also reported that he was being woken up every four hours to appear on camera for an inmate roll call. "They do not let me sleep," Chapo said, according to the psychiatrist's report. "Everything has become hell." Guzmán claimed to be taking a cocktail of thirteen pills daily—for pain, insomnia, and constipation. His sleep deprivation and hallucinations were so severe that he felt he was on the verge of death. "They have not beaten me," Chapo said. "But I would prefer that."

On October 24, 2016, Emma Coronel filed an official grievance with the National Human Rights Commission, alleging that the new prison conditions were inflicting "irreparable" psychological damage on her husband. She claimed that being confined in the Juárez prison would either kill Chapo or make him "go crazy" in a matter of months. She also complained that her conjugal visits with her husband had been reduced from four hours a week to only two hours.

Mexican officials denied that Guzmán's rights were being violated—he was being treated as a high-profile prisoner who'd made two previous prison escapes—and suggested that the reports of mistreatment were merely a legal strategy on the part of the cagey drug lord.

AND WHAT OF CHAPO'S status as arguably the most powerful narco-trafficker of all time? The truth was, Chapo's hold on his sprawling narcotics operations back in Sinaloa was beginning to crumble.

His most trusted sons—Iván, Alfredo, Güero, and Ratón—remained at large, but they did not command a modicum of the respect accorded their father. Many integral members of his inner circle were either dead—like Bravo—or in custody, like Condor, Cholo Iván, Picudo, and Araña.

Even Chapo's mother was no longer seen as untouchable. In mid-June 2016, it was reported that some 150 gunmen stormed into Guzmán's hometown of La Tuna, killing three people in the community and even looting Chapo's mother's home, stealing several vehicles. Eighty-six-year-old Consuelo Loera de Guzmán wasn't harmed, but the ransacking of her son's childhood home, the mountain hacienda at which Chapo had often taken refuge, was viewed as incontrovertible proof throughout the narco world that Guzmán no longer had power over his cartel.

Chapo was facing numerous legal cases in Mexico, primarily for drug trafficking and murder, but the government indicated they no longer had interest in prosecuting him at home; in early 2016, President Peña Nieto announced that he'd directed his attorney general's office to "make the extradition of this highly dangerous criminal happen as soon as possible."

Guzmán faced US federal prosecution for alleged involvement in cocaine, marijuana, and heroin trafficking, racketeering, money laundering, kidnapping, and conspiracy to commit murder. Jurisdictions in Arizona, California, Texas, Illinois, New York, Florida, and New Hampshire all staked claims to prosecute him on various offenses related to his status as boss of the Sinaloa Cartel.

Most legal experts agreed that, once extradited, Chapo would likely be sent to the Eastern District of New York—the Brooklyn venue where infamous Mafia bosses like John Gotti stood trial in the 1980s and '90s.

Loretta Lynch, then US attorney for the Eastern District—later United States attorney general—had personally signed the indictment, filed on September 25, 2014, charging Guzmán and other alleged members of his cartel with conspiring to import tonnage of cocaine into the United States between 1990 and 2005.

The indictments allege that Guzmán employed sicarios to carry out hundreds of acts of violence in Mexico, including murder, torture, and kidnapping. Lynch called Chapo's Sinaloa Cartel "the largest drug trafficking organization in the world," responsible for the vast majority of drugs imported into the United States.

YET, GIVEN CHAPO'S REPUTATION as the king of modern-day escape artists, it was perhaps inevitable that in July 2016, Internet rumors claimed that Guzmán had escaped from the lockup in Ciudad Juárez.

The response of the Mexican government was instantaneous: Secretary of the Interior Miguel Ángel Osorio Chong released a photo on his Twitter account showing Chapo sitting alone in the brightly lit and desolate prison room, clean-shaven, surrounded by only a few hidden, shadowy guards, waiting out the clock before his extradition to face justice in the United States. *"Para los rumores, una imagen,"* Osorio Chong wrote. "For the rumors, an image . . ."

IT SEEMED AS IF Chapo's legal team would drag out the judicial process for many months, but then, on January 19, 2017—and without warning—the Mexican Foreign Ministry and the US Department of Justice abruptly announced that Guzmán was being extradited.

Chapo was transferred from the prison handcuffed and still in his gray jailhouse jumpsuit, wearing an oversize tan jacket, his face pale and his hair so closely cropped that he looked like a skinhead. Chapo was clearly agitated and frightened as he sat aboard the Mexican government's Challenger 605 jet, which departed for New York just after 5:30 p.m. Several hours later, the plane landed at MacArthur Airport, in Islip, Long Island; Chapo was taken into US custody and escorted off the plane by agents from the DEA and HSI.

The timing of the extradition seemed highly unusual, and the government of Peña Nieto offered no explanation for why it chose to send its most notorious prisoner to the United States on the last night of President Obama's term in office.

From Long Island, Guzmán was taken to his new temporary home in the heart of lower Manhattan, the Metropolitan Correctional Center, a blocky beige twelve-story complex wedged between the Brooklyn Bridge and the Manhattan Bridge on Park Row. One of the country's most secure federal lockups, this is the prison where other high-profile inmates have awaited their trials, among them the Gambino crime family boss John Gotti and terror suspects such as the Al Qaeda associates of Osama bin Laden and Ramzi Yousef, the mastermind of the 1993 bombing of the World Trade Center.

Guzmán was housed in the most high-security wing within the MCC—10 South—known as "Little Gitmo."

On January 20—while most of the world watched President Trump's inauguration in Washington—Guzmán was brought before a judge in the Eastern District, in downtown Brooklyn, where he heard the seventeen-count indictment, alleging that between 1989 and 2014, as the leader of the Sinaloa drug cartel, he'd run a "criminal enterprise responsible for importing into the United States and distributing massive amounts of illegal narcotics and for conspiring to murder people who posed a threat to the narcotics enterprise." The United States government demanded that Chapo surrender $14 billion "in drug proceeds and illicit profits" that he allegedly smuggled into Mexico from the United States.

"Today marks a milestone in our pursuit of Chapo Guzmán," said Robert Capers, the US attorney for the Eastern District. "Guzmán's story is not one of a do-gooder or a Robin Hood or even one of a famous escape artist. [His] destructive and murderous rise as an international narcotics trafficker is akin to a small cancerous tumor that metastasized and grew into a full-blown scourge that for decades littered the streets of Mexico with the casualties of violent drug wars over turf."

The US prosecutors claimed that Chapo had continued to run his narco empire even during his incarceration in Mexico's prison system. "He's a man known for a life of crime, violence, death, and destruction, and now he'll have to answer for that," Capers said.

IT DIDN'T TAKE CHAPO LONG to begin complaining about the harsh conditions in Little Gitmo. On February 3, 2017, a heavy police presence escorted Guzmán from the MCC to the Brooklyn federal courthouse. The scene was unprecedented in New York history, even by the standards of the city's biggest criminal trials. Not even notorious mobsters like Gotti or any high-profile terrorists had been transported under such heavy security.

A twelve-car caravan, with Guzmán hidden behind the heavy tint of an armored van, shut down the outbound Brooklyn Bridge for fifteen minutes during the height of New York's morning rush hour. Authorities said they were concerned that Chapo had the resources to launch a possible "military-scale" rescue.

Guzmán appeared before the judge wearing a navy prison uniform, turning at one point to smile at his wife, Emma, who was seated in the first row of the courtroom. It was the first time they'd seen each other since the extradition.

Chapo's defense attorneys sought to lighten some of the strict security measures at the MCC. They complained that Guzmán was on a twenty-three-hour lockdown in jail, allowed to leave his cell only to speak to limited members of the defense team and granted one hour of exercise a day. One of his court-appointed attorneys, Michelle Gelernt, called the security measures "extremely restrictive" and said that Chapo should at least be allowed to make phone calls to his attorneys and have face-to-face visits with his wife.

Chapo's lawyer argued that he had caused no security problems since he had come to the United States, and that the current restrictions were excessive.

But Judge Brian Cogan—without mentioning Chapo's two prior prison escapes—was clearly unimpressed. Regarding the extra security measures, the judge deadpanned, "We know the reason for that."

IT WAS A BREEZY midsummer Saturday evening. I was back in Arizona for a friend's wedding, and Diego picked me up at Sky Harbor International Airport in his Chevrolet Silverado.

It wasn't the old Black Bomber, but the booming stereo system quickly brought back memories of our time together—ten years earlier—on the Phoenix Task Force.

"Paraíso personal de la dinastía Guzmán entre bungalows y alberca,"

Diego was singing as he hit the gas onto the freeway. *"Lo querían asegurar al más grande de los grandes—Señor Chapo Guzmán."*

A personal paradise for the Guzmán dynasty
Among the palapas and the pool
They wanted to capture the biggest of them all
Señor Chapo Guzmán

It sure felt like old times as we shot west to the Maryvale neighborhood once again for *mariscos* and a few beers.

We drove into a nearly blinding sunset, the Phoenix Mountains and the towering saguaro cactuses welcoming me like old friends. Over his iPhone's Bluetooth connection, through the Bose speakers, Diego was blasting the narcocorrido "La Captura del Chapo Guzmán," by Jorge Santa Cruz. He sang the lyrics loudly—syllable for syllable—as he drove the Silverado west on Interstate 10.

I no longer needed help with the Spanish translation. And I remembered what Diego had told me in my early years at DEA.

You're no one in the narco world until you've got your own corrido.

I was impressed by the accuracy of "La Captura del Chapo Guzmán." Virtually every detail of the operation was covered in the verses of the song: the arrival of the marines to storm Chapo's personal paradise at Duck Dynasty; our plan B to catch Chapo unaware in his house on Río Humaya in Culiacán; Chapo's Houdini-like disappearance into a secret passage beneath the bathtub and into the city's drainage system; Picudo's confession that he'd dropped off *"el más grande de los capos"*—the biggest of bosses—on the road to Mazatlán, where El Bravo was there to protect him.

And, ultimately, how the marines closed in, in the predawn hours of February 22, for the surprise raid on Room 401.

A Mazatlán, Sinaloa
Un lugar paradisiaco
Elementos de Marina
Uno a uno fue llegando
Pa no levantar sospechas
En el Hotel Miramar
El 22 de Febrero
Cayó El Chapito Guzmán

"Man, this is all you," Diego said. "The fall of Chapito. Your own corrido, Drew. *Felicidades!*" He let out a loud laugh. "You made it, brother."

I nodded as Diego pulled off the 10 at exit 138, turning his Chevy onto 59th Avenue.

But as faithful as the corrido was to the details of the capture, there was no mention in the lyrics about Americans having boots on the ground, no shout-out to DEA—those three letters most feared by every narcotrafficker.

"Yeah, man," I said, "but it's missing something."

"What's that?"

"There's nothing about Las Tres Letras."

"True," Diego said. "They didn't know about Las Tres Letras."

"Como siempre," I said, smiling. "In the shadows. Like always."

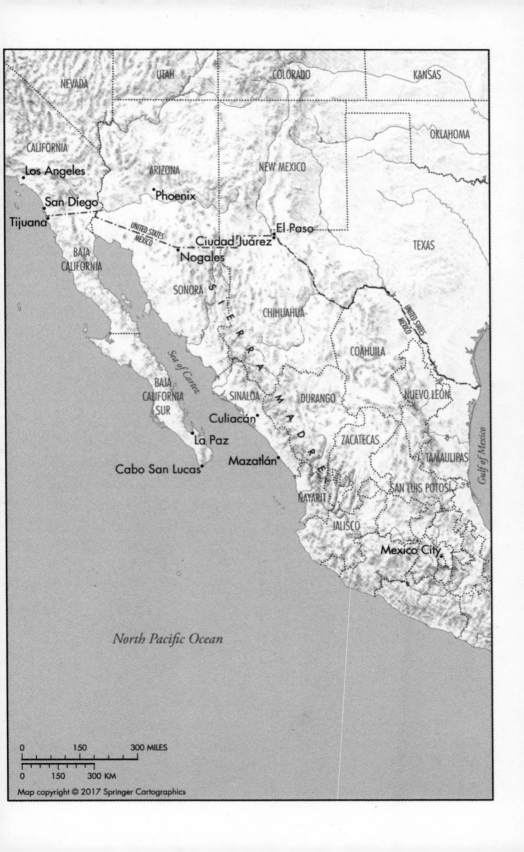

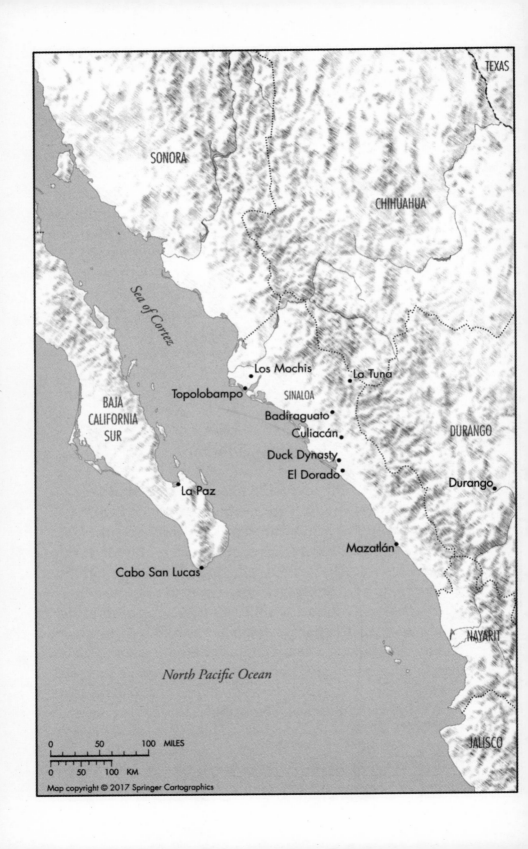

TEXAS

SONORA

CHIHUAHUA

Sea of Cortez

BAJA
CALIFORNIA
SUR

Los Mochis

La Tuna

Topolobampo

SINALOA

Badiraguato

Culiacán

DURANGO

Duck Dynasty

El Dorado

La Paz

Durango

Mazatlán

Cabo San Lucas

North Pacific Ocean

NAYARIT

0   50   100   MILES

0   50   100 KM

JALISCO

Map copyright © 2017 Springer Cartographics

ACKNOWLEDGMENTS

THE CAPTURE OF the world's most-wanted drug kingpin could never have been achieved by one man alone. During my law enforcement career, I had the pleasure to work with hundreds of men and women who deserve my deepest thanks here, but security concerns prevent me from directly naming them.

First and foremost, I owe immense gratitude to my wife for her unwavering love, support, and patience. The time she sacrificed over the years has been an essential contribution to my success, and I can only hope my continued love for her offers some solace for my constant preoccupations. My sons—the greatest accomplishments of my life—have put the true meaning of this story into focus. They will always be my inspiration.

Thanks also to my parents, grandparents, in-laws, siblings, cousins, aunts, uncles, nieces, nephews, and all my other family and friends who followed my journey so closely and were a constant source of love and support through it all. Special thanks go out to two very good friends, one who pushed me toward a career with DEA, back when I first had no intention of pursuing one, and a second who's been there at all the right times, graciously creating opportunities for my family and me to thrive after my days in law enforcement.

ACKNOWLEDGMENTS

Without Diego Contreras, my career at DEA would never have evolved as quickly as it did. We grew together, complementing each other's strengths—becoming a powerful team. I will forever be grateful for our partnership. Diego's cunning and savvy approach to investigation is remarkable; he was the initial driving force that ultimately led to the capture. His innate ability to infiltrate Mexican drug-trafficking organizations will mark him as one of the greatest undercover investigators in the history of federal law enforcement. Though miles may separate us, I will always consider him a brother and a partner for life.

The Drug Enforcement Administration is one of the premier law enforcement agencies in the world, and I'm honored and fortunate to have served alongside some of DEA's finest. Special thanks to former DEA administrator Michele Leonhart and her former staff at DEA Headquarters; Regional Director Tom McAllister and his entire staff, including my assistant regional directors and group supervisor, as well as my fellow special agents, pilots, intelligence analysts, and administrative support personnel. Special thanks to Nico Gutierrez for all his assistance with translating and for his frontline coordination.

This mission would never have been accomplished without the former SAC of the Special Operations Division and his staff, especially Don Dominguez and his team, my former ASAC and two Group Supervisors at NTF, as well as all my previous colleagues in Team 3. Finally, a very special thank-you to Snake for greasing all the right skids.

When I first ran into Homeland Security Investigations Special Agent Brady Fallon, it felt as if we'd known each other for years. His humility, good humor, and drive served as a catalyst for creating and sustaining HSI and DEA's relationship, which ultimately led to our success. No one will ever quite understand what it took to lead an investigation and operation of this complexity and magnitude—but Brady certainly knows, because we did virtually every step of it together. I owe Brady, Neil Miller, and Joe Dawson a world of gratitude; they were the workhorses behind the operation—and truly its unsung heroes. And I'm indebted to the tenacious team of HSI senior executive staff, supervisors, special agents, intelligence analysts, and translators; without their diligent work and coordination, the capture would never have happened.

United States Marshal Leroy Johnson and his team deserve far more credit than the space constraints of the story allow, and are rarely afforded the accolades they deserve for their bravery. Once we had boots on the ground in Sinaloa, it was the marshals' technical and operational expertise that proved essential. I give my sincere thanks to each and every one of them.

There are so many people within the US Department of Justice and US Attorney's Offices throughout the nation who deserve my gratitude—but none has been as instrumental to this operation as then–deputy chief Camila Defusio and her team of assistant US attorneys. Their relentless efforts provided us the perfect tools to track down and capture the most elusive drug lord of our age. I also owe many thanks to several former AUSAs from San Diego and Chicago with whom I had the pleasure to work closely over the years; their support had a defining impact on the investigation leading to the capture. We couldn't have done it without all of them.

At the Lincoln County Sheriff's Office, I'd like to thank all those—past and present—for opening the door to my law enforcement career and offering continued support in the years after I left.

Having the privilege to live and work in a country I've come to love almost as much as my own can be attributed to only one factor: the people of Mexico. Men and women who exude great pride in their land, who open their homes, share their culture, and believe in the common good. SEMAR admiral Furia and his marines are these types of Mexican patriots. *Todo por la patria.* All for the homeland. These Mexican marines live—and many good men have died—for those words. Admiral Furia and his brigade understood the importance of trust and embraced our partnership wholeheartedly.

Bonds between nations—even those as vast as the United States and Mexico—often boil down to just a handful of personal relationships. And I know of no better example of how both countries operated together as one team and achieved what most thought was impossible. It's been an incredible honor to work so closely with SEMAR; I'll never be able to pay back the debt of gratitude I owe to Admiral Furia and every single marine involved in this operation. They protected our lives—ensuring we returned home safely to our families without *once* having to fire a shot. They are warriors in the truest sense of the word, and I'll forever cherish their brotherhood.

A great deal of thanks go to the Mexican Federal Police, the Mexico Attorney General's Office (PGR), and all the specialized narcotics units throughout Latin America with whom Diego and I worked so closely in the early years. These men and women must fight against systemic institutional corruption every day— yet somehow manage to succeed and improve the quality of life for their citizens by disrupting some of most violent international drug-trafficking organizations. I'm honored to call many of them friends.

Thanks also to the members of Canadian law enforcement—

specifically, the Vancouver Police Department and the Quebec Provincial Police—for their efforts and support of DEA's mission.

I owe Douglas Century, my coauthor, an immense amount of gratitude. His complete submersion and selfless dedication were critical in capturing every detail, fact, and feeling of my journey. It has taken us several grueling years to fine-tune every line, paragraph, and page. Quite simply, I could never have written this book without him.

My agency, 3Arts Entertainment, was instrumental in bringing us together and helping us conceptualize how best to render this story; I owe everyone at 3Arts and the entire team at HarperCollins my deepest gratitude.

When I was in the DEA Academy, just before we graduated, we created a class T-shirt which read:

> Woe to the wicked! Disaster is upon them!
> —Isaiah 3:11

It wasn't that we were so religious, but we all felt that sentiment deeply: No matter how big or small the criminals, how distant or secretive the lair, there will always be lawmen and lawwomen dedicated to bringing them to justice. No criminal can operate with impunity forever.

Woe to the wicked! It's a phrase that has resonated with me since that academy graduation. So, my final note of gratitude goes out to all the heroes of our nation's law enforcement and military who, every day and night, commit their lives to delivering "disaster to the wicked" so that we can *all* sleep in peace.

—A.H.

A NOTE ON SOURCES

WRITING A BOOK set in the murderous *milieu* of contemporary narco-trafficking can be daunting. As with any criminal underworld, what passes for official history is often mere speculation or mythology. It's nearly impossible to separate fact from fable: urban legends, prison lore, and old war stories get repeated generation after generation—reprinted in newspapers, magazines, blogs, and books—to the point that they're often indistinguishable from verifiable fact.

It's no less true for the early days of Joaquín Guzmán than it was for American gangsters such as John Dillinger or Pretty Boy Floyd, Al Capone, or Bugsy Siegel.

The United States and Latin America are rife with narco-*porn* today—salacious films, paperbacks, websites, and magazines that often traffic in exaggeration, rumormongering, and glamorization of the exploits of grotesquely wealthy drug lords.

To be sure, there are hundreds of clear-eyed writers doing excellent and brave frontline reporting on narcotrafficking and government corruption, maintaining the balance of dispassion while cultivating direct access to primary sources. Gabriel García Márquez's *Noticia de un Secuestro*, a brilliant account of Pablo

Escobar's early-1990s reign of terror in Colombia, was an inspiration: for me it remains the exemplar of how a nonfiction author of the first order—through in-depth interviews, meticulous research, and novelistic technique—can capture the visceral terror wrought by criminals such as the Medellín Cartel.

I was fortunate in this book to have worked with a former federal agent who *lived* it, witnessed it, experienced it all firsthand. It's rare that someone of Drew's caliber leaves a federal law enforcement career at such a young age, while the story of his investigative journey is still so fresh and newsworthy. Together we've strived to write this book with an exacting eye, separating out all the hearsay, rumor, and dubious reporting that surrounded "the world's most wanted narcotrafficker" from the verifiable facts.

All too often stories of men like Drew remain untold. This historic capture operation, with all its remarkable twists and turns, deserves an accurate rendering for posterity. And the key participants—not just Drew, but the other DEA and HSI agents, US marshals, SEMAR troops and commanders—deserve to shine for the years of selfless sacrifice that would otherwise have remained cloaked in shadows.

My deepest gratitude goes to Drew, and to everyone who put in so much hard work—at 3Arts Entertainment, HarperCollins, and ICM Partners—for helping us bring his singular story to fruition.

—D.C.

GLOSSARY

abra las cartas: Literally "open the letters" or "open the books." In the context of a cross-national narcotics investigation, it means "to share all the intelligence."

ARD: Assistant regional director. DEA GS-15 rank in a foreign post.

ASAC (pronounced "EH-sak"): Assistant special agent in charge. DEA GS-15 rank in the United States.

ATF: Abbreviation for United States Bureau of Alcohol, Tobacco, and Firearms. (Now officially known as the Bureau of Alcohol, Tobacco, Firearms, and Explosives.)

AUSA: Assistant United States Attorney.

BDU: Battle-dress uniform. Camouflage fatigues worn by SEMAR.

Beltrán-Leyvas: A Mexican drug cartel run led by five Beltrán-Leyva brothers now based in the northern Mexican state of Sinaloa. Founded as a branch of the Sinaloa Cartel, the Beltrán-Leyvas became their own cartel after the arrest of Alfredo Beltrán-Leyva, a.k.a. "El Mochomo," in 2008, blaming Chapo Guzmán for the arrest.

birria: A spicy Mexican stew dish traditionally made from goat meat.

Caballeros Templarios, Los: A Mexican drug cartel known in English as the Knights Templar, composed of the remnants of the defunct La Familia Michoacana drug cartel based in the Mexican state of Michoacán.

cajeta: Literally "caramel"—DTO slang for high-grade marijuana.

carnal: Often abbreviated in text messages as "cnl," literally meaning "related by blood," it is a term of affection similar to "brother" or "bro."

chanclas: Sandals.

chilango: Mexican slang for residents of Mexico City or people native to the capital city.

cholo: Originally meaning a mestizo, or a Latin American with Indian blood, "Cholo" can now denote a lower-class Mexican, especially in an urban area; a gangster; or in the cartel underworld a particularly tough individual (such as "Cholo Iván" Gastélum, the plaza boss for the coastal city of Los Mochis).

CI: Confidential informant.

Cisne Negro: Spanish for "black swan." The name of the top-secret SEMAR operation to recapture Chapo Guzmán in January 2016.

confidential source: DEA's term for a confidential informant.

cuete (pronounced kweh-TAY): Literally "rocket" in Spanish, is common slang for a pistol or other handgun.

deconfliction: A common law enforcement check to reduce the risk of targeting the same criminals causing a potential "blue on blue" (law enforcement targeting law enforcement) incident.

desmadre: Literally, from "your mother," roughly translated as "mess-up" or "chaos."

DTO: Drug-trafficking organization.

el generente: The manager and a codename for Chapo Guzmán.

El Señor: A term of respect meaning "sir" or "the man," and a code name for Chapo Guzmán.

Gárgola: Spanish for "Gargoyle." The name of the top secret SEMAR operation to capture Chapo Guzmán in February 2014.

G-ride: Short for "government ride." Used by federal agents to refer to their official government vehicle, or OGV.

GS: Group supervisor, DEA GS-14 rank in the United States and in foreign posts.

Guadalajara Cartel: See page 16.

güey (pronounced "whey"): The equivalent of "dude."

halcón (los halcones): Literally "hawks" in Spanish, they are lookouts and street cartel associates who report activities, warning the drug cartels about movements from other DTOs, the police, or the military.

Inge: Short for *ingeniero*, literally "engineer" in Spanish and a code name for Chapo Guzmán.

jefe de jefes: Literally Spanish for "boss of bosses." The name applied to the highest leader of a drug cartel in Mexico and is most frequently associated with Miguel Ángel Félix Gallardo.

JGL: Initials for Joaquín Guzmán Loera.

La Paz: Literally "the peace," a Mexican city located on the southeastern edge of Baja California peninsula.

Las Tres Letras: Literally Spanish for "the three letters." Drug cartel slang for the DEA.

Lic: Short for *licenciado* (see below).

licenciado: Literally "one with a license," it may refer to anyone with a higher degree of education, such as a lawyer, engineer, architect, accountant; within cartel slang, this almost always refers to a lawyer or an educated adviser.

machaca con huevo: A Mexican dish of shredded dry beef that is scrambled with eggs often eaten for breakfast.

mariscos: Seafood, especially shellfish such as clams, oysters, and shrimp, very popular in Sinaloa.

más tranquilo: More calm.

Miapa: Slang for "my dad," and one of the code names for Chapo Guzmán.

mirror: A technique used by drug-traffickers to evade electronic surveillance by law enforcement—most commonly by having texts or messages manually retyped by a low-level cartel employee from one BlackBerry or mobile phone into another (creating a "mirror"), making it difficult for law enforcement to track the messages to the final recipient, and hindering wiretapping efforts.

Nana: "Grandmother"; another code name for Chapo Guzmán.

narco: General term for drug trafficker.

narcocorrido (pronounced "NARkoko'RIðo"): Literally a "drug ballad." An enormously popular subgenre of the Mexican norteño, traditional folk music from northern Mexico. Modern narcocorridos are considered to have started in 1974 with the hit "Contrabando y Traición" ("Smuggling and Betrayal")—the first hugely successful narcocorrido—by Los Tigres del Norte. Today's narcocorrido scene is immensely popular in both Mexico and the United States, with artists taking commissions from real-life cartel bosses and traffickers to celebrate their exploits. With a rollicking beat driven by tubas and accordions—and lyrics often celebrating murder, revenge, and violence—the contemporary narcocorrido scene is often likened to 1990s gangsta rap. It is now arguably Mexico's most popular form of music among young people—often despite a lack of radio airplay and attempts by the authorities to ban the music. The scene is thriving, with artists such as Roberto Tapia, Gerardo Otiz, Movimiento Alteradand, and El Komander drawing huge fan-bases with songs that often celebrate drug lords such as Chapo Guzmán and other high-level traffickers.

narco juniors: The children of the older drug traffickers—a new and often flashier generation of narcos. Unlike their fathers or grandfathers, narco juniors have for the most part been raised in urban wealth, with a higher level of education.

Navolato: A Mexican city just to the west of Culiacán in Sinaloa State.

NCAR: DEA's North and Central Americas Region, covering Mexico, Central America, and Canada.

Padrino: "Godfather," and one of the code names used for Chapo Guzmán.

palapa: A traditional Mexican shelter/structure roofed with palm leaves or branches, especially one on a beach or near a body of water.

pan dulce: Mexican sweet bread often eaten during breakfast.

PF: Policía Federal—Mexican Federal Police.

PGR: Abbreviation for La Procuraduría General de la República, the Mexican equivalent of the Office of the Attorney General, similar to the United States Department of Justice.

pinche cabrón (vulgar): Mexican slang for "motherfucker" or "asshole," it may also be used as a compliment in the sense of someone who is a "fucking badass."

plaza: Territory, turf, or primary smuggling route from Mexico into the United States. May also mean the taxes one must pay to use such routes.

pocket trash: Law enforcement term for anything found left over in pockets—could be receipts, miscellaneous notes, ticket stubs, SIM card remnants, gum wrappers, or anything else.

rápida: Literally "fast" or "high speed," Mexican slang for the armed pickup trucks of SEMAR.

raspados: From the word "scrapes," a cup of shaved ice and sweetened with various fruit juices.

Regional Director: The DEA's highest-ranking senior executive in a foreign post. The regional director is in charge of a foreign region (e.g., the Mexico City Country Office, which covers DEA offices in Canada, Mexico, and Central America). Reports directly to the DEA's chief of operations in Washington, DC.

SAC (pronounced "sack"): Special agent in charge, the DEA senior executive with the highest rank in charge of a specific division office in the United States (e.g., the Chicago Field Division, which covers Illinois, Indiana, Wisconsin, and Minnesota).

Secre: Short for *secretario*, or secretary, and a code name for Chapo Guzmán or his secretaries Condor and Chaneke.

SEDENA (pronounced "sey-DAY-nah"): La Secretaría de la Defensa Nacional, Mexican Army.

SEMAR (pronounced "sey-MAR"): La Secretaría de Marina. Mexican Marines.

sicario: Literally a "hitman" or assassin for the cartels.

Sierra Madre: The major mountain range that runs northwest to southeast through northwestern and western Mexico along the Gulf of California and primarily through the eastern portion of Sinaloa.

straw purchaser: Someone with a clean background who agrees to acquire goods or services—usually illicit—for someone who is unable or unwilling to personally purchase them. These goods or services are then transferred to that person after they are purchased. They are often hired by DTOs and gunrunners.

sugar skulls: Candied sugar in the shape of a human skull, decorated with colorful icing and glittery adornments representing a departed soul or particular spirit on the Mexican holiday known as Día de los Muertos, or the "Day of the Dead."

tacos de canasta: Homemade tacos served out of a basket, frequently from the trunk of someone's car.

tlacoyos: Oval-shaped tortilla pockets made of masa, stuffed with refried beans, cheese, or fava beans, and topped with queso fresco, nopales, and salsa. These are typically served by street vendors off a *comal*.

tolls: Call detail records from a phone.

Zetas, Los: A Mexican drug cartel formed when commandos of the Mexican Army deserted their ranks and began working as the enforcement arm of the Gulf Cartel. In 2010, Los Zetas broke away and formed their own cartel. Considered the most violent of today's cartels, they are also heavily involved in racketeering, kidnapping, and extortion.

INDEX

Page numbers in *italics* refer to maps.

Affleck, Ben, 132
Africa, 23
Agua Prieta, 102, 143
Alex (DEA agent), 33–34
Al Qaeda, 308
Alteradand, Movimiento, 321
Altiplano prison (Federal Social
    Readaption Center No. 1), 22,
    24, 292, 297–300, 304
Amsterdam, 39
Aponte Gómez, Manuel Alejandro "El
    Bravo," "El Negro," 249, 253, 279,
    293, 301, 306, 311
Araña (pilot), 70, 90, 92, 113, 154,
    300, 306
Arellano Félix brothers, 190
Argo (film), 132–33, 300
Associated Press, 70
Attorney General Exempt Operation
    (AGEO), 51
Australia, 40, 110
Ávila, Víctor, 66

Balboa Bank & Trust, 40
Baltimore, 31
Banco General, 40
Bank of Montreal, 40
Batallón de Infanteria Marina No. 10
    (BIM-10, Topolobampo), 193–94,
    196, 199, *314*
Beck (suspect), 14–16
Beltrán-Leyva, Alfredo "El Mochomo,"
    317

Beltrán-Leyva Cartel, 75, 85, 317
BlackBerrys, PINs, and line sheets, 68,
    65–72, 82–83, 90–92, 96–102,
    106–9, 113–43, 155–57, 164–67,
    173, 185, 220, 299–301
Bogotá, Colombia, 39, 42
Boston, 31
Bravo, El. *See* Aponte Gómez, Manuel
    Alejandro
British Columbia, 111

Caballeros Templarios, Los (Knights
    Templar Cartel), 75, 186–87, 317
Cabo San Lucas, 68–71, 75, 77, 82–83,
    93, 127, 138, 179–80, 226, 280,
    313–14
Calgary, 112
Cali, Colombia, 42
Calibre 50 (band), 71
Camarena, Enrique "Kiki," 78–79, 87, 183
Canada, 40, 59, 105, 110–12, 127, 236
Capers, Robert, 309
Capone, Al, 82, 191
"Captura del Chapo Guzmán, La"
    (narcocorrido), 311
Carillo Fuentes, Amado, 190
Carlino (filmmaker), 133
Caro Quintero, Rafael "RCQ," 79n,
    183–84, 190
Castillo, Kate del, 116, 301
Celis, 149
Centro Comercial de Los Andes, 40
Chaneke, 136–40, 163, 322

chaneques (Aztec spirits), 136–37
Chase Bank, 40
Chávez, Hugo, 92
Chávez Villalobos, Mercedes, 39–51, 62
Chiapas, 153
Chicago, 34, 105
Chicago Crime Commission, 83
Chile, 299
China, 23
Chino (SEMAR lieutenant), 243, 248–
    50, 256, 261–63, 268, 285–88
Chiqui (SEMAR officer), 248, 288
Cholo Iván. *See* Gastélum Cruz, Orso
    Iván
Chuy (operator), 97
CIA (los primos), 87, 90, 128–31, 158,
    165, 176, 187, 197
Ciento (gofer), 154
Cifuentes Villa, Hildebrando
    Alexánder "Panchito," 127–33,
    135, 189, 300
Cisne Negro, Operación (Black Swan),
    302–3, 318
Citibank, 40
Ciudad de Durango, 100
Ciudad Juárez, 2, 91, 304–5, 307
Clinton, Hillary, 69
CNN, 35, 144
cocaine, 5, 16, 23, 84, 90, 97, 110–11.
    See also specific countries and
    distributors
    fake bananas and, 235–36, 238, 251
    Mexico City International Airport
    and, 77–80
    price of, 110
    seizures of, 23, 63, 84
    transportation of, 23, 53, 58–64
    tunnels and, 143–45, 154, 157, 259
Cochinos, Los, 107
Cogan, Brian, 310
Colombia, 23, 42, 58, 90, 97, 105, 114
Colonia Libertad, 120–21, 136, 139, 150,
    157, 160, 189, 198–200, 201, 221
Columbia College (Vancouver), 111–12
Condor. *See* Hoo Ramírez, Carlos
    Manuel
Congressional Bicameral Commission on
    National Security (Mexico), 298
"Contrabando y Traicion"
    (narcocorrido), 320

Contreras, Diego
    background of, 4, 27, 28
    Blackberry PINs and, 68, 72
    Chapo and, 83
    indictments and, 118
    Jardines del Humaya cemetery and,
        121–22
    mentoring by, 4, 72–73, 98,
        100–101, 135, 277–78
    Mexico and, 67, 72
    money laundering investigation and,
        38–53
    narcocorridos and, 1–5, 231, 311–12
    Nueva Generación and, 31–38
    reunion with, 310–12
    Robles/Torres takedown and,
        53–62, 65
Cops (TV show), 133
Coronel Aispuro, Emma (Chapo's
    wife), 101, 287–88, 305, 310
Coronel Barreras, Inés, 101–2
corruption, 77–78, 94, 171, 298
Cortez, Sea of "El Charco," 168–69,
    188, 192–93, *313–14*
Costa Rica, 23, 57–59, 105, 299
Culiacán, 2, 4, 16, 98, 107, 111, 116,
    125–26, 129, 133, 138–39, 143,
    147–49, 160, 174–75, 190–91,
    195–96, 212–57, 261–63, 287, 311
    drug lord cemetery, 121–22
    map of, *313–14*
    Mercedes dealership, 255–58
Culiacán International Airport, 240, 243

Dawson, Joe, 106–8, 122, 126, 135,
    152, 194, 202, 205, 216, 254,
    268, 290
Day of the Dead (Día de los Muertos),
    115
D.E.A. en México, La (book), 247
deconfliction, 119, 127, 131, 318
Defusio, Camila, 108–9, 135, 202,
    268, 290
Deutsche Bank, 50
Diaz, Julio "El Toro," 182–83, 222,
    228–32, 235, 237–39, 240, 243,
    249–51, 255–56, 262–63, 274–75
Dillinger, John, 25
Dominguez, Don, 119–20, 129, 220, 291
Douglas, Arizona, 143–44

Doux, Hotel, 303
Drug Enforcement Administration
    (DEA), 105
    Chapo and, 151–53, 211–12, 293–95
    CIA and, 128–31
    FBI and, 127–28
    HSI and, 89
    job application and, 18–19
    language school and, 67
    as "Las Tres Letras," 27–29, 312
    Mazatlán and, 129–30, 193
    Mexico City and, 65, 68–72, 75–77,
        79–82, 277
    NCAR regional director, 76
    Panama and, 41, 105
    Phoenix Narcotic Task Force Team
        3, 4, 29–30, 33
    Puerto Peñasco and, 145–47, 175
    resignation from, 295–96
    San Diego Tunnel Task Force, 144
    SEMARs and, 142
    "six" report, 41n
    techies team, 120
    Training Academy, 19–21, 54
Duck Dynasty (Pichis, Pichiguila
    duck-hunting club), 148–50, 158–
    59, 162–66, 174, 177–79, 180,
    182, 184, 198, 252, 294, 311, *314*
Durango, 93, 100, 121, 126, 136, 188,
    301, *313–14*

Eastern District of New York, 307, 308
Ecuador, 23, 58–61, 90, 97, 105,
    112–14
Ecuador National Police, 60–61
Eisenhower, Dwight D., 150
El 19 (code for Culiacán), 139, 258
El 50. *See* Guardado Salcido, Carlos
    Adrián
El 70. *See* López Osorio, Edgar Manuel
"El Chapo Speaks" (Penn), 300–301
El Salvador, 11, 23
England, 110
Ensenada de Pabellones, 150, 174, 195
Escobar, Pablo, 23
Explosion Norteña (band), 27

Facebook, 111
Fallon, Brady
    background of, 89, 91

BlackBerry tracking and, 108–9,
    113–23, 126–27, 133–35, 137,
    142–45, 155–56, 165–67, 299
    core team of, 106, 135–36
    family and, 179, 205
    Chapo capture and, 141–42,
        148–52, 158–60, 165–67, 171,
        177–89, 192–243, 251–56, 259–
        64, 268–76, 278–80, 283–90
    Cifuentes arrest and, 128–32
    partnership begun with, 89–104
    Picudo capture and, 246–48, 250,
        252
    SEMAR and, 172–73, 175–76
Familia Michoacana, La, Cartel, 317
FBI, 68–69, 71–72, 89, 91, 128–32
Federal Police (Secretaria de Seguridad
    Publica, PF), 22, 53–54, 69–71,
    77–79, 83, 87, 102–3, 141, 145–
    47, 155, 300, 303, 321
FedEx, 31
Flaco (adviser), 155
Fonseca Carrillo, Ernesto, 79n, 190
Forbes, 42, 111, 254
Foreign Narcotics Kingpin Designation
    Act, 29
Fresa (Ecuador operator), 97
Furia, Admiral. *See* Reyes Aragones,
    Raul

Gallardo, Miguel Ángel Félix "El
    Padrino," 22, 79, 121, 190, 319
Gambino family, 308
García Rodríguez, Enrique, 130
Gárgola, Operación, 198, 230, 262–63,
    319
Garra, Admiral. *See* Reyna Marquez,
    Antonio
Gastélum Cruz, Orso Iván "Cholo
    Iván," 107, 172, 194, 199, 302–3,
    306, 318
Gelernt, Michelle, 310
Gerardo, 38
Gotti, John, 306, 308
Greene, Tom, 85–86
G20, 77
Guadalajara, 25, 39, 78–79, 98
Guadalajara Airport, 9–10
Guadalajara Cartel, 22, 79
Guadalupe, Doña, 38–40, 62

Guardado Salcido, Carlos Adrián "El
   50," 107, 227, 236
Guatemala, 11, 23, 30, 90, 97, 105
Gulf Cartel, 75, 142, 324
Gutierrez, Nicolás "Nico," 164,
   176–78, 181, 183, 185, 188,
   193–94, 197–207, 209, 211, 217,
   217, 225–26, 228, 240–41, 248,
   253–54, 259, 263, 273–74, 276,
   281, 284, 288
Guzmán, Arturo (Chapo's brother), 22
Guzmán, Edgar (Chapo's son), 3–4,
   98, 121, 231
Guzmán, Tocallo (Chapo's son), 154
Guzmán Loera, Joaquín Archivaldo "El
   Chapo," 1
   agencies targeting, 76–77, 89–90, 95
   arrest of 1993, 21–22
   background of, 286
   ball cap of, 233
   bathtub tunnels and, 157, 201,
      209–18, 221–27, 232–33, 238,
      249–50, 252, 294, 311
   birthday at La Tuna, 94
   BlackBerry chain and, 65–72,
      82–83, 90–92, 96–102, 107,
      118–28, 137–43, 172, 301
   business style and, 110, 113–14, 153–55
   Cabo San Lucas raid and, 68–72
   Canada and, 110–12, 127
   capture mission in Culiacán,
      193–207, 219–23, 240–54,
      261–62, 268
   capture mission in Mazatlán,
      253–254, 263, 269, 271–84,
      281–89, 291–93
   capture mission planned, 95–96,
      116, 141–42, 147–49, 151–53,
      151–58, 158–68, 171–92
   capture of 2016, 301–5
   CIA and, 128–29
   Cifuentes and, 127–30
   Colt Super gun, 251–52
   daughter Grisel and, 134
   Diego flips inner circle member, 68
   drug empire of, 22–24, 105, 110,
      112–13
   Duck Dynasty and, 148–59
   escape of 2001, 24–26, 142–43
   escape of 2015, 297–300

   escape of, in Los Mochis, 302–3
   extradited to US, 304–10
   fame of, 5, 9–11, 29–30, 82, 92
   FBI and, 127–29
   film and, 116, 132–34, 300
   Forbes and, 42
   Gallardo and, 22, 79
   go bag and, 238
   imprisonments and, 24, 292–93,
      304–5
   indictments in US, 99, 307, 308–9
   leaks to, 155–56, 165–67, 185
   lieutenants and, 23, 114, 122, 163
   misspellings and, 272–73
   money laundering and, 47, 50–57
   NADDIS file on, 29
   names of, 1–2, 5–6, 206, 209, 213, 240
   narcocorridos and, 1, 5–7
   pattern of life and, 125–26, 137–39,
      158, 160, 229
   photo of, 92
   Rolling Stone and, 301
   sons and, 3–4, 99, 135, 148, 231
   Torres takedown and, 59, 62, 65–66,
      101
   tunnels and, 143–45
   US Attorney's Offices and, 108–9
   violence and, 107, 118–19, 181,
      292–93
   wife Griselda and, 134, 232
   women and, 115–17
Guzmán López, Grisel (Chapo's
   daughter), 134, 232
Guzmán López, Joaquin "Güero"
   (Chapo's son), 134–35, 148–50,
   154, 232, 305
Guzmán López, Ovidio "Ratón"
   (Chapo's son), 134–35, 148–50,
   154, 232, 240, 253, 305
Guzmán Salazar, Iván Archivaldo
   "Chapito" (Chapo's son), 98–99,
   102, 135, 254, 256, 258, 305
Guzmán Salazar, Jesús Alfredo
   (Chapo's son), 59, 98–99, 135,
   255–56, 258, 305

Hells Angels, 111
heroin, 23
Herrera Esperanza, Jesus "Hondo,"
   111–12, 235–36

Hogan, Brandt, 11, 264, 266, 282
Holder, Eric, 294–95
Hollywood, 133
Homeland Security Investigations,
    US Department of (HSI), 66,
    151–52, 212
  El Paso Field Office, 89–90, 96, 99,
    108–10, 122–23, 127, 135–36, 143,
    194, 195, 201, 202, 205, 228, 236,
    237–38, 240, 247, 253, 254, 257
  San Diego Tunnel Task Force, 144
  US attorneys and, 108–9
Honduras, 181
Hoo Ramírez, Carlos Manuel
    "Condor," 119–23, 125–26, 130,
    136–38, 156, 163, 221, 223,
    230–31, 236, 238, 240, 249,
    252–53, 257–58, 269, 271–73,
    287–88, 300, 306, 321
Hoyos, Los. See tunnels
HSBC, 40
Humo, El, 75

India, 23
Inge (ingeniero), 117–19
intelligence community, 119, 131
Interpol, 299
Inzunza Inzunza, Gonzalo "Macho
    Prieto," 145–48, 175
Iranian gangs, 111
Iusacell, 126

Jaguares de Culiacán, Los (band), 2
Jalisco ranch, 10, 21
James Bond tunnel, 143–44
Jardines del Humaya cemetery, 121
Jenkins, Fred, 17–19
Jenkins, Tom, 19
Jesús María zone, 155
Johnson, Leroy "El Roy," 157–60, 164,
    177–79, 183, 187–88, 193–94,
    197–201, 211, 217, 219, 230, 240–
    41, 243, 248, 253–54, 258–59,
    262–63, 271–73, 280, 284
Jones, Nick, 32–33
Juárez, 158

Kansas Highway Patrol, 13, 16–20
Kansas State Troopers, 12, 16
Kansas State University, 13

Kava, 144–45, 148, 154, 217, 223,
    258–59, 277, 298
Kennedy, Robert F., 294
Knights Templar Cartel. See Caballeros
    Templarios
Kommander, El, 321

La Cienéga airstrip, 154
Laden, Osama bin, 308
La Paz air base, 70, 166, 167, 177–86,
    319
La Tuna, Mexico, 6, 94, 132, 306
Leonhart, Michele, 21, 151–52,
    293–95
Lic-F, "El Licenciado", 24, 142–44,
    155, 165–67, 185–86, 199, 205,
    236, 250, 252–53, 257–59,
    262–63, 306n
Lic (licenciado), 100, 319–20
Lic Oro, 101, 116
Lincoln County, Kansas, 13–14
Lizzy (madam), 116
Location One, 226–27
Location Two, 221–25, 227, 251
Location Three, 206, 219–24, 230,
    237–39, 251, 257
Location Four, 219
Location Five "El 5," "La Piscina,"
    206, 209–10, 213, 217–18, 222,
    228–29, 232–33, 235
Loera de Guzmán, Consuelo (Chapo's
    mother), 306
López Osorio, Edgar Manuel "Picudo,"
    "El 70," 70, 83, 107, 142, 154,
    225, 227–30, 236–37, 240–53,
    306, 311
López Pérez, Griselda (Chapo's second
    wife), 134, 231–33
Los Alegres del Barranco (band), 155
Los Angeles, 50, 105
Los Angeles Times, 10
Los Mochis, Sinaloa, 107, 155, 172,
    194, 199, 301–3, 314
Lucia (cook), 201, 287
Luciano, Lucky, 22
Luis, "Lucho" (Chapo's cousin), 181
Lynch, Loretta, 307

Macho Prieto. See Inzunza Inzunza,
    Gonzalo

Maestro (pilot), 153
Malverde, Jesús, 121
marijuana, 23, 31–32, 98, 102, 145, 235
marines. *See* Secretaría de Marina-Armada de México
Marsh, Warne, 205
Mayo, El. *See* Zambada García, Ismael
Mazatlán, 113, 155, 193, 227–28, 249–54, 263, 269, 271–84, 311, *313–14*
McAllister, Thomas, 76–77, 152, 164–65, 290, 293–94
McKenzie, Kenny, 53–56
McMahon, Jim, 11
Medellín, Colombia, 42, 121, 127
Mercantile Bank, 40
Mérida soccer team, 5
Mesa Police Department, 4, 27, 31
Metallica (band), 5, 13
methamphetamine, 5, 23, 38, 155, 222, 225, 239, 243
Metropolitan Correction Center (MCC, Manhattan), 308–10
Mexican Army. *See* Secretaría de la Defensa Nacional
Mexican Attorney General's Office (PGR, La Procuraduría General de la República), 78, 259, 292, 300, 323
Mexico, violence in, 65, 78, 86
Mexico City, 10, 30, 39–41, 59, 145
  application for position in, 66–68
  earthquakes, 114
  money from Canada and, 43–56
  move to, 75–77, 79–81
  return to, after Chapo's capture, 290–91
Mexico City International Airport, 77–78
Mexico-Guatemala border, 23
Miller, Neil, 122–23, 126, 135, 152, 194, 202, 228, 254, 268, 290
Miramar, Hotel, 269, 271, 275–84, 287–88, 294, 311
mirrors, 72, 93, 97, 100, 102, 109, 122, 126, 152, 254, 320
money brokerage and laundering, 31, 38–57, 60, 75, 99, 255

Montreal, 112
Moreno, Nazario "El Más Loco," 186
Motor (SEMAR officer), 229

Nana (code for Chapo), 240, 320
narcocorridos, 2–3, 5–7, 25, 27–29, 71, 311–12, 320–21
narco juniors, 3, 5, 6, 31–32, 99, 321
narco subs, 23
Narcotics and Dangerous Drugs Information System (NADDIS), 29
Naris (courier), 116–16, 139–40, 156–57, 178, 189, 203, 205–7, 209, 221–24, 227, 230–32, 235, 251, 268
National Action Party, 299
National Football League (NFL), 31
National Human Rights Commission, 305
Navarro, Pedro "Bugsy," 30–35, 37–38, 51
Negro, El. *See* Aponte Gómez, Manuel Alejandro
Netherlands, 110
New York City, 31, 50, 105
"Niño de La Tuna, El" (narcocorrido), 5, 29, 73, 237, 277
Nogales, Mexico, 38, 98, 143–45
Nueva Generación, La (New Generation) 30–32, 37–38

Obama, Barack, 151, 294, 307
Office devices, 96–100, 129, 138
  Office-1, 96, 98, 109, 126, 135, 240
  Office-2, 109
  Office-3, 96, 109, 236
  Office-4, 109, 126–27
  Office-5, 90, 92–94, 96, 97, 100–101, 106–7, 109, 110, 139
  Office-6, 109, 115, 140
  Office-10, 126
Organized Crime Drug Enforcement Task Force "La Nueva Generación" investigation, 30
Osawatomie State Hospital, 14
Oscar (accountant), 154
Osorio Chong, Miguel Ángel, 307
Otiz, Gerardo, 321

Palma, Héctor Luis "El Güero," 190
Panama, 105, 153
Panama City, 37–47
Panchito. *See* Cifuentes Villa,
    Hildebrando Alexánder
Patagonia, 299
pattern of life, defined, 125n, 321
Pattonville, Kansas, 11–13, 17
Pattonville's Firehouse Pub, 17–19
Payton, Walter, 11
Peña Nieto, Enrique, 304, 306, 308
Penn, Sean, 300, 301
Pepe (Colombia operator), 97
Perez, Marco, 145–47
Peru, 58, 77
PF. *See* Federal Police
PGP-encrypted smartphones, 111
PGR. *See* Mexican Attorney General's
    Office
Philippines, 110
Phoenix, 2–3, 110
Phoenix Field Division, 247
Phoenix Police Department, 28
Phoenix Task Force, 2, 98, 118, 310
Pichis or Pichiguila. *See* Duck Dynasty
Picudo. *See* López Osorio, Edgar
    Manuel
Pinguino, 154
Pinto (Culiacán worker), 154
plazas, 10, 22
pool house, defined, 32
Posadas Ocampo, Cardinal Juan Jésus,
    Archbishop of Guadalajara, 9–11
Potrillo, El (informant), 85–86
Primera División soccer team, 5
Proceso magazine, 247
Puente Grande (Federal Social
    Readaption Center No. 2), Chapo
    escape of 2001 from, 24–25, 83,
    96, 142, 143, 298
Puerto Peñasco takedown (2013),
    145–48, 247

Quantico, 19, 60, 67
Querétaro soccer team, 5

Raul (Panama operator), 153
RBC bank, 40
"Regreso del Chapo, El"
    (narcocorrido), 25

Reina del Sur, La (telenovela), 116, 300
Reyes Aragones, Raul "La Furia,"
    161–64, 166, 172–77, 182, 191,
    229, 289, 300
Reyna Marquez, Antonio "Garra,"
    182, 190–91, 196–98, 200, 203,
    209–12, 214, 220, 254, 258–59,
    262–63, 288
Robles, Ricardo, 51–53, 57, 62
Rolling Stone, 300–301
roving wire intercept, 202
Royal Canadian Mounted Police
    (RCMP), 110

Salazar Hernández, María Alejandrina
    (Chapo's first wife), 98
Salcido Uzeta, Manuel "Cochiloco," 190
Salinas de Gortari, Carlos, 10
Saludos a Generente, 134
Sánchez López, Lucero "La Diputada,"
    299
San Diego, 33–34, 105, 143–44
San Diego Field Division, 33
San Diego Police Department, 33–34
San Diego Tunnel Task Force, 144
San Luis Potosí ambush, 66
Second-Tier, 100, 109–10, 114–16,
    119, 122–23, 126–27, 129–30,
    136–40, 202, 228, 238
Secretaría de la Defensa Nacional
    (SEDENA, Mexican Army),
    130–32, 141, 155–56, 227, 322,
    324, 387
Secretaría de Marina-Armada de
    México (SEMAR, Mexican
    marines), 141, 152, 159, 161–67,
    171–91, 193, 196–200, 202, 204,
    207, 210–17, 220–25, 229–32,
    235–63, 271–85, 287–89, 291,
    300, 301–2, 323
SEDENA. *See* Secretaría de la Defensa
    Nacional
SEMAR. *See* Secretaría de Marina-
    Armada de México
Señor, El, 90–91, 101, 102, 137, 156,
    318
September 11, 2001, attacks, 89, 91
"Se Quedaron a Tres Pasos"
    (narcocorrido), 71
Sergio (adviser), 155–56, 199–200

sicarios, 86, 307
Sierra Madre, 26, 30, 118, 119, 299, 301, 323
Sinaloa, 2, 3, 23, 71, 83, 118, 121, 127, 300, *313–14*
Sinaloa Attorney General's Office, 24, 142–43
Sinaloa Cartel, 5, 9–11, 22–24, 26, 29, 42, 62, 75, 76, 101, 105, 143–46
Sinaloa State Police, 30
Sixto (pilot), 90, 91–93, 97
Snake (DEA agent), 19
Spain, 40
Special Operations Division (SOD), 119, 220, 291, 293
St. Louis, 31
straw purchases, 99
Suegro, El (father-in-law), 101, 102
Super Bowl, 11
Super Troopers (film), 28

Tandy, Karen, 21
Tapia, Roberto, 5, 321
Team America, Operation, 51, 67, 92, 101
Telcel, 100, 126
telecommunication service providers, 120, 126
Tigres del Norte, Los (band) 320
Tigre (SEMAR lieutenant), 262–63, 268, 273–80, 285, 287–88
Tijuana, 2, 72–74, 98, 144, 154
Tijuana Cartel, 9–10
Tocallo, 98, 102, 117–19, 149, 154
Tocayo (namesake), 98
Top-Tier, 125–26, 130, 136–37, 143, 152, 157, 160, 162–63, 177, 185, 189–90, 194–95, 199–201, 228, 237–38, 250, 254, 259, 262–63, 268–69, 271–72, 278
Toro, El. *See* Diaz, Julio
Toronto, 112
Torres-Leon, Jasmine Elena, 59
Torres-Ramos, Carlos, 58–62, 65, 101
Trafficker Directed Funds (TDF), 52, 60
traps, 31–32, 54

Trump, Donald, 308
Tucson, 110
tunnels, 143–45, 154, 156–57, 258
Turbo (Chapo lieutenant), 113, 139, 153
Tweety (Bugsy's right-hand man), 34–35, 38

UPS, 31
Usacell (mirror), 126
US attorneys, 108, 118, 290–91
US Customs and Border Protection, 144
US Immigration and Customs Enforcement, 144–45
US Marine Corps, 19
US Marshals Service, 157
US-Mexico border, 23, 143
US-Mexico Transboundary Agreement, 69

Vago, 106–7
Vancouver, Canada, 50, 111–12, 236
Venezuela, 23, 92, 97
Vero (nanny), 287
Villa, Pancho, 25

Walmart, 74, 139–40
Washington State, 110
WhatsApp, 102
Winnipeg, 112
wire intercepts, 32, 119
World Trade Center bombing (1993), 308

Yousef, Ramzi, 308

Zambada García, Ismael "El Mayo," 105, 117, 146, 183–85, 187, 189–90, 197
Zapata, Jaime, 66–68, 87
Zetas Cartel, 65–66, 75, 142, 240, 323–24
Zona Rosa neighborhood, 85, 87
Zorro (SEMAR lieutenant), 223, 225, 229, 239–40, 251, 271

ABOUT THE AUTHORS

ANDREW HOGAN is the DEA special agent who led the investigation and capture of El Chapo Guzmán. He now works in the private sector and lives in an undisclosed location.

DOUGLAS CENTURY is the author and coauthor of such bestsellers as *Under and Alone, Barney Ross, Brotherhood of Warriors,* and *Takedown: The Fall of the Last Mafia Empire,* a finalist for the 2003 Edgar Award in the category of Best Nonfiction Crime.